I0731344

ALIEN WARRIOR
MATES III

GRACE KENSINGTON

THE ALIEN'S VOYAGE

1

Ivy glanced up as Maxim approached her, offering him a smile. She felt the relief flow through her knowing that she could look at him, reach out and touch him, and know that he was safe even among the Denynso warriors who had just recently been completely set on killing him. She wondered if she was ever going to get over that sense of relief, and just being close to the man who she had fallen so deeply in love with without having to worry that any moment he would be dragged out of her arms again. Even if she didn't ever get over that feeling, she knew that she would always appreciate that she had the ability to feel it, that she hadn't lost him in the dark, terrifying moments that she was positive Pyra would simply destroy the entire group of Mikana men who had come to the Nyx 23 settlement.

Her eyes drifted from Maxim to Pyra as he entered the hall. He looked tired and drawn and Ivy could only imagine that Eden had sent him out of the house to come join the revelry so that he could get a break from their new baby. Having only been around babies of any kind when he was extremely young and the other warriors were born, Pyra seemed to be taken aback by the realities of the tiny, needy creature who was at once the most beautiful and beloved thing that he had ever seen, and the most terrifying, by his own admission. Eden had stepped into motherhood with much greater ease and confidence than Pyra had stepped into fatherhood, and though he was completely in love with his newborn son and was as prepared as he was when they were on their quest to protect Lysander from anything, Ivy could see on his face that taking a break and returning to the world that he already knew and was comfortable in would do him good.

As she watched the leader of the Denynso warriors walk through the banquet hall and drop down onto the bench of one of the long tables and reach for a piece of bread, she couldn't help but still feel a touch of animosity toward him. She wished that she didn't and that she had the ability to shove the thoughts away, but even though Pyra had earned the forgiveness of his king and apparently the others in the community, Ivy was not as quick to extend her good graces toward him. The journey that she had gone on since arriving on Uoria just weeks before was far more difficult and trying than anything that she could have ever imagined, and much of that was the fault of Pyra and the warriors who followed him with such devotion.

When Ivy first planned on coming to the planet to be with the scientist whose research assistant she had been for a couple of years, she had envisioned an exciting and thrilling opportunity that would allow her to use her knowledge and skill in a useful way while also having the unique chance to explore a new planet and encounter a species that she had only ever heard of, but never seen. Being a part of a university exchange program didn't seem like anything that could possibly be threatening. In fact, it seemed like the safest option for venturing off of Earth and seeing and experiencing new things while also pursuing the career path that she was so passionate about.

Almost as soon as she arrived, however, she found that her thoughts of this experience were nothing like what she was actually going to experience. Within moments of the university shuttle landing, all of her expectations of her time on the planet and her plans for what she and George would accomplish together shattered. Creia and Theia, the king and queen of the Denynso compound, had not been the welcoming people Ivy had heard that they could be. Instead, they showed cold anger and distrust toward her because she had arrived without giving them the notification that they expected from all who arrived on the planet. She had accepted this reaction with as much grace as she could, understanding that in her rather spontaneous decision to join George on Uoria even after telling him that she wouldn't be able to because of the timing, she had gone against the strictly held rules of the Denynso and offended their sense of tradition and regulation. When George stepped forward and acted as her representative, asking forgiveness of the rulers and appealing to them to allow her to stay on the planet rather than facing punishment and exile as they could have done, she felt a sense of relief. Had she known what she was going to face after that moment, that relief might not have been so pronounced.

She had come to Uoria with visions of the massive warriors and thoughts of learning about them and the amazing physical abilities of their kind, as well as the plant life of the planet and what role the environment played in the truly astonishing strength and power of the Denynso. Instead, she arrived in a compound that had been largely emptied and that felt oppressed under a low-hanging sense of worry and urgency that made the entire atmosphere of the surroundings feel anxious. Very soon she learned that the warriors had left the compound in a quest to explore the rest of the planet and find out what other species lived there in an effort to protect themselves and the impending future generation from whatever threats might be there. Though the goals of the university exchange program were still there, she found that the efforts had largely halted because of the war with the Klimnu that had burned through the compound and the new urgency to learn more about Uoria.

Then rather than concentrating on creating lesson plans for those Denynso interested in learning more about Earth and the people who were there, and gathering information to bring back to Earth to share with the rest of the university and possibly publish into their first co-authored studies, Ivy and George found themselves working with the human women. The warriors had contacted them after finding a settlement in which all of the people were frozen in place, seeking help finding a solution. While it was exciting in a way to be working on such a dynamic and unusual problem, Ivy felt like she had been thrown into something that she hadn't anticipated all because Pyra had decided that the warriors should head out into the planet to find out more about it.

Though she didn't realize it then, that had been when the smallest seeds of animosity for Pyra had been planted. She had heard that he was a powerful and impressive warrior, a leader that no one could deny and who could bring down any army. She had been so excited to meet him and compare what she had heard of him to reality, but she almost immediately found herself disappointed. When they went to the settlement, there was no time to get to know the warriors and learn about the Denynso. Instead, they were thrown into conflict, saving the people who were dying in front of them and struggling to come to terms with the discovery that these people, the humans who were on the planet even though the common knowledge was that there had been no humans on Uoria until they started to arrive in the compound at the invitation of the Denynso decades after this settlement was established, were actually the survivors of a long-lost mission from Earth that had been sabotaged by a species that Ivy hadn't even heard of until then.

The true feelings of disgust and fury toward the Denynso leader, however, had built after she had met Maxim and they discovered through a horrible reaction of his skin that the Mikana, a group of ethereally beautiful men who had come from a kingdom that once had friendly relations with the settlement, were in fact the creatures that had turned into the Klimnu. Finding out that the beings that they thought that they had eradicated in their final painful battle in fact still existed, if even in their whole and beautiful form, enraged Pyra, and Ivy watched him dissolve from the strong, rational leader he was supposed to be to one so overcome with hatred and fear that he took all of the Mikana, including Maxim, hostage and threatened to kill them all to prevent them from ever having the opportunity to become the gruesome enemies that had caused them so much hurt and left them in even greater terror. However, the Denynso would never admit that it was fear that was influencing them.

Everyone seemed to have overcome this turmoil as soon as they had brought Maxim and the Mikana leader Rey to Creia and the focus turned from Pyra's violence and aggression to his admitting his wrongdoing in the wake of the shock of Creia admitting he hadn't told everyone the full truth of the origins of the Denynso, and Rey stepping forward to help Eden give birth to her son. Ivy had not been so quick to forgive. She wanted to. She wanted to be able to put it all behind her and move forward with the others, but when she looked at Pyra she still saw the man who tried to kill the man she loved, and who had been so quick to sacrifice an entire species just for the transgressions of some of their ancestors. It just wasn't in her to let go of the horror and the anger that it caused, even when Pyra sank to his knees in front of his father and king to ask for forgiveness, and even when she saw the tears in his eyes and knew that he truly was feeling regret at the way that he had behaved. She knew that he felt remorse, but it wasn't enough for her. She still didn't feel like she could trust him completely.

2

Ivy felt Maxim's hand cover hers and their fingers intertwine. She took her eyes away from Pyra and brought them to Maxim's beautiful face, but noticed that his eyes seemed etched with something slightly dark and troubled. Concern constricted her belly and she immediately felt herself become defensive again. She tightened her grip on his hand and turned her body slightly so that it faced him more than the table in front of her.

"Maxim?" she said, searching his eyes for some explanation of the expression. "What is it? Is everything alright?"

"I need to talk to you about something," he said and the sound of his voice reflected the strain on his face.

"What's wrong?"

"Rey and some of the others are leaving in the morning to go back to the settlement to free the rest of the Mikana and tell them about our new alliance with the Denynso."

"I know," Ivy said. "I'm sorry that the shuttle to go to Earth is going to be arriving too soon for you to be able to go to the settlement."

Maxim nodded slightly.

"That's just the thing," he said. "I want to go to the settlement."

Ivy shook her head at him, her eyes narrowing slightly.

"What do you mean you want to go? The university is sending their fastest shuttle. There's no way that you would be able to get to the settlement and back here in time in order to catch it."

"I know. It's just that I really feel like I should be there. I feel that it is my responsibility to be with my people and see this through. I was in there with them, remember."

"Yes, I know," Ivy said, her grip on his hand faltering somewhat, "and I'm the one that came and got you out of it so that we could run away."

"But we didn't get away, Ivy. We came back and because we came back we were able to help these two species come together. I want to be there when the rest of the group is freed from the meeting hall. I want to be a part of the rebuilding."

"What about all of the plans that we had?" Ivy asked. "What about Samira and Ty's wedding?"

"You aren't even in the wedding," Maxim said. "You barely know them."

"That's not the point," Ivy said.

She knew that her voice was rising and Maxim looked around at the other tables to see if anyone was listening in.

"Can we go outside?" he asked.

Ivy dropped his hand to the table and stood, stepping backwards over the bench so that she could walk out of the banquet hall and down the front steps of the main building into the clearing at the center of the Denynso compound. It felt strange to step out into the night and look around to see no one around them. From the time that she arrived on the compound it had been made clear to her that she was not to move about the compound without the guard and protector who Creia had assigned to her, and though she had spent time on her own and with Maxim once they arrived at the settlement, she had not been without Zsilvia in the time that she had spent at the compound.

"You told me that you understood why I want to get back to Earth. You said that you wanted to go with me."

"I do want to go with you, Ivy."

Ivy took off at a fast, long stride across the clearing, heading toward the small row of houses where she had settled after first arriving.

"Apparently you don't."

"Are you allowed to go back to your house without telling anyone?" Maxim asked, the sound of his voice only slightly teasing. "Don't you still have to tell Zsilvia or at least George that you're going somewhere?"

"I am tired of telling anyone where I'm going or not being able to go where I want to go and do what I want to do," she said, whirling around to face him. "That's exactly why I am so ready to get off of this planet and back home. I don't have to have a guard and protector there. I move about how I please and no one tells me what to do."

"I'm sure that they will not force you to keep with a guard and protector for much longer. The others do not have them."

"The others are mated to their guards. They don't need them anymore because they are locked into them for life. I don't belong here, Maxim."

"What do you mean?"

"I am not part of them. I am not Denynso, and I am not the mate of one of the warriors or other men like the other human women are. Even George came here and bonded to Zsilvia. I'm an outsider."

"Because you fell in love with me?" Maxim asked, turning away and taking a few steps away from where Ivy stood.

"No." Ivy regretted saying the words as soon as she heard them come out of her mouth and saw the hurt on Maxim's face. "I am just not one of them. Uoria, from what I've seen of it, is beautiful and there are wonderful things to learn, but I wasn't ready for all of this. There has just been too much war and confusion for me."

"That's exactly why I have to get back to the settlement and then back to the kingdom," Maxim told her.

"What do you mean?"

"I'm tired of being confused. I'm tired of not knowing what is happening, even in my own family. I need to get to my brother and talk to him about our father. He might remember things that I don't that might be able to help me figure out the Order and what they have to do with the Klimnu."

"You don't even know who's in it or who controls it. Why does it matter what they knew?"

"My father died because of the Order and it had something to do with the Klimnu. My mother has never been the same since then. I need to know what happened to him and what the Order has been doing." Maxim suddenly turned to Ivy and took both of her hands in his, pulling her closer to him and staring into her eyes. "My mother told me, told us, that if we were going to have a life we had to stand up for ourselves and we had to finish what we started. I have to go back, Ivy. I have to finish this. I want to be with you. Please believe me. I love you like I never knew that love existed and I do not want to spend a moment of my life without that love, but I have to do this. I won't be able to move forward with our life until I get the answers to my questions and I am truly able to put all of this behind me."

Ivy felt herself melting at his words. As much as she wanted to go home, she knew that Maxim was absolutely right. With everything that they had found out about the Order and their involvement with the Klimnu only came more questions. Creia's revelations about another Denynso compound that had existed right on the other side of the rock ledges along the edge of the current compound had only brought up more confusion and more gaps in their information. She knew that she couldn't ask him to put all of that aside just so that he could go to Earth with her. He needed to resolve those areas of his life so that he could put them behind him and move ahead with her.

"Alright," she said, returning the tightness of his grasp on her hands. "We don't have to wait here for the shuttle and go back to Earth with the others. We'll join Rey and go back to the settlement."

"We?" Maxim asked, some of the familiar sparkle returning to his eyes.

Ivy nodded.

"You don't think that I would let you go through this without me, do you?" she asked. Ivy leaned forward and touched her lips to his softly. "If it wasn't for how much I love you, you never would have come into contact with those flowers and no one would have found out about the Mikana and the Klimnu. I suppose that makes us largely responsible for this mess."

Maxim laughed and returned her kiss. In that kiss she could still taste the new and exciting warmth of him that she had indulged in with such pleasure and intensity when they made love in the flowers outside of the Nyx 23 settlement. It was the reaction of his skin with those flowers, just as it had been with the rogue Mikana who had split off from the rest of the kingdom so many years before, that had shown the evolution from the Mikana to the Klimnu and that had started the storm of backlash from the Denynso warriors.

"I suppose we are," he said, and then the darkness returned, "but they would have found out. Eventually the Order would have made it known, I just don't know how."

"It doesn't matter if you know how now," Ivy said. "We will figure it out together. Come on," she said with a sigh of resignation, "we should probably go tell Creia about our plans. I wouldn't want to cause another problem doing something impulsive."

Ivy saw a mischievous flicker in Maxim's eyes and felt him drop one of her hands so that he held her fingertips. He started backing toward the houses, guiding her with a gentle pull on her fingers.

"Do you think that they are going to notice that you're gone?" he asked.

"I don't think so."

"Not even Zsilvia?"

"She and George are pretty wrapped up in each other right now."

"Good."

Maxim gave a hint of a smile, bit into his bottom lip, and turned so that he walked forward toward the houses, still pulling her gently along behind him. They walked in silence until they got to her house and he led her inside.

"What are you doing?" Ivy asked as they stepped inside and Maxim turned to press her back against the door.

He leaned forward and pressed his body to hers, covering her with himself so that she felt the pressure of his entire body touching hers and the insistence of a hardening erection nudging into her belly. His mouth crushed down on hers, drawing her tongue in against his. He kissed her until she was breathless and then pulled his mouth far enough way that he could speak but so she could still feel his lips brush against hers as he spoke.

"I'm being spontaneous. If you are going to get into trouble for spontaneity, it might as well be worth it."

Ivy smiled into the kiss that returned to her mouth and wrapped her arms around Maxim's neck as his hands came to her hips and pulled her up against him so that the pressure of his erection was even stronger in her belly. The feeling made her mouth water and she felt her body responding to him, aching for him. They hadn't had the opportunity to be alone nearly enough in the last few days for her and now that nearly everyone else in the compound was at the meeting hall, she felt like she could barely control herself. She needed him like she could never have imagined needing anyone.

Her hands dug into Maxim's back and she felt him press her back so that their bodies parted. He was shaking his head and Ivy looked at him quizzically.

"What?" she asked.

"Slow," he whispered and eased her arms away from his neck.

"Why?" she asked.

"Slow," he repeated.

Maxim's mouth touched the side of her neck and made its way down to the curve of her shoulder. As he kissed along her skin, his fingers moved to the row of buttons along the front of her shirt. He moved with torturously slow precision, opening the buttons gradually from the hem up so that he revealed the trembling skin of her belly first, then her ribs, and finally her breasts. His breath brushed along the swells of her breasts above the low-cut lace cups of her bra and she felt her skin tingle at the sensation. Maxim brought his mouth further down and followed the trail of his breath with her lips. Occasionally his tongue slipped out to glaze along her skin. The touch was bringing her desire for him to a fevered pitch, but he continued his patient, exacting exploration of her as he carefully pulled her just far enough away from the door to ease her shirt off of her shoulders and down her arms.

Ivy wrapped her fingers around the bottom of his shirt and pulled it up, forgoing the ties at the front and tossing it aside as quickly as she could so that she could access the warm, smooth skin beneath. He stood still long enough to allow her to lean forward and touch a series of kisses along the center of his chest. She could feel his heartbeat beneath her lips and could smell his intoxicating scent on his skin. After a moment Maxim took her by her upper arms and led her back against the door again. His hands smoothed around her ribcage until they reached the hooks of her bra and could unlatch it. He drew in a breath as he peeled the lace away from her body, revealing her desire-swollen breasts and darkened, taut nipples.

Maxim lowered himself to his knees and Ivy buried her fingers in his hair as he covered one breast with his mouth. One hand came up to cradle the swell as his tongue flicked over her nipple, encircling it and sucking tenderly as his other hand ran down the center of her belly to release the button on the front of her pants and ease down the zipper. Ivy stepped out of her shoes and lifted her hips away from the door so that Maxim could undress her further. She had forgone wearing anything under the pants when she got dressed that morning and Maxim made a sound of appreciation when she was finally bare in front of him.

She groaned when she felt his mouth move to the other

breast and repeat the same attention that he had given the first, and then start his slow progression down the center of her belly. The tip of his tongue dipped into her navel and she whimpered as a new wave of intense desire shot through her body and settled between her legs. She could feel herself getting wet and warm, preparing for him as he continued his kisses down her body.

Finally his mouth reached the apex of her thighs and Ivy felt Maxim's tongue delve through her folds in a long, slow lick that nearly brought her to her knees. The strands of his hair felt soft and thick in her fingers as she tightened her grip and held his head steady, desperate for more of the dizzying feeling. His hands moved to her hips so that he could hold her as he continued to coax her with the tip of his tongue. After a few moments he moved one hand down so that it tucked behind Ivy's knee and urged it away, parting her thighs and giving himself easier access to her. Maxim's tongue slid deeper and Ivy cried out at the intense feeling, her hips lifting off of the door to meet his mouth. He responded by cupping her butt in his hands so that he could tilt her pelvis forward toward him, allowing him even greater ability to explore her core.

Suddenly Maxim's tongue delved inside her, eliciting a scream. Rather than relenting, Maxim continued, swirling his tongue within her as he brought one of his hands forward so that he could massage the hypersensitive pearl of flesh at her peak. Ivy's head fell back against the door and she closed her eyes, surrendering herself to the incredible feelings Maxim was creating within her. His tongue eased out of her body and moved up so that the tip mimicked how his thumb had touched. She heard the sound of him easing out of his pants and the sound only worked to make her need for him greater.

His masterful worship of her body was bringing her close to the edge at incredible speed and Ivy could hear her own sounds pouring out of her as her hips rolled involuntarily against his mouth. She could feel how attuned he was to her body, adjusting and changing his touch in the slightest ways but so that she felt herself rapidly losing control. Just at the moment when she could feel herself spiraling into oblivion, Maxim bounded to his feet, swept one of her legs up to his hip, and sank inside of her. As soon as his body entered hers, Ivy felt her walls contract around him and she let out a strangled cry as her orgasm washed over her, pulling him deeply within her as he rolled his hips in long strokes to meet each of the waves that pulsed through her.

She was starting to come down from her climax when Maxim lifted her higher and tucked her against him so that she could wrap her legs around his hips. He turned and carried her into the living room, carefully laying her down on the sofa. She gazed up at him, savoring the feeling of him so hard and deep inside of her. Ivy released her legs, allowing one to drape over the back of the sofa and the other to hang over the side so that her toes touched the floor. The position opened her to Maxim fully and she could see the intensity of his desire for her flare in his eyes.

Maxim moved his body up so that he hovered over her, allowing Ivy to gaze into his eyes as he drove deeper into her. The muscles on his arms on either side of her bulged and strained against his skin as he rocked against her, groaning with each intense thrust. Ivy brought her hands to his back, allowing them to glide over skin slick with sweat as she savored the feeling of his muscles tightening and shifting beneath. As Maxim's thrusts became more insistent, his pace quickening and intensifying along with the sounds that came from deep in his throat, Ivy could feel herself moving closer and closer to another climax. She lifted her hips toward him, adjusting the angle just enough that he touched her back wall with every stroke and created a sensation that hummed through her body. Suddenly he gave one hard push and held himself as deep within her as he could get, tossing his head back and roaring as Ivy felt his hard cock throb.

The sensation of him filling her sent her toppling over the edge into her own orgasm and she felt her body squeeze down on him, milking him until they both collapsed into each other's arms, their ragged breath rising around them and their bodies seeming to meld together into one existence. Ivy had never experienced this level of closeness to anyone; the sense that their very souls were connected as much as their bodies were, and that Maxim was now completely, inextricably a part of her.

Ivy felt Maxim kissing along the curve of her neck as he rested his head on her, his body pressing down onto hers so that she felt fully enveloped in him. She wrapped her arms around him and sighed, touching a kiss to his shoulder before letting her eyes drift close and the feeling of him take her away. The rest of the compound was just going to have to miss them for a little while.

3

"Are you alright?" Lynx asked, coming to sit beside Rain at the table where she was completely alone.

Rain looked up at him as if coming out of a deep thought and then at the empty places around the table like it startled her to realize that no one else was sitting at the table. He wondered how long she had been sitting there by herself and felt a hint of worry. His mate had seemed to be struggling slightly since they left the settlement, and he felt like she was holding something back from him that she didn't want to talk about, as if she was still processing through it so carefully in her own mind that she didn't feel like she could put the proper words to it, even to him. He touched her back with one hand and felt her relax into the touch. Even though it had been a few weeks since they were able to wake her from the locked state that the Covra had put her and the rest of the Nyx 23 settlement into using a recording of Samira's voice, he still felt privileged and relieved each time he saw her move or heard her voice.

It had seemed like an eternity for him while he was

waiting for her to wake up. From the moment that he first discovered her, lying in the bed where she had gone to sleep for a nap one evening and was attacked by the Covra, he had known that this beautiful woman was intended to be his mate. Though he didn't understand it, he simply knew that Rain was meant to be his, and that no matter what it took he had to either figure out a way to free her from the locked state, or live throughout the rest of his life alone and longing for her, knowing that he was never going to feel the love and connection of a mate with anyone else. The wait had been excruciating as he visited her day after day, sleeping beside her in bed though she never moved, and talking to her constantly though she never spoke, and he didn't even know if she ever would. What had been even more excruciating than wondering if they would ever find a way to overcome the locking of the Covra and bring her back into conscious existence, was wondering if she would ever be able to understand his feelings for her and return them.

He understood that she was from a different time, that she may be frightened and confused when she woke up and not be able to comprehend what had happened to her, or life in a time one hundred years after she tucked herself beneath her flowered blanket and closed her eyes, but he had to try. He couldn't deny then what he was feeling for her and the sense of duty and responsibility to protect her even as they discovered that the people of the settlement were being used by the Covra as incubators for their next generation. Lynx had been there at that moment, he had been one of the first things that she had seen when finally freed from the bonds that the Covra had put her in and held her captive for decades before Lynx was even born. He would never forget how he felt in that moment, hanging in it like her breath had crystallized around him and was holding him still while she gazed at him, evaluating him, trying to understand what had happened and who he was.

Even more he would never forget what it was like when she told him that even though she couldn't open her eyes or respond to him, that she had been able to hear him talking to her, and that the sound of his words had been an incredible comfort to her. They had soon discovered that the reason she was able to hear him but not wake up fully was that the only thing that would break the locking was listening to one of her own kind speaking. The voices of the Denynso were close enough that it started to draw her out of the frozen state, but it could not bring her fully back into consciousness. It was not until she had heard Zuri's voice through the compact as Bannack communicated with Loralia and the others that she had begun to show any signs of life. It had been Zsilvia who had suggested that they use the recording of Samira's voice that she had given her mate Ty before the men left the compound. They played the recording continuously for hours, and soon the words drew her out of her lock, she breathed, and the blood started to flow through her veins once again.

Lynx knew in his mind that the toxins that the Covra used to lock the people of the settlement into place were gone and that she would never fall back into that frozen state again, but the fear always lingered in his heart that one day he would wake up and she would be gone again, lost into the years that had been swallowed by the Covra and beyond his reach. He was reminded of it each time he saw her sleep, and reminded of the cruel use that the Covra had of the people each time she removed her clothing. The scar from where Ciyrs had had to cut into her body to remove the eggs stood out gruesomely against the paleness of her stomach, a vicious reminder of the mere moments that had once separated her from a death more horrible than Lynx could have fathomed.

Despite the horror that that scar held, Lynx never shied away from it. He didn't allow it to have control over his thoughts or power over his adoration of her. When he saw it, he made a point to touch it. He ran his fingers along it as he made love to her and kissed it softly when she lay sleeping beside him. He hoped that in some way the tenderness of his skin against it would heal it more quickly and take away the darkness that the slightly raised ridge still seemed to hold.

Now as she returned staring at the table, seemingly engrossed in the pattern of the woodgrain, the intense fear and dread that had defined him in the days before she awoke threatened to settle over him again.

"What is it?" Lynx asked, touching her back again.

Rain returned her gaze to him and sighed.

"I don't know if I can do this, Lynx," she said softly.

Feeling alarmed both at her tone and her choice of words, Lynx slid slightly closer to her on the wooden bench and rested his arm around her waist. He was relieved when she leaned into him and briefly touched her forehead to his.

"What don't you think that you can do?" he asked.

"Go back to Earth."

Relief flooded over him, but was then replaced by confusion.

"I thought you wanted to go back to see it again."

"I know," Rain said, running her hands back through her hair. "And I thought that I did. When I first heard that a shuttle would be coming to bring some of the Denynso and the women to Earth, I was so excited. I thought that it was the perfect chance for me to finally get home and finish the mission that I started so long ago. I had this vision of me returning triumphant and getting to tell the story of what happened so that the world could finally know and I could get back to the life that I left behind."

Lynx felt his heart constrict painfully at those words. He knew what she was saying, but it sounded so painfully like she wanted to just forget everything that had happened since she arrived on the planet that he was terrified she was saying that she didn't care if that meant him as well.

"Of course," he managed, replying just so that she would know that he was listening to her.

"But then I really started thinking about it." Rain turned to him so that she straddled the bench facing him and opened her hands toward him as if showing him something that wasn't really there. "I started thinking about everything that the people of Earth now think of us and what it would do when they do find out what happened. It will change everything, Lynx. Everything. It will change the course of Earth's understanding of history, it will create animosity for a species that the people of Earth don't even know exist as far as I know, and it will make it so that more scientists and explorers and treasure hunters will want to come here. It will ravage Uoria and whatever is left of Penthos. I don't think that I can be a part of that."

"Maybe it won't be like that," Lynx offered, trying to comfort her. "I'm sure that it will be a surprise to them and that they will want to know more about what happened, but maybe it won't be so awful. You'll just have to be careful with how you tell it and make sure that you do everything that you can to protect the team as well as the planet."

"That's the thing, though, Lynx. It's not just my story to tell. There were dozens of people on that team. Now there are marriages and children, families that only exist because of what happened to us. There are people who really did die when the ship crashed, and even more who died in the conflict with the Covra and then in the hatching. Those lives matter. Even if they weren't lost in the way that the people on Earth think that they were lost, those people are still gone and their lives, their memories, matter. What we were able to build in the settlement matters. That was our world, Lynx. For fifteen years after we crashed, that was the comfortable, peaceful home that we created for ourselves, and now we're just thinking about abandoning it like it never existed. We're just going to leave behind our homes, our belongings. We're going to leave the bodies of the ones who died just buried alone out in the middle of the planet where no one goes."

"Not everyone is leaving, Rain. There were plenty of people in the settlement who didn't even want to come here much less go back to Earth. They want to stay."

"I think I do, too."

"Are you sure?"

"Yes. Earth was my home, but I have been here far longer than I was there, even if I don't remember most of it, and my loyalty has to lie with what we built here. I can't just abandon it. I can't pretend that those years didn't happen, and I can't pretend that showing back up on Earth is going to make it go away or that it is going to put things back to the way that they were before we left. That life that I left behind..." she sighed, looking down at the bench for a moment before lifting her eyes back to his, "that life is over. It will never be the same. It's behind me now and I will never be able to live that life again." She paused and reached up to cup Lynx's face with one delicate hand. "I wouldn't want to even if I could."

Lynx covered her hand with his, turning to press a kiss into her palm.

"Are you sure?"

"Yes. I love you, Lynx. I've loved you since before I had even seen you, and I will love you always. There is nothing that is waiting for me on Earth that could even begin to compare with what I have right here with you. I would love to have you live with me in the settlement, but even if we split our time between there and here at the compound, I will be happy as long as we're together."

"All I want is to be with you," Lynx said, leaning forward to rest her forehead against hers.

"It's also important to me to be there when they free the rest of the Mikana. It wasn't quite the same, but we were held captive by the Covra and our conflict with them for so long. We were sabotaged and threatened by the Valdicians and tormented by the Covra. We know what it's like to be taken over and to have no power, and I want to do for them what you and the rest of the Denynso did for us."

Lynx felt guilt wash over him.

"Even though it was the Denynso who are holding them captive?" he asked carefully.

Rain looked at him softly, the expression in her eyes telling him that she didn't hold any anger or judgment for him or for the rest of his kind despite everything that Pyra and some of the others had done.

"I will say the same thing now that Zuri said in the settlement about the Mikana and the Klimnu. Everyone has the potential for darkness." Lynx tried to look away but Rain turned his face back to hers insistently. "Everyone, Lynx. It wasn't the right way to go about it, but Pyra was doing what he thought was right for his kind. The way he went about it was completely wrong, but that's what makes situations like this so difficult. Sometimes it is hard to tell where what is right to one person ends and what is wrong to another person begins, or if, in truth, they are the same thing. What the Covra did was right and the way of perpetuating and protecting their kind in their eyes. That doesn't make it right and that doesn't mean that the suffering that they caused us wasn't real or should be forgotten, but it does give me more empathy than others might have."

"I don't understand."

"I went to Penthos with the rest of the Nyx 23 team because I knew in my heart that there was something going on on that planet that I believed was wrong and I felt like it was my responsibility to find out about it and end it. Ever since I found out that the military units went to the planet after they thought we disappeared and eradicated the Valdicians, though, I've been thinking about why they were doing what they were doing. We never found that out. We never even knew who the prisoners were, just that they were being held in an illegal prison camp. What we were fighting so hard against because we felt it was wrong, was something that was completely right to them, and what we did was wrong."

"So you don't think that the Valdicians should have been punished or that the Covra should have been killed?"

"No," Rain said, shaking her head, "that's not what I'm saying. All we have in this world is what we think is right, what we believe, and all we can do is live our lives the way that we think is right, knowing that along the way we are going to encounter others who see everything from their own perspective and think that what we are absolutely convinced is the right thing is actually the worst that could happen, and trying to see both sides."

"How could you be so generous?" Lynx asked.

It truly astonished him that this woman who had witnessed the brutality of a species holding another prisoner in horrific conditions, had her ship sabotaged and sent to a planet that she didn't know even existed, lost people she cared about in the crash, and had to rebuild her life thinking that she would never return to the country she knew and the people she loved, only to be taken over by a vicious species who inflicted pain by compelling the men to fight against one another and then left them for dead as the incubators and first meals of their children, could be so understanding. He would have thought that she would have been filled with hatred and wanted to seek revenge against every species that had hurt her, but she was looking at him with sincerity in her eyes that showed that even after everything she had gone through, even after she herself had been forced to fight and kill, she was willing to admit that there might be more to even the worst of creatures.

"I'm not being generous, Lynx. I don't like what happened to me. I don't feel love and kindness toward the Valdicians or the Covra, but I don't think that Pyra and the Denynso are comparable to them. The Mikana might argue with me about that, but that is what I want to help avoid. I don't want there to be another war. I want what we were trying to accomplish before we saw the reaction on Maxim's skin and everyone realized that the Mikana became the Klimnu. I want this planet, the planet that I have devoted the majority of my life to and the planet that I now consider my home, to finally come together."

"That's a beautiful thought."

"I don't mean it to be beautiful."

Lynx was taken aback by the sudden harshness in Rain's voice.

"What?"

"I don't mean it to be beautiful. Yes, it would be wonderful it all of the species who live on Uoria could come together and cooperate, that the species could love each other freely and not have to worry about what anyone thinks." At that, Rain took Lynx's hands in hers and he intertwined their fingers, holding her hands tightly as he thought of the negativity that the couples had faced as the different species came together. "But the truth is the conflicts aren't over. The Denynso thought that the Klimnu were gone, completely eliminated from the planet, didn't they?"

"Yes, but we didn't know about the Mikana. We didn't know anything about what they were before they were Klimnu except for what Leia was able to tell us from her time in the prison."

"That's my point, though, Lynx. You didn't know. You believed that the threat was gone, so when you found out that it might still be there, even if it was in a form that wasn't truly threatening at all, it created absolute panic. What if that's the same for the Covra or the Valdicians? I don't think that Uoria is safe."

"Then why do you want to stay?"

"Because I believe if we all came together and stopped letting misunderstandings and fear get in our way, that Uoria could be safe. We could protect it and ensure that it stays protected. There is more to this galaxy than Earth and Uoria, and we have to be ready for that. Besides, would you want to live on Earth?"

Lynx thought about the question for a moment. He had never considered living anywhere but on the Denynso compound. It had never even crossed his mind as a possibility.

"No."

"Exactly. This is your home. This is our home. I may want to visit Earth again someday just to see it and see how it's changed since we left, but for now I just want to go back to the settlement and finish this so we can move on."

"Alright," Lynx said, leaning forward to kiss her forehead. "If that's what you want, we'll go talk to Creia and tell him that we are joining the group going back to the settlement rather than going with the others."

"And you're ok with this?" she asked. "You don't want to go to Earth?"

"Like you said, we'll go there someday to visit. We don't need to go now. We're needed here."

4

Creia sat on the platform overlooking the banquet hall, his eyes moving from face to face as he watched the warriors, their mates, the humans, and the Mikana interacting. His children were among those faces, the most powerful and impressive of the warriors and those who had been destined from birth to lead just as he had. Up until now he had never thought about which of them would take his position when he was no longer king, or even if it would be one of his children. Though the original Denynso had passed the monarchy through birth, that had changed when the group divided and the current clan established themselves in this compound.

Rather than knowing who would ascend to the position of king after the end of the reign of the current king simply by birthright, it became a matter of earning that role. The man who would take over had to prove himself and demonstrate without realizing what he was doing that he was the only one within the clan who could rightfully rule. It was a tremendous feat and one that Creia simply assumed would occur without issue. Now in the wake of everything that had happened after the warriors and other men had left the compound for the first time to explore the planet, he wasn't as sure. He found himself worrying about when the time would come for the new king to step into his role and how that future king would prove himself. For the first time since he took over when he was even younger than his sons, he wondered if he had truly proven himself and if he had really been ruling the clan in the way that was truly best for them.

"Sir?"

Creia heard a voice speaking up at him from the foot of the platform. He recognized it as that of Maxim, the young Mikana man who had been the start of Pyra's rage about the Klimnu when he came into contact with the flowers that caused the same reaction that had begun on the Klimnu so many years before. He looked down and saw Maxim standing beside Ivy, his hand lightly holding hers between them as they gazed up at him. Looking down at him like that Creia could clearly remember the faces of the men who had come to him for help when they were going through their own horrific transformations. He could still see how their beauty was being ravaged by the quickly spreading reaction that left skin that was once smooth and soft pale, slimy, and sickly looking. He heard their voices reverberating through his mind, asking him to cure them.

He remembered the thoughts that had burned through his mind as he looked at them. They had already caused pain and heartache, and he had heard the plans they were making to take over the planet. He knew that the plan included his own compound. He didn't think that his clan would be safe if he healed them and allowed them to continue going about their lives after returning from the desolate planet that they had already all but destroyed. In those moments, he made the only decision that he thought he could. He told them that he would only heal them if they left Uoria and promised never to return.

He knew now that in that decision he had put himself, his children, and all of the Denynso, in incredible danger. Looking at Maxim, however, he knew that he had done what was right. Healing their skin wouldn't have changed what the Klimnu were. He could see the difference in Maxim's eyes. There was life and energy there that wasn't in the cold black eyes of the Klimnu. It was a difference that could seem so subtle but that meant everything.

"Yes, Maxim?" Creia said, stepping closer to the edge of the platform so that he could lean down to talk to the young man.

"Ivy and I have decided that we don't want to go to Earth on the shuttle when it comes."

"Oh?"

"We want to go back to the settlement so that I can be there to release my brother and the rest of our kind."

"Sir?"

Before Creia was able to answer Maxim, he heard Lynx. The warrior approached with the woman who he had released from the lock of the Covra and who he had taken as his mate.

"Yes, Lynx?"

"I'm sorry to interrupt, but I overheard Maxim saying that he wants to return to the settlement rather than joining the others going to Earth."

"Yes, that's what he was just telling me, and I –"

"We'd like to go, too."

Lynx cut him off and Creia closed his mouth slowly. He evaluated both of the men, searching their sincere, earnest faces and the way that they stood confidently in front of him.

"You want to join the group going back to the settlement to release the members of the Mikana kingdom?" Creia said, carefully repeating the sentiment that Maxim had expressed to ensure that Lynx really understood what he was volunteering himself for.

"Yes. I think that I could offer more being here than going to Earth right now."

Creia nodded. He looked from Lynx to Maxim, and then to Rain.

"And you?" he asked.

Rain nodded and Creia found himself caught by the strangeness of her lovely eyes, coppery hair, and smooth, unaged skin. It was somewhat unnerving to look at someone who he appeared so much younger than he was, only to remind himself that she had been alive, if not suspended for much of the time, for more than a century.

"I know that I come from Earth originally, but I have come to think of Uoria as my home and I don't want to leave it. I want to go back to the settlement and work on rebuilding it now that the threat of the Covra is over."

"And you, Ivy?" Creia asked.

Though his first impression of the young, willowy girl had not been positive, he had grown to admire her strength and fortitude. When faced with challenges and demands that would have sent many people running back to him and begging for the first shuttle off of the planet, she had confronted them fully and been an integral part of the resolutions. Even though he knew that she hadn't become a part of them like the other women had and was not comfortable on the compound, he felt a level of respect for her and wanted to ensure that she was making a decision that she felt comfortable with.

"Yes, sir," she responded. "It is important to Maxim that

he be there now and my place is with him. I'll stay here for as long as he needs to."

Creia gave a single nod, accepting the selfless gesture.

"I will allow all of you to join the group returning to the settlement. If you change your minds and want to go to Earth to join the others," he took a breath, "or to stay, I will make the arrangements for you."

"Thank you," Maxim and Lynx said together.

The two women smiled and nodded at him, reaching out to take their mates and guide them away from the platform. Creia had a strange feeling as he watched them walk away, Maxim and Ivy walked toward the table where the others who would be departing the next morning for the settlement sat, discussing their plans, and Rain and Lynx toward the main door to the building, likely heading back to Lynx's house to begin preparing themselves.

"You're worried about them, aren't you?" Theia asked, coming to his side and wrapping one hand around his arm.

Creia turned to his mate and accepted the kiss that she offered him. He nodded, turning his gaze back to the room.

"They're fighting my fight," he said.

"What fight is that, Creia?"

"They are trying to protect the planet."

"Is that your fight?"

"Hasn't it always been?"

"I don't know, Creia. I've never known."

Theia touched a kiss to the side of her mate's neck and walked away. Creia replayed her words in his mind. His mate had always been able to read exactly how he was feeling, but rarely would she tell him what she thought. Instead she would turn the situation around so that he was forced to truly think about it himself and interpret what he was thinking and feeling. While this often helped him to go deeper into what was happening and figure things out from a perspective that he might not have had otherwise, at that moment it only worked to make him more uncomfortable. He didn't want to delve any further into what he was feeling or the memories that these feelings were dredging up. The last few days since the group arrived back from the settlement had been difficult enough and forced him to confront issues that he thought would remain buried forever. He didn't know if he was ready to have to deal with even more.

5

"I promise you, you're going to be fine."

Samira reached out and patted Johnathan's hand, trying to offer the aging man comfort. He looked at her with pale grey eyes and gave a slightly weak smile. She was sitting at one of the long tables in the banquet hall with several of the people who were planning on heading to Earth on the shuttle that was scheduled to arrive in just a few days. Most of her thoughts were on her wedding and the excitement of finally having that experience with Ty, but she was also feeling concern for the members of the Nyx 23 group who had decided that it was time that they return to Earth. Only a few of the Nyx 23 group had come to the decision that they would return to Earth and try to start their lives again. Even though there was a sense of great excitement about their long-awaited trip back home, there was also a sense of worry and nervousness.

"How different is it going to be?" Johnathan asked.

Samira tried to come up with an answer. The idea of being gone from the planet for more than one hundred years and then returning was something that she couldn't even begin to fathom. The truth was that she had been on Uoria for only a matter of months and she was already concerned that Earth would be different when she returned, or that she wouldn't remember how to go about her life not living on the compound with the Denynso. She couldn't imagine what these people were going through wondering if they would ever be able to fit back in on the planet that they had left behind anticipating only being gone for a few weeks and instead crashing on an unknown planet and having to recreate their lives there. The thought was frightening, but she didn't want to let that on. They were already unnerved enough and she didn't feel like she needed to make it even worse for them.

"I can't really answer that," Samira said truthfully. "I only know what your time there was like from books and movies. I can tell you that it is most certainly different, and that you will have to get used to it. With all of the attention that you are going to get just from coming back to the planet alive after all of this time, though, you will definitely not be alone. Everyone will be there to help you figure everything out."

"What if we don't want the attention?" Brandy, a woman sitting near the end of the table asked.

Samira looked at her and felt a pang of compassion for her and for the others. She could see the nervousness in Brandy's eyes, but could also hear the defensiveness in her voice. In their excitement to discover that the team that they had been taught throughout their entire schooling had disappeared during their most dangerous mission had actually survived, Samira and the other women had just assumed that the Nyx 23 team would be looking forward to getting back to Earth and telling their story. It hadn't occurred to her that they might be reluctant to share what had happened to them, and that they might not be ready for the world to know everything that they had gone through, or to handle all of the attention that would come with their return.

"Then you don't have to have it," Samira told her. "No one is going to force you to tell anyone what happened or even to tell anybody who you are. You can just go back to Earth and settle in, and then after a while when you think that you might be ready, then you can tell them. You are going back home for yourselves, not for anyone else, and you don't have to do or say or live up to anything."

She could see the relief in Brandy's eyes as the woman looked at her for a few beats and then turned to exchange glances with the other people from her team sitting around the table. They leaned in close to each other and she heard them starting to whisper about the situation, discussing amongst themselves how they wanted to handle telling people who they were and what they would say about what had happened to them.

Samira felt a touch on her back and looked up to see Ty standing beside her. She smiled at him and took the hand that he offered to her. The group at the table was exploring the idea of going back and not saying anything to anyone until they were able to really talk to the rest of the crew and create a united front when Samira stood, stepped over the wooden bench, and let Ty lead her out of the meeting hall.

The evening was deepening into night as they walked across the empty center of the compound and toward Ty's shop. She remembered the brief time that she had spent in the small visitor house chosen for her by Creia after Zuri had contacted him to let him know that she was going to come back to Uoria with her. Though she had originally

thought that she would be in that visitor house for the dura-
tion of her time on the planet, she had in fact only spent a
few days there before she realized how deeply in love with
Ty she was and convinced the tremendous man to admit
that he loved her just as much. Though he had been reluctant because of her age, once Ty relented to the feelings that
he had for her, his passion and devotion were unlike
anything Samira had ever known existed.

They stepped into Ty's shop and she took a deep breath
of the lingering smell of fresh bread that hung in the air.
Despite his massive size, incredible strength, and rare and
special ability to move things with his mind that was
completely unique to him among the Denynso, Ty was not
truly a warrior. Just as the warriors were born to fulfill the
duty of fighting to defend the compound and their kind, Ty
was born with the purpose of being the nurturer of the clan.
His role in the clan was to prepare food and take care of the
warriors when they returned from battle injured. Ciyrs did
the actual healing, but Ty was the one who would make sure
that they had the care and support they needed to get better.

Ty guided her through the shop and into the attached
house that they had shared since they completed their
bond. They walked through the darkness and up the tall
flight of steps that led from the main room of the house up
to the long hallway that featured their bedroom and bathroom. Once they were in the bedroom, he turned her
around and started undressing her. He still hadn't said a
word to her, but she gave herself over to him completely,
allowing him to quickly remove her shirt and then untie the
knot at her hip that held her skirt in place as she stepped
out of her shoes. She released her bra and dropped it to the
side as Ty slid her panties off of her hips and down her legs.

As soon as they were off, Samira sank down to her knees

and went to work releasing the laces on Ty's pants while he removed his shirt. Wrapping her hand around his already surging erection, Samira took him into her mouth and luxuriated in the deep groan the stroke of her tongue drew from his throat. His hand tucked around the back of her head and she took him in further, letting her tongue stretch to the base and then swirl around the tip, gathering the salty-sweet fluid. Letting the pressure of his hand guide her, she used her hand to stroke the base of his cock while she concentrated the slow, worshipful sucking of her mouth on the tip.

Ty's hips were rolling subtly, pressing her deeper into his mouth and his sounds were growing more intense when he suddenly took her by her upper arms and pulled her to her feet. His mouth crushed down on hers and their tongues tangled as Ty led Samira back toward the bed with the pressure of his body. Just as Samira felt the backs of her thighs touch the edge of the mattress, Ty pulled his mouth away from hers and tipped her forward so that she landed on her stomach on the bed. She felt him climb over her, his body enveloping hers and his tongue running up her spine as he used one knee to nudge her thighs apart.

Ty's hand tucked beneath her hips and lifted them slightly. She groaned as she felt the tip of his erection stroke along her wet core, coaxing her to open up further for him. Samira pressed back with her hips, encouraging him to enter her, and felt him finally fill her. Her body stretched to welcome him and she gripped the blankets in front of her, moaning at the deep, fulfilling sensation of their bodies coming together. As soon as he settled completely into her, Samira felt Ty start to move his hips. His first few strokes were long and deep, nurturing her as he kissed along her shoulder. Then his pace quickened until he was pounding into her with such intensity she couldn't control the cries of pleasure pouring out of her.

A shattering orgasm shuddered through her and she arched into him, pressing him even deeper into her until she felt him surge forward and spill into her. Ty held himself in place for several long seconds then collapsed down onto Samira's back, gathering her into his arms and rolling onto his side so that he cradled her against his body. She could feel him still nestled within her and she wriggled her hips back against him to enjoy more of the feeling.

Ty kissed her temple and wrapped his arm around her so that their bodies entwined completely.

"I love you," he whispered.

Samira sighed contentedly and turned her head to kiss his arm.

"I love you, too."

"I can't wait to marry you." Samira's heart fluttered and she nodded. She felt Ty's arm tighten around her slightly. "Is something wrong?" he asked.

"Should we really be doing this?"

Ty sat up suddenly on his hip, causing Samira to tip back so that she was on her back staring up at him.

"What do you mean? Do you not want to marry me anymore?"

Samira reached up and cupped his cheeks with both hands.

"Of course I want to marry you," she said. "I've always wanted to marry you. I'm just worried that with everything that has been going on if planning a wedding is really what we should be doing."

"Why?"

"You don't think that it feels disrespectful or tasteless to come home after all the fighting and death, and then go back to Earth for a big party? Should we postpone it for a while to give everyone a chance to get over everything that we've just gone through?"

Ty pulled her up so that she was sitting facing him and rested his forehead against hers for a moment.

"I think that it is exactly what we should be doing," he said.

"Really?" Samira asked, pulling back so that she could look into his glowing orange eyes.

"Absolutely," he said. "After everything that we've gone through, what we need is something hopeful. We all need to be reminded of what it is to be just happy. This wedding isn't just for you and me. It's for all of us. This is something that no Denynso has ever experienced. For our kind, bonding with your mate is a very private thing. We watch our friends and family members go from being single, to experiencing the attraction of finding their mates, to being mated. It's a process that happens outside of the view of anyone else. We don't get to celebrate the joy of them coming together. Our wedding is going to let them celebrate with us, and it's going to be a fun and happy distraction from everything else. It will represent hope and unification. I think that it is exactly what everyone needs."

6

"It feels different down here now," Loralia said, gazing around the cavern.

Bannack dropped down from the vine he had climbed down so that he stood beside Loralia where she was pressed to the stone wall of the cavern. She reached for his hand, taking it in hers so that she could feel the connection between them as she tried to get used to the new feeling of the space that had always been her home. This system of caverns and chambers had been her home since birth and she had lived there completely alone for several years before the Klimnu came and then the Denynso waged war against them right in that cavern. That is when she met Bannack and made the impulsive, love-compelled decision to climb out of the caverns for the first time in her life and experience the world above her.

"Why?" Bannack asked.

Loralia shook her head. She couldn't quite explain what was going through her mind. She knew that there was something that was not the same and that would never be the same.

"I never knew why my kind came down here," she said. "I knew that we weren't always down here. My grandmother had told me that we weren't always here and that there was a time when we lived above ground, but were forced to come down here because of another species. I didn't know what that meant until now. I didn't know what had caused the plague that they ran from or that killed all of them, and even though I still don't really understand how the arrival of the Valdicians caused it, everything that Creia told us has changed what I think about them and their memory."

Losing everyone that she knew and loved had been horrific, but Loralia had forced her feelings and memories to stay behind her. She had pushed them into the back of her mind and continued forward in her life alone, resigning herself to be the only one that would ever know about her kind and that the knowledge of their history would die with her. Now she didn't feel the same way. She had survived for a reason. She had gotten through the plague that had burned through the cavern and destroyed her species, which meant it was her responsibility to make sure that they were never forgotten.

"You're still wondering why the plague didn't kill you."

"Of course, I am. It doesn't make any sense. I was right there with everyone else. I didn't go anywhere different or do anything different. So how did I escape it? I don't even remember being sick at all. Not even a little bit. Everyone else got sick and were dead within just a few days, but I always stayed just as healthy. It doesn't make sense."

"What about Ty?" Bannack suddenly asked.

Loralia glanced at him quizzically as she removed the compact from her neck and opened it so that she could create a solid floor across the reflected sky in front of them.

"What do you mean?" she asked.

She held the compact in her palm and tilted it so that the mirrors reflected the stones across the reflected sky and created a path where she could step.

"How do you feel when you are near him?"

"I can't honestly remember spending much time with him," she admitted. "I know that I have, but not really enough that I could tell you if it made me feel any different. Why do you ask?"

"Don't you remember what Creia said?"

Loralia stepped off of the final stone of the path onto the ground across the sky and turned sharply back to look at Bannack who was making his way carefully across the stones. She hadn't thought about it until that moment, but suddenly she remembered more of what Creia had said. He hadn't just talked about her kind and how they had abandoned their home on the compound that the Denynso now inhabited to create their own home beneath the ground. He had also talked about the original Denynso compound just on the other side of the rocks at the edge of the compound and the two strange children that had been born to two Denynso women once the clan split and half moved onto the land above them now.

"He's a descendent of the Valdicians," she murmured.

"Distantly, but yes. He is the first one of the line that has shown any of the abilities of the Valdicians. That means that the bloodline is strong in him."

"So I might have some kind of reaction to him?"

"I don't know. I don't know how that worked, but Creia said that the sickness started when the Valdicians came, ended when they went away, and then came again when the Valdicians returned."

"How, though?" Loralia asked, the desperation growing

inside her. "It doesn't make any sense. My kind came down here to escape from the plague. No one even knew that we were down here. How did the Valdicians cause the plague to come back if they never came down here?"

Bannack shook his head and reached out to take her into his arms. She tucked her head against his chest, holding herself as close to him as she could so that she could take comfort in the strength of his arms and the beating of his heart. In that moment it felt like those were the only things that would stay the same, the only things that she could rely on.

"Do you want to skip the wedding?" Bannack asked.

Loralia thought about it for a moment, and then shook her head.

"No. I can't avoid him forever. Nothing has happened yet, and I've been living in the same area as him for far longer than my kind was near the Valdicians before they got sick."

The embrace ended and Loralia started deeper into the caverns. She didn't know what she was looking for or even why she had come down there with him. Something about getting the new information from Creia had drawn her back into the home that she had always known. It was like she could feel them more strongly than she had in years. She could almost hear their voices coming at her through the rocks, reminding her of the days of her childhood growing up there and never imagining what the world outside of the caverns held. In the months after the final death of the plague Loralia realized that she had separated herself so much from her kind and the life that she once had. She no longer followed the traditions or carried on with the ways that her parents had taught her.

Now that someone else had acknowledged them, now

that she knew the torment that her ancestors had gone through and the courage that they had shown as they recreated their lives in the chambers that they manipulated to mimic the land above them that they loved so deeply, but that they knew they would likely never see again, she felt as though she were stepping back into that existence. She no longer wanted to separate herself from who she was and where she came from, and it suddenly felt extremely important that she carry with her the legacy of all those who came before her.

She turned to Bannack.

"Do you remember when we first bonded and you asked me how my kind made their pairs?"

He nodded.

"Yes."

"I told you about the tying ceremony and you told me that you wanted us to do that someday."

"I remember."

"Do you still want to do it?"

"Of course I do, if you want to."

"I do," she said. "I didn't know if I did before, but I know how important it is to me now. I already feel completely bonded to you and wanting to have this ceremony has nothing to do with not feeling like you and I are connected. I just realized that I am all that is left of my kind now, but that if we ever have children, those children will be part of my line as well. They will carry on my species, at least in part, and they deserve to know who they are and where they come from. I am dedicated to the Denynso and I want our children to be proud of their lineage, but I also want them to be proud of my side as well. I owe it to my family and to our future to carry on the culture and traditions of my kind so that they are never forgotten."

Bannack ducked his head to kiss her.

"Then we will. We will get married the way that your family would have and when our children our born, they will know everything that came together to create them."

Eden tucked Lysander into the crook of her arm and nestled him close to her to nurse. His tiny hand rested against her chest and she felt the warmth of him settle through her skin. She sighed, feeling content in a way that she had never imagined, and ran a finger along her newborn son's soft cheek.

"Is he alright?"

Eden looked up to see Pyra standing in the doorway of the nursery, looking at her nervously. She smiled at her mate and nodded.

"Of course he is. He's just eating. How is everyone at the meeting hall?"

"They're fine," Pyra said, pushing off of the doorframe and stepping into the room. "They all asked about you and the baby. I talked to people about him who I haven't spoken to in probably a year."

Eden laughed.

"Babies will do that. There's something about a brand new little one that suddenly makes everyone feel closer."

Lysander's mouth fell away from Eden's breast and she looked down to find him asleep, the last remnants of milk bubbling out of his satisfied-looking mouth. She covered herself and took the small cloth from over her shoulder to wipe away the milk. Pyra came to her side and reached down for him with his tremendous hands. Just as she had envisioned when Lysander was still tucked comfortably within her, Eden could place the baby into Pyra's hands and he was fully enveloped, rested as safely in those palms as he was when his mother held him in his arms.

She watched as Pyra leaned down to touch a kiss to Lysander's head and felt a surge of tenderness rise within her. When she was on Earth she had never thought of herself as the type of woman who wanted to be a mother. She wasn't like the other girls who played with dolls and spent hours meticulously brushing and styling their hair, dressing them in those tiny clothes, and pretending to feed and change them. And she had never been the type of teenager or young woman who envisioned getting married and having children of her own one day. She had always been so much more invested in her schooling and then in her career, thoughts of anything else just weren't something that she felt like she had the time to entertain. That all changed when she met Pyra.

Though their initial meeting and the first bit of time that they knew each other had not gone smoothly, when they finally came together, she knew that he was everything that she had been missing in her life, and that she wanted to create her life there on Uoria with him. When she discovered she was pregnant, she had been incredibly shocked, but even more surprising to her than the fact that she was carrying the warrior's child was how happy and excited she felt about it. She had an unexplainable sense of pride knowing that she had his baby within her and that she would be the one who would bear the first member of the new generation of the Denynso. It felt like an incredible honor, but more importantly it felt like she was creating a family with Pyra that she had never known that she wanted, but now knew that she never wanted to live without.

Seeing Pyra cradling their baby and whispering to him with gentleness and sweetness that belied his huge body and rough impression made the world feel calm, comfortable, and complete. She now knew that everything she had gone through in her life leading up to the moment when she stepped onto the shuttle to come to Uoria, everything with her family, everything with Ryan, had been absolutely worth it.

"Lynx isn't coming to the wedding," Pyra said, looking over at Eden.

She stood from her chair and crossed to the basket of baby clothes that had been sitting on the changing table Ero had built for them.

"He isn't?" she asked, picking up one of the tiny blankets that the midwives had made for her and folding it carefully.

"No," Pyra said, adjusting his grip on Lysander so that the newborn was draped on his chest, his father's tremendous hand nearly engulfing his body as Pyra held him in place, "He, Rain, Maxim, and Ivy have all decided that they aren't going to go back to Earth. They're going to leave with the group tomorrow morning and go back to the settlement."

"I suppose that makes sense," Eden said. "There's still so much that they have to figure out and with everything that we found out when we were on the settlement, and then even more when we talked to Creia, uniting the species and piecing the planet back together is going to take time and effort. Besides, I don't blame Rain at all for not wanting to go back to Earth."

"You don't?" Pyra asked.

"Of course not. What does she have there? She left so long ago that she wouldn't even be able to recognize it now. Everyone who she has ever known and loved is dead now and she doesn't have a home or a career or anything to go back to. She has a home here, and Lynx. Going back to Earth would just be a reminder of everything that she's lost and would put her right in the spotlight, which I know that I wouldn't want. Her life is here now."

"Is your life here now?" Pyra asked.

Eden folded another blanket and looked over her shoulder at him.

"Of course it is," she said. "Why would you even ask that?"

"I was just wondering if you ever thought about moving back to Earth. You left everything behind there without thinking that you wouldn't ever go back. You left all of those things that you said that Rain doesn't have to go back to; your home, your career, your friends. Do you ever wish that you were back there?"

"I don't wish that I was there, Pyra. There are times when I miss things that are there, but not enough that I would ever want to leave what I have here. Uoria is my home now. I feel more settled and comfortable here among the Denynso than I ever did when I was living on Earth. I want to be a part of everything that is happening here. Just think about it. I came here thinking that I was going to be on one small compound for no more than six months. I was going to do a little bit of studying, do some research, and then go back to Ryan hoping that somewhere along the way I could come up with an excuse as to why I didn't have any warrior blood to give him."

"So you never actually intended on trying to get blood from one of us for him?"

"No. I think I told myself that I did, that I was going to be the courageous scientific pioneer who helped make some of the most groundbreaking discoveries and advancements of our time by braving the fierce Denynso and coming away with my life and some blood." Pyra gave a short laugh and Eden grinned at him. "But when it came right down to it, I knew that I couldn't do that. Not only was it so incredibly stupidly dangerous that it would have essentially been suicide, which, of course, Ryan knew the whole time which is why he decided to force me to do it in the first place, but I also had a really terrible feeling from the first moment that he told me that he wanted to do experiments with Denynso blood."

"What kind of terrible feeling?"

Eden folded the last blanket and tucked the stacks of blankets and clothes back into the basket so that she could put it on the floor beside Lysander's cradle. She sighed, trying to come up with the right words to explain to Pyra what she had been thinking and feeling when Ryan first started talking about his plans for experimenting with the highly sought-after, and highly illegal, blood of the Denynso warriors.

"I worked with Ryan for a long time. It gave me a chance to really get to know him, both inside the lab and out, and he was not the person that everybody thought he was."

"I know. You told me about the things that he did to you, or at least tried to do to you."

"It's more than that," Eden said, walking over to Pyra and resting her hand briefly on the back of her baby son's head. "I think that people underestimate him. They think that he is a bit eccentric, but I think that it is something much darker than that. I think that he is capable of far more than anyone has imagined."

TBC

(To be continued in book II...)

THE ALIEN'S CONFLICT

1

Pyra drew his tiny son closer to his body, resting him directly over his heart and tucking his head so that he could envelope him completely and draw in a breath of his scent. Eden's words had struck him deeply and he couldn't shake the thoughts that they had inspired in his mind. His mate had always spoken of the man who had been her boss on Earth and sent her on the scientific expedition to Uoria with a sense of disgust and anger, but he had never heard the level of fear and apprehension in her voice that he did then as she revealed that she thought that Ryan was capable of far more than anyone had ever imagined. She stared at Lysander as she said it as if she were revealing something that she had held within her for so long but was only now willing to put a voice to because of the fragile baby that was now in the world, vulnerable to everything and needing the protection of his parents.

"What do you think that he could do?" Pyra asked, trying to keep his voice as calm and steady as he could so that he wouldn't frighten his mate any more than she already was.

The last several weeks had been incredibly illuminating

to the lead warrior of the Denynso. He had left the compound for the first time in his life with determination to find out what else lived on his beloved planet, identify any threats that might exist, and find ways to resolve them so that they could not harm the baby that was not yet born at that time. What he thought would be a simple journey had turned into something complex and horrifying, showing him not just the creatures that lived on that planet and what threats they held, but also the hidden threats that he never thought he would encounter again, and could never have imagined existed. What was just as, and possibly even more horrifying than the creatures he had found and what he had learned about the history of the planet was how much he had changed after learning everything.

Pyra, like all Denynso warriors, confronted threats with aggression, violence, and fury. This was what had earned them the reputation as being the most fearsome, powerful, and effective warriors in the galaxy. As he learned about the Covra and what they did to the people of the settlement, and then the Mikana and their unexpected disturbing connection to the Klimnu that he thought they had eliminated in that last terrifying battle, a change came over Pyra that was unlike anything that he had ever experienced. He felt a level of anger, disgust, and vicious desire for vengeance that he had never felt.

In an instant he went from wanting to help the humans who had been locked by the Covra and being willing to accept the help of the strange but beautiful people from the nearby kingdom that had once maintained good relations with the settlement to wanting to destroy and eliminate all of the Mikana and anyone who had stood in his way. In them he saw not just the Klimnu that had tormented his kind for years and been the cause of pain, fear, and death for as long as he could remember, torturing not just the Denynso warriors who engaged in battle with them, but also the human women who came to the planet and became the mates of several of the Denynso men, but as a deeply disturbing form of betrayal from his planet.

The Mikana were beautiful, seemingly kind creatures who had immediately welcomed Pyra into their kingdom and offered their assistance when he told them what they were facing with the people of the settlement and the Covra. He had trusted them, relied on them to help him protect the humans of the settlement as well as the warriors and themselves. Soon, though, this trust began to unravel as he learned of the secrets that their leader, Rey, had been withholding and the truth behind their lovely faces and helpful hands came to light.

He had begun to feel wary of them when he found out that Rey had lied to him when he told him that his kind had not had contact with the Covra. They had, in fact, been locked in aggressive conflict with the Covra well before the humans that eventually built the settlement even arrived on the planet. It had been them who had built the prison where the Covra held them captive and where eventually the Klimnu imprisoned and tortured both Leia and Elianna. Though it had made him angry that Rey had willingly lied to him, he could understand the unwillingness to talk about a period of his kind's history that was both horrifying and embarrassing. Rey hadn't meant any harm by not telling Pyra about the conflict and had been forthcoming in telling the truth when it became evident that the information was important to them understanding the humans that turned out to be an assumed lost expedition from Earth called Project Nyx 23.

When the young Mikana who had fallen for the new

human woman who had arrived on the compound after the men had left, Maxim, revealed the reaction that his skin had to some flowers outside of the settlement, however, any sense that he could trust these people, or that they could offer any good to the efforts and existence of the Denynso disappeared. The instant he saw the slimy white change of Maxim's skin, he knew what had happened to the group of the Mikana that Rey said had split off from the rest after the conflict with the Covra ended. They had not just gone off onto the planet with goals of taking over and disappeared. They had become the Klimnu.

As soon as he came to this realization, Pyra felt the level of hatred and disgust toward those creatures that still lingered inside him even after weeks had passed since the final battle, he felt a new level of intensity and voracity that seemed to burn away every bit of compassion and reason within him. If a species that appeared so beautiful and so kind could actually be hiding the capacity for the greatest level of evil and cruelty that Pyra had ever seen behind their lovely faces and gentle words, there was absolutely nothing on the planet that was safe. He couldn't trust or believe in anything. The world around him suddenly went from a place in which he felt dominant and strong, where he felt confident that he would be able to protect his child and raise him well, to a place where the seemingly most inno-cent and trustworthy of species could turn into a loathsome enemy in a moment.

He had left the compound knowing that he would likely encounter species that he had never seen and may even uncover threats and challenges that would force his warriors to fight and to come up with strategies to protect the rest of the compound now and well into the future. Never had he thought, however, that he would not be able to decipher these threats or that they would appear suddenly and without warning after he had already entrusted them and allowed them in close to him and the rest of those who he was duty-bound to lead and protect. The realization that he was no longer in absolute control and had been misled, even if unknowingly, was at once terrifying and infuriating to Pyra. He was accustomed to being a leader that never stepped down and never shied away from any sort of danger or threat. He was accustomed to being the one that knew when their aggressiveness was needed and creating strategies that kept him in as much control over the situation as was possible.

In those first moments of realizing that all of his beliefs about their defeat of the Klimnu and everything that he thought he knew about the Mikana were completely wrong, something within him had turned like a switch and he was filled with a blazing fury that drove him to capture the entirety of the group of Mikana who had come with him to the settlement, and promised death on them. When Maxim escaped with the help of Ivy and they fled onto the planet only to encounter Pyra again as they made their way through the ruins of the Nyx 23 crash site, he had nearly struck down the young man himself.

It had taken Rain, Ivy, Loralia, and George turning against him amongst the broken, disintegrating pieces of the ship that were being reclaimed by the plants of the planet to force Pyra to realize he didn't have total dominion over all of them, and that he couldn't make the final decision of their life or death. He had to rely on the guidance of his king to tell him what he should do about these creatures. He had been positive that Creia would agree with him and authorize the elimination of the Mikana and, therefore, the final and complete elimination of all future threat of the Klimnu.

After all his father and king had been the one who had been the focus of the beginning war between the Denynso and the Klimnu. It had been Creia's decision not to help those who had first come into contact with the flowers and started to experience the gruesome transformation that had fueled the epic hatred of the Denynso by the Klimnu and the vow of those creatures to not only destroy the warrior race and take over the planet, but to utilize their anger, aggression, and, finally, their blood to make them the most powerful and formidable species that had ever existed.

He was so certain that Creia was going to side with him that Pyra had even permitted the release of Rey from the meeting hall where he had quarantined the rest of the Mikana so that he could come along with them on their journey back to the compound. Having their leader there would be even more influence to Creia and would ensure that there was no argument when he returned to the settlement and then to the kingdom to follow through with the elimination.

When they met with Creia, however, the king had admitted that he himself had been withholding secrets about the origins of the Denynso and when they had come to live on this compound. He had revealed for the first time that they had once inhabited a land on the other side of the rock ledges where none of the Denynso ever ventured, and he had brought them there, allowing them to look out over the devastation caused by those who had confronted the Denynso trying to either become their allies or conquer them and take over their land, and had encountered only defiance. On the top of that rock ledge is where Eden had given birth to Lysander, aided by Rey. As Pyra had watched the leader of the species that he was so ready to destroy without a second thought so carefully and gently tend to his mate and ensure that his son was brought into the world safely, Pyra truly realized the extent of the darkness that had built within him.

The thought frightened and sickened him even now as he cradled that baby to his chest and remembered falling to his knees in front of Creia to ask for forgiveness for what he had done. It terrified him that he could reach that level of cruelty and disregard for life, and it occurred to him that if he was able to fall victim to those thoughts and feelings, then others could as well. He knew that he had failed all those who followed him and could have failed his own son, but through that disturbing transformation he had also illuminated the realities of the world around him. Him feeling capable of that level of destruction meant that he had to protect his son, and all others, from the possibility that someone else could feel that way as well.

2

E den could hear the emotion in her mate's voice as he asked her what she thought Ryan was capable of doing. She wished that there was a way she could tell him what she was thinking without frightening him or inspiring the aggression in him that she heard he had exhibited when he was out of the compound. She had known from the time that she met him that he had a short temper and was prone to anger and violence, but she had a difficult time envisioning what the others had told her had happened when they were on the settlement.

She watched him cuddle Lysander protectively and felt her heart squeeze. Almost as soon as she stepped off of the shuttle onto Uoria for the first time she had made the decision that she was going to put Ryan and everything that she had been through with him behind her. From then she had done everything she could to not think about him or the way he had treated her. Being with Pyra and concentrating on her pregnancy had helped her to rid her mind of the horrible thoughts of him and the nightmares that she had for weeks before her voyage. Now that her child had been born, however, the thoughts were creeping back in and she found herself worrying about what could be waiting outside of the compound.

"Eden?" Pyra said, looking at her sternly. "What do you think that he is capable of doing?"

"I don't know for certain, Pyra. It's not like he ever told me about the horrible things that he was going to do. All I know is the way that he made me feel and the way that his eyes looked. There was something there that I can't really describe. It was something deeper than just his arrogance and his complete disdain for other people. I hope that I don't have to see him while we're there."

"What do you mean you hope that you don't have to see him while you're there? You aren't going to Earth."

Eden looked up at Pyra sharply. Her mate was staring at her with his jaw set, his massive hand stroking Lysander's back with a gentle touch that stood in stark contrast to the intensity on his face.

"Of course I am," she protested. "I'm in Samira's wedding."

"Absolutely not."

"Excuse me?"

"You heard me, Eden. You are absolutely not going. You are staying right here with Lysander and taking care of him while we are on Earth. I'm sure that Samira will understand."

"Samira isn't going to have anything to understand because I am going."

Eden spoke the words slowly and clearly, making sure that he heard and understood each of them.

"Eden, I'm not arguing with you about this. You just gave birth. You need to stay here to heal and get back to normal, and he needs to be here so that he'll be safe. Traveling for days in the shuttle and then being on a new planet just isn't something you can do right now."

"Earth isn't a new planet for me, Pyra. I know that planet far better than I know Uoria, but that's not the point. The point is that I want to go back and see the people I left behind. There aren't many people that I really care about, but those who I do have I want to introduce to you and to Lysander. I want to show them that I am doing well and that I found a new life."

"Are you sure that you don't want to just go back and stay?"

Eden sighed, letting her head hang so that she could massage her temples to ease the tension that was building there.

"Please don't go back into that, Pyra. We've had that discussion already. We went through all of that. I don't want to run away back to Earth. I just want resolution. You have no idea what it was like to just walk away. I don't regret it. Not for a second. I love you more than I could ever tell you and I am completely devoted to my life here on Uoria, but that doesn't mean that I am just going to pretend that my life on Earth never happened. I can honestly tell you that I thought it wasn't going to bother me to be here and never even think about that life again. I thought that I would be able to just carry on without thinking about it or missing it at all. Now that Lysander is here, though, I am realizing how important going back there is to me."

"But why?" Pyra asked, carrying the baby across the room toward his crib. "Why do you need to go back there? You are Denynso now. This is your home and your people."

"I know, Pyra. I know that I'm Denynso, but that doesn't mean that I wasn't once human and that there isn't some human in Lysander. Everyone around me is finding out more about who they are and the history of their kind. Even you have learned more about the clan and how they came to live here on this compound. You can see how much it means to the rest of the clan and to Loralia. Don't you want that for Lysander? Your son deserves to know who he is and where he comes from. Even if he spends his life here and only identifies with the Denynso as he grows up, he should still know the planet where his mother was born and how she came here. You don't know what he's going to want when he's an adult. By then the relations between the Denynso and Earth will be far better. It will likely be common to travel back and forth between the planets and there may even be Denynso settlements on Earth."

"You think that my son will want to leave Uoria?"

"I don't know, Pyra, but neither do you, and it's not our job to tell him who to be or want to want. Our job is to make sure that he has all of the opportunities that he can possibly have and that means teaching him from right now what is beyond the compound."

Pyra tenderly lowered his sleeping infant into the crib and Eden watched him rest his hand lightly on Lysander's belly for a moment as if finding comfort in the rise and fall of his belly as he breathed.

"I don't want him to be in danger, Eden. I don't want either of you to be in danger."

"You must know by now that hiding from the danger doesn't mean that it isn't there. Things are changing. They've been changing. The threats that exist out in the universe are not going to stop existing and they aren't going to stop coming to Uoria. The Denynso have left the compound. You know now about the dangers that are out there, but they know about you, too, and they know more about your vulnerabilities than ever before. You can protect your son from a lot of things, but you aren't going to be able to protect him from everything forever. He has to live."

Pyra turned to her, his glowing orange eyes filled with emotion. He crossed to her and opened his massive arms to her. Eden stepped into them and allowed her mate to curl her against him. Being enveloped by his body was comforting and she allowed herself to relax into him. Having him away from her for so long at the end of her pregnancy had been incredibly difficult. She never could have imagined the devotion that she would have felt for this man, the level of adoration and attachment that she would feel even after knowing him for just a matter of a few days. That passion grew exponentially the longer they were together, and when he was away from her it was as if a part of her heart had actually gone with him. She ached for him in a way that she never could have imagined was possible, and now that he was home again she finally felt like she was complete.

She felt Pyra rest a kiss to the top of her head and she smiled.

"Alright, Eden," he said softly.

She could hear the resignation in his voice. She knew that he hated the words that were coming out of his mouth and that he almost didn't want her to hear them so that he wouldn't have to follow through with them, but that he understood what she had said to him.

"Alright?" she asked.

"Alright. We'll all go. As much as I wish that you didn't go through anything that you went through when you were still on Earth, I will never be able to change how you came to be on Uoria or to be with me. Lysander deserves to know both sides of his heritage. To be honest, I don't want to leave you again. It was horrible being away from you for that time and I was just outside of the compound. I can't imagine how hard it would be to be on a completely different planet from you and from the baby."

"I never want to be anywhere but with you."

"I also don't want to be like my father," Pyra said after a pause.

The words struck Eden and she stepped back to look up into Pyra's face.

"What do you mean?"

"Creia has spent his entire time as king hiding things from the entire clan, and that means hiding things from his children."

"I don't think I've ever heard you refer to yourself as his child," Eden said.

Even though she had known since early on in her time on the planet that many of the impressive warriors in the clan were in fact the children of the king and queen, it was very rare that the relationship was ever mentioned. Creia and Theia interacted with all of them in much the same way and they all referred to the monarchs by their first names or by formal titles. It wasn't that they didn't have the familial love that she had for her son, it was simply a part of the structure of the clan and how they operated within the roles they were duty-bound to uphold.

"I know," Pyra said. "But after finding out that he has kept so much from us and let us believe so many things about the origins of our kind that aren't true, it's hard to think of anything but being betrayed by my father. It's almost like I feel like he should have told us. Even if he wasn't going to tell the rest of the clan, even the rest of the warriors, he could have told my brothers and me. He could have let us know who we really are and how he came to be king. One day there will be a new king and it doesn't seem fair that he was willing to just let the new one take over without knowing everything that he knows."

"Do you think that you will be king one day, Pyra?"

"I don't know. But whether I am or not, Lysander is not going to grow up wondering who he is. Even if that means he might someday want to leave Uoria and live on Earth, which is a decision that I'm going to have to let him make. I can't shield him from everything. You made the choice to come here and to stay here with me. I wouldn't have wanted someone else trying to steer you away from that, so I'm going to have to start preparing myself now to not make decisions for him.

3

"It's so strange," George said, running his hand along Zsilvia's ribs and down into the dip of her waist.

"What is?" Zsilvia asked.

She was lying beside him on their bed, relieved after a particularly boisterous night at the hall to be in the quiet of the home that they had been sharing since returning from their journey. She enjoyed being with the others in the banquet hall, eating and talking, finally feeling relaxed after the hardships of the journey had come to an end, but after having spent so much time traveling and in unfamiliar surroundings, she had longed for more time just with her mate in the privacy of their home. She wanted to lie there beside him, look into his eyes, and be able to enjoy the space that they shared without having to feel like they were always being watched.

George's hand moved onto her hip and she lifted it slightly so that she could press into his touch. Even the simplest of touches from him were thrilling to her. She had waited for so long and had lost hope of ever finding a mate of her own to love. George had come along so unexpectedly and though she had fought hard against what she knew she felt from the moment that she met him, she had finally allowed herself to fall and had tumbled fully, completely, and unendingly in love with him. Having waited so long for him seemed to make every moment with him even more precious and she savored each second that she had to look at him, touch him, and fill her lungs with the scent of him.

"It's strange that I left Earth thinking that I was going to come here, be here on the compound for about six months, and then go back to Earth and maybe teach a seminar at the university about all of the wonderful thing that I discovered while I was on Uoria. Now here I am less than two months later getting ready to go back to Earth without having done a single one of the studies that I had actually planned."

She nuzzled closer to him and brushed the tip of her nose against his.

"And all of those wonderful things that you were going to discover here?"

George ran his hand from her hip back over her waist and onto the side of her breast. His thumb dipped down to stroke across her nipple through her shirt and she immediately felt it tighten at the sensation.

"I won't be sharing the wonderful thing that I discovered here with anybody," he said, bringing his hand to the front of her shirt to release the row of ties down the front, "much less teaching it to a seminar of university students."

George lowered his head and brought his mouth to one of her breasts. Zsilvia gasped at the feeling of his tongue stroking across her nipple, teasing it as he sucked it further into his mouth. As he continued to suckle at her, his hand slid down her body to the hem of her skirt so that he could draw it up her legs until it pooled around her hips. He removed his mouth from her for long enough to remove her shirt and release the knot at her hip that held her skirt closed. The fabric opened, revealing that she wore nothing beneath, and George groaned, dropping his mouth to her other breast so he could repeat the attention that he had given the first there.

Zsilvia allowed the pressure of his mouth to guide her onto her back and George sat up on his knees so that he could remove his shirt. She struggled to maintain control as he brought the tip of his tongue to her navel and swept it up, tracing a line up the center of her stomach, between her breasts, and along the side of her neck. He blew a cool stream of air onto the trail that he had just created, sending a shiver through her body that settled between her legs and made her writhe against the bed. George rose up over her, straddling her hips so that she was staring at his beautifully chiseled body. She lifted a hand up to run it through the thick dark hair that covered his chest and belly, biting her bottom lip as the coarse strands made the desire surge within her just as it always did. She had never before seen a man with hair on his body and it was something about George that made him even more irresistible to her.

He rested his hand over hers and drew it down to the front of his pants. She could feel his already intense erection pressing through the fabric toward her and she let her hand run along it adoringly. After a few seconds she released the button and eased the zipper down, allowing his cock to spring out into her hand. George's hands cupped her breasts, kneading into them as she stroked him. Fluid collected at the tip and she gathered it with her palm, using it to allow her hand to glide more easily along his length so that she could move at a faster pace.

George groaned and his head fell back, making Zsilvia's stomach clench with even greater need for him. She loved the deep, primal sounds that poured from his body when she touched him. They were at once completely unchained yet kept private only for her to experience. She held him with both hands, cupping him gently with one while she continued her smooth, even strokes with the other. His hips began to rock into her touch, bucking against her as more of the silky fluid slipped across his skin. Finally she couldn't take the temptation any longer and released him with one hand so that she could prop herself up and draw her tongue along the length of his erection.

The taste of him was intoxicating. The more of the sweet-saltiness of him touched her tongue, the more of it she desired and she took him fully into her mouth, letting it fall into the same rhythm as her hand as she savored the feeling of every ridge and vein against her lips and tongue. As she nurtured him with her mouth, she felt George's hand come around his hips so that it could touch her, his finger-tips slipping through her folds to brush against her most sensitive peak. She parted her legs as much as his position would permit her, and tilted her hips into his touch.

George rested his other hand onto the back of her head so that he could guide her into a faster pace, responding with small thrusts of his hips so that he plunged into her throat. After a few moments he gently pulled back, with-drawing from her mouth and easing his hand from between her thighs. He caught her mouth with his and kissed her deeply, entrancing her with the ministration of her tongue with his so that she barely noticed that he was guiding her backwards until she lay on the pillows. His body stretched out over hers so that they touched from their chests down and he continued to kiss her languidly, building her need for him with each tender press of his mouth.

Finally George took his mouth from hers and met her

eyes. Not taking his gaze away from her, he ran his hand down the side of her body and to her leg so that he could catch the back of her thigh and use it to lift her leg up and onto his shoulder. He pressed forward with his body so that her leg came beside her head, opening her up to him fully and allowing him to enter her. Zsilvia moaned as George's impossibly hard cock pressed into her body, causing her to stretch to accommodate him and then tighten around him again so that she cradled him completely within her. Once he settled as deeply inside her as he could get, George paused and Zsilvia closed her eyes so she could savor the feeling of their bodies melding into one another.

She lifted her hands to his face, resting her palms to the curve of his jaw and letting the pads of her thumbs run across his skin tenderly. He turned and touched a kiss to the center of one palm, keeping his mouth close even as he lifted his lips away so that the warmth of his breath rippled down the inside of her wrist. She opened her eyes again and found George gazing at her, focusing on her face as if he were memorizing every delicate lash and the tender bow of her lips. Their eyes melted into each other and he leaned forward, capturing the mouth that she offered up to him and slowly beginning to roll his hips.

His body moved within her as if crafted for that very purpose and Zsilvia struggled to control the emotions that the intense sensations inspired. She moved her hands to his shoulders and then onto his back, holding him close as he shifted so that he could ease her leg off of his shoulder and guide both of them up so that they hooked over his hips and held him firmly. George placed his hands on either side of her ribs and pushed up, giving himself greater leverage, and Zsilvia felt him slide even deeper into her. Her back arched and her fingers dug into his back as a strangled cry escaped her lips.

The feelings were almost overwhelming as soon as he started to move, but she welcomed each deep, intense thrust and allowed her hips to buck slightly with each stroke so that their bodies met. Sweat started to beat on George's forehead as growling sounds poured from his throat. She could feel the muscles in his back shifting beneath his skin, making him feel even more powerful. The beautiful balance of his primal intensity and the tender way that he enveloped her made her feel safe, desired, and loved. It was an incredible combination of burning need and intense seeking of the pleasure he so deeply desired from her, along with a sense that he was reaching into her very being, connecting their hearts and souls as much as their bodies.

His thrusts grew harder and faster, pushing her closer to climax. She tried to hold back, wanting the feeling to last longer, but George's incredible body was irresistible. His groans told her that he was getting close to his peak as well and she let go, crying out as her orgasm washed over her, her body clenching down on him to pull him even deeper within her. George's head fell back and she felt his cock throb as he roared with the climax that hit him. Her body milked him, each of her tremors meeting the pulses that spilled into her.

When the waves ended and her body relaxed, George rested down onto her, kissing along the side of her neck and softly stroking her breast and the side of her ribs with his fingertips. Zsilvia's body hummed with the intense, delicious feeling and she nuzzled closer to his warm, sweaty body. He lowered onto his side and scooped her against him so that her leg draped across his hips and her head tucked into the curve of his neck and shoulder. She listened to his heartbeat, letting the rhythm lull her as it gradually slowed. They breathed in gentle opposition, her filling her lungs as he released his so that their chests and bellies rose and fell with one another and it was as if they exchanged their breath between them.

Zsilvia could think of nothing more perfect than this. She would travel to Earth with her mate, learn of his life there and meet the people who were close to him, and then they would return here so that they could continue building their lives together.

4

_____

Zuri stepped out of the meeting hall and took a breath of the cooler evening air. It had gotten rather close inside with everyone gathering in the banquet hall and for the first time Zuri had realized just how much the compound had grown, if only temporarily, with the humans and Mikana that had joined them. Though their number wasn't a huge addition to those who already lived on the compound, it still seemed tremendously bigger, louder, and more confusing with all of the new faces and voices that filled the space.

Ero had left the hall a few moments before she had and she searched the moonlit open area in front of the hall to see if he was still out there, taking in a few breaths of fresh air like she was. To one side she saw the dark form of her mate hovering at the edge of the center of the compound, his hands on his hips as he paced, occasionally turning toward the forest as if tempted to start running. If he did, there was no way that she would be able to catch up with him.

"Ero?" she called out to him, gathering her skirt in her hands so that she could walk faster across the open area.

Ero looked up at the sound of his name, but then turned and started toward the forest. He wasn't running, but he was walking fast enough that Zuri quickly lost sight of him. She picked up speed, jogging toward the dark edge of the forest and continuing to call out to him. Finally she found him standing in the darkness of the shadows beneath the trees, staring up at the pattern that the branches made across the dark blue night sky.

"I need to get in better shape if I'm ever going to be able to keep up with you," Zuri joked as she walked toward him. "At least you weren't running this time. There's no way I'm ever going to be able to match that."

"You'll never have to."

The darkness in Ero's voice took all of the humor out of Zuri and she stepped toward him, touching her mate's shoulder tenderly.

"What do you mean?"

"I mean I'm never going to run again."

"Ero, running is a part of you. It's something you've always done. It's one of the first things that I found out about you. What do you mean you aren't ever going to do it again?"

Ero shook his head and turned away from her, the movement shaking her hand away from him. She allowed it to lower to her side, not wanting to upset him any further than he already was. He had seemed fine when they were in the banquet hall, laughing and talking with the others as they planned their trip to Earth, but now it seemed like all of the light that was in him had been drawn out and he was an empty shell standing just feet from her.

"You heard why I'm able to run as fast as I am," he said, his voice dropping even further.

"You can run fast because you were born to. It's something special about you that sets you apart from all of the other Denynso."

Ero gave a mirthless laugh and turned so that his back was completely to her.

"It's not something special about me. It sets me apart because I'm not like the others. As if I hadn't been reminded of that my entire life, now I know that I am even less a part of them than I ever thought."

"That's not true, Ero," Zuri said, trying to comfort him with the sound of her voice now that he had stepped away from her touch. "You are just as much a part of them as they are a part of you."

"I'm part Klimnu, Zuri," Ero shouted.

The sentence came out of him explosively, harshly as if he had been fighting putting a voice to what he had been thinking. He whipped around as he said it and Zuri could see the pain and fury mingled in his eyes even in the faint glow from the moonlight. She knew her mate's eyes. She knew the rich orange color that they had assumed as soon as they had completed their bond as a way of showing anyone else who looked at him that he had found his life-long mate and was linked to her for the rest of his life. She knew the light in them that usually sparkled and danced even when he was just talking with her as if there was so much energy and life inside him that it couldn't stay calm. That light wasn't there now. The happiness had been dampened out of him and it made her ache.

"I know," she said, not knowing what else to say.

The revelation from Creia that generations ago two Denynso women gave birth to children who were half other species was shocking, but it was even harder when he continued on to tell them that one of those children was the progeny of a Klimnu. It had disturbed Ero deeply when he learned the closely-held secret of his ancestry. He had always felt like an outsider in his own clan. An orphan from the time he was just a young child, Ero was far smaller and less powerful than the other warriors of the clan. Though he had been adopted by Creia and Theia, the position of his new parents had done nothing to ease the pain and struggle that he had been through. It had merely put him in even closer contact with the biggest and strongest warriors, growing up with them as his brothers.

This meant that he grew up with an even greater sense of inferiority, tormented by his adopted brothers for being smaller, weaker, and less aggressive. It was this lifelong torment that had nearly cost him the love of Zuri, who he turned on and made fun of cruelly because of her size. Though he hadn't shown any of the sense of self-hatred and self-consciousness since he had come to Earth to bring her back, the revelation that his smaller size and the incredible speed that he could maintain when he ran came from Klimnu heritage emerging after decades of being hidden seemed to have drawn out all of these painful feelings again and now he was suffering. Zuri hated to see the pain and self-doubt in his eyes, but she didn't know what she could do to ease it.

"How could I ever want to run again when I now know that the only reason that I can do it is because of the Klimnu? I can't believe I was so stupid as to never make the connection. They were always so fast when we fought them. I thought that being able to move as fast as them was an advantage. I could take them out more easily because I could keep up with them in a way that the other warriors couldn't. Now I know that the only reason that was possible is because I was using the same heritage as they were."

"Why does that have to be something that you hate, Ero? I know that the Klimnu have been the greatest enemy of the Denynso, but hasn't everything that has happened in the last few weeks taught you anything?"

"What could it have possibly taught me other than to hate the Klimnu even more? They destroyed the planet that they took over when they left Uoria, and then they burned the entire Denynso compound to the ground, killing all of them. This all happened even before they decided to wage war against our half of the clan."

"Do you know what I see when I look at you, Ero?"

Ero looked at her, his jaw twitching slightly.

"What?"

Zuri stepped up to him and rested her hands on his cheeks.

"I don't see Klimnu. I see the beauty, the kindness, and the intelligence of the Mikana."

"They were beautiful when they caused the volcanoes to erupt and burned the other Denynso compound."

"And they're beautiful now. Don't forget that we know some of the Mikana. You know Maxim and Rey. Do you see Klimnu in them?"

Ero hesitated for a few seconds.

"No. But the potential is there, Zuri. You know that. You saw Maxim change just like I did."

"And I also saw him healed, and I see the way that he looks at Ivy. I don't see evil there. I see love and tenderness and strength, just like I see when I look at you. Sure the potential to become Klimnu is in him just like it was in every single one of the Mikana that lived at the time of the split. The difference is that most of them chose not to let greed, darkness, fear, and hatred take over them. Most of them remained hopeful, led by their intelligence and by the beauty within them."

"But the man I come from was part of the Klimnu."

"Because he was born into it. He wasn't one of the men who separated from the group. He was born into the family, but what if just like the potential to become Klimnu existed in all of the Mikana, the potential to be Mikana existed in all of the Klimnu? What if he chose to be led by that part of him?"

"How can I know that?"

"Does it matter? You have within you the ability to choose just like every one of them did. You can choose to hate the part of yourself that could be led by darkness and hatred, or you could choose to embrace the part of you that is strong enough to overcome the power of that darkness even in the face of adversity."

5

"A re you sure that you don't want to come along with us?"

Creia looked at Gyyx, the bright orange eyes of the young warrior making something inside him feel even more painful than it already did, and shook his head. He tried to smile, but he wasn't sure if the expression was actually come across on his lips.

"No. As wonderful as it sounds to visit Earth and see what it's like outside of Uoria, my responsibilities are here. Someone has to be here in order to take care of the compound and those who aren't leaving, and to make sure that if any emergencies arise they can get handled as quickly and effectively as possible. "

"It won't be the same without you, though. We already left the compound for the first time without you. We shouldn't be leaving the planet for the first time without our king."

"Don't you worry," Creia said, resting his hand on Gyyx's shoulder to try to calm his protests, "there will be plenty more opportunities to travel and I fully intend that one of these days I am going to be on one of those shuttles to Earth and these women can show me some of the things that they carry on about. This time, though, my warriors are just going to have to be strong and carry on without me."

"You'll miss Ty's wedding."

"I don't even know what a wedding is Gyyx," Creia said, finally able to muster a soft laugh.

"I know, but it seems that it's something that you should be there for."

"Gyyx, there are decisions to be made and wounds to heal. Right now is not the time for the compound to be without its king. As much as I would like to be there to witness whatever this ritual is that Samira has convinced Ty to undergo, and that I suspect a few of the other warriors will fall into place doing as well, I have to think of my responsibilities and my role here first. There are others who are leaving the compound in the morning and I have to make sure that I am here for them when they return. As for now, you should be making your preparations to leave and that starts with getting your mate home so that she can get some rest. She looks asleep on her feet." Gyyx glanced down at Leia who was leaning on his arm with her eyes nearly closed. She was a tiny, delicate creature and sometimes it still startled Creia to see her with Gyyx, but the two were incredibly passionate about each other, devoted in a way that warmed his heart each time he saw them, especially when he thought of the horrific experiences that Leia had to endure just to get to where she was. "Go on, Gyyx," he said. "Go home and start getting ready for your journey."

Not looking convinced, but knowing that he was fairly well out of arguments, Gyyx swept Leia up into his arms, cradled her against his chest, and started out of the nearly empty hall. All that was left at the tables was two of the humans that Creia recognized as being members of the settlement that the warriors had released from the bonds of the Covra and the two warriors who were acting as their guardians though Creia had made no formal proclamation that those who were visiting from the other locations needed such guards.

As Gyyx disappeared through the main door of the building Creia felt his mate's hand rest on his shoulder. He glanced back to look at her and saw the knowing look in her eyes.

"What are you really thinking about, Creia?" she asked.

"What do you mean?"

He knew exactly what Theia meant, but he figured that he could delay answering, giving himself more time without having to put a voice to what was really happening in his mind. Finally the four men at the last table stood and made their way toward the door to the hall. They turned back to wish him goodnight and he waved at them, watching until the door closed behind them.

"I know you, Creia. You may be able to convince Gyyx that you want to stay behind here just so that you can hold down the fort while everyone is gone, but I know that isn't true. Something is bothering you and you are just waiting for that shuttle to leave for Earth for you to be able to do something about it. What is it?"

"I meant what I said to Gyyx, Theia. My first responsibility, as it always has been, is to the compound. I can't leave it without its rulers while the warriors are gone either on a completely different planet or on the other side of this one. If there is one thing that we've learned in the last few weeks it is that we never know what's going to happen. We can't assume that everything's going to be ok and that the compound is going to be secure. I can't leave it knowing that at any moment there could be another threat that comes and invades. This is our home and I can't put it at risk by leaving it."

"I understand that, and I agree with you. With things as fragile as they are right now, leaving the compound without any leadership or protection would be a terrible idea. But I also know that that isn't the only thing that is on your mind right now. You could easily assign one of the warriors who plans on going to the settlement to stay with me, or arrange for a shuttle that will bring you there and back in as short a time as possible without having to travel with the others, but you didn't."

Creia stared at his mate for several long, tense seconds, and then stepped down from the platform, stalking toward the back of the hall to the large tapestry that covered the curved stairwell to their living quarters. He didn't want to be in the hall any longer. He needed the privacy of his own space so that he could feel safe, so that he could relax out of the leadership role that he always had to take, and the tension that he had been feeling around his people since they returned from their quest across the planet. He had always tried to rule in a different way than the kings of his childhood. They had been far more distant from the people of the clan, avoiding meeting with them personally and maintaining a sense of formality with them that made them highly respected and formidable leaders, but made it so that they lacked the warmth that he wanted to offer the members of the clan when he stepped into the role of king. In choosing to rule this way, however, he had allowed himself to become far more attached to the individuals of the clan, caring for them well beyond the traditional responsibilities and relationships of a king to his subjects. While this had allowed him to enjoy what amounted to a tremendous extended family and a much greater sense of love and connection than had existed in his time with his own king, it also meant that he experienced a level of pain, fear, and disappointment that he didn't believe his king ever would have felt.

At the top of the stairs Creia released the latch at the front of the cloak he wore and let it fall from his shoulders. Theia was close behind him and scooped it up before it even touched the floor. After being bonded for decades, they existed in an easy and comfortable pattern that allowed them to predict each other in a way that was peaceful and comfortable, even if some of his habits were frustrating to his queen.

"Creia, how many times..."

"I failed them, Theia."

Creia cut her off, the words coming out of him like he could no longer hold them inside and it was as if they took all of the energy out of his body as they emerged. He sank down onto one of the large circular cushions in the center of the room and hung his face into his hands. He could feel Theia cross the room slowly and lower herself onto the chair in front of the cushion. She sat silently for several long seconds, giving Creia time to process what he was thinking and feeling before she reached forward and rested her hand on his head, gently stroking his hair back from his forehead.

"Who did you fail?"

"All of them," Creia said mournfully without lifting his head up out of his hands. "I've always thought that my greatest responsibility was to protect them and the compound, and so I hid things from them that I never should have hidden. I kept them within the compound borders and let all of the danger and the threats come to them rather than allowing them to venture out and find the dangers for themselves."

"But they defeated them, Creia," Theia soothed, sliding down off of the edge of the seat so that she could sink down onto her knees and pull Creia's face into her hands. "When the dangers came, your warriors were ready. They were able to protect the compound and the entirety of the clan."

"But they never should have been here. I never should have allowed the enemies to come into our compound and put the women at risk."

"The women are more than capable of taking care of themselves, as has been proven to us over the last few weeks."

"The warriors fought without ever knowing really why they were fighting. They knew that they had built a reputation of being fearsome warriors, but they didn't know why, and they didn't know why the other species would want to come here. I kept all of that from them."

"Even you don't know everything. You don't know why some of them came, but you do know why they stayed away, and that's because of the warriors."

"But they came because of a history that I never shared with them. They came because they knew of the wars with the Covra, the Klimnu, and the Valdicians. How do we know that some of them hadn't built alliances with those species and have been trying to carry on those wars all this time? I feel responsible for all of the pain and heartache that those men and their mates have had to go through because I didn't take care of them like I should have. I let them go off into areas of the planet where they had never been and that I didn't prepare them to experience. I didn't give them the warnings that I should have given them."

"What could you have warned them about? You didn't

know what the Covra had done any more than they did, and you didn't know that the Mikana still existed. You closed yourself off from the world as much as you closed them off. They wanted to go out of the compound and find out what else could be threatening us. All you did was honor those wishes and allow them to go. There was nothing more that you could do."

"I knew about the species that went underground, Theia. I knew that they existed before the Denynso moved onto this compound."

"Did you know that there were still there?"

Theia's voice carried a hint of the betrayal that Creia had never wanted to hear coming from her. Even worse than the thought that he had failed the rest of the clan was the thought that he had betrayed and disappointed his mate.

"I didn't. I wasn't even completely positive that they had gone beneath the same ground. We never fully knew what happened to them. I didn't know that they were right beneath us."

"When did you figure it out?"

Creia sighed. He hated admitting any of this to Theia, but he knew that he had to. He no longer had the choice to stay silent. It had caused too much pain already.

"I began to suspect it when the women went down into that tunnel and found the section that transported them down into the cavern. There would be no reason for that type of technology to exist if there wasn't a species that was going to utilize it regularly. It occurred to me that it might be there to help people who lived down there be able to get around more quickly without being detected. But it is not the type of technology that their kind created. That is from another kind, so I convinced myself that it wasn't the people who had lived here and were driven underground by the Covra and the Valdicians."

"What were that species called? Who were they?"

Creia looked into his mate's eyes and shook his head. He felt uncharacteristic tears building in his own eyes, but he didn't bother to fight them or even to wipe them away as they started down his cheeks.

"I don't know," he whispered. "I don't remember who they were or what they were called. We never even asked Loralia. She is the last of her kind and I never even asked her what that kind was."

The realization ached within him as Creia let the realization that if it hadn't been for the war with the Klimnu that brought his warriors down into the cavern, an entire species would have been lost and would be forgotten forever. He wondered if he could have done anything. If he could have figured out that they were down there, was there anything that he could have done that might have saved them from the horrific plague that killed so many only to return later and destroy all but one of their once prolific and strong number?

He knew that he had not done what he needed to do, what he had been entrusted to do when he was chosen as king, and it was time to rectify it.

6

L eia sat in the corner of the living room, her knees pulled up toward her chest so that she could use her thighs as a support for her sketchpad. The pencil balanced in her hand like an extension of herself and when the tip touched the paper and the lines began to form on the creamy surface it was like the embodiment of her breath. It had been that way since she had first begun to draw and discovered that those lines, those tangible versions of her thoughts and emotions, were the most effective way that she could express herself. It was through these lines that she could explore the pain and confusion that defined her life while keeping her safe. No one knew what she was thinking when she drew, and even when her pieces were complete, those who looked at them weren't able to interpret them as anything more than the shapes and objects that they could see.

She was feeling that way again now, tucked away from everything and existing only in that corner through the pencil and paper she held. Her hand was shaking as she drew and she couldn't completely focus on what the lines were going to become, but what mattered was that she was making them. Just that small amount of control gave her comfort and peace. She could hear the sound of a door opening and closing above her and she knew that Gyyx had finished with his shower and was making his way toward the bedroom. Her mate would expect her to be waiting for him in bed, but she hadn't been able to sleep. When she laid down and closed her eyes, all she could see was the cold, wet walls of the prison.

"Leia?"

Gyyx's voice came down the staircase at her and she felt it wash over her comfortingly. Even if she needed to retreat to the security of the corner and her sketchpad sometimes, simply hearing her mate's voice could make her feel safe and secure. When she didn't call back out to him, Gyyx started down the stairs toward her and by the speed of the sound of his footsteps she could tell that he was worried about her. It had been quite a while since the last time that drawing had been a salvation rather than just something that she enjoyed doing, and just as long since she saw the prison walls when she closed her eyes. Now, though, she feared even blinking because she worried that the next time she saw those walls she would also see Klimnu that held her within them.

"Are you alright?" he asked, lowering his tremendous body down to sit beside her on the floor.

The presence of him on the floor with her was as powerful as his voice and she started to feel her body pulling out of the corner toward him. No longer did she feel like she had to find her protection by retreating. If Gyyx was near her, she felt like she was protected.

"I think that everything just got to be too much," she said.

"Are you seeing them again?" he asked.

She could hear the concern in his voice. There was a time in her life when any type of emotion like that would have frightened her, making her feel like she was going to suffer serious repercussions for causing anything unpleasant. She would have struggled to apologize, to explain away how she was feeling, and to make the other person forget. Gyyx, however, had taught her that she didn't have to feel that way. He always allowed her to feel any way that she was going to, and simply let her know that he was there to hold her up.

"I haven't in so long, but then knowing that you were there, that you saw it again..."

Her voice trailed off and Gyyx nodded. She knew that she didn't need to say anything else. He understood exactly what she meant without her having to give any more words to it. She had stayed behind at the compound with Eden while the other women had left with George to help the men at the settlement. It had hurt her that she had not been able to reconnect with her mate the way that the other women had, but at the very end of a pregnancy that had already been tense and frighteningly filled with a sense of the unknown, Eden couldn't have been left alone. She had formed a close bond with the pretty scientist and it seemed only right that she be the one who would stay behind and take care of her. She had been overjoyed to see Gyyx again when they returned to the compound, but soon she realized that his return was not the happy occasion that she had wanted it to be. Instead, the return was filled with darkness that brought up memories so painful they took Leia's breath away.

Leia hated that Gyyx had seen what was left of the prison again. Even though she hadn't been there, she had for a few moments before he closed them off his thoughts to her, the thoughts that he was having as he stared down at the remnants of the destroyed building. She knew that he felt an indescribable level of anger and sorrow when he stood on that land and looked down at the blackened, skeletal remains of the foundation and the subterranean floors of the building. It was there that the Klimnu had brought her after taking over the shuttle that she was riding to Uoria. They had tortured and tormented her, keeping her in a tiny, grimy cell for nearly two months before she managed to escape and was discovered near death in the middle of a hallway by Elianna.

The battle that had broken out at the prison that night had been like nothing she had ever experienced. Though she only remembered brief slivers of it, moments like the few seconds of illumination in a flash of lightning, she distinctly remembered the intensity. She later learned the details of it and found out that the Denynso warriors, these men who she had come to the planet to draw, had fought the Klimnu bravely and burned their prison to the ground, destroying as much of it as they thought existed. They hadn't known about the basement rooms, however. They didn't know that she remembered them distinctly from the few but horrible times she had been taken out of her cell and brought down there.

Even worse than hearing about the prison again and finding out the grisly history of the building, starting with the fact that it had not, in fact, been built by the design of the Klimnu, but by the design and desire of the Covra and the hands of the Mikana, was hearing the extent to which Pyra had changed during the journey and the bloodthirsty way he was treating the Mikana. She knew what they were. She knew what had happened to the young man named

Maxim who had proven to them that the Klimnu still lived but in the beautiful, kind form that had existed so long before. But even she had been able to see past that when she looked at Maxim and Rey and not think of them as the brutal creatures that had held her captive for so long. When she looked at these two beautiful men she could still see the stains of the blood of their ancestors on their hands and had even felt a pang of compassion for them. There was something strangely poetic about being enslaved and forced to build something horrible, only generations later to have the descendants of those who suffered reclaim the space, even if for their own cruelty.

There was nothing poetic or understandable about Pyra's behavior, however. She couldn't justify what he had done and even though in his mind his determination to kill off all of the Mikana had been as a source of protection for the rest of the compound, Leia could only see it as a start and painful reminder of what she had gone through. He hated without limitation and without qualification. By merit only of being born into the same species as a group of rogue extremists who caused widespread pain and panic, these men would have to die, just as the Klimnu hadn't cared who she was or what her intentions on the planet were after she arrived. They only cared that she was human and that she was going to be in contact with the Denynso.

"Are you looking forward to going back to Earth?" Gyyx asked her.

The question shook her out of her thoughts and helped her to draw her focus away from the darkness within her.

"I think so," she replied.

In truth, she hadn't really thought much about what going back to Earth meant or what she might encounter when she was there. She had been so lost in everything that was happening around her, and the thoughts that were tormenting her as she tried to make sense out of everything that had been learned on the journey that it still hadn't really sunken in that in just a matter of days she would be getting back onto a shuttle and heading to the planet that for 57 days of captivity she thought she would never see again, and then since bonding with Gyyx never really wanted to see again.

"Is there anything that you want to do while you're there?" he asked.

Leia knew that Gyyx understood her past. It had been a brutally difficult conversation that they had had to have extremely early in their relationship, but one that was absolutely integral to their ability to come together and share their lives. Gyyx knew that there was little on Earth that she actually cared about, and even less that she would ever want to see or do again, but at the same time, she couldn't forget completely who she was before she had found him.

"I want to see Samira get married," she answered. "Never in my life have I known a happily married couple that stayed happily married for more than a few weeks. I want to be able to see that from the beginning and I know that they will be happy together for the rest of their lives. I'd also like to show you where I grew up."

"Are you sure?" Gyyx asked, sounding surprised that she would want to revisit those painful memories.

Leia nodded. She looked back down at her sketchpad and realized that she had continued to draw even as they spoke. The smooth page was now covered in a weaving, knotted vine studded with lethally pointed thorns.

"I feel like I need to see it again now that I have you. I want to face it. It still has power over me and I can't stand that. I feel like if I can see it again, if I can walk into those places that are such dark, looming forces in my life but I can have you with me, I can take away the power that they have and I can really move on."

"Then I'm willing to go anywhere that you need me to go," Gyyx said, pushing himself up from the floor and reaching down for her. "Now let's get to bed. The others are leaving early in the morning and I want to be able to be there to send them off."

Leia placed her sketchpad and pencil on the floor beside her and rested her hands in Gyyx's. They were so small compared to his, but that only made her feel safer. He could fully envelope her, completely surround her so that nothing else in the world could get close to her. With him, in him, she was safe.

7

"I still feel like I should go with you."

Lynx reached out and took the canvas bag from Ciyrs' hand and slung it over his shoulder to join his own bag.

"No," said Lynx simply. "You go with the others to Earth and enjoy the wedding. We're going to be fine. We're just going to free the captives, pack up some of the belongings, and bring people back here. There aren't going to be any battles this time."

"We didn't think that there were going to be any battles before," the healer protested. "What happens if the Covra aren't really gone or the Mikana are combative when they're released?"

"They won't be combative," Maxim said.

Lynx nodded toward the young man and then look at Ciyrs.

"See? From the lips of one of them himself, the Mikana won't be combative. This isn't like the first time. We aren't there to imprison them or to question them. We're there to let them go. That's all. If they want to come back to the compound and work with the rest of us to start rebuilding positive relations, that's great. If they want to go back to their kingdom and go about their lives, that's great, too. They have the choice. They won't have any reason to be combative."

"What if someone gets sick or injured?"

Lynx patted the bag that he had taken from Ciyrs.

"You packed enough supplies that we will be able to handle it. We have Rey with us, and as he showed us on the top of those rocks, he has some skills when it comes to taking care of people who need it."

"He helped deliver a baby. He didn't handle an injury or an illness or a war wound."

Lynx reached out and took his friend by the shoulders.

"We are going to be fine," he said.

Ciyrs still didn't look convinced. This was an uncomfortable situation for all of them. They were not accustomed to the clan splitting off into so many directions. Their time in the settlement when Pyra led the small group to the kingdom where they encountered the Mikana was the first time that they had purposely divided for more than a few hours, and now they were planning not just to divide, but for several of them to go to a completely new and unknown to them planet while the others stayed behind and returned to the site that had been the center of all of the turmoil that they had experienced. Lynx understood what they were dealing with, but he also knew that it was important that each of them went where he was needed, and even though the warriors and their mates were planning on going to Earth for a wedding, Lynx felt deep in his gut that what they would encounter on earth had the potential to be much more challenging than what he was going to encounter back at the settlement. It was far more likely that they would need the healer, though Lynx hoped with everything in him that they wouldn't.

"Is everyone ready to go?"

They all turned to see Creia approaching from across the clearing in front of the meeting hall. He had the same warm, proud smile on his face that he carried most of the time, but Lynx could see new signs of age wearing on his face. The last several weeks had impacted him just as it had impacted the rest, but it seemed to be especially hard on their king. He knew that it had to have been extremely difficult for Creia to admit that he hadn't been completely forthcoming with the clan, and to show them the ever-burning remnants of the old compound that he had held as a torturing secret within himself for the entire time that he had been king.

Around Lynx the rest of the group that was traveling back to the settlement called out their affirmations and Creia nodded. He stopped a few feet away from them and looked at each, his eyes lingering on their faces for a few moments before he gave a short nod.

"This time you are facing something even more than you faced the first time. The dangers may no longer be there, but the damage that they left in their wake is. It is your responsibility now to start repairing that damage. We all have to come together now, and that starts with just one person taking a step forward and closing the space between us." He reached into one of the deep pockets of the tunic that he wore and held out a rolled piece of parchment toward Lynx. "This is my official proclamation releasing the Mikana and restoring their absolute sovereignty over their kingdom and their own kind. It never should have been threatened. Please carry this and my apologies back to them. Let them know that they are welcome here and that I look forward to working toward making new connections and building a new and cooperative relationship with them."

Lynx nodded and tucked the parchment into his bag. He felt the tremendous sense of responsibility on him. He had been chosen to lead this group, building off of both the assignment that Pyra had given him when they were in the settlement and the trust that his leadership had inspired in the rest of them. Though none of them had voiced it in those exact words, there was a great sense of relief when he had told the group that he and Rain decided to go with them rather than going to Earth with the others. It seemed that having him as well as a leading member of the Nyx 23 humans and the Mikana created a mutually cooperative balance within the group that allowed them to feel like a united force as they started into this new chapter together.

Creia stepped back and allowed the others who were gathered behind him to step forward so that they could say their goodbyes to the group. Ty was the first to approach Lynx. He reached out and took his friend's hand, feeling a twinge of guilt in his stomach as he looked into the gentle baker's eyes.

"I'm sorry that I'm not going to be there for your wedding," Lynx said.

Ty shook his head with a soft smile.

"You're doing what you have to do," he said. "As much as I would like all of my warrior brothers there with me, I know that there is still so much to be done here and I feel better knowing that you are here to make sure that it gets done."

"I can't do it all."

"No," Ty agreed, "but you can make those first steps that Creia was talking about. You can be the one that starts building the bridges between all of us. Besides, you are just staying here and going where we've all gone before. I get to go to Earth."

Lynx laughed at the childlike excitement in Ty's voice. Visiting Earth had been something that they had all talked about and wondered about when they were younger. It seemed like such a distant dream to visit the huge and complex planet that had for so long been considered the center of the universe. Without technology to travel off of the planet, however, it had seemed like it would never happen, and even when the humans started to visit with frequency, the thought of the Denynso being able to simply climb aboard one of the shuttles and visit a planet where none of their kind had ever stepped seemed out of the realm of reality. Now it was not only possible, but imminent and the excitement among those who were going on the journey was palpable.

Ty stepped away to go talk to others in the group and Lynx leaned down to kiss Samira on the cheek. Pyra stepped up to him and pulled Lynx in for a hug.

"I'm proud of you," Pyra said in a voice low enough that only Lynx could hear it. "I know that you will be the leader that I wasn't able to be."

The sentiment sent a pain through Lynx's heart. He hated to hear Pyra, the man who he had admired for his entire life, talk that way about himself.

"You have always been an amazing leader, Pyra," Lynx told him. "You have led us through all of our battles and you will continue to lead us through whatever we face in the future."

Pyra was shaking his head as he stepped back.

"I wasn't the leader that any of you needed, but you were. You will be strong for them and they will follow you because you earned their trust. I will continue to work to earn the trust that I once had back."

"You will, Pyra."

Lynx stepped back toward Rain and took her hand. He looked over his shoulder at the rest of the people traveling with him and let out a long breath before turning back to the group that was staying behind.

"Safe travels to all of you," he said. "We'll see you when you return from Earth. For those of you who won't be returning to Uoria, I am glad to have met all of you and I'm happy that you're getting to return home. I know that it won't be easy for you, but I hope that you find the happiness there that you've been missing. Remember that you will always be a part of Uoria and that you will always have an ally in the Denynso."

Rain squeezed his hand and Lynx returned the gesture. He looked into the faces of each of the people standing in front of him for a few more seconds and then turned, starting across the compound toward the forest. The dark edge of the trees had always seemed mysterious to him when he was younger. He had known that the far boundary of the compound was beyond those trees and he had always known that he wasn't to even approach the boundary much less go beyond it. Now the trees were only a part of the journey, a peaceful section of the long walk that would bring them beyond the boundary and out onto the planet that was just now showing its secrets to them.

8

The banquet hall felt empty and quiet now that so many of the warriors were missing. Even though their number had been replaced by the humans and the Mikana who were still with them, the presence of the warriors was so strong that being without it made the space feel strangely abandoned. Zuri hadn't visited the hall for meals during the time that the men had been on their quest, preferring instead to eat with the other women in their homes so that they didn't have to face the continuous reminder of their mates being away from the compound. Now that they had returned, however, the clan wanted to gather in the hall as they always did so that they could eat together and continue with their preparations for their journey.

The long wooden table in front of her was empty, reminding her of the group that had stayed behind at the settlement and those who had left the day before to return to them. The table where she sat, however, was filled with the warriors and their mates who were preparing to travel when the shuttle came in two days. She could feel the tension that they were feeling even beneath the excitement. She and the other women had been doing their best to comfort the warriors, to explain to them what it would be like to travel on the shuttles. Zuri thought back to the first time she rode the shuttle to Uoria and how she had felt during the trip. It was a strange experience, but one that she was always happy she had taken.

"How many shuttles are coming?" Bannack asked.

"Creia said that there would be at least two. The university tried to arrange for two of the newest shuttles. They accommodate more passengers and are faster, but he hasn't heard from them since the planned day of dispatch so I guess we won't know until they show up," Samira said.

"Have any of you traveled on the new shuttles?" Ciyrs asked.

The women shook their heads.

"The only one of us who has is Ivy."

"And she's not here."

"No."

"You're going to be fine," Zuri said, offering a small smile to Bannack. "The trip is really no big deal. You can have them sedate you if you want them to."

"Sedate us?"

Zuri nodded. She remembered that experience strongly. During her first five-day journey to Uoria she had rejected the service from the attendant that would allow her to sleep contained within her passenger pod from soon after take-off until just before their arrival. She wanted to stay awake for the experience and use the time to prepare for what she thought was going to be a few months of participation as a visiting professor in the university exchange program with the Denynso.

"They can put you to sleep so that you don't even realize

that the trip is happening. It makes it go by much faster and you don't even really have the time to be nervous about traveling. You get into your pod, they start the process, and the next thing you know they are waking you up to prepare for arrival."

Zuri tried not to think about why she remembered that experience. She didn't ever want to revisit those awful days after Ero had been so cruel to her that she insisted on leaving Uoria to return to Earth on the same shuttle that had brought her, less than 24 hours after she had arrived. During that trip she hadn't wanted to be able to think. She hadn't wanted to hear his voice repeating through her head. Instead, she rested back into the passenger pod, closed her eyes, and let the sedation take over.

"What about once we get there?" Bannack asked.

She could hear a hint of nervousness in his voice that he was trying hard to cover. The courage of the Denynso was legendary and the warriors never liked to show vulnerability away from private moments with their mates.

"What do you mean?" Zuri asked.

"No Denynso has ever traveled to Earth. What are they going to think of us?"

"That's not true." Zuri turned to Ero. He had been silent the entire time they were in the banquet hall and had spoken very little since their conversation in the forest. "I've been."

The warriors looked at him, the looks in their eyes saying that they had forgotten that Ero had once visited Earth. It had been such a brief, spontaneous trip that many of them hadn't even thought of it.

"You have," Zuri said softly, reaching to take her mate's hand. "Ero came to Earth to get me after I left. He traveled completely on his own and he made his way from the university to my house without any help."

"If it hadn't been for such an unpleasant reason, I would have really enjoyed the trip," Ero said, lifting his eyes to look at the rest of the warriors. "As for Earth itself, I only encountered one real problem."

"What was that?" Ciyrs asked.

Zuri saw Ero's eyes slide over to Samira as he wordlessly asked her permission to tell them. He knew exactly what he was thinking about, and she felt uncomfortable even without the words having been spoken. Samira nodded.

"It's alright, Ero," she said. "You can talk about it."

"Samira's stepfather," Ero said. "He was absolute vermin. You can't blame that on the entirety of Earth, however. He was just one person. Remember that Samira, Zuri, Eden, Leia, Elianna, George, Ivy, Rain, and the rest of Nyx 23 are all from Earth. That is far more people that have fully accepted us than the one who was cruel."

"And he wasn't cruel to Ero because he is Denynso," Samira explained. "He is just a horrible, vicious human being. He has never been truly kind to another living thing."

"You have to remember," Eden said, tenderly adjusting Lysander over her shoulder and patting him, "Earth is not sparse like Uoria. There are many different species that live or visit there. There aren't as many as there are humans, but there are enough that it won't seem unusual for you to be there. I would even venture to say that there are some people who will be excited to finally have the Denynso on Earth."

"Really?" Bannack asked.

"Absolutely," Zuri said. "The university was extremely excited to start the exchange program, and there have been humans visiting here for quite some time. Earth is curious about the Denynso and most are eager to find out more. If anything, you might find that they are a bit too excited to meet you."

Zuri laughed as Ero pressed in closer to her. She knew that the warriors who were mated would have no interest in the human women who would inevitably find them attractive, and that if any of those women got too close to them, they would experience the searing heat that radiated off of the men's skin to keep such unwanted attention away from them. The single warriors, however, would likely have more than enough available women to choose from, and she was sure that they would leave a trail of heartbreak in their wake.

She looked over at Ero and he met her eyes. The pain that was there when they were in the forest was still there, but it was softer now, veiled by something more, something that told her that he was beginning to understand what she had said to him about his heritage and that maybe, someday soon, he would run again.

TBC

(To be continued in book III...)

THE ALIEN'S PAST

1

For the second time Ivy had walked through the compound and to the boundary that kept it separated from the rest of the planet. She felt like she was repeating the same steps as she had, wondering if her feet were falling into the same places that they had when she made her first journey toward the settlement. When she looked down at the ground in front of her it was as if she could see the hint of the outlines of footprints still marking the rich, dark dirt where they had not yet been able to resolve themselves through time or rain. She wished that she could tell which of those steps belonged to her and which belonged to Maxim. Had she been able to, she would have taken the time to rest her feet into his prints, finding comfort in the guidance that they would offer. It was as though if she followed along in her own footsteps she would be making the same journey, heading into the unknown with the same sense of insecurity and hint of fear that was there when she made this journey for the first time. If she chose Maxim's steps, however, though they were facing in the direction of the compound rather than toward the settlement, she wouldn't be blind, she would know where she was going and his presence still in those steps would protect her.

When the wall was finally at their back and they were walking across the wide, open section of the planet, Ivy had a strange feeling that she hadn't had before. The thoughts that she had the first time that she left the compound and headed toward the settlement with the women and George repeated themselves through her mind, but there were like they were coming through water at her. Images and questions that she asked herself swam through a haze, occasionally coming close enough to her consciousness that she could examine them and explore them again in the context of what she had experienced and now knew.

At the beginning of her first journey toward the settlement her mind had felt out of control. Everything had happened so quickly from the moment that she arrived until they packed up and left to go help the men as they struggled to figure out what to do about the people who had been locked in place by the Covra that Ivy didn't even feel like she knew what he was supposed to be thinking or how she should handle it. She struggled to bring her mind into the present moment, to force herself to realize that everything that was happening really was. No longer was her visit to Uoria about being a part of a scientific expedition or helping George participate in the exchange program between the university and the Denynso. No longer was she going to be spending a few months at the compound doing research that she had been dreaming about doing throughout her entire education and compiling reports that would make her the pride and the envy of the science community.

Instead, she had been thrust into an exhilarating but frightening project that had them dealing with plants that she had never heard of and concepts that were so far out of her mind that she would never have believed them even possible much less something that she would actually be dealing with in her time on Uoria. She had done everything that she could to help throughout their long days and nights trying to find the resolution that the men so desperately needed. She had given every bit of input that she could and pushed herself to her absolute limits trying to come up with new thoughts and new angles that they could take to find the right help. They told her that she had been helpful and reassured her that they were glad that she had come, but Ivy knew deep within her that she was never completely convinced that they were telling her the truth. Even as they were all standing together leaning over the table in the healer's office going through the pages of his old books and examining the supplies and materials that he had left behind, she found herself wondering how much of the acceptance that they showed her was actually for her, and how much of it was because they had come to accept George and he had stood beside her to act as her advocate and representative during the struggle with Creia that happened as soon as her shuttle arrived.

The worst of the feelings of uncertainty that she had gone through during those early days had come from the way that the Denynso woman Zsilvia looked at her. Ivy didn't know anything about her, and hadn't even spoken a single word to her, and yet the woman glared at her with a level of hatred and distrust that she couldn't understand. Of course, now she knew that Zsilvia had felt that way about her because of her deep love for George and her misconcep-

tion that Ivy and George were somehow involved in a relationship that went beyond their professional link. Though
she was extremely fond of George and considered him one
of the most impressive and amazing men who she had ever
met, there had never been anything in their relationship
beyond the work that they did together and the closeness
that formed in that context. When she finally realized what
was happening she approached Zsilvia to explain what their
relationship really was, and now she and George had
become mates in the tradition of her kind, but there was still
the lingering feeling of her eyes burrowing into her, questioning her, wondering if her motivations for being on the
planet were really what she said they were. Even though the
Denynso woman didn't look at her that way any longer, Ivy
still struggled with feeling like she was somehow less than
them, not quite fitting in enough to be a part of the group
that was forming, and yet also a small piece that would
make it so that the group wasn't ever the same again should
she not be there.

That first trip she had been taken completely off-guard
by how quickly and profoundly her visions of her time on
Uoria had changed. She had been thinking about the settlement that she had only just found out existed, and what was
going to happen when they arrived, trying to force her mind
to focus in like the people around her seemed to be doing.
Ivy glanced beside her as she thought about this and saw
Maxim walking along beside her, the look on his face
serious as he seemed drawn into the horizon ahead of them.
She realized as she looked at him that in thinking about her
first journey toward the settlement it hadn't occurred to her
that when she took those steps, she didn't yet know Maxim.
The imprints that her feet had left in the dirt leading
through the settlement the first time where intrinsically

different from those that now layered atop the ones returning because they were made by steps infinitely more unsure of themselves, wandering along a path that she didn't know and had yet to begin to understand. Now, though, her steps were more solid because they moved alongside Maxim's, more confident because they fell into the prints that he made, and more secure because she knew that from now on, no matter where those footprints led, they would never mark the earth alone.

This thought settled her mind and helped it to feel more in control as they continued forward toward the sky that had taken on a deep pink color and was now streaked with the foggy purple clouds of impending night. Rather than feeling like she was walking into the unknown and wondering what she was going to encounter next, the surroundings were familiar. There was even the sense as she looked at Rain, Lynx, and the others who had joined them in returning to the settlement that she, in a way, was even more prepared for this journey than they were. They had only traveled from the compound to the settlement and back again. Ivy and Maxim had escaped the settlement and journeyed all the way to his kingdom and then through the areas of the planet that even the Denysno had not yet seen.

The sudden thought of Maxim's kingdom made the breath catch in her throat. She thought about what he had said to her when they were talking about the fact that he wanted to return to the settlement rather than immediately going to Earth like many of the others. She knew he didn't just intend to go to the settlement and free the other Mikana. He wanted to return to his kingdom and unravel the mysteries surrounding the Order and the death of his father. She could see it in the way he carried himself, in the way that he watched the planet as it unfolded in front of him. He was holding a deep sense of responsibility and duty in his heart, but those compulsions were balanced by feelings of distrust and wariness that made him want to go beyond what he was told to what really existed in those tunnels and behind the hidden doors that his kind walked over every day, yet didn't know they were there.

2

"Can you tell me more about the Order?" Ivy asked.

The light was nearly gone and they had finally settled down for the night, knowing that they wouldn't be able to get any further without having to use their light sticks to illuminate their way. Though this was a possibility, Rain and Rey had felt uneasy about the prospect of venturing through the darkness not knowing what could be lurking around them, watching them by the glow of their own lights. They had stopped close to the site where they had rested on their other journeys and created their camp for the night, the group dividing so that the two couples broke away from the rest to set up their tents.

Maxim was spreading a thick blanket on the ground to provide cushioning and warmth as they slept, but when he heard her question he sat back on his feet and looked around his shoulder at her.

"Why do you want to know?" he asked.

She heard the hesitation in his voice, but she needed to know, so she pressed forward, reaching into one of her bags to withdraw a pair of lighter clothing to wear to sleep so that she didn't have to continue looking at him as she spoke.

"It's important to you," she said. "I stayed here rather than going back to Earth because it mattered so much to you. I think that, that means I deserve to know as much as I possibly can about what's going on. If I'm going to help you, I need to understand."

"You're going to help me?" he asked.

"Of course," she said, sitting down so that she could start to undress. "If I didn't want to help you, I wouldn't be here. I would have gone back to Earth and just hoped that someday you would be able to join me. Instead, I stayed. You told me how important it was to you to tell your brother what you've found out and to find out more about your father and the Order. I just want to know what you know so that I can do everything I can to help you. I don't want this hanging over us for the rest of our lives. I want you to find out whatever it is that you need to know that will put your mind at ease and give you peace so that we can really start our life together."

She lifted her eyes to Maxim and saw him staring down at the blanket, his fingertips tracing along the stitches in the fabric absently.

"I remember the night my father died."

Ivy felt her heart clench. She hated hearing the heaviness in his voice that seemed to come from deep inside of him.

"You do?" she asked, not really knowing what else to say.

Maxim looked up at her and nodded slightly.

"At least, I remember the night that we found out that he was dead. I don't really know when he died."

"Who told you that he had died?" Ivy asked carefully.

"Athan."

"The old man at the gate in the kingdom? The one who showed us the tunnels?"

Maxim nodded again.

"He's known my family since long before I was born. He was the one who came to our house that night and told us that my father hadn't survived the mission that they had gone on."

"What mission?" Ivy asked.

She dropped her nightshirt over her head and lay on her side so that she was closer to him, somehow offering him protection and comfort with the curve of her body around him.

"They were doing something for the Order. They had left almost a month before and when Athan returned he looked battered and starved. He wouldn't tell us where they had been or what they had been doing. All he said was that my father was dead."

"Where is he buried?"

Maxim's eyes grew cold and dark. He shook his head, looking away from her and focusing again on the stitches of the blanket beneath him.

"We never got to bury him," he said, his voice suddenly hoarse with emotion.

"What happened?" she asked.

"We never got his body back."

For a moment Ivy regretted asking the question. She didn't want to cause Maxim any more pain than he had already had to go through in the last few weeks, especially when it came to his father. She couldn't imagine what it would be like to lose her father in such a way. Though they didn't see each other as often as she would have liked once she started working with George, she knew that he was there, that he was just a phone call away and that if at any moment she needed him, her father would have gotten to her as quickly as he could to help her with anything that was within his ability to do. The thought of him simply being gone, killed in some unknown place and not even returned so that her family could bury him properly was excruciating.

She knew, though, that this was not the only pain of Maxim's that she would experience, or the only time that he would have to confront his memories of his father's death. If he really was dedicated to peeling back all of these layers and discovering the truth, there were going to be many more moments when she would feel the pain coming off of him and hear the regret in his voice. It was excruciating, but she had to believe that in each moment of that pain he was getting stronger, and together they were getting closer to the life that she wanted so desperately for them.

"Do you know what happened to it?" she asked, reaching out to rest her hand on his leg comfortingly.

"No."

"Athan didn't tell you?"

Maxim sighed and shook his head again. There was a flicker of emotion across his face that was close to anger, but it was fleeting and when he spoke she didn't hear it in his voice.

"He was only allowed to tell us that my father died, nothing else. Remember, we aren't even supposed to know that the Order exists. Even though we are from the original line, we weren't supposed to know until we were selected."

"But he helped us in those tunnels."

"It was expected that my brother and I would be selected for the Order. No one knows why or how anyone got selected, or even who is the one that does the selection, but because every other generation of men before us had been in it, my father just assumed that we would be, and he told us what he could to prepare us. Athan has been much the same way. He's told me what he could, but he is still very much under the control of the Order. The consequences of someone finding out that he had even known that we knew and didn't do anything about it could be dire."

Ivy suddenly remembered something that Maxim's mother had said when they were talking to her about the Order and her late husband when they were in the kingdom. She could remember the look in Ellora's eyes when Maxim started talking about the Klimnu and when she revealed that the rest of the Order already knew what had happened to the group that had split off from them, the segment of rogues that the rest of the Mikana had been taught had ventured out onto the planet and died, but who Ivy and the others now knew had actually become the gruesome and detested enemies of the Denynso and all others they encountered.

"Your mother said that your father died because of the Klimnu. What did she mean by that?"

"I don't know. The way she said it sounds like he went against the Order in some way, but if they were forming alliances to fight against the Klimnu, what could he have done to incite them to kill him?"

"Maxim," Ivy said carefully, hesitating saying the words that were weaving through her mind and tormenting the backs of her thoughts, "could your father..."

"Have been one of the Klimnu?" Maxim finished after her voice trailed off. "That thought has been killing me since my mother mentioned that my father was killed because of the Order and what they knew."

"Do you think that it could possibly be true?" she asked.

She couldn't bear the thought that this amazing man,

this beautiful, courageous man who she loved so fully and completely, could have come from one of those horrific creatures, but she also couldn't forget the way his skin dissolved beneath the touch of the flowers and the violent reaction that he'd had to Pyra when they encountered him among the wreckage of the Nyx 23 ship.

"It could be true that they killed my father because they were trying to fight against the Klimnu after they destroyed all of the allies of the Order and threatened the rest of the planet and he was one of those creatures or betrayed the Order and its allies to the Klimnu."

"But?" she asked, hearing the hint of hesitation in his voice that told her that he was thinking something else.

"But what if there's more to it than that? What if it wasn't that he was aligned with the Klimnu and trying to infiltrate the Order as part of their efforts to take over the planet...?"

"But that he wasn't..."

3

"Why do you think that they chose us?"

Rain was lying on her back staring at the roof of the tent above her and imagining the stars just beyond it. She could feel Lynx close beside her and the warmth of his body made the darkness of the tent feel comforting and protective rather than frightening. She was glad that they had stopped for the night rather than continuing onward as Ivy and some of the others had suggested. Not only did it mean that they weren't roaming the large, open area of the planet completely vulnerable, but she also felt like she needed as much rest as she could get before they got back to the settlement. What awaited them there was still unknown, and she wanted to be prepared for whatever they might encounter.

"What do you mean?" Lynx asked, sliding over slightly so that his shoulder touched hers and she could feel his hip against her.

"Why do you think that the Valdicians chose us to send here?"

"I thought that they sent you here so that the Covra could use you."

"Was that always the plan, though? The Valdicians didn't know that we were going to the prison planet. They would have had no way of planning that they would send us to Uoria for the use of the Covra, and I don't think this was something that they just came up with during our struggle on the planet. So did they always have the plan of sending some hapless crew to become enslaved by the Covra and help them with their quest to take over Uoria and it just so happened that we were the ones that showed up at the right time to be the ones that they sent, or did they always have a target on Earth humans?"

"A target?"

"Humans are a commodity, they always have been. We're strong, advanced, and plentiful, but seem to have a much stronger concept of justice and humane treatment of other species than others do." She looked over at Lynx. "I'm sorry. I didn't mean to imply..."

"No," he said, "it's alright. You're right. The Denynso are far bigger and stronger, but we are nowhere near as plentiful. We are, however, ruthless and violent when necessary. It's no big secret that the humans are far less likely to fight and more likely to try to save others than the Denynso."

"That is exactly why so many other species have come for us, though," Rain said. "They know that capturing some of us would give them a much better chance of taking over Earth. Could they really have just planned to send any group that happened to be close enough to take over, or did they somehow know that with what they were doing on that planet that eventually a team from Earth would arrive and they could send them to Uoria with the intention that that crew would not only become the slaves of the Covra and the

Valdician allies, but that they would lure others from Earth who would come hoping to find and save them?"

"How, though?" Lynx asked. "You said yourself that the people of Earth didn't even know that Uoria existed when you left. If the Validicians wanted to lure others from Earth, why would they force you to crash on a planet that the people who would be out looking for you wouldn't know was there much less think to look for you on, while also disabling all of your communication technology so that you wouldn't even be able to let others know that you were in trouble and possibly ask for them to come rescue you?"

His words were at once painful and reassuring. She didn't want to think that the mission that she had so carefully helped to plan and execute had actually guided them directly into the path of the Valdicians, but at the same time it was comforting to think that the people of Earth didn't simply not look for them.

"Did you ever think that you would get rescued?" Lynx asked.

His voice was soft, hesitant as he asked the question that seemed just as painful for him as it was for her. She remembered the last time she had heard his voice sounding like that and her stomach felt sick. Then she didn't know what he looked like and had never touched his skin. That was when she was still locked in place and unable to move her body or open her eyes. Lynx didn't know for sure then that she was able to hear him when he spoke to her, yet every time that he was in the room with her he had talked to her, told her what was happening, and reassured her of how hard he was working to try to find a way to release her from the torturous bonds of the Covra.

It was listening to his voice that had brought Rain out of the deep darkness of the lock placed on her, but also kept

her just out of his reach. She didn't know then that it was
because he was Denynso, a species close enough to human
that his voice began to release the lock on her, but not close
enough to completely free her. So she continued to listen to
him, falling in love with him as she waited patiently,
knowing that he was doing everything that he could and
believing with everything that she had that he would one
day be successful and she would be able to live again. His
voice had stayed slightly sad, though, and it hurt her even
then to hear that painful hint in each word that he said. It
wasn't until she had heard the voice of the woman, a woman
she later learned wasn't even in the room with them but
communicating with them through a piece of technology
that she had never seen and didn't understand, that she had
felt her mind release and her body come back into her own
control. Finally she was able to open her eyes and see Lynx
for the first time and feel his skin beneath her fingertips.
Finally his voice didn't sound so sad.

Now, though, the sadness had returned and she knew
that he was thinking about the years before he had found
her, years before he even came into existence. It was still
difficult for her sometimes to wrap her mind around the
idea that she had lived the majority of her life before Lynx
was even born, yet she had been intended as his mate from
the moment of his birth. He knew the instant that he saw
her that she was meant to be his, and even finding out that
she had been locked in sleep for one hundred years hadn't
dissuaded him from knowing that they were meant to spend
their lives together. He knew that if she didn't come out of
the lock or if she didn't fall in love with him, that he would
live his entire life alone and longing for the mate that he
never bonded with.

She hated that the sadness had returned to his voice, but

she understood why it was there. As painful as it was for her to think of the time that she had been without him, it was even more difficult for Lynx because he felt that he had failed her. Even though he wasn't even born for most of her life and he had no way of knowing that she existed, he felt that he hadn't lived up to his responsibilities to guard, protect, and nurture her. Part of him felt that he had allowed the lock to happen, had allowed her to languish in the bed that she had simply laid down on to rest and then didn't leave for more than a century. They had talked very little of the time before he had found her. Though she had told Pyra and the others everything that they had wanted to know and helped them to understand the Covra, Lynx hadn't asked her to tell him about what she had gone through. Now it seemed that he was ready to know more and she had to be courageous enough to tell him.

4

R ain took a breath and nodded.

"There was a short time when we first arrived on Uoria that I really believed that we would be rescued. I don't even remember if I told any of the others, but I just had this feeling that they were going to come for us. Of course, this was before we found out about the Covra."

"Why did you leave Earth in the first place?" Lynx asked.

She looked at him strangely, rising up onto her elbow so that she could look at him more closely.

"I told you. I was part of a team that left on a mission to explore beliefs that a species was utilizing a planet as an illegal prison camp."

"I know about Nyx 23," Lynx said. "I know that you had a job, but you never really explained why you did it, or what happened after you left."

"Do you really want to know?"

"Yes."

"When I was on Earth I was part of a small paramilitary operative that focused on illegal and unethical activities by other species and on other planets. We had received intelligence that what was widely accepted as a barren and unexplored planet was actually being used as a prisoner of war colony designed and operated not in compliance with the intergalactic agreements. The information came from a source that wasn't recognized and many people in our faction didn't believe that it was accurate. They thought that it was a conspiracy theory that had no basis in reality."

"How could you not know, though?"

"What do you mean?"

"How could you have not known that that planet was being used that way?"

Rain suddenly felt extremely defensive. She sat up sharply and stared at him.

"You didn't know that there was another species living right beneath your feet for your entire life, or that there was an entire settlement of people locked in place right on the other side of your planet, or that the enemies that you thought you had eliminated actually still existed and was living perfectly contentedly less than a four day's journey away from you. How did you not know any of that?"

"It wasn't my job to know any of that," Lynx said, the defensive tone rising in his voice as well.

"It was your duty, Lynx. As a Denynso warrior, you are bound to protect your planet and your kind, and that means knowing the threats that are there so that you can fight against them."

Lynx looked stung and his jaw hardened.

"You're right," he said. "I failed at my duty, and I will never be able to forgive myself for it."

"You shouldn't have to forgive yourself for anything," Rain told him, the anger starting to melt out of her. "You did everything that you knew to do. It wasn't your fault that you weren't given all of the information that you needed to know what you were up against."

She stopped short of mentioning that the blame actually fell on his king Creia, the powerful monarch of the Denynso clan who purposely avoided telling his people everything that he knew about the risks and threats that lurked on the planet. He hadn't known everything that was going on, on Uoria, but he had known enough that he should have told his people more. He expected that the warriors would devote their lives to protecting the planet and guarding their kind, and yet he hadn't told them everything that he knew about the origins of their kind or the other species that had built the planet as it was today.

"Tell me what happened," Lynx finally said, sounding as though he wanted to distance himself from his own failures and the lingering questions and doubts that kept him feeling somewhat off balance.

"You have to realize that the people of Earth knew far less about the galaxy then, than they do now. There were still many planets and species that we didn't know anything about, and a lot of people were unwilling to take risks to find out more. When we heard about the prison colony, the group that I worked for was divided over what we were going to do. Some didn't want to give it any credence and thought we should just move on. Some even thought that it was a setup and that if we did anything about it, it could lead to a war. The rest of us thought that it was worth the lives of whoever was being held on the planet to find out what was going on. We figured that there were two possible negative outcomes that could happen if we went. We could get to the planet and find that it was, in fact, deserted and that we had wasted the time and resources of the department. Or we could get there, find out that the information was accurate, and be put into a dangerous situation with the Valdicians."

"Did you know of the Valdicians before then?"

"Vaguely. We had heard of them and knew that they were not exactly the friendliest of species, but until then we hadn't had any contact with them."

"So you just left?"

"Not quite. The group of us who knew that there were dangers that we would likely face if we went on the mission and still knew that it was worth it split off from the rest and formed our own committee within the department so that the others could focus on the other projects that they felt were more promising than this one. Fortunately we had the support of the majority of the heads of the department and they enabled us to spend some more time gathering as much information as we could and prepare for the mission. When we left, we were using some of the most advanced technology available. Our Star City ship was exactly what it sounds like, a little city that could travel through space. It had everything that our group of more than 200 needed to survive the journey. It would take weeks to get to the planet, and that was in a ship that was among the fastest available."

"What happened when you got there?"

"The plan was that we would approach the planet in an orbiting pattern so that we would be more difficult to detect. We would be able to recognize any abnormalities on the surface of the planet that might indicate large buildings as we approached. We would gather as much information as we could, then land and infiltrate. The hope was that we would be able to free the prisoners and capture the Valdicians. If we weren't able to, we would send communication back to mission control and leave. When they arrived with more units, we would all return to the planet to complete the mission."

"When did you realize that something wasn't going the way that you wanted it to?"

"Everything seemed fine as we approached the planet. As we got within the orbit of the planet it didn't take long for us to see that the information about the prison colony was absolutely true. There were dozens of buildings spread across the center of the planet and massive walls surrounding them." Rain stopped, suddenly feeling her lungs closing, making it more difficult to release and draw in breaths. She gathered herself, pushing forward. "As soon as we saw it, we knew that we couldn't wait to collect information before we landed. We found a place as far from the buildings as we could and landed. I will never be able to forget what it was like when we stepped out onto the planet for the first time."

Rain felt her mind travel to that first moment when she left the Star City ship the first time. She could still feel the crunching of the dry, pebbly ground beneath her boots and the searing of the intense, almost oppressive heat on her skin. Her eyes closed and she felt her body sway as the overwhelming memories of the screams washed over her. She could hear the voice's cutting through the still air and seeming to sink down to her bones, trembling across them until she felt sick. She wished that she could forget those screams, that she didn't have to continue to hear them reverberating through her mind and reminding her of everything that she saw when they stormed the prison colony and encountered the Valdicians and the prisoners that they held captive on that horrible planet.

The warmth of Lynx's hand against her cheek brought Rain out of the darkness of her thoughts and she turned her face so that she could touch a kiss to his hand. The scent of his skin and the familiarity of his touch soothed her, quieting the disturbing sounds that ricocheted through her mind and shook deep within her soul. She focused on the sound of his breathing, imagining the air moving through his body and back out into the close space of the tent so that she could breathe it in.

"You don't have to tell me anymore," he said, rubbing the pad of his thumb across her cheekbone. "It's alright."

Rain nodded and brought her hand up to cover his, letting her fingers slip between his so that they intertwined lightly on her cheek. She drew her fingertips down along the back of his hand and along his arm until they reached his shoulder. As she traced his arm with her fingers, Lynx brought his hand down from her cheek so that it trailed along her jawbone and then onto the side of her neck. The touch of his fingers on this tender, vulnerable skin made her shiver and she tilted her head slightly to offer him more access. He took the invitation and continued his slow, careful exploration of her neck, bringing his fingers around to the front so that he could trail the tips into the soft dip between her collarbones.

As Lynx's fingers traveled down the front of her chest toward the swell of her breasts Rain could feel her breath quickening. Her hand had fallen away from his shoulder and she brought both to his lap now, running them along his thighs with the same slow, precise attention that he was giving her skin. She wasn't wearing anything beneath her nightgown and she could feel her taut nipples pressing against the thin fabric as if trying to reach Lynx. He didn't make them wait long. His hands came to the blue satin ribbon at her neckline and pulled on one end, releasing the bow and loosening the crossed pattern along the front. This caused the gown to become slack enough that it slipped from her shoulders and Lynx guided it the rest of the way off so that it pooled around her ribs.

Rain drew her arms out of the gown slowly. Her mate looked at her with such intensity, such hunger and adoration in his eyes it was as if she could feel the gaze as it brushed across the skin of her shoulders and her chest and then fell to her breasts. He dipped his head and gently ran his lips along the upper swells of each breast, not kissing but merely stroking the skin with his mouth so that his breath joined the evening air that swept across her nipples. Rain fought to control herself as desire for him flooded through her and settled in her core.

Lynx's mouth opened and his warm tongue glided over her breast and onto one tightened tip, encircling it and drawing it in so that he could suck it gently. His hand came up to cup the other, supporting its weight in his palm so that his finger and thumb could tease that nipple as his mouth did the other. Rain ran her hands up his thighs again, tightening slightly as they reached the juncture between his legs and his hips.

Finished with lavishing attention on her breasts, Lynx ran his hands up her sides so that he guided her arms up in the air beside her head. Rain held them in place as he took the gown that was bunched at her waist and led it up over her arms and off. He tossed it aside and she saw his eyes travel along her body luxuriously. With a soft moan of appreciation he reached forward and trailed his fingers down from the soft dip of her neck along her breastbone and onto her belly. She could feel her muscles shake and jump beneath his touch and her body tingled with growing need for him.

Keeping his eyes trained on her, Lynx peeled off his shirt

and tossed it over to join Rain's gown. She sighed at the sight of his beautifully chiseled body. She had grown accustomed to how much bigger he was than human men, but looking at his smooth skin and defined muscles still made her mouth water. As he brought his hand back to her belly, Rain lifted her eyes to look into his. She was still enraptured by the bright orange coloration of those wide orbs and she wondered if the color would ever lose its appeal for her. It wasn't just that it was so unusual for her, even though it was completely commonplace among the Denynso. Instead, the flicker of joy that came through her when she looked at them stemmed from knowing that he had not been born with eyes that color. Instead, it was finally completing his intended bond with her, his lifelong mate, which transformed his eyes to the color of the sunset. They were a visible signal to anyone who looked at him that he was bound to her and would be devoted to her throughout his entire existence.

Lynx rose to his knees to remove his pants and Rain couldn't resist reaching forward and wrapping her hand eagerly around the surging erection that was already pressing toward her. He drew in a sharp breath at the touch of her hand and she increased the pressure, slightly tightening her grip and running her hand down the length of him and then back up to the head so that she could gather the drops of slick fluid that were forming at the tip. She used them to help her hand slide quickly and smoothly along him, enjoying the feeling of his skin sliding across the hardened muscle beneath it. Lynx lifted his knees carefully and pushed his pants off, kicking them away without pulling away from her adoring touch.

His hand came to her cheek again and he stroked it softly, letting his thumb brush across her lips. Rain parted them slightly and touched the tip of her tongue to his skin. He slipped the pad into her mouth and she sucked on it gently. Lynx moaned low in his throat and Rain felt her stomach clench with the depth of her desire. He withdrew his thumb from her mouth and without needing any more of an invitation she leaned forward to replace it with the head of his erection. She sighed at the taste of him, allowing it to coat her tongue as she slipped her tongue into the slit and then ran it around the edge of the head, stopping to concentrate on the sensitive bundle of nerves on the underside.

She could heard Lynx groan at the attention she was giving him and after a moment she felt his hand tuck beneath her chin so that he could gently pull her away from him and guide her up onto her knees. When her body was touching his, she tilted her head to offer her mouth to him and he accepted it eagerly, drawing her closer as he kissed her so that his tongue explored the furthest reaches of her mouth and her breasts crushed against his chest. She felt one arm wrap around her waist firmly and guide her off of her knees and onto her back. Lynx came down over her, staring into her eyes as their bodies melded together.

Rain accepted him into her, drawing back her legs to open further so that he could sink in fully. He fit inside of her with such perfection it was as though he were part of her that always belonged there. She wrapped her legs around his hips, holding him as close within her and against her as she could. Lynx rested his forehead against hers and she saw his eyes close briefly before opening again to look into hers. He rolled his hips against her with incredibly control, nurturing her with long, slow strokes.

Bringing her hands to his back, Rain ran her fingers from his shoulder blades down to his hips, taking them in her hands so that she could pull him even deeper inside of her. The movement caused him to hit an achingly sensitive place within her and Rain cried out. The sound seemed to inspire Lynx and he thrust into her again, lifting up onto his knees to give himself even more leverage. Rain gasped with the intensity of the sensations that he was building within her and her body started to shake. Lynx continued, moving within her harder and faster until she felt her pleasure spiraling out of control and her walls closed tightly around him.

The squeeze of her body pushed Lynx over the edge and he buried his head down into the curve of her shoulder and neck so that her skin could muffle the scream of bliss pouring out of his chest. Rain could feel his cock throbbing within her and the thought of him spilling into her, filling her as he never had with anyone else pushed her even further, seeming to renew her orgasm so that her body milked his with each deep spasm.

Lynx remained buried deeply within her as they both came down from their earth shattering climaxes. When they had finally cooled enough that they could move, Rain reached beside her and pulled a blanket roll beneath her head while Lynx pulled another blanket up and over them. He was still nestled inside her body and she savored the feeling, not wanting it to end. Her eyes drifted closed and she fell asleep not to the sound of screams, but to the sound of Lynx's slow, even breath and deep, steady heartbeat.

5

They were walking before the sun touched the horizon the next morning. In the shady, purple-blue light of near dawn they walked as a loose cluster with the goal that since they knew where they were going this time, they would be able to make it to the settlement by nightfall that night rather than having to camp again and devote more of another day, leaving the captive Mikana in their state of unsureness for a moment longer than they truly had to.

Lynx felt at peace as they walked. He loved this time of day. He savored the softness of the air around him and the quiet of a world that had not quite yet woken. It was in these moments that a day always had potential and he felt like he could accomplish anything that he needed to.

"We didn't just leave immediately, you know."

Lynx turned toward Rain's voice as she suddenly spoke, breaking the silence among them.

"What?" he said.

"When we got to the prison planet, the one that they call

Penthos now. We didn't just leave as soon as we got there and noticed trouble. We stayed and fought."

"Rain, you don't have to talk about this," Lynx said, touching his mate's hand reassuringly.

"I know I don't," she said confidently, "but I feel like everyone, especially Ivy, deserves to know what really happened on that mission."

"Why especially me?" Ivy asked, sounding slightly taken aback by the assertion.

"You and the other humans are the only ones who even knew that we ever existed before the Denynso found us. They know what we've told them, but you've grown up going through school and being told all sorts of stories and legends about us. I think that you deserve to know the real story of what happened from someone who was actually there. Even though we say that when the others get back to Earth they can be discreet and stay anonymous, we all know that it is not going to stay that way for long. Eventually someone is going to figure out who they are and then chaos will ensue. The story is going to get even more complicated than it already is and there are going to be those people who villainize us and get angry because of the myths that other people created. I want to be able to tell you right from my own mouth everything that I remember about my time on the prison planet, my interaction with the Valdicians, and how we ended up on Uoria."

"Do you still remember everything after all this time?" Ivy asked.

"You have to remember," Rain said, "it has been far longer in your eyes than it has in mine. It has been only 15 years for me, and what I went through, 15 years is by far not long enough for me to forget. I don't even know if I would have forgotten if it had been more than 100."

"Are you sure?" Lynx asked quietly.

After seeing the look of horror and pain on her face the night before as she attempted to tell him what had happened, he didn't want her to feel like she had to go through all of that again. He had wanted to know more about what she went through so that he could feel like he knew her even better and that he could be there for her in the way that she deserved her mate to be, but he didn't want to put her through the turmoil of reliving those moments if he didn't absolutely have to.

"I am," she said, squeezing his hand as she turned to give him a small, reassuring smile. "Last night I started bringing forward memories that I hadn't let myself think about in a long time, and even though it was really difficult to think about them again and to face those demons and those questions, I feel like it was something that I needed to do. If I never talk about them, and I never tell anyone else so that they can know what actually happened, they will continue to eat at me forever and the same things or even worse could happen again because no one knows what to look for or what to do to prevent it."

"Things are different now," Ivy contended. "What happened to you wouldn't happen anymore."

"Every generation thinks that they know so much better than the ones that came before them and that they are going to be the ones that end all of the hardships and tragedies that exist in the universe. They think that they are the ones that would never do anything wrong or cause any pain to anyone. The problem is that they are always wrong. Death and suffering never change, and the curse of those who think that it does is that they rarely see what is happening. They think that everything is perfect until something horrible happens and then they are able to look back and condemn those who caused the pain, and even those who they think allowed the pain to happen. We will always be a step behind those who come after us. I am getting to see that in a way that you never will, but you have to trust me when I tell you that the generations that come after you are going to look back and wonder how you could possibly do things so wrong. All you can do is put all of your effort into doing as little wrong as you can and fixing as much of what happened before you as possible."

"I'm sorry," Ivy whispered, her head lowering to look at her feet as they crossed the open area of the planet rather than keeping eye contact with Rain.

"I know that I would be very interested in hearing more about what happened," Rey offered. "Now that we know that so much of the history of this planet and its species is inter-twined, I would like to know more about what happened. Especially considering what we know about our kind and its interactions with the Covra, it might help us understand everything more if we know how the first humans came to be here."

Lynx saw Maxim nod in agreement. Even as he nodded, though, Lynx noticed that the young Mikana man reached out to take Ivy's hand, offering his comfort and support to his partner. Though neither of them were Denynso, Lynx could see much the same attachment between those two as he did between mates of his kind. He knew that they didn't have the bonding ritual that the Denynso did, an experience that ensured that the members of his kind would only ever commit themselves to the person who they were intended to be with and that once the bond was complete they would never be apart, but they looked at each other with the same passion, intense connection, and total devotion that he did when he looked at Rain.

Rain looked at each of them and nodded as if making an agreement with them that she would continue her story. Adjusting her bag on her shoulder, she focused her eyes ahead in the direction they were walking and continued.

"As soon as we stepped off of the ship, we knew that the conditions on the planet were far worse than we ever could have imagined. The air smelled like smoke and blood, and there was never a moment of silence. All around us we could hear the screams of the prisoners and the shouts of the Valdicians who were holding them captive. We didn't know how many prisoners there were or what types of species they might be. We didn't even know how they had come to be on the planet. The intelligence that we had gotten only explained that they were prisoners of war, not prisoners of any type of crime, and that many were reported stolen from other planets without any concept of where they might have ended up. We knew that finding them and being able to release them,back to their own planets would help to prevent an intergalactic war that would have likely had devastating consequences that would still be reverberating through existence even now."

"You mentioned last night that there were walls around the buildings," Lynx said. "How did you get through them and into the colony?"

"Sheer force," Rain said. "The walls were massive, but they were poorly guarded considering the purpose of the colony. I suppose that the Validicians figured since they were the only ones that even knew that that planet existed and that there was little chance of anyone being able to find them by accident, they didn't really need the level of extensive security that most prison compounds have. We were able to approach the walls without even being noticed, and by the time that any of the Valdicians had realized that we were even there, more than half of those of us who had left the ship to go into the colony had already scaled the wall."

"How could they not notice a Star City ship landing on their planet? Wouldn't they have seen it orbiting and known it was landing?" Maxim asked.

"I really don't know," Rain said. "I would think that at least some of them did notice, but the Valdicians are single-minded, cruel, and conniving creatures. It is possible that those who noticed knew that they would have the upper hand against us and so rather than attacking immediately they took the time to tell others and prepare themselves. All I know is that when I landed on the ground on the other side of the wall, none of the Valdicians were anywhere near us. It wasn't until we had gotten close to the first building that they came after us."

"What did they look like?" Lynx asked.

All he could think about was Ty. Now that they knew that he came from a line that had Valdician blood, he wondered how many of the traits and characteristics he got from those creatures. He knew that the cruelty was not one of them, but Ty was brilliant and had inherited the stunning ability to move objects with his mind from a father he had lost far too soon.

"They were very tall, like the Denynso, but not as big. Their skin was pale to the point of almost being translucent, but their eyes and hair were like coal. As soon as they started toward us, we realized that we weren't contending with anything like what we had prepared for, and this mission was not going to be anywhere near as fast or seamless as we had hoped. Rather than using weapons, the Valdicians simply picked members of the crew up and tossed them. The only way that we could fight back was to get behind them and attack with our own weapons. I knew that there was little that I could do in terms of fighting them off, but I was still determined to help any of the prisoners who I could, so I broke away from the battle and ran into the colony."

She stopped talking and Lynx looked at her. The struck, terrified look had returned to her face and he knew that she was reliving the horrors that she saw within that prison camp.

"What happened, Rain?" he asked, trying to gently guide her forward.

He truly didn't want to hear anymore, but he knew how important it was to her to tell her story and he wanted her to know that he was there beside her, protecting her.

"I found them," she said. Her voice had become dull and even, sounding almost as though the words weren't coming from her at all. "I have never seen anything like what I found in that compound and I hope with everything inside me that I never will. I expected to find the prisoners in cells, possibly chained within the buildings. Instead, many of them were chained along the outer walls of the buildings, suspended several inches off of the ground so that they had to either pull themselves up by their arms constantly or suffer the cutting of the cuffs into their wrists and the drag of their entire bodyweight on their shoulders. Some you could see had already dislocated their joints and were merely dangling from the chains. They had given up."

"What did you do?" Maxim asked.

"I knew that I didn't have much time, so I released the shackles of the ones that looked the healthiest and the most capable of fighting and getting out alive."

"Their chains weren't locked?"

Lynx saw Rain shake her head. The darkness in her eyes made it seem like she wasn't even there and he found himself praying that it wouldn't always be there, that she would come back from the memories.

"It was part of the Valdician's torture. They used shackles that connect with a latch rather than a key, but the latch was just out of reach so even though all the person in the shackles would have to do is flip the latch in the right direction, they weren't able to. They had to hang there knowing that they were just a few centimeters away from being able to get out, and staring at the others knowing that there was nothing that they could do for each other. I released a few of the prisoners and gave them the supplies and weapons that I had carried in. By this time the Valdicians had started back into the colony and were starting to fight against the prisoners I had freed. At some point one of them lifted me off of the ground with his thoughts and threw me against one of the buildings.

Everything after that moment is very disconnected. I remember opening my eyes and all I could see was flames and smoke. I don't even know what was burning, but the air was so thick I could barely breathe. When I did manage to get a breath in, it burned in my lungs. I couldn't stand, but I felt someone grabbing my arm and yanking me to my feet. Everything around me was fire, smoke, and screams as I ran. We barely made it out of the colony. It was like I could feel them at my heels and as I ran all I could think was that at any moment I was going to be in the air again and this time I wasn't going to survive the impact of my landing. But we made it to the ship and back inside. When I think back on it now I wonder if they were chasing us on purpose, not to catch us but to get to our ship. They could have incapacitated us at any moment, but instead they just chased after us until we got to the ship and inside. I could hear things hitting the sides of the ship as we tried to take off. Then I thought that the Valdicians were hitting it, but now I know that it was the weapons.

The weapons that they used were unlike anything that any of us had ever heard of. It wasn't until much later that we realized that they were throwing these tiny spheres at the ship. They latched on and turned into robotic creatures that were able to infiltrate the actual structure of the ship, bypassing the control system and setting into action a course programmed by the Valdicians."

"How long did it take you to realize that you weren't going back toward Earth?"

"It didn't take long. We weren't far from the planet when we realized that our commander was no longer in control of the ship. We tried to reach out to mission control, but all of our communication systems had been destroyed. I think that I knew then that nothing was ever going to be the same. I just didn't want to admit it to myself. For the rest of the journey the crew tried to figure out what was controlling the systems and override it, but they couldn't. By the time that we got close to Uoria, most of us were in survival mode. Obviously none of us knew where we were or what was happening, but we knew that if we were going to land, we were going to have to figure out how to get through it."

"Did you know that you were crashing?" Lynx asked.

"I felt the control of the ship leave. I don't know how to explain it any other way. I could feel it carrying us and then suddenly it just wasn't anymore. Not all of us had the chance to get into our seats before the crash. It seemed like it was only a few seconds, but I'm sure that it took longer. It just seemed like we were flying one moment and then the next we were plummeting and then the ship hit the ground. I've never heard anything sound that loud. The impact destroyed all of the systems inside so it was suddenly pitch black. Even the emergency lights wouldn't turn on.

I remember scrambling to take off my safety straps and trying to claw my way through the darkness to get out. I could hear the hissing of the electronic systems and the fuel tanks, and I knew that there was going to be an explosion. As I was climbing through the control room trying to find my way out I felt something grab my ankle and I kicked it away thinking that it was a piece of the controls. I wondered every day after that if it could have been one of the crew that we later found dead in the wreckage trying to get me to help him escape. When I was nearly at the exit, I felt my feet slip and I fell. I cut my arm, but later I found blood on the bottoms of my boots and I knew that's what made me slip.

When the explosion finally did come it was like the world was ending around me. I had managed to run far enough away from the ship that I wasn't seriously injured, but I knew that there were many of my crewmates, my friends, who had been in the recesses of the ship and there was no way that they would have been able to get out. I heard them screaming and it brought me back to the prison colony and the screams of the prisoners. It all became one sound in my mind.

I wish I could tell you that I remember everything that happened after we crashed, but the truth is that the first few days, maybe even weeks, are so blurred together I can't remember what really happened then. I know that despite what I really knew deep in my heart, I kept telling myself that someone would come for us. Even while we were sending out scouts to try to figure out somewhere we could place our camp. Even as we were going through the wreckage and pulling out the bodies so that we could bury them. Even as the sunrises and sunsets blended together and we realized that we needed shelter so we started breaking down what was left of the ship to build the settlement. I lived in a state of balanced torment. There were moments when I felt like I was going along with life on this new, strange planet absolutely fine and that we would all be OK, and then there were moments when I started thinking about it and I became desperate to find away off of the planet. I knew that someone had to be looking for us and that eventually they would find us, or that we would find a way to rebuild our ship and send at least a few people back to Earth for help.

Finally I let it all go. I realized that no matter how much I wanted to think that the people of Earth wouldn't simply let us disappear and never come find us, that that is exactly what happened and we were never going to leave. I was never going to see my parents again. I would never see my sister get married or have children. I would never again see all of the places that I loved. This empty, unknown planet was my home now, and gradually it started to look more beautiful. I was fortunate. I realized the truth and settled into living my life out on Uoria far earlier than some of the people. I don't think that it was until the first baby was born on the settlement that some people really got it through their minds that that was it. We were done. Earth and its people were only a memory and this was where the rest of our lives would play out."

6

"They didn't forget about you."

Maxim felt his mate's hand slip from his and watched as she stared at Rain, her face tense with an emotion he couldn't quite identify.

"What?" Rain asked, turning to look at Ivy.

"The people of Earth didn't forget about you. You said that you realized that they had just not bothered to look for you, that they didn't come to find you and that's why you had to stay here on Uoria. That isn't what happened."

Maxim could feel the tension rising between the two and he looked to Lynx, the appointed leader of the expedition, to gauge how he was reacting. He seemed calm, watching the interaction without saying anything.

"That's how I felt, Ivy."

"But that's not what happened. You act like you don't remember what Zuri told you. They named the entire planet after lamentation and mourning because of how deeply they felt about losing you. There was no way for them to know what happened to you. You didn't even know where you were, how did you expect for them to know how to find you? We've lived our entire lives hearing about the heroics of Project Nyx 23 and you are making it seem like you were just tossed aside."

"That's not what I meant. You have no idea what it's like to be on a completely unknown planet, have no idea why you are there, or what you are going to do, and then to have a species that you have never even heard of come after you and try to destroy you. That's what we went through. It would have been impossible for us not to think about mission control and the rest of the people on Earth and wonder why they didn't come for us. It might not have been logical, but it was what we went through. We looked up into the sky every night and knew that somewhere out there, among all of those stars, was our planet, and we wondered if we would ever see it again. We wondered if anyone out there had realized that we were gone and how long it would take for them to start looking for us. Eventually those thoughts and all of the hope that came with them faded."

"It wasn't their fault," Ivy said. "They did come for you."

"What did you learn about what happened to them and how the military responded?" Lynx asked.

"Mission control alerted the government as soon as they realized that they had lost communication with the ship. It was a clandestine mission so not everyone knew that it was even happening, but that also meant that it was especially dangerous. Any changes in protocol were taken very seriously. Less than 12 hours after mission control was not able to get in touch with you and was not getting a response, a team of special operative military units were sent to Penthos. That was when they told the rest of the people of Earth what was happening. Everyone was put on alert. There was some concern that the ship had been high jacked and that it would return but with the crew being held hostage. The government instructed the people of Earth to be prepared in case the ship landed in their area. Of course, it never did.

The military units got to the prison colony as quickly as they could, but you weren't there. We were taught that there was a massive conflict and the Valdicians were destroyed with Earth taking over the planet and declaring it uninhabitable."

"What happened to the prisoners who were still there when we left?" Rain asked. Her voice sounded slightly desperate and her eyes were wide as she searched Ivy's face for any detail. "I know some of them had to have survived. Some of them had to have made it out of the colony and survived on the outskirts of the planet long enough for the military units to arrive and rescue them."

"We were told that the military units liberated them and sent them back to their original planets."

"Sent them back?" Maxim asked.

"The military operative traveled in several different ships so that they could arrange a more complex attack. After destroying the Valdicians, one of the ships was rerouted as a rescue ship to bring the freed prisoners home."

"Did you ever find out who those prisoners were? What kind of species or what planets they came from? Anything?" Rain asked.

Ivy shook her head.

"No. The military never released that information. They said that they didn't want to cause any more pain to those who had suffered by rehashing what had happened to them."

"What did they do to the planet? To Penthos?"

"What do you mean?"

"After they named it, what did they do with the planet?

Is there a memorial there or anything? Has anyone gone back there since the military units left?"

"Not that I know of," Ivy said. "The government announced that it had declared the planet uninhabitable and off-limits to everyone within the galactic federation. There are memorials on Earth, but as far as I know no one is allowed to travel there."

Maxim thought over what Ivy had told them. Something about the stories that Rain and Ivy had told didn't make sense to him, but he couldn't quite figure out what it was.

"No one ever found out who sent the intelligence about the prison colony?" he asked.

"No," Rain responded. "It was anonymous. One of the members of our organization brought it to our commander, but wasn't able to tell us where she got it."

Maxim made a soft sound of acknowledgement.

"What is it, Maxim?" Ivy asked.

"I'm not sure," he said. "It just all seems so strange to me. If the Valdicians really were as ruthless as Rain says that they are, who could have possibly found out about the prison colony and sent the information to Earth without getting caught? And how could they have suddenly made the decision to send you to Uoria? Did they just happen to have the technology to override your ship's operating systems and disable the communication devices sitting around at such easy reach that they were able to grab it in the midst of a battle?"

"What are you saying?" Rain asked.

"I don't know," Maxim responded. "It just doesn't make sense. They would only have developed that technology if they intended to use it. Could it really be a coincidence that when you arrived they just decided to use it and it perfectly led to them sending you to their allies?"

"We were lured there," Rain said.

Maxim could feel the startled emotions coming off of Rain as she started to piece together what he was telling her.

"What do you mean 'lured'?" Lynx asked.

"Whoever sent the intelligence that the Valdicians had an illegal prison colony on that planet knew about our department. They were trusting the fact that when we heard about the colony we would send a team to investigate," Rain said. "They wanted us to come. They weren't surprised by us. They were expecting us. This wasn't an accident. Us getting stranded here wasn't some convenient event for the Valdicians. They planned it. They wanted to send us to the Covra. They didn't realize that our voices would be their greatest weakness."

Rain sounded angry now, as if emotions that she had long suppressed were starting to come out of her.

"Maxim," Rey said, stopping him before he was able to respond to Rain.

Maxim looked up and saw the outline of the settlement wall against the horizon in front of them. His feet stopped moving as if by their own volition and he felt his breath pause in his lungs for a moment. They had finally made it. They were only a matter of steps away from the arched entryway that would lead him back to his people, to his brother who was suffering in the captivity of the meeting hall, not knowing what had happened to Maxim or if he would ever return. For now, questions about the Valdicians and who had brought Nyx 23 to the prison planet would have to wait.

Without saying another word, Maxim pushed forward. Everything around him seemed to fade as his steps quickened until he was running toward the settlement, no longer feeling the weight of the packs on his back or slung over his shoulders. He could hear the pounding of the footsteps of the rest of the group running to catch up with him, but he didn't stop. When he finally reached the arched entryway built into the worn, weathered stone wall surrounding the settlement he paused and glanced back over his shoulder. Just as he was turning back around he felt a hand clamp down on his other shoulder.

"So you've come back," a voice growled.

Maxim looked up to see Vax, the Denynso who had so vehemently agreed with Pyra's intention to destroy the entire Mikana clan, standing only inches from him, his massive hand gripping Maxim's shoulder painfully. Rather than feeling intimidated, Maxim was angry. He shrugged out of Vax's grip and squared his chest to him. Though his size was no match for the warrior, he refused to back down.

"I'm here to release my clan," he said calmly and evenly.

Vax laughed, his hand moving to his hip and the hilt of the knife that Maxim could see tucked into a sheath at his waistband. The move was subtle, but threatening, and Maxim felt his muscles tense in response.

"You will do nothing of the kind," Vax said through gritted teeth. "We are under the command of Pyra to keep the filthy creatures quarantined in the meeting hall."

"And we are under command of Creia to have you release them."

Maxim turned when he heard Lynx's voice behind him. In his intense standoff with Vax he hadn't noticed that the others had caught up with him. Now Lynx was holding the letter that Creia had given him before they left and staring down Vax. There was seething tension between the two warriors as they both stared at each other with expressions that said they still felt the other was wrong and a betrayal to his kind.

"What did you say?" Vax asked.

"Creia has sent us to release the Mikana and welcome them back to our compound if they want to come. If not, they are free to return to their kingdom. The warriors are to report back to the compound as soon as possible to perform guard rounds while the others are on Earth."

"They still went?" Vax asked, sounding both shocked and infuriated.

"Yes. Now bring us to the meeting hall."

"Let me see that letter."

Lynx handed the letter over to Vax, who glared down at it. His strong hand gripped the edge of the parchment so hard Maxim worried that it would tear it before they were able to get it to the warriors standing guard outside of the meeting hall. After a few seconds of examining the letter, Vax shoved it back at Lynx and made a huffing sound. It was obvious that he hated the situation that he was now in, but as a Denynso warrior his first loyalty was to the king and he was not able to deny him. No matter what he thought of the Mikana, he was at the mercy of the monarch's command and had to help the appointed group release the captives and then return to the compound.

Vax stepped out of the way and the group entered the settlement, stepping into the aftermath of Pyra's reign.

7

The streets of the settlement were unnervingly quiet. If he hadn't known that they were there, Maxim would have thought that none of the humans had remained when they left the settlement. They followed behind Vax and Maxim looked around intently, trying to find any hint of the people who lived there, of life continuing on after they started for the Denynso compound.

"Where is everyone?" Rain finally asked from behind him.

"They are in their homes," Vax said sternly.

"All of them?" Rain asked. "Why?"

"They have finished their services for the day and are at home where they belong."

"Where they belong?" Rain snapped, pushing past Maxim so that she was walking closer to Vax. "Where they belong according to who?"

"Pyra," Vax said simply. "You were here. You know the schedule that he created for the people of this settlement when they came under his command. They perform their services during the day and they spend the rest of their time in their homes. By controlling them, we keep them safe."

"Safe from who?" Maxim asked, the anger starting to build inside him. "The only ones who these people need to be kept safe from is you."

"They aren't under Pyra's command anymore," Rain said. "You have no right to keep them locked in their homes. They spent enough time stuck where someone else told them to stay. That's over now."

"I promised my allegiance and obedience to Pyra. This is what he wanted."

The words made Maxim's stomach feel sick. The blind, unwavering level of devotion and following of the lead warrior was disturbing.

"Pyra isn't here," Rain said, "and he isn't in command of anyone any longer."

"Creia disagreed with Pyra," Lynx said. "He told him that what he did here was wrong and that he had failed all of us. If you continue to insist that you will follow Pyra's commands, you are going against your king, your people, and even Pyra himself. He has denounced his actions and expressed deep regret for what he did while he was here."

Maxim could see a vein in Vax's neck throb and his jaw tighten even further. He didn't say another word to them, but as he approached the meeting hall Maxim saw him step up to one of the guards.

"Tell the people of the settlement that they are no longer under our control and that they may leave their homes and go about their lives as they wish."

The words carried hopeful sentiment, but the sound of his voice was still gruff. Maxim knew that regardless of how Creia, and even Pyra, felt, Vax was still firmly in the belief that the Mikana were not worth allowing to live. He could not be trusted, and Maxim was looking forward to the slightly older warrior leaving to return to the compound.

The other warrior looked at Vax strangely and then evaluated the group that had followed him. He met eyes with Lynx and Lynx stepped forward to show him the letter from Creia. After reading it, the warrior handed the parchment back to him and started down the main street, stopping at homes as he went to pound on the doors. Vax started around to the back of the building and as they followed him Maxim could hear the other warrior relaying the same message to the people who were streaming out of their homes that Vax had given him.

When they reached the back of the meeting hall they found two warriors flanking the door. They had a slightly worn look as if the days of standing guard on a continuously rotating schedule that offered precious little time to sit and even less to sleep was starting to drag on them. Lynx started to step forward and then came back and turned around to face Rey.

"I think that it is your place to do this," he said respectfully, offering the parchment from Creia to the leader of the Mikana kingdom.

Rey looked at him for a bit and then took the parchment from his hand slowly. Maxim could see the light in his leader's eyes, the light that had slowly disappeared while they were in the settlement and had gone completely the morning that Maxim discovered the changing of his skin, start to return. Rey stepped up to the warriors, both of whom turned their heads only slightly and glared at him.

"I come with a proclamation from your king releasing the Mikana from your control and your guard. They are to be let out of the meeting hall immediately and permitted to do as they wish."

One of the warriors took the parchment from Rey's hand and examined it before handing it off to the other, who also read it. He handed the parchment back to Rey who gave it to Lynx and then looked into the eyes of each of the warrior guards in turn.

"Now, men," he said, his voice sounding firmer and more confident than Maxim had heard it in a long time.

The warriors stepped away from the building and one of them released the large, heavy latch that kept the door in place. There was a rush of sound as soon as the door swung open and for a moment Maxim thought that it was the sound of air moving through the tight hallway, but then realized that it was voices from deep inside the building. Rey stepped inside and Maxim came up behind him, wanting to get in to the others as quickly as possible.

They had only taken a few steps down the close, stale-smelling hall when Danye, one of the young members of the kingdom, stepped out of one of the rooms that led off of the hall and faced them. He was holding a small bowl in his hands but he dropped it as soon as he saw Rey and Maxim. A smile broke across a face that looked weathered despite being trapped inside a room for days, and aged well beyond his years.

"Rey?" he said, sounding unsure of himself as if he thought that he was conjuring up the image of his leader and friend. "Maxim?"

Rey stepped forward and gathered Danye in an embrace, patting him on the back. When the hug ended, Danye turned down the hallway and shouted to the others.

"Rey and Maxim are back!" he yelled. He seemed to

suddenly notice the flow of evening light coming into the hallway from the open door and his smile only widened. "The door is open! The guards are gone!"

The hallway filled with the members of the Mikana kingdom. Their voices blended and lifted in the tight space, surrounding Maxim until he felt nearly overwhelmed by them. He made his way through the men gathering in the hall, pushing through in search of his brother. Finally he emerged from the hall into the room where they had been gathered when Pyra brought the decision down that they would be quarantined there until a final decision was made about their fate. Just stepping into the space brought back the panicked memories of standing there helplessly, watching as Loralia created a wall without windows or doors that cut the meeting room in half and blocked them in that small portion of the building.

"Maxim!"

Kyven's voice cut through the din created by all of the others and Maxim felt his heart lift. By the time he turned toward the sound, his brother was gathering him into his arms. Maxim held Kyven to himself tightly, gripping his shirt and rocking him slightly.

"Are you alright?" he asked, pushing back and looking at his younger brother's face carefully.

"Yes," Kyven answered.

"Are you sure?"

"Yes. I knew you'd come back for me."

Maxim felt a sudden pang of guilt. Escaping from the meeting hall with Ivy and running away from the settlement had been one of the most difficult decisions that he had ever made. He had left his brother behind, not knowing if he was ever going to see him again, not knowing if Kyven was even going to survive the ordeal. Maxim was glad he had done what he did, though. Had he not listened to Ivy and gone with her when she had come for him, they wouldn't have encountered Pyra in the wreckage and forced him along with the others to agree that what happened to the Mikana wasn't his decision to make.

"I didn't abandon you," Maxim said, holding his brother's face in both hands and looking at him in the eyes. "You know that, don't you?"

"I know, Maxim."

The sound of the voices in the hallway was lessening and Maxim realized the men were finally leaving the building. He started toward the hallway, but felt Ivy pull him back.

"I need you to stay in here with me for just a minute with no one else," she said.

Maxim looked at Kyven and held up a finger.

"Just one minute," he said. "Go outside. Breathe some fresh air. I will be right out."

Kyven nodded and hurried toward the door. Even though he was only slightly less than a year younger than Maxim was, Kyven suddenly seemed so young and vulnerable. When the voices all dissipated and the room fell silent, Maxim let Ivy pull him toward her.

"What is it?" he asked.

"There's something we need to do," she said.

Releasing his hand, she stepped up toward the wall that Loralia had created. It had been the most astonishing thing that Maxim had ever seen, and even now he didn't understand how she had done it, or how Ivy had managed to bypass it to bring him out onto the other side with her. He saw her lift her hands and rest them for a moment on the surface of the wall, her shoulders falling with a sigh.

"What are we doing?" he asked.

"Come here."

Maxim walked up to her and Ivy turned away from the wall to take both of his hands in hers.

"Do you believe that I'm here?" she asked.

"Of course I do," he said, leaning forward to touch his forehead to hers.

"Even if someone told you that I wasn't, would you still believe it?"

"Of course I would."

"Kiss me," she said.

As their lips touched Maxim could feel her take him by the arms and start to lead him away from the wall, guiding him along and up the steps of the well in the center of the floor until they were halfway up. She pulled away from him and looked at the wall.

"What are you doing, Ivy?"

"Do you believe that you can keep me safe? That you would never let anything happen to me?"

"I would never let anything hurt you?"

"Do you really believe that? Completely?"

"Yes. Ivy, what are you talking about?"

She was starting to scare him, and the fear only increased when she released his arms and started running down the steps toward the wall. She picked up speed as she went, but just before she would have crashed into it, she seemed to pass right through the wall. An instant later, he was looking at her on the other side of the room, the wall now gone. She smiled at him slightly breathlessly and they ran towards each other, meeting in an embrace on the platform in the center of the room.

"It was just a reflection," she said to him. "It was only real when you thought it was, but if we believed that it wasn't, it wasn't. You believed that no matter what, if you were with me, I was going to be safe, which means that I wouldn't hit that wall."

"What did you believe?"

"That when I turned around, you would be there."

TBC

(To be continued in book IV...)

THE ALIEN'S MATE

1

The air smelled like smoke and fire again, but this time as Ivy leaned against the stone wall at the back of the settlement, the smell didn't make her stomach turn. She remembered that first night that she had breathed in the acrid, burning smell of the flames that licked the sky. It was painful then, a harsh reminder of the funeral that was happening in the settlement below. That was the night that they had honored the dead that the settlement had lost to the Covra. She had run from the flames that night, wanted to get away from the mourning that made the air as thick as the smoke. That was the night that she had met Maxim.

The smell of the flames was celebratory now, but she had still run from them. The people in the settlement below lit the fires to burn the final reminders of the Covra and to celebrate the release of the Mikana from their captivity in the meeting hall. A mix of Denynso, Mikana, and humans swarmed the main street, dancing, singing, and feasting. Ivy stood on the hill that rose at the back of the settlement, her back against the stone wall. She had run from the flames, but not because she wanted to escape them. Not because they frightened and sickened her the way that the funeral fires had, but because she craved the darkness and privacy of that distant wall. Like the night of the fires, Maxim stood in front of her.

She was still enraptured by his intense beauty. Even though he was completely familiar now, known to her heart, mind, and body unlike any other man had ever been, she still found herself stopping sometimes just to look at him. His incredible beauty was by merit of being a part of the Mikana tribe. Every member of his kind had the ethereal appeal, and it was that appeal that made it even more shocking to find out that they were the predecessors of the grisly, slimy Klimnu. She had seen only part of Maxim's skin dissolving away as a reaction to the flowers that he had touched the first time that they had made love, and even that small amount of change had been truly terrifying. She couldn't even imagine what it was like to see the full Klimnu, creatures who had transformed under the power of the flowers and their own greed and hatred. The other women had tried to describe the creatures to her, pulling on their own horrifying memories of their encounters with them, but Ivy didn't think that those descriptions ever could have done justice for what those gruesome beings truly were.

In that moment, however, none of that mattered. She didn't care what Maxim had the potential to become. She cared only what he was, and that was the man who she loved with a depth that was almost unimaginable even as she was feeling it, the partner who she had chosen and who she was willing to face fear, danger, and hardship for by staying on Uoria rather than going home. Maxim was every-thing to her, and even though she ached to return home to

Earth and put the horrors that she had experienced on Uoria behind her, she knew that as long as he was here and as long as he was still searching for the answers to all of the questions that had come up once the Denynso arrived at the settlement, she would be by his side.

Ivy reached out for Maxim and took him into her arms. His body pressed against hers, pushing her back more firmly against the wall so that he enveloped her as his mouth took over hers. He kissed her languidly, his hands grazing down the sides of her ribs and into the dip of her waist. She could feel the rhythm of his heartbeat against her chest where the rhythm of her own responded, drumming against her as if reaching through their bodies toward one another. She wanted to stay right in that moment forever, to not have to let him go or even relinquish the indulgent taste of his tongue in her mouth, but she knew that she had to. They were waiting for him down in the settlement. There was a banquet happening and he was expected to be a part of it alongside his brother and the others of his kingdom.

She took her mouth slowly and reluctantly from his and touched the tip of his nose with hers.

"We should go back," she said softly.

Maxim gave a deep sigh and nuzzled his body closer against hers.

"I know," he whispered back. "I would rather just stay up here with you, though. Maybe take a little walk outside of the settlement."

He leaned around to nibble at her ear with his suggestion and she gave a soft laugh.

"I don't think that we need any more skin dissolving emergencies," she said.

"I'm sure that we could avoid the flowers this time."

"They are throwing a banquet down there in honor of

your people. Don't you think that you should be down there?"

He tilted his head as though he were thinking through his options.

"No," he said with a smile. "I would still rather be up here with you."

"What about your brother?" she asked, laughing as Maxim tucked his head to kiss along the side of her neck.

"He can find his own woman. I've never liked sharing and I'm not going to start now."

He ran the tip of his tongue in the curve between her neck and her shoulder and Ivy shivered slightly. She wanted to take that walk with him. She wanted to push their way through the old, forgotten gate as they had that night several days after the funeral fires, and disappear into the darkness of the fields and hills beyond the settlement. She wanted to feel his body against her skin and welcome him into her body in the way that made her feel safe, comfortable, and alive. She knew, though, that it was his responsibility to go back to the celebration. He had been instrumental in ensuring that the rest of the Mikana were released from the meeting hall where Pyra had ordered that they be put into what he called quarantine, but what Ivy knew was simply imprisonment. The leader of the Denynso warriors had been overcome with anger and hatred that day, and had let his power over the other warriors and the intimidation of the humans force them to enclose all of the Mikana in half of the main room of the meeting hall. If it hadn't been for Maxim's courage and determination, they would likely have all died there.

Ivy smiled as she thought of the wall that Loralia had made in the middle of the meeting hall room. It had truly been a reflection of the ceiling, put in place to prevent the captive Mikana from leaving that portion of the building. Though at the time Ivy couldn't understand the level of cruelty and disregard for life that had influenced the strange and beautiful creature to make that wall, she soon learned that it was how Loralia ensured that Ivy would be able to free Maxim. By suggesting to her that she simply not believe that the wall was there, she would be able to get him out so that together they could figure out what they were to do next. What she had learned, however, was that she didn't need to believe that the wall wasn't there, but that Maxim was. It had gotten him out of the room the night that he had been put into captivity, and just the night before it had made the entire wall disappear, leaving the room open again and removing the tangible reminder of Pyra's misguided decision.

"Come on," she said, playfully pushing on his shoulders to move his exploring mouth away from her even though the last thing she wanted was to lose the feeling of those lips and that skilled tongue on her skin. "There's a lot to be done."

Maxim stepped back from her and nodded.

"I know." He paused and reached up to brush a strand of her thick blond hair away from her face. "I love you."

Ivy felt the same shiver through her body that she always did when he said those words. They were wonderful and precious and inextricably hers. Each time that she heard them it was a reminder that he was real, the he felt the same passion and devotion for her that she did for him.

"I love you, too," she said.

Ivy lifted her lips up to accept the kiss that Maxim touched to them before he took her hand and started leading her down the hill back toward the revelry in the settlement. As they walked down past the meeting hall she noticed a dark shape lingering close to one of the walls, staying in the shadows rather than stepping out into the light created by the fire.

"Hello?" she called to the shape.

It stepped forward and she could see that it was Vax, the warrior who had followed so closely behind Pyra during his brief but terrifying reign over the settlement, and who had stepped in to ensure that Pyra's commands were upheld even as they left the settlement to return to the Denynso compound for Creia's guidance. Ivy fought the urge to step back away from the huge man. As much as she didn't want to admit it, she feared this warrior, possibly even more than she had ever feared Pyra. Even though the lead warrior had been vicious and single-minded in his determination to destroy the Mikana because of their link to the Klimnu, he had recanted. He had knelt before Creia and asked for his forgiveness for the choices that he had made and for losing the faith and the trust of his people. Though Ivy hadn't yet been able to bring herself to fully forgive him, she at least knew that he had recognized the wrong that he had done and wanted to change his ways.

Vax, however, had made no such move. Even after they told him that his leader had changed his mind and had gone back on his assertions that the Mikana should be killed, Vax would not back down. He had had no choice but to follow the proclamation from Creia that officially freed all of the captive Mikana. Even as he did it, however, he had shown nothing but contempt and fury. Ivy could still see in Vax's eyes the darkness and empty, sullen stare that told her that he had not let go of the fury that he had felt, or the desire for vengeance that he had thought he passionately shared with Pyra. In holding onto these feelings and now knowing that he was no longer supported and validated by his adored leader, Vax became unpredictable, and that was unnerving for Ivy.

Giving into the intimidation and stepping back away from Vax, however, would have given the warrior too much power and only reinforced his sense of superiority and control. She wouldn't give him that.

"Why did you have to come back?" Vax asked in a low, gravelly voice.

"I came back for my brother and the rest of my kind," Maxim said, tightening his grip on Ivy's hand slightly.

"Not you," Vax said. He turned to Ivy and she felt the animosity radiating off of the warrior. "You," he said. "Why did you have to come back?"

"I am here to be with Maxim," Ivy answered.

Vax gave a mirthless laugh and stepped toward them. Ivy still refused to back up.

"Why?"

"I love him."

"How could you do that?" Vax asked. "He isn't one of us."

"I'm not one of you," Ivy replied defensively.

"You came to the Denynso compound. You made the agreement to follow our ways."

"I came to the Denynso compound to learn your ways and find out more about your kind. I made no agreement to be anything like you, or to change in any way."

"The other human women who came here joined the clan."

"The other human women found their mates among the Denynso. That has nothing to do with me. Pyra had no power over me and you don't either. I have no obligation to the Denynso."

"Creia will feel differently about that," Vax said. "There are laws and regulations."

"Don't start that again, Vax. That's been done. I have followed the laws and the regulations. Creia released me from my guard. Pyra thought that he was going to agree with him about the Mikana and order them be destroyed, but he didn't. He is ready to welcome them into the compound and build alliances again. It's over. It's time to let it go."

"It will never be over."

axim's eyes squared on Vax. The huge warrior's words were cold and threatening, but Maxim wouldn't let himself react. It was what Vax wanted. He could see in the Denynso's eyes that he was hoping that Maxim would lose control and attack him, proving that he and his kind really were as vicious and uncontrollable as Pyra and Vax had said they were from the beginning. Maxim refused to give him that satisfaction and to feed into the hatred that drove Vax into the shadows and made him seethe with an anger that had nowhere to go.

Maxim held Ivy's hand tighter and pulled her back away from Vax. Without saying anything, he turned and led her back onto the main street and toward the celebration that was still going toward the center of the settlement. The warrior's provocation continued to burn in the back of his mind as they approached, but he pushed it away when he saw his brother standing among others of their clan and some of the humans, a large cup in one and a chunk of bread in the other. Kyven took a deep sip from the cup and then tore off a piece of the bread with his teeth. Maxim didn't want to think about how hungry and thirsty his younger brother was. He knew that some of the human women had tried to bring them food and water, but he would be very surprised if he found out that the Denynso guards actually permitted them to go to the men more than a few times since they had left.

Kyven looked up and caught sight of Maxim. Maxim saw a smile break across his face. A moment later his brother rushed toward him and Maxim let go of Ivy to gather Kyven into his arms. He had been free only one day and Maxim was still thrilled every time that he saw him able to move around as he pleased, alive and safe. There was still guilt deep in his chest for leaving with Ivy, even though he knew that it was only his leaving that made it possible for them to rescue the Mikana. When his father died he had promised his mother that he would take care of Kyven and make sure that he stayed safe. He felt like leaving him in that room rather than trying to get him out along with him was going against his promise to his mother and a dishonor to the memory of their father. As Kyven grinned and took a deep swig from the stein in his hand, however, Maxim felt a sense of relief. Everything worked out exactly as he would have hoped it would and he knew that his brother was safe.

"Have you had anything to eat?" Kyven asked, looking between Ivy and Kyven.

Maxim realized that in all of the chaos he hadn't actually introduced the two of them.

"Kyven, this is Ivy. Ivy, this is my younger brother Kyven."

"It's wonderful to meet you, Kyven," Ivy said.

"It's great to meet you, Ivy," Kyven said, giving Maxim a knowing look.

Maxim wrapped his arm around Ivy's waist and gave her a squeeze, leaning forward to press a kiss to her temple.

"Have you had anything to eat?" Kyven asked again.

Maxim laughed.

"You never change, do you?" he asked. "Always thinking about food."

As soon as he said it, Maxim regretted it. He didn't want to think about his brother being hungry in the meeting hall, and more than anything wanted to know that he was happy and comfortable. He gave him the biggest smile that he could manage, trying to press forward before Kyven could notice what he had asked and comment on it.

"What is there to eat?" he asked.

Kyven smiled again and gestured for them to follow him. They wove through the crowds filling the street, moving closer to the massive fire they had built near the wall created by Loralia to block the Covra when the warriors were still fighting them before the others from the compound arrived to help. The wall stood in the middle of the street, a reminder of everything that they had gone through and the efforts made to save the humans at the settlement from the fearsome creatures.

When Maxim had first arrived at the settlement with the rest of his kind and heard about the struggles that the Denysno had had with the Covra, Maxim had wished that he had been a part of the battles, had been able to witness the incredible tactics of the Denynso warriors. Now, though, he was glad that he hadn't been there. He didn't know then that it wasn't actually the Denynso warriors but a woman, the last of her species, who had been able to utilize her incredible abilities from the compound to create the towering wall of spikes that destroyed the advancing Covra. Had he known, Loralia creating the wall that had held them within the room of the meeting hall would have had a deeper, more painful impact. Standing beside them as they created a wall to defeat a hated enemy only to watch as the same people who he had fought alongside imprisoned them in the same cruel way.

Several people seemed to have dragged tables out of their homes and arranged them near the fire, piling them with food and full steins. The celebration wasn't like the banquets held in the kingdom, but there was something exuberant and informal about it that made Maxim feel energized and excited. He grabbed a stein and took a long swallow of the thick, spicy drink inside. He took a moment to look around at the people celebrating in the street. He noticed a few people standing at the outskirts of the celebration, seeming disconnected and distanced from the rest of the people in a way that was obvious and uncomfortable. Though there were only a small number of them, the expressions of ill feelings on their faces seemed to link them even across the space between them.

"I see that not everyone is as happy as they should be," Ivy said beside him and Maxim looked down at her.

He kissed the top of her head and gave her waist another squeeze.

"It will pass. Soon they will learn that we are moving forward and they have little choice but to come along with us," he said, hoping that he could convince himself of the same thing. "The future will be different for everyone on this planet and anyone who ever visits it. But we will face that when it comes tomorrow. Tonight, we celebrate."

By the time Maxim awoke early the next morning, the celebration felt like a distant memory. Even the sweetness of Ivy's naked body pressed against his in the predawn light wasn't enough to take the thoughts of his torturous dreams out of his mind. In those dreams he saw the face of his father, the details hazy and indistinct over time, and heard the sobs of his mother in the days, weeks, and months after they found out about his death. He saw the anger in Pyra's eyes, and the cold disconnection in Ciyrs's expression when the healer pressed his fingers into the dissolving place on Maxim's skin, revealing once and for all that he was reacting to the flowers as the Klimnu had. The dreams were brutal, painful flashes of shattered memories interspersed with thoughts of what could have been and what could still be if they didn't find out more about the Order and what had happened leading up to his father's death.

He knew that they couldn't wait any longer. He had come back to the settlement not just to free Kyven and make sure that the rest of his kind were safely freed. He had come back to dedicate himself to resolving the questions that lingered over him and the shadowy secrets that he felt some people would rather leave in the shadows.

Maxim climbed out of bed carefully, trying not to disturb Ivy. He dressed and turned to take a moment just to look at her. The sun was just started to creep up the horizon, allowing a small amount of blue light into the room. It was just enough to illuminate her where she lay on her belly on the bed, her hair spread around her and the blanket flung down low over her body so that he could see the swells of her breasts pressing to the bed and the soft curve of her hips just revealed by the edge of the cover. Her full lips, still slightly swollen and darkened by his kiss, were parted as she breathed and he reached to run his fingertips along them.

Ivy's eyes opened at his touch and she smiled at him sleepily before realizing that he was fully dressed and getting a confused, concerned look on her pretty face.

"I'm sorry, my love," he whispered to her. "I didn't mean to wake you. Go on back to sleep."

"What are you doing?" Ivy asked. "Where are you going?"

"I'm just going to talk with Kyven," Maxim told her, running his hand down her back tenderly. "It's alright. Sleep."

Ivy sat up and Maxim's eyes fell to her breasts. His stomach clenched, but he forced himself to concentrate on what needed to be done.

"I'm going with you," Ivy said insistently. "I agreed to be a part of this, and that means being a part of all of it. You can't just decide to leave me out of things."

"I wasn't leaving you out," Maxim told her. "I'm just going to talk to him and find out if he knows anything else about our father or the Order that he hasn't told me."

"I'm coming with you."

Maxim knew that he had little chances of convincing his partner of anything that she didn't want, so he waited as she climbed out of bed and padded around the room dressing. Even with the heaviness that had settled back over him with the taunting of his dreams, Maxim felt an overwhelming sense of gratefulness for her. He knew that no matter what he was going to face in the journey that lay ahead of him, she would be what was going to make it worth it, and what was going to give him the strength to carry it through.

3

Eden trembled slightly as she approached the shuttle, with Lysander tucked against her chest. She could feel Pyra's hand rested protectively against her lower back and felt comforted by its presence, but the gleaming shuttle positioned in the circular platform still sent a strange shiver of nervousness through her. It had been less than a year since she had first arrived on Uoria, but it felt like it had been a lifetime. She could no longer imagine living anywhere but in the Denynso compound with Pyra and the rest of the clan, and she felt oddly uncomfortable with the thought of getting back on the shuttle and traveling days away from the home that she had adopted as hers.

She had argued so passionately against Pyra to convince him that her and their son traveling to Earth with the rest of them was what was right for them, but even that conviction didn't change the anxiety that was starting to build in her stomach. At once she knew what was waiting for her on Earth and had no idea what might have changed. She knew that back at the research center Ryan was still working on his potentially less than ethical projects, and she knew that even though she had never returned and had made no effort to contact him, he hadn't done anything to make sure that she had even survived the trip to the planet, much less if she was still doing well there.

This didn't really surprise her. She had already resigned herself to the knowledge that Ryan hadn't sent her to the planet because he believed in her scientific abilities or really thought that she was going to be successful with the mission that he had created for her. Instead, he had sent her to the Denynso with the mission of collecting some of their blood in hopes that she would be caught by the warriors. Attempting to gather some of the highly desirable, incredible powerful blood from the fearsome Denysno warriors was the single most serious crime that a visitor to the Denynso compound on Uoria could commit. This single offense could result in imprisonment, exile, and even death. That was what Ryan was counting on, Eden had come to realize. She had rejected his advances and threatened to tell his superiors how he treated her and how much of the work that he presented as his own was actually hers. By sending her on this mission he was hoping that she would make a mistake and get caught, never having the chance to return to Earth and make good on her threats.

She wondered what he had been doing in the time that she had been gone. The impression that he had given her was that most of the research that he had been doing when she left had been hinging on her coming back with the Denynso warrior blood. He convinced her that it was that blood that would allow him to complete the research projects that they had started and complete some experiments that could completely change the face of weaponry. Eden hadn't really understood what he meant by that then, but now that she knew the Denynso warriors, the thought of someone utilizing their blood to craft weapons was truly terrifying. These were massive, fearsome warriors prone to aggressive, violent reactions and capable of relentless battle. Their blood held the source of this power, and if Ryan got hold of it the results could be disastrous.

"What are you thinking about?" Pyra asked softly as they gathered at the base of the platform to await boarding.

Eden's eyes were trained on the second shuttle beside the first and she shook her head slightly.

"Just Ryan."

"Why are you thinking about him?" he asked.

She could hear the defensiveness in his voice and regretted saying anything. Her mate was incredibly protective of her and their son and he hated to hear anything about the man who made her life so difficult when she was on Earth and then sent her to what he figured would either be her certain death or his ticket to fame and wealth.

"He sent me to Uoria because he wanted me to try to steal blood from one of the Denynso warriors," she said.

"I know," Pyra responded. "We've already talked about this. But you made the very wise decision to not go through with that and to stay with me instead," he said with a smile.

"But now I'm heading right back to Earth with a whole group of warriors."

The smile faded from Pyra's face and his hand slid around her waist to hold her more closely.

"He wouldn't try anything," Pyra said. "He might have thought it was a good idea to go after our blood when he wasn't anywhere near us and when he could send a woman to do it for him, but he will think differently when he is actually face to face with us."

"I hope that we don't end up face to face with him at all," Eden said.

"You don't need to be afraid of him, Eden," Pyra said. "We're going back to Earth for Ty and Samira's wedding. We aren't there to see Ryan and we aren't there as part of the university program. He doesn't even have to know that we are back on Earth."

Eden nodded, not wanting to talk about it anymore. The thought lingered in the back of her mind, however, that she doubted they could arrive back on Earth and not have Ryan find out. The task would be to avoid confrontation with him.

Creia stepped up in front of the group and Eden lifted her eyes to the king rather than continuing to dwell on her own thoughts. He held out his arms to all of them and offered a smile that looked softly sad, but also extremely proud.

"Another historic day has arrived," the king said. "As some of our number have returned to the settlement to free the Mikana and begin our journey toward long-awaited reconciliation and building of a new and meaningful coop-eration among the species who call our beloved planet home, you will embark on a journey that only one of our kind has made before. You will step on these shuttles and travel off of Uoria and to Earth where you will not only witness the also historic marriage of the first Denynso warrior who has undergone such a ritual, but you will learn more about the planet that we have been working toward creating an alliance with and learning more about. What you learn there will be instrumental in our continued efforts to eradicate the myths and misconceptions that the humans there have of us, and that we have of them so that the lines of communication and cooperation can truly open for the first time in our history. This is a precious and exciting time, and I cannot tell you how proud I am of each one of you. Even though I will be staying behind here with Theia so that we can protect the compound and be waiting in the event that the group from the settlement returns before planned, know that my spirit and my thoughts are with all of you, and that I'll be excited to hear everything that you experienced when you come home."

There was a scattering of applause and Eden realized how nervous everyone around her looked. It was comforting to know that she wasn't the only one who was coping with anxiety related to the trip, but she felt that as one of the few of them who had actually made the trip between the planets it was her responsibility to help soothe and reassure the others who had not ever been off of Uoria, or who had been away from Earth for so long that the thought of returning was almost like going to a foreign planet. She stepped up to Brandy's side and touched a hand to the human woman's back.

The woman turned to look at her and offered a shaky smile.

"It's really happening," Brandy said.

"It is," Eden said, wiggling her newborn son up higher on her shoulder and patting him gently to soothe his soft fussing as he started to awake from his nap. He quieted quickly and she felt his tender belly start to rise and fall slowly with deeper sleep. "Are you excited?"

Brandy looked at the shuttles and then back at her with a sigh.

"I think so. I know it's going to be different. I just hope that I recognize at least some of it."

"You will," Eden reassured her. "It is different, but it's still the same planet. And you'll have us there with you to help you."

Before Brandy could answer, the pilot of each of the shuttles stepped out of the doors of the shuttles and looked out over the group waiting to board.

"All of your cargo is securely packed. The attendants have lists of which passengers should be on which shuttles. Whenever you are ready, you are welcome to come aboard."

The group shifted as they formed a line to approach and climb the steps onto the platform where two attendants stood in the space that connected the two landing bays. They each held notebooks that Eden assumed had lists of the names and other details of the passengers so that they could arrange them into the two shuttles. When she traveled to Uoria from Earth the first time she had been the only one other than the crew who had been aboard. Now both shuttles would be filled to capacity.

Her family approached the first attendant and she checked through her list, then pointed them in the direction of the first shuttle. It looked newer and more complex than the one she had ridden to Uoria the first time. She stepped inside and took a breath of the starkly clean space of the first lounge.

"If you will proceed to your assigned passenger pod room we can begin preparing for takeoff," the attendant said from behind them.

"Will I have my baby with me?" Eden asked, suddenly worrying that they would take Lysander from her and she would be forced to be away from him throughout the journey.

"Yes," the attendant said. "You can keep him in your passenger pod with you. Everyone else, however, must be in individual pods. Please decide if you are going to undergo sedation so that we can begin the process."

The attendant stepped back out of the chamber and

Eden looked around at the people who were gathered in the lounge with her. Zuri, Ero, Elianna, Ciyrs, Ty, Samira, Loralia, and Bannack stood close together in the lounge as if unsure of whether any of them were ready to comply with the instructions from the attendant.

"Are we going to do the sedation?" Bannack asked.

"Did you do it?" Ero asked, looking at Zuri.

"I did on the trip back to Earth the first time," Zuri said.

"What was it like?" Loralia asked.

Zuri shook her head.

"I did it because I didn't want to think about anything on the way," Zuri answered and Eden could see an uncomfortable, guilty look cross Ero's face. "To be honest, though, I didn't like it. It was unnerving to close my eyes and then wake up a few days later. I knew that I was just lying there in my passenger pod, but at the same time, I didn't like knowing that the world was just going on around me and that the crew was awake moving about the shuttle while I was just lying there with no idea what was going on. Now that I know what the flight attendant that was there was actually up to, it makes me even more hesitant to want to be at the mercy of anyone for several days."

Eden nodded.

"Not to mention what happened to Leia."

There was a brief moment of tense silence and then Pyra nodded.

"So we're in agreement. None of us will undergo the sedation. We'll stay awake so that we can stay vigilant about what is going on around us."

"Have you made your decision?" the flight attendant asked as she stepped into the room carrying an armful of blankets.

"Yes," Pyra said. "We don't want to be sedated."

"Very well," she said. "I'll get you situated in your pods and let the captain know that we are prepared for travel."

"How long do we have to wait in the pods until we are able to get out?" Lynx asked.

"Just long enough for the shuttle to get far enough out of the planet's orbit to get into the planned journey path. Should be no more than an hour. When we are traveling safely, the doors to your pod will release and you will be able to get out and move about the shuttle as you please. Refreshments and entertainment will be available then."

Satisfied, Eden and the others followed the attendant into the first passenger pod chamber. As the attendant unlatched the two pods, checked the insides to ensure that they were properly prepared, and draped a blanket across each, Eden turned to Pyra.

"Just an hour," Pyra said, reaching forward and taking Eden's shoulders in his hands.

"I know," she answered.

Pyra pressed a kiss to the top of Lysander's head and then to Eden's lips.

"We'll see everyone in the lounge when we get out," Pyra said to the rest of the group.

They all affirmed and started out of the chamber into the next. Once they were gone, Eden walked over to one of the pods and carefully handed Lysander into Pyra's hands so that he could hold him while she got settled into the pod. This pod was far more comfortable than the seat that she remembered from her first journey, and she felt her nervousness start to dissipate. She settled in and secured her seat belts, positioned her carry-on bag at her feet, then reached for Lysander. Pyra settled the baby into her arms and then draped the blanket over both of them, tucking it in tightly around them.

Eden tilted her face up for one more kiss and then took a deep breath. She looked to the attendant who was standing beside Pyra and nodded.

"I'm ready," she said.

"Just relax," the attendant said. "Enjoy your trip."

Eden smiled and patted Lysander on the back as the large cover of the pod closed over her and clicked into place.

4

L eia felt herself shaking with fear as she stared down at the passenger pod. She wished that she and Gyyx were in the same shuttle as the other warriors, the human women, and Loralia, but she wondered if even that would make her feel any less fearful of climbing into that pod.

"It isn't the same shuttle, Leia," Gyyx said comfortingly from behind her, running his hand down her back.

"I know," she said back to him, trying to force her voice above a trembling whisper. "I know it isn't Gyyx, but I can't stop thinking about it."

"Everything is going to be fine this time, Leia. I promise. I'm here."

Leia nodded and took a breath, trying to calm herself. She couldn't help but think about the last time that she was in a shuttle much like this one. Though that shuttle was older, she could just as easily see the image of the interior of it super-imposed over this shuttle. She remembered getting onto the shuttle from Earth headed to Uoria, filled with the excitement of knowing that there was a new adventure waiting for her on the strange and distant planet. She wanted to create art inspired by the planet and the plants and creatures on it, and was dreaming only of the growth that she would experience as an artist on her visit to the planet when she stepped onto the shuttle.

She had never left Earth before and didn't know what to expect from the journey. When the pilot had asked her if she wanted to be put to sleep so that she didn't have to experience the entirety of the five-day journey, she had immediately declined, thinking that it would be so much better to just stay awake and maintain control. She had spent far too much of her life under the influence of men and the substances that they plied her with, and she didn't want to allow herself to spend any more time that way after she had worked so hard to rid herself of this control and shake herself free of the addictions that had defined her for so much of her life.

The pilot had promised her that the takeoff would be the worst part of the journey. He told her that all she had to do was sit in her pod and relax until it released her, and then she could move around the shuttle however she pleased until it was time to land. Though she knew that he thought it was strange that she wanted to stay awake for the full five days rather than just letting it pass easily while she was sleeping, he didn't seem at all concerned about the experience. This flight was going to be no different than any of the other ones that he flew, and he was accustomed to flying on a nearly continuous basis.

What she didn't know when he smiled at her and made his way out of the passenger chamber and into the control room was that it was the final time that she was going to see him. On the second day of her journey the pilot and the attendant who had helped her were slaughtered when the

Klimnu attached their ship to the shuttle and took over. They thought that she was a scientist who could help them with their efforts to take over Uoria. When she told them that she was only an artist who was part of a university exchange programmed designed to allow students from Earth to travel to Uoria and others from Uoria to travel to Earth as well, several of the vile, slimy creatures simply wanted to consider the entire mission aboard the university shuttle a wash and kill her as they had the other two aboard.

The leader of the group, however, hadn't wanted to kill her. Instead, he had taken a strange and disgusting liken to her and decided that he was going to keep her as his own personal pet. She had spent the rest of the trip dangling from a hook hanging from the ceiling of the shuttle. The wounds created in her skin had been so deep that even months later they were still painful and not fully healed.

It had been after this painful, torturous journey, however, that the true torment of the Klimnu had begun. She had no way of knowing then that she was actually the first of the humans who had visited the Denynso compound to encounter the disgusting creatures who were the most hated of the enemies of the warriors. She would later find out that the Denynso didn't even know that she had arrived. The university had lost contact with the shuttle and thought that it had gone off track. They had sent a recovery team to search for the shuttle, hoping that they would simply find that they had gotten lost and needed to be redirected.

Of course they never found them. That was because the ship had gone to Uoria, it had simply landed outside of the barrier of the Denynso compound. Leia didn't remember much of what happened after the shuttle landed. She assumed that the Klimnu had brought her over the boundary and destroyed the shuttle so that no one would find it. Now that she knew more about the planet and the mirrored realm that existed just beneath the ground of the compound, however, she knew better. Even the Denynso didn't know about what was going on under their feet at the time. They didn't know that there had once been an entire colony that had lived there but that then it was used by the Klimnu to hide from the Denynso as they built their defenses.

Leia now assumed that it was through the chambers of that mirrored world that they brought her into the far reaches of the compound and into the dark, dismal prison where she would spend the next 57 days. During the nearly two months of her captivity the KIimnu tortured Leia in ways that left her mind even more scarred than her body, but it was also during that time that they told her information that she would later be able to share with the Denynso that would help them to understand the motivations of the horrific creatures.

She hadn't thought that it would bother her to get back on the shuttle. She hadn't expected that the gruesome memories would flood back to her with the level of intensity that they had as soon as she stepped over the threshold of the lounge and into the passenger chamber. As soon as she had taken that step, however, her bag had slipped from her hand and she felt like she couldn't breathe.

Leia was incredibly thankful that she and Gyyx had been the last of the passengers to take their positions in the shuttle. She didn't feel comfortable enough with the others on the shuttle for them to see her in such paralyzing fear. Gyyx stepped up closer behind her and she could feel his body mold against hers. He was incredibly large, big enough that her head came to rest just beneath his chest and one of his arms was able to fully wrap around her without Gyyx having to reach. It had been this immense size that had immediately attracted and frightened her when she first met the man who had saved her from the coma that she had been in after the Denynso had found her in the prison.

Now it was this size that made her feel safe and protected. She had been completely alone except for the crew of the shuttle the first time that she was on it. There had been no one and nothing to guard her from the Klimnu. This time she was on a full shuttle that held three warriors in addition to her own mate. If something happened, she knew that they would be there and give her more of a chance of getting through the journey unscathed.

"Miss? I'm going to have to ask you to go ahead and get into your pod now," the flight attendant said.

Her voice was calm, but Leia could hear a hint of frustration in it that told her that the woman was eager to get them prepared and off of the ground.

"Do you want them to put you to sleep?" Gyyx asked softly. "It might help if you aren't awake for the next few days."

Leia thought about it for a moment. It was tempting to just lie down and not have to think about anything until they arrived on Earth, but at the same time she didn't relish the idea of giving the Klimnu such power over her, especially now that that iteration of the creatures had been eliminated by the Denynso. She had fought for so long to escape the darkness of her past and prove that she could overcome the torment that she had gone through even before leaving Earth the first time. She didn't want to give up now and resign herself to a life of fear.

She looked up at Gyyx and shook her head.

"No," she told him. "I want to be awake for this."

Leia settled into the pod and focused on Gyyx's face

until the cover came down over her and clicked into place. She closed her eyes and focused on the movement of her breath until she felt the shuttle lurch beneath her and knew that they had taken off. It was truly happening. They had left Uoria and in a matter of days they would be back on Earth.

An hour later she heard the familiar click and hiss of the lid of her pod releasing. It bounced up a few inches and she clambered to release the safety straps holding her against the plush seat and get out of the pod. Gyyx was already standing in the middle of the chamber and she ran into his open arms. He swung her up and held her against his chest, pressing kisses to the side of her neck. When she had first bonded with Gyyx she had hated the way that the massive warrior had picked her up and carried her around like a rag doll. Now, though, she loved to feel the total support and protection of his arms.

Gyyx lowered her to the ground and they walked together toward the long, wide windows that covered the entirety of the far wall of the passenger chamber. The windows of the shuttle she had ridden on her first trip had been smaller, and Leia liked the way that these almost made it seem like there was no window at all, just them floating together through the stars outside.

5

"Kyven," Maxim said, grabbing hold of his brother's shoulder and shaking it. "Kyven, get up."

Kyven groaned and gave a half-hearted attempt to roll over away from Maxim's grip, but Maxim held tight to him and gave him a harder shake.

"What?" Kyven moaned, partially opening his eyes.

"You need to get up. Ivy and I need to talk to you."

"What's wrong?" Kyven asked.

His younger brother pulled himself up to sit as he rubbed his eyes. As Maxim watched him his mind flashed to when they were younger. Kyven had woken up in that exact same way since he was just a baby, rubbing his eyes so hard sometimes that their mother had worried he was going to damage his vision. Kyven always said that he was just rubbing the last of his sleep out of them and that he never really felt awake until he had done it enough.

"We just need to talk. Come on. Get up."

Maxim walked out of the bedroom and went back downstairs to where Ivy was waiting in the living room. The house was still quiet in the dawn light and Maxim knew that with the revelry that had occurred the night before it was likely that most of the people in the settlement would be sleeping in for several more hours. Even so, he didn't trust that there weren't ears listening wherever they were in the main portion of the settlement so he knew that he was going to have to bring his brother further out before they could talk.

"What are you going to tell him?" Ivy asked as Maxim sat down on the sofa beside her.

He took her hand from where it rested on her thigh and examined her long, slim fingers.

"Everything. I don't think he even knows as much as I did before we talked to my mother, and now I know so much more. He deserves to know, and he could help us find out everything else."

"What if there is no everything else?" Ivy asked.

Maxim stared at her.

"Please don't start this again, Ivy."

"What do you mean? I am just wondering what if everyone who knows everything is already dead and you are just digging up the past?"

"Sometimes the past is worth digging up. That past is my past, and without that past I don't really have a future. I need to know everything that I can about my father and what caused his death. Him dying changed my life, my brother's life, and my mother's life more than I could ever tell you. I need to know why he died and who caused it. Especially now that I know that it had something to do with the Klimnu and everything that the Klimnu caused on this planet."

He was starting to feel worked up, but Ivy looked at him

with her cool blue eyes and lifted a hand to tenderly stroke the side of his face.

"Alright," she said softly. "I won't ask again. If this matters to you, then it matters to me. I will do whatever I can for you."

Just then, Kyven came down the stairs loudly and walked into the living room still looking like he hadn't managed to rub all of the sleep out of his eyes. He was dressed, but his thick hair hadn't been combed. The wild effect made him look even younger and Maxim felt a surge of protectiveness toward him.

"What did you need to talk to me about?" Kyven asked through a yawn.

"We can't talk here," Maxim said.

He stood up and stalked out of the house, needing to get as far away from the buildings and everyone in them as quickly as he could. He was trying, but he still didn't know who he could trust. He wondered how long it would be until he could truly relax again.

Several minutes later Maxim stopped at the back of the settlement near the wall. It was the place where he had met Ivy and where they had spent many of their early moments together. Here he felt calm and peaceful, and here he knew that there was no one who could get close enough to hear them talking without one of them seeing the person first.

He paced back and forth for several seconds and then looked directly at Kyven.

"Have you ever heard of the Klimnu?" he asked.

"Of course," Kyven said, looking at his brother strangely. "I was right there with you listening to that crazed Denynso ranting about them before he locked us up in the meeting hall."

"I mean before that," Maxim said.

Kyven shook his head.

"No."

"Are you sure? You never heard anyone mention them, even once?"

"I'm sure," Kyven said. "You heard Rey. None of our kind knew that the group that split off went on to become those creatures. Everyone thought that they had just gone out onto the planet on their own and died off."

"Mom knew about them."

Kyven stilled and Maxim saw his eyes widen slightly and then narrow as if he was searching his older brother's face for emotion or explanation.

"What do you mean that Mom knew about them?"

"She knew. She knew that the Klimnu existed and she knew that they came from the group that split off from the rest so long ago."

"Was Rey lying about that, too?"

"No," Maxim said, stepping closer to Kyven. "He doesn't know. According to him, the fate of that group was a complete mystery until we showed up at the settlement and my reaction to the flowers made the Denynso realize that we are the species that transformed into those loathsome creatures."

"I don't understand. How did Mom know? If our leader didn't even know, how could our mother possibly know?"

Maxim took a breath.

"It has to do with the Order." Maxim could see the darkness that rolled over his younger brother's face and he pressed on before Kyven could walk away from him. "When Ivy got me out of the meeting hall we were going to escape to some other part of the planet, but I changed my mind and decided to go back to the kingdom. I thought that it might be safe there. When we got there, we found Athan. He let us into the tunnels."

"We're never supposed to go into the tunnels."

"I know that," Maxim said. "I've spent a lot more time down there than you have. More than I ever wanted to admit to you."

"Why?"

"Because I was curious. I wanted to know what Papa had always talked about when he told us stories about the Order."

"I mean why did you not want to admit it to me?"

Kyven sounded hurt and slightly angry, and Maxim felt a slight pang of guilt.

"You never wanted to know as much as I did," he tried to explain. "You were always satisfied to listen to Mom when she told us that we should stay out of the tunnels and away from anything having to do with the Order. It wasn't enough for me. I needed to know more."

"I don't even understand why Athan would let you down into the tunnels. The Order is gone now. Those tunnels are probably dangerous."

"The Order isn't gone," Maxim told him.

"What?" Kyven asked, sounding shocked at what Maxim had told him.

"The Order isn't gone. It didn't end with Papa dying and it is still going strong."

"Then why aren't we in it?"

"I don't know. That's part of why I wanted to talk to you. Athan was really nervous to let us down in the tunnels, which means that he is still a part of and afraid of the Order. When we were down there we heard two men coming toward us. I couldn't recognize either of their voices, but they almost caught us. We barely made it up through a hatch into one of the hidden entryways before they got to us."

"Does Mom know that the Order still exists?"

Maxim nodded. Kyven seemed to be coming around. The sleepiness was gone from his voice and his eyes, and he was starting to pace slightly back and forth as he listened to Maxim.

"I'm pretty sure that she does," Maxim said. "When we got back home we told her what was going on and she talked about the Order like they are still around. She told me that they knew the entire time what the group had become. They knew about the Klimnu and the horrible things that they did."

"Why didn't they do anything about it?"

"She said that they tried to. She told us that they made alliances with some other species in the badlands and that they tried to fight them off before they left Uoria. It didn't work. By the time that they came back, the generations had forgotten about the Order and even about the Mikana. They only remembered warfare and they destroyed the alliance."

"Who was the other species?"

"She didn't know. That's when she kind of pulled back from us, like she realized what she was talking about and didn't want to do it anymore."

Kyven stared at Maxim for a few long seconds and then suddenly seemed like he had broken out of the spell that his brother had put over him and shook his head.

"What does this have to do with anything, Maxim? So what if the Order still exists? What if they knew about the Klimnu? That is all over now."

"What if it's not?" Ivy asked.

Kyven turned to look at Ivy, the expression on his face like he had forgotten that she was even there.

"What do you mean?" Kyven asked.

"Don't you think that it's strange that every male generation of your family since the beginning of the Order was a
member, but neither you or Maxim is?"

Kyven hesitated.

"Our father's dead. Maybe a living relative has to be a
part of it when the new people are inducted."

"Mom implied that Papa's death had something to do
with the Order and the Klimnu."

"What?"

"When she first told us that the Order knew about the
Klimnu, I questioned it and she said 'Why do you think that
your father died the way he did?'"

"What did she mean by that?"

"I don't know, but she also said that some members of
the Order tried to fight against the Klimnu when they came
back after being on Ynn for so long. She said that there was
a violent conflict."

"You think that that's when Papa died?"

"I don't know, but I want to. I want to know what
happened to him and why the Order tried to cover up the
existence of the Klimnu."

"What do you want to do?"

"We need to go talk to Mom again. We need to find out
everything that she knows, and then find out everything else
that we can."

Kyven looked unsure.

"Maxim, we aren't supposed to know that the Order
exists much less anything that they have done or might have
done. It is incredibly dangerous for us to even be talking
about this. I don't think that we should push it any farther."

"We have to know, Kyven. We have to know why we are
the only men in our family who haven't been in the Order.

Papa knew something. Something happened that he knew about and that's why he's dead and why we've been cut off from the Order. We have to know what that was."

"No. You have to know, Maxim. You're the one that this has always mattered to so much. I never cared about the Order or what it meant or when we were going to be a part of it. The only reason I cared when Papa would bring us into the tunnels or show us the secret doors was that we were spending time with him. Now that that's over, I don't think that there could be any benefit in us continuing to dig. We would just be putting ourselves and our mother in serious danger. I just got out of imprisonment because one group wanted to destroy us, I don't need to give another group reason to feel the same way."

"But don't you want to know why the Denynso did that? Don't you want to know what drove Pyra to keep us all captive?"

"He told us. The Klimnu have been the enemies of the Denynso warriors for decades."

"But why? What drove them to that level of cruelty and greed?"

"Maxim, it's over. We're out and the king of the Denynso compound has extended his welcome to us. He wants the conflict to be over, and I think that we should give him that wish. You need to learn to let go."

Kyven turned and started back down toward the settlement. The sun was fully up now and Maxim knew that their privacy would soon be broken as some of the people who had left the celebration earlier got up and started their days. He needed to convince Kyven to join him now or he might lose him again.

"We never got his body back."

Kyven stopped and kept his back to Maxim for a moment before turning to face him.

"What?" he said evenly.

"We never got Papa's body back. Don't you want to know what happened to it? Don't you want to know what could possibly have happened to him that we wouldn't be able to bury him the way he deserved to be buried, and why?"

"It won't change anything, Maxim."

Kyven's voice was softer, almost pleading for Maxim to stop so that he didn't have to think about the painful memories any longer.

"What if it could, though?" Ivy asked, stepping up beside Maxim. He felt her take his hand in hers and he intertwined their fingers familiarly. "So much is happening on Uoria right now, Kyven. The species aren't separate anymore, and they never will be again. Everything that happened here changed that and there's nothing that could happen that will put it back again."

"Everyone is learning more about the planet and how the different settlements and species came to be. People are finally coming together and have the chance of really benefitting each other," Maxim said. "But it isn't over yet. There are things that we don't know, that other people don't even realize that they need to know, and we are the only ones who can really figure it all out. If we don't do it now, if we don't really find out what happened and figure out a way to fix it, Uoria won't ever truly be safe."

"Alright, Maxim," Kyven said, finally sounding resigned to what Maxim had told him. "What do we do?"

6

A zra closed his eyes and pressed his hand over them, trying to force his mind to calm down. He was still sitting in his passenger pod even though the top had released and he could hear the voices of the other passengers drifting into the passenger chamber from the lounge where they had gathered. Anyone who looked into the pod right then might have thought that he was afraid of the trip, or that he was feeling sick because of the unusual, unknown movements of the shuttle. What they couldn't know is that the trip didn't bother him at all. Unlike some of the others who had climbed aboard the shuttle for their first venture off of Uoria, he was excited about the adventure and had absolutely no anxiety about the unknown that awaited them. The feelings that he was dealing with were something far more unexpected, and far more frightening, than any space travel could be.

The door to his pod opened and Azra took his hand away from his eyes to look up at who opened it. Elise, the beautiful flight attendant who he had first seen standing on the platform directing passengers into the shuttle, stood over the pod, smiling down into his face.

"Azra?" she said brightly. "Are you alright?"

Azra forced a smile and nodded.

"I'm fine," he said.

"All of the other passengers are out in the lounge and I was getting ready to serve breakfast if you'd like to join them."

Azra nodded again but didn't move.

"Thank you," he said. "Maybe I'll join them in a minute."

Elise looked at him strangely.

"Are you feeling alright?" she asked. "Have you rethought about being put into sleep so that you don't have to actually experience the flight? If you have, that's alright. It can still be done."

"No, no," Azra said, waving his hands as if trying to convince her that, that was not the case. In fact, the last thing he wanted was to sleep through the entire time that he had on the shuttle, and with Elise. "I'm going to be fine. I guess I'm just getting used to the whole idea of space travel."

The smile returned to Elise's plush red lips and she pushed the lid of his pod completely open.

"Come on. You'll feel much better once you have some-thing to eat."

Azra released the safety straps that held him to the seat inside the pod and climbed out, carefully pulling his blanket along with him and wrapping it around himself before turning around to face Elise. She laughed slightly.

"Chilly?" she asked.

"A little bit. I'm not used to being inside places like this."

"I can ask the captain if he can increase the temperature in your pod a little if you would like."

"No, that's alright," Azra answered quickly. "I don't really plan on spending much time in there, and if I am, I'll have my blanket. No reason to go to any trouble for me."

Elise smiled again and started toward the lounge. Azra followed behind her, trying as hard as he could to keep his eyes from only focusing on the sway of her hips and the deep curve of her waist. When they got into the lounge Elise disappeared into a crew area and Azra crossed the room to where Gyyx sat at one of the tables against the window. He was eating what looked like small nuts out of a bowl and he looked up at Azra with a confused expression when he approached.

"Are you going for some sort of fashion statement with that?" Gyyx asked, taking the shell of one of the nuts out of his mouth and tossing it into a cup beside him.

"No, I am not going for a fashion statement," Azra replied, the aggravation evident in his voice. "I'm trying to be...subtle."

"Subtle?" Gyyx asked. "What the hell could you be subtle about wrapped up in a blanket like....oh, damn." Azra nodded at him. "Who is she?"

"The attendant, Elise," Azra said.

Gyyx chuckled and took another shell from his mouth.

"Well, she's a good one, at least you've got that."

Azra felt his hands clench and his jaw tighten almost painfully with a surge of defensive anger that flowed through him at Gyyx's words.

"What do you mean by that?" he snarled.

"Calm down, Azra," Gyyx said. "My mate is standing about twelve feet from you. There's nothing for you to be so defensive about."

Azra tried to calm down, but he couldn't seem to control the waves of emotion that were moving through him at unnerving speed.

"Don't talk to me like that, Gyyx."

"What's going on over here?" Reston asked, crossing the lounge to stand beside the table.

"Why don't you tell him, Azra?"

"I want to kill him," Azra growled.

It was the most overwhelming blend of emotions that he had ever experienced. The intensity of his aggression toward Gyyx was blinding, even though in the logical part of his mind he knew that the fellow warrior posed no threat to Elise. Combined with the fierce arousal that seemed to be getting more and more evident by the moment, these violent emotions only further confirmed what he had realized only moments after seeing Elise for the first time. She was meant to be his mate.

"Why is that?" Reston asked.

"I mentioned that Elise seemed like a good woman," Gyyx answered.

He was continuing to work his way through the bowl of nuts and something about his incessant crunching and tossing of the shells into the cup beside him only made Azra's feelings of aggression toward him increase.

"The flight attendant?" Reston asked.

"Yes," Azra said through gritted teeth.

"Damnit," Reston said. "You are seriously going to leave me as one of the last maybe six warriors without mates, aren't you?"

"Just make sure that you are being careful, Azra," Gyyx said, his tone suddenly serious as the teasing disappeared.

"What do you mean?" Azra asked.

"Be sure that you are completely positive about this woman before you do anything with her."

"What are you saying, Gyyx?"

The other warrior sighed and looked into Azra's eyes intently.

"Look, Elise seems like a really nice girl. She's sweet and she's pretty, but so was the flight attendant who helped Ullie betray us to the Klimnu. I just want you to know what you're doing."

Azra made an adjustment so that the surging erection that he'd had since climbing aboard the shuttle wouldn't be as obvious and walked away from the table. He didn't want to listen to any more of this. He had been part of plenty of good-natured ribbing when the other warriors had mated, but now that he was going through the almost painful signs that he was close by his intended mate, it no longer seemed like something that they should be laughing about. This wasn't a Denynso woman or even a human woman who had come to the compound with the intention of staying for a while. This was a flight attendant who he would have only a matter of a few days with and the thought that she was meant to his mate sent a sinking feeling through his gut.

Holding the balled-up blanket in one hand, Azra stalked through the lounge and back into the passenger chamber. He dropped into his pod and let his head fall back against the seat.

"I guess that being in the lounge didn't agree with you as much as I thought that it would."

Azra looked up and saw Elise standing beside him again. She was carrying a tray balanced on one hand and a folded stand in the other. In one swift movement she propped the stand up and rested the tray on it.

"That was pretty impressive," Azra said.

Elise laughed and nodded.

"I've gotten a lot of practice," she said. "You don't want to know how many of these trays I've managed to splatter across the floor, or even worse, on a few passengers."

"I want to know everything about you."

The words came out of Azra's mouth before he was able to control them and he wished that he could gather them up and push them out of the way before she heard them, but the softly startled look in her eyes told him that Elise had heard. She opened her mouth slightly and then closed it again. Azra didn't know what to say to her, but started to apologize. Before he could, she looked down at the tray and spoke again.

"I made this for you," she said. "It isn't exactly what was on the menu for breakfast, but it's what I ate on my very first trip. I was really nervous and something about this made me feel better. I don't know if it was actually the food or not, but I've eaten it every first breakfast on every trip since and it keeps me calm for the rest of the trip."

Azra felt his heart swell slightly and he gave her a small smile.

"Thank you."

She nodded and walked away. After a few steps she stopped, turned back around to him like she was going to say something, and then turned sharply back around and left the chamber, closing the sliding door behind her. Once she was gone, Azra slid forward in his seat and looked at the plate on the tray in front of him. He didn't recognize most of the food, but the smell was delicious and he realized in that moment how hungry he was. Taking a swig first of the hot, rich drink in a mug beside the plate, he dug into the food, savoring every bite and wondering if it tasted so incredibly delicious because the food itself was so good, or because he could imagine the delicate, pale hands of his intended mate carefully crafting it for him.

7

"So what do we do now?" Kyven asked.

He was pacing back and forth in front of Maxim and Ivy in large swathes now, taking longer steps the faster the thoughts in his mind spun. Everything seemed to be coming at him too quickly and he didn't know how he was supposed to process it all. This was the first time that he had left the kingdom, just as it was with Maxim, but Maxim was older than he was and had a confidence and sense of calm that exceeded even the extra years that he had on his brother. Maxim was the one who would be able to handle all of this. Not him. Not Kyven. He had always been perfectly fine with being the younger brother and living somewhat in Maxim's shadow. At least living in Maxim's shadow enabled him to escape the expectation that he would live in his father's, or grandfather's, or great-grand-fathers.

The truth was that Kyven had listened to the stories that their father had told them more with a sense of fear and dread than one of excitement like Maxim. He wouldn't consider himself cowardly and it wasn't that he didn't want to do anything, it was simply that the thought of being a part of the Order and the mysterious activities they were involved in wasn't something that appealed to him. The thoughts that Maxim and Ivy had conjured of his father, however, had made Kyven realize that his connection with the Order was far from being over. He owed it to the memory of his father to find out really what happened and ensure that it never happened again.

"We have to go back and talk to Mom again," Maxim said.

Kyven shook his head.

"No."

"Why not?"

"She isn't going to tell us anything, Maxim. She is going to be too afraid. She already told you far too much and she's not going to be willing to put herself at any more risk."

"But she told me in the first place," Maxim said. "That means that the hold that the Order had on her is starting to fade. Remember when we were younger. She would never even mention the Order. I don't honestly think that I heard her say those specific words until Ivy and I were there talking to her last."

"She always just spoke after Papa or made references that she hoped we would understand," Kyven said.

"Exactly. But when we were talking to her, she said it. She said it right out loud. She is probably still afraid, but that fear is letting up. We're adults now, Kyven. She doesn't have to hide things from us anymore."

"Of course she does. It doesn't matter how old we get, we are always going to be her only children. She has never wanted us to know about the Order. Why would she start now?"

"I didn't say that she wanted us to know," Maxim said. "I

just said that the fear that she has had for so long is starting to lessen and the control that the Order has always had on her is starting to go away. That means that she is going to be more willing to tell us what we need to know."

"And what if she doesn't? What if she just shuts down and won't tell us anything?"

"She loved Papa more than anything in the world, Kyven. Losing him absolutely destroyed her, and you know it. You remember what it was like when she had to tell us that he was dead. It was like it ripped her heart out and she was never really the same."

"I don't think that she believes the story that they told her about how he died," Ivy said.

Kyven looked at the small blond woman and cocked his head slightly. She was difficult to figure out. She was quiet much of the time and didn't seem to mind disappearing into the background when he and Maxim were talking, but in the next moment she would interject herself in a way that was bold and almost unnerving. Coming from a family that revolved around secrets, it felt strange when a new face arrived who was so intertwined with everything even though he barely knew her.

"Why would you say that?" Kyven asked.

"There was something about the way that she said it to Maxim. There was a catch in her voice when she said 'Why do you think that your father died the way that he did.' It was like she was having to convince herself of something in her mind. What did she tell you about how he died?"

"We've already talked about this," Maxim said, stepping closer to Ivy and looking at her strangely as if she had forgotten a conversation that they had. "Remember? When we were on the way here from the compound I told you everything about that night."

"I know," Ivy said, looking at Maxim. She paused briefly and then looked back at Kyven. "I want to know what he remembers."

"Why?" Kyven asked. "If Maxim already told you about that night, why do you need to have it rehashed again?"

"What you remember about that night and what your mother told you and what Maxim remembers might be very different. If we compare the two, we might be able to learn more just from that."

"She's right," Maxim said. "You were younger, but I'm sure that you remember that night. Tell us what you remember."

Kyven sighed. He didn't want to have this conversation. He didn't want to think through that horror again.

"I remember Athan coming to the door. Papa had been gone for so long, and for a minute I thought that it might be him knocking on the door trying to be funny. I was in the kitchen when Mom opened the door and when I looked around the corner I could see Athan standing in the living room with her. He looked like he had been dragged through hell and back. His clothes were tattered and there was dried blood on his skin. I remember hoping that Papa didn't look that bad and wondering if Mom had enough of the herbs that he liked in his baths when he usually came home from those missions. I knew where the herbs grew and I could go get them for her if she didn't have enough to put in the water for when he came inside."

"So that's why you were putting on your shoes that night when Mom came in the room and told us that she had to talk to us," Maxim said.

Kyven nodded.

"I was lacing my shoes when I heard Mom make a sound like she was choking. I looked into the living room and she was standing there with her hand on her chest, pressing down as if she were trying to hold her heart in place. I guess in a way she was. I was so wrapped up in listening to what Athan was saying to her that I completely forgot to tie my shoe. I just sat there holding the laces."

"You could hear them talking?" Maxim asked.

He sounded surprised by the revelation and Kyven realized that Ivy might be right. He could know more about that night than Maxim did, and it could make a difference.

"Yes," Kyven said. "I was listening to them before you even came into the room."

"I couldn't hear them at all. I just saw them talking. I just thought that he only told her what she told us."

"You were so young," Ivy said. "She probably told you what she thought that you could handle. She was trying to protect you."

"What did Athan say to her?" Maxim asked, seeming to ignore the attempted comfort by his partner.

Kyven let his mind wander back to that night. He could still see Athan standing in the living room, part of his body obscured by his mother standing in between them. She was drying one of the dishes from dinner with a white towel and he remembered thinking that everything about her at that moment, the moment before their world shattered, seemed so peaceful and calm.

"He told her that Papa was dead. She asked him what happened, and at first he didn't want to say anything else. I didn't have any idea why, but he seemed scared, like he thought that there was someone who would hear anything that he said and that it could cause serious problems. Mom pulled him further into the room and turned so that her back was to the door and Athan was facing it. I guess she thought that that would help keep his voice from traveling through the door just in case someone was standing right outside. She asked him again what happened and he just looked at her and said 'They found out, Ellora. He knew what was happening and he couldn't fight it anymore.'"

"Was 'they' the Order?" Maxim asked.

"Or the Klimnu?" Ivy asked.

Kyven looked up at her again and saw that she was staring at Maxim.

"Remember what we talked about when we were on our way from the compound? Your mother said that your father died because of the Order and the Klimnu, but she didn't say which one was the one that was actually responsible for his death. He could have been evolved into Klimnu and been eliminated by the Order because they were fighting against the Klimnu and seeking vengeance for that group destroying their allies."

"But it also could be that he knew too much about the Klimnu because the Order was changing and he wasn't," Maxim said.

"Athan knows what happened," Kyven said. "He knows why Papa died and what happened to him."

Suddenly Kyven was feeling less distant from the situation. He could remember that night so powerfully. He could see the look in Athan's eyes, and hear the tremble in his mother's voice. Everything changed that night. He hadn't really made the connection before, but the kingdom became tenser after that. There was a sense of guarded distrust and the hint of danger that seemed to underscore everything that anyone in the kingdom did, especially his mother. She had started to disappear for lengths of time and her insistence that they not talk about the Order became even more aggressive. It was like she was trying to eliminate them in her children because they haunted her so much already in her heart.

"How long will it take you to get ready to leave?" Maxim asked.

"I only need to pack the few things that I brought with me."

"We need to make sure that we have enough supplies to get us through the journey," Maxim said. "We'll leave this afternoon," he said. "We're going home."

8

Azra leaned against the wall of the observation dome staring out into the endless blanket of stars that stretched around the shuttle. It was deep in the night, not that he would have noticed any difference had it been in the middle of the day. They were too far from either planet for either sun to impact how the sky looked. Instead, he was surrounded by continuous, almost tangible blackness and stars.

He didn't know how long he had been standing there, unable to sleep as all the others were doing, when he suddenly felt the presence of someone else step into the observation dome with him. Azra turned and saw Elise standing in the doorway timidly like she was unsure if she should enter or not. He noticed that she was no longer wearing the prim flight attendant's uniform that she was always wearing when she was interacting with them in the pods or the lounge during the day. Instead, she was wearing a long, flowing white gown with wide sleeves that closed tightly at the wrists. Hair that was usually pinned up and away from her neck and face tumbled down around her shoulders and a strand that fell in front showed that it stretched down to her waist.

She was even more breathtakingly beautiful than he already knew and he felt his stomach clench as his uncontrollable desire for her reached a new peak.

"Am I bothering you?" she finally asked softly.

"Of course not," he said, gesturing for her to come closer. "Please, join me."

Elise stepped inside and came to Azra's side. He breathed in the full, sweet smell of her and felt his mind go slightly dizzy.

"Is it true that you've never left your planet?" she asked after they stared together into the stars for a few moments.

Azra nodded.

"It is," he said. "Only one of the Denynso have left Uoria, and that was an emergency."

"An emergency?" she asked, sounding worried.

"His mate is from Earth. He offended her horribly within the first 24 hours of her being on Uoria and she promptly got back on the shuttle that hadn't left yet and went back to Earth. He knew that he couldn't live without her, so the king called for another shuttle and he met her there."

Elise laughed.

"I guess a man will do anything when he realizes that he has done something wrong to the woman he loves."

"Yes," Azra said.

The heat that was building between them was increasing and he felt his erection pressing almost painfully against the front of his pants. If the aggression and violence that he was feeling toward his friends didn't tell him what he already knew about Elise, his arousal did. It was perhaps the most potent and disruptive of the signs that a Denynso man was near the woman who was intended to be his mate and lifelong partner.

"How did he know that she was going to take him back?"

"She is the only person who he will ever love. She is human so had no way of knowing for sure that she felt the same attachment to him that he has for her, but he really had no other option but to go after her. If he didn't, he would be alone and wondering about her for the rest of his life."

"How did he know that she was the only one for him?"

"How much do you know about the Denynso?" Azra asked.

"Not much," she admitted. "I've heard of impossibly large, gorgeous men born to fight and who mate for life."

Azra gave a short laugh at the description and nodded.

"I can attest for the 'born to fight' and 'mate for life' elements of that," he said.

"I can attest to the others," Elise said softly, her eyes drinking in Azra standing in front of her in only loose sleeping pants.

Azra glanced away and then back at her, his heart pounding in his chest.

"Elise, I-" he started, but she cut him off before he could say any more.

"How does a Denynso man know that he has found the woman who is meant to be his mate?" she asked.

Her voice was low and sultry, making her seem innocent and incredibly sexy at the same time.

"He can feel it," Azra answered. "He gets aggressive and defensive, even more so than usual, as he prepares to protect his mate and their future children. He will lash out against anyone but her. This frequently causes issues among the warriors, but fortunately so many of them are already mated that they understand what's going on and are more willing to help the warrior who is in that phase get through it rather than fight back."

"What else?" she asked.

"His eyes start to change. They will shift from the color that he was born with to orange and back again up until he is fully mated to her."

Elise looked up into his eyes and Azra knew that she could see these changes happening as he stared back at her. She stepped closer to him and he felt his breath catch. She was only a few inches away now and his body ached for her. He could barely control himself and he looked away into the stars again for a few moments to quiet his thoughts.

"What else?" she asked.

Azra looked back at her and the tip of her tongue slipped out to run across her bottom lip just briefly. He reached down and took her hand, bringing it up to flatten it against his bare chest.

"His skin gets hot to the touch. Eventually it will get so hot that any other woman around him will not be able to stand being close to him because the heat actually radiates off of his body, forcing them back."

"It is only that hot to other women?" she asked.

"Yes," he answered, applying gentle pressure to her hand so that she stroked his chest. "His mate will only notice that it is warm."

She made a soft, appreciative sound and nodded lightly.

"Is there anything else that tells a Denynso warrior that he has found his mate?" she asked.

Azra could barely breathe for the intensity of the need for her that was pulsating through him. He wanted to control it, but he knew that he couldn't deny what was happening deep within him. He wanted her like he had never wanted anything, like he didn't think was possible to want someone, and he couldn't resist that need any longer.

"His body tells him," he said quietly.

"How?" Elise asked.

"He becomes hungry for her," Azra said, "Needing her in a way that is completely overwhelming, and it won't go away until he finally mates with her."

"Are you hungry?" Elise whispered.

Azra took her hand again and led it down his body, not breaking the connection between their eyes, until it reached the front of his pants. He turned her hand carefully and pressed on it to cup it around the hard swell that continued to push toward her. She gasped slightly and he felt a surge of strength within him. Elise stepped forward to completely close the space between them and touched a kiss to his chest, running her parted lips across his skin and occasionally allowing the tip of her tongue to follow the path. He groaned, touching her hair softly as she continued the attention along his body.

"Elise," he said, trying to control his voice. "If this is happening too fast for you..."

His mind was spinning. He didn't want to think about what Gyyx had said. He wanted only to listen to what his mind and body were telling him, and that was that Elise was meant to be his mate.

"I know what I'm doing, Azra," she said. "I've known from the moment I saw you."

At that, Azra reached forward and swept Elise into his arms, lifting her up his body so that he could capture her mouth with his. Her legs wrapped around his hips and she welcomed the kiss, parting her lips under the insistence of his tongue so that he could explore her fully. Azra held her close to his body and lowered himself to his knees, supporting her and protecting the back of her head as he carefully lay her back on the floor. He would have wanted to be in a bed with her, but the closest thing that he had was his pod and that was in a room he was sharing with Jonathan. The best he could do was lay her beneath the stars and bond with her surrounded by the most spectacular beauty that he had ever witnessed.

Azra used one hand to release the ties at the front of his sleep pants and then kicked them off. Just that quickly he was completely bare, but she was still covered from her neck to her ankles. The soft fabric of her gown against his skin was enticing, and he spent a moment resting on top of her, kissing her languidly. Finally he felt her reach down and take hold of either side of her skirt. She gathered it in her fingers so that it crept up her legs, gradually causing more and more of their skin to touch. With each new inch Azra felt like his control was disappearing.

Finally Elise lifted her hips slightly and pulled the gown out from under her so that it pooled around her waist. This movement revealed that she had worn nothing beneath the gown and Azra couldn't hold back any longer. Gently pressing her thighs apart with one hand, Azra positioned his hips between them and let the tip of his erection slide along the warm wetness of her core. Elise moaned and arched slightly, but Azra didn't delve into her quite yet. As much as he wanted her, he also wanted this incredible moment to last as long as possible.

Wrapping his hand around the base of his cock, Azra used the tip to stroke Elise's folds, focusing on her sensitive pearl until she was nearly sobbing. At last he released his grip and allowed the tip of his erection to slide down to nestle just at her opening. Elise parted her legs slightly further and pressed forward with her hips, accepting him as he eased into her. She felt incredibly tight and hot, embracing him intimately as he sank further into her.

Azra sat back on his knees and pulled her hips forward so that they balanced on his lap. As he drove himself deeply into her, encouraging her to open to him, Elise took hold of the hem of her gown and slid it off over her head. Azra let one of his hands cup a full breast, massaging it tenderly. After a few moments he tipped forward so that he was hovering over her again and slightly increased his speed and intensity. Each stroke drew a whimper of pleasure from Elise's chest and she reached up to wrap her arms around Azra's shoulders. The incredible sensations created by her body were building up inside Azra intensely and when he leaned down to take one taut pink nipple into his mouth, her cry made him lose control. In a few final thrusts he toppled into a blinding climax and had to bite down into her shoulder to prevent himself from roaring in pleasure.

Elise's body began to spasm around him, each tiny pulse meeting his throbs and milking him as he spilled into her. She was trembling in his arms, her head tucked into the curve of his shoulder and neck so that she could kiss along his collarbone as she tried to regain control of her breath. As his body cooled and relaxed, an incredible warmth flowed through him. He felt more content and at peace than he ever had, and in that moment it felt like her heartbeat against his chest was beating for both of them.

TBC

(To be continued in book V...)

THE ALIEN'S MYSTERY

1

"Maxim?"

Maxim turned away from the bag that he was packing toward the timid voice behind him. A woman stood several feet back from him, looking nervous that she was even speaking to him. He recognized her as one of the human women from the settlement, but didn't know her name.

"Yes?"

"Can I speak to you for a moment?"

"As long as you don't mind that I keep packing while you talk. We are leaving the settlement shortly for the Mikana kingdom."

He turned back to his bag as the woman took a step toward him.

"That's what I wanted to talk to you about. I'd like to come with you."

Maxim reached for another loaf of bread that Ivy had baked the night before and tucked it into the bag.

"Why?" he asked.

He knew that he was being less than kind, but he didn't

really care at that moment. He was too busy concentrating on getting ready to leave for home that he didn't have the time to think about the others around him. Now that Kyven agreed that they needed to get back to the kingdom and talk to their mother and to Athan about the Order and everything that had happened, Maxim felt even more urgent to leave the settlement and start on their way.

"It's just that—"

"Is everything OK?"

Maxim heard Ivy come into the room, cutting off the woman as she spoke. His partner approached him and handed him the satchel of tools that she had gotten from Rain.

"She wants to come with us to the kingdom," Maxim said, gesturing at the woman by way of explanation.

Ivy turned to the woman and looked at her with an expression that said she was evaluating her.

"Hi," she said, stepping toward the woman as he strapped the satchel onto the front of his bag, "I'm Ivy."

"I know," the woman said. "I'm Emerie."

"It's nice to meet you," Ivy said. She didn't sound convinced, but Maxim appreciated that she at least was attempting to understand the motivations behind Emerie asking to accompany them out of the settlement. "You want to come with us?" she asked.

"Yes," Emerie said. "Very much. My brother and our neighbors would like to come along as well."

"You do know that we are leaving the settlement for the Mikana kingdom. It is a long journey and we don't know what is waiting for us there."

"We understand that."

"Then why do you want to come with us? Many of the others are going back to the Denynso compound in just a few days. The king and queen, Creia and Theia, are waiting to welcome everyone."

"We know that," Emerie said, "but we don't think that that is the right choice for us. With all of the turmoil and uncertainty that has happened here recently, we don't think that staying in the settlement is right, but we also aren't sure that going to the compound and associating with the Denynso is right, either."

"We will have Denynso with us," Maxim said, latching the bag closed and putting it on the floor beside the other bags that he had already prepared that morning. "If you do not trust them, then you will not be away from them by coming along with us."

"There will be Denynso with us?" Ivy asked, sounding slightly surprised.

"Yes. Zyyr and Oro want to come along so that they can extend their personal apologies to the rest of the Mikana and ensure that the group gets to the kingdom safely. We'll have them and a few of the Mikana men with us."

"It's not that we don't trust the Denynso," Emerie said. "We know as well as anyone that the actions of a few do not dictate the actions of the entire group. What matters to us is that we don't believe that the original sentiments of the settlement apply anymore. It just doesn't feel the same. We think that it's time to move on, and that if the majority of the group is either staying in the settlement and trying to continue or going to the Denynso compound and attempting to build positive relations, we need to choose a different path."

Maxim looked at Ivy, wanting to gauge her reaction to the other human woman's explanation. Ivy looked back at him and nodded subtly. Maxim nodded back and looked at Emerie.

"You can come. But be aware that we aren't going to slow down or make any accommodations for you. We are aware that you haven't made travels like this in some time, but our reasons for going back to the kingdom now are urgent. We have to get there as quickly as we can, and that may mean a grueling journey. You will need to be prepared to keep up with us and handle the terrain as well as everything that goes into making our temporary camps when we stop at night."

"We understand that," Emerie said. Even with the stern warning, her voice sounded slightly more buoyant now that he had agreed to allow the small group of humans to come along with them. "Thank you."

"Please get whoever is coming along ready and meet us back here in one hour."

Emerie nodded and rushed out of the house, leaving the door open just as it had been when she came inside.

"That was a little harsh, Maxim," Ivy said when Emerie was gone.

"It wasn't harsh," Maxim said. "It was realistic. We can't be responsible for them just because they want to come along with us. We have to go at our pace and do what needs to be done for ourselves. If they want to come along with us, they need to be able to handle our pace and take care of themselves."

Ivy looked at him like she was able to see through his eyes and into his being, and he fought the urge to look away.

"You don't trust them, do you, Maxim?"

He walked past Ivy toward the stairs and climbed them toward their bedroom. He could hear Ivy following behind him. That was fine. He wasn't trying to avoid her or get away from her, he just needed some time to come up with the right answer to her question. He had thrown her off by asking if he trusted the humans. The truth was that he hadn't really spent any time thinking about how he felt about them. He was too invested in his thoughts and questions about the Order and his own people, and the lingering feelings of distrust and anger that he had toward Pyra and those who had supported him. It hadn't occurred to him to ponder what feelings he might have about the humans. Now that she had forced him into it, however, he realized that there were difficult feelings about that group that were hovering just beneath the surface of his thoughts.

When he got into the bedroom he pulled another bag out from under the bed and started digging through it to see what was still left inside from their last journey. For a moment he stared longingly at their bed. He felt like he had been doing nothing but traveling for weeks and he wanted so badly to be able to settle into place again. He longed for the comfort and ease of being at home and knowing calm and peace. A moment later, however, he forced the thought out of his mind. He knew that calm and ease were no longer an option for him, at least not for the foreseeable future. He had new responsibilities now, and even though he wished to be able to settle in with Ivy and start a life together that would be as happy as the life that his parents shared, that was something that he had to earn. It wouldn't be until he had resolved why his parents were no longer able to live that life together that he would even be able to begin to create that life for himself and Ivy.

Maxim took over several of the items from the bag so that he could fold and reorganize them. He knew that he wouldn't be returning to the settlement. When he left to go home to the kingdom, it would be the final time that he would walk through that gate, and walk among the houses built from the wreckage of the ship that crashed on Uoria so long ago. He needed to take everything that he and Ivy would need with him, but he also needed to make sure that he could carry it comfortably and safely. As he rearranged the items in his bag, Ivy came up to the side of the bed and perched beside him.

"What is going on in your mind right now?" she asked quietly.

Maxim shook his head.

"You're right," he said. "I don't trust the humans." He could see the hurt flicker in her eyes and he reached out to take her hands. "I'm sorry. It's not that they are humans. I know that you are human and of course I trust you. I trust Rain and George, and the other human women that have mated with the Denynso. It isn't that the people from the settlement are human that has made me not trust them."

Ivy leaned closer to him so that she could look into his eyes again.

"What is it then?" she asked.

"They did nothing," he answered, finally giving voice to what he realized that he had been holding inside of him since Pyra had taken over the settlement. "They watched while Pyra and the men who were following him took over the settlement and started forcing everyone to do whatever he wanted them to do. This was their settlement. They built it, they worked and they fought to come out of the adversity of the crash and the horror of the Covra. They went through all of that to establish this settlement and make sure that they had somewhere to live and to thrive even though there was so much working against them. Then Pyra shows up and suddenly they are completely weak to do anything."

"He saved them, Maxim."

"No, he didn't," Maxim protested. "He didn't do anything. He came here with an entire group of Denynso. While half of them stayed here to try to figure out how to unlock the people, he and several of the others came to our kingdom to get our help. They knew that our kind had once been friendly with the people of this settlement and they wanted to find out if there was anything that we knew about them being locked or if we knew how to unlock them. It was while he was gone that Lynx and Bannack spent their time with Rain. They are the ones that reached out to the women on the compound and who convinced them to work together and then with George to help them find a solution. They are the ones who were talking to all of you through the mirror when they realized that the sound of the human voices was what was helping to bring Rain out of her sleep. None of that had anything to do with Pyra.

"But even that doesn't matter," he continued, finishing packing that bag and turning to leave the bedroom before turning back to Ivy, "When he came back here he should have allowed the humans to figure things out for their own and offered his assistance however they needed it. Instead, he put himself in the position of leadership. Then when everyone found out about..." he hesitated. It was still painful for him to talk about the incident with his arm and how quickly things had changed in those few moments that terrible morning. "When everyone saw what was going on with my arm, he snapped, and there was absolutely nothing to stop him. None of the humans did anything to keep him from pushing us all into that space and closing us up like animals. Even though it still infuriates me, I can understand why the warriors were only able to voice their dissent rather than doing something to stop him. He's their leader and they are loyal by birth. The humans, though. They just let it happen. They let him take over and force them into his service."

"What were they supposed to do?"

"Anything. They could have done anything. This was not a military mission. Pyra was not sent here to avenge the humans or to find the Klimnu. The Denynso left the compound just because they wanted to find out what types of threats existed on Uoria and how they could stop them from getting to the others. That's all. It just so happens that they were able to find threats, and what they perceived as threats, on this settlement. That shouldn't have given him permission to take over, though. This settlement belongs to the humans. They should have been the ones who determined what should be done, and as soon as he decided to begin his reign of terror, they should have been the ones to stop it, but they didn't."

"But they tried. Rain spoke up, so did all of us from the compound."

"That's the thing though, Ivy. It shouldn't have been your job. You are not a member of this settlement. You are human, but you are different. There are enough humans left in this settlement after the wars and even after the hatching of the Covra young that they should have been able to overthrow one Denynso warrior. They simply chose not to. They decided that they would sit by and allow us to be imprisoned without any form of council and without breaking any form of laws. And what would have happened if you hadn't gotten me away and Rain and Lynx hadn't been able to convince Pyra that he needed to talk to Creia before he made any decisions about us? The humans would have just let us all die. I can't trust a people who would do that."

"I wouldn't have let that happen, Maxim."

Maxim turned sharply and saw Lynx and Rain standing at the door to the bedroom.

"We're sorry to eavesdrop," Lynx said, stepping forward toward Maxim, "but we heard you talking."

"I wouldn't have let Pyra destroy your clan, Maxim," Rain repeated. "You have to believe that."

"What could you have done?" Maxim asked. "Everyone was against us. Even those who didn't think that we had done anything wrong and didn't think that we should be imprisoned in the meeting hall didn't do anything to try to stop it."

"I would have done something. We would have. I know that my crew didn't handle the situation as well as we should have, but I'm not going to let that happen again."

"We aren't going back to the compound with the others," Lynx said. "We're going to stay here on the settlement and start to rebuild. It's time that the people who are still here remember where they came from and what they have gone through. Rain has already made the decision that she does not intend to go back to Earth."

"Really?" Ivy asked. "You don't want to go back home?"

"That's not my home anymore," Rain said. "This settlement is. Uoria is."

"Don't you miss Earth, though? And everyone that you left behind there?"

As soon as Ivy said the words Maxim could see the flicker of anxiety and regret across her face.

"I don't have anyone left, Ivy," Rain said gently, obviously hurt by the thoughtless statement but not feeling the need to make the situation more difficult than it already was. "Of course I miss Earth, but I miss the Earth that I left behind so long ago. Everything has changed, and I know that. I wouldn't be going back to the home that I knew or the people or the places. I would be going back to a place nearly as strange as Uoria was when we first arrived. That was the greatest challenge that I had faced up to until then, but I persevered. We all did. We knew that there wasn't going to be a way for us to get back to Earth. We held out hope in our hearts, but we never spoke about it. We never shared our thoughts or our hopes that we might somehow find a way to overcome the challenge that had been put in front of us and make it back to our planet. Instead, we resolved not to let the Valdicians destroy us. We put everything into creating a new home, and that is the home that I have come to know and appreciate. It may not be like Earth and it may not be everything that I would have wanted for my life, but it is what I have, and I'm not going to abandon it. I owe it to everything that we put into it, and to the lives that were lost, to continue on and to make this settlement everything that we intended it to be and more."

"I'm going to stay here with her," Lynx said. "As her mate it is my responsibility to help her accomplish what she wants out of life, even if that means leaving the life I know behind."

Maxim's eyes slid over to Ivy and he saw her back straighten as her expression changed from shock to resolve. Something Rain had said had gotten to her and changed something within her, and in that moment he felt truly prepared for the journey ahead of them.

2

Gyyx gave Azra a knowing look as he sat down and settled Elise into his lap. It was the morning after he had completed his bond with her and as he sat down at the table in the main lounge with the others, he realized that he had never felt so complete and at peace in his entire life. Of course he had heard the other men talk about what it was like to finally find their mate and bond with them. They had talked about the incredible buildup of tension, aggression, and need that would signal that he had found the woman who was meant to be his, and then the feeling of control, calm, and fulfillment that would come after he had bonded with her. It all seemed just too good to actually be accurate, however. Azra always felt like the men were exaggerating, especially the ones who had just recently found their mates. Nothing could be as wonderful as what they were describing.

Now that he had experienced it for himself, however, Azra knew that this was truly the defining experience of his life. No battle that he had ever fought, no accomplishment that he had ever made, could even begin to compare to what it was like to look at Elise and know that she had been intended for him since the very beginning, and that they would remain as devoted to one another for the rest of their lives as they were now.

He nestled her closer and touched a kiss to the side of her neck. She giggled and patted his hands where they rested on her stomach.

"I have to go to work now, Azra," she said softly. "I have to get everybody breakfast and go through all of the safety protocols."

"And when you are finished with all of that?"

"Then I have to clean up the ship, wash linens, and prepare for lunch."

"And then?"

Elise laughed again.

"And then I have the afternoon to be at the beck and call of all of my passengers until it is time to prepare supper."

"Can you be at my beck and call?" he asked, bending his head forward to kiss the curve of her neck and shoulder.

"I have to be available to provide assistance to everyone who is traveling with us," she said.

"You are so professional," Azra teased. "What about the other attendant? Can't he take care of everybody else and you can just be my personal...assistant?"

"I don't think that I would get anything accomplished," she whispered, turning her head slightly toward his as if she wanted to make sure that the others who were sitting at the table wouldn't hear her.

"I think that we would get plenty accomplished," Azra said, giving her stomach a suggestive squeeze.

Elise turned and pressed a quick kiss to his lips before sliding off of his lap and adjusting her skirt.

"I'll have everyone's breakfast shortly," she announced.

Azra noticed that everyone at the table stopped talking and turned to stare at her, some of them obviously fighting the urge to laugh. Color splashed across Elise's cheeks and he immediately regretted giving her so much attention in front of everyone else on the flight. This was her job and he was likely making it extremely uncomfortable for her to do it as she was supposed to, not to mention possibly putting it at risk by making her act so unprofessionally. He would have to remind himself to stay controlled and keep his distance from her at least while there were others around. The flight was only a couple more days. He would be able to get through that and then they could start building their life together without having to worry about what anyone else was thinking.

Just as he thought that, Elise stepped up beside the table carrying a large tray overloaded with plates. She rested it on a stand and started handing the dishes out. Azra stood to help her, but Elise looked him directly in the eyes, stilling him with just that single gesture.

"Sit down, please," she said. "This is my job and I can handle it on my own."

There was something slightly stiff and cold in her voice now and he felt it sink down into his stomach. He sat down and reached for a glass that she placed in front of him, taking a long sip so that the others sitting at the table wouldn't notice the painful emotion in his expression.

"Where does the ship go next, Elise?" Jonathan asked.

Azra's eyes snapped to the human man and then to Elise. Until that moment it hadn't occurred to him to think about the ship going somewhere else once it landed on Earth. He hadn't let himself think about anything but spending time with Elise.

"We have a two day break and then the ship is scheduled

for a research trip. I'm joining a crew on a leisure cruise to the outer shore of Agribella."

"How long does that take?"

"It's a luxury cruise, so the ship will take seven days to get to the planet, dock for five days, and then another seven days back to Earth."

"That's a long trip. It must be kind of strange spending most of your life on a ship."

"Not really," Elise said, placing the final plate on the table and lifting the tray up under her arm. "I'm used to it. I've been doing this for a long time. It would almost seem stranger to be on Earth for a long time." She gave a short laugh. "But I guess there are some things that I miss when I'm on long tours like this."

"Like what?" Jonathan asked.

Azra looked at the man and felt a sense of aggressive defensiveness wash over him. He tried to tell himself that the human man was just excited about the prospect of returning to the planet that he had left so long ago, but this entire conversation was making Azra feel uncomfortable. He was quickly realizing that the hopes that he'd had for his relationship with Elise weren't going to be as easy to accomplish as he had hoped.

"I like the beach. That's one reason that I'm really excited about this luxury tour. I'll get a few days to spend on the beach on Agribella, which is one of my favorite beaches that I've ever been to. I also really enjoy visiting amusement parks."

"Oh, I miss those so much!" Brandy suddenly chimed in, putting down the fork that still held a bite of her breakfast. "I used to go to them all the time when I was younger. I can't wait to go to one when we get back to Earth. I bet they are so different now."

Elise looked at her quizzically.

"How long have you been away from Earth?" she asked.

Brandy and Jonathan looked at each other and Azra could see the slight panic on both of their faces. Neither of them were prepared to talk about who they really were. They had already decided that they were going to arrive back on Earth anonymously and spend some time getting reacquainted with the planet before they decided whether they were going to come forward. Even though they knew that it was important that they were honest about what really happened to Nyx 23 so that the people of Earth would know the truth, they also knew that it would be completely overwhelming to them if they were to announce their arrival before getting there, or even soon after arriving. They needed time to assimilate and then they would work with the other members of the crew to determine how and when they should come forward.

"Long enough," Brandy finally said.

This seemed to satisfy Elise and she turned away from the table, carrying the tray and the stand out of the lounge toward what Azra assumed was the ship's kitchen. Everyone at the table went back to eating and talking, but he found himself without an appetite. The conversation was sitting heavily in his stomach and his chest, and he stared at the plate of food without really seeing it. The joy of finding his mate was suddenly feeling more like torment. He didn't know what their future was going to hold for them now and he started wondering about the other couples who found themselves divided between Uoria and Earth. Would the Denynso stay on Earth and try to assimilate to the new planet so that their mates could be surrounded by what they knew, or would those of Earth take this trip as their final goodbye to their home and return to Uoria knowing that it might be years before they saw their home planet again, if at all?

Azra grappled with the question, not even knowing in his own heart what was going to happen. Elise obviously loved her career and her planet, but he had never thought for a moment that he would ever live anywhere but on Uoria in the Denynso compound. Which one of them was going to have to make the sacrifice? Or would neither of them make the move...forcing him to spend the rest of his life alone and pining for her?

Kyven walked a few paces back from the rest of the group, his own thoughts keeping him from catching up with them. As he walked, his eyes occasionally lifted to the back of the woman who walked ahead of him, her thick dark hair coiled on top of her head and one hand gripping the strap of her bag that crossed her chest. He had been surprised by Emerie's presence when he arrived at the house where Ivy and Maxim had been staying in the settlement. He had thought that the three of them would be traveling back to the kingdom alone, or at the very most that a few of the other Mikana men would choose to go along with them. When he got to the house with his bags, though, he found Emerie and four other humans, along with several of the Mikana and two Denynso warriors gathered in the living room ready to travel.

Now that they were on their way toward the kingdom, Kyven was still struggling with the presence of Emerie in the travel group. When they were first talking about leaving and going back home, he had known that the journey would be challenging and that once they arrived in the kingdom it would only get more difficult. This was not going to be a happy reunion or a time for celebration. Instead, they were poised to venture into areas of their existence that they had always been warned to avoid and that could put them in very serious danger. He knew that he would have to focus completely on the mission that they were undertaking and that it would take all of his attention and energy to ensure that he was able to do everything that he was supposed to do. He couldn't let himself think about Emerie, even though for days she had been the only thing on his mind.

She had been one of the few human women who had tried to help the Mikana men when they were imprisoned in the meeting hall. Though the Denynso warriors didn't always allow the women in, when the more compassionate warriors were on duty, the women would come down the long, dark hallway toward the sealed area of the meeting hall bringing baskets of food and bottles of water and juice. Though the women generally changed on their visits, Emerie was one who came with every visit. Even on the visits that the warrior guides wouldn't allow them in, Kyven would listen at the door and hear Emerie's voice, trying to demand her way into the building. She was strong and forceful, but not enough to force her way past the warriors.

When she did make it inside the building, Kyven had never been able to keep his eyes off of Emerie. She would come over to him and look at him with her large brown eyes, a hint of a smile on her full lips even though they were near each other in the worst of circumstances. They barely spoke to one another. In fact, Kyven couldn't remember them exchanging any more words that him thanking her for the food that she brought and her accepting the thanks. It was always far too soon that the Denynso warrior guards would decide that they had been in there for long enough and demand that the women leave. He knew that they thought that the women would somehow be able to smuggle the rest of the men out the way that Ivy had been able to get Maxim out on the first night that they were trapped in place. This suspicion had meant that the women were only able to spend a matter of a few moments in the room with them before guards would shout for them to leave.

When they left, Kyven still couldn't get the thought of the beautiful, kind woman out of his mind. He longed to see her even more than he longed for the food and water that she brought with her. Each time that he saw her he wanted to talk to her, to spend a little more time getting to know her, but he never had the opportunity. Before he had even mustered up enough courage to ask her name, they would hear the shouts of the warriors, she would look at him with a touch of sadness in her eyes, and then she was gone. The only reason that he knew her name is because he had heard some of the other women say it in the time that they were there. As soon as they would leave, Kyven would go back to longing for her. He would lie awake at night thinking about her, and spend much of the day standing in the hallway straining to hear even the hint of her voice.

Now she was right there, walking in front of him, going toward the kingdom with the rest of the group. Though he was thrilled to be near her and know that the Denynso no longer had any power over them or the time that they were able to spend together, he still struggled with his feelings for her and the fact that she was now a fixture in the journey that they were taking to the kingdom, and the time that they would spend there. Having her there meant that he was distracted. He wanted to be able to put every bit of thought and energy that he had into focusing on the journey and the tasks that were waiting for them in the kingdom. Instead, his mind was wandering to her. He still longed for her and in the few hours that they had been walking, he hadn't been able to think of anything else. He hadn't spoken a word to anyone else in the traveling group and had progressively fallen behind. He wasn't prepared for the feelings that were coursing through him, but in the same breath he knew that there was very little he could do to escape them.

The sun had long set by the time that Maxim called back over his shoulder that it was time for them to settle in for the night. They had already determined that the glow from their light sticks would put them at risk of being seen by anyone who might be wary of them, so they walked in darkness, led only by the faint illumination of the stars reflecting off of the deep purple clouds above them. Kyven wondered who Maxim thought might put them in danger if they saw them walking toward the kingdom, but he didn't voice his concern. He had never seen his older brother as focused and determined as he was when he made the decision that they were going to return to the kingdom, and knew that it was futile to question him. Maxim was set in his plan and it was up to those who decided to go along with him to follow.

They walked a short distance further before selecting a place to create their temporary camp. As the men built the tents and started a fire in the center of the circle, the women opened the bags to take out food that they had brought along. As he watched Emerie carefully slicing loaves of bread, Kyven realized that they hadn't even stopped to eat since they had left the settlement. Hunger that he hadn't even noticed before gnawed at his stomach and he hurried to get the fire roaring so that they could warm up some of the food that they brought. He knew that Maxim would want the fire out as quickly as possible to keep their location undetectable.

Finally the air filled with the tantalizing scent of food and he turned away from the tent where he was building his pallet to see Emerie walking toward him with a plate. For a moment it was as if he were back in the meeting hall, waiting for the small amount of food that she and the other women were able to get into the building. He worried for a moment that he would hear the demand of the Denynso that would take her away from him, but as she approached, she could see the sparkle in her eyes grow brighter than he had seen it and the smile go from the slightest hint to a soft, but happy expression that made his heart thump deeply in his chest.

"I suppose that we should be used to this transaction," she said.

Her voice was slightly low as if she were trying to speak only to him without the others hearing them. He offered her a soft smile and took the plate from her.

"I suppose we should," he replied. "I'm Kyven, Maxim's brother."

"It's nice to meet you, Kyven," she said. "I'm Emerie."

There was a pause and Kyven worried that she was going to walk away from him. He took a slight step forward.

"I wanted to say thank you for what you did for me and for the rest of the men."

"You thanked me every time that I came to the meeting hall," she said, sounding slightly surprised.

"I know," Kyven said, "but I never really got a chance to say much. You had to leave so soon after you got there. We were always so rushed. Now that we have time, I want to tell you how much I appreciate what you did for us."

"For you."

Emerie had taken a step forward just as he had. She glanced down at the ground in front of her and then back up at Kyven.

"What do you mean?" he asked.

"The women who decided to help all of the men who Pyra kept in the meeting hall were supposed to rotate just like the guards. That way we could visit a few times a day and if the guards didn't let us in, another group would be able to visit a few hours later and might have the chance to get in. Each of the women were only supposed to go to the meeting hall once a day. I always insisted on going every time."

"Why?"

Though Kyven hoped he knew what she would say about her motivation, he needed to hear it from her. He wanted to hear the words come out of her mouth.

"I wanted to see you."

4

"We should almost be there by now, shouldn't we?" Ivy asked, lifting her hand to shield her eyes from the burning sun above her.

It was another day characterized by strange, shifting weather. What had started as a morning cool enough that she had added an extra sweater over her clothing was now blazingly hot and bright to the point that she could barely see Maxim's back ahead of her.

"Almost, love. Just keep going. We'll stop soon for a break if everyone wants to."

There were a few murmurs of agreement and Ivy nodded even though she knew that Maxim wasn't looking in her direction and couldn't see her. She felt like they had been walking for far longer than she and Maxim had walked in their first journey to the kingdom. Of course, during that first journey they were both filled with the adrenaline of the escape and of having to run from Pyra and the other Denynso warriors. She hadn't been aware of much during that experience but Maxim and the desire to be with him and protect him from everything that had been happening. Now, though, the journey was paced and deliberate. They were moving along toward the goal of the kingdom without fear of the Denynso or their retribution. Somehow the threat of unknown species or even a resurgence of the Covra were not as frightening as thoughts of the warriors.

During this journey had been the first time that Ivy had really thought about the threat of possible Klimnu still existing on the planet. There had been no sign of them and no indication that any were still living on Uoria, when Maxim had mentioned that he wanted to be wary of possible threats while they were traveling, that is where Ivy's mind went immediately. When she first arrived on Uoria and the women had told her of the conflicts that the Denynso had faced, she had been content to believe that the warriors had eliminated the species in that final battle in the mirrored realm. Even when she saw for herself Maxim's skin changing after coming into contact with the flowers as they made love for the first time in the field outside of the settlement, she believed that it was only the Mikana that still lived on Uoria, and though their skin reacted to the flowers in the same way that those who had eventually become Klimnu had, the creatures themselves didn't exist any longer.

As they started for the kingdom and the mysteries that awaited them there, however, her mind wandered to what could exist just outside of their knowledge and how they would handle it if they found it. She now knew that there were secrets in the Mikana kingdom, secrets that even the leader of the kingdom didn't know and that could change everything that Maxim and Kyven knew of their family and the death of their father. The Klimnu were at the heart of those secrets, and that made Ivy wonder if somewhere on the planet, in one of the abandoned compounds or hidden just out of view like Loralia had been, there were still some of the creatures lurking, waiting for the right moment that they would emerge again and continue on their mission to take over the planet.

If that was the case, she knew that she would have to fight. She would be right there beside Maxim, doing whatever she could to help him. Lynx's words back at the settlement before they left had affected Ivy deeply. She had been so resistant to Uoria and to the idea of ever making the planet a part of her regular existence. Even after finding Maxim and falling so deeply in love with him, she had still kept her heart blocked against the thought of living on Uoria and making her life and her home here. The challenges that she had faced as soon as she arrived and in the weeks following had seemed to sour her to the planet and to many who lived on it, but when Lynx said that he was willing to leave everything that he knew behind for Rain, Ivy realized that she had been incredibly selfish and truly hadn't thought about Maxim and the wonderful gift that he was in her life. She had been so willing to just pull him away from everything and assume that he would follow her wherever she went that it never occurred to her that there were more important things than just her being on the planet where she was comfortable, or getting away from what had been a challenging and emotionally draining experience on Uoria so far.

Now when she looked at Maxim she realized that really all that mattered was him. The need for him to stay on Uoria and uncover the secrets of his kingdom and his family far outweighed her needs, and now she knew that she was willing to follow him to the edges of the universe and beyond if she had to. She may have to learn to think of this planet as her home and to truly feel comfortable on it, but as long as she ways by Maxim's side, she knew that she was where she was supposed to be.

"Are you alright?"

Maxim's voice brought Ivy out of her thoughts and she turned to him. She hadn't even realized that they had stopped walking and that she had stopped right along with them. They were back on the bank of the small creek where she and Maxim had rested during their journey to the kingdom and several of the traveling group were stripping down to the least clothing that they could possibly wear so that they could step into the cool water.

"I'm fine," Ivy said.

"What are you thinking about?" Maxim asked.

Ivy sighed, watching Kyven laugh as Emerie splashed him with cold water and then turned away from the water that he sent back at her. Both seemed happier than she had seen them, and she wondered what was going on between them. Though they hadn't been showing obvious affection toward each other before now, it seemed that feelings were beginning to grow between them and Ivy wasn't sure how to feel about it. While she was happy to see Kyven smiling and laughing with the beautiful woman, their link meant more people closely involved in the dangerous mission that they had already begun. She worried that having him falling in love with Emerie would mean that Kyven wouldn't have the focus and determination that was needed and expected from his older brother to get through the challenges that awaited them. At the same time, however, she also knew that there was nothing more powerful and better designed to create strength and courage than finding that person to love.

"Are there more Klimnu out there?" Ivy finally asked, turning away from Kyven and looking at Maxim.

He stared back at her with an expression that she couldn't quite decipher.

"What do you mean?" he asked.

"You said that you are worried about there being possible threats while we travel. Is one of those threats the Klimnu?"

"The Denynso say that they're gone, but I don't know," Maxim said. "There are other species who live here that could be threatening to us, but with everything that we've learned about the history of my kind, I don't think that we can overlook the possibility that the Klimnu may still exist."

"So you do think that they have something to do with the Order?"

"I'm not sure. There's a reason that the Order still exists and Kyven and I aren't a part of it, though. That has to have something to do with our father and his death, I just don't know what."

"What would happen if we did come across Klimnu?" Ivy asked hesitantly.

She had spent many hours of their walking thinking about the creatures and trying to prepare herself for what it would be like should they encounter them. She had tried to remember everything that the women had told her about them and everything that Pyra had said when he talked about them in the meeting hall that horrible morning so that she could somehow ready herself for coming face-to-face with the gruesome, slimy, skeletal beings that they described. No matter how hard she thought about them, however, she didn't know if she could ever really be prepared for what it would be like to stand before them and fight, especially now that she knew how they had come to be.

"I would fight," Maxim said calmly.

"Would you?" Ivy asked. "Would you be able to look at them, knowing who they are and how they came into existence, and fight them? Wouldn't you, even for a moment, hesitate remembering what Pyra did to you and the rest of the Mikana men in the settlement?"

"They aren't Mikana, Ivy, they are Klimnu. They are the source of so much of the pain and turmoil on this planet, the reason that my father is dead, the reason that my mother is afraid and alone, and the reason that there is so much division even within the species. If they still exist, I will see to it that they no longer do."

5

———————

Kyven's hand brushed against Emerie's and he looked over at her. She glanced at him with a smile and intertwined their fingers for a moment before letting go. He felt a familiar shiver of disappointment and confusion go through his belly. This is how she had been since her confession that she had come to the meeting hall with the other women every day just so that she could see him. Though his feelings for her were obvious and growing more intense with each moment, she seemed to be hesitating to let herself go along with them. There was something that was holding her back from him, and he didn't know what it was.

Before he had a chance to ask her if there was something that was bothering her, he noticed her eyes widen slightly and her hand grasped his wrist. He looked ahead of them and saw a dark line breaking the horizon. Emerie looked at him with a questioning expression in her eyes as if she didn't want to trust herself to be excited that she was seeing their destination finally coming into view ahead of them.

"That's it," he told her softly. "That's our kingdom."

"I know," Emerie said, looking back at the wall slowly growing larger and darker in the distance as they walked.

"You do?"

Kyven was surprised at the revelation. He assumed that she didn't know where they were going, but now she was walking with greater purpose and confidence toward the kingdom.

"Yes," she said, tugging gently on his wrist so that he would speed up to catch up with her. "I've been here before. A long, long time ago, but I've been here."

The rest of the group had loosened into pairs and trios and dispersed out so that they walked a few yards apart, but now that the kingdom was getting closer, it seemed that they were drawn back together.

"You've been to the kingdom?" Kyven asked.

"You've been there?" Ivy asked, apparently hearing what Kyven asked as she and Maxim drew closer.

Emerie nodded, letting go of Kyven's arm and turning to look at each of the others in the travel group.

"You knew that the Mikana and our settlement cooperated. For years before the Covra people from each of the groups traveled back and forth regularly. I have been here several times before."

"Then why did you act like you didn't know how difficult the journey would be when you first asked to go with us?" Maxim asked.

Kyven could hear the suspicion and a sharp edge of anger in his brother's voice and he stepped forward slightly to create separation between the two of them. He knew that Maxim would never do anything to hurt Emerie, but he didn't want his aggression to frighten her or make her question continuing on with them.

"I didn't act like I didn't know anything and you didn't

ask me if I had ever been. You informed me of how challenging it was going to be and I told you that we understood that. You assumed that we had never been, but that's your fault, not mine."

"You didn't offer any help for how to get there," Ivy said.

"I didn't think that I needed to," Emerie said, her voice now holding defensiveness that made Kyven worry that their group would soon dissolve under the pressure of their conflicts. "I haven't been to the kingdom in more than 100 years. I would assume that the planet has changed since then. On the other hand, this is Kyven and Maxim's home. They left there only weeks ago, not decades. Why would I need to tell them how to get back to where they came from so recently?"

"She's right, Maxim," Kyven said. "You never asked if any of them had been to the kingdom before. We knew that the humans of the settlement used to maintain a relationship with our kind before the lock. It makes sense that she would have been here before. There's nothing strange about it."

"What did you do in the kingdom?" Maxim asked.

"Got supplies. Made friends. Learned about the planet. There was nothing mysterious about it. We were two neighboring communities that cooperated. Rey told you that they came for us when we were locked. They tried to find us and help us, but they couldn't find the settlement."

"I still don't understand that," Ivy said. "If the settlement was a place that the Mikana went to frequently, it just doesn't make sense that they wouldn't be able to find it."

"By the time that the Covra lock happened, the cooperation between the humans and the Mikana had become strained due to the war. It had been quite some time since the transit between the two was a regular occurrence," Emerie's brother, Nick, said.

"But Emerie remembers how to get to the kingdom after all this time," Oro pointed out.

Kyven looked at the Denynso warrior who had remained nearly silent throughout the journey and saw the suspicion in Maxim's voice reflected on his face.

"Didn't Rey tell us that it had something to do with the Covra?" Kyven said, trying to calm the tension that was quickly rising in the group. "Didn't he say that the Covra were able to confuse everyone and make it so that they didn't know how to find the settlement again?"

The truth was that Kyven didn't know if Rey had actually said that or if there was another explanation that had been given for why the Mikana hadn't been able to find the settlement when the humans ceased all communication. Even if there had been another explanation, he didn't know how much he would truly trust it considering everything that they had learned about the origin of their kind and the war that had a much further reach on the planet than they had originally thought.

"I chose to leave the settlement and come with you because I wanted to get away from the conflict and turmoil that was happening there. I didn't like the way Pyra acted and I am uncomfortable with what the crew has become," Emerie said calmly, looking directly at Maxim. "We all have our reasons for not wanting to stay there and for moving on. Don't become what we are trying to put behind us."

Kyven stepped up beside her and took her hand in his, intertwining their fingers tightly. He expected her to pull away from him, but felt a sense of strength and happiness when she didn't and instead gave his hand a squeeze as she continued to look at his brother. Ivy mimicked Kyven's gesture, taking her partner's hand with one of hers and resting the other on his shoulder.

"She's right, Maxim. I know that there is so much on your mind right now, but they aren't here for any reason other than wanting to start over. Please try to remember how you felt when you first left the kingdom to come and help the humans when they were still locked. They have nothing to do with anything that has happened, and if anything, knowing that she visited your kingdom so long ago should be a comfort to you. She has a connection to it that could be meaningful to you."

Kyven knew that Ivy was being careful with her words, wanting to relay her message to him without revealing what the three of them were really doing on their return quest to the kingdom. He turned his attention to his brother's face and watched as it gradually relaxed and Maxim nodded.

"I'm sorry," he said, looking from Emerie to Nick and the others. "I shouldn't have reacted like that. I appreciate that you chose to come along with us. We all need to be willing to show a little more tolerance." He looked at Oro, who Kyven noticed had taken a step back. "All of us." He looked back to Emerie and then to Ivy. "Especially me."

6

"**I**s everything alright?"

Elise stepped into the observation dome where Azra stood at the far end staring out of the large windows at the stars sprinkled across the inky sky. It was so much like the first night that she had found him standing there, but her heart didn't feel as light and her mind didn't feel as hopeful as it had that night. Though it had only been a few days, it felt like the time that had past was stretching, pushing the two nights so far apart that she wasn't able to reach those wonderful feelings again. As she stepped inside the room this time she felt nervous, the butterflies in her stomach coming out of anxiety rather than excitement.

Azra had seemed so upset after breakfast and had avoided her throughout the rest of the day. Even when she had tried to sneak away with him in the afternoon between serving the rest of the passengers their lunch and their supper, he had purposely engrossed himself in conversation with one of the other warriors so that she couldn't get him away. Even though she had tried to maintain her professionalism at breakfast she hadn't intended on pushing him away. Now she worried that she had accomplished just that and ruined the relationship that was just beginning to develop.

"Azra?" she said, stepping further into the room so that she could see his reflection in the glass.

Even in that faint image she could see that his face looked drawn, his jaw set as he focused out of the ship at something beyond him. Elise walked up behind him and touched a hand to his back. She could feel his muscles tighten under her touch and she pulled away from him instinctively. He was massive, so much larger than any man who she had ever seen, and even though she knew in her heart that he would never purposely hurt her, it was still intimidating to feel such tension and even anger built up within his body.

"Why didn't you tell me?" he asked.

His usually warm, comforting voice had a chill in it that only furthered her nervous, upset feeling and she shook her head.

"I don't know what you mean."

"Why didn't you tell me that you would only be on Earth for a couple of days and then you were going to be gone for three weeks?"

The question sank into her and she started to feel sick. It wasn't until that moment that she had even thought about her upcoming work obligations or what they would mean to Azra. It was simply the next step in her life, the event that had been on her schedule long before the time that she had met Azra or fell in love with him. That wasn't something that she expected when she climbed aboard the shuttle for the trip to Uoria, and it was only then that she began to think of what his sudden presence in her life might really mean.

"I-" she started, but felt like she couldn't find the words that she wanted to say. "I'm sorry, Azra."

"I'm only going to be on Earth for a short time. I'll be gone by the time that you get back from this leisure cruise of yours."

"It's work, Azra. I'm not the one that's going on the leisure cruise, the passengers are."

"So I suppose that it is work that is going to have you lying on the beach?"

"I get a break during the day while the ship is docked and the passengers are out on the planet. I work in the mornings and evenings every day except for my one day off in the middle of that week."

She was feeling slightly defensive, but she was also trying to understand Azra's upset. He had explained to her the importance of the bonding ritual for his kind and she had given herself to him openly and willingly. Now it seemed like she was just pushing him away, going about her life as if the time that they had spent together meant nothing.

"What happens after that, Elise? You'll have another job and then another and then another? There's never going to be time for us to be together."

"This is my job, Azra. I worked so hard to get this position and I am very good at what I do. Even if I didn't love my job, I am under contract. I have to uphold that. This is the life that I have built for myself and if you are the type of man who thinks that I should just give up my career and my home and everything that I have worked hard to accomplish, then maybe..."

"Shhhh," Azra said, turning to her and placing a hand on the side of her face. She tilted her cheek into the cup of his palm and let her eyes flutter closed. "I understand that you have a career and that you have accomplished amazing things in it, and if there is anyone that you ever meet that understands responsibility and duty, it is the Denynso. I just feel like I just discovered you and now I am going to lose you."

The words trembled through her bones and Elise gripped Azra's wrist to make herself feel steadier. She hated to think even for a moment that they wouldn't see each other again. She had known him for such a short time, yet she couldn't imagine living the rest of her life without him. Just as he had described that she was made for him and meant to be his mate from the very beginning, she felt like her mind and body were changed now that she had bonded with him, morphed in some incredible, beautiful way to match only him so that for the rest of her existence she would only ever be able to be happy with him and only ever find fulfillment in his arms.

"You told me that once a Denynso warrior finds the woman who is meant to be his mate, he will never not love her."

"That's true."

"And that he will be devoted to her for the rest of his life and completely committed to their bond for all of his existence."

"Yes."

"Then you can never lose me, Azra. I am bonded to you with everything that is in me and each moment that I am near you I feel more deeply connected to you. It is as if I have been looking for you my entire life even though I didn't know it until I saw you. We didn't find each other for no reason, and we weren't made to be together just for these few days and then to be apart. We will be together again."

Azra closed the space between them and reached down

with both of his hands to take hers and press them to his chest. She could feel the warmth coming off of his skin and the pounding of his heartbeat beneath her palms.

"I know we will," he said, his voice returning to his low, soothing timbre. "I know we will because I know that you are my mate and I have been waiting for you my entire life. We can't be apart."

"So you will wait for me for a little longer?" she whispered.

"It will break my heart every day that I am away from you," he whispered, "and I will miss you more with every breath that passes my lips, but I will always wait for you."

"My contract only lasts for another year before it is up for renewal. I know that during that time there are supposed to be a lot of trips between Uoria and Earth for the exchange program. I will request that the company assign me to as many of them as possible so that I can be close to you."

"Close to me is wherever you are."

Azra dipped his head toward her and Elise lifted her mouth to his, welcoming the warmth of his lips against hers and the touch of his tongue. She felt the overwhelming need for him take over her body and knew that she was trembling slightly as she pulled back from the kiss. Turning her hands so that she held his, she took a step backwards toward the door of the observation dome.

"Come with me," she said, leading him through the room and into the main lounge.

"Where are we going?" he asked.

"Shhhhh," she said, guiding him through the lounge and past the barrier that was meant to keep the passengers separate from the crew.

Elise tried to keep her steps as light and quiet as she could as she led him to a large three-part door and inputted her personal code in the keypad against the wall. A slot in the wall opened and a panel slid out. She rested her palm against it and waited until the blue light that passed beneath it stopped, flashed, and disappeared.

"What is that?" Azra asked.

"It is a safety protocol," she told him, stepping back slightly as the three segments of the door parted and sank into the walls, allowing them through. "It uses biometric measurements to make sure that I am really the one who was putting my code in to access this area of the ship. It is fairly new to these passenger shuttles. We used to only need the code, but recently they started increasing the security on them. We don't really know why, but there are rumors that one of the university shuttles was taken without proper authorization under the guise of being part of the university exchange program and didn't return. Some people believe that it was hijacked during its trip."

She fell silent again as they climbed the stairs toward the staff quarters. She knew that she could face serious consequences if the captain found her to have brought a passenger up to her quarters, but she wanted him with her that night. She needed to be with Azra and wanted their own space. The observation dome was beautiful and had given them a wonderful place for their first experience together, but she craved more privacy now, somewhere where they could be together openly and not worry that someone may walk in any moment.

Once they were inside her room and the door was closed behind them, she felt relieved. No one else had access to her room and as long as she was able to get Azra downstairs the next morning without encountering the other flight attendant or the captain, they could be blissfully alone together.

"Where are we?" Azra asked.

"My quarters," Elise responded, walking further into the small dressing area that was at the front of the room and resting her hand on the latch to the door in the opposite wall. "Do you want to come inside?"

Azra nodded and she opened the door, leading him into the private space that she had never shared with anyone. When they were inside, she turned to him and reached behind her back to slowly release the zipper along her uniform. She stepped out of her shoes as the zipper lowered and then carefully eased the uniform away from her body. Even without the lamps on, there was enough light in her quarters for them to see each other clearly and Elise wanted Azra to see every bit of her. The first time that they had been together had been incredible, but she felt like it had been rushed in a way, almost desperate in their shared need for each other. She wanted them to take their time now, allowing themselves to luxuriate in their enjoyment of one another. They had only a short time to be together before they were separated, and she wanted to make sure that she didn't forget how his mouth felt against hers, how his skin tasted on her tongue, or how her body felt embracing his.

When she stood bare in front of him, she reached her hands out to him, inviting him to come closer. He complied, the deep orange color of his eyes slumbering as he took in all of her. Elise released the ties along the front of his shirt and pushed the hem up as far on his body as she could reach before letting him take over and peel it off over his head, tossing it aside so that it joined her uniform on the floor. As he kicked out of his shoes, she untied the strings at the front of his pants and eased them off of his hips so that they fell down his muscular legs onto the floor. A thick, hard erection sprung forward toward her, making her mouth water.

Elise reached forward and wrapped her hand around Azra's erection, resting it against her palm and encircling it with her fingers as far as they would reach. Azra moaned at her touch and she stepped forward closer to him, wrapping her arm around his waist as she began to stroke her hand along his cock. She felt him lean forward to bury his face in her hair, using one tremendous hand to grip her hip.

"Keep doing that," he whispered into her hair.

The words made Elise's stomach tighten and she felt her intense desire for him surge between her legs so that the wet heat tingled along her inner thighs. She pressed her body closer to Azra and continued the long, rhythmic movements of her hand. She paused to gather the silken drop of crystalline fluid that had formed at the tip and used it to make her hand glide more easily along his skin. Azra's hips pushed toward her and he groaned against her hair, his fingertips digging into her hip as he continued to murmur encouragement.

After a few moments Elise stopped and turned toward her bed, leading him along with her. She climbed onto the fresh white covers and crawled forward until she was at the head of the bed. Azra followed her, lying down on his side when he reached her so that he was looking at her. Elise gently pressed on his shoulder until he lay on his back and ran her hand down his chest, along the smooth, chiseled expanse of his belly, and into the nest of hair around his erection. She let her fingers trace along it languidly for a moment, enjoying watching it as it rose and fell is response to her touch and more of the slick liquid developed, eventually slipping out and trailing down the head.

Elise climbed over Azra's leg and eased it away from the other one so that she could settle between his thighs. She sat on her knees and leaned forward so that one hand

braced her against the mattress and the other held his erection. Touching the tip of her tongue to the base, she ran it
up along the length until she reached the drop of fluid,
enjoying the hint of sweet, salty flavor as she gathered it.
Azra's hands gripped the covers on either side of him,
propelling her forward. Elise opened her mouth and took
him in, gliding him against her tongue until she couldn't
accommodate any more. She wrapped her hand around the
base and began a smooth, continuous rhythm so that her
hand and mouth glided along him in synchronized strokes.
She focused on the taste of him, the feeling of him against
her tongue. As she drew him through her mouth she felt
each vein and ridge, memorizing them so that she could
think of him in her long nights alone.

Azra's hand touched her outer thigh and then ran up
onto her hip. He applied gentle pressure, guiding her to
climb back over his leg so that she was on her knees beside
him rather than between his legs. The change of position
made his erection slip deeper into her throat, but it also
brought her to an angle where Azra could tuck his hand
around her hip and run his finger through her wet folds.
Elise whimpered and pressed back with her hips, seeking
more of the incredible sensation of his touch. Azra
responded by turning his hand so that he could slip two
fingers within her and use the pad of his thumb to massage
deeply into the taut pearl at her peak. Elise parted her knees
slightly to allow him greater access and mimicked the pace
of his fingers inside her with her mouth so that they were
nurturing each other in an intense, synchronized pattern.

Elise rolled her hips slightly in response to the delicious
movements of Azra's hand and soon she felt the sensations
he was creating within her spiraling out of control. She
pulled her mouth away from his impossibly hard, thick cock

and cried out as her climax overtook her, shuddering through her body so that she could barely hold herself up. Azra kept his fingers deep inside her as her body spasmed around them, tenderly massaging her upper wall to extend the nearly overwhelming pleasure that filled her. When the final waves of her orgasm ended, Azra slowly withdrew his fingers from her and sat up, pushing back so that he rested against the headboard. He reached for Elise and she let him take her into his hands, easing her forward and into his lap.

Wrapping her legs around his waist, she nestled into him, welcoming him into her body. Her eyes closed and her head dropped forward toward his as he filled her. Azra's mouth caught hers and he tucked an arm around her hips to hold her closer. She buried her fingers in his hair and rested her forehead against his. He moved slowly, tightening his hips slowly so that he stroked within her while still staying deeply buried inside her. Their bodies melded together in a way that she had never experienced and she knew that she would never feel such passion and connection to another man. Azra was everything that she would ever want or need, and she never wanted to let him go.

Elise let the pressure of Azra's arm around her hips guide her in a slow rocking motion against him. She wanted to remember every sensation that he created in her, every touch of him within her, and every brush of his lips against her skin. He groaned deep in his chest, pulling her closer and increasing the urgency of his thrusts slightly. Suddenly his head fell back and he made a growling sound as she felt him throb within her. The feeling of him spilling into her body sent her over the edge into an unexpected, but dizzying climax. The contractions of her body met his pulses, milking him and drawing him even more deeply within her.

When his body finally relaxed and she collapsed against him to rest against his chest, Elise felt Azra press a trail of kisses along her temple until his lips were settled close to her ear.

"I love you," he whispered.

Elise sighed, feeling complete in a way that she never could have imagined.

"I love you, too," she whispered back, knowing that those words were the most honest that she had ever said and that they would keep her tightly linked to him no matter how far apart they had to be.

7

Ivy expected the group to go through the same gate as she and Max did the first time that they visited the kingdom, but as they approached, Maxim led them around the opposite side of the large stone wall to a larger gate. An expressionless man stood on the other side of the gate as Athan had at the other gate when they first visited. He was younger than Athan and had an intense, severe energy about him that hadn't surrounded the older man.

The man's eyes widened slightly as the group approached and his gaze fell on Maxim. Ivy wondered if he had somehow heard of the struggle that had been happening in the settlement with the men imprisoned in the meeting hall and was surprised to see that they had emerged. A moment after that thought crossed her mind, though, she saw the tension in his face seem to fade and she shook her head, trying to force the suspicious thoughts out of her mind. She couldn't let herself be overwhelmed by questioning everything and everyone. She had to keep her mind clear and straight if she was going to have any chance of helping Maxim the way that she had promised that she would. Though she knew nothing about this man, she couldn't let herself make assumptions about him or his motivations. She would need to place her trust in Maxim and follow his lead as they ventured forward into the unknown.

"Sirrius," Maxim said as they approached the gate. "How is the kingdom?"

It was a question that Ivy hadn't heard him ask when they had approached Athan, but one that seemed to hold great meaning. The man he had called Sirrius nodded and stepped back from the gate, apparently a gesture that invited the group inside.

"It is well," he said in a deep monotone. "And your journey?"

"We're here now. Have you seen my mother?"

"I haven't seen Ellora in several days."

"I'll look for her at home," he said. Maxim stepped back to allow Sirrius to see the rest of the travel group. "These are my friends. They are in need of comfort and accommodations for the foreseeable future. Will you make sure that they are taken care of while I go to see my mother?"

He had assumed the somewhat formal, stilted speech that he seemed to have when he spoke to most of the other Mikana and Ivy found herself feeling slightly uncomfortable. When he spoke that way she felt like she should be anticipating something, preparing herself in some way for something. The fact that she didn't know what that something could be somehow made her feel even more uneasy.

"I will," Sirrius said. "You are welcome here," he said to the group and the words brought a softened, genuine tone to his voice.

Maxim nodded and turned to the Denynso and the humans.

"Wait here with Sirrius. He will make sure that you have a place to stay and help you to settle in for the time that you spend here. Kyven and Ivy will come with me."

"And Emerie."

Ivy looked at Kyven and saw him staring at Maxim with a steady expression on his face as though he anticipated some sort of opposition from his brother about wanting to bring the human woman along with them, but was prepared to stand up to him. Maxim paused for a moment and looked at Emerie, evaluating her. Kyven reached over and took Emerie's hand, and though Ivy saw a look of uncertainty cross the woman's eyes, she didn't take her hand from his.

"Fine," Maxim said. He took a step closer to Kyven and dropped his voice low enough that only he and Ivy could hear him. "She may come with us, but you know what we are walking into. You will not allow her to distract you and you are to keep her away from whatever we might encounter, do you understand me?"

"Yes," Kyven said.

Maxim stepped back again and looked to the rest of the group.

"If you are in need of anything in the time that you are here, speak to Sirrius. If he can't get it for you, he will find me."

Without another word, he turned away and started deeper into the kingdom. Ivy, Kyven, and Emerie followed, none of them looking back to the rest of the group that they were leaving behind. Though Ivy tried not to let the thought enter her mind, she wondered when she may see them again, and what may happen to them when they walked away from the gate and into the kingdom.

Because they had walked through the tunnels the first time that she had visited the kingdom, Ivy didn't recognize her surroundings as Maxim led them through the streets. It felt strange to just be walking through the kingdom without any sense of urgency or concern even though she knew that the mission that they were on put their very lives in danger. It was as if they were hiding behind masks, concealing their secret as they moved unsuspected, unnoticed along the street that led to Ellora's home. She looked into the eyes of each of the people she passed, trying to see beyond the smiles that they offered to what they may be harboring. Which of these people could be members of the Order? How many knew of the tunnels beneath their feet and the taunting lights that followed the steps of those inside, chronicling their progress as they moved through the segments so that there was no possibility of secrets within their recesses.

They made their way to the home Ivy knew belonged to Ellora and Maxim opened the door.

"Mother?" Maxim called into the home.

It seemed too quiet. The space was heavy with emptiness and Ivy felt nervousness prickle across her skin. She reached for Maxim's hand and gripped it tightly as they moved further into the space.

"Mama?" Kyven called from behind Maxim.

Ivy's heart was pounding in her chest so hard that she could hear it in her ears. Could the Order have already found out that they were there? Did they know about them going into the tunnels and had paid out their retribution on Ellora? There were a few more long moments of silence, and then she heard footsteps coming through the house toward them.

"Maxim? Kyven?"

The sound of Ellora's voice released the tension from Ivy's muscles and she felt relief flood through her. Ellora rushed into the front room, her eyes wide with surprise. She opened her arms and ran forward, gathering each of her sons into an embrace.

"Is everything alright?"

The concern in her voice was painful. When they had left her the first time that Ivy and Maxim had visited the kingdom together it had been with the understanding that they were going back to Pyra to seek resolution for the conflict that was happening in the settlement. Ivy could only imagine that she had been terrified for her children and had spent every moment that she had since then wondering what had happened since they walked out of the home.

"We're fine, Mama," Maxim said.

"What happened?"

"We met Pyra before we made it back to the settlement," Maxim told her. "Some of the others persuaded him to bring the situation back to the king of their kingdom and find out what he thought should happen. Creia was extremely welcoming and told Pyra that he had failed as a leader and that he was to release all of the Mikana immediately. We went back to the settlement to free them and several of the men as well as some of the humans are going to go back to the Denynso compound to meet with Creia. He wants to resolve the conflicts and rebuild the relations between our kinds."

"I am so thankful that you are both safe," Ellora said. She hugged each of the men again and then turned to Ivy. "Ivy," she said with a slight edge in her voice that Ivy couldn't quite decipher. "How are you?"

Ellora stepped forward and gathered Ivy in an embrace.

"I'm well, thank you," Ivy said.

"Mama?" Kyven said in a voice that told Ivy that he was

accustomed to seeking out the attention from his mother when his brother was in the room. "I want you to meet someone. This is Emerie."

Ellora turned to look at Emerie. She tilted her head at her, staring at her like she was trying to decipher something about her.

"Where are you from?" she asked bluntly.

"She's from the settlement, Mama."

"Are you one of the original humans?"

"Mother..."

"No," Emerie said, "It's alright. Yes, I was a part of the original crew that created the settlement. I have been to this kingdom before, but it was very different then."

"You've been here?"

"Before the conflict with the Covra," Kyven explained. "She was one of the humans that made journeys here frequently for supplies."

Ellora nodded, still not taking her eyes away from Emerie. Suddenly she turned to Maxim.

"Why have you come back here, Maxim? You have fallen in love with a human woman. Why have you not gone to Earth to be with her?"

Ivy felt like someone was squeezing her stomach. The distrust coming from Ellora toward her and Emerie was palpable.

"We want to know more about the Order," Maxim answered plainly.

Ellora took a breath and stepped back as if Maxim had struck her.

"Maxim," she said. "I thought that you had learned that nothing good could come of looking into the Order. You need to stay away from them."

"We deserve to know what happened to our father,"

Maxim said. "We want to know what happened to our kind and about the war."

"It's too dangerous, Maxim."

"I know that it's dangerous," Maxim said sternly, "but that won't stop me. I need you to tell me everything that you know and everything that you remember."

Ellora shook her head.

"No," she said. "I can't. I can't talk about it. You were never supposed to know. You already know too much. Please, just forget what you know and put it behind you. Go on with your life."

"I can't do that."

"Of course you can."

"No, I can't. Like you said, I know too much. I know too much to just walk away now. I have to find out the truth. This is more than me now. This is you and Kyven and Ivy. This is everyone in our kingdom and everyone that was involved in the war. This goes so much farther than just whoever is in the Order. I need to know what the Order is and what it has done. Don't you want to know what happened to Papa? Don't you want to know why he died and why we were never able to get his body back so that we could bury him properly?"

Ellora's eyes were misted and there was a hint of terror in them that made Ivy know that this went far deeper than they knew, and likely even deeper than Ellora was ready to learn.

8

Zuri took a deep breath to calm herself. The top of her pod being closed over her was having a much more serious impact on her this trip than it had in the past and she was struggling to feel in control. She had felt sick the moment that the flight attendant had told them that it was time for them to get back into their pods to prepare for landing. She knew that much of it was that she was no longer close enough to Ero that she wouldn't be able to touch him. It had been that way on her last trip from Earth back to Uoria, but that was before everything that had happened. That was before the battles with the Klimnu and before witnessing Jem's death. It was before the men had left the compound and found the settlement. It was before the horrors that had unfolded. Even though the planet had calmed, she still didn't want to be without her mate. She felt stronger and safer when she was close to him, and even the short time that she had to spend in the pod preparing for the ship to land back at the university felt far too long to not be able to be close to him.

There was something else that was bothering her, though. Something was lurking in her mind and tormenting her thoughts even though she was not giving herself the time or the permission to dwell on it. She forced her mind away from the thoughts, demanded of herself to think of something else and to push away the lingering questions and concerns that were making the journey more frightening than the ones before. When she wasn't vigilant and her mind was given a moment of free reign, it forced her to think about what was going to happen when they landed. They were going to have to face so many people and answer questions that she didn't know if she was prepared to answer. This was also what she knew was the moment of proof for her relationship with Ero. Though she didn't question their bond or her intention to spend the rest of her life devoted to him, this would be the experience that would prove that to him. She would stand on Earth again and face down the life that she used to have, seeing the people and places that were familiar to her, and have the opportunity within her reach to simply step back into that existence. That would be the moment when she would look at him and tell him that she was ready to walk away from all of that for the final time and truly begin their life together on Uoria.

She felt the dull thud of the ship settling into the landing platform and took a long breath to settle herself. The hissing sound announced that the door to her pod was releasing and she began to release the safety straps over her chest. As quickly as she could she pushed the top away from her pod and climbed out, running forward into Ero's arms as soon as he got out of his pod.

"I can't believe we're here," Ero said against her hair. "I

never thought that I was going to come back to Earth, especially not this soon."

"Me neither. Come on. I want to get off this ship."

They hurried toward the main door and stepped out onto the platform where the captain was already unloading their bags. Several yards away the other ship was settling into another landing platform and Zuri felt a sense of relief that everyone had made it to Earth safely. She stepped out of the way of the door to allow the rest of the passengers to come out of the ship. She looked at the faces of the Denynso warriors as they stepped out, watching as their expressions ranged from excitement to nervousness to tense defensiveness almost as though they were preparing to walk into battle. They would not be spending much time on Earth and Zuri hoped that the men would be able to relax and enjoy themselves while they were there.

Several people from the university approached the ship and smiled up at the passengers as they crowded the platform. Zuri noticed that a few of the women were staring at the Denynso men with looks in their eyes that bordered between shock and hunger. She wrapped her arm tightly around Ero's waist and rested her head on his shoulder.

"Do you think that the men are ready for this?" she asked.

"What are they staring at?" Simran whispered, not taking his eyes away from the group of people who were gathering in front of the platform.

Zuri laughed at the warrior's apprehensive tone and stepped away from Ero so that she could pat Simran's back reassuringly.

"It's going to be alright," Zuri said. "They aren't going to hurt you. Come on. I'll introduce you to some of my colleagues."

They were starting down the steps of the platform when she heard one of the women of the group squeal with excitement.

"Samira!"

Zuri watched as Samira rushed across the room toward a young woman who she knew wasn't a member of the university. The two embraced tightly and then Samira pulled back and looked up at Zuri, gesturing for her to come join them.

"Zuri," Samira said as she approached with Ero and Simran close behind. "I want you to meet my oldest friend, Jane. We haven't seen each other in about two years since she moved."

Zuri smiled and shook Jane's hand. With all of the pain that she knew Samira had gone through in her life, it comforted her to know that there had been someone to offer support, even if she hadn't been able to be there for her much recently.

"As soon as the university contacted me to tell me that Samira was coming back from Uoria and wanted me to be here to meet her, I knew that I had to figure out a way." Jane turned toward Samira and took both of her hands in hers. "I've missed you so much."

"I'm so excited that you're here," Samira said just as Ty approached them. "I have something to tell you." She took a breath, the smile on her face wider than Zuri had ever seen it and her wide eyes shimmering. "I'm getting married."

Jane let out a short scream before covering her mouth with her hand to muffle the sound. Zuri laughed and watched as the young woman took a moment to compose herself and then slowly withdrew her hand so that she could speak.

"Married?" she asked softly, as if worried that if she lifted her voice to a normal conversational tone she might scream again.

Samira nodded and reached behind her to take Ty's hand and pull him up beside her.

"This is Ty," she said, "my fiancé."

"What does that mean?" Simran asked from behind Zuri and she turned to look at him.

A smile came to her lips when she saw the look on his face and the faintest flickering of orange in his eyes as he looked at Jane.

"That is what humans say when they are engaged to marry someone," Zuri explained.

"What are you?" Jane asked, color splashing across her cheeks as soon as the words came out of her mouth.

"It's alright," Ty said with a soft laugh. "I'm Denynso," he glanced over at Ero and Simran, obviously seeing the same look on Simran's face that Zuri had, "just like Ero and Simran, here."

"Denynso?" Jane asked, sounding slightly shocked. "The warriors from Uoria?"

"Yes," Zuri said, nodding. "The university has been involved in an exchange program and several people have gone to the planet to learn more about it and the Denynso. This is my mate, Ero." She gestured toward Ero.

"The Denynso don't marry," Ero explained. "Samira and Ty's wedding is the first for our kind."

An idea suddenly sparked in Zuri's mind.

"Speaking of which," she said, taking Jane by the arm and gently pulling her away from Samira. "I wanted to talk to you about the wedding. I'm sure that Samira will want you to be a bridesmaid."

"Of course!" Samira said excitedly.

"Perfect," Zuri continued. "There is a lot to do in the next couple of days and since the bride and groom here will be busy inviting guests and packing Samira for her move to Uoria that leaves us to handle the preparations. I'm sure that Simran here will be happy to help us."

She looked up at Simran who was still gazing at Jane, the flicker of color in his eyes more pronounced now. He nodded.

"Anything," he said.

"Fantastic," Zuri said, then turned toward Samira and Ty. "Now you two go off and greet some of these people waiting for you. Let us take care of everything. We'll let you know if we need your input on something." As Ty and Samira walked away, Zuri stepped up closer to Jane and Simran. "I think that we should host a party for them to celebrate their engagement," she said, lowering her voice to as much of a conspiratorial whisper as she could while still making sure that they could hear her over the din of the voices and thudding of luggage around them.

"That's perfect!" Jane said excitedly. "We can even make it a combination celebration."

"Combination?" Zuri asked.

"Of course," Jane said, looking at her slightly quizzically. "Her birthday is in two days."

"Her birthday?" Zuri asked.

Jane nodded and made an affirming sound. The revelation hit Zuri hard. In the time that she had spent with Samira she had never known her birthday. Even as their friendship grew closer the young woman had been secretive and closed about that topic, insisting that she didn't celebrate her birthday. Now that Zuri knew when it was and how closely it corresponded with the date that Samira and

Ty chose for their wedding, the entire experience brought on an even deeper meaning that, despite all of the joy and excitement that came with it, also carried a hint of pain still left to resolve.

9

"Your mother doesn't like me."

Maxim turned to Ivy and saw her looking toward the ground, following the progress of her feet as they walked slowly along the back edge of the kingdom. It was just as in the settlement, the two of them seeking out comfort and privacy in the further reaches of the space while still staying within the boundary. He paused and reached for her hand.

"Why do you say that?" he asked.

"Did you see the way she looked at me?" Ivy asked. "She wasn't happy to see me back here with you."

"I don't think that it is that she doesn't like you," Maxim tried to reassure her.

"She looked at Emerie the same way, only worse."

"What do you mean?"

"She looked at her like she was waiting for her to do something horrible, or that she didn't believe she was who she said she was."

"What are you trying to say?"

"I don't think that your mother likes that her two sons are involved with humans."

The words stung when they fell on Maxim's ears and for a moment he didn't know how to respond. He never would have thought that his mother would even consider looking at his chosen partner in a different way because of her species, but now that he took a moment to consider how she had reacted to Ivy, particularly this time that she arrived along with Emerie, he realized that she did seem resistant to their presence. He knew that his mother had never had any contact with humans before them. The contact with the settlement had long ended by the time that his mother was even born. That alone, however, didn't seem to warrant the reservation that had been so obvious in the way that his mother spoke to both women even though she had greeted Ivy familiarly.

"I don't care if she has a problem with me being involved with a human. That doesn't matter to me. I love you and how she feels isn't going to change that."

"But what if she is even less willing to tell you what she knows because you have me around?"

"She was willing to talk as much as she did the first time that you were here."

"She didn't know that I could hear her, though. She was talking to you, I just kind of listened in. I don't want to think that I am going to keep you from finding out something that might help you."

"Listen to me," he said, taking her hands and resting a kiss to her forehead. "You are here to help me. Nothing is going to stop me from finding out what I need to find out. Even if my mother refuses to tell me anything because of you or because of Emerie, I will find another way to learn everything that I can."

Maxim was suddenly aware of another presence near them. He turned and saw Athan step toward them.

"Athan –" he started.

"Are you alone?" Athan asked, cutting Maxim off.

"What?"

"Are you alone? Is it just you and Ivy?"

"Yes. What's wrong?"

"Come with me."

As soon as the words were out of his mouth, Athan turned sharply and started walking quickly in the opposite direction. Maxim took Ivy's hand and pulled her gently so that they could catch up to the older man. They walked until they got to what Maxim recognized as Athan's house and the guard ushered them in quickly. Maxim saw him lean slightly out of the front door to the house and look in both directions as if checking to make sure that no one had followed them or was standing on the street watching them. He stepped back into the house and closed the door, turning the latch and settling a large piece of wood in place in a cradle that caused it to block the door so that no one could get inside.

The inside of the home was small and dark, lit only be a few candles scattered around the space. The windows had been covered with pieces of dark cloth that were tacked to the sides of the window frames so that they couldn't be moved. There was a sense of desperation and silence in the room that made it uncomfortable to stand in, and a moment later Athan pushed past them toward a door along the back wall, gesturing for them to follow him.

"Where are we going?" Ivy whispered nervously behind him.

"I don't know," Maxim replied honestly. "Just follow him."

As they walked further into the building memories

started coming back to Maxim. They appeared in his mind like brief flashes, sparking for just a moment and then fading, seeming to leave an faint impression on his thoughts as they came and went so that he could begin to piece them together.

He saw the inside of this house, but it didn't look as dark and cloistered. Light flooded through the windows and the candles on the surfaces were fresh and new.

He saw it again, darker this time, but not in the oppressive way that it was now. Instead, it was dark from the night that had replaced the shimmering sunlight that had filled the space. The candles were burning, but they were filling the room with warm, comfortable illumination rather than the trembling light that they seemed to be now.

Maxim remembered being in this house when he was much younger and listening to his father talking to Athan about the Order. It was here that his father told him the first stories of the Order and brought him down in the tunnels. It had all seemed like so much of a game then. He hadn't understood the significance of the tunnels or the secretive way that his father and Athan told him that he could never tell anyone what he saw down there, or even that he had been there at all. He had carried that secret like a treasure, guarding it within him even as he got older and began to wonder more about why there was so much mystery surrounding the tunnels and this group that his father and Athan would whisper about deep into the night. He had never felt compelled to tell anyone what he knew. This was the very best of secrets, one that was so exclusive that telling even a single person would have tarnished it.

He thought further and remembered a later visit. If he closed his eyes he could still see his father and Athan talking more heatedly. The space felt more tense then, and even then he knew that the game that he thought he had been playing throughout his childhood was somehow over. The conversation that passed between the men was far more serious now and Maxim wasn't allowed down into the tunnels. He strained for the words, wishing that he could remember even a single sentence that either of the men said, wondering if he did, if it would make a difference now.

Gripping Ivy's hand harder now Maxim continued to follow Athan until they ended up in a small backroom. The memories flooded back to him even more strongly now. He didn't have to concentrate to feel his father there. It was as though he could still see him sitting at the low wooden table in the corner, hunched over a piece of large parchment and slashing across it with his pen as he wrote unknown messages and codes across the creamy expanse. Maxim could still feel him in the air. His presence was strong around him and it made him feel even more determined to find out what had happened to him and bring resolution to the turmoil that had existed in his kingdom. In their last visit to the kingdom Ellora had urged him to do what his father had not been able to finish. He knew that when she said those words she meant that she wanted him to go out and help to establish peace. As those words repeated in his mind now, however, they were telling him to learn everything that he could about the Order and bring an end to whatever war his father had begun.

10

(TO BE CONTINUED IN BOOK VI...)

"What are we doing, Athan?" Maxim asked.

The older man had taken long strides around the perimeter of the room as if performing his guard duties just as he did at the stone wall. He stared into every corner of the space as though trying to seek out anyone who may have crept into the room when he was out searching for Maxim and Ivy. Finally he appeared satisfied that they were alone and he gestured for both of them to sit in two massive wooden chairs positioned close to a clod fireplace against one wall.

"I had to make sure that you came here alone," he said.

"Why not Kyven and Emerie?" Maxim asked.

Athan shook his head and leaned toward them from where he sat on a footstool a few feet in front of them.

"Kyven is not ready to hear what I have to tell you, and that woman has not yet earned her place in his heart. Until I can see in their eyes when they look at one another what I see in the two of you, I can't trust her."

"What is it that you need to tell me?" Maxim asked.

Athan looked around the room once more and then leaned slightly closer.

"I know why you have come back to the kingdom," he whispered conspiratorially.

"You do?"

Athan nodded.

"I can help you. It is time that you know the secrets of the Order and what really happened the night that your father died."

Maxim felt his heart begin to pound and he nodded, holding Ivy's hand in his lap for strength and comfort. He needed her there beside him more in this moment than he ever had and he was more grateful than he could express that she had chosen to stay on Uoria with him and walk along with him on this frightening and unknown journey.

"The Order knew about the Klimnu from the very beginning. As soon as the group split off, the Order began to track and monitor their movements and their actions. The men of the Order then already knew how dangerous the rogue group had become. Unfortunately, some were lured away from the focus of the Order and fell into the temptation of the Klimnu."

"Members of the Order became Klimnu?" Maxim asked.

His mind returned to Ivy wondering whether his father died either because he was Klimnu or because the rest of the Order was and he was not. Now that Athan had confirmed that some members of this ancient faction of the Order had actually split off from the Order to join the Klimnu, Maxim worried that his father's fate lay in his decision to join the slimy creatures.

"Yes," Athan said. "Soon after that, the rest of the Order entered the badlands and encountered new species that they had never seen before."

"Ellora said that the Order had allies in the badlands who helped them to force the Klimnu off of the planet the first time," Ivy said.

Maxim nodded and Athan reflected the gesture.

"That's true. Some of the species there were strange and completely unknown to the Mikana, but they knew about the Klimnu and the intentions that they had about Uoria. The Order connected with them and created alliances that would eventually succeed in forcing those original Klimnu off of the planet. They had no way of knowing that they would take over the planet of Ynn and destroy it to the point that they would have to return to Uoria generations later and resume their first goal of taking over the lush and beautiful planet that they had wanted all along. Later, when the Covra attacked the humans, the Order sought out their allies again. It had been so long, but they knew that if there was anyone who would be able to protect the vulnerable humans from the horror that the Covra was capable of utilizing, it was those powerful creatures."

"Who were they?" Maxim asked.

Athan shook his head and looked at Maxim with mournful regret in his eyes.

"I don't know," he said. "I have never known their names."

"But why could they protect the humans? We didn't see any sign of anyone having done anything to help them. The settlement was just sitting there alone and abandoned for all of those years just waiting for the Covra young to hatch."

"Exactly," Athan said. "It looked abandoned because no one but the Covra had gotten near it for more than 100 years."

"I don't understand," Ivy said.

"Do you find it strange that the Klimnu swarmed the Denynso compound determined that it was through the use of the Denynso warriors that they would be able to take over the entirety of the planet, but they didn't even for a moment consider utilizing the slaves that the Covra were already using for their human incubators? Even if the Klimnu had not passed the information about the Covra through the years to the subsequent generations, they still passed along their greed and their cruel, opportunistic approach. It wouldn't have taken long for them to find that settlement and to ravage it for everything that it had. They would have taken over and found themselves clashing with the Covra. Instead, they completely ignored the settlement and instead moved underground."

"Maybe they feared the Covra," Maxim suggested.

"No," Athan said. "They hated them. It wasn't about fear. Remember that the Klimnu changed because of them. They left everything that they knew and completely transformed themselves because of their deep-seated hatred and distrust. They took over the abandoned prison that the Covra had forced their ancestors to build for them but hadn't been able to use because they wanted to reclaim it. If they had known that the Covra had imprisoned another species for their own purposes, the first thing that they would have wanted to do was destroy that for them. They would have gone onto that settlement and found a way to either remove the eggs and capture the humans, or simply kill off all of the humans so that the eggs wouldn't stay alive. This, however, is not what they did. They went about their plan without even taking a moment to consider the humans. They acted like the settlement wasn't there at all."

"Because they didn't see it."

Maxim looked at Ivy and saw her eyes wide with realization. She looked at Athan and slid closer to the edge of her seat so that she could look him deliberately in the eye.

"Do you know what these allies looked like?" she asked.
Athan nodded.

"There were two species that cooperated closely with
one another. One was far more gentle and resisted fighting,
but had incredible abilities. The other was strong, a race of
warriors with massive wings growing from their backs and
skin that shimmered. They were truly beautiful, their wings
like shards of colored glass and their eyes a shade of purple
like none of us had even seen."

"What did the gentle ones look like?" Ivy asked.

"Lovely," Athan responded. "Long, silver hair and skin
that shimmered and glowed. They are the ones that hid the
settlement. The warriors protected them and ensured that
they stayed safe on their journey, but it was the others, the
gentler, softer ones, who protected the entire group of
humans by making the settlement disappear so that not
even the Mikana, their closest of allies, could find them
again."

"They didn't make it disappear," Ivy said. "They covered
it. They concealed it against the sky and the hills around it.
They built up a world around it so that no one else knew
what they were looking at and it would keep the rest of the
world out while also keeping the humans in."

"Just like a wall," Maxim said.

"Loralia said that her kind was at the mercy of the Covra
until they were driven underground and then the humans
came and saved them from further attacks by those
creatures."

"They saved them and they didn't even realize what they
were saving them from."

"That's why Loralia didn't die in the plague that took
over her family even though every other member of the
species did. She wasn't like them. In almost every way she

was like them. She looked like them with her long, silver hair and her ability to reflect the world around her to create what she needed it to be, and yet she didn't, with purple eyes that likely separated her from every other member of her kind. That's because she is like Ero and Ty...she's a hybrid."

"She must have been the first in the line that expressed the traits that she had inherited from the winged warriors. That is what kept her alive. Only the other species was vulnerable to the plague that eventually killed all of them except for Loralia. There must have been just enough of the blood of that creature moving through her veins that it kept her from falling victim to the illness."

"There is just one thing," Ivy said. "If her kind covered the settlement with a massive reflection, how did the Covra and the Denynso find it?"

"Remember what Loralia told you. The reflections only work when the person looking at them truly believes what he's seeing, but if you question what the reflection really is, or believe that you are seeing something that does not correspond with the reflection, it will falter. Both the Denynso warriors and the Covra were able to see the settlement because they already knew that it was there. The Covra had infiltrated it many times before, and they were determined that they would see where their young were being kept warm and preparing for their living dinner upon hatching. The Denynso knew because they had found the instructions that told them exactly where to find the settlement. They had no reason to believe anything but that the settlement would be there waiting for them."

"I don't understand, though, Athan. What does any of this have to do with the night my father died?"

"That is the night that your father told me that he had

uncovered something that pushed him beyond his control, that he knew that he was the one who had to do something about it. He walked into battled that night flanked by a glass-winged warrior angel on one side and a silver-haired soldier on the other. He ran into the battle and in a moment, he was gone. There was a bolt of lightning like nothing I had ever seen and I saw his body arch as if lifted by the light. By the time the sky calmed again, he was gone.

UNTITLED

(To be continued in book VI...)

THE ALIEN'S ENCOUNTER

1

"There was nothing left, Maxim," Athan said, his voice soft but leading as if he were trying to tell Maxim something without actually putting it into words. "I ran to the place where he had been, but there was nothing. There was no sign that he had ever been there at all."

"Where did they go?" Maxim asked. He was struggling to keep his voice calm, but he knew that there was a slight tremble in it from the anger that was beginning to course through his veins. "Where did the winged warrior and the silver-haired warrior go after my father disappeared?"

Athan shook his head.

"They walked away. They said nothing to me."

"And you just let them go?" Maxim asked.

"What was I to do, Maxim? We were in the middle of a battle. It felt like the world was crashing down around us and I had just watched my dearest friend, the man who I believed was going to save our kind and bring back the peace and the strength that we once had, die in front of me."

"You didn't watch him die," Maxim said. "You watched him get destroyed."

"And with him went all of my hopes for the future. You don't understand what it was like for us. None knew of the Order, so there was nowhere that we could turn for help to stand up against the corruption that your father was beginning to uncover. We were invisible in an already invisible world."

"He had a name," Maxim growled.

Athan looked at him strangely.

"What?" he asked.

"He had a name!" Maxim roared. He felt Ivy's hand touch his back. "Everything was taken from him. Don't take his name from him, too."

Athan looked at him for a long, still moment.

"Aegeus," he said calmly. "You don't understand, Maxim," he repeated, seeming to slow his words slightly as he said them to make sure that Maxim heard and understood each one completely.

"Of course I don't understand!" Maxim said. "How was I supposed to understand anything when all of this was kept from me for all these years? I was just a child when he died, Athan. I spent my entire life wondering what happened to him and what possibly could have led to him dying in such a way that we weren't even able to bury him so that my mother and my brother and I could go to visit him. Now I find out that my entire life not only you, my father's most trusted friend, but my mother knew that there was more to it and just never told me. How do you expect me to understand anything when you don't even give me the chance to know everything?"

"I'm sorry," Athan said. "I did what I thought was right at the time. Aegeus didn't tell me what he had planned for that battle, or even what he found out. I never had the chance to find out everything, and I didn't know what else to tell your mother. Ellora knew that it had to do with the Order, and I know that she knew about the Klimnu. We never talked about it since, and I don't know how much he told her, but I know that she did know about the group turning and about your father's determination to overcome them. Have you asked her what else she knew?"

"Yes, I've asked her. She won't tell me anything. She hates that I even know about the Order and she doesn't want anything to do with it. Even after all of these years she is still afraid to even talk about them. What could possibly have happened that would make her afraid of a group that is still anonymous for something that happened more than two decades ago?"

"The Order is powerful, Maxim. More powerful than Aegeus ever let you know. I know that you have memories of us talking and may remember much of what your father told you and showed you, but that is not everything. He kept so much of it from you because he knew that you were still so young and that you wouldn't be able to handle it yet. He didn't want to put the responsibility of that knowledge on you."

"Why not?"

"The Order doesn't discriminate. The fact that you were just a boy doesn't mean anything to them. If they were to find out that you had known about the Order and anything that we did, it would not just be Aegeus's life that would be in danger."

"Why would he choose to be a part of a group like that? Why would you?"

"It's not a choice. The Order is not something that a man chooses, it is something that chooses him, and if you do not answer that call, you are giving up your life and likely the lives of your family. This is a tradition that has persisted well beyond history. As long as there have been Mikana, there has been the Order. Much of what it has done has been good. Our men have protected the clan and the planet in ways that others will never know. But in every fight for good there is always the potential for evil. It is up to those who still believe in the good and who are strong enough to resist the temptations of the darkness to stand up and fight.

That is what your father did. Aegeus believed very strongly in the good of the Order. Even though there were aspects of it that were harsh and frightening, he was committed to all of the good that it had done and all of the good that he believed it could still do. He dedicated himself to not allowing the Klimnu to overtake the Order and transform it the way that they had transformed themselves. Had they succeeded, the Klimnu would have power beyond your imagination. They would have been able to take over all of Uoria and the rest of the species of this planet would be their slaves, even the Mikana. Those who didn't comply would have been forcibly transformed and would either allow the potential within themselves to build up until they were fully Klimnu and went along with what the rest of the army wanted, or they would live out their lives tortured by what they had become. Your father's death might not have eradicated the Klimnu from Uoria, but that sacrifice did prevent them from being able to take over the Order. When he died, the battle raged harder and the men who had once stood beside him fought in his name.

We fought against those who were once our brothers, Order against Order, fighting until they all lay dead and we could return home with only the knowledge that we had done what we could. There was no hero's welcome for us. The clan went along with their lives just as they had before, quiet and unassuming, unaware of everything that had happened. And that is exactly what we had wanted. Our reward was seeing those who didn't know about the Order continuing on as if nothing was strange, nothing was out of place. Those families who had lost people in the battle created stories to explain their loss, and life went on, just as Aegeus and the others would have wanted."

Rage filled Maxim and he felt himself lurch toward Athan before Ivy grabbed onto him and eased him back down into his seat.

"You think that this is what he would have wanted?" Maxim demanded. "He would have wanted for his family to have no idea what happened to him, and to spend our entire lives missing him and wondering if there was anything that we could have done to help him. He would have wanted for us not to be able to even go to the side of his grave and pay our respects to him, or just visit with him in the only way that we would ever be able to again? You think that he would have wanted to give up his life only to have the Klimnu come back and continue to ravage an already destroyed planet?"

"The planet hasn't been destroyed, Maxim."

"What about the badlands? How about all of the Denynso who never made it out of the compound they half abandoned? What about Loralia's kind? She is the only one left. And the winged warriors? No one even knew that they ever existed. Where are they now? What happened to them?"

"The Klimnu didn't do all of that," Athan said.

"Then who did? And even if the Klimnu wasn't responsible for everything that has happened, they are still what started it, and are still what continues all of the hate and division and violence on this planet."

"There are no more Klimnu," Athan told him.

"Yes, there are," Maxim said. "They are here. They are inside each and every one of us. The potential to become those creatures is just waiting inside each of us to take the wrong step, to feel the wrong thing, and to fall under the wrong influence."

"As long as we don't come into contact with the toxins that dissolve our skin, we can't transform."

"Do you really think that, Athan? Do you really believe that the transformation of the Klimnu was about some flowers?"

"That's what started it," he said, sounding slightly defeated.

"If that is what you truly believe, that the Klimnu happened just because their skin reacted to a plant, you are not what I thought you were, or what my father thought you were."

Maxim's hands felt cold and shaky as he stood up. He looked down at Ivy and she stood up beside him.

"Maxim," she said gently, but he held up a hand to stop her.

"We're leaving," he said. "At least I am. I can't stay here and listen to this anymore. I'd like to have you with me, but I won't force you. You can stay if you wish."

Ivy shook her head and reached up to touch his face gently.

"No," she said, her voice sounding slightly tremulous. "I'll come."

Out of the corner of his eye Maxim saw Ivy look at Athan and Athan give her a pained expression in return. Maxim felt heaviness in his chest and belly, but he couldn't force himself to sit down again and listen to more of what the man had to say. He knew that Athan knew more about the last days and moments of his father's life than he did, and that he would be the one that might be able to help him to uncover what had really happened, but he couldn't bear to listen any longer. What Athan was telling him was just too painful, and infuriating in a way that he couldn't explain. He knew Aegeus. Even though he had been just a child when his father had died, Maxim could remember enough of him that he knew that this is not what he would have wanted for his family or for the rest of the planet. There was more to his disappearance in that battle than just an instant and complete decimation. And Maxim knew that it had something to do with the soldiers that flanked him when he walked onto the field.

2

"Maxim, please slow down," Ivy called, rushing as quickly as she could to try to catch up with him as he walked in long, aggressive strides away from Athan's house.

"I'm sorry," he said, pausing and turning around so that she could get to him.

He reached out to her and Ivy curled into his arms, resting her head on his chest and sighing at the sound of his heart beating beneath his tunic. The smell of his skin rose up to her and she let her eyes close so she could focus completely on the presence of him. He pressed a kiss to the top of her head.

"I'm sorry," he said again, but this time it didn't sound like he was just apologizing for rushing out of Athan's house and away from her.

"You don't have any reason to be sorry," Ivy answered, turning her head so that she could touch a kiss to the expanse of skin revealed by the open ties of his tunic. "No one knows what you are going through and no one, including you, would know how to react in a situation like this. How could you expect to know what to say or do? You didn't even know that any of this was happening or that it had happened, and now you are having to face it all. I can only imagine how overwhelming and upsetting that is."

"I just wish that there was something else that I could do."

"What do you mean?"

"Like you said, I feel so overwhelmed. I feel like there's nothing that I can do. I talked to my mother, and she doesn't want anything to do with any of this. She is completely content to just go on living her life thinking the exact same things that she has been thinking this whole time and not for a moment worry about anything else, or even consider that there could be more to it than what she thinks."

"It might just be too hard for her, Maxim."

"What do you mean?"

"Your father was everything to her. She loved him with her whole being and when she found him she thought that she would be spending her entire life with him. She believed that they would have children, watch those children grow up, enjoy playing with their grandchildren, and just continue throughout life until they faded away together. Never could she have imagined that she would be left so suddenly and with two sons to raise on her own."

"How do you know that?" he asked.

Ivy pushed back so that she could look up at him, her eyes meeting his so that he could see the look on her face as she gazed at him.

"Because that is how I feel about you."

Maxim pulled her closer and rested his cheek against the top of her head, exhaling deeply.

"I guess you're right," he said. "Now that I have you I

couldn't imagine a single second without you. I don't know what I would do if you were suddenly taken away from me."

"Exactly. The suffering that she went through having to mourn your father while also taking care of you and Kyven, and staying alive herself, and also carrying the burden of keeping the Order and everything that she did know about Aegeus's death a secret was a pain that I don't even want to begin to think about. When you ask her about it and you try to get her to tell you what she might know about the Order, or even bring up things that she might now know about your father's death and try to get her to confront them, you are not just putting her at risk because of what she shouldn't know. You are also forcing her to relive those moments without him. I'm not saying that it has gotten easy for her to live without your father, or that she doesn't still miss him and wish that he was here with her, but I'm sure that it is not as fresh and raw as it was when it first happened. She has learned to go about her days and her nights without him. She has learned to think her own thoughts and to consider herself as her own person rather than thinking in terms of herself and your father together."

"She's right, Maxim.

Ivy pulled away from Maxim's chest and turned sharply to see Ellora walking toward them. Even at the distance she could see tears sparkling in the spectacularly beautiful woman's eyes.

"It is only in the last few years that I have learned to not reach for your father's hand when I am walking through the kingdom, or to roll over in the middle of the night to kiss him when I am having trouble sleeping. It has been so long, and yet to me it is still right here, right now. I am just begin-ning to know what it is to have a life without him, and when you came back here and started talking about him, it was like Athan had come to my door all over again. It's not that I don't want to think about Aegeus, because I think about him all the time. There isn't a breath that I breathe that doesn't have a thought or a memory of him in it. But I have learned to live with those thoughts and those memories. They have become as much a part of me as my blood. What you are looking for and the things that you are trying to find out are threatening those thoughts and memories.

It's not that I don't think that there isn't more to this, and it's not that I believe that I know it all, but what you are trying to do is putting everything at risk. If the Order found out, we could all lose our lives. If they don't, I will still lose what I have left of your father. Those are not risks that I am willing to take. I'm sorry if that hurts you in some way, but I just don't see the purpose in any of what you are doing. It won't change anything. It won't bring your father back or heal any of the old wounds."

"But what if it can help prevent further ones?" Maxim asked, taking a step toward his mother.

Ivy caught hold of his hand before he got too far away from her. The emotion in him was still so high and she didn't want him to upset Ellora any more than he already had. She didn't know exactly what was going on or what Maxim had in front of him to discover, but she did know that this was not the moment for him to delve any further into it. Ellora didn't look strong enough to handle any more.

"Where is your brother?" Ivy asked, guiding Maxim back toward her.

Maxim looked at her and then back at his mother, and then back at her.

"I don't know."

"He is showing that woman the rest of the kingdom."

"What is it that you have against her?" Maxim asked.

Ellora shook her head.

"Neither is Ivy," he said.

"Maxim, I don't want to have this conversation."

Ivy could feel her partner tense beside her and reached down to intertwine their fingers. She gave his hand a reassuring squeeze, hoping to offer him some of her strength.

"We should find Kyven," Ivy said softly, holding Maxim close to her side.

"Athan said..."

"We should find Kyven," Ivy repeated,

She knew that Athan had said that Kyven wasn't ready to hear everything that he had told them, but Maxim had already decided that he wasn't going to fully trust Athan. All that they could do was tell Kyven what they had learned so that he would be able to help them in any way that he could. This may be a journey that they would have to take without the guidance of the people who Maxim had loved and trusted the most when he was young, but that only meant that he was going to need to support and encourage of those that he did have even more.

3

———————

"What are you doing?" Samira asked, reaching ahead of her.

Eden laughed and looked over at Zuri who stood on the other side of Samira. Zuri checked the knot on the back of the blindfold that covered Samira's eyes and placed a hand on Samira's back to help guide her down the steps off of Zuri's house. Ero and Pyra were standing at the bottom of the steps to catch hold of her arms and guide her the rest of the way down. When Eden made it to the bottom she offered a kiss to Pyra and smiled up at him.

"Are you sure that Lysander is going to be alright?" he asked.

Eden laughed softly at the roles within their relationship yet again changing. She and her mate went back and forth frequently with how they felt about their son and their protectiveness over him. There were some moments when Pyra wanted his son to be brave and strong and was willing to be a bit more permissive with what he would do, but Eden felt afraid of letting their tiny son out of her sight. At other times Eden would choose an activity or make a choice that she thought was completely safe, and Pyra would be the one who would suddenly be afraid for Lysander's safety. Now that she had asked her grandmother, one of the few family members on Earth who she had a relationship with that was close enough to want to see her much less to trust her with her son, to babysit while she and Pyra attended Samira's surprise birthday party and engagement celebration, it was one of those moments when Pyra was feeling uneasy and unsure

"Lysander is going to be just fine," she reassured her mate. "I spent a lot of my childhood with Gramma. There are no two hands on this planet that I would feel safer putting our son in than hers."

"How old is she?"

Eden laughed again. She had specifically chosen not to introduce her grandmother to Pyra yet. She knew that she would have to eventually, but she felt like it might take a bit of time for her blunt, upfront grandmother to get through the intensive questioning and examination of her mate that Eden was positive was going to come.

"Old," Eden admitted, "but still sharp as a tack. Nothing gets past that woman."

They were now guiding Samira down the slight hill in front of Zuri's house toward the long luxury vehicle that they had rented for the evening. Her footing was unsteady and Ero and Zuri were having to support nearly all of her weight while Eden and Pyra stood behind them ready to catch any of them that happened to topple over before they made it all the way to the vehicle. This entire adventure was just beginning and already Eden was starting to see flaws in the plan.

"So tell me again why it is that you didn't want me to

meet her?" Pyra asked. "If she was so important in your life, wouldn't you want her to meet your mate?"

"Of course I do," Eden said, reaching forward to offer a bit of support to Samira as she tipped precariously backwards for a moment before continuing ahead. "And she is still extremely important in my life. I just haven't been able to see her as often recently for reasons that I am sure that you understand."

"You don't think that she will like me," Pyra said.

Eden looked at him and noticed the saddened look on his face. Even though he would never admit it, Eden had seen over his first few days on Earth that Pyra was not entirely comfortable with being away from his home planet and around so many humans. On Uoria he was accustomed to being extremely important and leading with an unwavering confidence and strength. The rest of the clan admired him and even when he faltered as he did in his leadership of the expedition to the Nyx 23 settlement, they were willing to forgive him and help him to rebuild himself. He was comfortable around his own kind and was accustomed to being engaged in battle with those that he didn't know and didn't understand. He was just starting to get used to the idea of creating true alliances with other species and being able to live and cooperate alongside them.

Being on Earth had forced him into a situation that was unknown and felt, in a way, unsafe. The humans who he had met recognized him as one of the exotic and alluring Denynso warriors who they had studied and been so fascinated with. They didn't, however, know him by name or understand his station within his clan. Eden could see that he was feeling unsure of himself, insecure in the thought that the people around him, who far outnumbered the Denynso who were on Earth, might not appreciate his presence or might not be willing to accept them. He felt judged and scrutinized for the first time in his life and it was making him feel off-kilter.

Eden reached out and rubbed his arm comfortingly.

"It's not that I don't think that she will like you," she said. "In fact, it might be more than I know that she will like you a lot. When my grandmother likes someone, she feels a sort of possessiveness toward them that fairly often results in conversations that are hours and hours long and have very little hope of escape. She will want to know everything about you and Uoria and your kind. She'll want to know how we met and what our relationship is like."

Pyra reached out to hold onto the door to the vehicle that Ero had opened so that Zuri and Ero could guide the still-protesting Samira into the backseat.

"She'll want to know how we met." Pyra asked.

Eden looked at the somewhat terrified look on her mate's face and had to laugh.

"We can just tell her that you were the very first Denynso warrior I saw when I stepped out of the ship on Uoria and that it was love at first sight," she told him.

"So you are going to lie to your grandmother?"

"Do you want me to tell her that I hated you when I first saw you and I tried to get you to leave me alone because I wanted nothing to do with you, but that the king forced me to have you as my guard and protector, which led to you watching me take a shower and then ravishing me?"

"You are going to lie to your grandmother."

"I thought so."

"Come on, guys," Ero called from inside the vehicle. "We have a...." he glanced back at Samira, who was still blind-folded and reaching around the inside of the vehicle from her seat, "...something to get to."

Eden and Prya climbed in and Eden was immediately awestruck by the colored lights and mirrored interior of the vehicle. Plush seats lined all sides and there was enough space for the five of them as well as the rest of the group that they were supposed to pick up along the way. They settled back onto one of the seats and Ero started pouring champagne into glasses and handing them around.

"And you're sure that she won't have a problem with the fact that I'm Denynso?" Pyra asked.

"Absolutely not," Eden told him. "In fact, Gramma was the one who encouraged me the most when I said that I wanted to be a scientist and find out everything that I could about the world. She told me that that wasn't enough. I should set my sights on finding out everything that I could about the universe and beyond."

"And in all the universe, you found me," Pyra said.

Eden reached for the glass of champagne that Ero was holding out to her and raised it toward Pyra.

"Yes," she said with a smile, "and that is more than I ever thought that I would know."

She touched the rim of her glass to his and took a sip. He followed suit, giving a strange look to the glass as he swallowed his first mouthful. Eden remembered then that this was the first time that the Denynso had, had Earth-originated beverages such as champagne. She hoped that it wouldn't impact them the way that it had a tendency of impacting humans. If they all started feeling a bit out of control, there was no way that the human women would be able to rein them in.

4

Zyyr leaned back against the curved stone of the wall and closed his eyes, letting the warmth of the sun heat the skin of his face. He wondered if he was ever going to get fully used to the strange weather on this portion of Uoria. He was so used to the weather patterns of the compound and it hadn't occurred to him when he planned on leaving the first time on the quest with Pyra and the other warriors that one of the most challenging things that they would encounter would be the strange and unpredictable weather. A hint of a smile came to his lips as he thought about how strange it was that after everything that they had gone through in the last several weeks that it would be the intensity of the sun, the temperature of the air, and the frequency of the precipitation that would be what would linger with him.

"It is nice to see such a lovely smile on a Denynso warrior."

The sweet voice opened Zyyr's eyes and he found a woman looking down at him from a few feet away. She was the most stunningly gorgeous woman he had ever seen, and for a moment he wondered if he was imagining her. She simply seemed to perfect to exist, but suddenly it occurred to him that she must be one of the notoriously beautiful and entrancing Mikana. Until that moment he had met only the men, but now he saw how the appeal of the man translated into a woman so incredible he couldn't even bring himself to speak.

"Did I bother you?" she asked, sounding concerned and taking a step back.

She was holding a large basket tucked close to her hip and as she moved it started to slip out of her grasp. Zyyr jumped up and rushed forward to help her stabilize it before she dropped it. As he did he forced the expression on his face to look less startled and more friendly.

"No," he finally forced past his lips. "No, you didn't bother me at all. I just didn't realize there was anyone here."

"I was just going to gather some fruit from the orchards," she said by means of explanation for breaking through his private thoughts. "My name is Lila."

She held her hand up in front of her, but Zyyr didn't know what she wanted him to do. He thought of the greeting rituals that he had learned from the humans of the settlement and took her hand, resting her long, slender fingers against his palm so that he could bring the back of her hand to his lips and tenderly touch a kiss to her pale skin. As soon as his mouth touched her skin, his body felt like it lit on fire. Tightness in his belly formed until it was like he was being tied in a knot, and he could feel the front of his pants straining against an erection that was almost painful in its intensity.

It was a strange and overwhelming feeling, something that he had not been prepared to experience. In all of his years he had heard the men of his kind talking about the sometimes excruciating physical and psychological experience of anticipating their mates. They spoke of dealing with days of unbreakable physical desire and a level of aggression and anger that threatened to overcome them. Brothers and best friends had engaged in fearsome fights during these times, the feelings within the man who was close to meeting his intended causing him to nearly tear the other to pieces.

In this moment, however, Zyyr felt absolute peace and calm. Though his body and his mind were telling him with absolute certainty that this woman, this incredible, almost unbearably beautiful woman, was meant to be his, he wasn't feeling any of what he had expected throughout his life. He didn't know what to make of it, but he knew that he wanted very much to continue to enjoy the aura of relaxation and contentment that Lila seemed to create around him.

"You are looking at me strangely again," Lila said, her pretty face scrunching slightly as she looked back at Zyyr with an expression like she was searching within him and trying to understand what was going on in his thoughts.

"I'm sorry," Zyyr said, looking down briefly and giving a short laugh. "I don't mean to look at you strangely. My name is Zyyr."

Lila looked down at her hand and then back at him expectantly.

"I liked the way that you greeted me before," she admitted softly.

Zyyr slowly lifted her hand again and touched his lips to it in another kiss, not taking his eyes away from hers.

"May I come along with you to the orchards, Lila?" he asked.

Lila nodded, her thick waves of dark, glossy hair moving around her shoulders and waist almost like liquid.

"I would like that very much."

Zyyr reached for the basket and she handed it over to him. He realized as he took it that it wasn't empty as he had expected it to be. Instead, it held a piece of red and white fabric draped over something.

"I brought along a picnic lunch," Lila said as if explaining the fabric even though he hadn't asked her about it.

"I'm sorry," he said, feeling suddenly awkward. "I didn't mean to intrude on your picnic."

He started to hand the basket back to her, but Lila smiled and shook her head.

"I brought along enough for the two of us," she said.

"You did?" Zyyr asked, shocked by the revelation.

"Yes," she said simply and started walking.

Zyyr followed her in silence as they walked along the edge of the stone wall that surrounded the kingdom much like the one at the settlement. He noticed as they walked that the wall was belling out. Though he had expected for it to maintain a close and relatively uniform shape like the settlement, this one seemed much larger toward the back, particularly to one side, than in the front. It had appeared relatively small as they approached it first, but now Zyyr realized that it was far, far larger than he had anticipated.

They had walked for several minutes before he saw the orchards. The trees grew in neat, uniform rows, the ground beneath and between them clean and smooth. He paused slightly and stared at the trees, trying to understand their perfect pattern.

"How do they grow like that?" he asked.

Lila turned around and cocked her head at him slightly, a look of questioning on her face.

"What do you mean?" she asked.

"They are in such straight lines and there are no other plants or trees or anything around them."

"It's an orchard," she said as if that explained everything. "Don't you have orchards on your compound?"

Zyyr shook his head.

"No," he told her. "I'll admit that I was not entirely sure what an orchard was when I asked if I could go with you."

"So why did you ask?" Lila asked coyly, glancing down at her feet and then back up at him.

"So that I could spend more time with you," Zyyr said.

She smiled and looked down again briefly.

"An orchard is where we plant trees of a specific kind so that we can grow and harvest their fruit. Where do you get food on your compound?"

"There is a forest," he told her, "and gardens. I have never heard of someone raising trees."

He felt a sense of awe and admiration for these unusual and truly amazing people. He found himself wanting to know more about them, craving a deeper understanding of Lila and her kind nearly as much as he craved her touch. They walked on for a few more yards before Lila stopped again and instructed him to put the basket down. She reached in and pulled off the cloth, revealing that it was a small blanket covering an abundance of food that Zyyr didn't recognize but that looked and smelled delectable.

They settled onto the blanket and Lila began to unpack the basket.

"Why did you bring enough for two people?" Zyyr asked.

He hated to think that she might have had plans to meet someone else in the orchard, but immediately assumed that if she had, she probably would not have been so willing, and even eager, for him to come along with her. Lila looked up at him with a hint of shyness in her eyes and gave him a smile.

"I've been watching you since you first arrived here with the others," she admitted.

"You have?" Zyyr asked, even more surprised by this revelation than he was by the first.

"Yes," she told him. "I noticed that you spend a lot of your time out by the wall, and I wanted to have a chance to talk with you. Was that dishonest of me?"

He smiled at her.

"No. I'm glad that you did."

They spent a few moments eating in silence and then Zyyr noticed that Lila was gazing over the wall with a wistful look in her eyes.

"What are you thinking about?" he asked.

She sighed and looked at him.

"Just...." she trailed off, looked at the wall again, and then back at him, "What is it like out there?"

Zyyr swallowed a bite of a rich, flaky bread that reminded him of something that Ty would have baked, and looked at her quizzically.

"What do you mean?" he asked.

"The planet," she said, leaning toward him. "What is the planet like outside of the kingdom?"

"You've never been outside of the wall?" he asked.

Lila shook her head and sat back, suddenly looking faintly sad.

"No. I've spent my entire life here. It's only the men who are permitted to leave the kingdom at will, and even then they have to be of age before they do. Of course, some do their best to sneak out and do a little exploring. For me, though, my life has been within this boundary. I've always wondered what it was like outside; what I might find and what it would be like to just be able to go anywhere and do anything without having a wall to stop me." She paused and looked down, picking at the last bit of food that she had in front of her as if embarrassed of what she was saying. "I guess you really wouldn't understand that."

Zyyr shook his head and reached out to touch her hand. The feeling of his skin against hers was electrifying, but he concentrated instead on her eyes as they lifted to look at him.

"I do understand," he told her. "Up until the Denynso left the compound only a few weeks ago and found the settlement, we weren't permitted to leave. We spent our entire lives within the boundaries of the compound. The difference is that most of us never even considered the possibility of leaving. I know I didn't. I never even thought about what might be outside of the compound or what it might be like to go to other areas of the planet."

Color splashed across Lila's cheeks and she glanced away from him.

"You must think that I am completely out of my mind or really silly to have thoughts like that," she said softly.

"No," Zyyr told her, tightening his grip on her hand so that she would feel the connection between them and know that he was there, in that moment, with her. "I think you are very brave."

5

"Surprise!"

Eden held onto Samira's shoulders while Zuri pulled the blindfold away from her eyes, revealing the crowd of people standing in the small bar. A strange conglomeration of birthday and wedding decorations covered the space and Eden noticed that a few of the guests wore shiny metallic birthday hats while others sipped drinks from novelty glasses featuring tiny faux pearl necklaces around the stem and little tulle veils attached to the sides. It was a hilarious, if confusing, combination of the two events that they were celebrating that night.

"What happened here?" Eden asked, leaning toward Zuri as Samira stepped away from them to greet her guests.

"I told Jane and Simran to handle some of the details. I have a feeling that the decorations got delegated to some Denysno and they might have raided a party supply store with only the words "birthday" and "engagement" to go on."

Eden covered her mouth to muffle her laugh and watched as a delighted Samira accepted a bouquet of roses from Ty and got on her toes to kiss him.

"I know that I'm not familiar with all of the traditions and customs of your kind," Ty said, stroking her cheek and gazing at her lovingly, "but the others have been trying to educate me on them so that I can understand what we are celebrating. Tonight I know that we are not just celebrating our plan to come together in marriage, but also the day that you were born. The people who knew you best when you lived here, before you came to Uoria and found me, tell me that your birthday is not something that you celebrated willingly, and many didn't even know when it was. I don't know why that is and I won't ask you, but I do want you to know that this day marks the first of what I hope will be many, many days that I will celebrate the most precious gift that has ever been given to me, and feel unexplainable gratitude that on this day you came into existence."

Eden felt tears forming in her eyes and Pyra's hand came around her waist to pull her closer to him. She rested her head against his arm, taking a moment herself to feel grateful that he was there with her and that she had discovered him. She knew that she had gone through a series of complex and often painful decisions in the days and weeks leading up to meeting him, and if she had made a single one differently, she wouldn't be standing there with him, the feeling of their child still lingering in her arms.

From behind her Eden heard someone say her name. The voice was familiar, but the word sounded surprised, almost shocked. She turned around and saw a woman who she vaguely knew from the university staring back at her.

"Hello, Evangeline," Eden said with a smile.

"It is you," Evangeline said, her voice somewhat powdery now as if the surprise of seeing Eden had taken away all of her energy.

"Yes, it is," Eden said, unsure of what else she should say. "How are you?"

Evangeline just continued to stare at her for several seconds, and then looked up at Pyra.

"Hello," he said, extending an enormous hand toward Evangeline in the handshake gesture that Eden had taught him on their way to Earth. "My name is Pyra. I'm Eden's mate."

"Nice to meet you," Evangeline said.

She turned her questioning gaze back to Eden and then turned away, walking deeper into the party without saying anything else.

"That was strange," Eden said.

Eden accepted a glass of champagne from Zuri as she approached.

"What was strange?" Zuri asked.

Eden brought the rim of the glass to her lips and gestured with her eyes for Zuri to look over toward the bar where she could see Evangeline leaned close to a few other women, whispering animatedly.

"Do you know Evangeline?" she asked.

"No," Zuri said, shaking her head. "Who is she?"

"She is someone who I knew kind of from a distance from working in the lab. Even though I wasn't technically part of the university program, working with Ryan meant that I came into contact with people from the university fairly often. She was one of the women who came into the lab every now and then to share research with Ryan. She just came up to me and acted like she had seen a ghost. She was completely shocked that I was here."

"Why?" Zuri asked.

Eden shrugged.

"I don't know. She didn't really say anything. Just 'it is

you' and then she said hello to Pyra and that was it. She just kind of walked away."

Zuri took another sip of champagne and smiled as Ero wrapped his arms around her waist from behind and pressed a kiss to the side of her neck.

"Come on, everybody," he said. "Ty baked a cake and we are just about to cut it."

The rest of the group started toward the table where Samira and Ty stood, but Eden stayed in place for a moment longer, slowly sipping her champagne and staring at the women at the bar. She knew that there was something more to the strange way that Evangeline had interacted with her. There was something behind the look in the woman's eyes when she saw her and the way that she was conspiring with the other women from the university now. Eden just didn't know what it could be.

6

"I don't understand," Kyven said, turning away from Maxim for a moment and then turning back sharply. "Athan knew all of this all along and never told anybody?"

"He's not supposed to," Maxim said. "This goes even deeper than just the fact that outsiders aren't supposed to know about the Order. This is corruption and conflict within the Order itself. Athan knew that our family was at enough risk because Papa told us about them in the first place. He says that he didn't want to put us in any more danger by telling the truth."

"So he thought it would be better if we just didn't know anything?" Kyven asked, new anger building within him.

It was bad enough that Athan had excluded him from the conversation that he had had with Maxim about their father, but now that he was finding out what it was that they had talked about, a sense of betrayal was forming low in his belly. As the younger brother he had always been the one that felt like he was being left out or that he was always a step behind Maxim. Maxim had always gotten to spend more time with Papa and with their grandfather. He had always been the one to find out more about the Order and what they were doing. When their father had died Kyven thought that the days of him lingering behind his older brother might be behind him, but now he was realizing that it was the same as it had always been.

"I think that there's more that he didn't get a chance to say," Ivy said.

Kyven turned to her and stared into her wide eyes for a moment.

"What do you mean?"

Ivy looked at Maxim tentatively and then back at Kyven.

"Maxim got angry and left before Athan was finished talking. I think that he had more that he needed or wanted to say."

"I couldn't keep listening to him," Maxim said, his voice low and angry. "You know that."

"Why not?" Kyven asked.

"What he was saying about Papa and the way that he died..." Maxim paused and Kyven saw him draw in a breath, "he was sitting there telling me that he never told us what really happened because he felt like this was the way that Papa would have wanted it."

Kyven thought about those words for a moment, letting them sink in so that he could truly process them.

"What if it is?" he finally asked cautiously, knowing that it would infuriate his brother but needing to express the thought.

"What do you mean?" Maxim asked, his voice holding as much anger and ferocity as he thought that it would. "How could it possibly be what Papa would want?"

"You know as well as I do that we were the most important thing in his life. You, me, and Mom. We were everything to him. What if he knew that everything he had found out about the Klimnu and the Order was putting all of us at risk and the only thing that he could do to protect us was to sacrifice his own life."

"Even if that were true," Maxim said. "Why would he not want us to know? Why would he want to make it so that we couldn't even have his body?"

"I don't know that, Maxim." Kyven took a breath and glanced over at Ivy who looked back at him as if she knew what he was going to say and thought that it was exactly what needed to be said. "But you know that Athan does."

Maxim's eyes slid up to Kyven's and he could see an intensity in his brother's glare that spoke of emotion Maxim didn't want to put voice to. Kyven knew then that there was more to what Maxim was feeling than just anger. Just as Kyven was, Maxim was feeling the loneliness, the empty, cold gnawing within him that had started when they learned that their father was dead. Aegeus had been everything to them, more precious than either one of them ever understood. In fact, it wasn't until Kyven knew that he was never going to come back that he really realized just how important his father was to him and how prevalent in his life he really was. He decided to use that now, hoping that it would speak to something inside of Maxim, something buried deep within him that he didn't want to let out; that he didn't even want to admit was there, and could help to push his brother forward on this journey that he had laid out for them.

"Do you remember what it was like when we were younger, Maxim?" Kyven asked, taking a step forward so that he could close the space between himself and his brother. "Do you remember what it was like to spend time with Papa? Can you remember his eyes? The color of his hair?

What it felt like when he scooped us up and gave us those hugs that were like they were never going to end?"

"Yes," Maxim said.

"I don't," Kyven admitted, his voice painful as it pushed through the tightening in his throat. "I miss him every single day and I feel an emptiness in every moment that I know that he should be a part of, but I don't remember those things. I don't remember what he looked like. I don't remember what he smelled like. I don't remember the texture of his skin or the way his hair felt. I know that I should. I know that those memories are somewhere inside me, but it's like they are getting washed away. When we found out that he was dead, it was like part of me had died right along with him. Suddenly I really knew just how much he was a part of our lives and just how important he was to me."

"Me, too," Maxim agreed.

"Up until that moment I never really thought about eating breakfast with him, but that first morning after Athan came and Mom had to tell us what happened, it was like I couldn't stop staring at his chair. Part of me was still waiting for him to come sit down and I felt like I couldn't take a bite until he did."

"It was hard getting dressed without listening to him talking to Mom in the kitchen."

"I couldn't focus on training without his instructions. I couldn't finish any of my chores because I knew that he wouldn't be there to..."

"Rest his hand on the top of our heads and tell us that he was proud of us. I couldn't fall asleep because I couldn't hear them whispering in their bedroom."

Kyven nodded.

"He knew that if he didn't come back from that battle

that he would be leaving a tremendous emptiness in our lives. He knew that it would be difficult enough for us to cope just with not having him around anymore. Maybe he thought that it would be easier for us if we didn't know everything that had happened. What he didn't think about, though, was how long those questions were going to linger with us. He thought that eventually we would forget about him and move on with our lives, and with the thoughts of him would go the questions that we had about the Order. He might have thought that his death would end everything. He had no way of knowing that the Klimnu would continue and that the planet would still be in danger. We have to be the ones to find out what happened and to finish what he started. If we let this go now, the planet will stay at risk and Papa would have died for no reason. There is only so far that we can go on our own. Athan is the closest thing that we have left to Papa, and if he knows more than he has already told you, we need to listen to him."

There was a pause as Kyven tried to gauge his brother's reaction. Maxim's shoulders squared and he took a long, steeling breath.

"I know," he said. "He deserves our memory. He deserves for people to know what happened, not just to him, but to everyone who fought. If Athan is the one who can help us do that, I will trust him."

7

"They are still acting weird," Eden murmured to Zuri as they leaned over the gift table and tried to rearrange the conglomeration of packages, bags, and envelopes into some semblance of order.

"Who?" Zuri asked.

Eden pretended like she was reaching for one of the gifts on the other side of the table so that she could gesture over her shoulder at the women who were still huddled at the bar, whispering conspiratorially and occasionally glancing her way.

"It's like they know something that they aren't telling me. Maybe they are just really surprised to see you with a Denynso like Pyra," Zuri said.

Eden shook her head and gave the women the briefest glance she could so that she could check in on what they were doing without making it obvious that she was looking at them.

"If that was it, wouldn't they be surprised about all of the women? Especially the ones they know better than me, like, oh, I don't know, the bride who they are celebrating tonight and who is marrying one of the warriors?"

She knew that she was starting to lose her grip on her emotions and her self-control, but Eden was starting to feel the same uncomfortable tension around her that she used to feel when she was working in the lab with Ryan. It always felt like there was something going on that she was a part of even though she wasn't privy to what was actually happening. It was a closed, heavy feeling that made her feel like she was being scrutinized from every angle and judged for something that she had nothing to do with and at the same time had contributed to.

Eden was reaching for an envelope someone had placed on top of one of the brightly wrapped gifts when something suddenly occurred to her. She turned so sharply that she brushed that envelope and a stack of others onto the floor, but she didn't take the time to pick them up. Instead, she stalked across the bar toward the women and stepped up close to them.

"You didn't think that I was coming back, did you?" she demanded.

The women looked at her with shocked, somewhat frightened expressions. Evangeline opened and closed her mouth a few times, and turned to stare down into her drink.

"Did you even know that I was going to Uoria? What did he tell you?"

The women continued to stare at her with expressions that told her that she wasn't going to get any information from them. Eden made an angry, exasperated sound and stomped away from the women, looking around the bar for Pyra. She didn't see him, and she didn't have the patience to look around for him. Instead she took several long strides directly over to Zuri and pulled her by her elbow to get her away from a few of the other guests who were starting to crowd around the gift table as if in an effort to convince the birthday girl to start unwrapping.

"If you see Pyra, tell him that if I'm not back here by the end of the party that I will meet him back at the house. He knows how to get to my grandmother's house and he can pick up Lysander on the way."

She started to turn away but Zuri grabbed her hand to stop her.

"Wait," Zuri said, "where are you going? What's wrong?"

Eden shook her head.

"I can't tell you now. I just have to go take care of something."

She pulled out of Zuri's grasp and moved quickly through the rest of the guests at the bar. She had come to the party with the others in the rented car and for a moment she didn't know how she was even going to get across town. Just as she was starting to give up, one of the sleek public transportation vehicles slid into place at the stop across the street. Whispering a few words of thanks at the serendipitous timing, she ran across the street to the stop and jumped into the car. The driver handed her what looked like a small, clear screen and she looked down at it. The image of the city appeared on the glass, showing her where she was and the route that this particular vehicle would take. She moved the image around with her finger and then pressed one of the pulsating red dots to indicate her final destination. She handed the screen back to the driver and he settled it into the port on his dashboard.

Immediately the car shot forward, moving smoothly and comfortably despite its incredible speed. It was only a few moments later that the car pulled up to the low stone bench that Eden had indicated as her destination. She thanked the driver and jumped out of the car. Eden waited until the driver had pulled away to go any further. She didn't want anyone to know where she was going.

Her feet pounded against the pavement as she ran down the empty sidewalk and through a narrow opening in a fence. She hoped that the security codes hadn't changed since she had been gone. She skidded to a stop at an unassuming looking door at the back of a tall building and touched the palm of her hand to the front of the door to access the keypad. In the year that she had been gone there should have been several new codes, but if her assumptions were correct, they wouldn't have changed at all. Not just because she was the only other person who knew of the code, but also the fact that Ryan was just conceited and arrogant enough to make his own birthdate and hiring date the sequence of numbers used to access the labs.

Eden punched the numbers into the keypad and an instant later she heard the low click of the locks within the door releasing. The door slid open slightly and she grabbed the edge to push it completely out of the way. The familiar smell of the laboratory hit her as soon as she stepped into the building and for a moment she felt like she had never left. Everything felt exactly as it had, but she didn't know if that was comforting or if she should be angry. She had suddenly realized exactly why Evangeline and the other women had been so confused, and a little frightened, to see her, and she wanted to know what had compelled Ryan to do it.

The tall heels of her shoes clicked loudly on the polished linoleum floor of the hallway, the sound reverberating off of the walls and making the building feel even more empty than it had when she had first gotten in. She knew, however, that it wasn't empty. Though the section of the hallway that she was walking down was shadowy, but light spilled from under one of the doors at the far end of the corridor and that told her that she was not the only one who had come for a visit in the laboratory late that night. Eden slowed as she got further down the hallway. She stopped and leaned against the wall so that she could take off her shoes and put them aside. The sound was loud enough that if she got much closer to the lit room that anyone inside would be able to hear her approach and she didn't want to give enough advance warning to allow for whatever was going on in there to be stopped before she got there.

Nervousness rolled through her belly as she continued to creep down the hallway. When she was on her way to the lab she had been so filled with anger and frustration that she hadn't thought completely through what she was going to do when she got there. The fears about Ryan that she had expressed to Pyra were building even more intensely inside her now and she wondered if it had been the right decision for her to come here on her own without any true plan of why she was there or what she hoped to accomplish.

She reached the partially open door and took a moment to brace herself. When she stepped in, however, she didn't see anyone. Pausing for a moment to listen for any of the sounds that would indicate that Ryan was somewhere in the back of the lab, she rushed forward to the tall tower of drawers in the back corner. This had been one of Ryan's many strange idiosyncrasies. Though his research had always been devoted to the next advancement and improvements in technology, he had always insisted on taking his notes by hand and keeping hard copies of all of the papers that he submitted. He was never able to give her a clear explanation as to why he did it, but in that moment, she was glad that he did.

Dropping down to her knees in front of the case, she checked to make sure that the lock was the same as it had been when she had left. Again, she wasn't surprised to find that it was. Ryan was too wrapped up in himself to think about something like changing the locks that he had chosen himself. He would simply assume that the plan that he had come up with was going to work perfectly, and when it did there would be no reason for him to change the locks or the codes. A truly arrogant man in everything that he did and thought, Ryan never thought beyond his own goals and plans to imagine that someone might interfere.

Eden typed the series of numbers and letters that she remembered from the many times that Ryan had made her dip into the stacks of paper in the drawers to find pieces of research for his reference. It was truly infuriating to her, and often she felt like that was part of the reason that he did it. She would show him the handheld screens that she used for her own research, the banks of computers that the other researchers used, and he would scoff at her as if she was simply too dumb to understand his viewpoint. Once he took a computer and input all of his notes, performed a few calculations, and utilized a program to coordinate the outline for a project that he was planning simply to show her that he was fully capable of using the same technology, and then erased it all. There was a level of almost psychotic secretiveness to his ways, and a level of meticulousness that showed a mind she was positive was capable of nearly anything.

"Not as capable as mine," she murmured as she pulled an envelope out of the drawer and carried it over to one of the gleaming tables in the center of the room.

She opened the envelope and pulled out the papers. Spreading them out across the table she scanned through them. She didn't understand what they meant and she had read through several of the pages before she glanced at the top and noticed that it was dated for several months after she left. Assuming that these notes were for a project that he had started after sending her away, she pushed them aside and went back to the drawers to pull out another.

This envelope had a scribble on the front that Eden recognized and she felt her heart start pounding as she pulled the older pages out and spread them across the table. Her ears started to ring as she went through the pages line by line. They were so familiar that she felt like she could have recited them word for word as she went. The last time she had read those words, however, she had been the one who had written them. Now, however, they were in Ryan's tightly controlled, precise hand. These notes had been about her own original research into a concept that Ryan had told her was worthless until she had started to delve into it and he realized that she was rushing headlong toward far more impressive advancements than he had been able to accomplish in the time that she had been with him. They had been her thoughts, her innovations, and her research. Now they had been stolen from her.

"You didn't think that I was just going to let all of that research go to waste, did you?"

Eden whipped around so fast that she knocked many of the pages off of the table and across the floor. Ryan was leaning against the doorframe peeling off a pair of gloves as he stared at her.

"How dare you?" Eden said, her hand tightening on the edge of the table as new anger surged through her.

"You know," Ryan said, his voice still sickly smooth,

"when I heard that the university had sent two of their newest shuttles to Uoria so that a group could return here, I had just a moment when I thought that you might be onboard. Then I said to myself, no, that's not possible. You've been gone for a year now. I had very little intention of you surviving the initial arrival on the planet. You see, I am very familiar with the laws of the Denynso, and with their rituals. I knew that they would send a warrior guard who would escort you directly to the king and queen of the compound. I figured that you would try to prove yourself by stealing the blood of the first Denynso warrior you saw and that your impulsiveness would have you dead by sunset. Even if you had somehow managed to get through that first day and none of them had found out about the real reason that you were there, you would only be allowed to be on the planet for six months before they sent you back. There was simply no way that you would be on those ships. Imagine my surprise when I heard that not only did you survive and somehow finagle more than six months out of your stay on Uoria, but that you were one of the group that was returning for a visit."

"Yeah," Eden said, her hand still wrapped tightly around the edge of the table. "It seemed to shock the hell out of Evangeline when she saw me. Why do you think that is?"

She was struggling to keep her voice sounding calm despite the range of emotions coursing through her.

"Perhaps," Ryan said, stepping further into the room, "it's because they didn't even know that you went to Uoria in the first place."

Eden gave him a quizzical look.

"How is that possible? The university knew that I was on that shuttle and they knew where it was going."

GRACE KENSINGTON

"They knew where it was going, yes," Ryan said. "That doesn't mean that they knew that you were on it."

"I don't understand."

Ryan shrugged.

"I suppose that I could have told them that you were going as part of the university exchange program or that you were doing specialized research for me. That might have made it easier for them to understand why I requested a commission of a shuttle and hired my own staff rather than utilizing members of the actual university flight program."

"What?" Eden gasped, taking an involuntary step back.

"That was the beauty of this whole plan. You had spent just enough time working with people from the university that if you had mentioned to anyone that you were going to be going to Uoria, they would automatically assume that you were going as part of the university exchange program without me even having to tell them. Then if they questioned it as not making sense, I could honestly say that I had never been the one to say that you were part of the program, and instead that you were doing some research for a project that I was spearheading for the university."

"That's a lie," Eden said.

"Of course it is," Ryan said with a laugh. "The thing is, I didn't have to tell them either one of those things. Instead, I commissioned the shuttle, I hired the crew, and I set it up so that it looked like an approved visit, even going so far as to contact Uoria and make sure that the Denynso knew that you were coming to perform scientific research."

"You never intended on me coming back," Eden said.

Even though she had already known it, now that Ryan was confessing that the purpose of sending her to the planet was to kill her, the reality was hitting her harder.

"Oh, I never intended it, no," Ryan said. He was within

just a few steps of her now and Eden felt her heart pounding even harder in her chest. "I figured that you would be dead within hours of getting to the planet. That's why I told the women that you had joined an exploration crew for one of the string of planets that were recently discovered on the edge of the fourth galaxy and weren't planning on returning to Earth any time soon."

"And why would I do that?" she asked.

"Because you were so devastated when I rejected your advances, of course," Ryan said, looking particularly proud of himself.

"Excuse me?"

"Well, Eden," Ryan said, running his fingers along the table in a way that made Eden's skin crawl, "everyone around here knows just how crazy you are about me. It's so obvious, and I'm sure that my lunchroom stories didn't hurt the matter. You spent all those long hours helping me in this quiet, isolated laboratory, all the while your heart longing for me and your imagination running wild with a blissful imagined relationship between the two of us. You convinced yourself that one day I would sweep you off your feet and you would no longer be my assistant, but my wife." He gave a deep, whimsical sigh and Eden felt her stomach lurch. Ryan turned a sharp look back to her. "It is completely understandable that when I arrived at the laboratory one night to find you naked and waiting for me on one of my tables, ready to give your body to me and proclaim your love, and I had to let you down gently that you were out of your mind with grief. You just couldn't take the humiliation or the thought that you were going to have to go through the rest of your life pining for me, tortured because your subpar scientific understanding and lack of vision were going to force you to remain in my laboratory as my assistant for the remainder of your career."

"Subpar scientific understanding?" Eden said back to him, keeping her voice low to stop herself from screaming at him. "Lack of vision? These notes are all mine!" she said, gesturing at the papers around her. "I came up with these concepts and designed the experiments. I did the research. You were so busy obsessing over having Denynso blood so that you could weaponize it that you lost all of your focus on any of your actual work."

"And how amazing it would have been if you were able to get that blood for me," Ryan said. "I thought of that, you know. I didn't want to leave anything to chance, so I thought about the possibility that you would actually be able to integrate yourself into the Denynso population enough that you could somehow get the blood and smuggle it back to me. Then I would have exactly what I have always wanted, but I could never let anyone know that it had been you who had gotten the blood." His look grew darker. "Just like I can't let anyone know anything now."

Before Eden could really process what was happening, Ryan lunged toward her. He grabbed her around the neck, tackling her to the ground and pinning her down with his knee in the center of her chest.

"What are you doing?" She managed to gasp out.

"I can't let you tell anyone what you know. I know that you were planning on going to my superiors to report me. I also know that given two seconds you would tell them that this research was yours and why I sent you to Uoria. I just can't let that happen." He tightened the grip on her throat and ground his knee deeper into her chest. "I have too much left to do. You could have been a help, but I'm going to have to just do it without you."

Eden refused to give Ryan the satisfaction of dominating her. She brought her hands up to his chest and shoved with all of the strength that she could gather into her arms. Ryan look stunned as the force of her shove sent him tumbling back off of her.

"What would you tell the people from the university?" she asked, scrambling to her feet. "You have gotten yourself into a hole that you are never going to be able to dig yourself out of, Ryan. They are going to figure out that you lied to the university, you lied to the Denynso people, and that you lied to everyone in the scientific community. They know that I'm back. They'll notice if I disappear again."

Ryan rushed toward her again and Eden caught him by his arms before he could grab her by her throat again.

"Of course," she said, "that would mean that you would have to kill me, and that isn't going to happen. Not here. Not ever." She shoved against him as he pushed back against her so that they were locked in the battle for dominance. "I won't let you."

"How are you going to stop me?" Ryan asked. "You couldn't hold your own while you were here, and you won't be able to now."

He pushed her and Eden felt herself stumble. She stepped back to catch herself and her foot landed on one of the papers on the floor, causing her to slip and fall onto the table. Ryan was on her immediately. His body draped over her back, pressing her so hard into the edge of the table that pain shot down her legs. Ryan's hand came to the front of her throat and he wrenched her head back.

"There were a lot of fresh young girls who would have loved to be in your position," he hissed. "I chose you because you were a hot piece of ass to look at, but you also knew what the hell you were talking about. I thought it would be fun to get to mix a little business with pleasure."

"You're delusional," Eden said. "No one would want to work with you, and there were certainly no young girls who would have any more interest in you groping them and making indecent proposals every day than I did."

Ryan pulled her head back harder and Eden felt herself starting to choke.

"You never would cooperate with me. You were much too full of yourself and just couldn't be bothered to just go along with me. The thing is, you never seemed to get it through your head that you weren't going to get anywhere in this career without me. Say what you will about me, but I have a respect and a standing in the scientific community that you could never even hope to achieve."

"You only have that because of your family."

Ryan whipped her around and pressed his body to hers again so that she was forced to bend back away from him. Taking her shoes off in the hallway had brought her down so that Ryan towered over her. She knew that there would have been a time that that would have been intimidating, but she had become so accustomed to Pyra and the other Denynso men that it didn't even faze her.

"My family hasn't achieved anything of note in decades. That's my job," Ryan continued. "I'm the one who is going to make the discoveries that are going to change the world."

"You mean that you are going to be the one who will steal the discoveries that are going to change the world," Eden said.

The pressure of Ryan's body on hers was cutting off her air and she was starting to feel dizzy.

"You have no idea what you are talking about," Ryan said, the low, gravely quality of his voice making the words terrifying. "You have no idea what I've accomplished and what I'm going to accomplish. All you know is about the little experiments that we were doing here when you left and this pathetic research."

"Pathetic research?" Eden said, gathering the strength to pull her hands up and press them to Ryan's chest, forcing him back. "It is my 'pathetic' research that started everything that you have supposedly accomplished in the time that I was here."

She gathered the strength that the Denynso blood coursing through her veins gave her and Ryan looked at her with fury and shock in his eyes.

"You don't know anything about the research that I've been doing," Ryan said. Suddenly his eyes sparkled with what Eden could only describe as a dark and vicious laugh. "Maybe I could show you a little of it. Now that you have spent some time with those creatures, it might interest you."

Those words sent Eden over the edge and she forced all of her strength against Ryan in a push that made him stumble away from her. She straightened and glared down at him, her breaths coming out of her in rough, ragged gasps.

"Those *creatures*," she said, "are my clan."

"What do you mean by that?" Ryan asked.

"She means that she is one of us."

Pyra's voice broke through the heated tension in the room and Eden stepped back as her mate lunged at Ryan, tackling him to the ground and pinning him there. His tremendous body dwarfed Ryan and the smaller man had an expression of pure terror on his face.

"What?" Ryan gasped, his hands coming up to grip Pyra's forearms on either side of him.

Eden knew that Ryan had absolutely no chance of overpowering Pyra. The Denynso warrior was not just taller and broader that the human man. He also had the intense, indescribable strength of the warrior kind. When combined with protectiveness for his mate, this strength was something that would be insurmountable for any human.

"She is Denynso," Pyra growled at Ryan, forcing him harder into the ground until Ryan choked with the lack of breath getting into his lungs. "She is also my mate and the mother of my son."

8

"Pyra, get off of him," Eden said.

"No," Pyra said back.

Every bit of anger and animosity that he had ever felt toward this man was pouring out of him as he held Ryan to the ground and pressed the palm of his hand to Ryan's throat. He remembered everything that Eden had told him about the way that Ryan had treated her when she worked with him on Earth before she had ever left on her journey to Uoria, and the fears that she had relayed to him before they left on this trip back. He had held that anger inside of him before, unable to do anything about it and knowing that in those moments Eden needed his strength and love more than she needed to see the aggression that burned within him each time that he thought about Ryan. Now, however, the man was lying on the ground beneath him and he had seen for himself what he was capable of when it came to Eden. He had seen the look in Ryan's eyes and heard the sickening blend of hatred and unrequited desire in his voice when he spoke to her.

"Pyra, stop," Eden said again. "You are going to kill him."

"Maybe I want to."

"Pyra, that's not how things work here. You can't just kill on Earth. Especially not like this. You are not at war," Eden told him. "You are in a laboratory and he is unarmed. If you kill him, the government will come after you."

"What can they do?" Pyra asked dismissively.

"They can take you from me and from Lysander."

Pyra's grip on Ryan eased slightly at those words.

"What do you mean?"

"There is no treaty between Uoria and Earth," Eden said. "That is part of what the exchange programs are working toward. If you commit a crime here, you will be taken and put into one of the prisons or in a prison camp. Things work differently here, Pyra."

Pyra's mind wandered to the now-destroyed prison on the edge of the Denynso compound on Uoria. He thought of the cold hallways and dirty, stained cells that they had explored. He thought of Leia and Eliana and what they had told him about their time within the fearsome stone walls of that building. Those images, however, didn't frighten him enough to take away his desire to simply snuff out the life of the man who had made his mate's life so miserable. Instead, it was the thought of being without her and without their son that forced him to release Ryan and stand up.

"I will let you live now," Pyra said down to Ryan, who had made no move to get up from the floor, "but you are never to get near my mate or our child. You have no claim on her life and she will be returning to Uoria with us when we leave. I don't want to see your face again."

Pyra stepped back from Ryan and felt Eden's hands come to his waist. She guided him back further into the laboratory toward the door, but he wouldn't take his eyes off of Ryan until they had backed out of the room and into the hallway. Part of him expected Ryan to get back up and come after them again, but the look of fear on the other man's face told him that he had taken Pyra's words to heart and was going to let them leave without any further resistance.

They walked out of the building quickly and Pyra remained silent until they had gotten outside again. When the door to the laboratory slammed behind them, he turned to Eden and scooped her into his arms. He buried his face in her hair and held her close to his chest. Soon he felt the heat of her tears soaking through his shirt and her body beginning to tremble.

"Shhhh," he murmured, trying to soothe her. "It's alright now. I'm here. I've got you. He can't get to you now."

She clung to him for several more long seconds and then pulled her face back to look at him.

"How did you find me?" she asked through the tears that were still falling down her cheeks and over her lips.

"I came to look for you at the party and Zuri told me that you said there was something that you had to take care of. I knew that you weren't going after Lysander because if you were you would have come to tell me and we would have gone together. The only other thing that I could think of was that you were coming here to see Ryan."

"You say that like you think that I wanted to see him," Eden said.

"No," Pyra said, shaking his head, "I didn't mean it like that. I know that you didn't want to see him. But there was something that led you here. I will always come find you when you need me."

He eased Eden down to her feet and she brushed the

hair out of her face, trying to regain her composure. She shook her head, took a deep breath, and he saw her eyes flicker back to the door to the building. He reached for her hand and led her away from the door toward the sidewalk.

"Why did you come here?" he asked.

He didn't want his voice to sound angry and potentially upset her any further than she already was. The truth was that he was angry. After all of the anger and fear that she had expressed to him about his man she had still just gone to the laboratory to face him completely alone. Even with the strength that she had gotten from becoming Denynso after her first vicious encounter with the Klimnu, Pyra worried that if he hadn't gotten there when he had, she would have been in very serious danger. Her strength was one thing, but it didn't make her completely invulnerable to other attacks. Had Ryan decided to pick up any kind of weapon, she could have been killed without Pyra ever knowing what was happening.

"He lied about the entire mission that he sent me on," Eden said as they walked toward the public transportation stop.

"What do you mean he lied?"

Pyra felt discomfort roll through his stomach as the sound of the sleek vehicle told him that it was approaching. He hated the strange and uncomfortable mode of transportation, but it had been the only way that he was able to get to Eden in the middle of the party. Zuri had explained to him how to use it, but it had been an unpleasant situation from the moment that he stepped inside. All of the other passengers looked at him with a combination of fear and morbid curiosity as he tried to take his seat in the cramped space. He had been unsure of where he was supposed to get out and had had to explain to the driver where he needed to go. Though he had ended up where he needed to be, the entire ride he had felt like the driver was doing his best to ignore him.

Eden waited as the door to the vehicle opened and she stepped inside. The driver's eyes went from her to Pyra and then back to her as if he was evaluating whether Eden was in danger. A sudden surge of defensiveness washed through him and Pyra reached up to rest his hand on Eden's shoulder. She immediately turned her head and touched a kiss to his hand, which seemed to at once assuage and unnerve the driver.

When they had finally settled into their seats, she turned to him and lowered her voice.

"I thought that there was a formal research trip planned and that Ryan had coordinated with the university and some of the department members who he had already worked with on other projects. Even though this was a new project and the aim that he had for me was completely unethical, as you know, I figured that he had at least found someone else from the university to back him up and get him the necessary clearance to use the university shuttles and connect with Creia in an official capacity."

"That's what we were told," Pyra said.

He still remembered when Eden arrived and Creia assigned him the role of being her guardian and protector. The king had told them that she was a scientist coming to the planet to research Uoria's plants, animal life, and other features. Though he hadn't actually told them that she was a part of the innovative exchange program that he had devised with Earth, it had been the assumption of all of the warriors. They had been receiving researchers and journalists for some time, but most of them arrived with little fanfare and soon left. This woman was highly anticipated, which was why it was even more of a surprise when she arrived and he discovered that she was his intended mate.

Eden shook her head and leaned closer to him.

"It was all a set up," she said. "Which makes it even more conniving because he told me that even though the trip itself was official, my mission to get the blood of the most powerful of the Denynso warriors was a secret. It was a set up within a set up."

Pyra felt his stomach tighten painfully at the words that Eden didn't even seem to realize that she had said.

"You were after my blood?" he asked, continuing to force his voice to remain calm.

Eden looked up into his eyes sharply, her mouth falling open slightly. Though he had known since the moment that she arrived that her underhanded mission on Uoria was to retrieve Denynso blood and bring it back to her boss, she had never told him that he had been specifically named as the warrior whose blood it was she was meant to take. It felt uncomfortably close to a betrayal even though he knew that she hadn't known him when she made the agreement and that she had never made any efforts to hurt him in any way.

"I'm sorry, Pyra," she said. "I didn't know you. I didn't even know that it was going to be you who Creia assigned to watch over me when I got to Uoria. All I knew was what Ryan told me about you."

"What did he tell you?"

"That you were mean and violent. That you would kill anything that crossed your path without a second thought and that you would bed any woman who came close to you and then toss her aside without even bothering to learn her name much less worry about what she was feeling. He told me that your blood was the most powerful substance in the universe, that it could make weapons that no one could defend themselves against."

"And you wanted to be a part of making that kind of weapon?" he asked.

The thought that she was willing to be a part of a project that vicious was completely against everything that he knew about Eden. She was a bit rough around the edges, especially after he met her, and he wouldn't say that she was the gentlest or even the most compassionate of women he had encountered. She was not cruel or uncaring, however, and he found it very hard to believe that she would have been complacent to something as horrific as not only stealing the blood of another creature, but then using that blood to create weapons to destroy as many other living beings as possible.

Eden hung her head and Pyra saw tears dripping onto her lap.

"No," she whispered. "Of course I didn't. Why do you think that I confessed to Creia and Theia as soon as I met them?"

"Because you lost your nerve when you saw me and you knew that if you tried it and they found out what you were doing that they could execute you?"

She looked up at him and the expression in her eyes cut into him.

"Do you really think that, Pyra?" she asked.

"I don't know what else to think."

"I confessed because I didn't want to be a part of it. I wasn't afraid. I could have gotten away with it if I tried, but I didn't want to be a part of it."

"Then why did you come in the first place?"

"I've already told you," she said, the familiar anger starting to build in her voice. "Ryan threatened me. I had already rejected his advances more times than I can count and then I started working on research that he knew was more complex than what he was doing and he wanted it for himself. I had no choice. If I didn't agree to go, I was throwing away my career. He was going to go to the head of the lab and tell them that I was the one who was harassing him, and that I had stolen his research. It would have destroyed my professional reputation and kept me out of any position for the rest of my life."

Pyra knew that the situation was escalating and that he needed to bring it back under control. He reached out and touched her face gently.

"I'm sorry," he said. "I know that you told me all of that. It just hurts to know that you came to Uoria with the intention of stealing my blood."

"I didn't know you, Pyra."

"I know that," he said, "but you were intended for me from the moment that you were born, so it still feels like a betrayal."

"But if I hadn't been sent to Uoria to steal your blood, then I never would have met you. We never would have had a reason to come together."

Pyra realized that she was right. If she had not been sent for that particular mission, they never would have met. She would not have ever come to Uoria, and he would never have had a reason to travel to Earth. He would have spent his entire life aching for the woman who was meant to be his mate and never would have found her.

The vehicle pulled to a stop and Pyra and Eden climbed

off. When it zipped away into the darkness, he reached for her wrist and turned her around so that he could wrap his arms around her waist and look down into her face.

"No matter why it happened, I am happier than I could ever tell you that you came to Uoria when you did."

"I am, too," she said.

Eden's voice still sounded strained.

"Why did Ryan set you up?" he asked.

"He wanted to steal my research. That's why the women were so surprised to see me. He didn't tell them that I was going to Uoria. Even though he told me that he knew that I was sneaky enough to pull off getting the blood that he wanted, he was positive that I was going to mess up and be killed. He told all of the women that I had been devastated by his rejection and moved to a developing planet. That way he could take all of the research that I had already done and all of the notes that I had already made, and didn't have to worry about me coming back and telling anyone what happened. He knew that if I was killed on Uoria, though, that the university would cause serious problems for the planet and everything would come out anyway. So he faked the entire thing. He rented a ship and hired a crew that I would think belonged to the university. That way there would be no questions when I didn't come back."

"Is everything alright?"

Pyra looked up to see Zuri running across the street toward them. She hugged Eden and looked at Pyra as if for explanation.

"Everything's fine," Eden told her. "Pyra just came to get me, but everything is going to be perfectly fine."

Though Eden's voice sounded stronger now, Pyra wasn't convinced. What Ryan had done, and his violent reaction to seeing Eden, was far too complex just to cover up some stolen work. Something more was going on, but he wasn't sure yet what it was. He knew that he would have to be on guard to protect Eden and Lysander, without upsetting her or letting any of the others know his concerns until there was something more that could be done.

9

"I don't understand why you are doing this," Theia said as Creia crossed the room to a tall bureau and removed several tunics to tuck into his satchel along with the pants that he had already packed inside.

"Because I have to," he said.

"Why?" she asked.

Creia turned to his mate and saw the look of worry and fear in her eyes. He hated that she was feeling that way, and even more that it was him that was causing it, but this was something that he knew that he had to do and he couldn't let her stop him.

"I have to find out more about what happened," he told her. "I have to do more to understand the original Denynso and what happened to them after the clan split and my half came here."

"But why, Creia?" she asked, her voice more imploring as he reached into the drawer at the bottom of another large piece of furniture and pulled out the dagger that he had not touched in many years. "Everything is going so well now. We have already found out so much and everyone is trying to make sense of it all together. The others are coming back from the settlement and soon we'll be able to rebuild all of the relationships that our kind used to have with the others of the planet. Isn't that enough? Can't you just let it go?"

"Let it go?" Creia asked, stunned that his mate would make such a suggestion. "Don't you think that letting it go for so long has caused enough trouble as it is?"

"What do you mean?"

"You see all of the species coming together and making amends. I see the shattering of those bonds that happened to begin with. Something more happened that we don't understand yet, and it is the cause of the turmoil that tore Uoria apart. This compound didn't used to be the only one of the Denynso on the planet. You know that."

"Yes, I do," Theia said, sounding slightly sad as she was forced to remember the difficulty that came when the clan split so many years before.

"So what happened to the others? Why has there been absolutely nothing from them in decades? How did we not know about Loralia's kind right beneath our feet? Why did the Klimnu decide to leave Uoria for Ynn in the first place? If they were so determined to take over the planet, what happened to change their mind?"

"I don't know," Theia admitted, looking taken aback by the sudden stream of questions that he had asked her. "But what good will it do for you to go out there in search of all of these answers? What do you think that you will find?"

"Exactly that," Creia said, putting a few final items into his bag and lifting it over his shoulder. "Answers."

"Will that help anything?" Theia asked.

"There's no way to know that until we find them," Creia said. "We didn't know what the men were going to find out when they left the compound and found the human settlement, or that they would discover the Mikana settlement and make the connection between them and the Klimnu. What I find in the badlands could completely change everything that we know about our own kind, and about the other species on Uoria. I have already let my people down so much. I owe it to them not to keep them in the dark any longer."

"What am I supposed to do while you're gone?" Theia asked.

"You are to lead," Creia said, stroking the side of her face, "just like you always have. You are not alone. You have the few who remained here, and the ones who went to the settlement to release the Mikana should be back soon. If they arrive back before I do, reassure them that I will return and allow them to make themselves at home in the compound. Let them move into the homes that we had set aside for the university program. You are completely safe, my love. The compound is secure just as it always has been."

He leaned forward and kissed his mate deeply, allowing himself just a moment to indulge in the feeling of her so that he could memorize it even more completely than it already was and carry it with him during his travels. Though he had reassured Theia that she was safe in the compound while he was gone, he didn't feel as sure about his own safety. The reality was that he didn't know what was waiting for him in the badlands. He hadn't been on that side of the ridge since he was a very young child, and from what he saw when he brought the others up to look at it just weeks before, it had undergone a brutal and devastating change. The damage that the Valdicians and their allies had done to the land was excruciating, and Creia wondered what other secrets could be hiding down in the smoldering remnants just waiting for him to discover them.

"I will be back," he reassured her. "Everything is going to be just fine."

He kissed Theia again and then walked away, keeping his back to her as he moved toward the back corner of the compound even though he wanted more than anything to turn around and get one more glimpse at her. Part of him knew that if he did, he would run back to her and stay in the palace, allowing his mind to remain cloaked in darkness. He couldn't allow that to happen. He wouldn't fail his people again, no matter what he had to do to make sure that they knew the truth.

Creia felt like the way to the ridge was far longer than it had been the last time that he had been up there. It was as if every step that he took extended the distance and it was nearly mid-afternoon by the time that he climbed the last bit of the loose, steep path to stand on the plateau over-looking the badlands. Out of the corner of his eye he saw the small cave where Eden had given birth and he took a moment to feel the happiness that came from that space. It was right here on this ridge where he had become a grandfather. It had also been here that they had learned of the compassion and care that were still so evident in the Mikana as Rey stepped forward to help Eden through the delivery of her tiny son even though he had mere moments before been at the mercy of Pyra. And it was here where Pyra had confessed that he had been overcome by the power that he had in the settlement and by his own fear of the Klimnu and that it had led him to mistreat those who he had been entrusted to lead, and those who he had gone to for help. So much had occurred right in this spot, but Creia couldn't help but also think of all that had happened here long before those moments had even begun.

This was the very ridge that half of the Denynso clan that had inhabited the space that was now the badlands had crossed when leaving that compound behind to begin a new one. This was where Creia had followed his family, clawing their way up the much rougher terrain of the other side in hopes of finding peace and comfort in the more fertile and beautiful land beyond the boundary of the ridge. When he closed his eyes he could still feel the grit in his mouth and the digging of the rocks in his hands as he had clawed. When he opened them it was as though he could see the lingering images of the two times superimposed over each other, still happening, still repeating in the dark orange glow of the afternoon sunlight.

Not all of them had made it to the other side, and he remembered the feeling of watching those who had died slowing, become weaker, and finally no longer moving when they hit the dirt. He didn't realize then that there was more to their deaths than just the journey. Though arduous, the trip had not been so difficult as to kill these strong and powerful men. Instead, something far more ominous had gotten to them. This was part of what had brought him back here so many years later. He needed to know what had happened to them. He wanted to know what had driven that half of the clan away from the others and why they had been kept safe when the others were destroyed.

After resting for a few more minutes on the plateau, Creia gathered his belongings and started the more challenging way down the other side of the ridge. Where there was a path on the other side, the face closest to the badlands was predominantly rough stone and jagged edges. When he was a child he had ridden part of this way on his father's

back and the rest of the way he had climbed with his brother's hand supporting him from beneath, helping to lift him
up each section so that he wouldn't tumble down again. In
those moments as he climbed, he never once imagined that
he would be going down the other way one day. His parents
had told him that this move was important, something that
would change their lives completely and that he was never
to look back. They never wanted him to think of the original
compound or the others again, and he, along with all of the
other young ones and everyone who came after them, had
been strictly instructed to stay away from the ridge. That is
when the rocks had become a boundary for the compound.
They were not to go past the foot of the path, and even then
they had to get special permission to even proceed that far.

To ensure that the Denynso who had taken up residence
in the new compound didn't stray far from the center of the
new land, the king of the time also established boundaries
on the other sides so that every member of the clan would
know where they were expected to go. It was he who
decided that there needed to be a wall along the furthest
boundary, and designed that wall to be made of stones
taken from the base of the ridge so that everyone who saw
them would remember the ridge and the prohibition of
going beyond it. Even though he was king now, Creia felt a
strange sense of nervousness in his belly as he made his way
down the first layer of rocks. Being contained within the
compound had become such a reality of life, so much a part
of being in the clan, that it had become engrained in their
existence. Though he could now acknowledge that it had
been merely a measure of control by the reigning king at the
time, a way for him to restrict and manage the movements
and abilities of the Denynso he ruled, Creia had grown to
appreciate the feeling of separation that it created and

continued the restrictions when he stepped into the role of being king of the compound.

He knew that things were changing, however, and that soon it was likely the times of the boundaries would be over and the members of the clan would have greater freedom to move about the planet as they pleased. It was a tremendous deviation, but one that Creia knew needed to happen. This was his first step, his first moment of rebellion against the fierce regulation of his youth and the systematic secretiveness and omission that had created the widespread distrust, hatred, and breaking down of bonds throughout the planet.

Night had fallen by the time that Creia had made his way to the bottom of the ridge and was standing at the edge of the badlands. The air around him was glowing with the flames and ash still pouring from the ground, and for a moment he was mesmerized by the heat and the dancing of the powdery debris in the light. Creia walked carefully around the edge of the fiery expanse close to the foot of the ridge. He dug into his memory, searching for anything that would tell him which direction that he should go. He wanted to find whatever may be left of the original compound and the buildings that had been a part of it, but much like the desire to return, he had blocked much of his memory of the compound out of his mind. He struggled to remember what it had looked like before they had left and before the Valdicians destroyed it so fully and completely. He looked into the distance, following the pattern of the flames, and realized that there were areas that were not engulfed in the fire.

Creia lowered his bag to the ground and reached inside for one of his tunics. He folded the fabric carefully and then wrapped it around his face so that it covered his nose and mouth and tied behind his head. Strapping the bag higher on his back so that it wouldn't catch fire if he slept too close to the flames, he held the fabric to his face and started further into the space. Though he walked on ground that was black rather than glowing red, he could still feel the residual heat coming up through the soles of his feet and tingling on his skin. Creia told himself that he would become accustomed to the heat and pressed forward, looking around himself for any sign of the compound or the Denynso who used to live there.

He had been roaming the space for a few moments when he realized that there were outlines in the blackened ground. They were faint and he had to focus intently into the darkness in order to see them, but he knew that he was seeing what were once the foundations of the Denynso houses that had once filled this area. As he let himself feel the grief and sadness that filled him at that sight of the foundations, the tangible representations of the lives that had once been centered on this compound, Creia also began to feel the exhaustion of his journey pressing down on him. He knew that he needed to sleep or he would never be able to get through another day of his mission.

Creia made his way across the open space, walking around the fires with as far a sweep as he could to avoid the intense heat. Finally he reached the far side and was able to walk away from the strongest of the fires and onto ground that was far cooler. This side of the original compound also had a tall ridge and Creia knew that in the daylight he would be able to see the natural entryway to the compound that was created by the gap between the two ridges as they came toward one another. He moved toward the foot of the ridge and saw a darker outline that indicated a cave. His feet felt heavy as he walked toward the cave and with each step it was as if the bags that he carried dragged on him more intensely. Finally he made it into the cave and stepped far enough in that he no longer felt the searing heat of the flames. The cooler air was soothing and somehow at once made him more tired and more alert. He felt that he wanted to lie down and sleep for hours, but at the same moment his mind was continuing to churn and he wanted to delve deeper, go farther, explore more so that he could feel closer to the answers that he was so desperately seeking. Finally the need for sleep won over and he spread out his blanket roll, laid down, and allowed himself to drift away.

Creia didn't know how long he slept, but when he opened his eyes the sky outside the cave was still the dark blue of the hour just before dawn. Despite the early hour he knew that he couldn't keep sleeping. He got up, rolled his blanket away, and ate some of the food that Theia had prepared for him. As he was finishing the sun started to come up, filling the space at the front of the cave with its glow. Out of the corner of his eyes he noticed something sparkling in the wall. Creia turned his attention toward it and saw what looked like pieces of shattered glass embedded in the stone.

He ran his fingers along the glass shards and immediately realized that they were not a natural part of the ridge. They had been placed there. Creia looked more closely at the glass and at the wall surrounding the shards. Pale markings in the stone seemed to note what those pieces of glass were and what they meant, but Creia didn't understand them. He pulled a sheath of paper and a pencil from his bag and did his best to copy them, hoping that somehow he would understand them later. He was beginning to turn away to head back out of the cave when he noticed that the cave went deeper than he had originally thought. He took a few steps further, his hand running across the embedded glass in the wall. The further that he walked into the cave, the sharper the pieces of glass became until he felt them biting into his fingers as he walked.

The cave fed into a tunnel and as Creia walked the space grew darker and darker until he wasn't able to see anything ahead of him. He pulled his light stick out of his bag and illuminated it, filling the tunnel with a bright, leading glow. He didn't know where the tunnel led, and no matter how hard he searched the recesses of his memory he couldn't recall this cave or the tunnel from when he was a child living in that compound. He knew that it must have been there. It was not simply created out of nothing, but he felt that he had never seen it before, and certainly had never walked down it. He wondered if this was part of the compound where he hadn't been permitted to go when he was younger, somewhere where the elders of the clan restricted the movements of the others for reasons that stayed shrouded in mystery even among many of the adults.

The further he moved down the tunnel the more that Creia thought of the tunnel that led from the ridge of his compound down to the mirrored realm beneath. It had been that tunnel that had revealed that realm, the place just beneath the compound itself, where Loralia's kind had lived and died, leaving her the only one left of her species. She had lived there for many years completely alone and unde-tected even by the Denynso who lived just above her. It wasn't until the Klimnu invaded that she saw another crea-ture, and soon she was inundated with others, including Denynso who streamed in to fight what they thought would be the final battle with the gruesome creatures. It bothered him still that every day of his life that he had lived on that compound he had been living above those people, going about his days mere feet above a deep cavern designed as a reflection of the compound above. They had loved that land dearly in the time that they had spent there, but were driven underground by the attacks of other species and a plague that threatened their existence, the same plague that would eventually kill all but Loralia.

The tunnel that had led down to that realm had been hidden away in a ridge just as this one was, but none of the Denynso were small enough to get all of the way down it. Instead they had had to rely on the human women to follow it down until it led them onto the reflected branches of the realm below. Creia felt the ground beneath his feet change and in that instant he realized that just like with the tunnel that led down to where Loralia lived, there was a transporter in this tunnel and he was now much farther away from the cave than the distance that he had walked would entail. The thought made the breath catch in his throat and he lifted he focused ahead of him to the sunlight that he could see faintly in the distance. He walked a little further and the light became bright enough that he was able to put his light stick away and follow the rest of the tunnel by the sunlight alone. After a few more moments he crossed through another cave and out of the mouth into what looked like an abandoned village.

Creia walked out of the cave and across an open space in front of another ridge that was strikingly similar to the ones that bordered his compound and the badlands. He stepped out into the center of the village and looked around, trying to gain his bearings. He had never been to this area of the planet and it was nothing like what the warriors had described when they told him about their mission out of the compound and across the planet. That meant that he had traveled further than they had in a matter of steps, obviously utilizing the same technology that had been put into place in the tunnel that led down to the mirrored realm. He thought back to when they realized that the technology existed in that tunnel and how they immediately assumed that it had been put into place by the human flight attendant and the traitor Denynso who had been aiding the Klimnu in their battles. Now that he realized it also existed in the tunnel that he had just left, Creia wondered if that assumption had been accurate.

He moved further into the village and stepped up to the closest building. The door hung off its hinges, dust coming from inside as though the years were taking over and were gradually washing the village away. Creia carefully moved the door aside and stepped into the building. It was cold and familiar. Low furniture filled the space and began to populate his mind with memories from his childhood. He knew that it wasn't this space that he was remembering, but something very similar, something that looked almost identical. He continued through the small house, touching the forgotten surfaces and letting his eyes travel across personal objects left strewn around as though still waiting for their owners to return and complete the moments that they had been living when those objects had been dropped or placed aside.

The memories continued to come to him as he entered a small room to the back of the house and saw that it was a bedroom. A thick blanket was folded back and there was still a wrinkle in the sheet indicating where the inhabitant slept. Where could that person have gone? Did he know when he climbed out of bed that final morning that he wouldn't be getting back into it that night?

Creia saw a book resting on the table beside the bed and reached for it. The pages were thin and frail, filled with jagged writing. His heart began to pound as he read the words. They were written in a language that he hadn't heard in many years, a language that formed his memories of his mother's voice and whispered the bedtime stories that his grandfather had told him before he fell asleep at night. It was a language that was spoken long ago, before the assimilation that faded the demarcations between the species throughout the galaxy and brought uniformity to spoken and written words. The book was written in ancient Denynso.

Creia flipped through the pages of the journal, forcing his mind to link the sounds and the words until their meanings flooded back to him through the years that had separated them. He could understand them again, read through them with the same speed and comprehension that he had when he was young and that he used now to read the core language. The words spoke of a different time, a time long ago before he was even alive. Creia knew now that he was in a Denynso home from long before his lifetime, before even his parents. The home looked like the home that his grandparents had lived in when he was just a child, reminding him of the afternoons that he had spent there watching his grandmother bake for the clan much the way that Ty did now.

The realization sank into him as he read through the journal that chronicled a life that had been so normal and then had taken a stark and terrifying turn. The words became more irregular and rough on the page as the date on the top of each progressed. He read of an enemy, a darkness that had overtaken the planet, and the ties between the Denynso compounds that were being threatened. Creia had never known about the cooperation between the clans, or the connections that had once existed between the compounds. This compound had ceased many years before he was born, long before the clan had split and formed the new compound, yet he had never even known that they had existed.

What could have happened to them? Where did the clan that had called this compound home go, and what did it have to do with the fear and concern that filled the words on the journal pages?

He knew then that the technology that had existed in the tunnel that brought them down into the mirrored realm had not been the work of the human flight attendant, at least not the original work. It had existed more than a century before in the tunnel that had brought him from the badlands here, which meant it had once been used to allow the Denynso to move from compound to compound quickly and undetected.

A sound in the front of the building made Creia pause. He carefully tucked the journal into his bag and turned to walk toward the door to the bedroom. Before he could take a step, however, a dark figure descended on him and the world around him went black before he hit the floor.

10

"What more do you have to tell us?" Maxim asked.

Ivy cringed at the straightforward bluntness in her mate's voice, but she understood the emotion behind it. Maxim was tired and worn, brought down by everything that was happening around him and the perception that he had nothing that he could do about it. She knew how desperately he wanted to unravel all of the tangled, confusing situations that were building around them, and truly understand once and for all what had happened to his father and what that had to do with everything that had unfolded on Uoria since. Fighting so hard against everything that stood in his way and forcing himself to confront the fact that he didn't know as much about his childhood, his family, and even his species as he thought, however, was draining everything that was inside of him.

The man who she loved was as beautiful inside as he was out, and the gentleness of his heart was making it difficult for him to pick up the burden that he felt Aegeus had left behind and finally bring it to resolution. As challenging as it was for him, however, Ivy knew that he was never going to give up. No matter what he had to face or the pain that he had to put himself through, Maxim was going to do everything that he had to do to find out what had happened and ensure that his home, his planet, and his kind were protected.

Athan stepped back from the doorway and gestured for the three of them to enter. Kyven had gone to Emerie in the home that she was sharing with some of the other women and told her that he would see her later that night. Ivy had watched as the woman's face changed from confused to worried, to saddened. She could almost feel the emotions that were pouring off of her and she ached for the past that Emerie was still struggling to overcome. Though Ivy didn't know Emerie well and didn't know who she was in the years before she left Earth as part of Nyx 23, she did know that there was something the woman was carrying that she hadn't yet come to terms with, and wasn't yet ready to reveal to Kyven. It was hurting her deeply, but she was fighting to push its influence away even as she eased into the relationship that was gradually building between the two of them.

When they had settled into the main room once again Athan took a moment to look at each of them in the eyes carefully.

"Are you sure that you want to know?" he asked, pausing with his eyes locked on Maxim's. "Are you sure that you are prepared to hear what I have to say this time?"

His tone was slightly scolding and Ivy felt herself tense. She worried that Athan would set Maxim off again and she didn't know if she had the energy to cope with the emotions that seeing her mate go through these sudden and intense swings caused in her. She wanted to be there for him, to offer him the support, encouragement, and help that she had promised when they first discussed not going back to Earth but instead heading back to the settlement to free the other Mikana from the meeting hall where Pyra had secured them. As they were sitting there, however, and she realized just how deep this situation was spinning, she felt like she wasn't able to live up to that aspiration and was in a way letting Maxim down. All she could do was sit beside him, hold his hand, and hope that somehow her presence was enough.

"I'm ready," Maxim said.

The vitriol was gone from his voice and his tone seemed to satisfy Athan. The older man glanced at Kyven.

"I take it your brother has told you what I told him?"

"Yes," Kyven responded.

"I told you that your father found out about the Klimnu influencing the Order," Athan said. He looked at each of the men for affirmation before moving on. "Aegeus wouldn't tell me the names of the men, but he did say that some of the most powerful of the Order, men who were rarely seen and only by invitation, had transitioned and were now fully Klimnu. The level of secretiveness within the Order is something that I don't think you could ever understand. This organization is meant to be unknown to any who are not within it, but even within the number of the Order there are secrets. Many have never seen the men who are at the highest ranks. I am one of them. When Aegeus told me that he knew that some of these men were now Klimnu and had begun to influence the Order, even those who had not transitioned, he wouldn't tell me the names of the men, only that it was their words that was arranging our movements within the Order, and that they were going to use that tactic to get the rest of the kingdom under the command even further. The final goal was to take over the entire planet with the Klimnu at the helm and the Mikana close behind."

"If Papa knew who these men were, why didn't he just tell someone so that something could be done?" Kyven asked.

Ivy looked at him and saw an expression in his eyes that was almost painfully hopeful, like a little boy who just didn't want to believe that there could be anything wrong with the choices that his heroic father made so many years ago.

"Who was he to tell?" Athan asked. "Remember that even the leader of the kingdom doesn't know about the Order. It was the same then. The Order has long acted as a check of power, a balance in a way. As long as the Order existed, the king would not be able to rule with too extensive of authority or too aggressive of a hand. If Aegeus had mentioned the Klimnu and what they were doing, it would have caused mass hysteria and would have revealed the existence of the Order. That would have put the entire clan at risk. He knew that if something was to be done, he had no choice but to handle it himself."

"You didn't offer to help him?" Maxim asked.

Ivy could hear the familiar softness returning to his voice and she slid closer to him. She couldn't imagine what he was going through.

"Of course I did," Athan said, looking at Maxim and then Kyven with sincerity in his eyes that cut through Ivy and made her chest ache.

As deeply as she felt the pain that her mate was feeling, she also couldn't help but feel compassion for the older man who was sitting in front of her. He looked worn and some-what broken, as if he had been carrying a tremendous burden for years and it was pulling him down even as he struggled to hold himself up.

"What did he tell you?" Ivy asked.

Athan turned to look at her as if he had forgotten that she was there.

"He wouldn't tell me anything," Athan said. "I knew what he had learned about the Klimnu and the members of the Order, but he wouldn't tell me anything about what he planned to do. We already knew that there was going to be a battle and I assumed that he was going to put whatever plan he had into action during that battle, but he wouldn't tell me what it was. It was only moments into the battle when the Valdicians, the Klimnu, and their allies descended on him and he was gone. He never had the opportunity to tell me what he was going to do. If he had, I would have done it for him. I would have done anything to avenge him and ensure that the hopes that he had for the planet were fulfilled."

"What did the others of the Order do when you told them about his death?" Kyven asked.

"Nothing," Athan said. "They told me that it was my responsibility to inform your family, but that that was all that I was to do. I was barred from delving any further into the situation or doing any kind of investigation of my own. I wasn't even permitted to go back to the battlefield to see if there was any way that I would be able to find any sign of him, even his armor. I wanted to have something to bring back to your mother to keep of him since I couldn't bring back his body."

"Why wouldn't they want you to look into it anymore? Didn't they want to know what had happened to him?" Ivy asked.

"I have no explanation for that," Athan said. "When the battle ended and we accounted for the lost, it was only Aegeus whose body couldn't be recovered."

"What happened to the others?" Maxim asked. "How did you explain to those families what had happened to them?"

"The Order had protocol for how to handle these situations. Since they didn't want to discuss the wars with those who weren't in the Order, they had a process for explaining deaths and other problems that would assuage the families without revealing the presence of the Order or the conflicts with the others. It wasn't as difficult as you would think. Aegeus was a bit of an anomaly when it came to the Order. He was the only man who had a wife and children and was still in the Order. It was the same with his father before him. In the past there had been more men who had come into the Order with families or who had started families once they were already in the Order. In more recent years, though, it became tradition for only men who were unmarried and had no families of their own to be a part of it. It made situations like this far easier. It is much less difficult to explain away a grown man going missing when he has no ties than it is to tell a wife and young ones that their husband and father are gone."

"You have never married, have you, Athan?" Ivy asked.

Athan shook his head.

"No. My life was devoted to the Order. I think that is why Aegeus and his family meant so much to me. I knew that I would never have a wife and children of my own, so in a way it was as if I could enjoy the feeling of having a family when I could be with all of them."

"You were a part of our family," Kyven said.

Athan looked to him and Ivy saw Maxim nod.

"You still are," Maxim said. "You meant so much to Papa. I know that he would be proud that you have stayed with the Order and have done what you can to finish what he started."

They were the words that Maxim had used to describe what he meant to do, and Ivy felt their meaning sinking into her as Maxim said them.

"I didn't know that the Mikana married," Ivy said softly.

She knew that it was out of context and didn't really matter to the conversation, but somehow it bothered her. The Denynso knew nothing of marriage and instead had bonds created in truly beautiful but private ways personal just to each couple. It startled her in a way to find out that this species, the species that had borne the man who she loved with every fiber of her being, not only understood but apparently participated in marriage as hers did. She didn't know if it should bother her that Maxim had never mentioned it or if she should simply accept that no matter how deeply she had already invested herself in him that they were still getting to know each other. This may simply be something that she would have learned later.

"It's not quite the same as humans," Athan told her. "The ritual itself is different and from what I learned from those who had the opportunity to interact with the people of the Nyx 23 settlement before it was locked by the Covra, there are some complex legal issues related to marriage on Earth that don't fit in with our kind."

Ivy had never heard marriage described in such harsh terms and she was taken aback by it. She looked to Maxim, who stroked her cheek gently.

"The Mikana and humans are different, my love. This is all something that we will talk about in time."

11

"If you could leave the kingdom right now, would you?"

Zyyr stroked his fingers through Lila's hair as he stared up at the purple and green sunset above them. It was that breathtaking time of day when the evening had night quite ended but the night was already beginning, putting him in the strange, somewhat ethereal mood of wanting to make the most of the last gasps of the day while also wanting to let the soft impending darkness of night soothe him to sleep.

Lila sighed beside him and nuzzled closer.

"I don't know," she said softly.

"You said that you wanted to know what was outside," he said, looking down at her.

"I know," she said, her hand running softly across his chest as her leg came up to drape across his. "But what if I got out there and it was dangerous? What if I have had these amazing images of the planet outside of the kingdom but when I got out there, I didn't like it?"

"What if you did?"

Lila took a deep breath.

"I don't think that I'm ever going to have the opportunity to find out. We are meant to stay within the boundary of the kingdom. It's just the way that it is, Zyyr. Dreaming isn't going to change it and sometimes I wonder if it hurts too much to even let myself wonder."

Zyyr felt his heart tighten in his chest. He hated to hear her talk that way. They had been out by the orchard for hours after they had eaten the last of their picnic and in that time he had only become more sure that his mind, heart, and body were telling him that this incredible woman was meant to be his mate. Love that he couldn't explain surged through his veins and he felt himself more drawn to her with each breath. Hearing the sadness and longing in her voice hurt him deeply. He had been telling the truth when he told her that most of the Denynso had never questioned the fact that they didn't leave the compound and were expected to simply live their lives in the place. As Lila had said, it was just the way it was and the warriors had been bound by their sense of duty and loyalty to such an extent that they never thought to wonder what could be beyond the life that their king had created and dictated for them.

Now that they had come out of the compound, however, Zyyr could understand what Lila was feeling. He could no longer imagine not being able to leave and not knowing what else the planet had to offer beyond the small area where he was born. He could hear that sense of tension in her voice now, the pull between loving her home and still wanting to step beyond the walls that stopped her and gain a new perspective.

"What is stopping you, Lila?"

Lila sat up and looked down at him, her eyes searching his.

"The expectations of everyone in the kingdom."

"And if you broke those expectations?" he asked, sitting up and resting his hands on her waist. "What would happen?"

"I don't know," she responded quietly after a short pause.

Zyyr smiled at her and leaned forward to rest his lips to hers. The touch ignited something inside him and he jumped to his feet, taking her by her hands to help her up.

"Let's find out," he said.

Lila's eyes widened and she shook her head slightly.

"What do you mean?" she asked.

"I mean let's find out," he said. "There's nothing to stop you, Lila. There are no laws, no formal restrictions to keep you here. Like you said, it is only expectations, and no one ever got anywhere by always following expectations."

"How would you know?"

Zyyr knew that she didn't mean the words as aggressively as they had sounded, but they sank into him painfully. He took a breath and pulled her a little closer.

"I know because I followed them my entire life and I never did anything that every other warrior of my kind hasn't done. I never saw anything or did anything. I never accomplished anything or experienced a single day that was anything different than the life that my brothers and father lived. When that ended, though, when I finally got to step onto the other side of that wall and do the things that I thought that I would never do, that I didn't even know were available to do, that is when I started to live. I was expected to follow everything that Pyra said when we were in the settlement, and I went against that. Instead, I joined those who stood up against him and helped to ensure that the Mikana stayed as safe as possible. I was expected to go back to the Denynso compound after the Mikana men were freed, but instead I chose to join Maxim, Ivy, and the others coming here. And I met you."

"Does that matter to you?" she asked softly, lowering her eyes and then looking back up at him.

Zyyr felt his heart swell and his stomach clench. He didn't know how much longer he was going to be able to resist her. He was thankful for the quiet time that they got to spend together away from the others, away from any of the Denynso men who may have ignited the fury and violence in him that was one of the hallmarks of the warriors finding their mates. This allowed him to enjoy being close to her rather than focusing on keeping others away until they could complete their bond. He stepped up closer to her and ran his fingers through her hair, letting his fingers graze around the curve of her cheek.

"It matters to me more than I can tell you," he said. "You are something that I never, ever expected, but I want to break these expectations more than I have ever wanted anything." Lila smiled and he could see the willingness and desire in her eyes. "Come on," he said.

Lila allowed him to take her hand and guide her away from their picnic into the orchard.

"Where are we going?" she asked.

"How far have you gone into this orchard?" he asked.

"About halfway, I suppose," she answered. "Why?"

"There has to be more beyond that," he said, "and beyond that is the boundary to the kingdom. We'll go that far, and then we'll see how you feel."

Lila took a breath and nodded. They walked along quietly, each enjoying the cool shade of the trees and the sweet scent that the fruit added to the air. Zyyr could feel the desire coiling in his belly intensifying with each step that they took further into the darkness and isolation of the orchard. Beneath his feet he could see the paths worn by the steps of the Mikana women who came into the trees to gather food, the trails as straight and consistent as the growth patterns of the trees. The further that they moved into the orchard, however, the less defined the paths became and the more wild the trees appeared.

Though they still grew in the even, meticulous lines. The trees further into the orchard seemed to reach into the sky with more abandon and spread branches laden with heavy, vibrant fruit. Lila lifted one of her slim, graceful hands and ran her fingertips along one of the pieces of fruit that hung low enough for her to reach.

"Everything looks so different back here," she said almost as though she were speaking to herself.

"No one ever comes back here," Zyyr said, "so there are no expectations holding the trees back."

He had meant the comment playfully, but Lila looked back at him with a serious look in her wide eyes. She didn't say anything to him, but Zyyr felt as though something had changed within her as they continued forward at a slightly faster pace. They had walked on for several more minutes and the sky above them had shifted from the bright colors of sunset to a velvety blue that somehow seemed to make the space around them feel warmer and more secure. Finally Zyyr looked ahead of him and saw the wall.

Unlike the wall at the front of the kingdom, the stones of this boundary were covered in vines and leaves. His mind immediately returned to the first time that the Denynso warriors had seen the wall of the Nyx 23 settlement. It had looked very much like this one, old and forgotten, left to offer itself up to the planet around it as if the last hands that had touched it had been the ones that had forged it. There, however, the wall had been the same around the entirety of the settlement; at least, as much as Zyyr had seen. Here the wall at the front of the kingdom was clean and well-maintained, beautiful and new even though he knew that it had been built many generations before. It was as if the wall itself was the embodiment of what he was learning about the world around him since he had left the compound. What he saw at first could be lovely and pristine, but he never knew what he would discover if he just delved far enough.

Lila approached the wall and reached out to rest her hand on one of the stones. He expected her to pause there for a few moments, to think about the significance of this moment. Instead, she looked over at him, gathered her skirts, and started to climb. Zyyr closed the space between them and reached out for her, grabbing her by her waist and lifting her up so that she could grab the top of the wall with her arms and pull herself up. When she was sitting securely at the top of the wall, he scrambled up after her.

"There it is," he said to her when he settled into place beside her.

"It is," Lila said back, her eyes trained on the night-cloaked expanse of the planet beyond the wall.

"Do you want to go back?" he asked.

"When you got to the top of the wall of the Denynso compound for the first time, did you want to go back?" she asked.

"No," he answered.

Lila's face turned to him and he saw that she was even more breathtaking in the light of the stars that touched her now that she was out of the cover of all of the trees.

"Neither do I."

Zyyr jumped down and opened his arms to her. She leapt forward, allowing him to catch her and gather her close to his chest for a moment before lowering her to her feet.

"Where do we go now?" she asked.

"Anywhere you want to," Zyyr responded.

The air around them seemed cooler and softer now that they were out of the orchard. He wondered if this moment was as heavy for Lila as his first moment outside of the compound had been for him. It had been a strange feeling, something that he didn't know if he would be able to explain. It was as if he was struggling with himself as he took his first breaths in the openness of Uoria. At once he felt liberated and out of control. The compound had never felt restrictive to him when he was young, it had simply been home. Leaving had never crossed his mind until Pyra began to talk about going out onto the planet to explore and find out what else was out there, so he had never had the opportunity to feel like he was being held back or kept from something. It was exhilarating being beyond the boundary for the first time, but he had also felt somewhat unsure, like he was distancing himself from something that would never be the same. It was almost like a tiny child taking their first steps from their mother. The compound had always kept him safe and protected, and though he knew that what they were doing was important and necessarily for the growth and survival of their kind, he still felt somewhat unsure and as though he would never really be able to feel that sense of blind, trusting protection again.

The grass was high around their legs as they walked, but after a few moments Zyyr felt the ground beneath his feet grow softer and more difficult to traverse. In the light glowing from the sky he was able to see that the grass was giving way to loose sand and in the distance he could hear the whispering of water lapping onto a shoreline.

"What is this?" Lila asked as they got closer to a tremendous body of water stretching from the sandy bank.

Zyyr thought of the water in the Denynso kingdom and the last time that he was there, gathered with the others as they said goodbye to Jem. It was so similar he felt like he could almost see the outline of the women kneeling at the water's edge as the men stood and watched his raft disappear.

"It's a lake," Zyyr told her. "I can't see how big it is right now, but it seems like it goes on pretty far."

As they approached the water the air suddenly felt thick and filled with electricity. The weather was shifting again and Zyyr worried that there was a storm building.

"Maybe we should go back," he said.

"Why?" Lila asked. "We just got out here."

"I know," Zyyr said, "but it feels like there's –"

Before he could get the rest of the sentence out of his mouth there was a massive crack of thunder and it seemed like the sky above them was torn away as a deluge of cold, stinging rain poured down on them. Lila gasped and curled into him. He tried to shield her from the rain, but within moments they were both drenched and he could feel the intense chill of the water seeming to seep into his skin. They ran back to the wall and he clambered up it first, turning around to grab her by her wrists so that he could pull her up and over with him. The branches of the trees provided some cover from the rain, but the drops were still able to get to them and with each step Zyyr felt colder and more dragged down by the heaviness of his wet clothes.

He was heading back toward the houses in the front of the kingdom, but they were nearly out of the orchard when Lila gave his arm a pull and directed him in the opposite direction.

"Where are we going?" he asked.

Another blast of thunder drowned out her answer, but a few moments later he saw a small building hunkered close to the ground several yards away. It didn't look like anybody had gone near it in years, but the door opened smoothly and easily beneath Lila's hand and she was able to reach for a lamp within just a few steps of the door and fill the space with a soft glow.

Zyyr looked around himself, taking in what looked like an old yet carefully preserved and maintained home.

"This was my great-grandmother's house," she told him. "Her father build it for her as a gift for her wedding."

"Why is it so far out here away from all of the rest of the houses?" Zyyr asked.

"She was...," Lila paused as though carefully considering her words so that she could choose exactly what she wanted to say, "different from the others of the kingdom in her time."

"What do you mean?" Zyyr asked.

Lila didn't respond but moved across the house toward a large fireplace. She looked comfortable in the space and he knew that this was not the first time that she had visited the home recently.

"You spend a lot of time here, don't you?" he asked, walking toward the fireplace and watching as she reached into a brushed brass box to pull out tools and start building a fire.

"I'm different from the others of the kingdom, too," she said simply.

12

S amira realized that she was gripping the front edge of the backseat of the car so tightly that her hands were cramping and she let go so that she could stretch and rub them, distracting herself from the nervousness that rolled through her belly by trying to bring the feeling back to her fingertips. She looked out of the window to the car and saw a grey, foggy world beyond. It was only the day after her party and yet she felt like the merriment and fun of the celebration was so far distanced from where she was now that it was barely even her own memory. It was more as though she were looking into someone else's memory and trying desperately to live vicariously through it so that she didn't have to really come to terms with what she was doing.

"Are you sure that you want to do this?" Zuri asked her from the driver's seat.

Samira looked up into the rearview mirror and saw her dear friend gazing back at her through the reflection. She tried to look calm and give a confident smile, but all she could muster was a vague nod of her head.

"Yes," she said. "Well," she looked out the window again, "no. I don't want to do this," she admitted, "but it's something that I have to do. I won't be able to go through with the wedding until I have."

She felt Ty's hand slide onto her thigh and give it an affectionate squeeze, and Samira covered his hand with hers to squeeze back. Having him sitting beside her, just knowing that he was there and that she wasn't going to be going through this without him was comforting. It made her feel stronger to know that when she climbed those steps again, so soon after she ran down them and told herself that she never wanted to see the house, much less the man inside it, ever again, she would have Ty by her side to reassure her.

"You know that we are all here for you and that we won't let anything happen to you," Ero said from the passenger seat beside Zuri.

"I do," Samira said.

Zuri smiled at her in the reflection again.

"Well, it's good to hear that you have your line memorized. You just keep practicing that in your mind and this will be over before you know it."

Samira smiled but even as the rest of the car chuckled she couldn't help but let her mind wander back to the last time that she had been in her mother's house and how horribly the situation had unfolded. Zuri and Ero had been there that time as well. They had brought her to the house to help her get a few things so that she could be ready for her journey to Uoria, but instead it had turned into a tense, violent battle between Ero and her stepfather. Though it never would have been an even match even had her stepfather been completely sober, the clash had been awful to watch and she knew that it had taken all of Ero's restraint just to prevent him from destroying his unworthy opponent.

She didn't know if he would be able to exhibit the same level of control this time and could only hope that when they arrived at the house she would be able to spend some time with her mother in peace. Perhaps this would be one of the many evenings that her stepfather spent bellied up to one of his favorite bars and she would be able to escape the situation without even having to see him. If she was truly fortunate, she would never have to see him again.

The car pulled up in front of her mother's house and Samira felt everyone in the car turn to look at her expectantly. She wasn't sure what they thought that she was going to do, and as she looked up at the darkened, quiet house, she didn't really know what to do, either. Part of her wanted to just tell Zuri to drive away, to let her put that house and everyone and everything in it behind her so that she didn't have to think about it anymore and could just focus completely on the new life that was ahead of her. The other part, however, actually did have the compulsion to go through with this. Even though the thought of facing him again made her stomach turn and reminded her of the dark and terrifying nights that she used to spend cowering from him in her bedroom or escaping through her window so that she could hide away in the garage without him being able to find her, she was different now. That part of her wanted him to see her strong and happy, standing by the side of her mate and telling him that he didn't break her and that her life was going to go on just fine without him being a part of it, no matter what he had done to her.

Suddenly the front door to the house opened and a figure darkened the pale blue rectangle of light that indicated the only thing that was on in the house was the ever-present television. Samira felt her muscles tense. She knew not only that silhouette, but its stance. Not only was her stepfather most certainly in the house, but he had already stumbled home from the bar and was now toppling head-long into the rows of beer he kept on the bottom shelf of the refrigerator. This would make him even more impulsive and mean, bringing her back to days that she would much rather forget.

"Who's that?" he shouted into the quickly darkening evening air.

"You're alright," Ty said soothingly, squeezing her thigh again as if in response to the defensive tightening of her muscles. "Everything is going to be fine."

"We're here with you, Samira," Zuri said. "There's nothing that can happen to you now."

Samira took a breath and nodded, then reached for the handle of the car door. As soon as it opened, a flood of anger surged through her. It was an unexpected rush of emotion, a burning intensity that felt like the suppressed feelings and reactions of her lifetime finally releasing inside of her so that she could feel them fully now that she knew that she didn't need to be afraid. She stepped out of the car onto the street and slammed the door, ensuring it was loud enough to startle her stepfather standing at the door.

"Who parked their damn car in front of my house and is disrupting my relaxing time with all of that noise?" he demanded.

Samira came around the back of the car toward the end of the walkway that would lead up to the door and she saw another figure appear in the light of the doorway. It was smaller, though far from slight, and she felt her heart swell a little.

"Samira?" her mother's faint voice said.

"Yes," Samira said, starting up the walkway as fast as she could on her shaking legs.

It was no longer fear or even worry that was making her tremble. Instead it was the surge of adrenaline and anger that was making her muscles twitch and her body shake with the pent-up energy and aggression she was finally allowing herself to feel. Behind her she could hear the footsteps of Zuri, Ero, and Ty coming after her and she felt empowered by their presence. She realized then that it was not that she wanted them there to protect her. Instead she felt strengthened just by the reality of their existence and the new life that she had begun on Uoria. They were proof that she was capable of getting through life on her own and that she was not broken down or destroyed by her stepfather, no matter how hard he had tried. By them being there with her, she was showing him that he didn't own her and that she was not under his command; that she never would be again.

"What are you doing here?" her stepfather demanded, taking one step out of the house so that he leaned against the outside of the doorframe and she could see the beer bottle dangling in his hand.

"I'm here to talk to my mother and get my stuff," Samira answered.

"There's nothing of yours here," he slurred viciously.

"That room is still hers," Valerie said.

"Keep out of my conversation," he said, turning just enough that he could push Samira's mother backwards further into the house.

That single move galvanized Samira and she took off running toward the house. She could hear the others coming up behind her and in moments Ero had overcome her. The warrior surged up the front steps to the porch and dove toward her stepfather, causing him to stumble back and crash onto the floor. The bottle of beer flew from his hand and shattered, sending glass a spray of dark, dank-smelling liquid out onto the porch. In an instant Ty was past Samira and trying to pull Ero up.

"What the hell do you think you're doing?"

"I thought you would have learned the last time that I was here," Ero growled, shoving the man harder onto the floor. "I told you to never put your hands on your step-daughter or your wife again."

Ty finally succeeded in dragging Ero to his feet and Samira helped to push him backwards into Zuri's arms. She knew that it was her time to step forward. This was not the time for her to rely on other people to speak for her. She couldn't settle for just being ushered through the house and then back out to the car. This may be her only opportunity to confront the man who had tormented her and her mother for so long, and to know that she had been the one to look him in the eye and ensure that he knew that her heart, her mind, and her spirit hadn't been lost, even if there were times when she felt like she could no longer reach them.

Samira walked across the room to her mother and crouched down to wrap an arm around her shoulders.

"Are you alright?" she asked.

Valerie looked up into her eyes, staring at her as if not really believing that she was there.

"She's fine."

Samira rubbed her mother's arm comfortingly and stood up, turning calmly to face her stepfather.

"I wasn't speaking to you," she said.

"What did you say?"

"I wasn't speaking to you, Trevor."

The word came from her lips like fire. She hadn't even allowed herself to think of her stepfather's name in so long, much less said it, and now that she had it felt as powerful as a physical blow. He couldn't control her any longer. He didn't have the right or the power to control what she thought, did, or said, and she wouldn't let him think that he did for another moment.

"What did you say to me?"

Samira squared her shoulders toward Trevor and looked him directly in the eyes. For the first time she realized that he was not as much bigger than her as he had always seemed.

"I said that I wasn't speaking to you. I was speaking to my mother. She is a grown woman and she has the ability to speak for herself. She doesn't need you to do it for her."

"Don't tell me what to do in my house, you insolent child."

"This isn't your house," Valerie said. Samira whipped toward her mother, shocked at the sudden sound of strength in her voice. "This isn't your house," she said again, standing and facing off against Trevor, "and she isn't your child. She is my child and this is my house. They were both mine well before you came along."

Samira was startled by her mother's assured stance against Trevor, but also thrilled to hear her finally speaking up for herself after so many years. She hoped that it would be enough to make the man step down, but instead he turned to Samira and took a threatening step forward toward her. Ty stepped forward, but Ero and Zuri took him by his arms and guided him back carefully. The energy in the room was high and tense, but Samira wasn't backing down.

"How dare you come in here with these," he looked back at Ero and Ty and looked them up and down with an expression of disgust on his face, "things and get into my wife's head? We were doing just fine with you gone and now you come back here and get her acting up."

"She's not a child, and they are not things. These are men, and this," she took a step backwards and took Ty's hand so that she could pull him forward beside her, "is Ty. He's my fiancé."

"Your what?" Trevor said with pure vitriol in his voice.

"We are getting married this weekend," Samira said.

She looked over at her mother and saw the sparkle in her eyes. Even beneath all of the pain and anger in the expression, there was excitement and happiness. Samira offered a smile and looked up at Ty.

"We met when she came to my planet with Zuri," Ty said. "She is my mate."

"The Denynso don't marry," Samira explained. "Ty is the first."

"He's willing to do that for you?" Valerie asked.

"I asked her," Ty responded. "I love her and I want to do anything that I can to make her happy. I'm not sure what all of this entails, but I am willing to do anything that she would want me to do so that we can spend our lives happily together."

"What kind of man does whatever a woman would want him to?" Trevor scoffed.

"One who is worth spending your life with," Samira said.

"I'm a real man," Trevor said. "My word is law here and your mother is perfectly happy with me. She knows what's good for her and she stays in her place."

Samira saw Valerie look to Trevor, her eyes wide and frightened, and for a moment she worried that her mother was going to hand herself back over to her husband. She worried that her mother would feel that she had exerted herself enough and that just as she had so many other times before, she would stand up to protect Trevor rather than thinking about what was good for herself.

"No," Valerie finally said. "Not anymore."

"Stop talking, Valerie," Trevor said.

"No," she repeated. "I'm not happy and I haven't been in nearly as long as I've known you. A real man doesn't treat a woman, or a child, the way that you have treated us. Get out."

Samira could see her mother shaking, but she was standing tall, her shoulders as strong and squared as Samira had ever seen them. She stepped up beside her and wrapped her arm around her shoulders to hold her steady, and met Trevor's eyes.

"I believe she told you to do something," she said. "You've given enough commands in your day that I'm sure you know how to follow them."

"I don't have to go anywhere," Trevor said. "I'm your husband and that means I have the right to be here whether it is your name on the deed or not."

There was an arrogant hint in Trevor's voice and Samira felt her fists clench.

"She told you to get out," Samira said.

"Samira," Zuri said. Her voice was calm and even, offering the same soothing effect that it always had. "Unless your mother is going to call the police and file charges against him, she can't force him out of the house. He's lived here with her for long enough that he has the right to be here. The only thing that she can do is evict him, and since he is her husband, that will be difficult."

"See?" Trevor said. "There's nothing you can do about me being here, so you might as well just shut your mouth and get them gone so that I can deal with you."

"You won't be dealing with anybody," Ero said. "Either

you leave now or we will take Valerie with us and see to it that you get a formal escort out of here tomorrow."

"I'll go with you," Valerie said. "It will be nice to spend a night away from this house. I'll go to the judge tomorrow."

Samira felt her heart soar with pride as Valerie stepped away from her and started down the hallway toward her bedroom. Trevor watched after her with a dumbfounded look on his face. For a moment Samira worried that he would go after her, but instead he crossed the living room and dropped down into the worn recliner where he spent the majority of his life. A few minutes later Valerie came back into the room carrying two bulging suitcases.

"Is there anything that we can help you with?" Ty asked.

"There's another suitcase in the bedroom," Valerie said.

Ty headed down the hallway and Valerie turned to Trevor. Samira watched as her mother's eyes scanned the man to whom she had devoted her life for so many years and had been rewarded only with pain and disappointment. She said nothing, but turned away and walked out of the front door, her face directly ahead and her focus not wavering until she climbed into the back of the car.

As soon as the door closed and Samira settled into place beside her mother, she felt Valerie's shoulders drop. It was as if all of the tension that she had held within her since the beginning of her marriage to Trevor had just released and for the first time in all of those years she was able to relax.

"Are you alright?" Samira asked.

"I will be," Valerie said, offering a hint of a smile that would be the first that Samira had seen on her mother's face in as long as she could remember.

"I'm proud of you," Samira said.

"So am I," Zuri offered, glancing back at them in the

rearview mirror. "It couldn't have been easy for you to say that to him."

"It might have taken me a longer time than I would like to admit to finally realize all of what I said to him, but Samira made me see it."

"I did?" Samira asked.

Valerie reached over and took Samira's hand, giving it a squeeze that was as much to reassure her daughter as it was to reassure herself.

"Yes," Valerie said. "I realized that if you were strong enough to not only leave the planet, but to leave and find a man who truly loves you and is willing to change his entire life for you, then I am strong enough to give myself a different life."

13

"Why are you different?" Zyyr asked.

Lila looked back at him from the roaring flames that had built up in the fireplace.

"Take off those wet clothes," she said.

"What?"

He was taken aback by the departure from his question and her sudden, forward request.

"That rain isn't going to be stopping any time soon. There's no reason for you to stay wet, cold, and miserable while you wait. Let me put your clothes by the fire so that they can dry."

She was obviously avoiding his question and he wondered if she had meant to say what she had about her great-grandmother or if it had simply come out. Whatever the reason, she didn't want to continue the thought, and instead was slowly releasing the ties of her dress. She wasn't looking at him as she did it and Zyyr wondered if he should be watching. He tried to divert his eyes, but his intense, nearly overwhelming desire for her kept pulling them back.

The lamp suddenly went out and Lila gasped, turning to look over her shoulder at the darkened lamp.

"I must not have set the solar panel last time I was here," she said. "There wasn't enough energy conserved to keep the lamp going."

"It's alright," Zyyr said. "The fire gives us plenty of light."

Lila nodded and turned her back to him again. The light of the fire framed her, creating her silhouette against the dancing orange and red flames. As he watched her carefully undressing he complied with her request, starting by peeling away his sopping shirt and resting it on the table beside him. They undressed cautiously; apart yet together in their slow, careful revealing of their bodies.

When Lila was completely bare she remained facing the fire, her hands coming up to move through her wet hair, lifting it so that the heat from the flames could work on drying it as it was her skin. Zyyr watched until he couldn't resist her any longer. He walked up behind her and stood close enough that he could just feel the front of his body lightly grazing the back of hers. Lila's hands slowly lowered to her side and she took a breath, synchronizing with his so that the only sound in the room was their shared exhalations.

Finally Zyyr brought his hands to her hips and guided her back a few steps away from the intensity of the heat. When they were further in the darkness of the room he turned her gently in his hands and then let his fingers run down the full swells of her hips until they fell away from her soft, warm skin. He lowered himself to his knees in front of her, the new position bringing his face level with her breasts. He leaned forward to rest his cheek against the front of her ribcage. Her hand settled onto the side of his head as he paused, listening to the rhythm of her heart and enjoying the soft rise and fall of her breaths. After a few moments he turned his head so that he could touch his lips to her skin. It was more a brush of his mouth than truly a kiss, but he could feel her shudder lightly.

He moved his mouth down, resting a slightly more insistent kiss against her belly. He continued his slow, patient progress until he reached the soft valley between her hipbones. The heightened senses that came with knowing that she was his mate meant that he could smell her body responding to his touch and it threatened the control that he was working hard to maintain. Zyyr kissed his way to one of her hip bones and drew the tip of his tongue across it softly. She drew in a breath and Zyyr waited until she calmed to repeat the tender touch on the other hipbone. When finished, he rose higher on his knees again, letting his nose glide up the center of her belly until his face was nestled between her breasts again.

Zyyr took a deep breath and lifted both hands to cup her breasts, slowly filling his palms with her soft flesh and letting his fingers mold around them. Her back arched slightly and he kneaded into her, gently kissing her skin. Lila's hand ran along the back of his head and onto his neck, her fingernails softly dragging along his skin until a shiver ran down his spine. She slowly eased herself onto her knees in front of him and for a moment they were suspended, their breath lingering between them and their hearts beating in time, pounding toward each other.

Gradually, each moving with the caution of the unknown and yet absolute certainty, their faces drew closer to one another. Her eyelashes brushed his cheek and Zyyr smiled softly. He moved slightly so that the tip of his nose nuzzled hers. His body was trembling slightly, but he wanted to savor every moment that he had with her. Each second, each breath was precious and he didn't want to hurry a single one of them. Their lips drew closer to each other and finally they touched. They melted into the kiss and Zyyr felt his soul reaching out to hers, seeking the connection that he so desperately wanted. As their mouths moved across each other Zyyr coaxed her lips apart with the tip of his tongue. She allowed them to open, welcoming his tongue in to explore her mouth more deeply.

Taking her by the waist, Zyyr eased backwards, drawing her with him as he laid back on the floor. He felt his erection press against her belly, her soft skin grazing across it so that intense sensations flowed through him. Lila pulled her mouth away from his and sat back so that she straddled him on her knees. Zyyr ran his hands up her thighs and over the swells of her hips to rest into the deep curve of her waist again. She began to rock her hips subtly, the movement causing the wet heat of her core to brush against his hardened shaft. He bit his bottom lip as his eyes closed and he focused in on the feeling of her body so close to his.

Zyyr felt Lila's hand flatten on the center of his chest just above his heart and he rested one of his over it.

"What are you thinking right now?" she asked breathlessly.

Zyyr opened his eyes and looked up at her. She was gazing down at him with a soft, irresistible blend of desire and innocence in her eyes.

"How incredible you are," he answered. "How much I want to slide inside of you right now."

Her hand tightened slightly on his chest and he felt the soft brush of her hair on his skin as she leaned forward to bring mouth close to his ear.

"Please, Zyyr," she whispered, her lips touching his ear as she spoke. "Make love to me."

"Are you sure?" he asked, his body aching for her now but not wanting to take advantage of her.

"Yes," she said. "I have heard rumors that the Denynso men are incomparable lovers."

Zyyr sat up sharply, grabbing Lila around the waist as he did so that he could continue to hold her close even without lying down.

"I don't want to be your lover, Lila," he said.

"You don't?" she asked, sounding both upset and embarrassed.

"No," he said. "I want to be your mate."

Her eyes widened and he nestled her a little closer, craving the closeness and needing her to be as focused as possible as he spoke to her. Even as many of the other warriors had spent their younger days bedding unbonded Denynso women prior to finding their mates, he had made the conscious and purposeful decision to not do that. The emotions that he was feeling were nothing like he had ever experienced, and he knew that this moment was everything that he had waited for. It would not just be another bedding that happened to result in his bond with his mate. This was something transcendent, powerful beyond even the words that he was trying to form for her, and he needed her to fully understand it.

"I don't want to claim just your body," he said, leaning forward to kiss the soft curve between her neck and her shoulder. He couldn't resist touching her. "I want to claim all of you. You were intended for me from the day of my birth and right now, in this moment, if you still want me, you will be devoting your life to me, and accepting the devotion of my life to you. You will be my mate, the most cherished of any person in my life, and there will be nothing that will ever come between us."

He realized that as he spoke his voice became quieter until he finished in nearly a whisper. When he was finished he looked up at her and saw a shifted emotion in the gaze she returned. The softness and affection had deepened now, creating something beautiful and intense that told him she had understood everything that he said to her.

"I would never want you to just be my lover," she whispered back. "I've known since I first saw you."

"Will you be my mate?" he asked.

Lila nodded, looping her arms around his neck and leaning forward to rest her forehead against his.

"Yes," she said.

Zyyr used the arm that was looped around her waist to lift Lila's hips and then lowered her down, sinking into her as he settled her into his lap. Her body was hot and tight around his cock and he heard her whimper slightly. Holding her still, he lifted his hips slightly so that he pressed deeper into her so that her body could become accustomed to holding him. Soon he felt her relax and her body open to him more so that he could press deeper still. Lila rolled her hips against his slowly and Zyyr felt a groan pour from his chest. Their bodies melded with indescribable perfection, creating a closeness that he could never have imagined. It felt as though her every curve was crafted to cradle him and his every hardened plane and sharp angle was designed to complement her softness.

Zyyr wrapped Lila's legs around his hips and tucked his own legs forward so that he held her tightly in his lap and she was fully engaged around him. He took her hips and changed their movement slightly, guiding then into a rocking motion that kept him buried deep within her but created long, deep strokes that had him feeling like he was rushing headlong into oblivion. Lila's head fell back and her back arched slightly, thrusting one taut pink nipple up toward him. Zyyr caught it in his mouth, drawing it in between his lips and nipping at it lightly with his teeth. He continued to suckle her as Lila rocked harder and faster against him. Her hands gripped at his back, digging harder into his skin the more passionate her pace became.

"Look at me," she suddenly gasped.

Zyyr pulled his mouth away from her breast and looked at her, catching her eyes. The instant that their gaze met, he felt the pleasure that had been swelling inside him spiral out of control. Pressure that had built through his thighs and stomach tightened even further until it was almost too much, and then released in a shattering climax. He felt his cock pulse and Lila cried out. Her body contracted around his, meeting each throb with a tightening of her own so that he could feel her milking him as he spilled into her.

He felt completely spent when the waves of his orgasm finally stopped. Lila's body draped over his, sweat making their skin slick and hot against each other. Zyyr held her as close as he could and kissed the top of her head, drawing in the scent of her hair. Everything had changed. The world was different now and he felt a greater sense of joy and fulfillment than he ever had. With that joy and fulfillment, however came a tremendous sense of responsibility. Lila was his, now, and it rested on his shoulders and in his heart to ensure that she was safe and protected no matter what type of threat she might face.

14

"**A**re you sure that you want to talk to her again?" Maxim looked over at Ivy and nodded.

"I have to," he said. "Just one more time."

"She said that she doesn't want to talk about this."

"I know," Maxim said, "but I have to try one more time. Especially after everything that Athan told us, I have to give her one more opportunity to tell me what she knows, even if just to find out what she thinks happened and if there is anything that she might know that Athan didn't tell us."

"Why would Athan not tell you something? If he wanted to tell you what happened in the first place, especially with the threat that it poses to him, why would he hold anything back?" Ivy asked.

"It's not that I think that he would hold anything back," Maxim told her. "My father and mother were extremely close when he was here. I have never seen two people love each other the way that they did, and they were always whispering in their room. Athan was my father's best friend and he confided in him a lot, but I can see him not telling him everything, especially when it came to the Order, because of the turmoil within the organization and the always-present possibility that Athan could fall into line with the members of the Order who had transformed into being Klimnu."

"Do you really think that that was something that could have happened?" Ivy asked.

"I don't know," Maxim said. "That isn't a situation that I can even begin to imagine. I'm sure that Papa didn't want to think that Athan could ever betray him and the rest of our kind that way, but he also had to be cautious. He didn't know exactly what was happening or why, and he had to be suspicious of everyone. The only person who he could trust completely was my mother. She had nothing to do with the Order, so she would have no reason to use what he told her for any ulterior motive. I have a really hard time believing that he would hold all of that inside of him and wouldn't tell her anything at all. What if she knows something that even Athan doesn't?"

"She was surprised by what you told her, though, Maxim."

"Maybe. I have to at least ask her one more time."

"Maxim?"

Maxim turned to her and saw tears sparkling in Ivy's eyes. He reached forward and took her hands, pulling her closer so that she could feel the comfort of his body against hers.

"What is it, Ivy?" he asked.

"All of this is starting to scare me," she said.

"Why?"

"If the Order is so secretive that even Athan, one of the oldest and most respected members, is frightened of them finding out that they were talking to you, what do you think that they would do to us if they found out what he told us?"

"I will always keep you safe, my love. No matter what happens, you know that I am always here to protect you."

"What do you hope to accomplish with all of this, Maxim? Do you want to find your father's body? Do you want to find out who the members of the Order were that became Klimnu? I thought that we came back here because you wanted to know more about the Order, but now I don't know what good could possibly come of it."

"There is something that we don't know, Ivy. Something that even Athan doesn't know. My family deserves to know what happened to my father and why he would fight so hard. This can't just be as simple as he wanted to fight off the Klimnu and they killed him in battle. There has to be something else."

"Why?" Ivy asked. "Why does there have to be something else? Why couldn't it just be that simple? Why couldn't it just be that Aegeus found out about the Klimnu, knew that members of the Order had changed, he wanted to fight them off so that they couldn't threaten the rest of your kind, and the rogue members of the Order found out so they targeted him? If they were so determined to take over the planet, they would want to do whatever they could to prevent someone who was as powerful as your father from pushing them back. I just don't understand why you want to make it more complicated than that."

Maxim felt the words fall into his stomach like stones. He let her hands fall away from his and took a step back from her.

"You think that I want this to be this way?" he asked, feeling the pain in his throat that came from fighting the tears that had wanted to fall since he had returned to the kingdom. "You think that I am enjoying finding out all of this about my father?"

"Maxim," Ivy said, trying to reach for his hand, but he pulled away, "I'm sorry. I didn't mean to upset you. I just hate to see you this way. I wish that we could just put it all behind us and move on with our lives."

"Maybe you should stay out here while I talk to my mother," he said, turning away from her and stepping into the house.

Ivy hand touched the back of his shoulder as he walked away, but Maxim continued forward, letting her fingers run down his back and ignoring her voice as she called for him. He couldn't let himself focus on that pain in that moment. He couldn't allow himself to fall into her words and let the comfort that they offered to pull him away from the task that lay ahead of him. Maxim knew that he was doing what he had to do. His father would have wanted him to be strong and follow in his footsteps. It didn't make sense that he and Kyven weren't part of the Order. Though most of the contemporary Order was not hereditary, that was not the way that it used to be, and he couldn't help but wonder if part of the reason that they had been kept out of the tradition was to prevent them from ever finding out about what really happened to their father. If that was true, it meant even more than that he needed to find out what Aegeus had learned but had never told Athan and what had actually happened to him. If nothing else he would understand what had motivated his father in his last days and what he had envisioned for the world that his sons would grow up in.

He could only hope that soon Ivy would understand.

Ellora was standing in the kitchen braiding a loaf of bread on the counter when Maxim walked in.

"Hello, Maxim," she said.

Her voice sounded tired and worn, and for the first time Maxim let him think about his mother before Aegeus died.

She had been brighter, more energetic then. Her eyes had sparkled when she looked at him and there was light around her that seemed to carry her through everything she did. When his father died, that light faded. She was still kind, loving, and encouraging of him and of Kyven, but there was something missing. Over time he had put the thoughts of her before his father's death behind him, knowing even at that young age that things would never go back to the way that they were. He had resigned himself to the changed woman that his mother had become and eventually stopped thinking about those early childhood days. He couldn't help but think of them now, and he felt like they were stolen from him just as much as his father was.

"I need to talk to you," Maxim said.

Ellora stopped weaving the dough and hung her head, giving a deep sigh.

"Please, Maxim, don't start again. I already told you that I don't want to talk about any of this. It won't do any good."

"What do you know about the Klimnu? What did Papa tell you?"

"I don't know anything more than you do, Maxim. They used to be Mikana and then something happened to them and they changed. It had been happening for generations before your father became involved, but no one talked about it."

"What happened to get the Order involved?"

"I don't know, Maxim," Ellora said, going back to weaving the dough. "The number of Klimnu was becoming higher and they were getting more aggressive. I don't know why."

"And Papa didn't tell you anything at all about what he planned to do? You didn't know anything?"

"Where's Ivy?"

"She's outside. He didn't tell you anything?"

"What are you doing, Maxim?" she asked.

"What do you mean?"

"You are letting yourself get so wrapped up in the past that you aren't even looking into your future. Instead of thinking about that woman who obviously loves you, you are so determined to find out things that no one needs to know and that will do no one any good."

"I thought that you didn't want me to be with Ivy."

"I never said that, Maxim."

"You said as much."

"I'm sorry," Ellora said. "I am trying. Really I am. I just want you to be with someone who will make you happy, and who you can build a life with here."

"Right now all I am thinking about is Papa and finding out what happened. I can't even begin to think about having a future or a family if I don't even know my own history. He was doing something, Mama. He knew something and he had a plan to handle it, and something happened to him. That has impacted the entire planet since then, and I need to figure it out. If I have to do that without your help, that's what I'm going to have to do."

"I already lost my husband. I don't want to lose the rest of my family."

"If you know anything, you can help make sure that we stay safe."

"I don't know any more than what you already do. He wouldn't tell me anything. All I knew was that he was going into battle that day, but he assured me that he was going to be safe. He wasn't. He never came home. I don't know anything else."

15

S imran kept his back to the wall as he sipped the dark, earthy beer in his hand. It was similar to some of the drinks that they had on Uoria and it made him feel slightly homesick as he looked out over the party that was unfolding in front of him. It was yet another celebration of the wedding that would be happening in just a few days and he was starting to feel overwhelmed. The bonding of his kind on Uoria was something that happened quickly and only in the privacy of the space the two chose to share with one another. The marriage ritual of Earth, however, was complex and long, focusing far more on the people around the couple and their role in the community and their families rather than just the relationship of the couple itself. He wasn't sure how he felt about the contrast. As much as he liked the idea of friends and families having the opportunity to celebrate the union of two people, it somehow seemed that the union itself got lost among all of the parties, events, and preparations that he was witnessing.

Even as he thought this, his eyes wandered across the room to Jane. She had told him that this party was going to be different than the engagement party that they had hosted for Ty and Samira when they first arrived on Earth. While that party was more about toasting their plan to marry and letting friends and family greet and congratulate them, this party was about having the couple having fun before they "settled down". Simran wasn't entire sure what that was supposed to mean, but he went along with it, wanting to do anything that he could to spend more time with Jane.

Though he hadn't told any of the others yet, he had known since before they even landed that something incredible was going to happen to him during this visit to Earth. In the hours before the ship docked at the university he could feel the tension building in his belly and the heat starting to radiate off of his skin, telling him that his mate was waiting for him and that he would soon find her. He never would have expected to find his mate on Earth. Like the other Denynso warriors, it was just his assumption that he would find the partner who had been intended for him since birth among the women of his clan. Now as he looked at Jane, however, he knew that that was not the way that his life was going to happen.

He had done everything that he could to hide how he was feeling from the rest of the warriors and even from Jane. He knew that most of the warriors pursued their passion for their intended mate as quickly as they could from the moment that they found her. For some they completed their bond in a matter of hours. Though this created a strong, life-long connection between them just as it did for any pair of Denynso mates, it meant getting to know each other after they had already devoted themselves to one another. Simran struggled with the idea of finding that closeness with a woman that he didn't know, even though everything inside of him had compelled him to do just that since he first stepped off of the ship and met Jane.

He had spent the last several days with Jane, and the feelings that he had for her were almost overwhelmingly intense now. He knew now that the desire for her was more than just the urges of his body, but also the longing of his heart and his soul. Though his existence was so incredibly different than hers and he couldn't truly envision what it would mean to spend their lives together, he also couldn't imagine spending the rest of his life without her.

As if she could hear him thinking about her, Jane turned away from the women who she was talking with and smiled at him. She lifted the glass of sparkling wine in her hand like she was waving at him and he returned the gesture with his beer. Jane glanced back at the women and said something, one hand lifting to touch the arm of the woman in front of her. The woman nodded and Jane started across the room toward Simran. The warrior could feel his ever-present erection pressing toward her and was thankful for the tighter undergarments that he had put on so that she didn't notice as she approached him.

Her beautiful face grew brighter the closer she got to him, and when she was only a few steps away she glanced down like she was trying to hide the size of her smile.

"Hi," she said.

"Hi," he replied.

"Are you having fun?"

She took her place beside him, turning so that her back touched the wall like his did, and lifted her glass to her lips.

"Um," Simran said, looking out over the party again. "I think so." His eyes fell on a few of the women from the university climbing up on top of the bar and starting to

dance, the men standing beneath them shouting and cheer-
ing. "Not as much as they are, I'm fairly sure, but fun, yes."

Jane laughed, pulling her glass away from her mouth
and covering it.

"I don't think that anyone has ever had as much fun as
they are," she said.

"It's kind of hard to envision any of those women
working at the university," Simran said. "They don't exactly
seem...academic."

"I wouldn't know," Jane said. "I don't know Samira from
the university."

"That's right," Simran said, remembering what she had
told him about her friendship with Jane. "I keep forgetting
that you and Samira go further back than the university."

"Nope," she said, shaking her head as she watched the
women stumbling across the top of the bar, "and that means
that I don't get the joy of being a part of that delightful
social group."

"Well, that's just a shame."

Simran laughed and nudged her with his elbow. Though
the gesture was playful, it sent a tremble through his body.
Jane seemed to feel something, too, because she looked up
at him with slightly wider eyes and then looked down at her
glass sharply.

"So, there's something else that not being a part of
university has caused for me," she said.

Her voice was slightly softer now and the words came
out almost cautiously, like she suddenly felt nervous about
speaking to him.

"What is that?" he asked.

"I don't know much about you," she said.

"Me?" he asked.

"Your kind," she said by way of explanation. "Samira

mentioned learning about the Denynso a few times, and I know that there was an exchange program set up between the university and Uoria. That's all, though. I don't know anything else about the clan or even your planet."

The tone of her voice sounded like she was really telling him something else, but Simran wasn't sure what that could be.

"Is there something that you'd like to know?" he asked.

He took another sip of his beer as Jane turned to him and let her eyes travel across his face, following the curves of his jaw and then settling into his gaze. She stared at him for a few long moments.

"You remind me of something," she said.

"Of what?" he asked.

She shook her head and narrowed her eyes, staring deeper into him as if he was a filter allowing her to look into memories she couldn't quite touch.

"I don't really know. You just look so familiar, but I can't figure out why. You just remind me of something."

"I hope that it isn't anything bad," Simran said, trying to bring some levity into a moment that was feeling progressively more tense and heavy.

Jane made a sound like she was thinking through what she had said.

"I'm not sure."

16

"Maxim?"

Maxim turned toward Athan's voice and nodded at the man as he approached where Maxim was sitting on the wide back porch of Ellora's house.

"Hello, Athan."

"I came to tell you that I'm leaving."

Maxim stood sharply and took a step toward Athan.

"What do you mean you're leaving? Where are you going?"

"I don't know, but I can't stay here. Now that I've told you everything that I know about your father's death, it isn't safe for me to stay in the kingdom any longer. If the Order finds out, I will be targeted first."

"You can't just leave, Athan. You can't just walk away now."

"I have to, Maxim. It wasn't an easy decision to tell you everything that I have. I truly believed that I was going to bring all of that to my grave with me. When you came back here, though, I knew that that wasn't my choice to make.

What your father told me and what I experienced with him didn't belong to me. Those moments belonged to him, and that means they belong to you and to your mother. I struggled with telling you because of the danger that I knew even saying the words would create, but in the end it is something that I had to do. You deserved to know, and I believe that you will do with it what needs to be done."

"I need your help," Maxim insisted.

"No," Athan said. "You don't need me. I have done my part. There's nothing more than I can do for you."

Athan turned to leave and Maxim took another step forward.

"You owe this to him," Maxim said. "He trusted you. He might not have told you everything, but whatever it is that he chose to keep away from you, he did it for a reason. You know more than anyone, including my mother."

Athan turned back to look at him.

"Aegeus didn't tell your mother what was happening?" he asked.

"No. She only knew that you were going into battle that day and that Papa promised her that he was going to return safely. That's all. Anything else that you know and that you experienced is unique to you. You still hold all of those moments. You might have shared them with me, but that doesn't mean that they left you. You owe it to the trust that my father had in you and everything that you experienced with him to see this through. I understand that you are in danger, but so am I. All of us are now, Athan, and running isn't going to change that. They will come for you. They will find you. You say you didn't have a choice but to tell me what you knew. Now you don't have a choice but to stay and finish this for him."

Before Athan could respond Maxim heard loud footsteps pounding toward them and the door to the porch
swung open. Kyven and Emerie ran out onto the porch and
Maxim saw the frantic look in his brother's eyes.

"Kyven," he said, walking around Athan toward his
brother. "What is it?"

"You need to come with me," Kyven said.

Panic rose in Maxim's chest and he felt a sick feeling roll
through his stomach.

"What is it? Is something wrong with Ivy?"

Despite the hurt and anger that still burned in his chest
for her, his first thought was still to protect the woman who
he deeply loved.

"No," Kyven said. "It isn't Ivy. Just come with me. You, too,
Athan."

Maxim turned to look over his shoulder at Athan. The
older man met his eyes and gave an almost imperceptible
nod, offering his agreement to what Maxim had said. He
nodded back and they followed Kyven back off of the porch
and through their mother's house. He briefly thought that
they were going out the front door, but Kyven suddenly
turned and led them down a narrow hallway that held
Aegeus's private rooms. These had been spaces that they
had rarely been allowed to enter when they were younger
and Maxim felt slightly uncomfortable entering them
even now.

"I started thinking about these rooms and how much
time Papa spent in them when we were younger," Kyven said
as though responding to Maxim's thoughts. "He used to
bring us to Athan's house and down into the tunnels, especially you, but these rooms were off-limits most of the time.
That made me think that there had to be something in here
that was too dangerous for us to ever see."

"Why is she here?" Athan asked, pointing at Emerie.

Maxim saw Emerie's eyes flicker to Kyven and then her take a small step back like she was going to leave, but Kyven reached for her and took her hand.

"Because I asked her to be."

"This isn't the place for human women, Kyven," Athan scolded, but Kyven remained steadfast.

"She is not just a woman, Athan, and you don't have any authority to tell me who I can and can't be with. I'm not a child anymore and you don't need to keep trying to raise me in the place of my father."

The statement fell heavily and painfully around them and Athan took a step back.

"You're right," he said.

"What did you want to show us?" Maxim asked.

Kyven stepped into the second of the small cluster of rooms at the end of the hallway and the others followed him. He walked directly to a narrow door in the corner and opened it. Maxim stepped up close to the doorway and looked into the shallow closet. Kyven flattened his hand on the back wall and pressed. Maxim heard a click and then the wall moved aside, revealing a steep set of stairs leading down into darkness.

"What is this?" he asked.

Kyven looked back at him.

"There's more."

"You went down there?"

Kyven nodded. He reached into the pouch at his hip and withdrew a light stick, illuminating it as he handed it over to Maxim. Maxim took it and held it forward so that the light cut through the darkness of the stairs before starting down them. The air of the staircase was dense and thick. It felt like it carried all of the energy of the years that it had been closed and when Maxim filled his lungs with it he felt a surge of emotion rush through him.

"What is this, Athan?" he demanded.

"I don't know," Athan responded from behind him.

Kyven and Emerie had waited at the top of the stairs, allowing Maxim and Athan to go down first.

"You don't know?" Maxim asked.

"I promise you, Maxim. I have never seen this before. I don't know what this is or what's down here."

Maxim let his hand trail down the wall beside him as he walked down the stairs. He had gone down several steps when he felt the texture of the wall change. He paused and turned the light of the stick to the wall. His fingers followed the shape of a designed carved deeply into the wall and he felt a memory surfacing.

"This symbol," he said, looking back at Athan, "it has something to do with my grandfather."

Athan took another step down the staircase and leaned forward slightly to look at the design more closely. He nodded.

"It was his symbol within the Order," he said. "He must have built this."

"One of his hidden doors," Kyven said.

Maxim turned away from the symbol and continued down the stairs, keeping the light stick ahead of him to illuminate as much of the space as possible. Finally the walls beside him opened and he stepped off of the stairs into what looked like a small, low bunker. When Kyven joined him in the room he touched a panel on the wall beside him and the space filled with light. On the wall in front of him Maxim saw a larger version of his grandfather's symbol painted in gold across a black field. Just beneath it was another symbol painted in silver.

"Do you recognize that symbol?" Athan asked.

"It's my father's," Maxim said. "Kyven, is this what you wanted to show me?" he asked.

Kyven walked past them and Maxim watched as he lifted his hand to touch the symbol that represented their father. For a moment he thought that he was simply touching the shape to feel closer to Aegeus just as he wanted to do, but after a few seconds Kyven drew his hand down from the shape to a section of the wall just beneath it and pressed with his fingertips. A sound behind him made Maxim turn sharply. In the back corner of the room a section of the wall had shifted and moved aside, revealing another doorway.

Maxim crossed to the open section of the wall and looked in. He stepped into the short passageway and immediately the ceiling began to glow much like the tunnels beneath the kingdom. He moved down the passageway as quickly as he could, feeling like he was chasing the light as it glowed briefly above him and then extinguished as it lit up the section in front of him. He felt like he had only gone a few yards when the passageway ended and he found himself in another room, this one even smaller than the first. He stopped in the middle, the breath feeling like it had been torn from his chest and his heart beginning to beat so hard that he could hear the rush of his blood in his ears.

All around him the walls of the room were covered in weapons and armor. He turned slowly, trying to take it all in, trying to make sense of what he was seeing. Athan, Kyven, and Emerie came into the room with him, but he didn't acknowledge them. Instead, he reached forward and ran his fingertips along the edge of one of the long swords suspended on the wall with thick, heavy nails. Even after all of the years that had passed since Aegeus had stepped into that room, the edge of the weapon was still sharp enough to sting on his skin.

"What is this?" Maxim asked, repeating the question that he had asked when they first entered the stairwell, but now directing it to no one in particular. He was answered only by silence and he whipped around to look at the others in the room. "What is this?" he demanded.

"This is how I found it," Kyven told him.

"How did you find it?" Maxim asked.

"It was an accident," Kyven told him. "I went into the room just to see what was there. I thought that maybe I could find something that would help us. When I opened the closet, I noticed that the wall looked too close to the door, like the closet was too small. I touched it and it opened."

"How did you know to open the passageway to this room?"

"I just wanted to touch Papa's symbol," Kyven said softly, affirming what Maxim had felt when he first saw the shape on the wall. "I hadn't seen it in so long. Mama took all of them out of the house after he died and—" his voice trailed off and he took a breath, "I just wanted to feel close to him again."

"Why is all of this still here?" Athan asked, his voice low. "Why wasn't it with him?"

Maxim turned to him, struck by the question that he seemed to be asking himself rather than them.

"What do you mean?" he asked.

Athan looked up at him with questions lingering in his gaze.

"If he built this bunker and prepared it for war, why didn't he bring the weapons and armor with him when he went to war? When we walked into that battle, he only had one sword with him. He went to all of the trouble to build this, but then when he went to face down the enemy, he had nothing."

"What did it look like?" Maxim asked.

"What?" Athan asked.

"His sword. What did it look like?"

"It was just a sword. Just like the ones that the rest of us carried."

"Was it my grandfather's?"

"It might have been."

"My mother always told us that whenever he left home to do something with the Order, he carried my grandfather's sword."

"That's true. It's what he always had with him, so it must have been what he had that day."

"Where is it now?" Maxim asked and watched as Athan's eyes widened slightly, but he didn't respond. "Athan? Where is my grandfather's sword?"

"I don't know," Athan finally replied.

"Had he drawn it before he died?" Maxim asked.

Athan nodded and Maxim watched him walk up to the wall so that he could touch the same sword that he had.

"Yes," Athan said. "He stepped out onto the field and drew his sword. The last thing I saw was him pull it back as the Klimnu descended on him."

"Then he was gone."

"Yes."

"So where is the sword?"

"The Klimnu and their allies could have destroyed his body," Kyven said, "but they couldn't make a sword disappear completely. There would have been something left."

"Did you seen any part of it when you went back to the field to look for his body?" Maxim asked.

Athan turned away from the wall and met Maxim's gaze. "No."

TBC

(To be continued in book VII...)

THE ALIEN'S FINDING

1

Consciousness came to Creia in layers. He felt himself lifting out of the darkness gradually, first aware of the cold air touching his skin and the presence of a soft humming sound somewhere near him. He fought to bring himself further, to remember what had happened to him and what had thrown him into the depth of the darkness and to convince his body to move. He could remember walking through the abandoned remnants of the lost Denynso compound, exploring the houses that had been left behind so suddenly it still felt like there were moments of life lingering there. In the back recesses of his mind he remembered hearing someone come into the house and turning to face them, only to be attacked.

Creia fought to remember something else. He reached for details, to bring anything else into his consciousness that would tell him what was happening to him. Feeling was slowly returning to his body and as it tingled along his fingers and through his blood, the image of the person who had attacked him gradually etched itself into place in his mind. He could see only the silhouette of a being. It was not as tall as him, but still taller than most of the other beings that he encountered, including the humans and the Mikana. The being wore a long, thick cloak that stretched to the floor and covered his hands. A hood came over his head and shadowed his face so that all Creia could see was a black recess. It was a terrifying image that made Creia feel like he wasn't looking at something that was living at all, but the breath and thought of death itself.

The memory of that image brought the panic in Creia's chest to a fevered pitch and he fought harder to bring himself back into his own body. Finally consciousness returned fully and he was aware of the feeling of a cold surface on his back, something beneath his feet propping him up at an angle so that it was as if he were lying down and standing up at the same time. He could feel something hard and tight around his wrists and around his neck, and when he strained against them they only tightened, pulling him back. Finally he was able to open his eyes. They ached as though they had been closed for far longer than he thought, and at first his vision was blurred so that he wasn't able to see where he was.

Creia blinked, squeezing his eyes shut as hard as he could and then opening them again. The action had helped to clear his vision, but he still couldn't tell where he was. The room was so dark he couldn't see anything beyond a few feet in front of him. He looked down at himself and saw that he was chained to a metal bed that was tilted, only the chains and a platform beneath his feet holding him in the near-standing position.

"Where am I?" he shouted into the darkness.

Though he felt like he had forced the words out as loudly as he could, they came through his tight, painful throat sounding hoarse and quiet. He drew in a breath and felt his lungs burn as they expanded. He forced himself to shout again, but only silence responded. He started feeling dizzy and his body trembled against the metal of the table that propped him up. Creia tried once more to scream out to anyone who may be nearby, but the words tumbled from his dry lips like powder and he felt the darkness descend on him again like a black cloud rolling up his body, stealing first his feeling and then his consciousness.

The next time that Creia awoke it was in one sudden, frightening moment. Rather than each little piece of himself coming back gradually, everything hit him at once so that he was suddenly aware of a hand on his forehead, shoving his head backwards and forcing it to tilt. Water rushed across his lips and down his neck, seeping back into his nose so that he choked and gasped. Gasping opened his mouth so that some of the water rushed inside and slid down his throat. Even with the painful choking, the wash of the water was soothing and he began to swallow eagerly.

When the flow of the water stopped, Creia opened his eyes and found himself staring up into the dark recess of the hooded cloak. He tried to reach forward to push away the cloak so that he could see who it was who was holding him there, but the chains on his wrists were still there, shackling him in place so that he could move only a matter of inches.

"Who are you?" he asked, the water having softened his mouth and throat enough that he could speak more loudly and confidently.

The cloaked figure didn't respond, but stepped away from the metal bed into the shadows that surrounded him. Criea dropped his head back to try to see where the hooded creature had gone, but he saw only a dim light hanging a few feet above him. He noticed movement on the edges of the illumination around him and realized that the creature had come behind him. A dark-gloved hand reached across the faint light and grabbed a device that hung beside it. Creia struggled as he saw the hand bringing the device closer to him, trying to fight it, but he couldn't get his head far enough away. The metal cuffs around his wrists cut into his skin as he thrashed against them, but the pain didn't matter to him.

"Who are you?" he demanded again. "What are you doing?"

The creature again didn't respond, but pulled the unknown device down closer and turned it so that Creia could see that it was a flattened screen and a set of diodes attached to long black cords. He brought the cords down on either side of Creia's head and pressed the diodes into place on his temples.

"Stop," he demanded. "Get those off of me. What are you doing?"

The creature didn't heed anything he said. He reached above Creia's head again and took the screen down so that it was in front of Creia's face. For several long moments the screen was completely black. In an instant, though, a bright image appeared on it, stinging Creia's eyes with the intensity of the light and forcing him to squint to filter it. When they grew accustomed to the glow, Creia slowly opened his eyes all the way again and looked at the image.

The screen showed what looked like a large, brightly lit room. The floor was a shiny white expanse flecked with grey and shimmering brushed metal tables sat along the center. He didn't recognize the space and couldn't figure out what he was supposed to be getting out of the image. The longer he stared at it, the more details he noticed. The far wall of the room was lined with white boards covered in indecipherable notes and shapes. Bottles and vials covered one end of one of the tables and another seemed to hold several boxes that glowed from the inside.

Creia noticed something in the far corner of the room, seemingly out of the bright lights of the rest of the room, and he narrowed his eyes at it, trying to make out what it was. It appeared to be a rounded tube that stretched from the floor to the ceiling. It had a faint blue glow that came from the bottom and in that glow Creia could see that there was something within the tube. Whatever it was inside the tube was chained around its wrists and neck like he was, but there was no table at his back to support it. Instead, there was an additional chain around the being's waist and another around its legs.

For a moment Creia was not sure that whatever was inside the tube was still alive. It hung from its chains as if it had no strength within it, its head forward and its arms pulled slightly up from its shoulders. The thought made a tremor of fear and disgust roll through him and he tried to look away. Turning his head, however, just meant that the screen went with him and as he watched, the thing moved slightly. As if in response to Creia's acknowledgement of his existence, the creature straightened just a small amount and lifted its head just enough so that it was above his shoulder height.

Creia wished that he could see more detail of the creature. He wanted to know what it was, and why it had been captured as he had. He didn't understand who could be interested in imprisoning him and what whoever it was could possibly think that he was going to get from him, or from the other creature that was dangling, seemingly only moments from death, in that strange room.

2

"Do you want to dance with me?" Jane asked.

Simran looked down at her and then back out over the rest of the group crowded into the bar as they celebrated the impending wedding. He looked back at her and saw a hint of a sparkle in her eyes.

"You do know what dancing is, don't you?" she asked.

He opened his mouth and closed it again, trying to come up with some kind of response, but then realized that there was nothing that he could say and shook his head.

"No," he admitted. "Not really."

"You don't dance on Uoria?" Jane asked.

"No. I've heard about dancing. The human women talked about it while they were on the compound and they even tried to teach a few of the warriors."

"How did that go?" Jane asked with the hint of a laugh in her voice.

"Not terribly well," Simran responded. "The Denynso warriors are made for power and fighting, not really so much for grace and smoothness."

Jane laughed and turned so that her back was to the

others and she faced him. She reached her hands toward him and smiled.

"It isn't hard," she told him. "Just come try."

"I don't know," he said.

He had done many things in his life that would have terrified others to their bones, but this was something that he didn't feel like he could face. The thought of being so close to her, even touching her, in front of others was something that he didn't want to contemplate.

"Come on," Jane said. "It's fun. Besides, just about everyone here is so drunk that they probably won't even notice that you are dancing, much less if you are doing it well or not." He hesitated and she gave him a slightly pouty look. "Please?"

He knew that he couldn't resist her. There wasn't anything that he wouldn't do for her, even if that meant risking certain humiliation not just with his completely out of control dance stylings, but with the arousal that was becoming increasingly obvious with every passing moment. Hopefully she was right and the rest of the party-goers had gone beyond the point of compromise when it came to their alcohol consumption and wouldn't really be paying attention to what was going on around them. He did take some comfort in knowing that even if the Denynso who were in attendance weren't able to consume enough that they would be impaired, if they did notice that he was experiencing the intense, unrelenting erection that came from being near his mate for the first time they wouldn't really care. He still wanted to be able to keep the reality of Jane private until he was able to tell her how he felt about her, but if a few of the warriors noticed, at least he wouldn't be completely humiliated.

Jane shook her hands slightly as if giving the gesture of

offering her hands more insistence and Simran reached forward to rest his hands in hers. She smiled and moved backwards a few steps toward the dance floor before turning around and taking just one of his hands to guide him the rest of the way. A few other couples were scattered around the floor and Simran noticed that he was not the first of the Denynso to be lured out onto the floor to attempt dancing. A couple of the other warriors were with their mates or other of the partygoers and attempting to follow the rhythm of the music that was thumping around them in whatever somewhat spastic ways they can think of. The image was reassuring and he let Jane pull him a little closer.

"Just move," she said. "It doesn't really matter how. You can just stand there and sway if you want to."

Simran laughed and started moving around in what felt like completely odd and nonsensical ways, but Jane nodded.

"There you go," she said, starting to move in ways that closely mimicked his own but that seemed a bit more controlled.

They kept going through the rest of the song and then into another. Simran saw her take a step toward him.

"Guess what?" she said.

"What?" he said, his movements faltering for a moment as he worried that she was going to tell him how ridiculous he looked.

"You're dancing."

Simran laughed and reached for her, taking her by her hips and pulling her up against him without thinking about what the motion would mean. Jane gasped as her body came into contact with his and she looked up at him with eyes filled with wonder. For a brief moment Simran tried to figure out a way that he could explain away the pressure of his erection that he knew she was feeling in her belly, but the words didn't come. Instead, he felt his eyes slumber and his body responding to hers even more strongly.

"Jane..." he started.

"Your skin is so warm," she murmured.

Simran nodded. They had stopped moving and he started again, swaying ever so slightly to the beat of the music. It was just enough so that he could feel her breasts moving against his chest and her hips brushing his. The feeling was pushing him closer and closer to the edge of his control and he took a breath to quiet the need surging through him.

"Only you can touch me right now," he said softly.

"What you do you mean?" she asked, not taking her eyes away from him.

"My skin only feels warm to you, but to any other woman that tried to touch me it would be so hot that it would burn her."

"Really?" Jane asked.

Simran nodded and dipped his head down slightly so that he could speak to her more easily without having to raise his voice enough that others might hear what he was going to say to her.

"You are the only woman in existence that could be this close to me right now, and you are the only one who I will ever want to be this close to me."

Jane glanced back toward where Ty was sitting on a stool by the bar with Samira in his lap and then back at Simran.

"Will you come back to my house with me and explain it?" she asked her voice softer now and filled with an emotion that sounded slightly nervous.

She was running her hands along his arms, watching their progression across his skin as if transfixed by this strange new ability that she had just learned that she had.

Simran nodded and she stepped back from him, taking his hand again and guiding him away from the dance floor and toward the exit. He didn't bother to let anyone know that they were leaving. He didn't care if anyone noticed they were missing or not. All that he could focus on in that moment was the need for her that was coursing through his body and the feeling of her hand in his.

3

They rode in silence through the city and out into one of the tightly packed neighborhoods that stretched out from it. Simran was amazed at how heavily populated the areas of Earth that he had seen were. It wasn't like Uoria where parts of the planet were open and barren, beautiful and strange in how untouched they were, and where the compounds where the species did live were made so that there were still sections where there are no buildings or interruptions to the natural layout of the land. It wasn't like that here. Instead it seemed that every foot of the planet had been touched and changed in some way. If there wasn't a home, a store, or a government building there, there was a paved road, a monument, or some other reminder that the humans had taken over the land completely and irreparably. It was at once fascinating and unnerving. Simran found the complexity and surrounding feeling interesting, but at the same time it was overwhelming to never feel like he was away from others. He couldn't imagine living in a place where he couldn't open his eyes without seeing someone else who was so close it was almost like they were using his very space.

Finally Jane pulled her car into the driveway of a small house and pressed a button above her to open the door to the small building in front of her. She drove directly into it and pressed the button again and Simran watched the door slide back into place. The engine quieted and Jane turned to him.

"Here we are," she said softly.

"This is your house?" he asked.

"Well," she said, "kind of. I live a couple hours away. This is my cousin's house, though, and he always lets me stay here when I'm visiting."

"He won't mind if we are here?" Simran asked.

He felt a slightly sick feeling settle in his stomach as he worried that the house not being hers would mean that they wouldn't have any privacy. Even if this wasn't the night when they were meant to complete their bond, he still wanted to be able to spend some time just with her. Jane shook her head.

"No," she reassured him. "He isn't here this week. It'll be just us."

They looked at each other for a few moments before she reached down and released the button on her seatbelt. Simran followed her lead and they both climbed out of the car, closing the doors behind them. Jane led him up a short flight of wooden steps and unlocked the door at the top. They stepped into the house and Simran looked around.

"Does this look anything like the houses on Uoria?" she asked.

"Not really," Simran said. "Similar, I guess, but not quite. We don't use electricity or have the appliances that you do."

"Really?" she asked. "I always thought that other planets were so much more technologically advanced than Earth."

She got a shocked, embarrassed look on her face and he heard her stumbling like she was trying to backtrack what she had said. He laughed and shook his head.

"It's fine," he said. "Uoria is very different from Earth. There are many different species and each kind of lives their own life. There isn't much cooperation or interaction. At least, there hasn't been until recently. The Denynso have an understanding of the technology and could use it if we wanted to, I suppose, but we have always lived this way and I guess we just don't see the point in changing it. We use the sun to fill batteries that power our lights and heat our water. We have luminescent plants for when the weather has been bad and there hasn't been enough sun to completely recharge the batteries. We use other fuels for our cooking and other tasks. It works for us."

Jane nodded.

"That's good," she said. She walked further into the house and Simran followed her. "Do you want to sit down?" she asked, gesturing to a large sofa in the middle of the living room.

"Sure."

They sat down together and Simran turned to her, ready to finally tell her what he had been feeling for her and what she meant to him. It was a conversation that he had never really thought his way through. Like the other warriors, he had always assumed that he was going to mate with a Denynso woman who would already understand the ways of their kind and have no questions about it. Now that he was faced with the reality that his intended mate was not one of the Denynso women but a human woman, he realized that he was going to have to explain the ways of his kind to her and simply hope that she was able to process and accept it. Though it was all he had ever known before the humans arrived, and not something that ever seemed odd to him, he was coming to realize that the mating traditions of the Denysno were not anything like those of other species, particularly the humans. Having to try to put words to the process and its meaning suddenly felt daunting, but he knew that he might as well just dive in and let it unfold in the way that it was going to. Her rejecting him would be the most painful and inescapable thing that he would ever experience in his life, but that was simply something that he was going to have to face. He wasn't going to know if she would accept him if he didn't give her the opportunity to. He drew in a breath.

"Jane," he started.

"Tell me how Samira and Ty met," Jane said, her voice overlapping with his.

They laughed.

"I'm sorry," Simran said. "What were you saying?"

"Um," she said, looking down at her lap, "I was just asking how Samira and Ty met. She just told me that she met him while she was on Uoria, but I didn't really understand the whole situation. Could you tell me?"

Simran nodded.

"She joined Zuri when she returned to Uoria after coming back to Earth briefly."

"Why did she come back? I thought that the exchange program was supposed to last for a few months for each of the participants."

"It is," Simran said, "but there was a special circumstance."

"What special circumstance?"

"She had only been on the planet for one day when she

was attacked by our greatest enemy." Jane gasped and Simran nodded again. "The reason that the Klimnu attacked her, however, is that she had run into the woods after hearing the man who was her intended mate was making fun of her because of her size."

"Her intended mate?" Jane asked.

Simran realized that he had unintentionally broached the very topic that he had wanted to discuss with her.

"Yes," he said. "Just like Ty is for Samira, Ero is Zuri's mate. Each Denynso warrior has one and only one intended mate. It is that person who he is waiting for from the moment that he is born and the person who, if she accepts him, he will remain devoted to throughout the rest of his life. She is his world and his meaning for being. She becomes the central focus of his life and every choice, every decision; every breath for the rest of his life will revolve around her."

"There's only one?" Jane asked.

"Yes," Simran replied. "In all the world, in all of creation, in all of existence, there is only one other person who can be the mate of each Denynso warrior."

"And if he doesn't find her?"

"He will live out his life alone, longing for her."

"And when he does?"

"It is one of the most important moments in his life."

"How will he know?"

"There are signs," he said.

"Tell me," she said.

"His skin will become intensely hot, especially when she is nearby. It will be so hot that no other woman will be able to get close to him, much less touch him."

"Like yours is right now," she said.

"Yes."

"What else?"

"His eyes will start changing color. They will shift from the color that they have been since he was born to bright orange."

"Look at me." Simran lifted his eyes so that he was looking directly into Jane's and heard her take in a breath. "Is there anything else?"

"Yes," Simran said. "He will need her. With every fiber of his being he will need to be with her. He will ache for her until he is able to be with her. Once he is, their bond is complete and nothing can separate them."

"Ache for her?" Jane asked.

Her voice was breathless now and when Simran focused in on her with his elevated senses he was able to hear her heartbeat pounding rapidly in her chest. She licked her lips and Simran trembled slightly. He couldn't hold himself back from her any longer. He slid closer to her on the couch and reached for her hand. Meeting her eyes with even more intensity, he brought her hand forward and pressed it to the swell of his erection. She gasped, but he didn't feel her pulling away. He let his hand fall away from hers and felt her stroke her hand along him cautiously, almost experimentally. An involuntary moan fell from his lips and he saw a hint of color cross her cheeks.

"Jane, I don't want you to feel like I am trying to..."

"I don't think that you are trying to do anything," she said, cutting him off. "I know what I am feeling for you, and if you are feeling anything even close to that, then I want to know why."

"I know why," he said.

"Tell me," she said. "I want to hear you say it."

"You are meant to be my mate, Jane. I have known since

the moment that I saw you and I have wanted to tell you every moment that we have spent together since then."

"Why didn't you tell me sooner?" she asked.

"I wanted a chance to get to know you better. I didn't want you to think that I was trying to force you into anything, or that I had just come here for this wedding with the intention of having fun with some random girl and then going home to my planet and going about my life without ever thinking about her again."

"I would never think that you could do that," she said. "I would never believe that you would be able to hurt someone that badly."

"You might be surprised at what the Denynso are capable of doing," he said.

She shook her head.

"No," she said. "I don't care what you do when you are in battle. I can look into your eyes and know that you would never pretend to care about someone if you didn't. I also know that I have never seen Samira as happy as she is now with Ty, and that she told me that she knew as soon as she met him that they were supposed to be together. She was feeling for him what I am feeling for you now."

Simran leaned forward and softly touched his lips to hers. It was a cautious kiss, purposely brief as to give her the opportunity to evaluate what she felt when he did it and then chose how she wanted to proceed. Even though she had expressed that she was having feelings for him, he didn't want to make any assumptions and press too far. He let his forehead rest against hers and they both took in a few slow breaths. Finally he felt her come forward and press her mouth to his again. He wrapped an arm around Jane's waist and drew her closer to him, coaxing her lips apart with the tip of his tongue so that he could deepen their kiss.

Their mouths explored each other for several seconds before he pulled away.

"I never told you how Samira and Ty met," he said.

"Do you really want to tell me now?" Jane asked.

Simran smiled and shook his head.

"No," he said.

"Good," she replied and caught his mouth again.

Jane's arms reached up to wrap around his neck and Simran swept her up and into his lap. Their kisses were deep and exploratory, but without any rush behind them. Each movement was careful and precise, enabling them to savor every moment that they were experiencing together. Suddenly this incredible woman was sharing his space and Simran not only didn't mind it, he didn't want it to end any time soon.

Their kiss parted again and Jane looked into his eyes.

"Would you like to come upstairs with me?" she asked.

Simran didn't reply, but scooped her up into his arms and started for the stairs that they had walked past on their way through the house. He rushed up them three at a time and when he got to the landing at the top she directed him where to go until he got to a partially open bedroom door. He pushed the door the rest of the way open with his foot and stepped inside the room. It was decorated in shades of white and blue, creating a feeling of peaceful calm.

Simran lowered Jane carefully to her feet and looked down at her with seriousness in his eyes.

"I need you to tell me that you understand what I told you," he said. "I need to know that you know what all of this means."

"I understand," she said.

"You understand that this is a life-changing and inalterable decision? Once you are my mate that will never change."

"I never want it to," she said. "I am not going into this lightly, Simran. I want to be with you. I have felt since the moment that we met that there was something about you so familiar. Maybe it wasn't that it was familiar, but that it was something in you reaching out to me. That part of you that has always been waiting for me spoke to a part of me that I didn't even know about; a part of me that somehow knew that there was something more for my life than what I thought. I know that this is a decision that will alter my life, but my life was changed the moment that I met you. I never want it to change back. I never want to be away from you."

Simran felt overcome with emotion. He had always known that the experience of finding his mate would be something powerful, but he never expected it to be like this. This was more than he could have ever anticipated, and more than he truly knew how to process. All he could do was let himself fall into the rush of emotion and need that was threatening to overwhelm him and let life change around him.

He dipped his head down and captured Jane's mouth. She willingly opened it to him, letting her tongue glide across his. They undressed each other slowly, allowing their fingers and lips to trace the skin that they exposed as each button opened and each garment fell away. Soon they were bare in front of one another and Simran traced her body with his eyes. She was the most beautiful thing that he had ever seen and he wanted to just stand for a moment and drink her in.

Jane looked away shyly and Simran lowered to his knees in front of her. He brought his mouth down to her belly and kissed it softly. The tip of his tongue slid along her skin and he moved his mouth up to her breast, taking it in and licking a tight circle around her nipple. She gasped, her fingers burying themselves in his hair and holding his head in place. Simran continued to lavish attention on that breast for a few more moments before moving over to the other to repeat his actions. When her nipples were taut with desire and he could see the flush of arousal across her chest, he moved his mouth down, kissing a path along her belly and occasionally stopping to blow a stream of cool air along her newly damp skin.

He finally made it to the valley between her hipbones and brushed his face along the soft curve of her belly there. His hands came to her hips to hold her still as he nipped his teeth playfully on her skin. The smell of her need for him rose up to him and Simran felt his body clench. He lowered his face down and dipped his tongue into the apex of her thighs, groaning as he gathered the taste of her into his mouth. He repeated the action, bringing his tongue further into her folds, and was rewarded with a gasping cry from Jane. Her hands dropped to his shoulders and he could feel her fingertips squeezing into his skin as he continued to explore her hot, wet core with his tongue.

After a few moments Jane's legs began to tremble and Simran took his mouth from her body, replacing his tongue with the pad of his thumb on the tight pearl he had coaxed forward with his patient attention. He circled his thumb slowly as he led her back toward the bed and then lifted her so that he could position her with her head rested on the pillows. She reached her arms up to him and he lowered himself over her, enveloping her body with his.

Using his legs to ease her knees apart, Simran stared down into Jane's eyes and finally allowed his hard, seeking cock to slip into her. They both moaned as he sank slowly within her and he had to bite his lip to maintain control as the feeling of her tight walls closed around his erection. She fit him tightly but perfectly and he settled completely within her until their bodies melded as one.

Simran rested his forehead to hers and remained still for a moment to give her body a chance to become accustomed to him. When he felt her relax just enough that he could move easily, he began to roll his hips. Jane writhed beneath him, her silky skin gliding across his and the scent of her raising around him so that he was completely surrounded by her. She lifted her leg and hooked it over his hip, granting him greater access to her and making each long stroke deeper and more intense. Soon he couldn't control himself any longer. Simran increased his pace and pushed harder, deeper into her until each thrust was greeted with a high, sharp cry and Jane's eyes closed as her back arched so that her breasts crushed into him.

Suddenly she screamed out and Simran felt her body squeeze tightly around him as her climax washed over her. The feeling of her pleasure pulsing around him overcame Simran and he felt himself spiral into oblivion, crashing into a series of strong pulses that met each of her spasms as he spilled into her. He felt the change come over them. The passionate feeling for her had increased indescribably and now instead of just knowing that he would feel the unbreakable connection to her and absolute devotion to her safety and happiness, he felt it. She had fulfilled a place within him that had always been empty, and for the first time he felt truly complete. He had never realized that it had been there, but now that the emptiness within him was gone, he felt just how deep it had been.

Simran curled onto his side and pulled Jane in close to him so that he cradled her against him with no space between their bodies. He could feel her relax into him and her breaths gradually slow and deepen as she fell asleep in his arms.

Several hours later Simran woke to the cold feeling of Jane's body no longer being tucked against his. He sat up sharply, but found her sitting on the end of the bed, a large book sitting in her lap. He slid toward her and curled on his side so that his stomach touched her back and he could look around her at the book she was examining.

"Hi," she said.

"Hi," he said, kissing her arm. "What are you doing?"

"This was my great-grandfather's scrapbook. I looked at it all the time when I was a little girl. It's full of all kinds of pictures and documents and notes. He loved to keep things. He lived with my grandparents who watched me when my parents were working. When I was over there my great-grandfather would sit with me and we would go through all of the pages together. I was really young, but I can still remember him telling me stories about the things that he kept in here. When he died, my grandfather gave it to me."

"Why are you looking at it?" Simran asked.

"He seemed to have a story for just about every little thing that was in here. Even the tiniest ticket stub or piece of napkin or pressed flower had a tale attached to it that he would tell me in elaborate detail. There was a picture, though, that he would never talk about. He completely avoided it when we were going through the book together and the one time that I asked him about it, he just stared at it for a minute, touched it, and then told me that he didn't remember what it was or why it was even in the book."

"He never took it out, though?"

"No," she said, turning another page. "I always figured that that meant something, but he died before I was ever able to get him to tell me what it was or why he kept it in his scrapbook."

"So why are you looking for it now?" Simran asked.

"Do you remember when I told you that there was something about you that was so familiar but that I couldn't figure it out?" she asked.

"Yes," Simran said, "but then you said that you didn't think that it was actually that I reminded you of something that you couldn't figure out."

"I know, and I still believe that much of it is simply that we were supposed to be together, but that isn't it. It occurred to me when I woke up what I had been thinking about."

She flipped another couple of pages and then paused, resting her hand to one of the pages. She took a breath as if the memories of that book had filled her. Sliding her hand off of the page, she turned the book slightly so that he could see it clearly. Simran felt the breath catch in his throat as he looked down at it. The picture was yellowed with age and the clothing on the people in it told him that it was many decades old. It showed three men standing against a blank wall, and in the middle of them stood a far taller, broader figure with the long white hair and piercing eyes of a Denynso.

4

"You have to listen to me, Mama," Maxim insisted, following his mother into the kitchen and watching as she looked around, struggling to find something to do that would distract her from the conversation.

"No, Maxim," she said, her voice tense with emotion. "I don't have to listen to you. We've had this conversation and I have told you more times that I care to think about that I don't want to talk about this. I didn't want to talk to you about it then, I don't want to talk to you about it now. I will never want to talk to you about it and I would thank you to show me the respect of accepting that and just leaving me alone.

"I can't just leave you alone about this," Maxim said, stepping up closer to her. "We found a secret passage off of one of Papa's rooms that had Grandfather's symbol on the wall."

"You know that your grandfather delighted in making those passageways. There are more of those throughout this kingdom than I think that anyone would ever be able to find."

"But this one led down to a room that had his symbol and Papa's. There was a hidden room that Kyven found accidentally." Maxim took a breath. He knew that his mother wasn't going to respond well to his continued story, but he couldn't stop now. He had to keep going. "It was full of weapons."

"Weapons?" Ellora asked, looking at Maxim with a softly startled expression in her eyes that told him that, if only for a moment, he had gotten through to her. Then she shook her head and waved her hand like she was trying to wave him away. "Your father died in battle. That was something that he and every other member of the Order knew was a possibility. It was their responsibility to take care of the kingdom, and that meant sometimes going to war. Of course that meant that they would have weapons. Don't you know that that is why the young members of the Order today are not allowed to be married or have families? It became too difficult to explain away their deaths."

"I know all of that," Maxim said. "Athan told me."

"You've been talking to Athan again."

It was said as a statement rather than a question and Maxim could see the painful blend of emotion in her eyes.

"Yes, Mama. He knows more about what happened to Papa than anyone else and I want to know."

"I know what happened to your father, Maxim."

"Do you?" he asked.

Ellora took a breath and looked away as if trying to gather the strength to continue with the conversation.

"When Athan came to the door that night, I already knew what he was going to tell me. I didn't want to believe it, but there was no other reason that he would be coming here. Before he left for that battle, your father promised me that everything was going to be fine and that he would come home to me just like he always did. There was something different about it that time, though. Usually when he left, he was incredibly serious and focused. The only thing that could break it was you two boys and saying goodbye to me. That time, though, he wasn't like that. There was a different feeling about him. It was almost like he was excited about something. He wasn't focused. He hadn't put himself into the mindset that he always said that he needed to when he was going to fight. It just didn't feel right. When I opened the door that night and I saw Athan, I felt like my heart had left my body. I knew then that your father was gone. His mind wasn't in the fight that day and they overcame him. That's all there is to it."

"Are you saying that it was his fault that he was killed in that battle?" Maxim asked.

"What?" Ellora asked.

She sounded hurt by the accusation, but Maxim didn't stop.

"You said that he was different before he left. That he didn't have his head in the battle like he always did and that it allowed the enemy to overcome him. Are you blaming him for his death?"

"That's not what I meant, Maxim. I can't keep talking about this."

She pushed past him and stalked back out of the kitchen, heading down the hallway toward her bedroom.

"He had Grandfather's sword with him."

Ellora stopped, but didn't turn around to face him.

"He did?" she asked.

"Yes. Athan told me. He carried that sword into battle just like he always did, but it disappeared the same way that he did. There was absolutely nothing of it left after the battle. You know as well as I do how strong that sword was. Grandfather forged it himself and there was nothing that could destroy it so completely that Athan wouldn't have been able to find at least part of it when he went back to look for Papa after the battle."

"Someone could have stolen it," she said.

"No, Ellora."

Maxim turned toward the sound of Athan's voice and saw him walking out of the front room of the house toward Ellora. She took a step back from him and Maxim could see emotion crackling between them.

"Athan, what are you doing here?"

"Your sons deserve to know what happened to their father, Ellora. And you deserve to know what happened to your husband."

"I know what happened to him. He died in that battle. Why dwell on it anymore? What good does it do to keep digging into it? You are doing nothing but hurt me and my sons."

"It's not knowing what happened that is hurting us," Kyven said, coming to Athan's side. "Maxim and I grew up wishing that we had a better idea as to what happened to our father. We didn't even have a body to bury and we never knew why. You said that it was different the night that Papa left for the battle and said goodbye to you. You're right. It was. Before each time that he left, he would tell us where he was going, why he was going, and when he was going to come back. Always."

"He didn't tell us that time," Maxim said. "He told us that he was leaving, but when we asked why, he just walked away."

"Some things just shouldn't be shared with children.

Maybe he finally realized that what he had been telling you boys was inappropriate and he didn't want to frighten you."

"You don't find it strange that he was so different to all of us that time? That the one time that he changed the way that he said goodbye to us was the time that he died?"

"Maxim, I don't know what your father was thinking the night that he left us to report to that battle. I don't know why he changed how he spoke to us or why he said any of the things that he did. Maybe he didn't actually change anything. Maybe he said different things and acted a different way each time that he left, but we are only remembering it seeming strange that time because he never came home."

"But you yourself said that he was always the same way. We were just little so it makes sense that we might not remember everything exactly the right way, but you weren't. You were an adult. You would remember what he said and how he said it when he left to serve with the Order, and you would remember why that particular night stood out."

"I don't want to talk about this anymore," Ellora said, sounding defeated. "That day in that battle those creatures didn't just kill your father. They killed me. The only reason that I have been able to keep going all of these years is because I had to be a mother for you and for Kyven. It distracted me enough that I was able to put most of that pain and emptiness in the back of my mind and pretend that it wasn't there. It never went away. I was just able to not feel all of it for a little while. Now that you are insisting on bringing all of this up again, and now I'm having to feel it all fresh. It is like he dies again every time that you try to talk to me about it. He's gone, Maxim. No matter what took him or why, he's gone. Talking about it and trying to get answers isn't going to bring him back. It won't fix anything. Why can't you just stop? Please, just stop."

"Listen to me, Ellora," Athan said. "I remember you. I remember you from long ago before any of this happened. I remember the sparkle in your eyes and the smoothness of your skin. I remember the way that you laughed and the light that came from your smile. When I knew you, I knew a woman who was stronger than most of the men I knew and more playful than the children. I also knew a woman whose heart was compassionate and open. You dreamed of a planet that was at peace, where everyone was united and no one had to be afraid. You wanted your children to grow up where they would be able to know the others that shared Uoria as their home and would have all of the opportunities that were available to them. What happened to that dream?"

"That dream was a ridiculous flight of fantasy from a young woman who didn't yet know what the world was really like."

"That dream was something that could have happened. Every time that you refuse to help us, though, you are making it so that it never will. You are making a planet that is already in torment worse, and ensuring that what your husband gave his life for will never come to be."

Ellora looked into the eyes of each of her sons and then looked back at Athan.

"It's gone, Athan. That dream and everything that I thought that I believed are gone. Please. I can't do this anymore. I can't keep living through this again and again."

"I'm sorry, Mama," Kyven said, "but we aren't going to stop."

"You might want to close your eyes and pretend that there isn't something more to this than what you see," Maxim added, "but we aren't going to."

"We are going to find out what happened and why, and we are going to figure out how to resolve it," Athan said. "Even if that means that we have to do it by ourselves."

Ellora shook her head and walked away from them, rushing the rest of the way down the hallway and slamming the door of her bedroom. Maxim could hear the sound of her sobs and remembered listening to her cry just like that for months after his father died. She wouldn't let her sons see the devastation that she was facing during the day, but at night when she went to bed and felt alone in the privacy and emptiness of her bedroom, she would pour out the emotion that she held within her, gasping out the tears until she finally fell asleep.

5

Feeling drained and defeated, Maxim followed Kyven and Athan out of the house and into the purple light of the setting sun. He missed Ivy more deeply at that moment than he could have imagined. He wanted to hold her, to lose himself in the sound of her heartbeat and the smell of her skin and to forget what was happening around him, if only for a brief moment. The lack of her presence was tangible, and so painful that it took his breath out of his lungs. In that way he felt he could commiserate with his mother more than he used to. He knew that Ivy was still somewhere in the kingdom, close enough to him that he could likely find her in a matter of minutes if he searched, and he still felt like he was barely existing. He couldn't even begin to imagine the level of pain that must come with his mother knowing that she would never speak to or hold her husband again. She could think of him and long for him, but she knew that he was completely out of her reach. The thought was overwhelming. He knew in that moment that he wouldn't be able to stay away from her.

He turned away from his brother and Athan to walk

toward the houses where he knew that the others of their travel group were staying. As if his longing had called out to her, Ivy was standing at the edge of the houses, her hands clasped in front of her. He stopped and stared at her. There was a moment when it felt as though time had slowed and they were being held in place. Finally it broke and she ran toward him, her arms held out. He swept her up into his arms, cradling her close and tucking his head into the curve of her neck and shoulder so that he could breathe in the scent of her.

"I'm sorry," she murmured against him.

"You have nothing to be sorry about," Maxim whispered back to her. "I understand what you are feeling. I know that you are just worried about me, and I can't tell you how much I love you. Not just for that, but for everything. Everything you are, everything that you have been for me. I love you."

"I love you, too. I love you for all that you have done for my life and all that you are doing to protect your family and your planet. I love you."

"I don't know what I'm doing or if it is going to accomplish anything, but as long as you are standing beside me, I know that I can keep going."

"I will always stand beside you. It tore my heart out to be away from you and I never want that to happen again. I don't care what I have to do or where I have to be. I will do whatever I need to do to be with you."

She pulled back away from the embrace and looked into his face.

"Were you just talking to your mother?"

Maxim nodded.

"I need to tell you about something."

He took her by her hand and guided her away from the

houses, not wanting to be close enough that someone might over hear them. Athan walked up beside him as he was telling Ivy everything that they had found in the bunker and about his grandfather's sword.

"Kyven has gone to get Emerie," he said, "I think that we need to go to my house and talk about this."

His eyes darted around them suspiciously and Maxim looked at him quizzically.

"Why did Kyven go get Emerie?" he asked.

"Just come with me," Athan said. "I'll explain when we are sure that we are alone."

They rushed across the kingdom to Athan's house and took the places that they had assumed more frequently in the last few days than Maxim could remember in his entire life. He reached over and held Ivy's hand in his, letting just the reality of her skin against his provide comfort and calm. Athan paced back and forth across the room until Kyven and Emerie finally came in. Emerie looked confused and frightened, but she settled down beside Kyven and turned her attention to Athan with an expression that held a complex blend of emotions that Maxim couldn't quite unravel.

"What is going on, Athan?" Maxim asked.

"I can't stop thinking about what your mother said."

"What did she say?" Emerie asked.

"She said that she knew that there was something different about that time that Aegeus left for battle, and that she knew that it wasn't like the other times."

"I don't understand," Kyven said.

"We said the same thing," Maxim said. "He was different when he said goodbye to us, too."

"That's the thing," Athan said. "He didn't talk to you the way that he did when he was going into battle. He always said the same things to you when he knew that he was going to fight. Why would he suddenly change what he said? What did he know about the enemy that we were going to fight that made him change how he looked at that battle?"

"And why did he have a bunker filled with weapons that he kept hidden, but didn't bring any of them with him?" Maxim asked.

"I don't know for sure about anything," Athan said, "but what I do know is that all of this has to do with the Klimnu. What we know about those creatures is limited. Maybe if we spoke to someone who knows more about them than we do we will be able to figure out what it was that Aegeus found out, and what he had planned."

"Are there any members of the Order who were around during that battle who are still alive and will talk to you?"

"No," Athan said, shaking his head. "Remember, Aegeus was extremely secretive about everything that he found out. The Order was highly divided over the issue of the Klimnu and no one wanted to talk about it. There wasn't even anyone then who I would have trusted to talk to about what was going on except your father."

"The Klimnu are gone. Who is left that we could possibly talk to?" Ivy asked.

Even as she finished asking the question, however, Maxim saw her eyes widen as realization settled in. She looked to him and he looked at Athan.

"Creia," he said.

Athan nodded.

"He has had interactions with the Mikana and the Klimnu for many years. He knows more of them than even I do, I would venture to say. Maybe he knows something that would help us to understand how the Klimnu fight."

"Any of the Denynso warriors could tell us that," Maxim

said. "I can probably tell you better than anyone that those warriors are fierce. They have fought the Klimnu extensively and they would know how they behave and how they operate in battle."

"But Creia knew them first," Ivy said. "One of the human women who came to live in the compound, Eliana, told us about being captured by the Klimnu. When she was imprisoned by them they told her how they used to be beautiful and happy," she said as she looked at Maxim and reached up to touch his face, the expression in her eyes telling him that she was thinking of the brief time of terror when they thought that he might be lost to the transformation of the Klimnu. "When they first started transforming, they went to Creia for help. By then he already knew that they were planning on taking over."

Athan stopped and turned to her.

"Say that again."

"By then he already knew that they were planning on taking over."

Athan let out a sound that was like a frustrated growl and curled his fists, slamming them on his thighs as he started pacing again.

"What is it, Athan?" Maxim asked.

"Don't you get it?" Athan asked. "Creia already knew that they were planning on taking over when they came to him for help because of their transformation. They had already started planning before they ever started transforming."

"We know that," Maxim said. "Mom said that after the conflict with the Covra, some of the clan never recovered. They wanted to exert power rather than ever letting anyone else exert power over them. That's when they left the kingdom."

"Exactly. All this time we've been thinking about the Klimnu, not the Mikana."

"What do you mean?"

"When the clan split, it was members of the Order who broke off and wanted to take over the planet. They weren't Klimnu yet. They didn't become Klimnu until after they had decided to split off. That means that it goes back further than I even expected. We shouldn't be thinking about the behaviors of the Klimnu. We should be thinking about the Mikana."

"What happened to the Klimnu after Creia denied his help for them?" Emerie asked.

"At first we didn't know. They were simply gone. Then we found out that they had left the planet and moved onto Ynn. It is brutal there. The climate is horrible and the ground is inhospitable. The ways of the Mikana, though, make it possible to survive and even thrive there. It wasn't until they found that they couldn't have the power that they wanted when they were on that planet that they decided to return to Uoria and try to take over again. That is when they were fully transformed. When we went into battle, though, they had just started. Not all of them were fully transformed. The more vicious they got, the faster they transformed. It wasn't the transformation that started them becoming greedy and cruel. They were already like that. It was being greedy and cruel that hastened their transformation, and then the transformation made it worse. It became a cycle."

"Papa knew," Kyven said. "He knew what was happening."

"And how he was going to stop it," Maxim said.

"We have to get to Creia," Athan said. "We have to find out what he knows. We have to find out more about his interactions with the Mikana and what he remembers from when he was a child in the original compound. This can't just be about the Klimnu. Even you said that the division happened because of the Covra. They were allies to the Valdicians. When and why did that begin? What happened to the compound that made the Denynso divide?"

"If we leave in the morning it will be several days until we are able to get back to the Denynso compound to speak with Creia."

Athan paused again and looked at him.

"Not necessarily," he said.

"What do you mean?"

The older man looked nervous, unsure that he wanted to continue. He looked at each of the four sitting looking back at him and his face took on an expression of determination.

"Leave," he said. "Leave now and go back to your houses. Eat. Talk to the others. But pack your bags. Come back here at midnight and tell no one what we are planning."

"What's going on, Athan?" Kyven asked.

"Just do it," Athan said.

Without another word, they stood and left the house, heading back to the houses that they were sharing with the others of the travel group. The hours ticked by slowly and Maxim couldn't pull his thoughts away from the tone of Athan's voice when he told them to come back that night. Finally it was time to return and he and Ivy met Emerie and Kyven behind their mother's home. They all exchanged glances that held questions along with their resignation to whatever was happening.

By the time they made it back to Athan's house, he was standing outside, two large bags over his shoulder.

"Did anyone follow you?" he asked.

"No," Maxim replied.

"And you told no one that we were leaving?"

"No one," Maxim confirmed.

"Come on. Move quickly. We can't risk the guards finding us."

They moved along quickly behind Athan as he walked in long strides across the kingdom toward the gate that Maxim and Ivy had used the first time that they visited. There should have been a guard standing there, but the entire area stood silent and empty.

"Athan, are you supposed to be on guard duty tonight?" he asked.

"Yes," Athan said back to him over his shoulder, keeping his voice just loud enough for Maxim to hear. "It is the only reason that we were able to do this tonight."

"Won't you be in serious trouble with the Order if they find out that you aren't in your post?"

"What I have already told you has already put me in serious danger. What I plan to show you tonight would have me killed if any of the Order was to find out. I have come this far. I might as well see it through."

They continued on through the gate and out of the kingdom. Rather than venturing out across the open space in front of the kingdom, however, he remained close to the wall, following it with one hand outstretched as if he was searching for something. Maxim's mind immediately went to the stones that Athan touched to open the Order tunnels that wound beneath the kingdom. They had followed the curve of the wall until they were nearly at the back of the kingdom when Athan finally stopped. He stepped closer to the wall and ran his fingertips across it again.

"Do you need light?" Maxim asked.

"No," Athan said. "I don't want to call any attention to us."

He continued to feel along the wall, and then Maxim heard a click. The ground beneath his feet trembled slightly and then the moonlight illuminated the grass in front of them just enough that Maxim saw a section slide open. It was much like the tunnel, except that it didn't seem the ground was creating a ramp. Rather, it was opening and a moment later the shape of something dark rose up out of the grass. Ivy gasped and Maxim reached for her, taking her by the hand and pulling her back behind him protectively. He didn't know what was happening, but a sense of intrigue flowed through him.

The shape rose only a few feet and then stopped. Athan stepped forward; paused briefly, and then walked up to what Maxim now realized was a small metal building. Athan reached into his pocket and withdrew a small piece of intricately shaped metal. He pressed it into a recessed section of the wall and the outline of it lit up in a bright blue glow. A moment later an area of the wall slid down and then inward, folding as it went to create a set of steps leading down.

"Follow me," Athan said.

They all moved forward, Maxim approaching the doorway first with Ivy close behind him. Though the building had only risen out of the ground a few feet, the metal steps that had formed led far enough down that Maxim only needed to duck his head for the first few steps. He moved down the stairs as quickly as he could to allow the others to get into the cover and protection of the building. As soon as Kyven's feet touched the floor, Athan touched a panel on the wall beside him and the steps folded themselves back up to create a solid wall in the building again. There was a low groaning sound and the building itself began to move, lowering back down. Though he knew that they were deep enough beneath the ground that the building frame wouldn't come close to them, it was still a strange sensation to watch the space around himself progressively shrinking and Maxim fought the urge to crouch down.

Finally the metal frame locked into place and Athan urged them to continue. They followed him down a hallway that illuminated in the same progressive color pattern that the tunnel did, and Maxim found himself watching ahead of them out of nervousness that he would see the ceiling brighten as someone approached. The panels remained dark, however, until they crossed under them and soon they exited the hallway into another room. There were several large forms hunkering in the center of the room covered with large cloths. Athan approached one of them with a nostalgic, reverent look on his face and flattened his hands to it.

"They're still here," he whispered almost to himself. "I was hoping that they would be."

"What are they?" Maxim asked.

"I know that you probably don't remember it, but there was a time when moving around the planet and even leaving the planet for brief visits to others was not completely out of the norm for the Mikana. We had some of the most advanced technology in the galaxy. That all changed, though, and the Klimnu were the last to leave and return. It has been many decades since we've utilized any of the technology that we developed for fast and reliable trans-portation. The kingdom leaders thought it was too dangerous to have transportation that allowed the people of the kingdom to move about as they pleased. They banned the use of the technology and destroyed all of the vehicles." He gazed down at the form beneath his hands. "Most of them. The Order preserved these, kept them aside out of the destruction pits to ensure that they were available in the event of an emergency." He gave a mirthless laugh. "I suppose that their idea of what may be an emergency is somewhat different than ours."

He stopped talking and grabbed onto the cloth, yanking it away to reveal a black vehicle that sat on the floor without wheels. It was unlike anything that Maxim remembered. If he dug deeply into his memories he thought that he might remember a few instances of his father talking about the use of transportation technology, but his lucid memories were all of everyone walking everywhere. He couldn't remember ever seeing, much less riding in, something like this.

"Do they still work?" Kyven asked.

Athan glanced at him and then back at the vehicle.

"I can't imagine why not. They were designed for absolute reliability. Their fuel cores could last more than a century before needing recharging.

"How do we use them?" Maxim asked.

His voice sounded strong and determined, and Athan turned to him with the hint of an approving smile on his face. He moved over to the next form and pulled away the cloth.

"Get in," he said. "Kyven, ride with me."

Maxim approached the vehicle and saw that the center was a deep well molded into seats. He helped Ivy in and then climbed inside, settling into the seat positioned in front of a bank of control panels. His heart started pounding and he was unsure of what he needed to do.

"Do you want me to do it?" Ivy asked from beside him.

He glanced over at her.

"I drive on Earth. Do you want me to try to pilot it?"

There was nothing judgmental or teasing in the question and Maxim touched her cheek gently.

"Yes," he said.

They switched places and Ivy settled into the control seat while he sat beside her. It felt both strange and liberating to hand over the control of the vehicle to her. He was accustomed to wanting to be strong and do everything himself, even when following the commands of the king. Ivy had offered herself to him as his partner, however, and that meant that he could lean on her when he needed her. Driving was a skill that she had that he didn't, and even though he assumed that these Mikana vehicles were very different than the ones on Earth, this was her way of offering her help, being there for him, and making sure that he was safe and had what he needed to do what they had to do. It was all that he had asked of her and he finally felt like they were truly coming together.

"Are you ready?" Athan called to them.

"Yes," Ivy called back.

"Do you have your restraints on?"

Maxim and Ivy adjusted their restraints and ensured that they were firmly in place.

"Yes," she called back again.

"Press the blue button in front of you and sit very still."

Ivy complied and they both sat still as a clear, bubble-like top slid into place over them. Despite its age, the material was still crystalline and he was able to see around him almost as though there was nothing there.

"Ivy?"

Athan's voice came at them from in front of Ivy and Maxim jumped.

"Athan?" he said.

"This is the inter-craft communication system. As long as your top is up you are fully protected, but you will not be able to hear me calling to you. If you have something that you need to say to me, just press the purple button in front of you and it will connect directly to my ship. It will work anywhere on Uoria no matter how far we are apart. Hopefully there won't be a time when we are out of each other's sight, though. Are you ready to go?"

"I am."

"Good. Touch your hands to the screen in front of you. It will measure size and shape so that it can customize the control bar for you. That way it will be as responsive as possible while minimizing discomfort and error. There is a way that you can tell the craft to pilot itself, but that requires you to know exactly where you are going and it does not account for sudden changes in your travel. It's best to just go ahead and pilot it yourself unless we are moving through large open places that don't really require us to make decisions."

"Alright," Ivy said.

Maxim watched her press her hands to the screen and a series of multicolored lights appeared beneath them. The screen scanned her hands in several directions and then made a low beeping sound. Ivy pulled her hands away and there was a faint glowing outline of them on the screen for several seconds before it disappeared and a curved black bar came out of the control panel toward her.

"I have my control bar," she said to Athan.

"Good. I'm going to go first. When I am in front of you and have gone a few feet, press the green button, take your control bar and we'll go. Follow me as closely as you can without bumping me, and do as I do. I'm going to have to trust you on this."

"I will, Athan."

"Here we go."

6

(TO BE CONTINUED IN BOOK VIII...)

"That's a Denynso," Simran said, sitting up and swinging his legs around so that they hung off of the end of the bed like Jane's. "At least, that's what it looks like."

"I thought so, too," she said, allowing him to pull the book off of her lap and into his so that he could look more closely at the picture.

"There are a few things that are little different about him," Simran said, "but it is unmistakable. The size, the hair, the eyes. I don't know what else it could be."

"It doesn't make any sense, though," Jane said. "This picture is extremely old. The Denynso and Earth didn't have any interaction when it was taken. I don't understand how it could possibly be a Denynso with human men."

"I don't, either," Simran said. "I can't help but think that it means something, though. The only thing that I can think of to do is bring it to show Pyra and Eden. Pyra is the leader of the Denynso warriors. Other than Creia, our king, he is the most knowledgeable and honored of us." He said the words with as much confidence as he could, trying to force his mind away from the horrors that had occurred on the Nyx 23 settlement at the hands of this leader. Pyra had acknowledged his wrong doing and asked for their forgiveness. Though he struggled like many of the others, Simran knew that he had to let go. "His mate, Eden, was the first human woman to come to the compound and end up staying with us. She has actually become Denynso."

"What?" Jane asked.

"Eden was a human woman but now she is Denynso."

"How did that happen? Does that happen to all human women who mate with Denynso warriors?"

There was a faint look of fear on her face and Simran felt his stomach sink slightly.

"The thought of that terrifies you, doesn't it?" he asked. "You weren't really prepared for the realities of being my mate."

"That's not it," Jane insisted. "I just don't know these things. You need to be patient with me. This was not something that I expected to happen in my life and I feel like I am navigating it by the minute."

Simran wrapped an arm around her waist and pulled her in for a kiss.

"So do I," he said. "Don't worry. I am right here with you. We're going to figure it out together." Jane laughed softly and he gave her a smile. "No," he told her, "most human women do not automatically turn into Denynso women when they mate with a Denynso man. Though Pyra was the first of our clan to mate with a human woman, there have been plenty others after, as you know, and they are all still perfectly human. No signs of altering DNA yet."

Jane smile and kissed him again.

"Then what happened?" she asked.

"When she was first in the compound, she was tricked by

a Klimnu. They were the greatest enemies of our kind and some of them had the ability to mimic the appearance of others. That particular creature took on the appearance of Pyra so that Eden would trust it and then attacked her. It nearly killed her, but the real Pyra found her in just enough time that he was able to get her to our healer, Ciyrs, and he saved her life. The healing that she needed was extensive, however, and in the process she was changed. We still don't know how it happened, or why, but she now has the DNA of a Denynso and has started exhibiting some of the characteristics of a Denynso woman. She hasn't grown any, though, so she is still quite small compared to the other women of the clan."

"And you think that showing them the picture will help?" she asked.

"Yes," he told her.

"Alright. Let's get dressed and we'll go find them."

After a long shower they got dressed and headed out. Simran directed Jane to the house where they were staying and carried the scrapbook inside. He found Pyra sitting in the kitchen sipping a drink called coffee that they had never had on the Denynso compound but of which Pyra had become quite fond of in their time on Earth. The warrior leader glanced over at them and swallowed hard, setting his mug down on the table.

"What happened to you last night?" he asked.

"What do you mean?" Simran asked, trying to look like he didn't know what Pyra was talking about.

"We went looking for you when the party wound down, but you weren't at the bar anymore. Someone said that they saw you leaving with Jane."

Jane stepped out from behind Simran and Simran wrapped an arm around her.

"I did leave with Jane," he said with a smile.

"Congratulations!" Pyra said loudly, getting up to shake Simran's hand.

"Thanks," Simran said, "but that's not what we're here to talk about. Is Eden around?"

"Yeah. She's upstairs with the baby. Is everything alright?"

"We're not sure. We just need to talk to both of you."

"Come on up."

Pyra led them up the stairs to a bedroom. Eden was sitting in a rocking chair cradling Lysander in her arms and singing quietly to him.

"I'm sorry," Simran said, "We didn't mean to intrude."

"No," Eden said with a wide smile, "it's fine. Come in."

They stepped inside and Simran looked at them both.

"Jane has been telling me that I was really familiar to her, that I reminded her of something, but she didn't know what. It wasn't until this morning that she figured it out." He showed them the scrapbook. "This belonged to her great-grandfather. It's full of every kind of memento imaginable and she said that he used to tell her stories about everything that was in it. Everything except for this one particular picture. That picture he wouldn't talk about and would even act like he had no idea what it was or why it was in the scrapbook."

"Is it OK if we look at the picture, Jane?" Eden asked.

"That's fine," Jane said. "That's why we came here. Simran thinks that it is significant but we don't know why. You and Pyra might be able to help us."

Simran lowered the scrapbook to the bed and flipped through the pages until he got to the picture. Just looking at it again sent new chills down his spine and he spun the book toward Pyra as quickly as he could. He gestured toward the picture and Pyra leaned down to look at it. Simran saw his eyes narrow and his massive hands come to the side of the book so that he could look more closely at it.

"Is that..." he started.

He brought the book over to Eden and held it so that she could look at the picture.

"A Denynso," she said, finishing his thought with her own surprised exclamation.

"That's what we thought, too," Simran said.

He saw Eden squint at the picture much like he had and she shook her head.

"I've seen this before," she said.

"You have?" Jane asked, sounding stunned.

"Yes," Eden said. "Not in this book, though. I've seen it somewhere else."

"Where?" Pyra asked.

Eden shook her head again.

"I can't put my finger on it. I know that I have though." She shuddered slightly and looked down at Lysander's face, looking as much like she just wanted to gaze at her son as she did like she didn't want to look at the picture any longer. "Something about it bothers me. I don't remember where or why I've seen it, but I know that it isn't a good thing that I have."

Pyra pulled the book back in front of him again and looked back down at the picture.

"There's something strange about the Denynso in this picture, if that's what he is, of course."

"I don't see what else he could be," Eden said. "He has all of the characteristics."

"Yeah, but there's some things about him that are a little

off. I can't really explain exactly what it is, but he just looks different."

"He's smaller," Jane offered. "Now that I've seen you in person I really notice it, but that Denynso is not as big in comparison to the men beside him as you would be if you were standing next to them. Could he be very young?"

"No," Simran said. "Look at his hair. You can tell what stage of life a Denynso is in by his hair. This is a grown adult. He is at full height."

"His face looks a little different, too," Eden offered. "I'm not exactly sure why, but it doesn't look like a Denynso face."

"Do you know when this picture was taken?" Pyra asked.

"No," Jane admitted. "I don't know anything about it. I mean, I know that it isn't a contemporary picture. It has looked old and worn ever since I was a little girl. And look at the clothing. It is definitely an old picture."

"Is there anything written on the back?" Eden asked.

"Written on the back?" Pyra asked.

"Yes," Eden said. "Remember how Lynx found out Rain's name because he saw it written on the back of a picture of her? That is something that people used to do here. If you put a picture in a scrapbook or a frame, you wrote who it was and when it was taken on the back so that you could remember later when you look at it."

"I don't know," Jane said. "I've only ever seen it in the book. My great-grandfather never checked, not even when I asked him about the picture."

"Would it be OK with you if we took it out?" Simran asked. "I'm sure that we can get it back in."

Jane nodded.

"Of course," she said. "It's about time I find out the real story behind that picture anyway."

Pyra put the book carefully on the bed and grasped the

corner of the picture. Holding the rest of the book down with his other hand, he gently started to peel the picture up and off of the page. It came more easily than Simran would have suspected, which only further confirmed to him the age of the picture. Pyra handed Jane the picture without flipping it over to look at the back.

"You should look first," he told her.

"Thank you," Jane said and accepted the picture.

She turned it over in her palm and looked down at it. She was silent for a moment and then looked up at Simran.

"Success," she said.

"Did you find something out?" he asked.

Jane nodded.

"Success," she repeated. "That's what it says on the back of the picture. Just 'success', nothing else."

She handed the picture to Simran, who looked at it, flipped it over, read the word, and then flipped it over again. He handed it to Pyra.

"What do you think that means?" he asked.

"I don't know," Pyra answered, handing the picture over to Eden so that she could take her turn.

"What's strange about it," Jane said, "is that it was obviously taken quite a long time ago and it is using Earth technology and has Earth fashion, so I would venture to say that it was taken here. That doesn't make sense, though. You are the first Denynso to visit Earth."

"Except for Ero," Pyra said.

"Zuri's mate," Jane said and Simran nodded. "OK, yes, but he was here for one day and didn't go anywhere but from the university to get Zuri and back. Other than that, you are the first to come here. Human visits to Uoria only started about fifty years ago, and those humans were tourists. The exchange program and the visiting scientists and journalists are really the only possible means of interaction with the Denynso except for those early tourists who I doubt would have staged such a picture."

"That's not true," Eden said.

"You think that they would stage the picture?" Jane asked.

"No," Eden said. "That's not what I meant. You said that those tourists were the first opportunity that the humans had to interact with the Denynso. That there weren't any other means of interaction before that."

Simran sudden realized what Eden was talking about. He felt his heart pound slightly. He met Eden's eyes and they both turned to look at Pyra, who was already staring at them. He shook his head and gestured slightly toward Jane.

"What is it?" she asked. "What's going on?"

"Nothing," Simran said, heeding the nonverbal warning from his leader.

"Yes, there is," Jane replied. "There's something going on. What is it?"

"It isn't our story to tell, Simran," Eden warned.

"This is my mate, Eden," Simran said. "I have to tell her. I can't keep anything from her. Besides, she deserves to know as much as she can about her great-grandfather, even if we can only help her to figure out what this picture is all about."

"What is it?" Jane asked again.

Eden finally gave a nod of permission and Simran looked at Jane.

"What do you know about Nyx 23?" he asked.

There was a pause and Jane looked at him strangely as if she wasn't following what he was saying.

"Nyx 23," Eden repeated. "The mission team."

Jane continued to stare at him like she didn't know what

to think, and then her eyes widened. He could see recognition sinking in and her lips parted slightly before she spoke.

"The team that left here and never came back?" she asked. "I remember reading about it in school when I was younger, but I never knew the whole story."

"No one did," Eden said. "The official take was that they left here on a mission to free an illegal prison camp and were lost in transit. There was never any further communication from them and no signs of them were ever uncovered."

"Alright," Jane said. "What does that have to do with the Denynso?" she asked.

"We found them," Pyra said.

Jane's eyes snapped to him.

"What?" she asked sharply.

"We found them," Pyra repeated. "Well," he said, "we came upon them."

"It is a very long story," Eden said, "but for now suffice it to say that Nyx 23 was not lost. They weren't killed when they went to that planet and they didn't spiral out of orbit. They crash landed on Uoria and have been there ever since."

"Did they stay with the Denynso?" Jane asked.

"No," Pyra said. "They were on a different area of the planet. That still means, though, that there was more opportunity for interaction between the Denynso and the humans than we might have thought."

"Do you think that this picture was taken on Uoria?" Jane asked. "Maybe those are crew members of Nyx 23 and this picture was taken during an encounter with the Denynso?"

Pyra shook his head.

"I don't think so," he said. "They don't look familiar."

"What do you mean?" Jane asked.

"Is there someone who we can ask?" Eden asked,

seeming to want to brush the question away. "Maybe someone who is a bit more familiar with what the team looked like?"

Simran nodded.

"I'll be right back,"

He took the picture and rushed down the stairs into the living room where Brandy sat. He crouched down beside her and held the picture so that she could see it.

"Were any of those men on the crew?" he asked.

Brandy looked slightly startled, but took the picture and held it carefully as she examined it.

"Where did you get this picture?" she asked.

"That doesn't matter right now. We're trying to figure out what it is. Do you recognize any of those men?"

She looked at it again and shook her head.

"None of them was on the crew," she said. "This one, though," she said with a slight laugh as she pointed to the man standing closest to the Denynso in the picture, "he looks like Captain Francisco."

"Captain Francisco?" Simran asked.

"Yeah. He was part of a military operative who we sometimes worked with. He was a good thirty years younger than this man, though."

She handed him back the picture and Simran took it, his fingers closing slowly around it as he let her words sink in.

TBC

(To be continued in book VIII...)

THE ALIEN'S SUFFERING

1

Kyven tossed another piece of dried brush onto the fire that they had built and sat back on his heels to stare into the glow of the flames. The light breeze that was blowing through the camp that they had set up was making the fire dance and spark, and he felt himself worry that someone was going to see the glow or the smoke and come after them. Even as the thought moved through his mind, however, he wondered who it would be that would have the most reason for pursuing them, and what would happen even if they did.

He knew from what Athan had told them that they were all now on the bad side of the Order, putting themselves at serious risk by stealing the vehicles and embarking on this journey to find out more about his father. The thought scared him. He didn't remember as much about the Order from his childhood that Maxim did, but what he did remember let him know that they would not take the betrayal of one of their own or the unauthorized use of technology that had been made out of bounds lightly. If they found out what was happening, there would be hell to pay and the Order wouldn't stop until they were satisfied that they had gotten proper vengeance. At the same time, however, Kyven felt that it was not just the Order who had the right to vengeance. Though there was nervousness deep in his belly when he thought about them finding out what Athan had done or what they were trying to find out, there was also a sense of responsibility and drive. More than ever now he wanted to know what happened to his father and was willing to face danger in order to avenge Aegeus the loss of his life, his mother the loss of her husband and the life that she should have lived, and himself and his brother the loss of their father and knowing who and what they really were.

The area around him was quiet and Kyven looked up, wondering where everyone else had gone. They had traveled for several hours and were nearing the Denynso compound when they had decided that it was time to stop and rest. The thrill of the incredibly fast travel had started to wear off, leaving exhaustion and hunger in its place, and Kyven reached into one of the bags that sat on the ground beside the fire and pulled out some of the food that they had brought along. He imagined that Maxim and Ivy had gone off on their own to talk through whatever had been happening between them in the last few days, and he hoped that they would be able to resolve it. He had never seen his brother as happy as he was with that woman, and now that he had found Emerie, he felt that he might be beginning to understand what Maxim was feeling.

That thought of Emerie brought a slight moment of panic to Kyven's heart and he stood, looking around as he realized that he had not seen her since they had stopped their vehicles and began to set up camp for the night. She had told him that she was going to go down to the small river that Athan said was nearby and bathe, but she had not yet returned and Kyven worried that something had happened to her in the time that she had been away. He didn't put it past the Order to capture the woman and use her as bait to lure the others to them. They wouldn't care that she was completely innocent in this matter and didn't even fully understand what was happening. They would care only that she was alone and vulnerable to them.

Athan approached from the other side of the fire carrying more brush to keep the flames going. His face changed when he saw Kyven's expression and he took a step toward him.

"Is everything alright?" he asked, his voice sounding concerned.

"Emerie hasn't come back," he said. "Maxim and Ivy are together wherever they are, but Emerie is alone."

"She said that she was going down to the river to bathe," Athan said.

"I know that," Kyven replied, sitting down to pull his boots back on as he prepared to go look for her. "She has been gone for a long time, though. What if the Order found her?"

"If the Order found her, we would already know about it," he said. "They have no use for her."

"They would know that if they had her, that I would come for her," he said, adjusting the knife attached around his hips.

"If they want us," Athan said, his voice becoming slightly gravelly as he spoke, "they will come for us. Go down to the river and look for her. I will go find Maxim and Ivy. We need to stay together as much as we can. Together we have much more of a chance against them or anything else that we may encounter here. We need to remember that this is no longer just a journey. We are not just exploring. The choices we have made are more dire than you might imagine now, but they are the ones that bind us. In their eyes we have gone rogue, and they have no tolerance for rebellion."

"Why would my father – or you – be a part of something so horrible?" Kyven asked.

"It wasn't always like this, Kyven. This is the brutality of war and the reality of deceit. The Order was always good. We fought, but it was for the protection of others. It only took the destruction of one heart to make that change."

"I don't understand."

"Everyone is fragile. Even if they won't admit it and even if they never show it, everyone is only strong enough to handle but so much. That time came and the Order changed, I believe that is what your father was fighting for, he wanted to restore what had been lost."

Athan dropped the brush to the ground and took a few steps backwards.

"Go," he said. "Find Emerie and bring her back here. From now on no one goes anywhere alone. We stay together at all times."

He turned and started away from the fire, his pace faster than what it had been when he approached Kyven just moments before. Something that Kyven had said had startled the older man, but he wasn't going to question it. Athan understand the Order and everything that they did on a level that Kyven and the others didn't. Even if he tried to explain it, they would never be able to truly understand it the way that he did. He had lived it, breathed it, and existed only within it for the vast majority of his life. Even though he wouldn't want to admit the connection, he shared heartbeat with the other members of the Order, a rhythm that controlled how they thought, felt, and responded to the world around them. The thought that those compulsions had become so twisted in some of their members had to be frightening for Athan, reminding him that he was always only a step away from becoming like them.

Kyven turned and ran toward the river, trying to remember the directions that Athan had given Emerie when she had asked. It shouldn't be far from the camp, and Kyven felt a surge of motivation when he heard the light sound of the bubbling water coming toward him from the darkness ahead. He continued at a faster pace, holding back the urge to call out her name. He didn't want to bring any more attention to himself than they already had just by settling in and building the fire. Finally the moonlight from overhead illuminated the surface of the water and Kyven felt relief wash over him as he saw Emerie walking through it. She was deep enough that the water came up nearly to her shoulders but he could see enough of her to know that she had undressed fully to submerge herself.

Her back was to him and as she moved her hair shifted, allowing the soft glow of the moon touch the smooth, pale skin of her back. She stretched her hands out to her sides, waving them slowly so that her fingertips just grazed across the surface of the water. Kyven felt struck by her. He paused where he was, several yards away from the bank of the river, and watched her as she continued to move gracefully through the night-darkened water. She looked so at peace, so calm as her body parted the water and allowed it to sweep across her skin. He didn't want to disturb her. In the time that he had known her she had seemed like she was holding something within herself, carrying a burden that she didn't want to share. Now as she bathed quietly in the river she seemed as though she had rested that burden on the bank and stepped into the water free from it, if only for a few moments.

The desire and adoration that he felt for her surged higher within him and he longed to be close to her. He knew that she had feelings for him. She had offered those feelings timidly, not going far enough to admit that she loved him and now allowing him close enough to her for him to show his love for her, and she had committed herself to coming along with him when he left the kingdom. Even though he knew that she didn't fully understand the implications of everything that was going on, he knew that she was aware that she was putting herself in danger just by agreeing to go with him. It put him in a strange and confusing place where he was at once ready to fully give himself over to her and unsure if she would ever be ready to do the same.

His need to be close to her overpowered any unsureness that he felt and Kyven walked slowly toward the edge of the water. He was nearly to the bank when Emerie turned. She gasped when she saw him, her arm coming up to cover her breasts even though they were not quite visible over the top of the water. Kyven held up a hand to calm her.

"It's just me," he said quietly.

"Kyven!" she said, not moving her arm away. "What're you doing? You scared me."

"I'm sorry," he said. "I didn't mean to intrude. I was worried about you when you hadn't come back and Athan said that I should come and find you."

"You didn't intrude," she said after a quiet moment.

She didn't look as startled now and she slowly lowered her arm away from her body. The water was high enough that only the top swell of her breasts was visible, but even that was enough to make Kyven ache for her. The water moved slightly, revealing more of her skin and all thoughts of Athan's warnings disappeared from his mind. Emerie was safe. The Order had not come for her and now they were peacefully alone at the water.

Kyven moved cautiously, removing his boots slowly. Emerie watched him and he knew that she was fully aware of his intentions. He wanted her to be. He wanted her to watch his every move and know exactly what he was doing so that she could control it if she wanted to. When she said nothing about his boots, Kyven took the hem of his tunic and pulled it off over his head. He saw her draw in a breath, her eyes grazing across his chest and stomach as she drank in the sight of him. Kyven paused for another brief moment and then released the ties on the front of his pants, easing them off without taking his eyes away from hr.

Now completely vulnerable to her, Kyven stepped forward. The cool of the water rose up to touch his toes and he felt a slight shiver move through his body. It was not as intense, though, as the shiver that she created within him and he continued forward, letting himself sink into the water as slowly as he could. Emerie watched him, her lips parting slightly. He could see her starting to tremble and wondered what emotions were causing the reaction. The water pressed in around his body, making his movements even more gradual as he made his way across the sandy bottom of the river toward her.

When he was finally only a few inches away, Kyven lifted one hand and lightly touched the side of her face. Emerie sighed softly and tilted her head to brush her face against his touch. He ran the pad of his thumb across her lips and felt her kiss it. The soft pressure of her lips brought a long exhalation from deep in his chest and Kyven took another step toward her. He rested his hand on her hip and reveled in the feeling of her bare skin beneath his palm. He applied pressure to her hipbone to pull her closer to him and felt the tips of her breasts brush against his chest.

"Kyven," she whispered softly.

He took his hand away from her hip and used it to gently lift her chin so that her face tilted up to his.

"Hmmm?" he murmured, bringing his lips down to hers in a soft kiss.

She sighed as she relaxed into the kiss, but then he felt her pull back from him. He looked at her and saw her shaking her head, looking down at the water and the arm that she had crossed over her breasts again.

"I can't," she said, her voice tight with emotion. "I'm sorry, Kyven. I can't do this."

Embarrassment rushed through him and he took a step back so quickly he nearly stumbled.

"I'm sorry," he said, looking away and turning around so that he could get back onto the bank and dress as quickly as he could.

When he turned back around she was several yards away from him, her back to him as she finished dressing. She straightened the bottom of her shirt and then crossed her arms, wrapping her hands around her upper arms and hanging her head slightly. Kyven could see her shoulders trembling and could hear the soft sounds of her crying. He finished dressing and approached her cautiously, breaking through the embarrassment and discomfort with his need to soothe her.

"Emerie?" he said carefully as he got close to her.

He wanted to rest his hand on her back, but didn't know if she would welcome the touch or it would only upset her even further. Instead he came up to stand beside her and ducked his head so that he could look at her better.

"I'm so sorry," she said through her tears before he was able to say anything.

"What's wrong?" Kyven asked. "Did I do something?"

Emerie shook her head and looked up at him. The moonlight touched her eyes, sparkling on the tears and illuminating the trails that they left on her cheeks as they fell. He reached up and brushed one of them away. He had touched her so similarly just moments before, but now the contact felt so different. He ached for her in a different way now, the pain centered on his desperate desire to find out what had happened to hurt her and do whatever he could to ease that pain.

"No," she finally said. "You didn't do anything. It's me."

"What do you mean?"

Emerie hung her head again and started to cry harder, bringing her hands up to cover her face. Her vulnerability suddenly made Kyven remember what Athan had said about them being alone.

"Come on," Kyven said. "Let's go back to the camp. Athan said that we shouldn't separate while we're out here."

Emerie nodded and allowed him to loop his arm around her shoulders and help her walk back toward the camp, supporting her as much as he could without feeling like he was overwhelming her with his presence. The others were around the fire when they got back. Emerie shied away from the light coming from the flames and after acknowledging them, rushed toward her tent muttering something about wanting to get to sleep so that they could get up early and finish their trip. Kyven walked to the edge of the fire and found the food that he had started to prepare sitting on a plate beside the pit. He took a bite of it but he was no longer hungry.

"Is everything OK?" Maxim asked.

Kyven looked at his brother, unsure of what to say.

"Everything's fine," he finally said. "I'm tired, too. I'm going to go to bed. Wake me up when you are ready to go."

He didn't wait for anyone to respond but went to his tent and ducked inside, closing the flap tightly. He changed his clothes and rested back on his bedroll, staring up at the top of the tent. Finally the others went to their own tents and the glow from the fire died. A few moments later he heard rustling outside of his tent.

"Kyven?"

Emerie's voice was startling but welcome in the darkness. He leaned forward and opened the tent, moving back so that she could come inside.

"Is something wrong?" he asked.

He felt like that question was becoming his default greeting, as though it was the first thing that his mind came up with when he saw another person. He wondered if there would ever be a time when that didn't happen, and hoped that it would come soon.

"I wanted to apologize again," Emerie said.

Kyven shook his head.

"You don't need to apologize," he said.

The truth was that he didn't want to think about the situation anymore. He didn't want to have to relive those moments any more deeply than he already was.

"Yes, I do," Emerie said, settling down on her knees on his bedroll as Kyven moved back to sit further up. "I need you to understand what happened."

"It's fine, Emerie."

"No, it's not," she insisted. "I care about you. I care about you so much, and that's why I need you to understand what happened back there."

"If you care about me so much, then why..."

"Because I'm married. At least, I was."

Kyven was startled by the revelation and he stared at her, unable to respond, willing her to continue so that she could clarify what she had said.

"When I left with the Nyx 23 mission, I was married. I believed, like everyone else on the mission, that we were only going to be gone for a short time. A few weeks, maybe. A couple of months at the very most. My husband was used to me going on missions, but he was nervous about this one. He didn't like that we were doing something so outside of the usual goals and actions of the department. He thought that it was dangerous and he asked me not to go. I told him that I had to, that I believed in what we were doing and that there was nothing to be worried about. I know that he was upset with me the morning that we left."

"What was his name?" Kyven asked.

"What?" Emerie asked, sounding surprised by the question.

"He had a name," Kyven said, remembering what Maxim had told him about his conversation with Athan and the older man's reluctance to speak Aegeus's name. "He deserves to be called by his name."

Tears came to Emerie's eyes and Kyven saw her lips tremble slightly.

"Jason," she said quietly.

The name came out of her mouth sounding powdery and hesitant, as if she hadn't said it in so long that her tongue wasn't sure how to form it any longer.

"How long were you married?"

"Just two years."

Kyven nodded. Hearing that she had spent years of her life with another man was painful and brought an uneasy, somewhat sick feeling to his stomach, but he couldn't pretend that it didn't exist. She had lived another life in another time, well before he was even born, and he couldn't simply act like it had never been. The man who she had devoted her life to then, Jason, had been precious to her and he had been there to care for her and protect her in every way that he could when she didn't even know that Kyven existed. He deserved respect for that.

"You've been thinking a lot about him."

He had meant it as a question but it came out as more of a statement, an acknowledgement of what she was suffering through. Emerie nodded.

"When I got on that ship there wasn't a single thought in my mind that I wasn't going to be getting back to him in just a short while and we would make everything fine again. It was just going to be another mission and then we would keep going with our lives together. We had a vacation planned for later in the year and had started talking about starting a family."

This revelation took the breath out of Kyven's lungs and he had to fight to keep himself from allowing the tears that were forming in his eyes to escape.

"I wish I had known," he said. "I'm sorry."

"There's no way for you to have known," she told him. "I didn't tell you and I should have. I have struggled with it since we woke up in the settlement. When we crashed he was my sense of connection back to Earth. I knew that he was there thinking about me and missing me and hoping that I was doing alright. I thought about him every day and it was what kept me going during those first really hard months. Finally I came to terms with the fact that we weren't going to get back to Earth, that our ship was destroyed beyond repair and that there was no way for anyone on Earth to know where we were or what had happened to us. I realized then that Jason must think that I was dead. For days I wondered what he was thinking about. I wondered if he had a funeral for me and if he was still living in the same home that we shared. I wondered about silly things like what he had done with my clothes and if he had ever painted the bathroom yellow like he had wanted to when we first moved in but I insisted that it stay white. Most of all I thought about his wedding ring."

"His ring?" Kyven asked, feeling confused.

"Yes. On Earth when we marry we exchange rings. I don't know if it's the same way with the Mikana."

"No," he told her. "That's not one of the rituals that we share with the humans."

Emerie held up her hand and for the first time Kyven noticed the thin gold band that she wore around her finger. It was so tiny, and yet its presence was intimidating.

"I kept wearing it the entire time we were in the settlement and I wondered how long he would wear his. To me, we were still married. Our relationship was just as real and just as committed as it had been the day that I got on that ship. I knew for him, though, it was different. He thought that I wasn't alive any longer. He had no reason to continue to think of us as married or to keep living his life as though we were. For years I tormented myself wondering when was going to be the day that he was going to take that ring off and start looking for a new partner. When was going to be the day that he was going to find someone else and start thinking of her the way that he thought of me. When was he going to get married again, when were they going to have a child? Even with those thoughts, though, I could never bring myself to think of our marriage as over. I was still just as much alive as I always had been, and that meant that my vows to him were still valid."

"I'm sorry," Kyven said again. "It was never my intention to offend you or to cross any lines."

He felt himself pulling away from her even in the small space, but she reached for him and rested a hand on his arm as if to hold him in place.

"That's the thing, Kyven. You didn't. I was on that settlement for 15 years before the Covra locked us. People age differently on Uoria than they do on Earth. I don't know how to explain it, but I know that I look and feel younger than those 15 years should have made me. Jason wouldn't. He would have aged just as he was going to. We married very young because of my intended career, but even with that, in those 15 years he would be older than you are now. His life would have been set. I know him." She took a breath. "I knew him. He still would have wanted a wife and children and the life that we had always imagined sharing. By the time that the Covra locked us, he would have had all of that. Our marriage was over to him, because he thought that I was gone. Then more than a century passed. I didn't change as I lay there, but again, he would have. He would have lived those years and they would have changed him, gradually fading him away until his life was over. He thought that I was dead when I didn't come back from that mission. I know that he is now. I don't know if he struggled with the idea of letting our marriage go and no longer thinking of me as his wife, but I know that I have been having a difficult time with it. The feelings I have for you are so strong, stronger than I would have ever thought that I would be able to experience again, and it is hurting me more than I could have imagined it would. I feel so guilty for feeling this way about you. I still feel loyal to Jason and to our marriage, and I'm scared that feeling these things for you is betraying him in some way."

"Emerie," Kyven said, taking her hands in his and pulling them up so that he could cradle them against his chest, "listen to me. It's alright. I would never want you to do anything that would make you uncomfortable or unhappy. You know that Jason has been gone for a long time. You also know that he would want you to be happy. No one could ever replace what he was for you. You can never expect to love anyone exactly the same way that you loved him. That doesn't mean, though, that you can't love someone else in their own way and let them love you in return. I will be respectful and patient for as long as you need me to. I have waited for you my entire life. I can wait longer. I want you to know, though, that I am not asking you to make a choice. There is no choice to be made. You don't have to decide to either keep loving him or to love me. One is loving your memories and one is loving your future. You know better than anyone that you can never predict what is going to happen in the next moment of your life. You can't live it thinking that you know and planning every breath around that, and you can't live it pretending that the past is still here with you. All you can do is just live."

2

—————

"**A**re you sure that you want to do this?" Lynx asked, stepping carefully around a sharply pointed rock that had risen out of the ground in front of him.

Rain was walking several feet ahead of him, her eyes fixed on the horizon, and he saw her nod.

"Yes," she said. "I have to. Avoiding a pile of metal and weeds just because there are some bad memories attached to them won't do anyone any good. I have to be able to do this for everyone on the team, even those who never made it out of the wreckage."

Her voice was tight with emotion and Lynx felt the urge to pick her up and carry her back to the settlement where he knew that she would be safe. The last time that they had gone to the wreckage was incredibly difficult for her, and then she had the distraction of convincing Pyra to let Maxim live so that they could bring him back to Creia. Now she didn't have that layer of protection that could keep her thoughts from wandering to the meaning of the scattered bones of the ship that had brought her and the rest of the team from Earth. Going there would mean that she was forced to come face-to-face with those memories again, reliving them a way that she hadn't in more than one hundred years.

They continued in silence for several more minutes and Lynx found his thoughts wandering to the rest of his clan. The Denynso warriors were a fiercely loyal people and had spent their entire lives together. It was simply the way of their kind. They lived, fought, and died on the compound. Things had changed so drastically in the past months that the clan was almost unrecognizable. Not only had they left the compound in search of greater understanding of the rest of Uoria and the types of creatures that inhabited the planet, but they were now scattered. They hadn't stayed together as they had all assumed that they would. When they first made the decision to leave and go on their mission, it had always been assumed that they would travel together and return together. Nothing really would change. They would find out what they needed to know, go back to their compound, and better their defenses for the possibility that they may someday come into battle with one of the species that they had found on their journey.

He wondered now as he walked through the tall grasses at the center of the land they had explored if that thought had been naïve. Could they have closed their eyes and their minds to the possibilities that were awaiting them on the other side of the wall that had contained them their entire lives? Maybe they should have realized that when they made the decision to change something so central to the way that they lived their lives, that they would be creating a ripple effect that would have implications for all other aspects and all other moments of their lives. Even as he thought about this, though, Lynx knew that he was just like the rest of the warriors. He hadn't wanted to think of a life that wasn't like the one that he anticipated from the time he was a child. He had been raised in the loyalty, duty, and tradition of the warriors and the idea of walking away from that life and willingly embarking on one that was so completely different was not something that he ever would have wanted to imagine. He knew that the others felt the same way and that they would never bring themselves to admit it.

Rather than being all together, protected in the compound that had always been their home but that they had only recently discovered was not where their clan had originated, they were spread across the planet and throughout the galaxy. Some had remained on the compound, others stayed in the settlement with those of the Nyx 23 project who decided that they wanted to remain on Uoria, others had traveled to the Mikana kingdom, and still others had taken the greatest adventure that Lynx could imagine and gone to Earth to be a part of Ty and Samira's wedding. Though part of him felt sad for not being with the others on Earth and experiencing the traditional wedding ritual of the humans, he knew that he had made the decision that was right for him. His mate had made the decision to remain on Uoria rather than returning to Earth, and his place was with her. If she ever changed her mind and decided that she wanted to visit her home planet, he would travel along with her. For now, though, she was committed to finding out more about why her mission had been diverted the way that it had and the actual events that had led up to them being stranded on Uoria at the mercy of the creatures that lived there.

Nothing around them looked familiar to Lynx, but soon he saw the faint outlines of pieces of wreckage in the distance. He had been to this place only once before, on that dismal afternoon when he stood behind Pyra and watched him stare down Maxim with hatred, fury, and fear in his eyes. Lynx had been terrified then. He had been afraid for Maxim's life and for the future of the interactions between the Mikana and the Denynso. He had been afraid that if Pyra had gone back on his word to Rain that she would completely turn her back on the Denynso and he would lose the mate that he loved so desperately. He had also been afraid that if he watched Pyra let the darkness that had appeared within him overtake his thoughts and killed Maxim as he threatened that he was going to, that he would lose the trust, faith, and respect that he had for the leader of the warriors. They were thoughts that were painful to bear then and that rushed back to him now as they approached what remained of the massive ship that had been state-of-the-art in its time but had been reduced to nothing but tattered steel and cast-aside components gradually being reclaimed by the planet.

Rain didn't hesitate when they approached the wreckage. Instead, she ducked down and walked right into the large opening that Lynx remembered led into what was left of the actual structure of the ship. Though she had told the others about what it had been like in those last moments on the ship and during the crash, she had been more reserved with them than she had been with him. For him she had reserved the most painful and graphic of the details, offering up memories that he had had to choke down and pretend that they didn't sear into his belly every time that he thought of them. He had spent his life preparing for war and surging into battle with the rest of the Denynso, yet what she had gone through had sent shivers along his skin. He couldn't imagine the terror that must have coursed through her when she realized that the ship was no longer under the control of the pilot and that they were headed for a planet that none of them had ever visited, that Earth didn't even know existed at the time.

In the quiet of their time alone together she had described what it had felt like when the ship began to hurtle toward the ground. She told him of turbulence that had made it nearly impossible to stand and had forced most of them into their seats. He could only imagine that most of them, if not all of them, were thinking that these were the last moments that they would ever live and were dreaming of the people they loved who they had left behind and who would never know what had happened to them. He wished he could take those thoughts from her, could remove the memories from her mind and replace them with happiness that would soothe the hurt that he knew still lingered there. At the same time, though, he would never ask her to forget who she was or where she came from. Those may be some of the most torturous of memories that he could imagine, but they were hers and that made them precious.

3

R ain knew that Lynx was behind her and it gave her the strength to continue into the remnants of the ship. She hadn't looked back at him during the last portion of the walk to the wreckage because she didn't want to see the emotion in his eyes. She knew that if she looked at him she would see the worry in his expression and it might chip away at the resolve that she had as she pushed through the grass and toward the site of the crash that had made Uoria, as much as she and the other members of the project hadn't anticipated or wanted it to be, her home.

Now that they were at the wreckage all she could think about was those last moments on the ship. She rested her hand on the wall beside her and closed her eyes, letting her senses come alive with the memories that swept over her in the space. She could remember the darkness that suddenly surrounded them as the power within the ship completely cut off over Uoria. It was darkness like she had never experienced, so deep and intense that she almost felt like she could reach out and scoop it into her hands and cast it away from her. The thoughts that had ran through her mind as they hurtled down into the unknown were fevered and terrifying. It felt as though everything had fallen out from beneath them and she had no idea what was going to happen in the next second.

Many of the crew had gone to their seats, strapping themselves in the way that they had as they prepared for launch and landing. For the first few moments Rain had sat in her seat the way that they had, but sitting there felt like she was even more out of control than she already knew that she was. She couldn't just sit there and allow whatever was going to happen to happen without trying to do something. She scrambled out of the chair and felt her way toward the pilot's cabin, using her memory of the ship to guide her through. The darkness around her seemed to amplify the screams of her crewmates, but she used them to fuel her forward, to push her ahead even through the fear that was building in her chest.

Her hand finally touched the hatch to the ship's control room and she pressed against it with all of the strength that she could, having to force it open because the power was not there to open it for her. She could see better in the control room by merit of the light filtering in through the wide, curved glass that covered the front of the ship, enabling her to see the outlines of what was inside. The pilot was sitting in his chair, his hands seemingly frozen over the controls. He didn't move as she approached and she felt her heart sink down into her stomach. A moment later the ship smashed into the ground and her body flew backwards, crashing into the wall and sliding to the floor. The screams stopped and there was a moment of intense, horrific silence.

A moment later the sounds returned, but they seemed to come to her through water. They were undefined and fuzzy, making it difficult to even understand where they were coming from or who they were. The impact of the crash had sent painful shocks through her body and she didn't feel like she could stand. Instead she began to crawl forward, using the faint light that was still coming through the front of the ship to guide her as she moved through the cabin. Sharp pain cut into her hands and she lifted them, watching as trails of blood slid across her palms and down her wrists. She forced herself to continue, moving toward the dark form on the floor that she knew was the pilot.

Rain touched the pilot's back, shaking him slightly to try to get him to respond to her. He didn't move and she shook him harder, still with no response. A sudden glow of green light filled the room and Rain turned toward the door to the room. Greyson stood in the doorway, blood streaming from a wound in his forehead and looking at her with wild eyes. The light stick in his hand gave her enough light that she was able to see that the pilot was crumpled, lying on his hip with his torso and face down on the floor. She grabbed hold of him and pulled until he rolled over and she could see his face. There was a large piece of glass embedded in his neck, but not enough blood trickled around it. Her breath came from her lungs in harsh, ragged gasps as she reached for the glass and touched it with her fingertips.

"Rain?" Greyson said from behind her.

"Rain?" He said it again and she heard his voice blend with Lynx's. "Rain?"

It grew louder and more insistent and she realized it was only Lynx calling out for her. Her eyes opened and she realized that she had lowered herself to her knees on the weed-covered floor of the destroyed control room. Her hands were rested exactly on the place where she had found the body of the pilot, his skin already far colder than it should have been when she touched him. She turned them over and looked at the faint white scars that marked her palms.

"Are you alright?" Lynx asked, coming to crouch down beside her.

She turned to look at him and saw the look of concern in his eyes that she had expected. Now that she saw it, though, she welcomed it. It started to fade the fear and sadness that had settled into her as the memories coursed through her mind. Knowing that he was there beside her comforted her and she nodded.

"Yes," she said. "I'll be fine."

"Did you find something?"

Rain looked back down at the floor, trying to decide whether she wanted to tell him about the memories that had just come over her. She wanted to share them, to take some of the burden off of herself by giving it over to him to bear, but at the same time she didn't feel like she couldn't bring herself to speak them. These were still hers to suffer, hers to bear, and it wasn't the time for her to release that yet.

"No," she said, shaking her head. "Not yet."

"Can you tell me why you wanted to come here? This isn't a happy place for you. It isn't a happy place for anyone."

"Exactly," Rain said.

"What?"

"This isn't a good place. There aren't happy memories here."

"I'm not understanding you," he said, straightening to his feet as she did.

Rain moved deeper into the ship, forcing thoughts of that day to stay away from her as she continued making her way over the wreckage.

"I haven't been able to stop thinking about what Ivy said."

"What did she say?"

"It's more what she didn't say. When she was talking about how the government on Earth responded to the team's disappearance and went to Penthos, something bothered me. It took me a while to realize it, but I figured it out."

"What?"

"What happened to the Valdicians and their prisoners?"

"What do you mean?"

Rain pushed a tangled piece of metal away with her foot and bent down to look into a large tear in the wall into what she remembered would be a corridor.

"I told you that the reason that we went on this mission was because the Valdicians had an illegal prison compound on the previously unexplored planet. That was not a minor infraction. You have to remember that this was a long time ago. This was when intergalactic cooperation was still in very early days. There was still a tremendous sense of suspicion and uneasiness, and the agreements and laws that had been put into place had been chosen specifically to create security and control. The fact that the Validicians had gone against those laws so blatantly would have made them a target. I would assume that the military would come in and kill off all of the Validicians."

"Maybe they did."

Rain tore away weeds and vines that had grown over the gap and crouched down further to move through the wall into the corridor. It was no longer intact. She remembered her own hands pulling away the pieces of steel so that they could use them to build their settlement. There were only fragmentary reminders of the shape of the ship, allowing her to follow it as if walking through those memories that she had tried so hard to keep out of her mind.

"No," she said, shaking her head. "They would know. It

would have been one of the first things that she would have told us. With a military maneuver that big there would be a statue or a holiday or a museum or something. They wouldn't just do nothing. It doesn't make sense that they wouldn't have done something to acknowledge the loss of our team and the heroic actions of the military if that is what had happened."

"You said that the cooperation between the planets and the species were still tenuous at that time," Lynx said. "What if Earth didn't want to say anything about that type of mass killing because they didn't want to get a bad reputation? Showing that this type of activity could go on and that it took that level of force to stop it, and could be used as proof that there shouldn't be any kind of federation, that all of the planets and the species should keep to themselves."

"Alright," Rain said, reaching a section of grass that would have been where two corridors would have crossed. "I may be able to accept that as an explanation for the Validicians, but what about the prisoners?"

"What do you mean?"

"It doesn't make sense that there is no mention of the prisoners or what happened to them. Earth has a habit of making memorials and honoring the innocent dead in lasting, highly visible ways. But they also have a habit of saving people. What happened to those prisoners? Where did they go?"

Something suddenly triggered in her mind and she spun around, trying to orient herself, willing her mind to build up the walls of the ship again so that she could see where she was and navigate her way through it to the specific room that she needed to find.

"What if there weren't any prisoners left by the time that the military got there?"

"No," Rain said, increasing her pace as she made her way through the overgrown wreckage toward a section that would have once been the largest, most important dormitory in the ship. "That would have likely caused even more of an issue. If the Valdicians had killed off everyone and the military found that when they got to Penthos, it wouldn't have mattered if they were trying to keep up appearances or gloss over what had happened. There would be something. Everyone would know that that had happened. There was nothing."

She found the area of the wreckage that she knew had been the pilot's personal quarters and began to dig through what was left. They had shied away from clearing out this area of the ship after burying the pilot. Even though they probably could have used more of the metal and components that they left there to build more in their settlement, but none of them felt right about dismantling the space that had been so private in the pilot's life. The loss of their leader had been devastating, and Rain knew that only she had been there to see what had happened to him. Only she knew that he had already been gone long before the ship crashed into the ground.

"What are you doing?" Lynx asked as she dug through the wreckage.

"I need to find the box."

"What box?" he asked.

"The pilot's box. Every pilot had a secure box that they kept in their quarters. It's where they kept all of their records and most valuable personal possessions. It was never recovered when we dismantled the ship. I hadn't thought about that until now. It might have something in it that will help us understand what happened."

4

———

The Denynso compound looked quiet and empty as they approached it and for a moment Maxim felt a sense of fear ripple through him. He didn't know what threats still lingered on the planet for the Denynso, and now that he knew more about the Order and what they had done in the past, he found himself afraid that someone had made a link between the Mikana and the Denynso and come for them.

The group brought their vehicles over the wall and landed, concealing them as much as they could in the trees. It felt strange climbing out of the vehicles and looking around himself realizing that they were in the territory of the Denynso without the accompaniment of even one of the warriors. He looked over at Athan and saw dark emotion brewing in his eyes. There was pain there that the older man wasn't putting voice to, and Maxim could only begin to imagine what he was thinking and feeling. From what he had learned from Creia in his first visit to the compound, if Athan had come here before, it would not have been when the warriors were living there, but when it was Loralia's kind who inhabited the beautiful land.

They walked through the trees toward the center of the compound with Maxim and Ivy leading those who had not been with them on the first visit. He reached beside him and took Ivy's hand. He had a rush of thankfulness for her presence in that moment. He loved her with an intensity that went beyond what he could have ever thought was possible, and the time that they had spent apart had only reaffirmed that for him. The touch of her hand gave him comfort now, and he allowed himself to feel reassured by knowing that she had spent more time in the compound and with the Denynso than he had. He was willing now to give himself over to trusting her. Despite loving her from the moment that he saw her, he had struggled within himself to completely make her a part of his journey. He knew that it was because of the loss of his father, the instability within him that came from the years of watching his mother try to navigate living her life without her husband by her side. He never wanted to feel that. As deeply and desperately as it had hurt him to think of a time when he would not share his days and his nights with Ivy, he had forced himself to keep that thought in the back of his mind. He told himself that if he believed she was a tentative presence in his life, something that could at any moment leave, he wouldn't learn to rely on her.

When she began to question his motivations for seeking out an explanation behind his father's disappearance and the actions of the Order, it seemed that he had come to the point that he had dreaded. He had released her so that she would feel like it was easy for him, so that it would seem that it was of little consequence and she could simply go back to the life that she had, had before she had met him. In reality it had felt like he was tearing his very soul from within him, separating a part of himself from the rest of his being. Now he knew that she had be inextricable from him from the moment that they met and that no amount of telling himself that she was not so precious to him would prove it. Instead he was putting himself in the very position that he had been fighting to avoid. Rather than protecting himself from a life of trying to find meaning in a reality without his partner he was creating that very reality for himself. As soon as she was back in his arms, it was as though the air had returned to his lungs. In that moment he knew that he had no choice but to give himself over to her, to accept that she was a part of him and that he would have to trust in everything that they meant to one another.

They moved through the woods as quickly as they could and Maxim was relieved when he heard voices coming from the edge of the trees. He could see the sun on the other side of the shade just before he noticed the three Denynso women standing beneath the first tree of the woods. They each had baskets tucked against their hips and were gathering fruit from the trees. The women looked up at him as they approached and he saw them take several steps back, their faces registering nervousness. One looked to Ivy and seemed to relax slightly as recognition took hold.

"Hello," Ivy said. "Please don't be afraid. Everything's still alright. Do you know where Creia is?"

The women exchanged glances and then looked back at Ivy.

"He isn't here," one of them said, sounding as though it confused her that they didn't know the king was not at the compound.

"What do you mean he isn't here?" Ivy asked. "Where is he?"

"We don't know," another of the women said. "He didn't tell any of us where he was going. Theia told us at breakfast one morning that he had left but should be back soon."

"When was this?" Maxim asked.

The first woman seemed to think for a few moments.

"A few days ago," she told him. "Is there something wrong?"

Maxim didn't understand why, but the response started a slightly panicked feeling within him. Without saying another word he rushed the rest of the way out of the woods and continued toward the center of the compound. He needed to get to the main hall and talk to Theia. Maybe the women had misunderstood what she had said. If nothing else, they needed to know where the king had gone and why he had chosen to wait until the warriors and humans had left the compound to do it.

When they finally made it to the main meeting hall they found Theia sitting in her chair, staring across the room as if completely lost in thought. When the guard announced their arrival she looked at them with an expression of hope blended with worry.

"Maxim," she said, standing and coming to the edge of the platform so that she could take his and Ivy's hands in greeting. "It's good to see you."

"It's good to see you, too, Theia," Maxim said. "This is Athan, my brother Kyven, and Emerie," he introduced, gesturing to the rest of the group.

The queen of the Denynso compound acknowledged each of them with a small nod and then turned her attention back to Maxim.

"Have you heard from Creia?" she asked. "Did he by chance come to your kingdom?"

Maxim felt confused and shook his head.

"No," he told her. "Where did he go?"

Theia looked panic-stricken. She gestured for them to draw closer to the platform.

"Please," she said, lowering her voice, "come with me. I need to speak with you but I don't want anyone else to hear."

The group followed her back around the platform to a spiral staircase that led up to what Maxim could only imagine were her and Criea's private quarters. They entered a lushly decorated room and she closed the door behind them, covering it with a thick tapestry. It seemed like an odd feature, but with everything he was learning about the ways of the planet before he was born and the types of conflicts that existed between the species unfurling before him with every new detail, he could understand the suspicion and caution that went into it.

"Soon after your group returned to the settlement to release those being held and the others left for Earth, Creia told me that there was something that he needed to do. He said that he was feeling guilty for not telling the warriors everything about the origin of our clan and our interactions with some of the other species of Uoria, and that it was time that he fixed everything, but in order to do that he needed to know more. I asked him not to go. I told him that I was scared and that I didn't think that he should be doing this."

"Have you had any communication with him since he left?" Ivy asked.

Maxim knew that the Denynso had the ability to communicate within their bonded pairs simply through their thoughts, enabling them to stay connected to one another even when they were not in the same area. This allowed them to share with one another without others hearing and kept them from being completely distanced from each other, even if they were miles apart. This should mean that Theia had been able to keep in contact with her mate while he was gone and would know where he was. The fact that she had asked them if they had seen him sent a shiver down Maxim's spine.

"No," Theia responded, the emotion making her voice crack. "He has only communicated with me once since he left. I've been trying to connect with him since he's been gone and I haven't been able to. I don't know what to do."

"What did he say when he communicated with you?" Maxim asked.

Theia looked at him with terror in her eyes, the tears trickling down her face and across her lips.

"Badlands."

Maxim felt his body tighten and the fear contract his heart. He remembered what Creia had said about the badlands. These were where his family had lived and where the clan had begun. They were also the site of some of the most brutal fighting that Maxim had ever heard about, fighting that forced half of the clan away and destroyed the other. He knew that if Creia had ventured into the badlands on his own and was not communicating with Theia, there was something wrong.

"We need to get to him," Maxim said. "We have to find him and make sure that he is alright. We're going to need to be able to communicate with Theia while we're gone."

"How?" Ivy asked. "None of us can communicate with each other the way that the Denynso can."

"Maybe one of the couples here on the compound can help us," Theia suggested. "Not all of the warriors left on the shuttle. Some are still here with their mates."

"Call the one you trust the most here. It is very important that he is completely loyal and trustworthy. No one else must know where Creia is or what might have happened to him."

Theia nodded and swept out of the room.

"Do you think that this is going to work?" Ivy asked.

Maxim reached over and took her hand, squeezing it tightly. He didn't want to respond. The truth was he didn't know how to. He could only hope that they were going to be able to find a way to communicate because he knew that he had to find Creia but didn't know what they were going to encounter when they left the compound for the badlands.

Several minutes later Theia came back into the room with two Denynso Maxim didn't recognize. Both looked apprehensive, obviously uncomfortable to be in the private space of the king and queen, a place where none of the Denynso had ever been permitted, even the sons of the king and queen themselves. They were permitted into other spaces of the monarch's quarters, but these rooms had always been reserved only for the couple so that they could have peace and protection only for them away from all of the pressures of their station.

Theia came around the pair and gestured for them to sit. The two stayed close together as they walked further into the room and then settled into place on the cushioned stool on the other side of Ivy. They exchanged glances and Maxim saw them holding hands tightly.

"Thank you for coming," Theia said. "This is Maxim, Ivy, Kyven, Emerie, and Athan. Please meet Nylek and his mate Mina."

The group exchanged half-hearted greetings and Nylek and Mina turned their attention back to Theia, looking at her expectantly.

"What can we do for you, Queen?" Nylek asked carefully.

Theia looked at Maxim.

"Please," she said.

He was stunned at the imploring sound in her voice. This woman was meant to be the strongest of the Denynso clan, and yet she looked frightened and almost as though she was fading away from them. He stood and turned so that he was looking at the pair.

"Before I continue I need to know that you understand that by coming here you are agreeing to be held under the strictest of confidences. Nothing that we discuss here or even the fact that you were asked to come here will be shared with anyone outside of this room. It is of the utmost of importance that you abide by that, and I can assure you that I will hold it to the strictest of adherence."

"We understand," Nylek said.

Maxim looked at Mina and she nodded, leaning slightly closer to her mate as she did it. He knew that they were likely confused and possibly even scared, but he didn't have the time or the patience to comfort them in this moment. He knew that Creia's safety, and possibly his life, rested in the balance and them being able to find him as quickly as possible was essential. It was not just about Creia. What the king knew and his connections with the history of Maxim's kind could make a tremendous difference in the fulfillment of his quest to understand what happened to his father. He could only press forward and pull those that he needed along with him, hoping that he could achieve what he needed to.

"The king may be in danger," he said. Their eyes widened, but he didn't pause for them to ask any questions. "I do not have the time to divulge the specific details. I can only tell you that he has left the compound in an effort to better understand his past and he may have found himself in a very treacherous situation. He has not been in communication with Theia for the majority of his time away and we have reason to belief that his life could be in imminent threat. My group will be leaving as soon as possible to hopefully find him and bring him back safely. In order to do that, however, we will need to remain in communication with the compound. I have asked that Theia select the warrior who she felt would be the most trustworthy to assist us in this mission and she chose you."

"What is it that you need me to do?" Nylek asked, standing.

"I ask that you come with us. Mina will stay here with Theia. Whenever there is need for us to communicate with Theia, you will send the message to Mina, who will relay it to Theia. The reverse will apply if Theia finds out something and needs to share it with us. You will be managing the most sensitive and confidential of information, so I trust you understand the importance of remaining discreet."

"Yes," Nylek said. "I would be honored to serve my king and queen this way."

He extended his hand to Maxim, who gripped it.

"Thank you, Nylek. I appreciate your service."

"Nylek," Theia said, stepping forward. "You will follow Maxim as you would Pyra or Creia himself. He has my full trust."

"I will, Queen."

"When will you leave?" Theia asked. "Will you stay the night?"

"No," Athan said. "That is too long."

"I agree," Maxim said. "We will stay here for a few hours to rest and replenish our supplies from our last trip and then we'll leave. We need to get to Creia as soon as we can."

5

Pyra stepped into the doorway of the bedroom and leaned against the doorframe to watch Eden as she put Lysander to bed. The room was shadowy, lit only by a small lamp on the nightstand that created a halo of light around her as she leaned over the crib and whispered to their infant son. He knew that this was a moment that he wanted to hold onto for the rest of his life. In all of the turmoil and pain that he had experienced in the past weeks, this treasured moment alone made him feel at peace.

Eden straightened and he crossed the room, gently placing a hand on her back. She knew his touch and wasn't startled by it, which brought an even greater sense of warmth to his chest. Even though he had spent his life waiting for the time when he would find his mate, he never would have imagined how it would have changed his existence. He knew that his parents loved each other deeply, but it wasn't until he had met Eden that he really understood what that meant. He never would have allowed himself to imagine the incredible dichotomy of emotions that filled him when it came to Eden and to their child, a child that he never thought would exist.

At once he felt a softness and tenderness that was totally foreign to him. From the time that he was old enough to understand, he was trained in the ways of the warriors. He was born to fight and to defend, and there was no secret throughout the galaxy that the Denynso took this responsibility very seriously. They were not kind when in battle and they showed little tolerance for any who crossed their paths. He was stern and fearsome, yet when she came into his life Eden had shown him that there was a place inside him that was completely vulnerable, if only to her. She could make him feel as though he was completely in her control with only a smile and the touch of her hand had more power on him than the mightiest of weapons that he had ever encountered on the battlefield. The arrival of their son had only brought a greater sense of gentleness and love. The fact that these two beings were tied to him in a way that was completely unchangeable, that even with the fear that she faced Eden was completely at ease with him, was at once empowering and humbling.

On the other hand, the vulnerability and tenderness that he felt when he was near his mate and child seemed also to intensify the feelings of defensiveness and aggression within him. The thought of anyone hurting them in any way infuriated him to a level that was almost unfathomable. In those moments when he felt that either of them was being threatened the world around him became hazy and everything that he saw was edged in red. He struggled to contain himself and he knew that in a single moment he could kill and never think about it again.

That tension was with him now as he curled Eden close to him and turned to kiss her head. The vantage point that his height gave him allowed him to see that even in her pajamas she was wearing the necklace that he had designed for her before the warriors first left the compound. It had been only weeks and yet it seemed a lifetime ago that they had made the decision to step over that boundary wall and see what else laid on the planet of Uoria. It seemed so long ago that he almost couldn't remember the day, just a few weeks before that, when he had met with Jem to design the necklace so that he could make it for Eden.

Just thinking about the friend that he had lost in what he thought was the final encounter that he would ever have with the Klimnu brought the pain and anger back in fresh waves. He had seen death on the fields before, of course. He could not have been a true warrior without knowing the taste and sight of blood, both that he drew and that was drawn from those who had stood beside him. Death among the Denynso was not common, however, and the way that Jem had died had been so much more painful than the deaths of any of the other warriors that he had seen. He did not run into battle and get struck down by another as he fought. He gave himself into death. He offered himself to it, ensuring that he grabbed hold of the last of the Klimnu and took them with him.

As Pyra stared at the pendant on the necklace, the piece of carefully hone metal that represented him cradling his mate and their child in his hand, he wondered if he had been wrong to encourage the other warriors to leave the compound. Their home planet had been a strange and forbidden mystery to them, but they had broken through the bonds of tradition that had held them within the compound and now the world was open to him, but he wasn't completely confident that it was the decision that he should have made. They had learned so much and ensured that at least most of the people in the Nyx 23 settlement survived. At the same time, though, he had caused pain and torment to the Mikana and now there was turmoil on the planet and within his own kind that hadn't existed before. Though he was glad that they had been able to help those that they had, he hoped that it was worth the damage that he felt like he had caused.

Eden let out a sigh and looked up at him.

"What is it?" he asked, stroking her cheek with his thumb.

"I can't stop thinking about Ryan."

"I don't think that he's going to be bothering you again after our conversation in the lab."

"I don't know, Pyra," she said, sounding nervous. "I think more than ever that he is capable of far more than anyone will give him credit for. You saw how he was. There is something going on. He is doing something and it's scaring the hell out of me." She sighed and looked down at the baby again. "And I can't get that picture that Simran and Jane showed us out of my mind."

"Why?" he asked.

She looked back up at him and shook her head slightly.

"There's something about it that really bothers me."

"What?"

"I don't know really. There's just something about it that seems off. I know that that big man in it is Denynso. At least partly."

"What do you mean 'partly'?" he asked, not liking the way that that word sounded.

"Like Lysander," Eden said.

"You are Denynso," Pyra argued. "You have been since Ciyrs healed you."

"I know," she said, "but is he? I didn't carry completely

like a Denysno, but I didn't carry completely like a human, either."

"What are you saying, Eden?"

"We had no way of monitoring how he was growing when I was pregnant with him, so we had no way of knowing how big he was or how developed. We didn't even really know when I got pregnant. What if I got pregnant with him our first time together, before I was changed?"

Pyra struggled enough with the memory of her being nearly killed by a Klimnu who came into the compound. The thought that it was not just Eden, but that she was also carrying their tiny son within her at the time of the attack made the rage soar inside him so that he felt like it was swelling in his muscles and tearing through his skin. He fought with himself to remain calm. His mate was obviously having difficulty with the situation and he didn't want to upset or frighten her any further. It was his responsibility to guard and support her, not to allow his emotions to overtake him.

"What would that have to do with the picture?" he asked.

"If we conceived Lysander during our bond that would mean that I was still fully human when it happened. Ciyrs would have changed me when I was already pregnant. I became Denynso but that doesn't change that the baby would have been made half of human and half of Denynso."

"I still don't understand."

"It means that it's possible, Pyra. It means that Lysander might not be full Denysno, which is proof that the two species can have a child together."

"So that man in the picture may look slightly different not because he is not Denysno, but because he is human as well."

"Yes, and that frightens me."

"Why?"

"Because that means that anything is possible. Every-thing that we know about the Dneynso and the humans is wrong. What does that mean for Uoria? Or just for the future of the species?"

Eden looked worn and scared and Pyra felt his heart aching for her. He hated to see her this way. He glanced down at his son and saw that he was sleeping peacefully, and then took Eden's hand and started leading her out of the room.

"Where are we going?"

"Just come with me," he said.

They walked together through the quiet house, moving carefully so as not to wake the others who were sleeping in the other bedrooms, and out into the back yard. Pyra had never seen anything like it and had been immediately fasci-nated when he first arrived at the house that had been set aside for them to live in during their time on Earth. On Uoria the homes were built very close together and had no barriers between them. While the outer portions of the compound were lush and rich, the center had been cleared out before they built their homes and main buildings, creating an expanse that was largely flat dirt and carefully mapped roads. This simplified and streamlined the area, but it did somewhat take away from the beauty that lay beyond. Here, though, the homes were much larger and further apart. Even the modest home where they were staying was considerably larger than the average warrior house and each had its own little segment of land that was partitioned off from the others with tall fences that did not permit those living on either side of the home to access or even see into it. Within this confine was soft green grass and towering trees, meticulously organized gardens of flowers and playthings that had once belonged to children who had lived there.

Pyra had been wary of the lawn when he first saw it. He appreciated the open, cooperative nature of the compound and the way that the closeness of the buildings connected all who lived there. After spending time in the grass and feeling the quiet peacefulness that came from being on the private section of land, though, he realized that he also very much valued that occasional time to be on his own and to not have to always live up to the outward behaviors and appearances that were expected of him. He could simple breathe and not have to think of anything but what was happening right there with him. He didn't know how he would feel about always being separated from everyone else and having the members of the clan isolate themselves rather than spending more time together as it seemed that many humans on Earth did. For the time of their visit, however, he was going to enjoy the lawn, and that started with spending some time in it with Eden.

Eden seemed to curl into herself slightly as they walked across the moonlight-dappled grass. She looked to either side of herself, wrapping the hand that wasn't holding Pyra's around her arm as if to cover herself.

"It's alright," he said to her. "It's just us out here. No one can see you."

Eden nodded and smiled up at him. They continued until they reached a thick tree that had slats of wood nailed along its trunk. Pyra released Eden's hand and started climbing up the pieces of wood. When he was nearly to the top he turned and glanced down at Eden, who stared up at him with a look of confusion on her face.

"What are you doing, Pyra?" she asked.

"I'm going up to the treehouse," he told her.

"What?" Eden said with laughter in her voice.

"Samira told me that human children like to play in these. I've never seen one before and I want to explore it."

"It's just a tree house Pyra," she said. "It's just a big wooden square with walls."

"I want to see."

Eden chuckled and started up the slats of wood behind him. Pyra continued until he reached the gap in the side of the treehouse that served as the door and slid his way inside. His shoulders barely fit and for a moment he was worried that he was going to get stuck and he was going to have the embarrassment of having to send Eden to get one of the other warriors so that he could help Pyra get out of the treehouse. Fortunately he made his way into the small space and was able to move out of the way for Eden to join him.

The inside of the treehouse was much too small for Pyra to actually stand up, but he was able to sit and lean back against the wall, curling his legs in to give Eden the room to come inside.

"We shouldn't stay out here very long," Eden said. "Lysander might need us."

"He's asleep," Pyra reassured her, "and if he does wake up and start crying one of the others in the house will hear him. He will be just fine."

He reached for her and pulled her into his arms, positioning her in his lap and cradling her against his chest. He tilted his head back and saw a rope tied from the center of the ceiling to a hook on the wall.

"What's that?" he asked.

Eden looked at it and shrugged.

"I don't know."

Filled with curiosity, Pyra reached up and unwound the

rope from the hook, giving it a hard tug. A section of the ceiling came down, opening up so that they could look up through the branches of the tree to the stars scattered above them.

"Did your treehouse when you were young have that?" Pyra asked.

Eden laughed softly.

"I didn't have a treehouse when I was young," she told him.

"You didn't?"

Pyra was beginning to truly recognize the variations that existed in the lives of human children on Earth. On the compound on Uoria lives were incredibly similar. Children had specific callings from birth and they discovered them fairly early. It was obvious who was meant to be a warrior and who would take on other roles within the clan, like Ciyrs the healer and Ty the baker and nurturer. When they were not training for those positions, they played in much the same ways. Since the clan was extremely cooperative in most ways, at least until the young warriors got old enough to begin feeling their strong urges toward the women and may choose to separate themselves in order to wait for their mate, there was little sense of those who had a lot and those who had little. Even he, the most powerful son of the king and queen, played with all of the other children and maintained a life virtually indistinguishable from theirs. The only real difference is that until he was old enough to be on his own he slept in the family quarters of the meeting hall. The realization that there were major differences in the opportunities and realities of the children of Earth made him sad and he was more thankful than ever that his own son was born and would be raised on their home of Uoria.

"No," Eden replied. "I didn't spend much time at home

when I was a child. Most of the time I was with my grand-mother and she didn't have trees in her yard that were big enough for us to build a treehouse. Even if she had, I'm not sure how we would have built one."

"Didn't you ever want to know what it was like to play in one?" he asked.

"Oh, I played in some of my friends'," she told him. "Not everyone had one, but the ones who did would usually invite groups of us over and we would play these elaborate games. That all pretty much ended by the time that we were eleven or twelve, though."

"What happened after that?"

"We just got too old for the games. Then people started using their treehouses for other reasons."

Eden giggled but Pyra didn't understand. He gave Eden a questioning look and she smiled at him.

"The girls used to bring their boyfriends up into their treehouses when they wanted to spend some time with them without their parents knowing," she explained.

Pyra was still getting used to the human concept of dating, but he caught on to what she was saying and imme-diately felt his stomach tighten in the way that it had since the moment that he sensed his mate was on her way to him.

"So you never got to do that?" he asked, running his hand up her back and feeling the slight ripples of her spine beneath the soft fabric of her pajamas.

"No," she said.

She sounded slightly breathless and he knew that she was feeling the same thing that he was. He ran his fingers along the back of her neck and around her shoulder so that he traced the neckline of her shift.

"Did you ever wish that you got to?" he asked.

"I never had anyone that I wanted to do it with."

"How about now?" he asked. "Can I make up that memory for you?"

Eden nodded and Pyra bent forward, capturing her mouth with his. It suddenly felt as if all of the tension and stress within him broke and he was able to completely lose himself in the feeling of her lips on his and her hips rolling subtly into his lap. He used the tip of his tongue to coax her mouth open and delved in, tasting her full as he used his hands to gather the hem of her long pajama shirt up her thighs and over her hips. As he did that Eden pulled at the ties on the front of his pants, releasing them so that she could free the erection that was pressing up toward her, aching for her.

She ran her hand adoringly along the length of him, applying just enough pressure that it sent waves of incredible sensation through him without pushing him too close to the edge. The combination was intoxicating and Pyra felt himself getting dizzy with his need for her. Eden had worn nothing beneath her pajama shirt and he could already feel the wet heat from her body pressing against his. He took her by her hips and lifted her, bringing her up so that he could enter her. She moaned as she settled back into his lap, taking him fully into her so that their bodies melded completely. Pyra leaned forward and touched his lips to the soft skin above the neckline of her shirt. Tucking his hands behind the small of her back he led Eden's hips into a deep rocking motion that kept him fully inside her but let him feel the intense sensation of her warm, tight walls massaging against his length.

Eden's head fell back and she let out a deep groan, her hands coming to Pyra's shoulders so that she could grip him as she picked up the rhythm of his hands. Pyra brought one of his hands around her hips so that he could use the pad of his thumb to stroke the taut pearl of flesh at her peak. The touch of his hand seemed to send her nearly out of control. She cried out and rolled her hips with greater insistence, at once pressing against his hand and driving him deeper inside her. Pyra had wanted to hold off, making their time together last, but he knew that he wasn't going to be able to control himself. He tightened his grip on her hip with one hand and continued to massage her with his thumb as he thrust up into her in a harder, faster rhythm.

He could feel his climax rushing upwards and he pulled her forward, crushing his mouth down on hers so that he could roar into their kiss as he poured into her. Eden gasped against his mouth, her fingers grinding down into his shoulders as he felt her squeeze him then contract around him in a series of pulses that pulled him deeper and drew each drop of him into her body. Finally their mouths parted and they panted against each other's shoulders, cradling each other in their arms as they let the preciousness of their reality together distract them, if only for a few moments, from the turmoil that existed just beyond that simple treehouse that they had made their fortress.

6

Creia felt like the life was slowly draining out of him and he fought to resist it. The room around him was dark and he could feel the table beneath him moving as it propped him up again, bringing him back to the position that had become so painfully familiar. He knew that in moments the hooded creature would come back and attach him again to the screen that would show him the strange laboratory room. He didn't understand the purpose of the ritual. The scene barely changed each time that he was forced to stare at it for hours. The only thing that he ever noticed that seemed to change was the position of the creature in the tube in the corner. There were days when it slumped and hung from its binds in such a way that Creia wondered if it was still alive. There were other times when it strained and thrashed, fighting against the chains with an almost terrifying fury.

As he waited for the screen to take its place in front of his eyes, Creia wondered when the last time that he ate was. The hooded being had come into the room a few times and poured water down his throat, but hadn't fed him.

Consciousness came to him randomly and without him knowing how long he had been awake or asleep so he didn't know how long he had been held captive. He could feel the weakness coming over him, however, and knew that he wouldn't be able to struggle much more. He had stopped fighting against the screen. His only hope was to conserve the strength that he did have so that he would have the best chances if he did happen to have the opportunity to get out of his binds and come up against the hooded creature, possibly allowing him to get out of wherever he was.

A moment later the hooded creature stepped into the room again and Creia gave himself over to having the screen attached to his head. The laboratory appeared in front of him again and he scanned it with his eyes to see if anything had changed. At first there was nothing different that he could see and he wondered if he was going to have to sit there and stare at the unchanging space again for several more hours still not understanding the purpose. After a few moments, however, the space changed. He noticed a long shadow cross the floor and the creature in the tube in the corner visibly stiffened. Creia strained to see who may have come into the room and a moment later saw a man in a stark white coat appear in his field of vision. The man at first acted like he didn't even realize that Creia was watching him. He moved around the space repositioning tubes and vials on the tables, then crossed to the creature in the back and slammed his hand against the thick glass that contained it. Creia saw the creature pull away from the glass as if startled by the sound.

The man laughed and then turned, looking directly at Creia. The king felt his eyes burning into him in a way that sent a tremor down his spine. The man approached slowly and gave Creia a vile, disturbing smile.

"Hello, king," he said, the last word have a distinct edge of disdain. "So kind of you to accept my invitation."

"Who are you?" Creia forced through his tight, dry throat.

Just the effort that it took for him to say that made him feel weaker and he could see spots bursting in his vision.

"Don't worry about that," the man said. "You don't need to know who I am. All that matters is that I know who you are and that I finally have you."

"What do you mean?"

"I have been so patient," the man said, the image of his face coming even closer. "I have waited so long and now, I finally have what I have been waiting for. It has been years. Years of my life that I have spent wanting to pay homage to my family and finish what they started. There were times when I was so frustrated, so angry. I felt like I may never actually succeed. I always thought that I was going to be the one who was going to be able to make my family proud. You see, they worked so hard. They were revolutionaries who were never accepted and respected the way they should have been in their time. Do you know how much that tormented me? How much I hated finding out that these incredible men who saw the world in a way that no one else did and could have completely changed the entire universe were shunned because of their brilliance? I didn't want that to continue. Even though they went to their graves knowing that their lives' work had not ever been fulfilled and that the scientific community had never found the place for them that they deserved, I was going to fix it. I was going to be the one who picked up where they left off and finished it."

"I don't understand."

"You don't need to. It has taken more work than you could ever imagine to finally get you here, but I managed it all. I will admit, though, I did almost lose faith for a short time. I thought that I had everything so perfectly planned out. I knew...I just *knew*... that everything was going to work out perfectly when I sent Eden to Uoria for her research."

"*Ryan,*" Creia growled, feeling a surge of anger flow through him as he realized that the face of the man in front of him was that of the man who Eden had described to him as being such a source of torment to her.

Ryan gave a malevolent laugh.

"I see no introductions were really needed. My reputation already precedes me."

"Where is Eden?" Creia asked.

"I don't know where she is," Ryan said. "For now. You see, I had this all planned out. It was all planned out. Eden didn't want to play nice with me when she was here. I could have made her a part of all of this and it would have been incredible. She would have had a life that she could never have imagined. It would have been amazing. Instead, she pushed me away. I didn't like that. For a while I was really upset about it. I wondered what it was that I did wrong and I let it really get to me. Suddenly, though, I realized that she had actually given me an opportunity. She had made it so much easier for me to get what I wanted. I told her that she would go to your compound and collect the blood of the most powerful of the Denynso warriors and then return here. Of course, I knew that that was not ever going to happen. Everyone knows how closely guarded you are and how aggressively you defend the blood of your kind. I knew that she would go and as soon as it was discovered what she was doing, you would see to it that she was either imprisoned or killed."

"I would never have done that," Creia argued.

"Of course you would have," Ryan said. "You would have

absolutely no problem punishing her in the exact way that you would have punished anyone else who was attempting to do that. And when you did, Earth would have responded. There would have been a military response and it would have been quick and fierce. I would have gotten exactly what I wanted...you presented to me for my own use. I would be rid of Eden, she would have paid for the humiliation that she had put me through, and I would have the chance to continue the work that my family had started. At least, that's what I thought was going to happen. That's what I had planned. I never suspected that she would admit what she was doing. She ruined everything for me. She destroyed the entire plan and made it so that I didn't feel like I had any options anymore. But now I do."

"I won't do anything for you."

"You already have," Ryan told him. "Of course it's not the same as it could have been. You are not here so that I can use you directly, but that doesn't mean that you aren't helping me. Every time that I have attached you to this screen I am also attaching you to the lab itself. I have been feeding your fear and your anger into my system, and that is exactly what I have needed. I will continue to use you until there is nothing left. It will be easy to go from there. It's not like I don't have other Denynso right at my fingertips now. In fact, I have your bloodline so close all I have to do is go after them. It is only a matter of time now before I am able to complete my plan." He paused and gave a low chuckle. "You know, it's a bonus that I get everything I wanted and still get to seek revenge on Eden."

7

"Are you alright?"

Ivy stepped into the bedroom of the small Denynso house that she had stayed in for the short time that she had spent on the compound as Maxim turned toward her. He was carefully unpacking everything in his bags and laying the items out on the bed. She knew that he was taking note of what he had and what he might need for the journey that lay ahead of them. The systematic concentration in his movements, however, told her that there was more to the process than just ensuring that they were prepared for the mission that lay ahead of them. He seemed to be distracting himself with the process, letting himself focus all of his energy and effort on going through their supplies rather than the thoughts that were really on his mind.

"Why did he leave?" he asked.

"Creia?" Ivy asked.

"My father."

"What do you mean?" she asked, walking further into the

room so that she could stand beside her partner and run her hand along his back.

"My mother and Athan both said that he was different before he left for that battle. He knew that something was going to happen. Why did he leave?"

Ivy let out a breath.

"I obviously never knew your father, but from what I have learned about him from what I've heard everyone saying about him, he was extremely dedicated to what the Order once was and to doing what was right. He knew something about the Klimnu and the heads of the Order, and it was important to him that he did what he needed to do to resolve it in whatever way that he could. I don't know what that was and I don't know what he had planned to do, but he left because he knew that he had to."

"Did he?"

"Do you?"

Maxim turned to look at her and she saw the familiar softness in his eyes that she had fallen so desperately in love with.

"I won't stop until I feel like I've done everything that I can for my father."

"And he was doing everything that he could for his kind and for you."

Maxim opened his arms to her and Ivy stepped into them, letting him draw her close so that she could feel his heartbeat against her chest.

"What do you think that Creia went after?" he asked.

Ivy stepped back and looked at him, shaking her head.

"I don't know," she admitted. "Theia said that he wanted to know more about the clan that used to live in the other settlement, but that compound was completely destroyed.

You saw it as well as I did. He said that the enemies came in and ensured that it would continue burning forever. What could he possibly find there?"

"There has to be something," Maxim said. "There has to be some reason that he left the compound, especially when most of the warriors aren't here."

"I feel like he did that on purpose."

"Why?"

"He might not have wanted the warriors to know that he was leaving. Maybe he thought that he was only going to be gone for a short time and that he would know what he needed to and be back before everyone returned. That's why he specifically waited until the group had left for Earth before he left."

"What do you think we're going to find out there?" Maxim asked.

"I don't know," Ivy said.

She felt like those were words that she was saying more now that she had in her entire life.

"There's something out there," he said. "Something that I'm afraid will link Creia and what happened to my father. It can't be a coincidence that both of them were drawn to the badlands right before they disappeared."

"Your father didn't die in the badlands, though. He was in battle."

"But my mother said that he had traveled to the badlands because of the Klimnu." He let out a breath and leaned forward to rest a gentle kiss to her lips. "I am going to take a shower before we leave," he said.

Ivy nodded and watched him walk out of the bedroom toward the bathroom. She heard the water running and turned to look at everything that Maxim had spread out across the bed. She wished that there was more that she could do for him. The brief time that she thought that she had lost him had made her feel as though her heart had been torn from her chest and she couldn't bear the thought of feeling like she could let him slip through her fingers again. Thoughts of returning to Earth were completely gone from her mind now and she hated that she had ever let them alienate him. She had been so insistent about not wanting to be on Uoria and wishing that she hadn't come, and now that she had felt what it was to miss Maxim she wished that she had never said them. It hurt her to know that she had ever made him think that she didn't want to be with him or that she wouldn't do everything that it took to stay with him. Now she couldn't even begin to think about leaving Uoria. Maxim was her home and wherever he was, was where she would be.

She listened to the sounds of the water for a few more moments before going into the bathroom. Maxim's clothing was scattered on the floor and she let hers join it. Ivy moved the curtain aside and stepped into the shower behind Maxim. She came up close behind him and wrapped her arms around his waist, leaning forward to rest her head on his back as her hands smoothed up his belly onto his chest. The warmth of his skin comforted her and she relaxed into the feeling of her body molding against his and the hot water washing down over them. Maxim's hand covered hers on his chest and his other came around to hold her hip, pulling her closer.

Ivy kissed his back and nuzzled his skin with her face, stroking his chest with her thumb.

"I love you," she whispered.

"I love you," he whispered back, leaning back so that his head rested on her shoulder.

Ivy pulled her arms from around him and filled her

palm with some of the thick, shimmering body wash that was still left in the shower from when she had first moved into the small home. She held her palm under the water briefly, allowing it to turn the gel into lush bubbles and the steam to carry the sweet smell throughout the space. She carefully spread the bubbles along his skin, washing him tenderly. It was a quiet gesture, one she hoped would show him how deeply she truly loved him and how devoted she was to taking care of him.

Her hands moved along his back and across his shoulders, then down his arms so that she leaned forward and pressed her breasts to his back as she washed his hands. Her fingertips followed the deep dip of his spine between his strong muscles and then along his hips.

Finally he turned and gathered her into his arms, pulling her under the water with him. He held her close, tenderly kissing his way down her neck. She could feel his body responding to her and subtly brushed against him. Maxim's hands ran along the side of her ribs and her waist then slipped around to grip her. Their mouths met and played across each other as Ivy indulged herself by running her hands along his body. The feeling of his muscles rippling beneath her palms was hypnotizing and she felt her craving for him building even more within her.

Maxim led her backwards until she was against the wall and parted their lips. He looked at her with hunger in his eyes and lowered himself to his knees in front of her. His mouth slid down her body, his tongue occasionally touched her skin, bringing shivers of pleasure through her. They settled between her legs and Maxim followed them, drawing his tongue through her core. Ivy's eyes closed and her head fell back against the wall as the feeling jolted through her. Maxim swept one up beneath her leg and lifted it up so that she opened more to him and pressed his mouth closer. She couldn't withhold the sounds pouring from her lips as he continued to nurture her with his tongue and lips. Her hand ran through his hair and settled at the back of his head.

She felt like she was spiraling out of control and she tilted her hips toward his mouth seeking more of the incredible sensations that he was creating within her. She was just on the edge of oblivion when he suddenly rose to his feet, lifting her leg higher and burying his long, thick erection in her in one smooth movement. Ivy cried out at the feeling of him filling her and wrapped her arms around him, pulling him closer. Maxim held her leg around his waist and rolled his hips to drive deeply into her. As he thrust into her, Ivy lifted onto the ball of her supporting foot and then lifted it, wrapping it around him so that both of her legs were around his waist.

Maxim grabbed her by her hips and drove into her harder, using the position to his advantage by stepping slightly away from the wall so that she was at an angle. This allowed him to move harder and faster, pushing so far into her that he created a delirious pleasure that was just on the edge of being overwhelming. He felt impossibly hard within her and her body cradled him like it was crafted specifically for him. It was a feeling so beyond anything that she had ever experienced, something beyond just the physical to a place that was truly transcendent.

Ivy felt Maxim thrust into her one final hard time and roared as he pulsed against her walls. The feeling sent her tumbling over the edge and her own climax responded to his, clutching him so that their bodies melded further and she welcomed his essence into her.

When the waves of their orgasms eased, Ivy lowered her

legs and they slid to the bottom of the shower, allowing the now cool water to wash over them as their bodies tangled and their mouths leisurely explored each other. Ivy rested her head on Maxim's chest and let her fingers trace along Maxim's body, enjoying the contrast between the heat of his skin and the cool of the water. Finally they knew that as much as they wanted to hang on to these precious moments and pretend that there was nothing else for them to be doing, their time was running short and they needed to leave. They climbed out of the shower and dressed slowly, reluctantly, before carefully repacking and leaving to meet the others at the main hall where Theia had gathered further supplies for them.

Ivy watched as each of the members of their group picked up their bags. Emerie had a somewhat frightened look in her eyes but kept her expression steady and strong. Ivy admired her courage. She knew how overwhelming and scary it was to be at the edge of a quest into a completely unknown world that held challenges and threats she couldn't even begin to imagine. Ivy remember how she felt when she realized that her time in the Denynso compound was going to be nothing like she had first imagined and that she would in fact be leaving it to help those on the outside. At least then there was a clear reason for them to leave the compound. They knew what it was that they were doing and why they were doing it. Now they were faced with a totally dark road ahead. They knew only that they needed to find Creia. None of them had ever been in the badlands or knew what was there.

As she looked at her, though, Ivy remembered that

Emerie was not a woman who had just come from Earth and found herself thrust into this type of experience. Instead she was a woman who had left home when she was very young, climbed aboard a spaceship, and left for a planet that she had never seen and that was filled with a cruel and unpredictable species. This was a woman who had found herself crashed and stranded on a planet that she hadn't even known existed until they arrived and had not crumbled. She had spent fifteen years rebuilding her life and then survived an attack that was meant to kill everyone in the settlement. This was a woman who could handle whatever may be waiting for them. Emerie might have fear in her eyes, but she had steel in her blood.

Theia stepped up to Maxim and took his hands between hers.

"Thank you, Maxim. Please, stay safe." She stepped back and took Ivy's hand in one of hers and Athan's in the other. "Stay safe all of you."

Nylek and Mina embraced tightly and Ivy could see Mina's hand gripping the back of his shirt as he held her. She could sense the pain coming off of her and Ivy felt a pang. Nylek was fulfilling his duty to the clan and to his king, but that didn't change how difficult it was for her to watch the man she loved walking away without knowing what he was facing and when, or even if, he would return.

They stepped out of the meeting hall and into the soft sunlight of a gradually deepening afternoon. Athan had told them that it wasn't safe to bring the Mikana vehicles and had hidden them before they gathered their supplies so they took off on foot as they had when Creia led them to the ledge. They walked in silence, their own thoughts fueling them forward. Finally they reached the ledge and climbed to the top, seeming to follow in the same footsteps that they had the first time. Maxim was the first to reach the plateau and Ivy came up to stand beside him. She followed his gaze and looked out over the burning destruction of the badlands.

TBC

(To be continued in book IX...)

THE ALIEN'S WINGS

"**I** found it."

Lynx tossed the broken piece of the ship that he held in his hand back to the ground and started back across the room toward Rain. She was crouched in the wreckage with her back to him but he could see that she was holding something in her lap. The room around them was in remarkable condition compared to the rest of the ravaged ship. Though it was still crushed and broken, much of the room was still standing and appeared almost as Lynx assumed it did when the ship was in service. This had been the private quarters of the captain of the ship that had brought the Nyx 23 crew to Uoria, and out of respect they had left it as it was after the crash rather than breaking it down to make into the buildings of their settlement as they had with the rest of the ship.

Rain turned around and showed Lynx the box that she held on her thighs. She looked like she was almost cradling the box as she looked up at him with difficult to decipher emotion in her eyes. He felt a deep, painful pull in his chest as he looked at her. He had known that she was different since the moment that he met her, that she had been locked in place by the vicious and vengeful Covra and had been lying in place for more than a century. Knowing this, however, didn't change how it made him feel when he looked at her and saw those years reflected back at him through her eyes. It was in that moment that he could really feel the differences in the lives that they had lived and realized just how distanced their realities were from one another. No matter how deeply the two of them loved each other and how much they truly wanted to be together, there was no arguing the reality that they would never completely and fully understand each other. What she had gone through in the decades before he was even born was something that he could never fathom, and it would be his struggle for the rest of their lives to not only do everything that he could to understand as much of her as possible, but also to show her that even if he didn't completely understand her, he still loved her fully, totally, and without reservation.

Lynx approached her carefully and lowered himself down onto the ground with her. She continued to hold the box reverently and he wondered what emotions were moving through her in that moment. After she shared the horrifying memories of finding the captain dead moments before the crash Lynx knew that there was much more to this experience than he had originally thought and he was determined to help her get through it in whatever way that would soothe the ache within her.

"Do you want to open it?" he asked after several long moments.

"I don't know," Rain said back softly. She looked down at the box and ran her hand along it. "What do you think that I'm going to find in here?" she asked, looking up at him.

"I don't know," he said, shaking his head. "I don't know what would be in there. I'm still not completely sure what it is."

Rain nodded as if what he had said was undeniable truth and glanced back down at the box.

"What if what we find in here is horrible? What if it tells me something that I really don't want to know?"

"What could you find out that would be so horrible?" Lynx asked. "What could be in there that would be something so terrible you just don't want to know?"

She looked up at him and he could see the thoughts churning in her eyes. He hoped that asking her that would give her the confidence to open the box that she had been so aggressively searching for and let her know that no matter what was inside, she would be able to handle it.

"What if the captain was involved in all of this?" she asked. "We always assumed that having our travel course manipulated so that we came to Uoria and crashed was completely the work of the Valdicians and that there was nothing that anyone on the ship could do about it. What if that wasn't the case at all? Maybe the captain actually knew about the prison colony on Penthos and created the entire Nyx 23 project as a ruse to get scientists up here so that the Validicians could use them as they pleased. Maybe he knew that they were allies with the Covra here and were looking for a powerful species to act as their slaves and help them with their mission to take over the planet and ultimately the rest of the galaxy so he created this entire project under the guise that it was about freeing the planet and saving everyone on it, when in reality he knew all the time that we were going to end up on Uoria."

It was a possibility that Lynx hadn't considered, and one that made him feel like there was ice water running through his veins. The thought that the captain, the man that the rest of the crew trusted above all others and without reservation, would have actually be one to betray them was something that Lynx couldn't fathom. Even when Pyra had been so cruel in the settlement and imprisoned the Mikana men, he had done it thinking that what he was doing was the right thing to protect his kind and guard the future for his son. He would never had given up the life, safety, and comfort of the Denynso for someone else. Lynx couldn't even imagine the level of pain and betrayal that that kind of revelation would have caused him and the other warriors.

"You said that he was dead when you found him," Lynx said cautiously. She hadn't yet said the actual words that the captain was dead when she discovered him in his control room right before the crash, but she knew and he had to force her to think about it so that she could understand. "What do you think killed him?"

Rain didn't look at him. She continued to run her palm along the box and suddenly let out a breath. She didn't respond to his question, but he knew that she was thinking about it. Finally she took the latch on the front of the box with a shaky hand and released it. Designed specifically to withstand a disaster, the box was unharmed and only small vines that had grown up around it indicated that it had been sitting among the wreckage for more than 100 years. The lid opened without resistance and fell back to reveal its contents.

Rain lowered the box to the ground and began to sift through the items inside. Nothing that Lynx saw had any meaning for him, but Rain touched each of them carefully and with respect. Even with her concerns about the pilot possibly betraying all of them, she still felt incredible loyalty to the man who had led then in their mission and who they had thought of and memorialized in everything that they had done on Uoria since the crash. Suddenly she moved aside a piece of paper and Lynx saw a small book sitting on the bottom of the box. It was bound in dark leather and a name was embossed in gold across the front.

"Etan," he read.

"That was the pilot's name," she explained.

She touched the name with her fingertips. There was no romance in the touch, just a deep sense of connection that reached the memories within her that she had until recently refused to allow herself to speak. Lynx knew that she had spent her time in the settlement trying to overcome what she had found in the pilot's control room before the crash, and never sharing it with anyone. Greyson had been there just a few moments after the crash and given her the light that confirmed that she was looking at the body of the pilot. She had never told him, though, that she was sure that Etan had been dead for some time before the crash. She had never told any of the crew what she thought had happened to him or what that meant for the rest of the team.

Rain opened the book and scanned a few of the pages. Lynx leaned closer so that he could look at the pages along with her. Each page was filled with close, tight handwriting that seemed to chronicle what the pilot was going through each day.

"What is this?" he asked Rain.

She turned the page and started reading the next set of tiny handwriting.

"It's his journal," she explained. "It's a book that people use to record what is happening in their lives and what they are feeling. Do the Denynso do that?"

Lynx shook his head.

"No," he said. "What does it say?"

"He recorded the entire mission from a few days before we left. He talks about what he was thinking about our goals in the quest and what he was hoping to get out of it."

"So he wasn't an ally of the Validicians."

Rain nodded, letting out a breath that sounded calm and relieved.

"I don't think so. This was his private journal. He never intended on anyone else reading it. He would have no reason to conceal what he was thinking or how he was feeling about his actual motivations if they weren't what we thought they were going to be."

"That's good," Lynx said. "Right?"

He felt strangely out of control in the situation. He wanted to comfort and support her, but it was like he was looking at her from the other side of all of the time that had passed since that moment when she crouched beside the pilot's body and realized that he was dead. Rather than being there with her and looking back through those moments alongside her, he felt as though she had somehow transported back to that moment and he was now separated from her in a way that he couldn't overcome on his own. He would have to wait for her to come back to him.

Rain nodded again and continued through the book. As the pages progressed Lynx realized that the handwriting was getting larger and more erratic. Some pages only had a few words while others were so full it was almost impossible for them to read them properly. She was growing close to the pages that would describe their arrival on the planet that held the illegal prison colony, a planet that would later come to be known as Penthos, when a sheet of paper slipped out from between the pages and fluttered onto the ground between them. Rain reached down slowly and picked it up. Lynx watched her stare at the folded paper for a few moments, her eyes looking as though she were nervous to open it.

Finally she lowered the journal to her legs and used both trembling hands to carefully open the fold and smooth the paper out so that they could read it.

"What is it?" Lynx asked.

"I don't know," Rain said softly.

She turned the paper around in her hands and continued to stare at the faint image.

"It looks like a map," Lynx said, reaching forward to run his finger along one of the lines that appeared to be a road.

"A map to what?" Rain asked.

Lynx took the paper from her hands and looked down at it, trying to decipher the symbols and shapes on the map. Something about the map looked strangely familiar. He continued to stare at it, turning it in his hands so that he looked at it from different angles as the memory that was lingering in the back of his mind continued to come to shape and deepen so that he could examine it further. Finally the memory came to the front of his mind and he realized that he was looking at a map that looked very much like the one that the Denynso warriors had discovered in the prison that had led them to the Nyx 23 settlement during their first exploration of the planet.

"I think it is Uoria," he said. "It looks like a primitive sketching of the planet." He touched an area toward the top corner. "This is where the Denynso compound is. This," he gestured toward another area of the map further down and to one side, "is where your settlement was built."

Rain reached over and took the map from his hands and gazed down at it. She touched her fingertips to the area of the map where he had said the settlement was found and ran them along toward the center of the paper.

"Then this is about where we crashed."

"What does that mean?" Lynx asked, pointing toward a symbol on the top corner opposite of the Denysno compound.

Rain shook her head.

"I don't know. Do you know what is in that area of Uoria?"

"No," he said. "Remember when we left the compound and came to your settlement was the first time that we had left the compound. I don't know of anything that is on Uoria except for what I have seen since then."

Rain looked at the map again and gestured toward another area of the planet.

"This is where the Mikana kingdom is," she told him.

"Why would the pilot have a map of Uoria in his journal?" Lynx asked. "I thought that you said that you didn't even know that the planet existed."

"We didn't," Rain said. "At least, I didn't. The rest of the project crew said that they didn't either. We had never come across it in our preparation for the mission. That was why when we crashed we didn't know where we were or what to do. It was a foreign planet to us and we didn't even have any context of what the planet might be like. It made building our settlement and learning what we could eat much more challenging than it would have been if we had known anything about this planet."

"If he didn't know that the planet existed, though, how would Etan have a map of it? What would he use it for if he didn't know what it was?"

Rain picked up the journal again and Lynx could see her eyes roaming rapidly across the pages, taking in the words as quickly as she could. She turned the pages harshly the further she read and he could see color creeping across her cheeks.

"He knew," she said, her voice now low and gravelly with anger.

"What do you mean he knew? What did he know?" Lynx asked.

"He knew that Uoria was here. He knew that we were coming here."

"I don't understand," he said.

Rain shook her head.

"*I hope that what I have discovered is not true,*" she read. "*In our time in the prison colony I was able to breach the inner quarters of one of the Valdician officers. In it I found what I believed to be the personal journal of the officer. I stole a map that I found in it. I didn't have the time to read everything that the journal entry said, but it led me to believe that the Valdicians anticipated our arrival. They do not intend on allowing us to go back to Earth. This map is to a planet that they call Uoria and I fear that they are planning to send us there. I don't know why they would want us on this planet or what awaits us there if we allow them to send us there, but I can only hope that if I am not able to overcome them that having this map will help me to lead my crew even there.*"

"How did the Valdicians know that you were coming?" Lynx asked.

"There must have been a leak. Someone on our crew must have betrayed us."

"But why didn't he tell the rest of you when you got back on the ship and left the planet with the prison colony? Wouldn't he think that all of you deserved to know what was going on?"

Rain turned the page and scanned the entry.

"*The ship is no longer under my command. I am terrified and do not know what to do. The rest of the team doesn't know and I am doing everything that I can to keep them from finding out. They believe that I am still piloting this ship and that we are on the proper course back to Earth. I do not know how much longer I will be able to conceal from them that the weapons the Valdicians attached to our ship have taken over our internal control system and are now bringing the ship off course and in what I can only assume is the direction of this planet Uoria. What will I tell them? How will I confess to them that I have guided them toward a fate that could be more horrible than any of us can fathom?*" She let out a breath and looked at Lynx. "He wanted to protect us."

"Is there anything else?"

Rain turned the page and Lynx saw that the handwriting had returned to the tight, controlled hand of the earlier entries as if the pilot had stepped back from the panic that had taken over his mind and was now able to think clearly again. The precision in the shape of the words showed a man who had pushed away fear and was now looking ahead with clarity and determination. Lynx could hear the tears in Rain's voice as she read the entry.

"*I had hoped desperately that I would be able to find a way to reclaim the ship under my own control and prevent it from going to Uoria. That hope is now lost. The technology that the Valdicians have used to take over the ship is beyond anything that I have ever seen and I cannot even begin to decipher it. It has not just taken over the control of the ship, but has also destroyed all forms of communication. We are not able to access any one in our mission control team or any of the other ships that are trav-eling through the galaxy. We are completely alone and there is nothing that we can do. I know now that we will never return to Earth. Never again will we see the planet that we have called home or the people who we love. I wish that there was more than*

I could do for the people who have followed me with such devotion and determination. I believe that the map that I found shows where the Valdicians intend for us to be when we find our way to Uoria. I can only imagine what horrors may await us there, if we even survive our arrival. I have decided that I am not going to tell the crew what I know. They already know that the ship is no longer under our control and that we have moved completely off course. I know that telling them about the map and what I think about the Validicians will only cause them to panic and ruin what morale we have left. There is no reason to do that to them. They followed me, Journal. They trusted me. I am responsible for what has happened to us. As I lead them toward death I know that it should be me that leads them into death. I can only pray for all of our souls and that one day someone will understand."

The tears were streaming down Rain's face by the time that she finished. She turned the page of the journal but all of the papers that followed were blank. Lynx rested his hand on her back and she turned to look at him.

"He killed himself," she whispered. "He felt so guilty because he thought that he was responsible for all of this and didn't believe that we would survive. He believed that he should be the first of us to die."

"I'm so sorry," Lynx said.

He knew that it wasn't enough. There wasn't anything that he would be able to say that would be enough in this situation, and those words were the only ones that he was able to bring forward. He wished that he could do something, anything, to ease the pain that he knew that his mate was feeling, and take away the guilt and the suffering that he could see crossing her face. Rain continued to look into his eyes for several more seconds and then he saw a sudden spark of light in them as if a thought had come into her mind.

"The map," she said.

He reached for it and handed it to her.

"What about it?" he asked.

Rain spread the map out over the journal and ran her hand across it.

"You said that this would be where the Denynso compound is," she said, gesturing to the area on the map that Lynx had showed her.

"That's right," Lynx said.

"And this would be where the settlement that we made is," she said, gesturing to that area of the map.

"Yes," Lynx told her. "And this is the wreckage," he said, pointing to the area of the map that was approximately where they were as they crouched among the final remnants of the ship ruins.

"Then what is this?" Rain asked, touching her fingertip to the symbol toward the opposite corner of the Denynso compound.

Lynx looked at it and shook his head.

"I don't know what's up there."

"Neither do I," Rain said. "And maybe that's the point."

"What do you mean?"

"This is the map that Etan found in the Validician officer's quarters, right?"

"Yes," Lynx said, narrowing his eyes as he focused in on Rain's rapidly increasing pace.

"If he took this map directly from the journal that it was in and put it in his journal that means that that symbol was drawn by the Validician officer. Now, Etan didn't say in his journal exactly what he read in that book, but he said that he knew the Validicians knew we were coming and they planned on sending us to Uoria. That means that there was a plan all along. It wasn't something that just suddenly came to the Validicians when we showed up."

"Which means that this symbol is part of the plan," Lynx said.

"Exactly," Rain replied, the tears now dry in her eyes as she looked at him. "But what if the plan didn't turn out the way that it was supposed to?"

"What do you mean?"

"The Validicians obviously had this planned out. We know now that they had an alliance with the Covra and that they sent us here as an offering to them. The Covra wanted to take over the planet and then the rest of the galaxy."

"Etan didn't know that, though," Lynx said.

"No, he didn't. But he did know that they knew that we were coming here, and if they knew that we were coming here, they had a plan for where we were going to end up."

Lynx looked down at the map again and his eyes locked on the symbol. Realization hit him and he felt his heartrate increase.

"You crashed in the wrong place," he said.

Rain nodded.

"All along they intended us to crash somewhere closer to whatever this symbol indicates. This is where the Covra expected us to be, and we didn't end up there. Instead, we crashed here and made our settlement on the other side of the planet. That's why it took so long for the Covra to find us and start their attacks. They thought that we were going to be in a completely different place."

"But what place?" Lynx asked. "What is in this area of the planet that made them choose this place specifically?"

"A Covra compound?" Rain asked.

"I don't think so," Lynx said. "Remember what we found out about the Covra. They can't build anything on their own. They have to use the power of other creatures to do anything. I doubt that they have any type of settlement or compound or anything that would be so obvious or extensive. They need to be able to move around easily and undetectably so that they can find other creatures to manipulate and to use as incubators."

"But the Validicians were the allies of the Covra. Wouldn't they want us to crash near them?"

"Not necessarily," Lynx said. "They were sending the Covra a group that they knew were going to be powerful tools in their mission to take over. You were here for 15 years before the Covra laid their eggs. That means that you weren't brought here just to be their incubators. It wouldn't make sense for the Validicians to send a group to the planet so long before the Covra would be ready to reproduce. You were sent here for another reason. Where they intended you to crash had something to do with that original intent. Wherever this place is," he said, pointing at the symbol, "it was where you were originally supposed to go and where the Covra thought they would find you. That means there is something there that had something to do with their goal of taking over the planet. Something that might have much more extensive impact than we know."

"We need to find out what is there," Rain said. "If we're right and the Validicians had this planned before we even got to Penthos, there was much more going on than just that. There could still be danger. Even after all this time, there could still be something there that could put Uoria and everyone on it at risk. We need to get back to the settlement and pack as many supplies as we can. We need to get there as fast as possible."

Lynx nodded and helped Rain to her feet as she put everything back in the box and tucked it under her arm to carry back to the settlement with her. He knew that there was a journey ahead of them that could be long and dangerous, but he would walk beside her and give her all of the strength and courage that he had within him. This was unlike any battle that he had ever faced and he knew that he would fight harder for her than he had ever fought.

2

They walked along the edge of the badlands, away from the flames that licked up toward the sky, but Maxim could still feel the heat of the burning compound beneath his feet. With every step he was reminded of the destruction that his ancestors had caused to this area of the planet. It hurt him to think of the pain that they had caused, the suffering that they had doled out to the Denynso who had once called this area of Uoria their home. He remembered what Creia had told them about the badlands and how they had come to be, but in his heart he felt that there was more to it than just what the king had said.

"What do you remember about the badlands, Athan?" he asked, turning toward the older man.

He could see in Athan's eyes that being in this area was painful for him and that the memories brewing within him were ones that he thought he would never have to face again.

"They weren't the badlands then," Athan told him, his voice slipping away into memory as he spoke. "This area of

Uoria was more beautiful than anything that exists today. It was lush and fertile. This is where the belief that the sunrises of the Denynso compound were the most incredible that existed and that the warriors gained their strength and courage from the light of those sunrises originated. There had already been extensive conflict here. Those who had divided from the kingdom had already come seeking alliances with the Denynso."

"This was before the Order became corrupted," Maxim said.

"Yes," Athan confirmed. "The first to split from the kingdom did so after the tragedies with the Covra. They broke away and traveled to Ynn, only to return later and continue with renewed efforts to take over Uoria. That is when the Order began to change."

"The Covra had already been here," Maxim told him. "Creia told us that the Covra and the Validicians had both come to this compound generations before to find alliances and the Denynso rejected them."

"That is when the Covra found out about us," Athan said. "There was no darkness or corruption or greed in our kind then. There was only gentleness and peace. We had good relations with the Denynso of this compound and some even cooperated with those of the other compounds."

"Creia told us that those clans disappeared and that no one knows what happened to them."

"That's right," Athan said. "They were not as friendly as the clan that lived here, but they still cooperated with us. I am convinced that when the Covra found that they wouldn't be able to align with the Denynso that they decided to enslave them, just as they wanted to do with the other species so that they could work toward taking over this planet and the others throughout the galaxy. In order to do that, though, they first needed to build up their army. Together with the Valdicians they went after the species that would not expect them and that could fulfill the work that they needed done. They came after us. It was that decision that many years later led to our kingdom dividing and the greed, avarice, and cruelty to build in those who left. That is the first time that the Order fought the Klimnu. That was when the Denynso divided and half left this compound to create the compound that is there now."

"Did they know what they were then?" Maxim asked.

"Of course," Athan answered. "Just like you said before we came here, their appearance hadn't changed at all yet. They wouldn't for more than 250 years. They left Uoria just as beautiful as they were when they left the kingdom. The Order aligned with the Denynso to combat the group and force them off of the planet, hoping that if they were to go somewhere else they would soon lose the viciousness that formed in them because of the torment our kind went through. The Order hoped that the time away would restore their kindness and purity of spirit so that they could return and reunite with the rest of the kingdom."

"That didn't happen," Maxim said. "It only got worse."

"Yes," Athan said. "Their time away from the planet only intensified the change that they had already gone through. Not their physical change. Remember that still hadn't happened. It was the change within them that was the worst of the transformations that came over them. Being away from Uoria and the connection with the rest of the kingdom took away the reminders of beauty, love, and perseverance that kept the rest of the kingdom going even through the darkness. As new generations were born they weren't taught about what had happened to the Mikana to turn their hearts cold. Instead, they only learned hatred and it was that hatred that would push the planet toward destruction. When they returned from Ynn, they went right back to where it had all begun and tried again to get the cooperation of the Denynso, hoping that over the time that they had spent off of the planet that the other species would have been successful in changing how they felt. Of course, you know that it didn't work that way."

"The Denynso on this compound didn't want anything to do with the Klimnu and told them to leave again."

"Exactly," Athan said. "They still remembered the invasions of the Covra, Valdicians, and Klimnu from years before. By then the memories of the Order had faded and only the fear of the Klimnu lingered. They told the Klimnu that they wanted nothing to do with them and that they needed to leave. This infuriated the group, a group that didn't even remember that the Mikana existed or that their kind had once been a part of a kingdom here on Uoria. These were creatures who believed that they had originated on Ynn and that they were the only ones of their kind in any form. I know in my heart that it was that belief that saved the rest of the kingdom."

"You think that if they remembered the Mikana that they would have come back and destroyed us?" Maxim asked.

"Absolutely," Athan said. "They would have wanted to kill off those who they felt were a betrayal because they didn't choose to let the darkness take over them."

"Instead they destroyed this compound."

"The Denynso refused to be their allies and help them to explore other planets and seek out slaves."

"Just like the Covra wanted to."

"Yes. And when they did that, the Klimnu were infuriated. All of the anger and pain that had built within them from all of the generations of Klimnu who had lived on Ynn poured out and they not only destroyed this compound but ensured that it would burn forever. They transformed what was incredibly beautiful into what we know as the badlands."

"But you saw it before they destroyed it."

"Oh, yes. The Order tried to stop the Klimnu from causing any trouble with the Denynso or with any other species. We confronted them and fought against them. We formed alliances with the other species that I told you about. We walked into battle against them several times. We didn't know then that each time we confronted them, the corruption within our very own was getting worse. It wasn't long before the members of the Order had started to change. Aegeus knew it. He knew something was going to happen. It was after that final battle, after he died, that the Klimnu destroyed the compound. It was as if his determination to protect Uoria and resolve what had happened within the Order had been what protected it. When he died, the Klimnu, both the outsider group and those within the Order itself, were able to rise up and destroy the compound. I watched it burn, knowing that with it burned all hope that Aegeus's plans would ever be fulfilled."

"The weapons," Ivy suddenly said.

Maxim turned to her and saw that her eyes were wide and her mouth slightly parted.

"What?" he asked.

"The weapons," she repeated. "Remember when Rain was telling us about how Nyx 23 ended up here? She talked about the weapons that the Valdicians used. They were able to control them with their minds, but some of them also threw them. They were powerful enough to destroy the inner workings of their ship."

"That is what the Klimnu used to detonate the volcanoes," Maxim said, realization settling over him. "How did they get them?"

Athan shook his head.

"I don't know," he said.

"What happened after the battle?" Maxim asked.

"I went back to the kingdom," Athan said. "I had to tell your mother..."

"No," Maxim said. "I know that. What happened to the Order? What happened to the members who were Klimnu?"

"Most left and joined with them. No one knows where they went or what they did, but within two years they had come into contact with those flowers and started their physical transformations. Some came back to the kingdom, but were so gruesome that they were sent away. Some were killed. The others remained with the Klimnu group and went with them to Creia to implore him to heal them."

Maxim shuddered at the horrific details and shook his head.

"I don't understand. Why would they go to Creia? They had just destroyed the compound where the clan had once lived only two years before."

"But it had been generations since the clan had split. Yes, Creia and many of the others had spent their childhoods going back and forth between the compounds to stay connected with the descendants of family who had remained in the original compound and there were many who felt that it was truly just one large compound now that they thought that the threat of the Klimnu was gone, but it was still a divided clan. They hoped to appeal to the honor of the Denynso, especially one who was both warrior and healer."

"I never knew that Creia was a healer," Nylek said.

He had remained silent throughout the entire journey

and it startled Maxim slightly to hear the voice of the warrior who he had nearly forgotten was accompanying them. Maxim remembered that this young warrior was not one of the men who had been a part of the group that had left the compound and had likely not heard everything that Creia had told them.

"You didn't know that the Klimnu asked him to heal them and he sent them away?" Maxim asked.

"When Leia told us about her time in the prison with the Klimnu she said that the Klimnu who tormented her the most told her that they had asked Creia for help, that they knew that he would be able to heal them. I didn't realize that meant that he was an actual healer."

Athan nodded.

"Creia is a Denynso of truly unbelievable power. He is the source of virtually all of the myths and legends that other species hear about your kind. In the Mikana kingdom it has been so long since there was any cooperation between our kind and the Denynso that the thoughts of the species had turned mostly to legend. Many of our young people did not even believe that the Denynso warriors really existed until Pyra and his men came into the kingdom. I suppose it is just like none of the young generations of the Denynso knowing that the Klimnu originated as Mikana. Time tends to blur lines and erase details until people aren't sure what to believe anymore. It takes away the truth and changes it until it is almost unrecognizable."

Maxim felt like he had been knocked off balance by everything that he had just heard. It seemed that every time that he thought that he was on the right path toward understanding what had happened or even just the origins of the different species that inhabited the planet, he learned something that made him question what he thought that he already knew.

Athan's description of the fire that had destroyed the compound and turned it into the badlands still rolling through his mind, Maxim turned to stare at the still-burning ground of the badlands. In the glow of the flames breaking through the dark ground and sending sparks up against the black night sky he could almost see the lingering presence of the men who had lost their lives there. Among the shadowy images of those who had fought so hard to protect it but were cut down and tossed aside he could see his father. He knew that Aegeus had walked on this ground, left his footsteps on the dirt that now burned. The thought of the ground where his father had lived, fought, died, and lain now engulfed by flames was almost too painful for Maxim to contemplate. He longed to know where his father had stood when he was cut down so that he could stand there and be more connected to the man who he had missed for so long. Even more now he ached to understand what had happened to Aegeus's body after he had died. It still didn't make any sense that he had simply disappeared. Especially now that Maxim knew that he had walked into the battle carrying the sword that his father had carried, he couldn't rationalize in his mind how his father's body and his grand-father's massive sword could just vanish without any trace leftover for Athan to find and bring home to them.

Now more than ever Maxim believed that there was far more to those last moments of his father's existence than he knew, and likely far more than even Athan knew. Part of him had wanted to distrust Athan. Despite him being so impor-tant to the family throughout his entire life, the older man had been the only link that Maxim had to the moment of his father's death. Even though that could have made him even more precious, in Maxim's mind it made him, in a way, a threat. Rather than feeling the connection and being grateful that at least Aegeus had had Athan with him until the end, Maxim felt suspicious of Athan and the information that he had shared with them from the time that Maxim and Kyven were children. He believed that there was more for Athan to tell him, and felt embittered by the fact that the older man seemed completely reluctant to share it. Faced with the reality of the burning badlands, though, the realization that Athan was the only one of the kingdom outside of his family who he could trust. He knew now that Athan had truly told him everything that he could and that if there was anything else that he hadn't told them, it was because he didn't know that the information mattered.

They had been roaming the edge of the badlands for long enough that the horizon had gone from inky blackness to a soft pink as the sun started to rise. Maxim remembered his father talking to him about the sunrises on the compound of the Denynso and how they were the most beautiful in all of the galaxy. Now that story carried even more meaning to him. His hand ran along the stone ledge that rose up around the former compound and suddenly he felt it dip. He looked at the wall and saw an opening he hadn't noticed before.

"What's this?" he asked Athan.

Athan came up to the wall and examined the opening, then shook his head.

"I don't know. I don't remember it from my time here."

"Nylek," Maxim called. "Do you know what this is?"

The Denynso approached the wall and stared at the gap in the stone. Maxim knew that like the other warriors of the clan Nylek had never been to the badlands. It had been forbidden just like the other areas outside of the compound and they had only seen it when Creia had brought them up to the top of the ledge and shown them the burning ground when they first returned from the human settlement. He hoped, though, that Nylek might have heard more about the badlands than he had. Perhaps his parents had told him stories that they had heard from their own parents, linking the generations to the years that the clan had been united and lived in the compound that was now the badlands.

Nylek shook his head, looking at Maxim with regret in his eyes.

"I'm sorry," he said. "I don't know. I don't know anything about the badlands. My family never talked about them."

"What is it, Maxim?" Ivy asked.

Maxim turned to his mate and held his arm open to her so that she could step up close to him. He gestured toward the opening in the stone.

"Do you have any idea what this might be?" he asked.

Ivy looked at the opening closely, her eyes narrowed as if trying to come up with something to tell him.

"It reminds me of some of the caverns on Earth," she said.

"Caverns?" Maxim asked.

Ivy nodded.

"They aren't all underground like Loralia's home. Some of them start at ground level or even up high on mountains and then they go deeper underground as you move further into them. There's one on the Denynso compound like that."

"There is?" Maxim asked.

Ivy nodded.

"That's how they first found the mirrored realm. Some of the warriors found a cave in the rock face of the ledge and when they went further into it they found a tunnel that led down into the caverns. They couldn't fit in the tunnel, though, and had to send the human women through it to find out what was in it."

"Were you there?" Maxim asked.

Ivy shook her head.

"No. It was before I came to the compound, before the warriors left on their exploration of the planet. Eden and the others told me about it."

"We need to go into it," Maxim said.

"We need to rest," Kyven protested. "We haven't slept in more than a day. We can't keep going without sleep."

Maxim looked at the others of the group and saw them nodding slightly. He looked down at Ivy who gazed into his eyes softly.

"I know that you are eager," she said, "but if we are going to stay safe and be able to do what needs to be done, whatever that is, then we have to have our strength. It is already morning. We need to get some rest and then we can keep going later."

Maxim nodded. He hadn't wanted to admit it to himself but he was feeling the pull of the hours of walking on his body and knew that getting some sleep would give him the strength and the energy that he needed to keep on their way. He didn't want to sacrifice the entire day, however, so he looked back at the rest of the group determinedly.

"We will set up camp and rest for a few hours. Just a few, though, and then we will keep going. We can't waste the daylight."

Maxim stepped through the opening in the rock and found himself in a cool, dark tunnel. He pulled out his bedroll and laid it down, then rested Ivy's beside it as the others stepped cautiously inside. Athan stretched a blanket across the tunnel to block as much of the sunlight from getting in as he could, and they all settled down to rest.

When Maxim's eyes opened he felt like he had been sleeping for years. His eyelids felt heavy and the rest of his body seemed to sink into the ground beneath him. Ivy curled against him, her head tucked against his chest and one of her legs draped over his. He leaned down to touch a kiss to the top of her head and she stirred slightly.

"We need to get going," he whispered.

Ivy nodded and they carefully disentangled themselves from one another. Around them Maxim saw the others starting to wake and gradually they got up and packed. Athan pulled the blanket down from where he had secured it, revealing the bright sunlight of midday. Maxim stood deep enough in the tunnel that the light barely touched him, but it illuminated the walls. That light allowed him so see carvings deep in the stone. He stepped toward them and touched them with his fingertips.

Athan saw what he was doing and came to his side.

"Do you know what these mean?" Maxim asked.

"I've seen them before," Athan told him, reaching up with his own hand to touch them. "Not here. They were in the inner quarters of some of the Order when I was younger. I can't decipher them fully, but I know that they are the same ones."

Maxim looked back down the tunnel, feeling drawn into the darkness.

"Could Creia have followed this tunnel?" he asked.

"He might have," Athan said.

"Nylek," Maxim said, "we need to get in touch with the queen. Can you please contact Mina?"

"Yes," Nylek responded.

Maxim felt slightly awkward watching as Nylek turned his eyes toward the wall and concentrated on the thoughts that he wanted his mate to hear. Even though it was something that the Denynso knew as commonplace, it still felt incredibly intimate to Maxim and he felt somewhat uncomfortable taking advantage of this connection, especially if it meant watching him as he did it.

Finally Nylek looked back to him again.

"I have her," he said. "What do you need me to ask her?"

"Please have her ask Theia to try to get in touch with Creia again," Maxim said. "We have found what appears to be a tunnel leading out of the badlands and I need her to ask him if he followed it."

Nylek nodded and went back to looking at the wall as he relayed the message to his mate back at the compound with Theia. They waited for several long moments with Maxim hoping that this would be the time when Theia would be able to get through to Creia. If they could confirm that he did follow this tunnel they might be able to get to him more quickly.

Nylek looked up at him, shaking his head.

"Theia isn't getting a response from the king," he said regretfully. "She said that she will keep trying, but that she hasn't been able to get to him again since he sent the message of 'badlands.'"

"Thank you, Nylek," Maxim said, "and thank Mina for me."

"What are we going to do?" Ivy asked.

"If Creia did go down this tunnel, it is going to be the only way that we are going to be able to find him and help him. If he didn't, though, and we follow it we could get lost and end up even further away from him. It could mean not being able to save him."

"We have to make a decision," Ivy said. "You have to choose."

Maxim looked at Athan. The older man looked into his eyes, the expression in his gaze telling Maxim that he didn't need this man's confirmation to know what he should do. He had to follow his heart and do what it told him.

3

———

Zyyr stared into the fire that Lila had built and cradled her closer to him. She curled familiarly into his arms, the curves of her body fitting into his as though each were crafted for the other. His body and mind felt satiated in a way that he could never have imagined, and now he truly understood what it was to be mated. It made sense to him now why the warriors were so aggressive about their mates while at the same time becoming more tender and softer with just the look of those women's eyes. Now that he had completed his bond with Lila he knew that he would never be able to be without her, and that he was irrevocably changed. She was all that mattered to him, and he would do anything to protect, comfort, and please her. Even as these thoughts rolled through his mind, however, something that she said lingered, bothering him.

"Lila?" he said.

"Hmmmm?" she said softly, the sound almost more of a sigh than it was an actual acknowledgement of him speaking to her.

"What did you mean when you said that your great-grandmother was different?"

Lila shifted slightly and Zyyr couldn't tell if it was because she wanted to get closer to him or if he had made her uncomfortable with the question.

"I'm sorry," he said, immediately regretting prying, especially in the calm and beautiful moment that they had been sharing. "I shouldn't have asked you that."

"No," Lila said as if trying to reassure him. "It's alright. I am the one who said that. You have every right to be curious. I'm just trying to decide what the best way to explain it would be. You see, I never really thought of her as strange. I guess that there are so many things about her that are like me that I didn't see her as odd the way that other people did. I just saw a woman who was beautiful and wonderful, a woman who always made me feel safe and understood. I was always comfortable when I was here with her. She never made me question the things about myself that other people did, or look at me with the curiosity in her eyes the way that I saw other people look at me. None of the things that were different about me when I was younger mattered to her."

"Maybe she loved you so much that she didn't notice that there was anything different about you," Zyyr offered, thankful that Lila wasn't angry with him and honored that she was sharing these things with him.

Lila laughed softly.

"No," she said, "she definitely noticed. In fact, I think that she might have noticed even more than other people did. Sometimes she would show me little things about her that weren't like anything I had ever seen in others and give me a little wink. She never said anything about it, but I somehow knew that I wasn't supposed to talk to other people about what she showed me or told me. It was like we had a special secret that was just about the two of us. Even though I knew that it was those secrets that made her an outcast and forced her to live out here away from the rest of the kingdom, they were the things that I loved the most about her."

"Why did they make her live out here? Just because she wasn't exactly like them?" Zyyr asked.

Lila sighed and shook her head.

"My mother told me that the people of the kingdom never told her that she had to live out here. They never forced her to. It was something that she chose to do because she knew how different she was and didn't want the other people to have any more opportunity to ridicule her than they already did."

The thought of the kind and welcoming Mikana people being cruel to one of their own simply because she was different in some ways didn't seem to fit in with his visions of these people, especially the soft and lovely Lila. He couldn't imagine people who were like her ousting another for no other reason that she didn't fit their exact concepts of what they should be.

"What did they ridicule her about?" Zyyr asked. "What was so different about her?"

"I never heard anyone be cruel about her," Lila admitted. "She never told me that anyone was mean or that that was why she lived out here. One time I asked her, and she told me that there were things that people didn't need to know because it might cause more harm than good, and she left it at that. When she said that to me I just thought that she was talking about me. After all, I was just a young child and she was already old. I thought that she was just worried that I wouldn't understand the things that she had gone through, even though I was so much like her, and that she worried if she told me that I would be afraid that the same types of things would happen to me."

"You don't think that anymore, do you?" Zyyr asked.

Lila shook her head and then turned in his arms so that she could look at him.

"What if she wasn't talking about me at all? What if she wasn't worried about what I would find out or what I knew, but about the other people in the kingdom?"

"What do you mean?"

"One time we were talking about my hair and she asked if my hair was like my mother's. My mother was the daughter of her son, my grandfather. She never went to see my great-grandmother. I never asked her why, but I know that it hurt my great-grandmother. When I told her that it wasn't, she just nodded, but there was something about the look on her face. It was almost like she was relieved. Like she didn't want to think that her granddaughter was different, too. Almost like she didn't want there to be someone who was different that was out among the rest of the people of the kingdom as often as she was. Maybe she didn't mean that there were things that I shouldn't know and that she wasn't going to tell me why she lived out here. Maybe that was the actual explanation. She was telling me why she lived here rather than in the kingdom itself. She lived here because the people of the kingdom didn't need to know some things about her."

Zyyr was starting to feel confused. He was trying to follow her, but he was struggling.

"Why was she asking about your hair?" he asked.

Though she was more beautiful than any other woman that he had ever seen, including the stunning Mikana women, there wasn't anything so distinctly different about

her hair that he would have thought someone would question it. She looked at him strangely.

"You didn't notice?" she asked.

He shook his head and she tucked an arm under her
thick mane of hair, lifting it up away from her back and
turning it over. There among the other strands, glittering
against them with their bold contrast, were strands of
bright, shimmering silver.

Zyyr reached up to touch the strands of silver, his heart
starting to pound in his chest as thoughts and questions
raced through his mind. This was something that he hadn't
seen on any of the others in the Mikana kingdom, but that
he had seen before. He knew that shade of silver and the
faint sparkle that came off of it. He didn't understand. How
could Lila have these streaks of silver through her hair?
What did they mean?

"Did your great-grandmother live in this house her
whole life?" Zyyr asked.

Lila shook her head.

"No. Just as an adult."

"Where did she live when she was younger?"

"I don't know. No one was ever able to show me the
house where she grew up. My grandfather only knows that
he was born in this house. He never met his father."

Zyyr knew that what he had just learned was important,
but he didn't know why. There was something about the
information that struck him and lingered in his mind,
creating an urgency to find Maxim and tell him everything
that Lila had said.

"Lila," he said, turning her around so that he could take
her hands and stare into her eyes, wanting to ensure that
she was listening to him and understanding what he was
saying to her. "Do you trust me?"

"Of course, I do," she answered, her eyes narrowing slightly as she looked at him.

"I need to find Maxim and tell him what you have told me."

She shook her head slightly.

"Why?" she asked. "I told you those things in confidence."

"I know that, Darling. I know you did, and I wouldn't tell anyone if I didn't think that it was important. There are things that Maxim, the Denynso, and even the humans are trying to understand, and I think that what you told me about your great-grandmother might be another piece for them."

"What do you think it means?" she asked.

"I'm not completely sure," he admitted. "I just know that it seems important and if there is even the slightest chance that that information could help them, we want them to have it. It could mean more to this planet than either of us know."

Lila looked as though she were contemplating what he had just said to her and then nodded.

"But why Maxim? I thought that a warrior named Pyra was the leader of the Denynso."

"Just the warriors," Zyyr told her, "and I have withdrawn my loyalty to him and given it to Maxim. I believe in him and want to do whatever I can to help him.

She nodded again.

"I trust you," she said. "If you think that what I've told you could help in some way, then you can tell Maxim."

Zyyr leaned forward and kissed her.

"Thank you," he said.

He climbed to his feet and dressed as quickly as he could. When he was finished he rushed out of the house to run back toward the houses so that he could find Maxim,

Lila right beside him. They searched the houses and the common areas, asking everyone who they passed if they had seen Maxim, his human partner, or his brother. No one seemed to know where they were or where they had gone, and Zyyr started to feel a sense of panic rising in him.

Finally they found Oro, the other Denynso who had traveled with them from the settlement to the Mikana kingdom. He stood with some of the Mikana men in one of the clearings, eating fruit out of a basket much like the one that Lila had brought with her.

"Oro," Zyyr called to him, gesturing for him to come away from the others and talk with him in private.

"Do you know where Maxim is?" Zyyr asked.

"No," Oro said. "Is everything alright?"

"We need to find him," Zyyr said. "I have something that I need to tell him."

"I know where his mother lives," Oro offered.

"Let's go."

Zyyr followed Oro through the kingdom, confident that they would arrive at Maxim's mother's house and find him there with her and Ivy. When a woman opened the door, however, the strained look on her face told him that she was not going to be able to help him. He had to do whatever he could to try to find out, though.

"Hello," he said. "My name is Zyyr. I traveled from the human settlement here with Maxim and Ivy."

"Yes," the woman who Zyyr assumed was Maxim and Kyven's mother said.

"Do you know where they are?" he asked.

She shook her head, looking weakened by his words.

"I don't know," she said, emotion in her voice making the words sound somewhat distant. "They left."

"Left?" Zyyr demanded. "When?"

"Yesterday," the woman said. I don't know where they went."

"Was it just Maxim and Ivy?" Zyyr asked.

"No," she said. "Kyven, Emerie, and Athan were with him, too."

Zyyr turned to Oro with the feeling of panic rising in his chest again. The warriors met eyes and Zyyr knew that without words even passing between them their decision was made. They had to find Maxim. If he left the kingdom it was for a very specific, very serious reason, and they needed to be with him.

4

P ain radiated through Creia's eyes as he struggled to open them. The sharp, piercing pain came as a relief. He had been unconscious for quite some time and briefly thought that the life had finally drained out of him. The pain came as a sudden, intense, and welcome reminder that he was still alive. No matter how long he had been latched to the table, staring into the screen that was in front of him, Ryan had not yet succeeded in killing him. He could continue to fight.

The hooded creature had not been back since the last time that he put the screen over Creia's eyes. This had forced him to watch Ryan as he moved through his lab, performing strange experiments and occasionally going over to the thing in the tank in the corner, glaring in at it as if examining it for some reason that may apply to whatever he was trying to accomplish with the tubes, vials, and bottles strewn across the tables. Sometimes he would open a notebook and scribble feverishly in it, his garbled mutterings to himself loud enough that Creia could hear his voice, but indecipherable as actually understandable words. That is what he was doing now, hunched over the notebook and writing so quickly that Creia could see the ink from the fresh words spreading across his hand as it slid across the page.

The process fascinated Creia. Though the Denynso were known for rejecting the technologies that many other species had and relied largely instead on craftsmanship, he knew that the humans didn't follow the same way of life. Instead they seemed to thrive on advancement and pushed to progress their technology and way of life as fast as possible. Some of the things that the human women had described to him were almost unfathomable, but it was the very reality that those items existed that made watching Ryan use a nearly primitive form of recording his thoughts oddly intriguing.

Suddenly Ryan stopped and dropped the pen he was holding. It hit the table and rolled across the smooth metal surface, tipping over the edge and falling to the floor. Something about the gesture sent a thrill of fear through Creia. He knew deep within him that the people he treasured the most were in serious danger, but there was nothing he could do to help them. He was tied to the table so that he couldn't move and his body was weakening more and more with each passing hour. He had already gone without food or water for long enough that he could feel everything within him failing. He wanted desperately to reach out to Theia, but with the diodes connected to his head and the screen in front of his eyes, he couldn't be sure that the thoughts he would send her would be completely his own. He knew that she had tried to speak to him. Even though he had forced his mind to block her out to protect her, he could feel the pull within his heart that told him that she had been thinking of him, reaching out to him with her mind. He wondered what she had wanted to say to him, but couldn't let his mind wander or it would take away the last grasps of control he had.

Ryan looked up at the camera sharply and Creia saw the wildness in his eyes. The man seemed to be slipping further and further into insanity, losing his own control over his mind and allowing his intense thoughts to take over him completely.

"DNA," Ryan said, taking a few fast steps toward the camera so that he was right up against it and Creia could only see his eyes. "Do you know what that is?"

Creia didn't know if he should respond. It didn't seem as though Ryan were truly taking to him, but part of him feared what may happen if the scientist intended for him to respond but he didn't. Ryan took a step back so that Creia could see the entirety of his face again and tilted his head.

"Hmmm?" he said questioningly. "Do you Denynso know anything more than war and bedding women indiscriminately?"

Creia squirmed at the accusation. He knew the reputation that his men had throughout the galaxy, and much of it was well earned, but the way that Ryan said it made him feel angry and provoked.

"I know of DNA," Creia managed to force past the pain in his dry, tight throat.

"Good," Ryan said with a mirthless chuckle. "Then you understand why I had to send Eden to your planet."

Confusion washed over Creia.

"You already told me that you sent her to get the blood of the Denynso. You sent her for Pyra's blood and with the hope that we would capture her and kill her."

"Yes, yes," Ryan said, waving his hand as if brushing away something inconsequential. "I did hope that if she wasn't able to get the blood of your most fearsome warrior that you would take her and punish her the way that everyone knows the Denynso love to punish. Not only would it be giving her something that she deserved, but it would mobilize Earth's government and force them to see you and your kind as nothing but a galactic threat." He gave another laugh. "And, of course, we all know how that would have turned out for you. Earth does have its way of going after those who they think have wronged them."

Creia found it strange the way that Ryan was speaking of Earth and its inhabitants in such a disconnected, cold way, but his mind was already struggling through the impairment of the exhaustion, starvation, and dehydration to understand anything that the man was saying to him so he couldn't stop to try to dwell on his motivations.

"You know," Ryan said, bringing a finger to his lips briefly as if the cruel smile there indicated he was pondering new thoughts running through his mind, "that is how this all began. Come to think of it, it was because of that little tendency of Earth's government that any of this happened at all. I suppose my mind just went right back to the beginning."

"What do you mean?" Creia asked, his voice soft and almost inaudible over the sound of Ryan's laughter. "How what all began?"

"DNA," Ryan said again, the laughter suddenly gone from his voice as he stared directly into the camera in a way that told Creia with certainty that just as he could see the scientist in his lab, Ryan could see him wherever he was secured to the table. "It's like little blocks. You know? Like the toys that little ones play with." He walked back a few steps so that he was standing at a table and grabbed a handful of small glass cubes from a box. He started to stack them into several individual towers. "You can make them into anything. You just start building and suddenly you have created something." He paused and looked at the towers of blocks contemplatively. "Why do those blocks always have to be the same, though? What would happen if you took them," he picked the top block off of one of the towers with his thumb and forefinger and dropped it into the top of one of the other towers, "and found out what else you could build with them?"

A horrifying reality started to form in Creia's mind and he felt the desperation to escape building through him again.

"What have you done, Ryan?" he demanded. Ryan continued to play with the tiny glass cubes, giggling to himself as he redistributed the cubes among the towers and then took them and started creating new towers. "What have you done?"

Ryan looked up.

"It wasn't me," he said, the look on his face suddenly innocent in a way that bordered on disturbing. "I didn't start this. I only intend to complete it. I've had to be so patient. So incredibly patient. It is all going to pay off soon, though." He smiled and Creia felt a sick feeling twist through his stomach. "Things are working out even better than I had originally planned and I am being rewarded handsomely for the sacrifices I have made and the devotion that I had shown all these years. You see, things don't always work out the way that you intend them to. Sometimes what you think you're building," he turned his attention back to one of the towers and used the back of his hand to push it over so that the cubes scattered across the surface of the table and down onto the floor, "topples. Or perhaps you come up with a better idea but all of your blocks are already being used.

Whatever the reason, it can be incredibly frustrating. There've been times when I felt like all of this was for nothing and that I would never be able to accomplish what I had planned to do. Then I just kept working. I sent Eden to Uoria to secure the DNA and the potent elements within the blood of your Pyra. She didn't accomplish that, or so I thought. Now I have access to something far more powerful than I could have ever imagined." He picked up one of the cubes and stared into it. "I have a hybrid baby and the milk that nourishes it."

5

"Is everything alright?" Lila asked.

Zyyr gave her an intense look and she noticed for the first time that his once green eyes were now a vibrant shade of orange. She could see in that stare that everything was most certainly not alright and that Zyyr was deeply troubled by what Oro had said to him.

"We have to leave," Zyyr told her.

Panic with a sharp edge of pain coursed through her and Lila resisted the urge to take a step back.

"Why?" she asked.

"Maxim is no longer in the kingdom," Zyyr explained. "He left with his mate, his brother, and two others. We have to find them."

"What is it about what I told you that upsets you so much?" Lila asked.

She couldn't understand what she had said about her great-grandmother that had gotten to Zyyr so much that he shifted from a passionate and tender man to one who seemed distracted and obsessive. The anxiety he was feeling radiated off of him and it made Lila feel as though she could barely breathe. Zyyr reached out and took both of her hands in his, pulling them up so that he could clutch them against his heart.

"I wish that I knew of a way to tell you," he said. "I wish that I could make you understand, but even I don't understand completely what's happening or what has happened. I can only tell you that we have seen so much more in the time that we have been out of the compound than we ever could have imagined, and every day it seems that we are finding out more. While I wish that it was all good, the truth is that it's not. We're worried that some of the things that we've found out could mean that there is serious danger for everyone on this planet. If we can find out what that is, we might be able to stop whatever it is from getting worse, or from happening at all."

"And you think that my great-grandmother has something to do with it?" she asked.

"I don't know," Zyyr said, shaking his head, "but it is something that I feel that we need to talk to Maxim about. Most of the Denynso warriors are not on the planet right now, but Maxim is and so is our king, Creia. They might have more insight into what you told me and be able to find the connections to everything else that we have uncovered better than I can."

Lila was trying to understand what Zyyr was saying, but it all seemed so strange to her. She knew that her great-grandmother had been different and had spent her life isolated from the others of the kingdom, but she couldn't fathom what impact that could have on anything that the Denynso or Maxim had learned. Idella had been reclusive nearly her whole life as far as Lila knew. Like most of the Mikana women she had lived in the kingdom her entire life and had not left it. She had had one son and then lived to a fairly remarkable age alone in the small home that she adored.

She tried to remember everything that she had told Zyyr when they were alone together in her great-grandmother's house, trying to find something, anything in her words that would have triggered the response that he had had. Suddenly she remembered telling him what her great-grandmother had said about living out in the house away from the rest of the kingdom, first with her son, and then alone after her son grew older and began his own life. Idella had told Lila that there were things that people didn't need to know because they might cause more harm than good. She was certain now that she hadn't been chastising Lila's question. Instead, she had been answering her. Her great-grandmother had stayed out in that house away from the others so that the people of the kingdom wouldn't find out something about her.

She rested a hand on Zyyr's arm and lifted her eyes to his.

"I need to show you something."

"I'm sorry, Lila, but I have to find Maxim."

"This is important, Zyyr," she told him. "I think that it might help you."

She saw him nod and they started toward Idella's house again, Oro following close behind them. When they arrived she closed the door tightly and pulled the drapes. Though she hadn't seen anyone come around the house in many years, she didn't want to take any chances that this would be the time that someone would wander out through the orchards for a peek into the windows of the strange and storied home.

Once confident that the house was secure, she walked over to the fireplace and counted out the bricks in the pattern that Idella had taught her when she was just a child. It was a game to her then, but now that she was older Lila realized just how serious it was that her great-grandmother had to be so secretive. She identified the right brick and wriggled it out of place. Inside was a gemstone, dulled by years and embedded so deeply into the stone around it that Lila could barely see it. She felt it with the pads of her fingers and the pressed it, holding it for a few moments just as she had been instructed. When she realized it she heard the dull scratching sound of the fireplace moving out of place and easing forward a few inches. Lila stepped carefully up to the edge, relieved that she and Zyyr had extinguished the flames before they left in search of Oro, and tucked her fingers behind it.

"Can you help me?" she asked over her shoulder.

There had been a time when even her small great-grandmother had been able to move the fireplace aside with ease, but that had been many years before and the time had settled the stones into place so much that they resisted being moved again. It was almost as if the house itself was trying to protect the secrets that the small room behind the fireplace concealed. The two warriors came up to the fireplace and tucked their hands around the edge just as she had. In one motion the stone moved out of place, revealing the door behind it.

Hoping that it would move more easily than the fireplace had, Lila grasped the large metal ring that acted as a handle and tugged it. The door relented fairly quickly and she pulled it open. The smell of forgotten years and captured breaths came out of the space toward them and Lila waited a tense, nervous moment before walking inside. Behind her Zyyr illuminated a light stick and held it up above her head so that the glow splashed across the floor in front of her and helped her to see as she moved further inside. Soon she found the lamp that had always sat on the small table inside the room and lit the flame inside, adjusting it so that it would burn brightly enough for them to see in the space, but not so much that it would do away with the precious oil within it, the last oil that Idella had ever put inside.

"What is this place?" Zyyr asked.

"My great-grandmother used to bring me in here when I was younger. It always felt like a secret passage, like this was where she could store all of the treasures of the world and no one would find them. Now, though, I wonder if it was her that she wanted to make sure that no one found."

"Why do you say that?" Oro asked.

"I was thinking about what I told Zyyr about my great-grandmother. Idella was an amazing woman. Perhaps the single most incredible person I have ever known. Yet she always stayed right here, and if anyone came close to the house, I would see her getting closer to the fireplace. Now that you've told me that there are secrets and dangers on Uoria that we don't understand, I wonder if she was preparing to hide in this room. Maybe she knew of one of the dangers and wanted to be able to come in here whenever she felt threatened."

"So that others wouldn't find out and cause more harm than they could good," Zyyr said.

Lila nodded.

"Is this what you wanted to show us?" Oro asked.

Lila stepped further into the room, holding up the lamp so that she could look at the shelves built along one wall in the small space.

"Yes, but the room isn't all. There's something else that I need to show you."

She saw the box sitting in the center of the middle shelf just as it always had been and reached out to carefully take it down. She carried it over to the small table and rested it reverently on the surface.

"I never got to know my great-grandfather," she said, pausing with her hands on the top of the box, "and there wasn't much that Idella would tell me about him. She would only say that he was the greatest love that she would ever have and that he was the reason that she was able to have the life that she did. She said that he was the only reason that she was able to have a family the way that she did."

"Of course he is if he was her son's father," Oro said.

Lila shook her head.

"I think it's more than that," she said. "The way that she always said it didn't seem like she meant it because their son was the only child that they had and that she wouldn't have had him had she not found my great-grandfather. Instead it seemed more like she was saying that without him she never would have had a family at all. Like he ensured that she was able to have a life." She took a breath. "This box was my great-grandmother's most prized possession. She used to take it down when we were in here and look at what was inside. She told me once that her husband carved it for her and that she used to keep their love letters in it."

"Is that what's in it now?" Zyyr asked.

She shook her head, feeling tears pricking the corners of her eyes as she thought of those letters. She could still remember the way that the paper felt beneath her fingertips and the curves of the words across the page.

"No," she said. "When she died I didn't think that she should be without them. They were with her when we buried her. I knew that I was perhaps the only other person who knew about those letters, so I made sure that they were tucked out of sight so that she could carry them privately with her and no one would ever know what she said to him or what he said to her."

"Did you ever read the letters?" Zyyr asked.

Lila shook her head again.

"No," she answered. "Idella would read them and then she would place them aside and go back into the box for this."

She reached into the box and withdrew the blue leather bound book she had seen at some of her favorite moments throughout her life. These were the moments when she was able to spend quiet time with her great-grandmother, the one person who made her feel like she belonged.

"What is that?" Zyyr asked.

Lila sat and lowered the book to her lap, running her hand along the cover. It had been so long since she had seen that book, but if she searched the corners of her mind she could still hear Idella's voice reading the story inside to her. She opened the cover and ran her fingertips along the words on the title. It simply said *Fairy Tale.*

"This is a book that my great-grandmother read to me. She said that it was her very favorite fairy tale."

"What is it about?" Zyyr asked.

There was a slight edge to his voice that told Lila that he was feeling impatient, wondering what it was that had led her to bring him and Oro to this hidden room. She turned the title page and looked at the detailed illustration on the first page of the book. It was a beautiful and lush scene of a place that Lila had never seen except for on those pages.

"This book," she said, turning the page again and looking at the next illustration, "tells the story of a woman who was born in a strange and foreign land and cruelly mistreated by an evil master. She often wondered who she really was and where she had come from, but the man who kept her would tell her that it didn't matter if she ever knew because the only reason that she was alive was to continue the work on a large and complex project." She turned the page again and looked at the stark image of a cold-looking room that had walls lined with tanks. "This woman thought that she was going to live out her life trapped there, kept for this evil man's whims. She was becoming an adult, coming to an age that she had always feared because it was the age at which the women that lived alongside her would be taken from that space and she would never see them again. She didn't know what was happening to them or even who took them, but she was terrified that it was going to happen to her."

"What happened?" Zyyr asked.

"It was nearly time for her to come of age and she was moved out of the space that she knew into a room connected to it. That is when she met a wonderful young man. He cared for her and prepared her for the experience that lay ahead of her, but wouldn't tell her what it was. She knew when she looked into his eyes that he was afraid of what he knew and didn't want to tell her anything about it. One night, just two days before she was to come of age, the young man came to her room and took her. He helped her escape from the building where she had been born and that she knew her entire life. They ran away together and he told her the story of how she came to be." She turned the page again and showed him a picture of two people sitting beneath a tall, overhanging tree that was nothing like Lila had ever seen. "He told her that she was not like other women and that this planet that she had known all of her life was not the one that she was intended to live on. It was not the home of her ancestors."

"Where was she?" Oro asked.

Lila could hear that the fascination was starting to build in the men and she continued on, letting the magic interwoven in the words of the story to draw them in so that they could understand what she needed them to know.

"It doesn't say," Lila said, "but the illustrations are not like anything that I have ever seen in the kingdom or in the drawings done by those who have left the kingdom and explored other parts of Uoria." She turned the page again and showed them a picture of the two stepping onto a small ship. "The young man told her that he wanted to bring her back to the planet where she should have been born, and yet would never have been born at all. She was afraid, but she had fallen so deeply in love with him that she knew that she could never resist him. They got onto a strange craft and it took them into the stars. It was something that this young woman couldn't have imagined. She had lived her entire life thinking that there was nothing beyond the building and now she was traveling off of the planet with the promise of a new life."

"I don't understand," Zyyr said. "What does it mean that he was going to bring her to the planet where she should have been born, but where she never would have been born at all?"

Lila smiled. It was the same question that she had asked her great-grandmother when she was young and would hear the story. Idella would smile at her and continue the story, and it was not until she got older that she began to understand it. She did the same now, turning the page again and letting her eyes move adoringly over her favorite picture of the book. It was of the young woman stepping into an incredibly lush and beautiful glade, welcomed by lovely people with flowing hair the same shimmering silver as half of the woman's.

"When they arrived on the new planet the man brought her to a place filled with people who looked very much like her. They welcomed her and began to teach her their ways. She felt comfortable there, but it still seemed as though part of her were missing. It was a strange feeling, something that she had never experienced before, but it was as though she was suddenly aware of a longing, a deep draw that wanted to lure her to something that she didn't even know she was missing. After a short time with the silver-haired people, the man told the young woman that she had somewhere else to go now. They left the beautiful place and traveled across the planet for some time. Finally they arrived at a kingdom that seemed so different from the place where they had just been, but also felt strangely calming and familiar to the young woman. This was the home of the young man's kind. This kingdom was less lush and natural than the first place, but rather filled with technology and people so incredibly lovely that it was almost breathtaking to look at them. Here she felt like the piece of her that she hadn't known was missing was suddenly restored.

Here she settled with the man. Though most of the people of the kingdom were kind and welcoming to her, there were some, a very few, who seemed to know that she was different. This made her worry that she was something that could put the others at risk. She wasn't like them in many ways and found herself wanting to hide these differences. She withdrew from the rest of the people and created a home deep in the woods where she began her family. She never spoke of what made her different and there she remained throughout the rest of her life, knowing that she was home but still carrying in her heart the spirit of the silver-haired people that she had left behind."

Lila closed the book and ran her hand lovingly across

the cover again. She felt tears forming in the back of her throat as she thought of her great-grandmother. The sound of Idella's voice faded from her mind and Lila longed to feel the soft kiss that she would always press to her great-granddaughter's forehead after reading the story to her. It was as though that kiss was an affirmation, an encouragement for her to take more out of the fantastical tale than just the delight of hearing it. Though she had never told her great-grandmother, Lila had always put great meaning into that story and knew that there was far more in the words than Idella had ever admitted.

"Is that book about your great-grandmother?" Zyyr asked.

Lila nodded.

"I think so. She never told me that, but I don't see how it couldn't be. She used to touch my hair as she read it to me, like she was trying to point out the silver streaks in my hair that were just like the ones in hers. Hers had far more silver in it than mine, at least when I was young, and she never fully looked like the other people of the kingdom. I can't tell you exactly what it was, but there was just something about her that was slightly different. Of course, to me she was just my great-grandmother. As I got older and heard this story over and over, and then after she died and I read it to myself to feel close to her, I really started to understand what she was trying to tell me with it."

"She didn't want to tell you where she came from or what had happened to her because she was afraid that the others in the kingdom might find out and it would put them all at risk," Oro said.

"I think so," Lila repeated, nodding. "I think that she used this fairy tale as a way to ensure that I would know the true history of my family. I'm the last of my bloodline, and if I didn't know what had truly happened, it would all be lost. I believe that she hoped I would understand and ensure that I carried it on to any future generations. Even if it was just through the fairy tale."

"No," Zyyr said. "No. It can't be just the fairy tale. The reason that she told you that story so many times was so that you could know who your family really is. Your great-grandmother recognized in you the features and characteristics that made her different. She knew that one day you would realize that they were more than you even know and she wanted you to be ready for it."

"What do you mean?"

Lila saw Zyyr give Oro a meaningful glance and then look back at her.

"You said that there were times when your great-grandmother would do things that were different and that she would smile at you, like you two had a special secret."

"Yes," Lila said.

"What would she do? What were some of those special things that she seemed to be able to do but that others couldn't?"

Lila thought back. These were the types of private moments that she had shared with her great-grandmother and never told anyone else about. They had been such an element of her time with Idella that it was difficult to separate them from other parts of their time together and exactly explain what it was that Idella did that was so different. She gave a sigh.

"I don't really know how to explain it. It was like she could make people believe things were happening that weren't. That's really the only way that I can describe it. She always knew exactly what someone was feeling and if they needed something, and sometimes she would do things that would make it as though she could make them see things or have things disappear."

Zyyr looked at Oro again and Oro nodded.

"Lila, when those things happened, was your great-grandmother holding anything?"

"What do you mean?"

Zyyr reached out and touched the book in Lila's lap.

"May I?" he asked.

Lila nodded and released the book so that he could pick it up. She watched as he carefully opened the cover and turned the pages until he came to a specific picture, then turned the book so that she could look at it. He rested his finger on the illustration.

"This picture is what I'm guessing is the place where the silver-haired people lived and they are greeting the young woman. They are handing her something. If we are right and this young woman is actually your great-grandmother, this might be a picture of them giving her a gift that she carried with her and used for the rest of her life. Do you recognize it?"

Lila had never made the connection before, but Zyyr pointing out that image made her remember something from her childhood with Idella. She stood and rushed out of the small room behind the fireplace, heading directly to the bedroom where Idella had slept and taken her last breath. She opened the small drawer in the table beside her bed and moved aside a small stack of handkerchiefs. Beneath them, just where she had tucked it years before after Idella's death when she had taken over the home, was a tiny silver compact. She withdrew it carefully and turned to the men who had followed her.

"This," she said, holding the compact up for them to see. "She used to wear this around her neck. When those strange things happened, she was always holding it. I never really thought of it before."

She heard Zyyr draw in a breath and his face take on an expression that she couldn't quite decipher.

"Do you believe that what this book says is actually about your great-grandmother?" he asked.

"Yes," Lila said, more confident about it now than she ever had been.

"Then we need to go."

"What? I don't understand."

Zyyr had run back toward the room behind the fireplace and Lila followed him, watching as he picked up the book and carried it out of the room and toward the table in the center of the house. He rested the book onto the table and flipped through the pages again.

"The young woman, your great-grandmother, and the man, her husband ---"

"Idella and Finean."

Lila felt a rush of strength and peace come over her as she said the names of her great-grandparents, finally acknowledging that this story was her history, the legacy that they had left for her. She felt connected to them in a new and powerful way, as though she were giving them a voice again after they had to go so long without one.

"Idella and Finean traveled back and forth from the place of the silver-haired people to the Mikana kingdom more than once. The first time that they came to the kingdom they walked and it took days of travel. The second time they visited they used some of the technology that the Mikana used at the time to travel and it was much shorter. But the last time that they made the journey, right before Idella decided that she could never go back there, they didn't use the vehicles. They traveled through tunnels that got them there almost as fast as the vehicles would have. Where are the tunnels?"

"I have no idea. I never knew of any tunnels."

"If the rest of this story is true, then those tunnels have to exist. At least they did when Idella was younger. Maybe that's where Maxim went."

"What do you mean?" Oro asked.

"Maxim is on a mission to understand what happened to his father. I don't know everything that he knows, but I have heard him talking to his mate, Ivy, about some of the things that he has uncovered."

"He talked about it a lot on the way here from the compound," Oro agreed. "He wouldn't explain it all and we haven't seen him since we got here."

"So you think that the secrets that he is keeping have to do with my great-grandmother?" Lila asked.

The thought was overwhelming in a way. Her entire life she had only thought of her great-grandmother as being different, but still her great-grandmother. There was nothing more extensive to it than that. Now she was realizing that the story of Idella and why she was so different than the others had much further-reaching implications that she could have ever imagined.

"They might. That is all we have to go on right now. He could have found out the same things that we just did and gone to this place, where the silver-haired people lived."

"Lived?" Lila asked, emphasizing the fact that Zyyr had used the past tense to refer to them.

His eyes grew troubled and a darkness came over his face that made her nervous. He gestured to the compact in her hand.

"We have seen a compact like that before," he told her. "Two of them. One was given to another warrior named

Bannack by his mate Loralia. It belonged to her father. The other is hers. If they are the same..."

His voice trailed off and Zyyr drew in a breath. Lila didn't ask him to continue. She didn't want to hear the rest. Her hand wrapped tightly around the compact and she held it close to her.

"How do we find the tunnels?"

6

Creia thrashed against his binds, fighting them with the wave of fury that gave him new strength. He knew that Ryan was referring to Pyra, Eden, and Lysander, and the thought filled him with an anger more intense than he had ever experienced.

"That is my son," he growled, "and his mate, and my grandson. He is not a hybrid."

The word came out of his mouth like poison, sounding vile and making his muscles tense. Ryan laughed.

"Of course he is," he said. "He is Denynso and he is human. He is not either one and he is both."

"Eden is Denynso now," Creia said.

He didn't know why, but it seemed that perhaps if he convinced Ryan that Eden was not truly human any longer, Ryan's aggression toward her, and perhaps his desire whatever it is that he planned on doing with her, Pyra, and their son, would fade.

"She was born human," Ryan said. "She was human when she conceived the child. That means that the baby has human DNA. I couldn't care less what species she is. I don't need her for anything but the milk that she produces. The rest of her is useless to me now."

The words sent panic through him and Creia fell silent. He knew now that his arguments were going to do nothing for him. He didn't know what Ryan had intended for the family, but he did know that it was not the first time that he had done it, and that he wouldn't be influenced by anything that the Denynso king had to say. Creia's eyes closed and he forced himself to reach deeply into his mind and release the blocks that he had put up. He focused in on Theia, gathering all of his strength and determination to reach out to her, to plead for her help.

"Theia," he thought. "Theia, please, are you there?"

Creia heard Ryan give a short laugh.

"Are you finally dead?" he asked. "Have you given up?"

Creia ignored the taunt and continued to focus on Theia, pushing past the defenses he had put up to try to reach his mate. The silence that greeted him was almost painful as it settled in his chest and seemed to swell with each second that passed.

"Theia," he thought again. "Theia, please, talk to me."

"Theia."

The cup that was in Theia's hand fell from her fingertips and crashed the floor, the water inside splashing out and spreading across the smooth stone. She gasped, her hand coming to her mouth.

"What is it?" Mina asked, rushing to her and kneeling down in front of the queen's chair to look into her face.

Theia didn't respond. Instead she closed her eyes so that she could focus harder on the soft, almost inaudible words she thought she had heard.

"Theia, please."

The words came again and she was positive then that they were in Creia's voice. Hearing her mate again after days of not being able to get in touch with him made her sob with relief.

"Creia, I'm here," she thought. "I'm here."

There was a moment of silence and she felt panic building within her.

"Theia."

She gave another sob at the sound of his response and reached out for Mina's hand. The girl took it and squeezed it comfortingly even though the queen knew that she didn't know yet what was happening.

"Oh, my love, I've been so worried about you," Theia thought. "Where are you?"

"I need you to listen to me," Creia said.

The sternness in his voice brought the smile from Theia's lips.

"What is it?" she replied. "What's wrong?"

"Is Maxim in the compound with you?" he asked.

"No," Theia told him. "He left searching for you. I can communicate with him, though. He brought Nylek with him and I have Mina with me."

"That was brilliant. I need you to tell him that I have been captured. I am being held somewhere outside of the badlands, but I'm not sure where."

"Are you alright?" Theia asked, terrified now that she knew that her mate was not just away, but in danger.

"I am alive," Creia responded. "That's the most I can say for now. Pyra, Eden, and Lysander are in serious danger."

"But they are on Earth," Theia argued.

"I know. Ryan ordered my capture. I don't know who actually did it or where I am, but it was done for Ryan. He told me himself that he has been waiting for Pyra's blood and now that he has the three of them he will be able to work on a project that he has been waiting to do since before Eden even came to Uoria."

"What project?"

"I'm not sure, but I know that they are in danger. Is Maxim alone?"

"No. He has Ivy, his brother, a human woman, and Athan with him."

"Athan," Creia muttered.

She knew that the name carried meaning for Creia.

"How will they find you?" she asked.

"Get in contact with them. When you are in touch, I will give them all of the information that I can. "

Maxim watched Athan as he walked ahead of them, running his fingers along the walls of the tunnel and using the illumination from the light stick that Maxim held to decipher the symbols carved into the stone. The frequency of the carvings had changed very suddenly and Maxim had the strange sense that they had traveled a very far distance in only a few moments.

"Do you understand what they mean?" Maxim asked.

Athan shook his head.

"Not all of them," he said. "Some of them, like these," he ran his hand along one section of the wall, "are familiar. This one says 'war'. This one says 'ally'. A few of these are names or family symbols. This one you might recognize, Maxim."

Maxim stepped forward and looked at the symbol that Athan was pointing to, tucked among many other symbols carved into the stone.

"My father," he said softly.

Athan nodded.

"Is your symbol here?" Maxim asked.

"No," Athan said. "I was never in this tunnel."

"I thought that you were always with my father when you went into battle."

"I was," Athan said, sounding slightly confused. "We stayed together when we fought so that we could back each other up or be able to tell our families what happened if..."

His voice trailed off as Maxim felt his spine stiffen.

"Could someone else have carved it?" he asked.

"I don't think so," Athan said. "Each symbol is very specific and the way that each member of the Order writes it is unique. Your father wrote this symbol."

Maxim looked at the name symbols more closely and noticed that they had been carved calmly, as though written there when the men were relaxing rather than in a hurried, hectic way. It seemed as though they were written out of the desire to entertain themselves rather than out of fear or the desire to be noticed.

"If you were always with him, how did he write his symbol here?"

Athan shook his head, continued to outline the carving with his fingertips.

"Maxim!"

The shout of his name from behind him caused Maxim to turn sharply. Nylek was rushing toward him down the tunnel. He, Kyven, and Emerie had been moving more slowly down the tunnel and Maxim hadn't realized how far behind them they had gotten.

"What is it, Nylek?" Maxim asked.

"Where did you go?" the warrior asked, panting as he stopped in front of him.

Maxim felt Ivy's hand wrap around his arm tightly.

"What do you mean?" Maxim asked. "We've been right ahead of you."

"Did you find him?" Kyven shouted moments before appearing in the glow of Maxim's light stick.

"He is right here," Nylek said.

"Kyven, we were only a few steps ahead of you. What's wrong?"

Kyven was shaking his head, a frightened look in his eyes.

"You were there and then you weren't. We had paused for a few seconds to drink some water and when we looked up again we couldn't see your light or hear you. It was like you disappeared."

"The tunnel," Ivy muttered.

"What?" Maxim asked.

She looked up at him, her hand tightening further.

"Remember when I was telling you about what the women told me about the tunnel that led down into the mirrored realm where they met Loralia?"

Maxim nodded.

"Yes. You said that it was like this one."

"Exactly. They said that there was a portal in that tunnel that led them down into the realm much faster than they would have been able to go without it. In just a matter of seconds they were able to get a distance that would likely have taken them an hour or more to walk."

As if the words have galvanized him, Athan took off running down the tunnel. Maxim followed, holding Ivy's hand with a sudden sense of concern that if he didn't keep her close he could lose her in the tunnel. After a few moments he could see sunlight ahead of him and they burst out of the tunnel into a quiet, empty space that looked like the forgotten remnants of an old compound.

"What is this place?" Kyven asked as he followed Maxim out of the tunnel and into the sunlight.

Maxim shook his head.

"Athan, do you know where we are?"

"I don't," Athan said, taking a few steps forward and looking around. "I've never been here before. It looks so familiar."

"It looks like the Denynso compound," Ivy said.

Maxim heard Nylek gasp behind him and turned to see the Denynso reaching out for him as if trying to get his attention.

"Nylek?" he said. "What is it?"

"Mina," the warrior said. "She says that Theia needs to talk to you."

Maxim saw Ivy's eyes widen and the other members of the travel group stepped in closer together.

"Alright," Maxim said.

Nylek nodded and turned his eyes away from them.

"She says that she heard from Creia."

Maxim felt a spike in his heartrate.

"Where is he?" Maxim asked

Nylek shook his head.

"She doesn't know. He says that he was captured."

"By who?" Maxim demanded.

"He doesn't know," Nylek said. "Theia wants to know where we are."

"Tell her that we don't know. Describe this place to her."

A few moments later Nylek nodded.

"Creia says that we are in the old Denynso compound. This is where he was when he was captured."

Ivy's hand squeezed Maxim's and he squeezed back.

"Ask him where he was when he was captured."

Maxim felt his heart pounding in his chest as he waited for the response from Creia. The moments dragged past, piling onto one another, intensifying his anxiety.

"Theia says that the king is weak. She is having difficulty understanding him. He said that he was exploring one of the houses and that he was taken by a hooded creature. He doesn't know where he is or how far he was taken from the compound. He only knows that Pyra, Eden, and Lysander are in serious danger, and he thinks that the others may be as well. He needs us to find him as quickly as possible. He says even if he doesn't survive, he needs us to do everything we can to help them."

"Tell her that we will find him," Maxim said.

"There's one more message from Creia," Nylek said, and then paused as if waiting for the message from Mina. "There may be more in the compound," he said. "They are extremely dangerous." His eyes snapped up to Maxim's. "Be careful."

7

"**D**o you have any idea where the tunnels could be?" Zyyr asked as Lila gathered items from the bedroom and then moved toward the kitchen to collect food for their journey.

"No," she said, shaking her head. "I told you, Idella never admitted that that story was anything more than a fairy tale. She wouldn't have mentioned the tunnels being real to me."

"And there's nowhere that you can think of that she liked a lot or that she visited often? Somewhere that could be where the tunnels are?"

Lila packed as much of the food that she had put in the kitchen of the house into her bag as she could and then turned to Zyyr.

"No," she repeated. "We rarely left the house when we were spending time together."

"Rarely," Oro said, taking a step further into the kitchen. "That means that you did. Where did you go when you did leave? Where did she take you?"

"The orchard," Lila said. "We would go into the orchard

to pick fruit. It's the same orchard that I brought you through, Zyyr. There are only trees, no tunnels."

Zyyr felt disappointment settle into his stomach. They didn't know where this place was, and the tunnels were the only way that they would be able to get there without having to spend days and possibly weeks traveling. The thought brought sudden realization to Zyyr's mind. He rushed across the house and spread the book on the table again. He sifted through the pages until he found the picture of the silver-haired creatures welcoming Idella.

"What is it, Zyyr?" Oro asked.

"What do the tunnels remind you of?" he asked.

Oro seemed to think for a moment and then stepped up to the side of the table, staring down at the book along with Zyyr.

"The tunnels to the mirrored realm," he said.

"Exactly."

"Mirrored realm?" Lila asked.

"The woman that we were telling you about with the compact, Loralia, she lived with her kind in a place under the Denynso compound. It is a mirror of the compound above it. We discovered it because of a tunnel."

"I'm sure that there are many tunnels around the planet. They used to be the most efficient way of moving around without being exposed to the elements," Lila said.

"Yes," Zyyr said, "but Loralia's kind didn't always live under the ground. Her kind, silver-haired people who use compacts to make things happen, used to live on the land that is now the Denynso compound."

"What do you mean they use compacts to make things happen?" Lila asked.

"I can't explain it," Zyyr said. "It's something that you would have to see. All I know is that it sounds exactly like what you were talking about your great-grandmother doing but on a larger scale."

"Do you think that the place that Idella visited was what is now the Denynso compound?" she asked.

Zyyr shook his head.

"No," he said. He pointed to the illustration. "This doesn't look like the compound. These plants are different and we don't have a river like this. Loralia mentioned, though, that the area that is the Denynso compound now was where they lived when they were above ground, but that then and when they moved underground they would still visit another place to gather food. She had never been, but her family would go into another place to gather fruit and other foods. It was close enough that they were able to travel there through their underground realm. None of us have seen it, though, which means that it is far enough from the compound that we have not been able to see it from the ridges."

"I don't understand what that has to do with Idella."

"What if where she visited was actually the place where the silver-haired creatures would go for food? She may have visited the actual settlement but not have included it in the book because, while beautiful, it is not like this."

"Where is the tunnel to the underground realm?" Lila asked.

"It is on a ridge in the Denynso compound," Zyyr said.

Lila made an exasperated sound.

"That is days away," she nearly shouted. "How does that help us?"

Zyyr turned to her, meeting her eyes in an effort to keep her calm.

"Because it tells me how to find the tunnels that led here."

. . .

Several minutes later they were walking into the orchard. Zyyr was carrying his bags as well as the bags that Lila had packed, and his eyes were locked on the ground in front of him. They walked deep into the orchard and he examined the base of every tree that they passed. He was beginning to think that his impulse might have been wrong when he noticed what he had been looking for. Lowering himself to his knees, he flattened his hand onto the patch of thick moss on the ground. It stretched a few feet from the base of the tree and felt warm beneath his palm. He looked up at Oro who stared down at him with a look in his eyes that told Zyyr that he was thinking the same thing that he was.

"Lila, did your great-grandmother come to this area of the orchard often?" Zyyr asked.

Lila looked around and then nodded.

"Yes," she said. "This tree," she flattened her hand on the tree across from the one with the moss at its base." She walked around the trunk and then looked at him. "Look," she said.

Zyyr got to his feet and went to the tree where Lila was standing. She had her hand rested on the trunk right beneath a set of initials carved deep into the trunk. *F + I.*

Positive now that his assumptions were correct, he moved back to the moss and grasped the edge with one hand. He pulled and felt resistance. Moving his hand a few inches along the edge he pulled again and felt the moss giving way beneath the pressure of the tug. Finally it rose up off of the ground, revealing a wide opening just like the ones in the orchard on the Denynso compound. He looked up at Oro and then to Lila, who stared down at the ground with widened eyes and her mouth slightly open.

"What is that?" she asked, her voice powdery as if she knew the answer to the question that she had asked but still felt as though she needed to ask it.

"It is an entrance to the tunnels," Zyyr told her. "There are several openings like this throughout the orchard in the Denynso compound. They lead down into the mirrored realm where Loralia and her kind lived."

"Idella was visiting the entrance to the tunnel," she said, sounding as though the realization was settling into her. "When she brought me here it was because she missed Finean and the other place. Why do you think that she never went back?"

"She said that the kingdom was her home."

"But she traveled back and forth before she settled here. If she loved that place so much, why did she never go back to visit?"

"Maybe she was afraid. Maybe she knew that if she continued visiting that the others would find out the secret that she wanted to keep from them. She said that people finding things out can sometimes cause more harm than good. That could be part of it."

Lila nodded. Zyyr's heart ached for his mate. He could see how hard this was for her, and there was nothing that he could do to help her. They couldn't stop now. He reached into his bag and pulled out a light stick. Pointing the illumination down into the opening, he took a breath and swung his legs over before letting go and dropping into the darkness.

For a moment he worried that there was nothing beneath him, then he felt his feet hit soft ground and he stumbled forward. Zyyr lifted his hands in front of him and caught himself on a wall a few feet ahead.

"Are you alright?" Lila called down.

Zyyr straightened and held the light stick so that he could look up and see her at the edge of the opening staring down at him.

"I'm fine," he called up. "Come down. This is it."

Oro helped Lila into the opening and Zyyr caught her, holding her close to his body as he lowered her down to the ground. He felt himself responding to her intensely in that simple movement and craved time when they could be alone together again.

Once Oro dropped to the ground, Zyyr lifted Lila so that she could move the moss back into place, covering the opening and preventing anyone else from finding it. As they started down the tunnel Zyyr's thoughts wandered to Jem and the horrific battle waged under the ground. They had thought that Ullie and the human flight attendant who had betrayed the Denynso and aided the Klimnu had been the ones to implement the technology that helped them to get down into the realm faster, but now Zyyr was realizing that this was not the case. Instead, the technology was in place in many other tunnels as well, helping those who knew of them to move around the planet undetected. The thought was unnerving, but at the same time thrilling as he felt that they were finally on the path to what Pyra had intended when they first left the compound to explore the planet.

Zyyr tried to remain aware of how far they had gone as they traveled, but after a few hours of walking he knew that they had passed through portals and were now far further from the Mikana kingdom than his awareness told him. Suddenly they came to a section of the tunnel that split off, leading in two different directions.

"Where do we go?" Lila asked.

Zyyr held up his light stick to shine the illumination down each of the tunnels. They looked identical, neither giving any indication of which would be the right option to lead them to the lush and beautiful land where Idella had found the first clues as to who she really was.

"This way," Oro said.

Zyyr turned and saw him gesturing toward one of the tunnels. He looked absolutely confident in his choice.

"Are you sure?" Zyyr asked.

Oro nodded.

"Yes. I can feel it."

Zyyr nodded and allowed Oro to guide then down the tunnel. The temperature in the tunnel was cool and the darkness surrounding them was making it difficult for him to interpret the time of day that it had gotten to in the time that they had spent below ground. They continued on for a little while longer before he realized that Lila was falling behind. Her steps had grown shorter and she seemed to be forcing her body along.

"Are you tired?" he asked, coming up behind her and wrapping an arm around her waist to support her.

She looked up at him and nodded, her long eyelashes falling heavily over her wide eyes. She was so incredibly beautiful and Zyyr felt a surge of even greater protectiveness toward her. He didn't know what they were walking in to, but he did know that no matter what, she was his greatest priority and he would do anything that it took to protect her.

"Let's rest for a few hours," Oro said. "It won't be too much longer."

"How do you know?" Lila asked as Zyyr lowered their bags to the ground and started setting up a meager camp for them.

He glanced up at Oro who was staring down the tunnel in the direction they were walking. He noticed the other warrior's hands clenching and unclenching slightly at his sides.

"I just know," Oro said, his voice taking on a tone of slight aggression that it had not held before.

Realization struck Zyyr and despite the uneasy feeling that it brought to his stomach, he couldn't help but feel the slight smile come to his lips.

8

The tunnel was quiet except for the sounds of Zyyr and Lila breathing deeply from their bedrolls several feet away. Oro lay on his back on his own blanket, his hands folded behind his head as he stared up at the top of the tunnel. They had turned down the light stick so that it only let off a slight glow but his eyes had adjusted to the dimness enough that he could make out the rough earth that formed the top of the tunnel. As he stared at it he wondered about the creatures who had created it. Though they knew now that Idella and Finean had used them to travel between the settlement of the silver-haired people and the Mikana kingdom, and that there was an entrance to the tunnels in the orchard of the kingdom, that didn't mean that the Mikana had built those tunnels originally.

From the way that Lila had described it, Idella and Finean were the only ones who knew about the tunnels, and their use of them had been extremely secretive. It was possible that the technology that allowed fast and easy passage was an innovation of the Mikana but that the tunnels themselves were not widely known.

Even as Oro tried to focus on these questions rolling through his mind, his thoughts continued to wander the intense feelings that had been building within him as they traveled through the tunnels. Something within him had changed as soon as he dropped down from the orchard floor and it had only grown as they had moved further and further away from the kingdom. It was a feeling of aggression and anger, a shortness of temper that made him feel ready to lash out at either of his traveling companions at the slightest word.

This alone would not have been strange considering the tension that was building around them and the stress that was forming as they headed almost blindly into the unknown. As he traveled, however, it was the changes that came over his body that kept his mind reeling. He could feel a need rising within him, a desire that was unlike anything he had ever experienced. His body was responding to that need intensely, making his shaft so hard it nearly hurt as it pressed against the front of his pants. It was something that he would never have anticipated experiencing while on this journey, and something that he didn't know that he was prepared to face, though he, like all of the other warriors within the Denynso clan, had been waiting for it his entire life. The change that had come over him and was causing the violent temper and constant arousal could only be explained in one way. He was close to meeting his mate.

The realization that his mate was somewhere nearby was one that had completely taken him by surprise. That thought had never even crossed his mind when he left the Denynso compound for the first time in his life and started on the venture that was intended to be an exploration of the planet. Like the other warriors he had been thinking only of what they would discover along the way and what that would teach them about the planet that they called home and the other species that lived there. It would never have occurred to him to think that the woman who had been intended for him from the beginning of his life would be waiting for him somewhere along his journey.

It seemed that he had just drifted to sleep when Zyyr shook him by his boot, waking him to tell him it was time to move along. Oro stood reluctantly and packed his bag, accepting the food that Lila held out to him before starting up the tunnel again. Though they had started this exploration with Zyyr clearly leading them, the positions had shifted and now he was the one that was ahead of the other two, guiding them along the tunnels with the powerful draw within his chest pulling him in the right direction as they went.

He continued to follow this feeling as they wound their way through the tunnels. The passage that they followed seemed abandoned and forgotten, but there were times when he thought that he heard movement through the walls or saw glimmers of light deep in the tunnels that they were not following, as if there were others down in the tunnels as well. The thought was unsettling. If there were others, he had to wonder if they were aware of this area of the tunnels, and how they would respond to knowing that the three of them were now following them.

The darkness and close space was slightly disorienting and Oro didn't know how long they had been traveling or even the time of day or night that it might be when he felt an intense, almost breathtaking surge of arousal within him. All of the muscles in his body tensed and violent aggression flowed through him as though moving in his very blood. He wanted to scream, to strike out at anyone or anything that got close to him. Oro struggled to suppress the feelings, reminding himself of the turmoil that those urges had caused other Denynso who were going through this difficult phase. Though it was one of the most difficult things that he had ever tried to do, he knew that he had to hold himself back. There would be no benefit to giving into them now. It would only work to distract them from their goal and possibly prevent them from accomplishing what they had set out to do.

Instead, Oro used the intensified feelings within him to fuel him forward, allowing him to push through the exhaustion that was dragging on him and continue forward. As he walked he was aware that the ground beneath his feet was gradually leading up so that they were climbing up toward ground level. He hoped this would mean that they would not have to climb out of the tunnel through a hidden hatch the way that they had gotten in. That would eliminate the concern that they would not be able to find the exit and all of this travel would have been for nothing. As they wound their way through the tunnels, the passages took on less and less of an abandoned feeling. Soon they appeared as though they had been used within just a few years rather than having sat empty for decades.

Finally he allowed his urges to guide him around a last corner and they entered a tunnel that felt fresh and alive, as though filled with air just breathed and touched by the presence of people still within his reach. Within moments he could see a milky shimmer of light coming into the tunnel from an entrance just ahead. He paused and looked back over his shoulder to ensure that Zyyr and Lila were close to him. He had pulled ahead of them hours before, preferring to be alone with his thoughts than having to fight to control himself around them. They soon came around the corner and he saw Lila's eyes brighten as she saw the light ahead of him.

"An exit," she breathed, sounding almost as though she were reluctant to put much volume to the word for fear that acknowledging it would somehow make the exit disappear.

As soon as the thought rolled through his mind Oro felt a sense of panic come to his chest. He realized that if they were right and these were the silver-haired creatures that had been Loralia's kind before the plague that devastated them, killing all but her, it was entirely possible that what they were seeing ahead of them was not an authentic exit at all. It could simply be a reflection, mimicking the safe exit in a way that would guide intruders in the tunnel into danger rather than to their intended destination.

Lila started to pass him, and Oro held up his arm to stop her.

"What are you doing?" she asked.

"Do you believe that exit is really there?" he asked her.

"What?" Lila asked, sounding confused and exasperated.

"That exit," he said, pointing at the gap in the stone ahead of them. "Do you believe that it is really there?"

"I don't understand what you're asking me."

"Is it there?" he shouted.

Lila took a step back, cowering closer to Zyyr, but Oro didn't care about her show of fear. She nodded.

"Yes," she said. "Of course, I do."

"Zyyr," he said, turning to look at the other warrior. "How about you? Do you believe that it is there?"

Zyyr looked over Oro at the shimmer of light and then back to Oro.

"Yes," he said.

His voice sounded reluctant and almost regretful, as

though he knew exactly what Oro was thinking. Oro nodded and turned to look at the exit again.

"Well, I don't," he said.

"What does he mean?" Lila asked.

Oro ignored her and stalked toward the exit, his eyes focused directly on it.

"I don't believe that it is here. I don't believe that this is really an exit of the tunnels. I think that it was crafted and that if we tried to go through it, we would end up somewhere far worse than where we intend."

"What do you mean it was crafted?" Lila asked.

"Just like your great-grandmother used to make things happen with her compact. I think that one of their kind crafted this as a final form of protection. It's not real. It's not an exit at all, and I'll prove it to you."

Oro stared at the shimmer of light and stepped up closer to it. He told himself again that it wasn't real, that it was just like the wall in the meeting hall or the mirrored realm beneath the ground. It was an illusion, though one that could be made very real just by the belief of the person perceiving it.

"It's not real," he told himself again and reached forward with one hand.

As soon as his hand drew close to what looked like the exit, the shimmer of light disappeared and his hand came into contact with hard, warm stone. Oro could hear Lila gasp behind him and he turned to look at her.

"That is what we meant when we said Loralia could do things. She can create things just like that, but in order for it to work, the person perceiving it has to believe in it completely. If you do not fully believe that it is there, it won't be. Can you still see the exit?"

"Yes," Lila said, "but it flickered."

"It's not real, Lila," Oro told her. "You need to believe what is real, that you are looking at a solid wall of the tunnel."

He watched her take a long breath and then her eyes widened slightly.

"It's gone!" She looked frantically between Zyyr and Oro.

"How are we going to get out?" she asked, her voice now high with fear. "If that wasn't really an exit, how are we supposed to get out of these tunnels?"

"You have to believe that we will," Oro told her. "You have to really believe it. Don't just say that you do. Don't just tell yourself that you do. You have to reach inside of yourself to that place that told you that that fairy tale your great-grand-mother read you was more than just a story, and believe with everything that we will find the way out. Question everything that we see and don't believe that anything is the way that you think it is."

"I think I know where it is," Lila answered softly.

"Where?" asked Zyyr, coming up to rest his hand on her back.

"You told me that what Loralia makes, like what my great-grandmother and the rest of her kind made, are reflections. If that image was created, then that means that it was reflected from somewhere."

She turned around and faced the wall opposite of where the image of the exit had been.

"Where do you think it is?" Zyyr asked.

"Here," she said, flattening her hands on the wall in front of her. "This is where the exit is. This is what will lead us to where Idella lived when she first came to this planet."

Oro felt the draw within his chest again, more powerful this time than it even had been before, and he nodded.

"Yes," he said. "That's it. That's where it is."

In an instant the wall disappeared beneath Lila's hands and the three were bathed in soft, milky light from outside. Oro stepped forward out of the tunnel and looked around. His eyes fell on the large trees and lavish plants that had been in the pictures in Idella's book. He breathed in air that was sweetly perfumed by flowers blooming among the leaves. He took another step out into the open space and suddenly heard a scream as something hit him, sending him crashing onto the ground.

9

Oro grunted as he hit the ground and felt something heavy come down on top of him. Lila continued to scream behind him and he heard Zyyr shout. The weight on top of him shifted as he heard Zyyr shouting at whatever was on top of him to get off. Oro felt a harsh blow to his head and pain radiated through his body.

"Anson!" a woman's voice said. "Stop this instant."

The weight on top of him eased and Oro was able to roll over onto his back as he gasped for breath. When he opened his eyes he saw a man standing over him, glaring down at him with a fury in his eyes that was chilling. He was not large by the standards of the Denynso, but was certainly larger than the Mikana men or the human men he had encountered. It was not his size, however, that took Oro aback. It was the huge translucent grey wings that stretched on either side of him.

The man who Oro assumed was Anson stepped back away from him and he felt the primal need within him swell as a new light appeared just before a stunningly beautiful woman stepped up beside Anson. She had the soft, glimmering light around her that Loralia did and wings like delicate pink glass. She reached a pale, graceful hand toward him.

"Let me help you," she said softly.

Her voice was like music and everything within Oro seemed to come alive as he place his hand in hers and climbed to his feet.

"Thank you," he said.

"Who are you?" Anson demanded in a gruff voice. "Why are you intruding here?"

"Hush now, Anson," the woman said in a softly scolding tone. "They aren't intruding. Can't you see," she stepped forward and Oro saw her take Lila by both hands and lead her carefully forward, "she is no stranger."

The woman ran her fingers through Lila's hair, bringing some of the strands forward as if to show off the silver streaks to the winged man. Anson's stiff stance relaxed slightly as he looked at Lila's hair, but he had the same suspicion in his eyes when he turned his gaze back to Oro.

"Who are they?" he asked. "Why are they with her?"

"Why don't you ask her," the woman said, "and allow her to tell you for herself? What is your name?" she asked, looking to Lila.

"Lila."

"Hello, Lila. My name is Ariella. This is my brother, Anson. I apologize for his less than hospitable greeting."

"It's alright," Lila said. She gestured toward Oro. "This is Oro." She stepped back slightly and turned to reach for Zyyr. "And this is Zyyr, my mate."

Oro noticed Ariella's eyebrows lift slightly at those words, but she continued to smile at them, the expression making Oro feel weak and somewhat out of control.

"You are welcome here," Ariella said. "Come with me. I'm sure you are hungry and tired after your long journey. You will stay in my home with me."

"Ariella," Anson protested, but the winged woman turned her brother and lifted a hand to silence him.

"Not another word, Anson. They are our guests. You will not offend the memories of our friends and family."

The words fell painfully on Oro. He didn't know what she meant, but the emotion in that message felt heavy. Anson nodded once and turned away from them. Ariella followed and the three fell into step behind her. The dress that Ariella wore fastened around her neck and then swung low over her hips, and Oro watched her graceful back as she walked, admiring the smooth expanse of her skin and the incredible wings that stretched from between her shoulder blades. Anson and Ariella led them through plants that looked richly green even in the moonlight that fell on them toward a series of gently sloping hills in the distance. As they got closer Oro noticed that there were doors in the hills and realized that these were their homes.

Anson ducked into one of the doors and closed it tightly behind him without saying another word to them. Ariella watched him and then opened another door, gesturing for them to enter.

"Please come inside."

They did as she asked and Oro found himself stepping into a home that was as unexpected as Ariella herself. Everything within the home seemed to be fashioned out of leaves and carefully bound branches with only small bits of fabric added in. There was no cut wood in the house, but rather elements of the world around them that had been thoughtfully salvaged and creatively utilized.

Ariella gestured for them to sit and Oro took his place

on a chair that rocked gently on curved legs. He used his feet to increase the rocking, allowing the motion to soothe him. Zyyr and Lila sat together on a small sofa.

"I have to apologize for my brother," she said. "He takes his position as guard very seriously."

"It's alright," Oro said. "Protecting you is the most important thing that he could do."

He felt heat creep across his cheeks as Ariella turned to look at him, her eyes registering slight surprise at his words. He could feel Zyyr looking at him now and he knew that the other warrior already knew what he was going through.

"Thank you," Ariella said softly. "Now, I am sure that you have a reason for coming here, but I think it is best that you eat and rest. There will be plenty of time tomorrow for you to tell me what it is that I can do for you."

The three agreed and Ariella walked out of the room, returning a few moments later with a tray of food that she settled onto the table in the center of the room. She left again and returned with another tray that she set alongside the first. She left a third time and returned with tall glasses and a curved pitcher. Zyyr reached for the food first and Oro followed suit, picking up a piece of something that he didn't recognize and looking at it. Though it didn't look like anything that he had ever eaten, knowing that Ariella's hands had made it made him immediately want to eat it.

They ate until they were satiated and then Oro sat back in his chair, feeling the exhaustion really settle into him now that they had arrived at their destination and his belly was full.

"If you have all had enough, I can show you to your rooms. There are baths in each and you are welcome to wash if you would like."

They followed her deeper into the home and Ariella

pointed out a room for Zyyr and Lila first. When they had thanked her and closed the door behind them, she gestured at him to follow her further down the hallway. She brought him to a door and opened it, stepping back so that he could enter. The room as far larger than he anticipated and in contrast to the wood and leaves of the first room, this one was light and soft, delicate like Ariella. A soft-looking bed piled with white blankets looked incredibly inviting, but he also felt the dirt and sweat of their journey sticking to his skin and knew that he should take her up on her offer of bathing before settling in for the night.

"Thank you, Ariella," he said, his voice coming out slightly powdery.

"Are you alright? Anson didn't hurt you badly, did he?"

Oro shook his head, somewhat embarrassed by the scuffle, but also enjoying the fact that she was concerned about him.

"No," he told her, "I'm fine. He mostly just knocked the wind out of me. It was a shock more than anything."

"Good," she said. She paused and their eyes met for a brief moment that Oro could feel coursing through him. "Sleep well."

"I will."

He stepped back and she closed the door. Oro waited a few moments and then crossed the room to the sunken bath in the far corner, disrobing as he went. He groaned as he let his pants fall to his ankles, finally releasing the pressure on his engorged cock. Being close to Ariella had only increased his arousal and now Oro felt like he couldn't handle it if he got any harder.

The water that poured from the faucet was the perfect temperature and Oro sank into it blissfully, letting the heat release the tension in his muscles and rinse away the reminders of the tunnels that clung to his skin. He filled his palm with soap from one of the bottles lining the edge of the tub and ran it back through his hair, then went through the process of washing his body. He submerged himself completely to rinse and when he came out of the water he was startled to see Ariella standing just steps from the edge of the tub.

"You are a Denynso warrior," she said simply.

Oro nodded.

"I am," he confirmed.

"I suspected as much when I saw you, but I knew when Lila described Zyyr as her mate."

"Yes," Oro said, not sure how else to respond.

"My mother warned me about Denynso when I was young," she said, stepping closer to the tub.

"She did?" Oro asked.

Ariella nodded, a soft smile coming to her lips. There was something fragile and innocent about her that made his desire for her even more intense and Oro fought to resist the urge to reach for her.

"She told me that the Denynso men are powerful in many ways and are fearsome in battle. Even more, perhaps, than our own warriors. When they meet their mate, however, they are insatiable until they have her and irresistible when they want her."

Oro found himself walking up to the edge of the tub as she approached and lowered herself to her knees. She reached out and ran her hand through his hair then gently touched the back of his head as if checking to make sure that he was not more severely injured than he had admitted.

"That's true," he said.

"Do you have a mate, Oro?" Ariella asked, her fingers wandering to the plane of his jaw.

"I think so," he said quietly, tilting into her touch.

"You think so?" she asked.

Her voice sounded nervous and he ached to comfort her, to show her that she was safer now than she had ever been in her life. He shook his head.

"I know," he whispered.

Oro tilted his mouth up to hers and Ariella met it. Her lips were soft and sweet against his and Oro felt like a flame had ignited within his belly. He reached up to tuck his hand around the back of her head and drew her closer to deepen their kiss. He guided her gently with the tip of his tongue and Ariella complied, parting her lips so that he could explore her mouth. When the kiss ended Ariella looked breathless and flushed, her eyes slumbering but also bright as though she couldn't decide what to do with the new feelings that she was experiencing. She dipped her hand down into the water beside Oro and filled her palm, lifting it up and tipping it so that the warm water slid down his chest. She repeated the gesture and he watched her eyes as they traveled with the drops along his skin. Her gaze stopped and she bit down on her bottom lip, color rising even higher on her cheeks. Oro looked down to see what had caught her attention.

He hadn't noticed that coming closer to the edge of the water had caused him to rise up out of it slightly and now the tip of his hardened cock sat above the water. Oro brought his hand to it, running his palm across the head and then stroking down over the shaft. He heard Ariella moan softly and he looked at her, waiting until she met his eyes to take her hand and guide it forward to replace his. The movement caused her to lean forward over the edge of the tub and he took advantage of the position to kiss her again and then reach around to the back of her neck to release the tie of her dress. The fabric fell away from her body and he ran his flattened palm down her back, letting the tips of his fingers touch the juncture of her back and her wings, but not venturing onto the wings themselves.

Ariella seemed timid about touching him, but continued to gaze into the water with fascination and desire. Oro wrapped his hand around hers, tightening her grip on his shaft and beginning to guide her in stroking him. She gasped softly and Oro moaned at the intoxicating combination of her hand on him and the sweet sound coming from her lips. After a few moments he felt her pulling her hand away. He was briefly nervous that he had moved too fast with her and that she was going to leave, but then he saw her stand and push the dress down her hips, allowing it to fall away completely.

She wore nothing under the dress so now she stood in front of him with her lush body bare and waiting for him. He had never seen anything as incredible as her, the swells of her hips full and sultry, her breasts gently sloped with taut pink nipples, and a tiny waist that seemed to accent all of her soft, enticing curves. Ariella looked at him with a nervous, questioning look in her eyes and he let out a long exhalation.

"You are beautiful," he said.

She smiled and reached for him, both delicate hands extending out to welcome him to her. Oro climbed out of the water and took her hands, allowing her to bring him forward toward her until their bodies just touched. Their marked height difference made it so that her mouth was just beneath the center of his belly and he drew in a breath as she ran her lips softly across his skin. He ran his fingertips along her arms, delighting in the velvetiness of her skin. The tips of her wings fluttered slightly and a moment later she rose off of the ground, coming up until she was able to look him in the eye. The impact was mesmerizing and Oro felt that he couldn't control himself any longer.

Grasping Ariella by the waist he leaned forward and captured her mouth with his, kissing her more deeply and insistently than before. He moved one hand to wrap tightly around her waist and slid the other down the curve of her belly until it dipped between her thighs. She cried out against his mouth as his fingers found her already hot, wet folds and began to explore them. Oro held her closer as she writhed against him, slipping one of his fingers within her and using the pad of his thumb to massage the taut pearl that his attention was easing forward. As her tight, untouched body started to relax, Oro slipped in another finger, taking his time to allow her body to take it in.

He kissed along her neck until his mouth reached the soft place beneath her ear.

"Are you ready for me?" he whispered.

She was nearly sobbing with the pleasure that he was already giving her and she nodded, tucking her head down onto his shoulder.

"Are you sure?" he asked.

"Yes," Ariella responded, touching a kiss to his neck. "Yes, I'm ready."

Oro slowly withdrew his fingers from her body and returned his hands to her waist so that he could carefully position her over his hips. He settled her at the tip of his erection and eased her forward, slowly sinking into her. Suddenly, unexpectedly, Ariella's head fell back and she cried out. The glow around her intensified for a moment and Oro felt her already tight walls squeezing around him as her climax drew him in deeper. He moaned, rolling his hips slightly to meet each of the delectable spasms as she rode the waves of the orgasm that had hit her so intensely as soon as he was fully inside her.

As the contractions slowed Oro carried her over to the bed and turned so that he could sit on the mattress. He lowered himself back, positioning her so that she was straddling his hips. Her body was even wetter now and relaxed by the climax, allowing him to press deeper within her. He gripped her hips and guided them into a rocking motion that let her grind against him without their bodies parting. Ariella looked uncertain and slightly taken aback by her own sexual response, drawing her arms up to cover her breasts and looking away.

"Don't cover yourself," Oro said, reaching up to take her arms and ease them away from her body. "You are so beautiful. I want to see you. All of you."

He led her hands down to his stomach so that she flattened her palms against him. Her long hair had tumbled down from the knot that had held it to her head and now hung wildly around her. Oro tucked one hand around her cheek and Ariella turned her face to touch a kiss to his palm. As if empowered by the kiss, she started to follow the guidance of his hand still on her hip, falling into a rhythm that threatened to send him into oblivion within seconds.

In an effort to prolong the almost overwhelming pleasure and remain as close to his new mate as he could, Oro sat up, pulling Ariella in close so that she cuddled into his lap. She responded by wrapping her legs around his hips and crushing her breasts to his chest. This position allowed them to stare into each other's eyes, elevating the intense emotions that were taking over Oro's mind and heart. Their skin moved across each other slickly with water and sweat, and he savored the feeling of her breasts rising and falling against his body.

He could no longer resist. He brought one hand up and ran it gingerly down the edge of one of her wings. It fluttered and he groaned slightly. He touched it again, amazed by the texture of it beneath his fingertips. As he stroked her wing with one hand, Oro slipped the other between their bodies so that he could mimic the touch on her most sensitive peak. She rocked against his hand, her eyes closing and tiny cries spilling from her lips. Oro lifted his hips, pounding into her in rhythm with the grind of her pelvis. He quickened the pace of his fingers on her body and she screamed out again, grasping his shoulders with both hands as she released into a cascade of new contractions.

Oro let out a growl and thrust into her with an almost frenzied pace. Within seconds he felt himself spiral out of control and plunged as deeply into her as he could. Letting out a gasping cry he gave himself over into his own orgasm, spilling into her with each pulse. As their bodies cooled he let himself tip back again, bringing Ariella down with him so that she lay across his chest, her head rested just above his heartbeat. He kissed her hair and watched as her wings slowly folded down and tucked against her body as she drifted to sleep in his arms.

10

Rain finished packing all of the supplies that she could into her bags and turned to watch Lynx secure his closed. She didn't know how long they were going to be away or what they would encounter along the way, so they needed to bring everything possible with them. They started out of the house, but were almost immediately stopped by another of the former Nyx 23 crew.

"What are you doing?" Jonah asked, starting intently into Rain's eyes.

"I can't tell you," she said, trying to step around the man to continue out of the settlement.

"Rain, you know something that you aren't telling me."

Jonah had been one of her dearest friends while traveling on the Nyx 23 craft and then on the settlement, and in that moment she realized that in the time since they had been released from the lock put on them by the Covra she had spent almost no time with him. The thought made her feel guilty and regretful, but she knew that she had to press forward. What she and Lynx had discovered was important and she needed to find out more as quickly as she could.

"I'm sorry, Jonah," she said, fighting off the tears that were starting to form in her eyes at the thought of leaving her friend behind again.

"I can help you."

"I'm not going to put you in danger."

Jonah stopped walking but Rain continued.

"What about our project?"

Rain stopped in her tracks and whirled around to face Jonah.

"What project?" Lynx asked. "What is he talking about?"

Rain couldn't answer her mate. Instead she rushed back to Jonah, her heart fluttering wildly in her chest.

"Our project," she breathed. "I don't know how I could have forgotten it."

"You seem to have forgotten a lot," Jonah said, his voice sounding slightly bitter as he watched Lynx walk up behind them.

"Please, Jonah, don't be that way."

"What project is he talking about?" Lynx asked again.

"Do you think that it's still there?" Rain asked.

She didn't want to get her hopes up thinking that the project that had not been touched in over 100 years was still intact where they had left it.

"I know it is," Jonah said.

Hope swelled in Rain's chest. Jonah turned and started toward the edge of the settlement where they had constructed a small, simple structure they hoped would function as their lab while they were on Uoria. At first a few of the others had been excited by the idea and used the space to perform simple experiments and run tests on the plants and soil of the planet, trying to glean as much information about it as they could. Rain knew that it was their way of keeping their hope alive. As long as they gathered this information they could believe that one day they would be able to share it with the rest of the scientific community back on Earth. Before too long, those who had joined them stopped coming and the lab was left completely to Rain and Jonah. Though Rain had seen it as a failure of the motivation and scientific devotion of the other members of the crew, Jonah was excited by the departure.

It was his enthusiasm for having his career-long dream of having his own dedicated lab coming true, no matter what the circumstances, that spurred them into starting their project. Neither had ever told anyone else about it and in the tragic, hectic weeks leading up to the final Covra attack they had abandoned it, choosing instead to focus their energies on the direct attacks and protecting themselves. Now she wondered if it was even possible for the makeshift lab to still be there, much less their only partially completed project.

She rushed through the settlement, trying to suppress the hope that was building in her but also not able to contain her excitement. Ahead of her rose the building that they had constructed largely out of the outer shell of the original ship. Though worn and covered with encroaching plants, the lab was still there, still standing. Jonah stepped up to the door and yanked on it. The door groaned but didn't move. He tried again but it still wouldn't move.

"Excuse me," Lynx said from behind them.

Rain and Jonah stepped out of the way and Lynx planted a perfectly aimed kick directly in the middle of the door, causing it to crash into the building.

"Thank you," Rain said, climbing onto the balls of her feet to kiss her mate. "I appreciate it."

"Any time," Lynx replied. "Now will you tell me what project you were talking about?"

"Just a minute," Rain said.

Lynx gave a grunt of frustration, but Rain ignored it. She looked around the space, letting the memories of that building wash over her. Jonah was already rushing toward a door on the far wall that led to the smaller room. This had been their private space and where they had conceived and begun to build their project. She rushed after him, relieved to see that he was able to open that door with greater ease. She didn't want Lynx to have to break down this door as well and risk damaging whatever was left inside.

The door opened and Jonah hesitated to go in.

"What if it isn't there anymore?" he asked.

Rain stepped up beside him and nudged him with her shoulder.

"And what if it is?" she asked. "What if this is our chance to finish it?"

"Would it help you?" Jonah asked.

Rain nodded.

"Yes. More than you know."

"I don't know anything. You won't tell me. You never kept anything from me."

Rain felt her heart squeeze. The truth was that she had been holding things back from him since the crash. She knew that no matter how much she had tried to avoid it, tried to protect others from what she knew, the time had come to tell Jonah what had really happened.

"You're right," she said. "I'm sorry. There are things that I should have told you from the very beginning that I didn't, and that is my fault. But I'm willing to tell you about them now."

Jonah immediately settled onto one of the chairs in the room, crossing his legs and propping his chin in his hand in the position that he always used to tell people that he was listening to them. If what she had to tell him had not been so serious, she would have laughed at the pose. Now, though, it only made her more afraid of how he was going to react. She settled onto another of the chairs so that she could look at him and gave a deep sigh.

"Etan killed himself," she said, deciding the best way to handle the situation was simply to throw herself into it and tell Jonah everything right out.

"What?" Jonah asked, sitting up and letting his hand lower down so his arm fell across his legs.

Rain nodded.

"When the ship lost power and started to crash, I went to the control room to see if he knew what was happening. The ship crashed before I could get there. When I got into the room I found him. He was barely warm to the touch already."

"He had been dead for some time," Jonah said.

Rain nodded again.

"I didn't know what happened, so I never told anybody. Even you."

"So how do you know that he killed himself?" Jonah asked. "Something else might have happened. One of the Valdician weapons could have –"

"No, Jonah," Rain said, cutting him off as his emotions sent his voice higher and faster.

"But Etan was so devoted to the project. He dedicated his life to being a captain."

"That's exactly what he did," Rain agreed. "This team, this mission, was everything to him. Being the captain and doing right by the crew was the most important thing in his entire life."

"So why would he kill himself?"

Rain lowered the bag on her shoulder to the ground and

dug through it until she found the journal that they had taken from Etan's quarters. She handed it over to Jonah. She knew now that he was a part of this, as he likely should have been from the beginning. He had been on the perimeter of everything that had happened from the moment that the Denynso had succeeded in starting to awaken the members of the settlement after being frozen in place by the Covra for more than a century. It was time now that she brought him in and benefitted from not only his brilliance and incredible understanding of science and technology, but from the emotions and memories that he had within him. So much of what she and Lynx, as well as the others, were learning was discovered simply through memory and intuition. Though much of Jonah's memories were shared with her, she knew that he had many of his own that may give them greater insight into what had actually happened to them and to the others affected by the Validicians and the Covra.

Jonah finished reading the journal entries that Rain pointed out to him and looked up at her, shaking his head.

"How could he do that to us?" he asked. "He abandoned us."

"He didn't see it as abandoning," Rain said. "To him, we were all going to die within just a short time anyway. It was his way of continuing to be our captain, our leader."

"If he killed himself before the crash, what good would our project do now?"

Rain handed him the map and pointed out the strange symbol.

"We need to go there," she said. "Lynx and I believe that that is where we were originally supposed to crash and something got off course somehow. We need to know what is there and why that was where we were supposed to end up."

"That's pretty far away," Jonah said. "If we can complete our project it could make that journey much easier for you."

"What project?" Lynx asked again and Rain could hear the frustration and growing anger in his voice.

She got up and walked to the center of the room where she had Jonah had propped several sheets of scrap metal years before. She took hold of one of the pieces and pushed it aside, then repeated the gesture with a few more pieces. Finally she turned to her mate and held out a hand in presentation.

"This project."

TBC

(To be continued in book X...)

THE ALIEN'S WAR

1

L ila walked slowly through the lush plants, allowing her fingertips to run across the smooth leaves. Around her the moonlight dappled the grass, trees, and thick carpeting of ferns and brush. She breathed in the sweet smell of the air around her and felt like she was coming into touch with a part of her that had been kept from her throughout her entire life, a part of her that Idella had tried to connect her to in the simplest ways that would at once protect her and let her know who she really was.

"You look like them, you know."

The soft, sweet voice behind her startled Lila and she turned sharply to see an ethereally beautiful young woman walking toward her. Gauzy wings stretched out from her shoulder blades and emitted a soft pink glow that seemed to sparkle lightly in the darkness of the lush woods.

"Like who?" Lila asked when her heart stopped pounding and the fear dissipated.

"The silver warriors," the woman said simply, as if it was a response that Lila should immediately understand.

"The silver warriors?" Lila asked.

The woman nodded slightly and continued to approach. She was evaluating Lila extensively, making Lila a feel as though the winged woman were searching for something in her eyes.

"They lived here many years ago."

"Did your kind live here, too?" Lila asked.

The woman shook her head.

"No. We had our own village several days' journey away. We kept in close connection with the silver warriors, though. They were our greatest allies, our friends. They fought alongside our warriors and for a time there were many blended families."

"What happened to them?" Lila asked.

The woman gave a hint of a shrug and walked past her toward the small pool of water in front of her. She reached forward and ran her hand beneath a waterfall that trickled down from moss-covered rock face ahead of her, and then sipped the water from her palm.

"I don't know," she said. "They were gone before I was born."

"Then how do you know that I look like them?" Lila asked.

The woman turned to look at her.

"How did you know where to find us?" she asked.

"My great-grandmother had a book that she used to read to me when I was a child. I realized that it was the actual story of how she came to be and her coming here to live with the species that lived here before moving to the Mikana kingdom."

"And you believe that she is the only one who has books?"

The woman's voice was soft and slow, almost as though it was made of the starlight that shimmered down around them. Lila felt entranced by it, drawn in by the sound even with the dismissive words. Lila watched as she walked away from the water and started out of the woods again.

"I don't understand," Lila called after her.

The woman's wings fluttered slightly as she made her way back through the trees and Lila felt like they were luring her forward. She followed them cautiously, staying several yards back, but always remaining close enough that she never lost sight of the soft pink glow as it wove its way through the rich green of the plants.

"Evangeline," a voice called into the trees, "where are you?"

"I'm here," the young winged woman ahead of Lila called back.

"What are you up to in there?" the voice asked and Lila saw Evangeline step out of the trees.

"I was talking," Evangeline responded.

Lila stepped out of the cover of the trees and saw another, older woman standing several feet away.

"Oh," the woman said when she saw Lila, "it's you."

Lila couldn't decipher the emotion in the woman's voice. There was something in it that was at once mournful and happy, as if she was both pleased to see Lila and saddened by the memories that seeing her created.

"Hello," Lila said. "I'm Lila."

"I know," the woman said. "I remember."

"Remember?" Lila asked.

The woman nodded.

"I suppose you don't. You were so young. My name is Valaria. I knew your great-grandmother?"

"You did?" Lila asked, taking several steps toward the older woman.

She searched the woman's face, desperately seeking any

recognition, anything that may remind her of what this woman might have meant to Idella and when she would have known her. No matter how hard she delved into the furthest recesses of her memory, however, she couldn't bring up anything that connected this woman to her great-grandmother and the precious time that they had spent together when Lila was younger.

"Yes," Valaria said with what sounded like a hint of a laugh. "Of course I was much younger then, but Idella was very important to me. I still remember when she came here. I was little more than a child then, but we became very close after that."

"I thought that your kind didn't live here when Idella was here," Lila said.

Valaria's eyes moved to Evangeline and she nodded softly.

"I see that Evangeline has been telling stories about the silver warriors," she said.

"So it isn't true?" Lila asked.

"Oh, no," Valaria said. "The silver warriors were very real and it is true that our kind, the Eteri, were their closest allies. We lived in the village then, but frequently came to visit the Irisa. There weren't the separations like there are now. You probably cannot even imagine a world in which the species flow back and forth, cooperating and enjoying their lives together. That was what it was then, though. At least among our kinds. There was tension and division among other kinds, but here there was peace. When we stepped out of our borders that peace didn't end. We fought alongside one another and did what we could to protect each other."

"What happened to them?" Lila asked. "Where did the Irisa go?"

Valaria shook her head slowly, the sadness in her eyes evident even from the distance that Lila stood from her. Evangeline approached Valaria and they both turned away from Lila, starting away from her toward where the homes were. She felt the same draw to follow them that she had when Evangeline had led her out of the woods. This time she stayed closer to them, watching in fascination as their wings seemed to flutter open and closed the tiniest amount with each step and the colors of the faint glow around them seemed to blend in the air between them. They stayed silent as they led her along to the gently rolling hills that contained the beautiful homes of these mysterious creatures. Each of the doors tucked into the hills was closed and the world around them was quiet. Lila knew that it was very late and that she was likely one of very few people in the hollow that was still awake.

Finally they came to the center of the hills and Lila saw a single building nestled among them. It appeared to be built entirely out of the stones that had been polished and tumbled by the small creek that ran through the hollow. Valaria and Evangeline stepped to either side of the door in the center and looked back at Lila.

"Go in," Valaria said. "You'll find your answers there."

Lila was unsure. She didn't know what was inside the building or what she would possibly find out. The Eteri were completely unknown to her and she wasn't entirely sure that she could trust them. Her mind wandered to Zyyr where she had left him as he slept in the home Ariella had welcomed them into when they first arrived. Lila had gotten out of the bed as carefully as she could so as not to disturb her mate as he slept, wanting to roam and be alone with her thoughts. Now that she was standing here looking at the strange building in front of her, however, she wished that he was with her. She knew that he would protect her and give her the strength that she needed to make the decision that was right for her, as well as for Oro.

She drew in a shuddering breath, letting her thoughts move from Zyyr to Idella. The book that had served as her bedtime story for so long was so engrained within her that she could see the words written across her mind. Lila let them roll through her thoughts like ribbon unwinding from a spool. As the story unfolded, straddling her memory and her current breaths, she felt herself growing calmer. Idella had been stronger and braver than Lila could ever have imagined being. Though she was still unsure of what much of the story meant, particularly the beginning when Idella had met Finean and they escaped, she knew that whatever her great-grandmother had gone through was far more intense than anything that she had ever faced. Idella had been purposeful and intent when she shared that story with her and Lila knew now that she had meant for her great-granddaughter, the end of her bloodline, to carry that story with her and make it meaningful. Lila knew that she was meant to do something with the knowledge that that story brought her, and that the only way that she was ever going to understand that knowledge or to know what it was that she was meant to do with it was to show the same strength and courage as Idella.

Lila resisted the urge to look at either of the winged women that flanked the doorway. To do so would have been to hesitate and to seek guidance from them. They had brought her far enough. Now it was time that she find the strength that she needed within herself and do what she knew needed to be done, even if that meant just taking the next step forward.

She rested her hand against the cool surface of the door

in front of her and pushed it gently. It moved out of the way, opening into a room so dark that she was unable to see anything in front of her. Instinctively she reached to either side of the door until her hand touched something that felt like it could be a torch. She pulled it down and ran her hands along it until she found what felt like small crystals inside the cupped piece at the top. Lila pressed down on them so that they crushed against each other and a faint light began to glow within them. Over the next few moments the glow intensified until finally its bright green illumination filled the space around her and she could see the room.

Lila turned and held the torch up so that the light spread around the room. She gasped as she saw that she was surrounded by a seemingly endless array of books. They were arranged on towering shelves that stretched from the polished floor beneath her feet to the curved ceiling above and scattered across tables, benches, and chairs arranged throughout the space. It seemed that every corner of the space was filled with books and the random assortment of furniture tucked at various angles and in seemingly chaotic positions as if placed there without any thought to the other pieces. It seemed that the people intended to sit in them were to have no awareness of anyone else in the room. They would settle into place on their chosen chair, bench, cushion, or sofa, and then simply disappear into their own existence as they browsed through the pages that filled the volumes surrounding them.

She took a few steps into the room and then turned to look over her shoulder at the door to the building. It now stood closed. She didn't know whether it had simply closed itself when she stepped inside or if the two Eteri women who escorted her there had closed it behind her. Lila took in a few deep breaths to calm her shaking and continued further into the room. She didn't know why she was there or what it was that she was supposed to discover in the stacks of books. The warm, powdery smell of the pages reminded her of her great-grandmother and the hours that they would spend reading through the book that she now knew was the history of Idella's life. Valaria had promised her that she would find the answers to her questions in this room, but she didn't know what that could possibly mean. There were innumerable books in the room. How was she to know which one she was supposed to choose, or the meaning of what she was going to read inside of it?

Lila moved slowly through the room until she came to an ornate chair positioned close to a dark fireplace. She sat on it and stared into the emptiness of the cold stone fireplace, wishing that she could light a fire in it to take the chill away from her skin. As if the thought had guided her, she looked to her side and found a curved metal basket that held what appeared to be narrow logs. She picked one up and held it closer to her so that she could look at it better in the illumination of the torch. As she looked at it more closely she realized that it was actually three lengths of thick, dried vine braided together. She glanced down into the basket again and saw that there were long, tapered matches tucked into the bottom. Lila rested several of the braids into the dark fireplace and picked up one of the matches. She struck the head of the match across the stone of the wall beside the fireplace and watched the dark tip spring to life in a large blue flame.

The color of the dancing flame transfixed her for a few moments and it wasn't until she felt the heat of it coming closer to her fingers as it burned its way down the length of the match that Lila tossed it onto the braided vines in the fireplace. The braids immediately burst into flame, taking on the hue of the match and filling the space around Lila with a lovely glow. It was not the warm, orange illumination that she remembered from when she was a child and would sit with Idella. The glow from those fires was surrounding in a way that made her feel protected, soothed, and guarded from everything outside of her immediate area. This fire, instead, was as ethereal as the winged people who she presumed were the ones who had created both the braided vines and the matches. It was comforting in the way that it provided expansive light in the deep darkness of the room, but its blue color and shifting, almost gossamer flames seemed somewhat fleeting, as though any minute they might just sweep out of the fireplace and flit away on their own.

The more that she stared into the flames, however, the more solid and less transient they seemed to become. She focused on them, trying to see beyond the softness of their initial appearance and glean the strength and comfort out of them that she needed. Soon they stabilized and deepened into a roaring fire that was still the beautiful shade of blue, but far more comforting and reassuring. It was as if forcing herself to see beyond just what the flames looked like initially and put her trust in them had brought them to a new level, making them more real and ensuring that she got from them what she needed.

She stared into the flames for a few moments longer, still wondering how she should know which of the books she was supposed to be reading and how she was going to get any meaning out of it. It had taken her most of her life to realize that the story that Idella had read to her when she was a child was the recollection of her life and was meant as a way to introduce her to the story of her family and their history. How could the winged women expect her to search through this massive collection of volumes and gain anything from reading them just once?

Suddenly the fire in the fireplace started to spark. It reminded her of the time when she was much younger and she had tossed a green branch into the fire. The flames had jumped and spat, sending orange sparks cascading across the floor and nearly igniting the rug on Idella's floor. Though Lila had been horrified by the situation and thought that her great-grandmother was going to be angry with her for doing something irresponsible and dangerous, Idella had carefully removed the green branch, immediately quieting the larger flames, and extinguished it, setting it aside on the hearth so that Lila would be able to look at it every time that she was at the house.

It was a reminder, Idella told her, of what it means to be ready for the challenges that lay before her. If she was like the green branch, young, unprepared, and unaware of the world around her, and tried to take on something beyond her, like being a part of the fire, it would cause chaos. Just like that green branch she could cause something carefully designed and built to fall apart. Her haste and inexperience could put others in serious danger and destroy everything that they had worked for. It was not until she was well seasoned by life like the dry, hardened wood that supported the flames that she would really be able to handle the tasks that life presented her. Then she could remain steady and strong with others and do what was needed to be done, just like the firewood burned smoothly and powerfully. At the same time, though, she didn't want to be like the wood that sat at the bottom of the pile, never to be used. It went beyond its readiness, beyond its peak, and began to rot away, becoming damp and ineffectual again. It was her greatest responsibility to know when she still had work to be done to be ready, when her time had come, and when she was waiting too long and letting the time when she is most needed pass her by.

The reminder of Idella brought her to her feet. Her great-grandmother had meant more by sharing that book with her than just telling her where she came from. She was more sure of that now than ever, and it was her responsibility to not only understand what it was that she was supposed to do, but to take it on fully and completely. She wasn't ready before, but she was now, and it was time that she step into the role that was always intended for her.

Lila looked around the room at the stacks of books illuminated by the glow of the fire. She tried to decipher which one she was supposed to read and finally her eyes fell on a thick book bound in pale purple. The sparks still streaming from the fireplace seemed to be reaching toward that volume, pointing it out to her. She walked over to it and rested her palm flat on its surface. The gold words across the front were written in a language that she didn't understand, but she felt as though she had found the correct book. Her hands trembled slightly as she picked it up and carried it back to the chair by the fireplace with her. The chill in the room had finally faded and she felt comfortable and relaxed as she settled into the chair and opened the book on her lap.

It was much the same as the book that Idella had read to her throughout her life. The illustrations were rich and detailed, drawing her into the pages. She was relieved to find that despite the words written across the cover being in a language she couldn't read, the text itself was in her own tongue and she could read it easily. As soon as she started to read, Lila felt as though the world around her slipped away. She absorbed every word that was written on the thick pages and ran her fingers along the curves of the illustrations, taking them in and gaining greater meaning in the messages that the book was offering her. When she finished, she rested the book beside her and chose another. The hours slipped past her as she hungrily read everything that she could. A swell of emotions began to build in her the more that she read. There was a deep, painful tangle of anger, sadness, loneliness, and fear that seemed to grow more with every moment that passed. Within those difficult emotions, however, was also a glimmer of precious meaning, something that made her feel more connected to Idella and whispered to her that she had found what her great-grandmother had been trying to tell her, her entire life. Now all she needed to do was take that information and understand what she was meant to do with it.

2

The sun was already high overhead when Lila rushed out of the building looking for the winged women. She wanted to ask them about what she had read in the books and find out if they could tell her more. When she stepped out of the building, however, both of the women who had been flanking the door were gone. She looked around, hoping that they were nearby or that she would see someone who would be able to guide her toward them, but everything seemed as empty and quiet as it had in the middle of the night when they had first brought her there.

Lila knew that she should be tired. She had read throughout the night and on into the morning without taking a break and without resting. Everything that she had learned, however, was coursing through her veins with such intensity that she wasn't able to even think about sleeping, much less bring herself to actually lie down. She needed to find out more. She needed to tell someone about the things that she had read and what she felt like needed to be done.

Not knowing where she should go or who she should be

looking for, she gathered her skirt and started running back toward the woods. That was where she had found the women the first time and it may be where she could find the right people now. As she wove through the trees, suddenly feeling more confident and secure in navigating the space, she could hear a voice in the distance calling her name. It was muted, faded as if the thick, lush plants around her were absorbing much of the sound, but as she drew closer to it she recognized it as Zyyr.

"Zyyr!" she called out to him, hoping that he would hear her and at least know what direction to come to meet her.

"Lila?" the voice called back.

"I'm here!" she returned.

"Lila!" Zyyr called, more insistently this time. "Stay where you are."

She paused as he had asked, leaning back against a tree thick with soft moss and letting her head fall back against it for a moment. She closed her eyes, but the darkness was filled with the images from the books and the longer she stood the louder the voice in her head read the words from the pages. Her eyes snapped open and she could see Zyyr running toward her, smashing through the growth as if desperate to be near her. She took a step away from the tree and he gathered her in his arms, lifting her up off of the ground so that he could hold her to his chest and bury his face in the curve of her neck.

"I was so worried about you," he said. "Where have you been?"

"I have so much that I need to tell you," she said as he lowered her to the ground. "That book, the one about my great-grandmother, is not the only one like it. I met two of the winged women last night and they brought me to a building filled with books like it. They told me that they knew that there were things that I wanted to know and that those books held the answers that I was seeking."

"Is that where you were all night?" he asked, taking hold of her shoulders as if trying to stabilize her so that he could look directly into her face. "I was so worried about you. I woke up and you weren't there in the house with me, and I couldn't find you anywhere."

"I spent all night in the building with the books. I just left there. I was looking for the winged women, Evangeline and Valaria. They told me that I would find out what I wanted to know in those books. I wanted to tell them what I read."

Zyyr looked concerned as he stared into her eyes, but Lila couldn't control the energy that was coursing through her. It was a strange blend of emotion that she hadn't felt before and wasn't entirely sure how to interpret. There was excitement there, thrilling her as she processed what she had learned about her family and the two species that had called this area of the planet home. There was also anger at the pain and misery that her great-grandmother had suffered and the emptiness that she must have experienced as she tried to put her past behind her and live a normal life, all the while knowing that there was no way that she was going to be able to do that. Despite everything that she had learned while she was reading, there was also confusion. Some of what she had read didn't make sense, but it was told just as though she already knew everything that she needed to know in order to fully understand it. She had read as many books as she could in those hours, but never had one of them completely illuminated all of the details of the stories that they told. Somewhere deep inside of her, however, Lila felt as though that was the point of her reading those stories to begin with. She was not meant just to read them so that she could find out more about family and the planet where they lived. It was also her responsibility to find out the other details and truly bring the stories together.

"I don't know where they went," Zyyr told her carefully, "but you need to get some sleep."

"I can't sleep, Zyyr," she said insistently. "There's more that I need to know."

"What did you find out in those books?" he asked.

His voice sounded as though he was extremely concerned about her, but even though Lila knew that her behavior had become erratic, she didn't care. She took a breath and dove into a recollection of everything that she had learned from the books. She told him of the beautiful silver-haired creatures, the Irisa, who had once inhabited that area of the planet and that she believed that it was those creatures that were in her great-grandmother's bloodline, and therefore her own. She explained the close alliance between the Irisa and the winged Eteri, and how they fought alongside each other. As she spoke she could feel the emotion building inside her. Lila knew that she was going to have to tell him the most painful details that she had learned, but she dreaded it. She didn't even want to put voice to the words that she had read deep in the night.

"They are all gone," she finally said.

"What do you mean?" Zyyr asked.

"The Irisa. They are gone. There was a tremendous war. The books said that it was as if all of Uoria was dying. The planet was folding in on itself and the sky was black with fire. Somewhere amid the fighting the Irisa began to die of a horrible plague and went into hiding. Only a few were courageous enough to come out of their hidden lair to find food and to continue engaging in battle alongside the Eteri.

They thrived beneath the ground, but even when the war ended, they didn't come back. By then the land that had been their home was no longer theirs and they were afraid of what might be to come. It seemed that they were right, because many years after they first went below ground, they all disappeared."

Zyyr's eyes were cold when she finished talking and Lila looked at him imploringly.

"What is it?" she asked.

"They didn't disappear," Zyyr told her. "They all died. Well, nearly all of them."

"What do you mean?" Lila asked, feeling somewhat startled by what her mate had just said to her.

"You already know that this is not where the Irisa spent most of their time," he said, gesturing around himself at the beautiful landscape. "This is where they would come for leisure and to find food. Their main settlement, however, was on the other side of the rock ledges, beyond the caves and tunnels that brought us here. That is where I come from, the Denynso compound."

"The creatures that took over the Irisa lands were Denynso?" Lila asked.

"Yes," Zyyr responded.

Lila didn't know how she was supposed to feel at that moment. She was only just coming to terms with the idea that Idella was not who she believed her to be and that she herself was not the Mikana woman who she always assumed she was. Now she was hearing that the ancestors of her mate were the ones who took over the precious land where the mysterious creatures who shared her blood had once lived before being forced underground by the ravages of a horrible plague.

"Why?" she asked.

She wanted to hear what he had to say, to tell her what the books had been missing about that part of the story.

"There were once several clans of Denynso spread across Uoria. One of them lived on the other side of the rock ledges that border the current compound, where the Irisa lived. During the battles of that war that you read about, the clan split. There was tension and turmoil among them, and some split off to form their own clan. They knew that the Irisa had abandoned the land and that it was fertile, lush, and beautiful. They settled there and have been there since. They didn't take anything from the Irisa. They didn't fight them or conquer them. They just came in when the silver warriors were no longer there."

"What happened to the other Denynso?" Lila asked. "I have only ever heard of your clan. I didn't know that there were others on the planet."

"There aren't any longer," Zyyr told her somewhat mournfully. "We are the only ones left. The other half of the clan that split off was destroyed and the entire compound burned to the ground. That is the badlands."

Lila shivered. She had heard of the badlands before. They were a place that was only whispered about and warned of when young people spoke of leaving the Mikana kingdom.

"What about the others? You said that there were more clans."

Zyyr shrugged again.

"No one knows," he said. "There was very little contact between the clans as it was, and by the time that our clan reached out in an attempt to align ourselves with the other clans, they were gone. We didn't even know where the compounds of some of them were."

Lila's heart ached that it wasn't just the Irisa that had

been obliterated by some unknown force. The anger that she had briefly felt toward the Denynso faded and she reached out to wrap her arms around Zyyr. She felt an even greater connection with him now.

"What could be capable of all of this?" she asked softly.

"The Valdicians."

Lila turned sharply and saw Evangeline walking toward them. It was the same strange, ethereal sight that it had been when she first saw the young wined woman the night before, but this time Lila was too overcome with the need to know more to be unnerved by her presence.

"Who are the Valdicians?" she asked.

"Did you find out everything that you wanted to know in the books?" Evangeline asked.

"No," Lila said. "What or who are the Valdicians?"

"They are the ones who drove the Irisa underground and then destroyed them. They killed whole species and did their best to enslave others."

"Do they live here?" Lila asked.

Evangeline shook her head.

"No. The Valdicians never wanted to live on Uoria. They only wanted to use it for its beauty and resources, including turning its inhabitants into their captors so that they could continue with their goals of becoming the most powerful creatures in the galaxy."

Lila was starting to say something to Evangeline when something that Zyyr had said to her suddenly popped back into her mind. She turned to him.

"You said that the Irisa aren't gone completely. You didn't know that I was part Irisa, so you must mean someone else."

Zyyr nodded.

"I told you that we had used those tunnels before to move through the mirrored realm. That is where we met

Loralia. She has long silver hair and lavender eyes. She told us that she was the last of her kind. It is strange, though..."

"What's strange?" Lila asked.

"There are things about her that are so unusual. They aren't anything like you or what I read about in your great-grandmother's book."

"What do you mean?"

Zyyr looked like he was trying to come up with the right words to express himself. Suddenly he looked up at Evangeline and his eyes grew wide.

"Like you," he said.

"Like me?" Evangeline asked in surprised.

Lila watched as Zyyr nodded and took a step toward the winged woman.

"She doesn't have wings, but she shimmers like you do. There is always this slight glow around her. We barely notice it now since we have been around her so much, but now that I see you I remember what it was like when we first saw her. It was almost as though the glow coming off of her skin was bright enough to light up the cave. It only gets more intense when she is angry. And she always knows what any of us are feeling. She says that she can't read our thoughts, only what we are going through and the emotions or fears that we are experiencing."

Evangeline nodded.

"Yes," she said, her voice sounding tremulous.

The winged woman looked back and forth between Zyyr and Lila, and then turned and took off running back through the forest. Lila immediately followed her, listening to Zyyr crash through the trees and undergrowth behind her. Evangeline ran until they made it back to the building full of books and turned to face them, the expression on her face saying that she had fully anticipated them following her.

"This woman," she asked. "She says that she is the last survivor from the Irisa?" she asked.

"She never told us what her kind was called," Zyyr said, "but she did tell us that the rest of her kind all died in a plague and that she had been left alone many years ago."

"A plague?" Lila asked.

"Yes," Zyyr said. "When the Valdicians came, the Irisa became very sick. They went underground to prevent any more deaths."

"I know that," Lila said, "but how could it have been a part of the plague if they remained underground even after the war and after the Valdicians had left the planet?"

"They return," Evangeline said ominously. "The Valdicians always return. Their destruction is something unfathomable to most and if their existence is what caused the plague that destroyed the Irisa it could get to them even if they did live underground."

"What does that mean about Loralia, then?"

Evangeline stepped through the door into the building of books and Lila followed her. They had only taken a few steps into the building when she noticed someone sitting in the chair that she had occupied.

"It means that she had enough of the Eteri blood to protect her from the effects of the plague. That means that she was not diluted by generations. She was the direct bloodline of a powerful Eteri."

Lila watched as Evangeline stepped cautiously toward the figure who sat hunkered in the chair near the dancing blue flames of the fireplace. They were far lower now than when they had burned for Lila, almost as though in reverence to the person sitting in front of them.

"Sir," she said, her voice nervous.

"Yes?" a deep, rumbling voice like the sound of water rushing across river rocks replied.

"There are people here who you need to meet," Lila said.

The chair shifted slightly and the massive figure of a man stood up out of it. Though not as tall as the Denynso, the size and visible strength of his body rivaled theirs and his presence was dominating. Lila could feel Zyyr tense beside her in the way that all warriors did when presented with the possibility of a worthy opponent.

As he turned to them the man's wings stretched out beside him. They were light blue edged with black, but what Lila noticed most about them was the tatters. It looked as though the man's wings had been torn by some form of intense violence, each of the damaged areas now tinged at the rough edges with the same inky black that created the frame of the wings. Unlike the sparkling glitter that came from the women and reminded Lila of stardust, when this man moved it created a shimmer like the mineral streaks at the deepest core of rocks.

"This is Lila," Evangeline said, gesturing toward her. Lila didn't know what she should do to greet the man, but he didn't move toward her so she simply stayed still. "And this is her mate, Zyyr."

"He is Denynso," the man said.

"Yes," Evangeline said. She took a breath and looked between the two of them and the strong winged man. "He knows your daughter."

3

"**P**ass me the power cell."

Rain looked at Jonah from under the hood of the hyper speed vehicle that she was trying to bring to life. She and Jonah had been working on building the vehicle out of spare parts that they salvaged from the crash site when the Covra came for their last attack. He tossed her a power cell and she took a breath before pushing it into place. Nothing happened and she dropped her head forward onto the open hood, discouraged by still not being able to complete the project that had been lingering for so long.

"Still nothing?" Jonah asked.

Rain shook her head and stared down into the vehicle again. They had been working on the vehicles tirelessly for weeks before the Covra came. The night before the attack they had covered it carefully, promising each other that it wouldn't be long until it was finished. She still remembered the hope in Jonah's eyes. He had been one that was not satisfied by the settlement or how complacent so many of their group had become. He wanted more. The part of his heart that had led him to be a part of the mission to the planet harboring the illegal prison colony was still burning inside of him like it was within Rain. He was far more verbal about his dissatisfaction with the way that the mission had turned out than she was. Even though she wouldn't talk about it and always did her best to show her support for the leaders of the settlement, feeling as though it was almost her duty and responsibility to the fallen captain, Jonah knew her better. He knew that she also still carried within her the great need for more. She hadn't settled when she was on Earth, and she didn't want to settle then. She wanted adventure. She craved the experience, the exploration, just as much as Jonah. Though they had had contact only with the one other kingdom on the planet beside their battles with the Covra, he didn't believe the leaders when they said that the rest of the planet was empty and barren. She knew that there was more, and she was eager to get out of the restriction of the settlement and discover it.

She had been thrilled when Jonah first showed her the pieces of the ship that he had smuggled away when they had broken down the crash scene to use the pieces to create the buildings of their new home. He had kept them hidden away for so many years, almost as though they were his security blanket, his backup plan for when he simply couldn't take being a part of the failed mission any longer. That moment seemed to come just over 14 years after they crashed on Uoria and established themselves as the newest settlement on the foreign planet. While the other survivors of the original mission had settled in, started families, and fully resigned themselves to calling the planet home for the rest of their lives, Jonah wanted out. He knew that there was more and he wasn't going to give up the rest of his life simply because of their circumstances. In his eyes, if they could take the parts that he had salvaged and integrate some of the new technology that he had managed to create during his own musings after the crash, he and Rain would be able to leave the settlement, explore the planet, and possibly encounter another species with the means of contacting Earth so that they could return.

For as long as she had known him, Jonah had been one of the most incredible people in Rain's life. His intelligence never ceased to astonish her and there were times when she was utterly convinced that he would be what would save them all. While those that they had elected as the leaders of the settlement had made the official determination that they would no longer consider getting off of Uoria and instead do everything that they could to be happy in the home that they had created, she knew that Jonah would never accept that fully. Though for the most part she remained quiet, she always put the most secret faith of her heart in the intelligence and ingenuity of Jonah to find the way that this would not have to be the life that was left for them. When he showed her the parts that he had salvaged and the power cells that he had designed, she knew that this was it. This was what was going to save her and give her back the life of discovery and making a difference that she had always envisioned for herself.

Together they had painstakingly planned out the creation of vehicles capable of traveling long distances at incredible speed using only the power cells as fuel. Finally it was time for them to begin building the vehicles and every opportunity that they had they crept away from the rest of the settlement to work. Rain often feared that they would be found, but Jonah reassured her that even if they were, there was nothing that could be done. The settlement had decided on very few laws for their new existence, deciding

to forgo the concept of creating their own form of government in favor of essentially carrying over the laws and structure under which they had lived when they were on Earth.
That meant that while they might have to endure the scru-
tiny and even the disdain of the others, and probably the
seizure and destruction of the work that they had done,
there was little else that the leaders could do. They hadn't
broken any laws.

There had been moments when Rain had felt like the
project was never going to come together, that she simply
wasn't the type of person that he needed to help him and
that she would be the cause of their failures. After more
than a month of working, though, everything finally started
to come together and she could see progress that told her
that it was going to work. They had nearly gotten to the
point when they could try the power cells that day when
they covered the vehicle and went back to their homes,
eagerly anticipating the next time when they would be able
to work on their project together. That had been more than
100 years before. The Covra returned the next day and
locked every member of the settlement into place.

The thought of the project languishing in the years that
they had been frozen in place was painful. For more than a
century the vehicle had sat, hidden away in the small
building at the edge of the settlement, and the time had
ravaged it. Unlike the people of the settlement, the vehicle
and all of its components had been vulnerable to the years
as they passed, causing extensive damage to the work that
they had already done. Now Rain felt even more desperation than ever to complete what they had started and get out
of the settlement. She needed to follow the map that she
had found and understand what had really happened. All of
this had to mean something, and at this point it seemed that

she, Lynx, and Jonah were the only ones who were going to be able to find out what that was.

"Are you sure that the power cells are still viable?" Lynx asked from where he stood partway across the room, watching them with fascination. "It has been more than 100 years since you built them."

"They are still viable," Jonah said without hesitation. "I crafted them specifically to have a lifespan that would withstand anything that we might encounter, including jumps through hyperspace that might compact time and overextend the cells. Even if we used them every day for the next century, they would still be viable."

Rain watched as her mate's face grew slightly dark. She knew that look. It was the anger and aggression of the Denynso coming through him. He had warned her of the reaction that his kind had when another man came too close to their mates. Even though she had tried her best to reassure him that there was nothing more than friendship between her and Jonah, the ferocity building within Lynx was evident. She knew that it was up to her to try to keep the situation between the two men calm. The last thing that she needed was for a conflict to rise up between the two of them and cause even more difficulty than what she was already going through.

"Lynx," she said, stepping around the side of the vehicle, "maybe you can take a look to see if there is anything that I might be missing."

"What would I know about it?" he asked. "The Denynso don't have things like this. We don't travel by vehicle or use power cells. We craft things with our hands and use the energy of the world around us when we need it."

"What do you think that these power cells are?" Jonah asked.

Rain watched as Jonah came around the other side of the vehicle holding one of the power cells in his hand. The green bar was nearly as long as his hand and emitted a very faint glow from inside. He had crafted a case around it using salvaged metal so that it would connect in place with the rest of the components that he had made. Now he was holding it by that metal and displaying it to Lynx.

"What do you mean?" Lynx asked.

"You said that your kind uses the energy of the world around you. What do you mean by that? How do you use the energy of the world?"

"Our lights and hot water uses the sun," Lynx replied simply.

"How?" Jonah asked.

Rain stepped back into place in front of the hood of the vehicle, deciding it was better if she invested herself in her work and let the men talk through their tension than trying to play mediator at that moment. If at any moment she thought that the situation was going to get out of control, she could be there to stop them. For now, she would let them talk and hopefully find the middle ground that they didn't see, but that she knew was there.

"It is contained until needed."

"This cell has fragments of a very particular mineral. It is exceptionally rare everywhere else, but I found that it is quite prevalent on Uoria. By itself it has tremendous potential energy, but it also has the ability to absorb massive amounts of solar energy and store it almost indefinitely. We are the same, Lynx. My kind might thrive on technology while yours prefers to use your hands, but in the end we all rely on the same thing."

There was silence in the room and Rain felt the

atmosphere shifting. It was as though the tension was gone. Lynx appeared at her side and she leaned into him slightly.

"So?" she asked.

He looked down into the vehicle with her and reached forward to run his hand across the internal mechanisms. Without saying anything, he walked back over to Jonah and Rain heard him ask if he could borrow the power cell. He came back to her side and Rain held up the cell that she already had.

"I have one," she said.

"I know," he responded, taking it from her hand.

He started for the door to the building and Rain rushed after him with Jonah close at her heels.

"What are you doing?" she asked.

"There are plants that we have in our homes that glow. They are not common on the planet any longer, but they once were. Now they are only in some of the furthest corners of the planet where no Denynso, at least no Denynso of my clan, as ever gone. That makes the ones that we have in our home even more precious. We have them not just because they are rare and beautiful, but because when the weather is bad and there hasn't been sunlight in some time, or if we have already used all of the contained energy in the home for the day and the sun has set, the plants produce light that lets us see within our homes and helps us to get around."

"What does that have to do with the power cells?" Rain asked, watching as Lynx walked around looking at the ground, and then up at the sky, and then back down at the ground. "Those plants are bioluminescent," she told him. "They glow naturally."

"That's right," he said, "but not because of themselves."

Lynx finally seemed to find what he had been looking

for and leaned down to rest the two power cells in a small patch of grass.

"What do you mean?"

"The mineral that Jonah was talking about is very well known to the Denynso. We rarely use it because it is very hard on the planet to remove it. There are many plants that rely on it to thrive."

"Including the ones that glow," Rain said, suddenly understanding what Lynx was saying.

"Yes," he said. "Most of the time our plants are bright and glow perfectly. Sometimes, though, especially those that are in the homes of the older Denynso and have been with the families for generations, the plants fade. They do not put out as much light when it is dark. That doesn't mean that they are not longer viable. It doesn't mean that they don't have the energy within them. It just means that they need to be reminded."

Rain looked down at the power cells sitting in the grass and noticed that even in the sunlight that bathed them, their glow seemed to be intensifying.

"They've been hidden away for a century," she said. "They forgot the potential that they had."

Her words seemed to hit Jonah and she saw his shoulders square as his face became more determined. He looked at Lynx.

"How long does it take?" Jonah asked.

"Not long," Lynx said. "It just takes a little bit to remind you of what you were meant to do."

It sounded strange for Lynx to be talking about the cells as if they were sentient beings, and yet it was incredibly appropriate. His words had been difficult for her to hear herself, and she wondered how much of it was really meant about the power cells, and how much he meant about her and Jonah, and perhaps the rest of the members of the mission still living in the settlement. They waited for a few more moments and then he reached down and scooped the cells back up. He carried them over to Jonah and rested them in his hand. The men met eyes and she saw what looked like a flicker of understanding and connection pass between them.

Without saying anything, Jonah accepted the power cells and turned back to rush into the building. Rain ran after him, stepping inside just in time to see him press one of the cells into place within the inner components of the vehicle. Almost immediately he stepped back and she heard him let out a happy shout. He ran around to the front of the vehicle, slipped in through the side hatch, and pressed the ignition button. There was a roar as the vehicle sprung to life.

Joy surged within Rain. She turned to Lynx and he scooped her into his arms. She kissed the side of his neck and squeezed him as close as she could considering her arms couldn't get all the way around him.

"Thank you," she said. "Thank you so much."

He lowered her down to her feet and touched a kiss to her lips.

"I love you," he said.

Rain felt her already joyful smile stretch even further.

"I love you, too."

He pressed another kiss to her mouth and patted her hip sharply.

"Now that this thing is working, we need to get going. Do we have everything that we need?"

Rain tossed their bags into the vehicle and nodded.

"Yes. We have everything. Let's go"

She climbed in and settled into the seat beside the steering wheel. Jonah rushed around and jumped into the

open seat. He pressed a button on the small control panel
on the front and the hatches on either side of the vehicle
slid down and snapped into place. A familiar feeling of
excitement and anticipation filled Rain as she secured her
safety harness and wrapped her hand around the bar at the
side of her seat. It was the same thrill that she had always
gotten when they left on missions. Though she had no idea
what the goal of this mission really was or what they were
going to do, it was enough to excite her again, to fill her with
the same sense of potential that she always felt when she
had something ahead of her to accomplish.

Rain took the map from her bag and spread it out onto
the panel in front of Jonah. He pressed it into place on a
small dip and closed a hinged screen over it. Pressing several
commands into the control panel, he shot her a look that
was somewhere between hard to contain excitement and
fear that after everything that they had done, the vehicle
still wouldn't work, or would malfunction and put them in
danger. She smiled back at him and saw the flicker of
mischief and always-churning thought sparkle back at her.

"Hold on," he said.

Rain tightened her grip and glanced back over her
shoulder to ensure that Lynx was properly secured in the
harnesses behind her. He didn't look extremely comfortable
thanks to the proportions of the vehicle, but she could see
that the harness was in place and his hands were tightly
gripping the bars on either side of the seats. He nodded
back at her and she took a breath. Jonah grasped the
steering wheel with one hand and flipped a switch. Before
Rain had a moment to release the breath, the vehicle surged
forward and she heard a catastrophic crashing sound as it
smashed through the back wall of the building. They were
moving so fast that the only indication that they had left the

settlement was another sound of crashing that she assumed meant that the vehicle had gone through the wall barrier. She didn't worry about the integrity of the vehicle or its ability to withstand the crashes. The vehicle's structure was made from the incredibly powerful walls of the space shuttle that had brought them there, walls that had been designed to withstand torrential downpours of asteroids as well as most of the known weaponry of their time.

The vehicle took a sudden turn and Rain felt her body press against the seat almost painfully before it finally relaxed when the vehicle settled into a forward trajectory again. She closed her eyes and rested her head back against the seat. They had done it.

4
———

S weat beaded along Creia's forehead and rolled down into his eyes. It burned, but he struggled not to close them. He feared that if he let his eyes close, even for a moment, that the darkness that had been threatening him for so long would finally claim him and he wouldn't be able to come out of it. Ahead of him he could still see the lab and Ryan shuffling around it, preparing what looked like complex equipment for yet another experiment. The hooded creature had completely stopped coming in and the king didn't know how long it had been since he hadn't been staring into the frightening space, or since he had had anything to eat or drink, or a moment's sleep. The world around him didn't seem real any longer. Ryan no longer seemed human as he moved through the lab, even when he walked up close to the camera and leered into it.

He hadn't said anything to Creia in some time. The Denynso king didn't know if that was better or worse. While he didn't want to think of what else the vile man had to say about his family or the plans that he had for them, Creia also felt as though not hearing him speak was just an indication that his mind was moving too quickly, coming up with whatever horrific experiment he was going to do next, to engage him. At least when he spoke Creia had some insight into his state of mind, but now he was a helpless and tormented onlooker.

Creia tried again to reach out to Maxim and the others. He knew that with his body growing weaker it was going to be more difficult for him to communicate effectively. He gathered everything within him and sent another message to Theia, asking her to relay instructions to the others through Mina. He tried to remember every step that he made the day that he was captured by the hooded creature, relating them to Theia so that she could use them to guide the travelers to the right place.

Thinking of that day filled him with emotion. He wondered what would have happened if he hadn't chosen that particular house to explore. Did Ryan have the hooded creatures stationed in each of the houses just waiting for him to come so that they could capture him? If so, how did he know that he would be coming? Creia tried to force himself to not think except for the words that he was sending to Theia. He knew that with every moment of anxiety, fear, or hatred that he was feeling, he was feeding whatever creature it was that was being held in the tank in the back of the lab. Creia didn't know what it was, but he knew that Ryan wanted it as powerful as possible and it was Creia's darkest emotions that were going to make it that way. The king wanted to do everything that he could to prevent that from happening.

Suddenly he got a message from Theia and felt his heart lift in his chest. Just hearing her words in his mind, regardless of what they were, elevating him and dispelled the painful thoughts and emotions within him.

"They want to know if you know what the symbols mean," Theia said.

"Symbols?" Creia asked. "Where?"

There was a brief moment of silence and then Theia returned.

"They said that they are in the compound, but that they are seeing symbols carved into the walls like in the tunnel. Athan is able to read some of them, but he is struggling with others. Were you able to decipher any of them when you were there?"

Creia searched his mind as carefully as he could, forcing past the fog and darkness that were trying so hard to prevent the memories from coming through. He wished he could remember the carvings or even if he saw them.

"Did they tell you were they are?" he asked Theia.

"What do you mean?"

"Did they tell you what the compound is?" he asked.

"No," Theia said, her voice sounding slightly hesitant.

"It is an old Denynso compound. It was where one of the other clans lived back before our clan split."

There was silence and Creia tried to determine if she was just processing what he had said to her.

"What?" she finally responded.

Even through his thoughts he was able to detect that her voice sounded powdery and somewhat startled.

"I can tell by the way that it looks. It's like home, only... different. I can't really explain it. I just know that that is one of the old compounds where one of the other clans of Denynso lived."

"But there weren't any there?" Theia asked.

Creia tried not to be frustrated by her response. The effects of being held for as long as he had been were short-ening his temper and he felt himself nearly lashing out at her, even though that was truly the last thing that he would want to do when he knew that at any moment he could take his last breath and the words that he had just spoken to her would be the last that she would ever hear from him. She knew that they had not heard from or come into contact with any other Denynso in their lifetimes. They knew that they at least had existed at one point, but there was never any indication as to where they had lived.

"No," he responded. "There was no one of any kind in the compound when I went there. Not until whatever the creature was that captured me surprised me in a house that I was exploring. In fact, it looked as though no one had been there in years, but that everyone had just gotten up and left. The homes, everything, looked like there were still people that could show up at any time. Everything was still in place, just aged. It was like everything was just waiting for the people who lived in the compound to come back and start living again."

"And there was no indication of what happened to them?" Theia asked.

"No. I wish there was. I wish there was more that I could tell you or that you could tell Maxim and the others to help them to get here. That's all I know, though. That's all I have."

Creia could feel the painful emotions welling inside of him again and in front of him his eyes caught a sudden shift in movement in the back corner of the lab. He still couldn't see it clearly, but he knew that the creature that was in the tank was moving. It was as though it was responding to the uncontrollable flood of emotion. Ryan had already told him that when he was upset or angry that he was feeding the creature. Now he realized that it was more than feeding it. He was sustaining it and strengthening it. Since Ryan had told him that Creia had struggled to control his emotions so that he wouldn't be supporting the thing, afraid of what it was and what it could do if he supported it any more. Now that he was seeing it move, however, something within him started to change.

The movements of the creature within the tank made the chains even more obvious than they had been before. Now instead of just a shadowy shape that was held in place by the vague impression of chains, he could see the details of the creature's body silhouette and how the shackles restrained him. It sank into Creia's realization that this creature was just like he was. It was a captive just like him and was likely going through the same types of torment that he had been. If Ryan was holding him for some sort of experimentation, then he may be holding that creature with the same horrific plans in mind. He felt a sudden wave of compassion toward the creature and then the realization that maybe, just maybe, it could be a way for him to escape. If he could strengthen it enough, it was possible that it could break free and he might be able to communicate with it enough for it to help him find some way out.

"Let them know to listen for me," Creia told Theia.

He balled his hands into fists and gathered all of the energy and emotion that he had within him. Focusing on the struggle of the creature in the lab and letting it remind him of everything that he had ever seen or gone through, the pain that his mate was suffering now, and what his people were seeing and experiencing because of the choices of others and the cruelty that existed on their planet and on others, Creia started to scream.

5

Zyyr felt his chest tighten as he heard the words that Evangeline spoke. The massive winged man in front of him straightened slightly and the look on his face darkened even further.

"How do you know that they are not lying to you?" he asked without taking his eyes off of Lila and Zyyr.

Evangeline took another imploring step toward him, holding her hands up slightly as if trying to keep this man calm. It reminded Zyyr of the way that the human women often tried to control the emotions and outbursts of the Denynso warriors, but this was different. With the Denynso, the angered, violent tendencies were simply part of their makeup, it was what they were and an intrinsic part of their being. This man, however, was carrying anger within him that was not a function of his birth. Instead, this simmering aggression and cold, intense darkness came from pain so deep within him that it might feel as though it was now part of his blood, but it was something so much harder, so much more bitter and damaging. It made him fearsome in a way that Zyyr wasn't accustomed to experiencing.

"Because they don't know," Evangeline said carefully.

She was obviously well versed in managing this man, and it made Zyyr wonder what type of relationship they had. She had referred to him as "sir", so he doubted that he was her mate, but there was definitely something close and personal about their interaction even if he was so resistant.

"I am Azrael," he said. "Tell me what you know."

It was a direct command rather than a request, but Zyyr tried to avoid bristling. Evangeline had mentioned the man's daughter in a way that suggested that he had not seen her in some time, or that he didn't know what had happened to her. Zyyr couldn't imagine what type of pain that would cause and how it might torment someone. He knew that he had to be as accepting of this man as he could and do what he could to help him, even if he didn't yet understand what was happening.

"I don't know what she means," Zyyr admitted.

He felt Lila's hand touch his arm and he looked down at her. She was gazing up at him with wide eyes filled with soft, deep emotion.

"Loralia," she whispered. "Tell him about Loralia."

Zyyr looked back up at Azrael, meeting his intense, dark eyes, and nodded.

"There is a woman that I know," he started carefully, choosing his words with as much caution as he could while still making sure that Azrael would understand what he was trying to tell him. "She is not of my kind. We met her after a battle with our greatest enemies. She is unlike anyone that we have ever known."

"He says the she has silver hair," Evangeline said.

Zyyr nodded.

"Long silver hair and lavender eyes. Her skin glows. She

is able to reflect objects and make them real, and she can feel the emotions of the people around her."

"Are you close to her?" he asked.

"She is the mate of one of my warrior brothers."

"She is alive?"

The question struck Zyyr as strange, especially with the even, still way that he asked it. His voice didn't sound desperate or imploring, but matter-of-fact, as if he only needed confirmation. Even though Zyyr had been describing her and speaking of her as knowing her now he needed to hear him say that she was truly alive.

"Yes," Zyyr said. "Very much so."

"Where is she now?"

Zyyr drew in a breath. He didn't know how Azrael was going to react to finding out that Loralia was not on Uoria at that time.

"She is on Earth." Azrael's eyes flared and Zyyr took a step forward. "Only for a short time," he reassured him. "She went with some of the other members of my clan to attend the wedding of one of the warriors and a human woman."

The anger drained from Azrael's eyes and he cocked his head slightly at Zyyr.

"A human woman?" he asked.

"Yes," Zyyr said. "Several of my kind have human mates."

"Are there children?" Azrael asked.

Zyyr nodded.

"Yes. One. Lysander. He was born not long ago. He is the son of the leader of the Denynso warriors and the first woman to join our clan."

"And that child is accepted."

"What do you mean?"

"He is loved? He is safe?"

"Yes," Zyyr said, slightly taken aback by the question.

"Come sit," Azrael said.

The invitation seemed far more significant than it would have been if it had come from anyone else. Zyyr took Lila's hand and they walked toward the small group of chairs where Azrael had been sitting. Zyyr didn't take his eyes off of the winged man as he settled into one of the chairs. Evangeline came up to stand behind him, her hands rested on the back of his chair in a gesture that was at once reverent and protective.

"What is her name?" Azrael asked.

"Loralia," Zyyr told him.

"Loralia," Azrael said slightly under his breath as if he was experimenting with the name, tasting it on his lips to see what it was like to say it.

Zyyr realized that what Evangeline had said was true and that this was the first time that Azrael had spoken the name of his child.

"She is the only one of the Irisa that survived," Evangeline said gently.

"Can you tell us more about her?" Zyyr asked.

"You already know that the Irisa and the Eteri were once very close allies. There were times when it almost seemed as though we were one species. That, of course, was not the case. There was a woman who came. She was Irisa, but not. There was something about her that was different and soon the Irisa and Eteri of the time realized that she was only half Irisa. She had come from Earth, but knew that she was meant to be here. She wasn't half human."

"She was half Mikana," Lila said.

"Yes," Azrael responded.

"Idella," Lila said. "That was my great-grandmother."

"She was the first hybrid that we had ever known," Azrael said. "Then she left. There was tremendous turmoil on the planet, and the Irisa had been dying at an incredible rate. We realized that there was an illness that was killing them within hours of them contracting it. We didn't know what was causing it or what could be done to resolve it. It was decided that they would go into hiding where they couldn't be harmed any longer. The problem was that the woman I loved was an Irisa. She was carrying my child."

"Loralia," Zyyr said.

Azrael nodded.

"She wanted to stay with me in the Eteri village, but I knew that that wasn't an option. It was far too dangerous."

"Because of the plague?"

"Because of the others on the planet."

"I don't understand."

"There were some of the elders of the Eteri that believed that the Irisa were cursed. They believed that they were being punished for something within them and that continuing to associate with them was only going to put our kind in danger. They felt that if even one Irisa was to stay with us, we would all be at risk. When they discovered that there was a baby coming, they were even more insistent. They said that the blending of the kinds was forbidden and that it would bring destruction to us and to the rest of the planet."

"But Idella was a hybrid," Lila protested, "and she was accepted."

"She did not have Eteri blood, and the elders said that she had to leave us because of the damage that she could cause if she stayed. This child was a blend of our kind and the Irisa, and the elders became threatening. The longer that Aiyla stayed with me, the worse the wars became and soon some of the younger of our kind started to believe what the elders said. I knew that Aiyla and our baby were in danger. I had to send her away."

"Everyone who I have spoken to has been nothing but loving about the Irisa," Lila said. "They have seemed so hurt that the Irisa are gone."

"Yes," Azrael said. "They are now. They know now that what they believed about the silver warriors was not the truth, that they were destroyed just as they feared would happen to us. By the time that we realized what had happened, they were all gone. I never even saw my daughter. I had fought for years. I walked into battle alongside the only silver warriors who had chosen to emerge to continue to fight in the war and watched as they fought until they died right on the field."

"You never tried to find your baby?" Zyyr asked.

"I couldn't. I didn't even know if I had had a son or a daughter, or when it was born. I didn't know where to look. I had devoted myself to ending the war, thinking that that would resolve the conflict and we could be reunited. I fought in what I thought was going to be the turning point of that war, when the greatest Mikana I had ever known stepped onto the battlefield ready to offer himself to the cause that he believed in more deeply than anything, but believing also that he was not going to die."

"What do you mean?" Zyyr asked.

"What do you know about how they died?"

"We only know that they went into hiding and things seemed fine for a while. Loralia was born in the mirrored realm and spent her entire life there. She told us that she knew of some of the men still leaving to gather food and other supplies. Then the plague returned and everyone but her died."

Azrael nodded.

"That's right. Those men weren't just getting food. They were also working with us and the Mikana to fight. There was a small group of warriors who were dissatisfied with the way that the leaders of our armies had managed the war. We knew that there was more happening than they told us. The Mikana man came to us and told us that he had information that could resolve all of the problems that we were having and save Uoria from the destruction that he knew was coming."

"What did he know?" Zyyr asked.

"He wouldn't tell us. He said that would put us in greater danger. We had to trust him and do what he asked of us just believing that what it would be was right. I was angry at everything that had happened and I believed strongly that there was more that needed to be done. I offered him my loyalty and did as he asked."

"What happened?"

Azrael let out a long breath.

"I don't know. We did exactly what was planned. Each of us used our capabilities to manipulate the battle around us just as he had orchestrated. We did as we were told. We fought as we were told. When the battle was over, we went to the meeting place that we had chosen before, but he never came. We didn't know what to do. We waited as long as we could, but he never showed up. Everything stopped right then. We divided up again and went home, knowing that there was more to come. It was never calm after that. There was never a moment of peace. I tried to find Aiyla and our baby, but they had put such defenses up around where they were hiding that I was never able to find them. Then the Valdicians returned, just as we knew they would. The defenses were suddenly gone and we knew that the Irisa were dead."

"But Loralia wasn't," Lila told him. "She lived."

"I held out hope for so long that that would be true. My

kind was immune to whatever plague had killed them, and I could only hope that it would be the same for her. I went down into the place where they had been hiding. I knew the moment that I stepped inside that it was where they had lived, where my child had been raised. I recognized the mirroring that they had created. It looked exactly like the land where they had lived. The fact that it was there meant that many of them had been involved in creating it, unlike the defenses. Only one of them had crafted those defenses, and when they died, the defenses went with them. The mirroring, though, had existed for so long in the hearts and minds of so many of them, and had been the reality of the generations that had been born there. It made it real."

"Loralia told us that in order for the mirroring to work, the person perceiving it had to believe it."

"That's true," he said. "I would have believed anything that I needed to, to search for my child. When I saw the mirror, the reflection of one of the places that I had spent so much time with the only woman I had ever loved, my mind latched to it. It was as real to me as those memories. When I didn't find my child, I was broken. I went above ground to see if somehow she had returned to their original home, but I found that it had been taken over."

"By the Denynso," Zyyr said.

"Yes," Azrael told him. "I made contact with no one. I left and dedicated myself to battle until there were no more to fight. Then I went home. By then the innocence of the Irisa had already been accepted, but it was too late. There was nothing that they could do to fix the damage that had been caused. The woman I loved had been torn from my arms. The child I loved but had never met was taken from me. People who had meant so much to me were now all dead.

And I had been betrayed by the one man who I believed, even for a moment, would have been able to change it all."

"How do you know that he betrayed you?"

"He told us that he knew what he was doing. He assured us that everything was going to be exactly as he planned. Then he failed us."

"Did you ever see him again?" Zyyr asked.

"No," Azrael said sternly. "I never saw him or spoke of him again."

"What if he died?"

Azrael's eyes turned to Lila and Zyyr could see a storm brewing in them. It was as though those simple words had unleashed emotions that he had not permitted himself to feel or consider.

"Aegeus is dead?"

"Aegeus?" Lila said, her voice suddenly softer.

"You know the name?" Azrael asked.

Lila looked to Zyyr and he saw tears sparkling on her cheeks.

"That is Maxim's father," she said quietly. She turned back to Azrael, shaking her head. "No one has ever seen Aegeus again. Athan came home after that battle and told his family that he had died in the battle. There was no body to bury."

"Athan," Azrael said. "I remember that name. He was there with us. Is he still alive?"

"Yes."

"It's not over."

Zyyr's eyes snapped to Evangeline where she stood behind Azrael. He had forgotten that she was there and her sudden comment startled him.

"No," Zyyr said, shaking his head. "There's more. Far more than you know."

"I know that my great-grandmother sent me here to find out more about her and my kind for a reason," Lila said. "There is something that she wants me to find out, something that I am meant to do. I think that you have something to do with that." She turned to Zyyr again. "We need to bring him to Loralia."

Azrael stood and his wings stretched out beside him, creating an imposing appearance.

"I will be standing beside you when the time comes. If there is another battle to fight, I will fight it alongside you."

6

The scream made Maxim's stomach turn. It had started faint when they were in the house exploring, so muffled by distance and obstacles that he almost wasn't sure that he was truly hearing it. When he ran outside, however, the sound got louder. He followed it, feeling it rush into his heart and make it pound with fear. The scream got louder and louder still until he found himself at the bottom of a flight of steps that led up to what looked like a smaller version of the main meeting hall of the Denynso compound. It stopped for a moment and an eerie, almost tangible silence fell over the entirety of the empty space. The others ran up behind him and they gathered at the bottom of the stairs, looking up at the massive doors at the top.

Another, even louder scream tore through the air and Maxim bolted up the stairs as quickly as he could. His hand moved to the dagger that he had at his hip as he reached for the latch on the door. It was badly rusted and it wouldn't move. The scream continued and he knew that someone was inside that building.

"Theia says we need to hurry," Nylek said, coming up behind Maxim. "She says she can hear Creia screaming but she doesn't know what's happening or if he's safe."

"I can't get the door open," Maxim said angrily.

"Step back," Nylek told him.

Maxim got out of the way and watched as Nylek lifted one foot and planted it in a perfectly-aimed kick directly on the rusted latch. The door bowed and he kicked again. This time the door around the latch splintered. Ivy ran up behind them with one of the bags that she had been carrying and dropped it to the top step, digging through it until she pulled out a small hatchet. She handed Maxim the hatchet and he ran forward, slashing at the door until the wood began falling down around him. Finally there was a large enough gap that he was able to push through and into the building. He tossed the hatchet behind him and continued to run toward the sound of the king's screams.

Now that he was closer to them he could hear the sound of the scream better. He knew that it was not a scream of pain or of fear. Instead, the sound was deeper, more animal. This was a scream of anger.

The meeting hall looked much like the homes had; as though it had been completely abandoned for many years. When he looked at the floor, though, Maxim noticed that there were paths in the coating of dust and dirt that was on the smooth stone. They were not footprints, but wide swathes following consistent paths through the building, moving just from one room to another. He was walking toward those paths when the scream went silent again. It ended with a choking, gargling sound this time and Maxim knew that now Creia was in serious danger.

Almost as soon as the silence fell, Maxim could hear a soft sound in the silence. It was almost like the rushing of wind, but a moment later he realized exactly what was making the sound. From one of the rooms stepped a tall creature, its long cloak pooled on the floor and brushing through the dust on the ground as it advanced toward him. Behind him Ivy screamed and Maxim turned to see another of the creatures coming toward him from the other room.

Pulling the dagger form it sheath, he spun back toward the first creature and lunged toward it. Behind him he heard Nylek follow his lead, attacking the other creature. Maxim's knife plunged into the thick cloak of the creature, but long, strong fingers wrapped around his hand and pulled him away. Ivy screamed behind him and Maxim fought harder. He forced all of his bodyweight against the creature, forcing it back against the wall behind it. Suddenly Athan was at his side holding the hatchet that Maxim had discarded. Together they fought the creature, and soon it lay motionless and bloodied on the floor.

They rushed across the open space to Nylek and the other creature. His larger size was giving him more advantage over the creature than Maxim and Athan had, and within seconds this creature was on its knees in front of them.

"Where is Creia?" Maxim demanded.

The creature wouldn't respond and Nylex tightened the grip that he had around its neck.

"Where is the king?" Maxim shouted again.

"Maxim!" Ivy screamed and he turned to see another, larger of the creatures advancing toward him from other side of the foyer.

He thrust his knife forward into the being's chest, but it didn't stop. Its strong hands wrapped tightly around his neck and Maxim struggled to draw in a breath. He grabbed at the wrists of the creature and kicked at it angrily. He could hear the two other men continuing to hold the other creature at bay behind him and then a gag that told him that creature, too, was now crumpled on the floor like the other. Darkness was starting to build around the corners of Maxim's eyes and he continued to claw at the creature's arms.

Suddenly the pressure of the hands around his neck released and he heard a loud grunt. Maxim opened his eyes and saw Ivy and the creature grappling on the floor at his feet. She had flung herself onto it, startling it so much that it stumbled to the ground. Maxim reached down and grabbed her around the waist, pulling her away from the creature. As he pulled her away, he realized that she was holding his knife in her hand, her skin now streaked with blood. Athan stepped up in front of Maxim as he pulled her further way from the creature and planted his foot on the creature's chest, grinding it down onto the wound that Maxim had created and Ivy had worsened.

"Where is Creia?" Athan asked through gritted teeth.

The creature stayed as silent as the others had and Nylek stomped forward. He reached down and yanked the hood off of the creature's head, revealing a face so gruesome Maxim knew it would be seared into his memory. He saw Athan straighten and stare down into the face of the creature.

"Valdician," he said, his voice registering shock as he realized what he was looking at.

The creature hissed at him through a grisly expression that looked almost like a vicious smile. An expression like Maxim had never seen him have rolled over Athan's face and he forced his foot harder into the Valdician's chest. Maxim heard the bones of the creature's ribs crack and it took one last gasping breath before going slack against the floor.

"That is a Valdician?" Maxim asked.

Athan nodded.

"I will never forget what they look like. If they are the ones who brought Creia here, we need to find him as soon as possible. They are cruel and vicious, and thrive on the torment of others. The only thing that could be worse than him being at their mercy, would be knowing that there is a reason for them to keep him alive."

"Why?"

"That would mean that there is something even worse waiting for him."

The words brought the sickness back to Maxim's stomach and he looked around the building frantically, wishing that Creia would scream again, anything that would let him know where he was so that he could find him. He looked at Nylek.

"Tell him to scream again," he said.

"What?" the warrior asked.

Maxim took a step over the body of the Valdician toward Nylek.

"Tell Theia to tell him to scream again. We need to find him *now*."

Nylek nodded and turned away so that he could concentrate on sending the message through to his mate, who would then relay it to Theia. Maxim stalked across the foyer to the door that would nearly coordinate with the door to the banquet hall in the main building back at the Denynso compound. Unlike the banquet hall that he had eaten in on the Denynso compound which only had a stone archway leading off of the entryway, there was actually a door leading into this room. Not bothering to reach for the latch, he kicked the door until it moved out of the way and he was able to look inside. The room was intensely dark and he reached into his bag to get out a light stick. The glow from the stick bit through the darkness of the room and showed that it was, indeed, filled with long tables that looked very much like the ones that were in the other compound. Other than the tables, though, the room was empty.

He was stepping out of the room when he heard a short shout. It didn't have the same level of strength and fury of the screams before, but it was strong enough that he heard it.

"Tell him to do it again!" he shouted, running back toward the others.

Several moments later there was another shout. He followed the sound and suddenly a thought occurred to him. He ran back over the body of the Valdician and through the door that he had come out of. Just as Maxim expected it to, it opened out onto the expansive room that would be the meeting hall where the king and queen of that compound would sit on their thrones and greet those who came to visit them.

"Maxim?" Ivy called from behind him.

"Come with me," he called back. "I know where he is."

He waited long enough for Ivy to get to his side and then surged forward again, holding the light stick high above his head so that he could spread as much illumination through the space as he could. Finally he saw a sagging tapestry on the wall and his mind went back to the day that seemed like a lifetime before when Theia brought them into the private quarters that she shared with Creia to talk about the mission that lay ahead of them. He glanced at Ivy and she looked back at him with widened eyes that told him that she had the same thought.

Maxim cupped his hand around her cheek and took a moment just to look at her. The chaos around them had made it so he felt like he hadn't had even a second with her in so long and right then, just for that moment, he needed to be with her. He leaned down and touched a kiss to her lips. The taste of her reinforced him and restored his determination.

Nylek and Athan came up behind him, each now holding a weapon at their side. Without another word they pushed past the tapestry and started up the curving stone staircase. The shouts have given way to grunts, but they were still strong enough to lure them to the top of the stairs where a door stood partially open. Maxim tightened his grip on the handle of the dagger he had taken back from Ivy and pressed the door open.

"Creia!" he shouted when he saw the king secured to a tilted metal table in the middle of the room.

Creia let out a low groan and tried to turn his head, but it was obvious that he couldn't.

"Maxim," he moaned. "Is that you?"

Maxim forced the knife back into its sheath and ran across the room toward Creia. He gripped the Denynso king's arm and leaned so that he could look into his battered, strained face.

"Yes, Creia. I'm here."

Creia's eyes drifted closed and a hint of a smile curved his lips. Ivy came to the other side of the table and grasped Creia's other arm.

"Creia!" she gasped.

"Ivy," he said softly.

"Athan and Nylek are here, too," Maxim told them.

Maxim and Ivy started pulling away the diode attached to Creia's head and pushed the small screen away from his face. He pulled at the metal cuffs around Creia's wrists but found that they were locked securely in place.

"The key," Creia groaned. "Get the key."

"One of the Valdicians has to have it," Maxim said.

Athan nodded and ran back out of the room.

"Do you know who did this to you?" Ivy asked, brushing her hand tenderly across the king's forehead.

The gesture was impactful and Maxim felt a painful blend of emotion tightening in his chest. He knew that Ivy didn't have a good start with the king, but she now looked at him with admiration and tenderness that showed just how much she had changed in the time that he had known her. He had loved her from the moment that he met her, but the woman who she had become was deeper and stronger in a way that reaffirmed his devotion to her with every moment that he spent with her.

"Ryan," Creia murmured.

"Ryan?" Maxim asked.

Nylek stepped up Maxim's side.

"The man Eden worked for?" he asked. Creia nodded and Nylek turned to Maxim. "Before Eden came to Uoria she worked in a laboratory on Earth for a man named Ryan. He was horrible to her and when she wouldn't sleep with him, he threatened her. He sent her here to steal Pyra's blood."

"He wanted her to die," Maxim said.

"Of course, I did."

The sudden voice in the room brought a new level of tension to Maxim's muscles. He looked around and then felt Ivy's hand clamp onto his arm. He glanced at her and saw her eyes locked on the screen that they had pulled away from Creia's face. A human man was staring through the screen at them, his eyes wild as if he had gone beyond the point of exhaustion but was fueled by some sort of frantic energy burning within him.

"Of course I meant for her to die," the man Maxim now assumed was Ryan said, his voice creeping a little higher. "She was ruining everything for me. Not only did she refuse my advances – advances that any woman would be lucky to have – but she was going to tell people about my work."

Suddenly he started laughing and Maxim narrowed his eyes at him.

"What do you think is so funny?" he asked.

"My work," Ryan said. "She was going to tell the authorities that I was working on a weapon. What's hilarious about it is that she had no idea. She had no idea what she was talking about."

"You weren't trying to create a weapon?" Ivy asked.

"I was," Ryan said. "I still am. She just didn't know what that weapon was. She never could have imagined what I was able to create. Of course, none of you will, either. Well, Creia will. I couldn't deny our most honored of kings the pleasure of being a part of my beloved experiments. As for the rest of you, my guards should be returning any moment now and they'll ensure you are no longer an issue for me."

Just then Athan came back into the room. He gripped a key in his blood-soaked hands and Maxim noticed a faint spray of blood across his face.

"I suggest that you rethink that," Maxim said. "It doesn't seem that your guards offered much protection."

Maxim watched as any sign of laughter on Ryan's face dissolved away, replaced by a look of shock, and then dark, brooding anger. Athan unlocked the cuffs around Creia's wrist and ankle and then handed the key to Ivy on the other side.

"No!" Ryan roared. Maxim heard a loud, metallic sound

as the scientist slammed his hands down on the counter in front of him. "No!" he shouted again.

"Nylek, help me," Maxim said as they released the last of Creia's bonds and the king's body slumped forward. "We're going to need to carry him."

Creia moaned something unintelligible and Maxim heard Ryan laughing.

"It doesn't matter now," he said. "You go ahead and take him. I have more than enough here to handle everything that I want to do. I hear that there's a wedding in town tomorrow. I wonder if there's room for me on the guest list."

Maxim and Athan hoisted Creia onto Nylek's back and they all started out of the room as fast as they could move.

"You can run," Ryan's voice taunted from behind them, "but you'll never make it. You'll never be able to get here fast enough."

7

"**K**yven!" Maxim shouted as he ran out of the meeting hall. "Kyven!"

Kyven and Emerie had stayed behind when they ran from the house to follow the sound of the screams, promising that they would continue exploring, but now Maxim needed his brother back with them. He was carrying the bags that had all of the healing supplies that Ciyrs created and that they would need to bring Creia back to enough health that he would be able to get back to the compound and heal. The rest of them needed to get to Earth as quickly as they could to stop Ryan from doing whatever it was that he had planned.

"I don't think that we should risk bringing him into any of the houses," Athan said.

He was walking behind Nylek with his hand on Creia, helping to stabilize him so that he would stay in place on the younger warrior's back.

"He's right, Maxim," Ivy said. "There could be more Valdicians around here. Creia said that he was captured in one of the houses. They could be in there. We need to get him healing as quickly as we can."

Maxim reached into his bag and pulled out a thick cloak he had packed to protect him from any serious weather that they might encounter. He had spread it on the ground and was helping Nylek lower Creia onto it when he heard the heavy footsteps of Kyven running up to them. Emerie came to his side a moment later, gasping when she saw Creia lying on the ground.

"Is that him?" she asked.

"Yes," Nylek told her. "This is my king, Creia. He's been held captive in that building since very soon after leaving the compound."

"Kyven," Maxim aid. "We need the healing ointments. Do you have any water?"

As Kyven pulled the jars of healing ointments and ingredients out of his bag, Emerie lowered hers to the ground and started taking out the food and canteens of water that she had packed. Ivy lifted Creia's head and started slowly pouring water down his throat. The king gurgled and choked for a moment, then started drinking eagerly. Maxim poured water from another bottle onto a cloth and wiped Creia's face, trying to remove as much of the sweat and blood that he could.

He was wrapping a bandage around Creia's wrist when he heard footsteps pounding toward them. Defensiveness surged within him and he turned sharply, ready to fight off more of the Valdicians. Instead, he saw Lynx running toward him, Rain and another man close behind.

"Lynx!"

"What's happened?" Lynx asked, dropping to his knees beside Creia.

"I'm alright," Creia managed to say weakly.

"You don't look like you're alright," Lynx said, picking up the cloth that Maxim had put down and continuing the efforts of cleaning the king's face and neck. "What happened to him?"

"He came out here after everyone left for Earth. He said that there are things that he needed to find out. He went through the badlands first, but found a tunnel with a transporter in it like the one that was in the tunnel that led down to Loralia's home. It brought him here. When he was –"

"I can speak for myself."

Maxim stopped talking sharply and they all looked down at the king. He still looked weak and tired, but some of the color was returning to his face.

"Yes, sir," Lynx said, tucking his hands behind Creia's shoulders to help him sit up.

Emerie offered Creia a piece of bread and some dried fruit and he took several bites before speaking again.

"There are things that I never told any of you," he admitted. "Things that you all deserved to know. I thought that I was protecting you by not telling you, but now I realize that I was only making the situation far worse than it ever was. For so long one of my greatest fears was having our kind leave the compound. I knew that as soon as any of us did, the problems that had driven me to keep everyone there would only come back to haunt me again. Now, though, I know that I was only delaying the inevitable and worsening a situation that should have been resolved a long time ago."

"Why didn't you tell us not to go when Pyra and Bannack suggested that we explore Uoria?" Lynx asked. "You seemed so proud of us for wanting to do it and encouraged us to find out as much as we could."

"I knew that I couldn't tell you not to go," Creia said. "You are grown men, the most fearsome warriors in the galaxy.

You deserve to know what you're protecting when you fight so fearlessly."

"We're protecting our compound. We all knew that," Nylek said.

"No," Creia said, shaking his head. "That's only part of it. If you were only fighting to protect our compound, the rest of the planet would already be destroyed. The truth is that every time that you fought a new enemy, the survivors brought word of you out into the galaxy and warned others not to come to Uoria and threaten the home of the Denynso. After you met the humans and the Mikana, and encountered the Covra, though, I knew that it was only a matter of time before the wars that were always promised to return would start again and you would be forced to fight a conflict that you didn't know everything about."

"What did you come here to find out?" Ivy asked.

"I thought that I understood what had happened when the Denysno split and took over the new compound. I thought that I understood the Klimnu. With everything that you found out, though, I realized that much more was going on than I thought and that maybe what I was protecting you from all along wasn't really the threat. I went back to the badlands to find out anything that I could, and I ended up here."

"Have you ever been to this compound?" Rain asked.

Creia shook his head.

"No. When there were multiple clans of Denyno on Uoria, we didn't associate with each other. It wasn't that there was animosity or competition. We just existed separately on our own areas of the planet and didn't have the need to engage with each other. It wasn't always that way. When I was very young I remember my grandfather talking about how the different groups used to be just one large clan."

"What happened?"

"There was an old tradition of the king of the Denynso exploring the planet once every two years to make sure that everything was doing alright and to maintain contact with allies. Usually the king traveled alone or with one specially chosen warrior. On one of these quests, the king decided that he was going to bring most of his warriors with him. At that time they were free to wander the planet as they saw fit, but they felt compelled not to because they felt that they should always be together and ready to engage in whatever conflict might arise. The chance to get out and explore the planet while still being together was too much for them to resist."

"Like us," Lynx said.

Creia nodded.

"When they left and began to explore the planet, some arguments arose over whether they should stay in the original compound or if they should take over another area of the planet. There were many different spots that some of the warriors thought would be better for the clan. The king disagreed and said that they would stay where they had always been, but he agreed that any warrior who felt compelled to was allowed to leave and start their own clan with the understanding that there was never to be any conflict of any kind between the separate groups. A few chose to go and brought loyal family and friends with them. It divided the original clan into several, but for some time they continued to interact with each other fairly regularly. The kings of the clans would continue to do their tours every two years. Then the tradition faded. Each clan developed its own traditions, laws, and customs. Though still

Denynso, they were each distinct. They stopped interacting. Alliances faded, and soon it was as if they had all forgotten about each other."

"That's why you didn't know where this compound was," Ivy said.

"That's right. By the time that I was old enough to be a warrior, there was no longer any communication between the clans and we rarely left the compound. I don't understand why that transporter was in the tunnel between the badlands and here. Or why the Valdicians knew that I was going to be here."

"They were already here," Rain said.

"What?" Maxim asked.

Rain pulled a small book and an aged sheet of paper out of her bag.

"I found this when I was going through the wreckage of the ship. It was in a box that belonged to the captain of the mission. Everyone thought that Etan died in the crash, but I knew that he was dead before the crash. I had never told anyone that, but with everything that has been happening recently I realized that it might have been more than just him knowing that we were going to crash and deciding to end his life first. I was reading his journal, and that's when I found this."

She handed the piece of paper to Maxim and he looked down at it. For a moment he didn't understand what he was seeing, then it occurred to him that it was a map. He followed some of the lines with his fingers. He rested them on the symbol at the top.

"This is here?" he asked.

Rain nodded.

"Yes. Etan tore this page out of a book that he found on

the prison planet. It belonged to one of the Valdicians. They always intended on us crashing here. The decision to send us to Uoria wasn't something that they just came up with when we were there. They intended it all along. They knew that having that prison compound was against galactic regulation and that that would get a response from an Earth team. The Earth government has a reputation of responding promptly and aggressively to any signs that we find of breaking regulations that involve cruel or inhumane treatment of any species, or the grave misuse of planets, claimed or unclaimed. Once they had that prison colony established, they weren't being excessively secretive about it because they wanted us to find out about it. They wanted our team to know what they were doing so that we would come to the planet and try to take over. They weren't surprised that we were coming. We might have taken them off guard for a few minutes when we first got there because they didn't know when we were coming, but that's it. They were ready for us. They had the weapons prepared and they knew what was going to happen next."

"I don't understand," Nylek said. "Why is the compound on the map? This isn't where you crashed."

"I know," Rain said, "but it is where they intended us to crash. That was the plan all along. Remember the Valdicians were offering us to their allies. The plan was for us to become slaves to the Covra so that we would help them take over Uoria first, and then the rest of the galaxy. The Valdicians thought that the Covra would be comfortable here and that it would be easy to enslave us here because it was already established. The Mikana had already been forced to build the prison for the Covra years before, but that wasn't good enough for the Valdicians. They wanted something more, something that would allow for a larger group so that they could capture more if they wanted to. That's why they chose this compound."

"But there were already Denynso on this compound," Creia protested.

Rain shook her head and Maxim could see the sadness in her eyes, emotion stemming from knowing that she had to tell him something that she deeply didn't want to tell him.

"That was the reason that the Valdicians knew where this compound was and knew that it would be perfect for the slaves. It was where their prisoners had lived before they captured them."

Maxim felt his heart sink painfully. He could see the hurt and anger flashing in Creia's eyes and felt the tension radiating off of Nylex and Lynx. There was nothing that he could see to make the admission any easier for them to handle. This was horror that they had to face.

"Are you sure?" Creia asked in a low, controlled voice.

"It's the only thing that makes sense. I knew when I first saw the men who came and rescued us that there was something familiar about them, but I couldn't quite place it. That's because the Denynso of that time and in this compound look slightly different from your clan."

"They would," Creia said. "We have changed over time and the clans would take on the appearance of the families that made them up. They would resemble us but not look exactly the same."

"What happened to them?" Maxim asked.

"What do you mean?" Rain replied.

"Ivy told us that on Earth they are taught that the military sent a special operatives unit to the planet after your mission went missing and liberated the planet. That's when they named it Penthos. They specifically mentioned liberating it. That means that the prisoners were still there when they got there. What happened to them?"

"They obviously never returned here. Where did they go after the military freed them from the prison? And what happened to the Valdicians?"

"They would have been destroyed," Rain said.

Ivy shook her head.

"We never learned what happened to them and we know for a fact that they are still here."

"It was the Valdicians that captured me," Creia told her. "They held me in the meeting hall."

"Why?"

"For a man on Earth named Ryan. Eden worked with him before she came to Uoria. He's the reason that she is here. He was trying to have her killed."

"What did he want with you?" Rain asked.

"I don't know for sure. He has been referencing experiments that he has been doing and that he plans on using Pyra, Eden, and Lysander, and maybe even others who are on Earth for the wedding for them." Creia said.

"We need to get to Earth as soon as possible," Maxim said. "We have to stop him."

He saw Rain look back at Lynx and the man who had come with them.

"Can they all fit, Jonah?" she asked.

The other man looked at the group and evaluated them. He nodded.

"I think so. It might be tight."

"That's fine," Lynx said. "We just need to get Creia back to the Denynso compound as quickly as possible so that we can arrange for a shuttle to Earth."

8

L oralia took another deep breath as she stared into the vanity mirror. Her mind was spinning and she felt like her body hadn't stopped trembling since she arrived on Earth. She reached up to smooth her hair, but accidentally knocked one of the small pearl pins out and sent it skittering across the polished surface of the vanity table. She closed her eyes and lowered her head, telling herself that she needed to calm down.

"Are you alright?"

She heard Bannack's voice from behind her and felt it calm her slightly. It was always a relief to have her mate close to her, but even he couldn't make her feel secure. It was the morning of Samira and Ty's wedding and while everyone else was buzzing around excitedly getting ready for the ceremony, she was still sitting in one of the hotel suites that they had rented trying to make herself feel anything but overwhelmed.

Bannack came up behind her and took her shoulders, leaning down to kiss the top of her head. She reached up and rested her hand on his, squeezing it slightly.

"I'll be fine," she said. "I'm just having a hard time getting accustomed to Earth. I thought that it would be easier to get used to being here, but we've been here for days and I'm still struggling."

"What's going on?" he asked, pulling a chair closer to her so that he could sit down.

Loralia turned to look at him and sighed.

"I wish that I could explain it to you."

"Try."

"You know that I am able to feel the emotions and feelings of the people around me."

"Yes," Bannack said. "It's one of the more frustrating things about you sometimes. No one can hide anything from you, even when they want to."

He chuckled, but she didn't smile. Instead, she nodded and gripped his hands in between them.

"Exactly. I don't do this on purpose. The others of my kind didn't understand me when I tried to explain to them what I was going through. It didn't seem like any of them could do it. Unless I am concentrating really hard on not tuning into a person, I can't help but feel what they are going through. That level of concentration, though, takes up a lot of energy and there's no way that I could block as many people as are around me all the time when I'm here."

"It is a little more crowded than Uoria."

Loralia nodded.

"I have never seen so many of any kind of species this close together. I don't know how the humans do it. It's like they live right on top of each other. You can never go anywhere where there aren't other people. There's no such thing as being in the quiet or being truly alone. While I think that I could get used to being around others, I don't think that I can ever get used to having to feel everything that all of these people are feeling all the time."

"Is it all bad?" he asked.

Loralia shook her head and reached up to brush a strand of Bannack's white hair away from his forehead.

"No," she said. "Some of it is wonderful. I love how happy Samira and Ty feel, and how excited her friends are. It's even fun to feel how in awe of everything the Denynso are. At least, those who weren't immediately appalled by the planet and have been wanting to go back since landing."

"Then what is it?" he asked.

"I'm not sure," Loralia admitted. "It might just be that there are so many different kinds of people and they are packed so close together. They have experienced and felt things that I have never been exposed to, so maybe I'm just overwhelmed. It might just be too much for me."

"Do you really believe that?"

"I don't know, to be honest. I just have this terrible feeling. I can't explain it. It doesn't connect with any one person. It is just a feeling of dread, like something is off. I wish that I could understand it better. I wish I knew why I was feeling this way. Maybe then I would be able to figure out what to do."

"What do you mean figure out what to do?"

"I feel like there is something that's going to happen. There is a heaviness here that doesn't have to do with anyone who is with us."

"Is there someone here that we don't know?" he asked.

She wanted to be offended by the question, but the truth was that she didn't know the answer to it and it made sense for her mate to be concerned that there might be someone nearby that could mean them harm. With the exception of the human women, George, and Ero, they were all on a strange planet that none of them had visited before. They didn't know anything about their surroundings or how they should know how to protect themselves.

Before she could answer, the door opened and Eden came in. Lysander gurgled playfully as she held him over her shoulder and patted his back.

"Have either of you seen Zsilvia?" she asked.

"I thought that I heard George say something about having to go to the lab this morning," Banack said. "He said that he wanted to check in on the progress of some of the work that he had been doing there and get some papers. I would guess that she is with him."

"Is everything alright?" Loralia asked, trying to withhold any sign of nervousness or tension in her voice.

"Oh. Yeah. Everything's fine," Eden said. "We're just running short on time so I was making sure that everyone was doing alright getting ready. She was nervous about the dress that she picked out for the wedding so I thought that I would see if she was feeling better about it. I was thinking about it last night and I think that there are a few things that I might be able to do with it to make her more comfortable about it."

"That's very nice of you."

"I just want her to feel beautiful. I know that she has a hard time sometimes." Eden turned away and then looked at Loralia again. "You look gorgeous, by the way. I love what they did with your hair. Those pins are perfect."

"Thank you."

Eden swept out of the room and Loralia looked at Bannack.

"She's different here," she said.

Bannack laughed softly and shook his head.

"No. She's different in general. You should have met her

when she was first on Uoria. She was...harsh. That's really the best way that I can describe it. She was still Eden. There were times when she was funny and warm, but she was extremely defensive. Since Pyra and Lysander, though, she has softened so much. I know that she is nervous being back here. Maybe she is just trying to cover it."

"Why is she nervous?"

"Pyra told me that they have already had a run-in with Ryan. It apparently wasn't pleasant and now she's scared that something else is going to happen."

"She's trying to pretend that she's not scared," Loralia said. "She doesn't want to make anyone uncomfortable or ruin Samira's day. And she doesn't want to give Ryan any more power over her life." Loralia said.

Bannack stroked her cheek with the back of his hand and leaned forward to kiss her. He rested his forehead briefly against hers and Loralia sighed with the contentment that settled over her when she forced herself to focus in on his feelings and the warm, comforting energy that surrounded her with his touch.

"I should go check on the groom," he said. "It won't be too long, now. I'm looking forward to seeing how this whole thing turns out. Maybe if we like it, we'll have one, one day."

Loralia smiled.

"We still have to have a traditional tying."

Bannack kissed her again.

"So many chances to show the world how much I love you."

9

"**T**his is where you work?" Zsilvia asked as George guided her along the long, stark-looking hallway.

"Yep," he responded. "This is my lab. Eden worked on the floor above us."

"Everything is so...clean."

George laughed and stopped in front of a door.

"That's important when you are working in a lab. If you think that this is clean, though, you should see some of the special authorization rooms."

He took a card from his pocket and held it up to a sensor beside the door. There was a low buzz and a click, and George turned the handle to push the door open. It led into a dark room that Zsilvia could only describe as smelling cold. He pressed on one of the several buttons along the wall beside the door and some of the lights in the space turned on. The artificial glow gleamed off of the bright surfaces throughout the room and Zsilvia resisted the urge to squint.

"I don't know if I'm ever going to get used to how bright the lights are here," she said.

"I never really noticed before, but since being on Uoria and not using electricity, I think I have to agree with you," he said as he sifted through some papers in a wire rack on a desk close to them.

"So what are you checking?" Zsilvia asked. "We aren't going to miss the wedding, are we?"

George shook his head.

"No, we have plenty of time. I'm just checking on the progress of some cultures that I was working on when I was gone. I had left them in the care of Ivy for the time that I was going to be away, but since she decided to surprise us by showing up on Uoria, I am not feeling as secure about it. She said that she assigned the project to some of the others that we've worked with before, but I don't know them as well. I figured that since I'm already here, I might as well just take a peek and see how things are progressing. I also wanted to grab some of my research papers and books to bring back to Uoria with us. They might be interesting to Ciyrs."

"So you are planning on coming back with me?"

Zsilvia wasn't expecting to ask the question, but now that he had she was eager to hear the response. George straightened and looked at her with a somewhat hurt look on his face.

"Of course I am," he said, lowering the papers that he held in his hand to the desk and taking a step closer to her. "Why would you even ask that?"

Zsilvia shrugged.

"You seem so concerned with your projects here and are so wrapped up in making sure that everything is working out the way that you want it to. I just started to think that maybe coming back here reminded you of everything that you have here and you might not want to leave it again."

"What I have here is a career and some friends. That's it. It doesn't even begin to compare to what I have on Uoria."

"What do you have there?" she asked coyly.

George stepped up closer and wrapped his arms around her waist to pull her close.

"I have the most incredible mate I ever could have asked for and a new home that I love almost as much as I love her."

Zsilvia smiled.

"Well, that sounds really nice. Do I know her?"

George tickled her playfully and Zsilvia laughed, wrapping her arms around his neck. He leaned forward to capture her mouth with his and Zsilvia relaxed into the kiss. She sighed as their lips parted.

"I love you, too."

"Good," George said, stepping back from her and going back to looking through the papers on the desk.

"So what are you going to do about your projects when you leave?" she asked. "Are you just going to end them?"

"No," George said, shaking his head. He picked up another folder and added it to the growing stack on the corner of the desk. "I have written extensive notes about every project that I have been working on and my objectives. Some of them I'm going to pass on to other research teams to continue for me. I plan on writing up a grant while we are here so that the university will support more time on Uoria for extended research about those projects that I can research while I'm there. When I'm finished with that research, I can plan a trip back here to present it and submit the write-ups for publication. I was thinking that maybe we could make a honeymoon out of it."

"A honeymoon?" Zsilvia asked.

"It's a trip that newlyweds take after they've gotten married to celebrate."

Zsilvia felt her heart swell in her chest. This was the first time that George had mentioned that they might one day get married in the way that humans did on Earth. They were already bonded in the way of the Denynso and until they had arrived on Earth Zsilvia hadn't even thought about getting married the way that Samira and Ty were. It wasn't her custom and it didn't occur to her that she would ever care about the possibility. After getting to Earth and being a part of all of the preparations for the wedding, however, she started feeling a tinge of envy for the celebration and joy surrounding the couple. She could see the pure happiness on Samira's face and had enjoyed watching as she chose a wedding dress, welcomed everyone to her parties, and talked about all of the details that would go into the wedding. Though she didn't think that having a human wedding would make her union with George feel any more legitimate, she had begun to think that she really would enjoy the experience, and that it might carry special meaning to George. Hearing him mention it thrilled her.

"Would you want that?" she asked softly, wanting to hear more confirmation.

George looked at her for several long seconds and then lowered himself slowly to one knee in front of her. He took her hand in both of his and turned it so that he could press a kiss to her palm.

"What are you doing?" she asked.

"On Earth when a man wants to ask the woman he loves a very important question, he gets on one knee to show his sincerity. And even though I didn't plan this to happen right at this exact time, in all of my life I have never wanted to be more sincere than this moment. Zsilvia, my life changed when I met you. I know that we didn't have the easiest beginning, but that only makes you more precious to me. I want to share every moment of every day of the rest of my life with you doing everything I can to show that to you. I wanted the moment that I asked you this question to be something special and memorable, but I really don't want to wait anymore. Will you marry me?"

Zsilvia drew in a breath through the tears that were forming and nodded.

"Yes," she said, overcome with greater emotion than she would have expected to feel. "Yes, I will marry you."

George got to his feet and swept her into a tight hug. She breathed in the scent of him and clutched him tightly, wanting to cherish every sensation of that moment. Things were changing. She knew that she no longer lived in the world that her parents had lived in, and even so it would be further changed when her children came into being. She wanted to remember exactly what these changes felt like so that she could share them with the future generations of her family, telling them about the time when it was unheard of for a Denynso to mate with anyone but another Denynso and how she watched that change, how she was a part of it.

She felt his lips touch the side of her neck and shiver rippled through her body. It felt like it had been so long since they were alone together and even that subtle touch made her body respond to him immediately. Zsilvia tilted her head to the side to grant him more access to her neck and George obliged by continuing the trail of kisses up to her ear.

"Remember how I mentioned the special authorization rooms?" he whispered.

She could feel his hands sliding around her hips toward the buttons on the back of her dress as she nodded.

"Mmm-hmmm," she affirmed.

"Well, those rooms need to be so incredibly clean that you have to have an extra set of clothing on over what you are already wearing to make sure that you don't bring in any foreign debris."

"Oh, really?" she asked.

George nodded as he started to kiss around the front of her neck and toward the other ear.

"We don't have that rule in this lab," he said. "I can do anything that I want in here and it most definitely doesn't require extra clothing."

"It doesn't?" she asked playfully, her hands moving to the front of his pants as he guided her back toward one of the tables positioned in the center of the room.

"No." She felt the buttons on her dress release. "In fact, I don't think that we need clothes in here at all."

George eased her dress forward and Zsilvia straightened her arms so that he could guide it off. When it pooled around her waist, she pushed it down over her hips, letting it fall to the floor at her feet. George moaned when he saw that she had chosen to wear nothing under the slim-fitting dress and reached forward to cup his hand around one of her breasts. Zsilvia went back to working at the fastening of his pants, finally succeeding in opening his belt and button. George stepped away from her and walked over to a rack sitting against one wall. He pulled a thick wool blanket from one of the shelves and spread it over the metal surface of the table. Coming back in front of her, he took her by her waist and lifted her, positioning her on the table's edge.

Zsilvia watched as George continued to undress, first slowly unbuttoning the buttons on his shirt to reveal the thick, coarse hair along his chest and stomach that always made her body ache for him. She reached forward and ran her hand along the hair, biting into her lip as she felt his taut muscles beneath the layer. He stepped back slightly and lowered his zipper. It was immediately obvious that he, too, had chosen to forego wearing anything beneath his clothing as his thick erection sprung free. She reached for it as he kicked out of his pants and George happily obliged, stepping forward so that she could wrap her hand firmly around the engorged shaft.

George's soft moan as she stroked him encouraged her even further and she lengthened her stokes so that her hand came up and over the tip. She could feel the fluid forming and knew that he was already eagerly ready for her. He stepped forward and used one hand to push her knees apart so that her legs opened. Capturing her mouth with his, George kissed her deeply and ran one hand up the inside of her leg until he reached the hot, damp core that told him that she was just as ready for him. He mimicked the motions of her hand on his cock with his fingers through her folds, coaxing her to be even more open and wet for him. Their tongues tangled as they continued to nurture each other with their hands.

Suddenly George pulled his mouth away from hers and lowered it to her breast, sucking her taut nipple in against his tongue. After a few seconds he lowered himself to his knees and ran his tongue down the center of her belly. Zsilvia spread her legs further and put her hands back behind her to support herself on the table. George held her thighs and dipped his tongue inside her, gathering some of her fluids and spreading them across her as he drew his tongue up through her folds. She cried out as his tongue hit her most sensitive peak and focused in on it. Intense waves of pleasure rolled through her and she felt her body already rocketing toward climax. Just before she toppled over the edge, however, George stood and walked around the side of the table. He tucked his hand behind her head and turned it so that she would take him fully into her mouth.

His hand continued to play along her aching core as she drew him into her mouth in long, eager sucks. She stopped at the tip, allowing her tongue to languidly trace along the edge and then concentrated the tip on the bundle of nerves under the head. George thrust into her mouth in time to her sucks, pushing her desire to an even higher level. Finally he gripped her hair and eased himself out of her mouth.

"You're going to have to stop that," he said through his ragged breaths.

"Why?" she said teasingly.

"Because I'm not finishing without getting to be inside you," he growled.

George walked around to the end of the table and grabbed her legs. He yanked her forward, plunging into her in one hard thrust. Zsilvia sat up straighter and wrapped her legs around his hips. She gripped the table on either side to hold herself steady and stared into George's eyes as he thrust into her deeply. His pace was fast and hard, almost painful in its intensity, but that fine edge only made it more deliriously pleasurable. His grunts grew louder as he continued to stroke her wet, tight walls faster and harder. Suddenly his head fell back and he let out an animal-like roar. She felt his cock throb within her and the sensation of him spilling into her completely took all of her control.

Zsilvia threw herself forward onto George, grasping at his back as she toppled over the edge. Her body clenched around him and she cried out, biting down into his shoulder to muffle some of the sound. As their bodies started to cool and relax she started to straighten. A sudden sound from the section of the room that was still dark startled her and she gripped George tightly to her again.

"What was that?" she gasped.

George held her around her waist and looked over his shoulder towards where the sound had come. There was another slight shuffle and the sound of a door closing in an adjacent laboratory.

"Is someone here?" she asked, feeling extremely uncomfortable at the thought of someone else being there and possibly watching them.

"It's alright," he said comfortingly. "I'm sure it is just a research assistant in one of the other labs. It's fine. They probably don't even know that we're here. Come on. We need to get going if we are going to make it to the wedding on time."

He kissed her lovingly and she slowly lowered her legs from around him. They got dressed quickly and George tossed the blanket into a laundry basket. As they were heading out of the lab, Zsilvia heard the rustling again and the low click of a door opening.

10

M̲axim felt exhilarated as the vehicle pulled to a stop in the orchard of the Denynso compound. They had gotten there almost unimaginably quickly in the vehicle that Rain and Jonah had built, and the possibilities offered by technology thrilled him.

"Do you think that you can fix those to do what your vehicle can do?" he asked Jonah, pointing at the Mikana vehicles that were still where they had left them when they arrived from the kingdom.

Jonah walked over to the vehicles and ran his hand across them.

"These are amazing," he said. "Rain and I can work on them while we're waiting for the shuttle and see what we can do with them. Having as much transportation as possible is going to help all of us."

"Where should we bring Creia?" Nylek asked. "Ciyrs's shop?"

"No," Creia said, his voice sounding slightly stronger. "Ciyrs isn't here. Besides, you've done everything for me that he would. I want to go home. I want to go to Theia."

Maxim turned and saw the king trying to climb out of the vehicle. The days that he had spent held captive in that room had obviously taken horrible effect on him and Maxim shuddered just thinking of what must have happened to him in order for it to reduce the powerful king to such a weakened state. He rushed to Creia's side and grasped him to help him to his feet. He handed him off to Nylek and turned to help Athan and Kyven pull everyone's bags out of the vehicle. Ivy, Emerie, Rain, and Jonah helped them collect the bags and they all waited while Creia found the strength in his legs again. He took a few steps leaning on the men on either side of him and then released them. His eyes focused forward, the king lifted his head, squared his shoulders, and began to walk out of the orchard.

The show of strength and perseverance was nearly overwhelming and Maxim's mind immediately went to his father. Aegeus had always been the strongest, most courageous man he had ever known, and in that moment Maxim longed for him even more than he had. They were walking out of the orchard when Maxim heard Theia's voice.

"Creia!"

Maxim looked toward the sound and saw the queen running toward them with Mina close behind her. Hearing his mate's voice seemed to ignite something in Creia and he started moving faster. They reunited just on the outside of the orchard and Creia took Theia into his arms with such ferocity it was like he never intended to let her go.

"You're alive," she whispered into his chest. "You're alive."

"You heard my voice," Creia said. "You knew that I was alive."

"It's not the same as being able to touch you. It's not the same as standing here with you, smelling you, feeling you close to me."

She reached up and ran her hand along the side of his face.

"I'm sorry, Theia," he said.

Theia shook her head almost aggressively.

"No. I don't want to hear you say that. You did nothing wrong. You were trying to protect us, just like you always do."

"Sir," Nylek said, stepping closer to the pair. "Would you like us to go ahead?"

Creia shook his head.

"No. I'll come with you. I will arrange for an emergency shuttle."

"Shuttle?" Theia asked.

"We need to get to Earth as quickly as we can," Maxim told her. "Eden's former boss Ryan is the person behind Creia's capture. He's threatening her, Pyra, and Lysander, as well as the others."

Theia gasped and stepped back to look at Creia.

"Why didn't you tell me this?" she asked.

"I didn't want you to worry," Creia said. "There was nothing that you could do. Now that we're here, we can put plans into place. We need to get to Earth, find Ryan, and make sure that he can't hurt anyone."

"You can't go," Theia told him.

"What?" he asked.

"In your condition? No. Creia, you can't take on that journey right now. You need to stay here and heal. Getting to Earth is a long trip and you have no idea what you would encounter if you did end up there."

Creia stared at his mate for several long, intense moments and then started toward the meeting hall again, obviously forcing his body as hard as he could to try to show that he wasn't as weak as she was saying that he was. Maxim could see his body shaking even from his position several feet behind him and heard him grunting softly with each step. Suddenly his legs buckled and the king collapsed to his hands and knees. Theia screamed and ran forward toward him. Maxim followed and reached down to Creia.

"Sir? Are you alright?"

Creia was drawing in long, deep breaths.

"Creia, please," Theia said, kneeling in the dirt beside her mate. "You have to trust your men now. You have led them well and Maxim has shown his honor and worth. He is as much a member of your warriors as the others. It is time that you let them serve you."

Theia's words swelled in Maxim's chest. He was touched by the sentiment, especially remembering the darkness of the time in the human settlement and the horror of his brief transformation into being Klimnu. Though he never would have imagined it as something that he would have encountered in his life, he was proud to be counted among the number of the Denynso and to offer his loyalty as much to Creia as he would his own leader, possibly even more.

"You can trust us, King," Maxim said. "You need to focus on taking care of yourself. All of us will still need you at your best when we all return from Earth."

Creia turned to look at Maxim, and then lifted his eyes to Nylek, Kyven, Athan, and Lynx. Finally he nodded.

"Thank you," he said. "My father always told me that it takes great courage to face the challenges that are in your path, and even greater courage to ask for the help that you need to face them. I will have to follow that now. Please help me to the meeting hall."

Lynx and Bannack tucked their shoulders beneath Creia's arms and helped him up off of the ground. Maxim took up the bags that the two had put down and the group moved forward toward the meeting hall again. When they arrived, Theia immediately started toward their private quarters.

"You need a bath and to sleep," Theia told him. "I will make you something to eat."

"No, Theia," Creia said. "I have to call for the shuttle every moment is important."

Theia nodded and the Denynso warriors helped their king toward a room at the back of the meeting hall. After they had disappeared into the room, Maxim walked over to one of the tables in the banquet hall and sank down onto the bench. As he sat there, memories of the building in the other compound, the aging, dilapidated version of this meeting hall, flashed through his mind. He couldn't get the sound of the Valdicians' screams and their bodies hitting the floor out of his ears. He didn't regret a single thing that he had done. The sound and the images of the dusty, near-forgotten building was more of a reminder, a startling lesson that everything was tenuous. It was just like it had been the day that his father left for battle. Life was as it had always been and as he always thought it would be until that moment when Athan arrived to tell them that Aegeus was dead.

He could still look back on that moment and feel the conflicting, tearing balance. Just like the building in the other compound was like an aged, forgotten, and tattered version of this one, the life that he was living now seemed like a tattered version of the one that he could have lived if his father had never walked into that battle, if he had stayed and they had been able to live their lives together as they were meant to. In that moment when he heard Athan at the door telling Ellora that her husband had died in battle, Maxim had, if only for an instant, lived both lives. Though the darkness and pain of the new existence without his father was already starting to build, until he really let the news settle in, Maxim could pretend that life was still everything that it had been and everything that it should be.

Athan lowered himself on the bench across from Maxim, but he didn't look at the older man.

"Did the Order ever do anything good?" he asked.

There was silence on the other side of the table for several seconds as if Athan was trying to process the question and come up with the right response.

"Why do you ask?" he finally said.

"When I was younger, I spent so much time with my father, and my grandfather, and you. I feel like I always knew about the Order as a thing that existed, but I never knew what you did. I never understood the point of the Order or why any of you would leave the kingdom for long stretches at a time without anybody knowing. I didn't understand why you were a part of something so amazing, but I wasn't allowed to talk about it. Now I know that you were fighting in wars. Wars that I didn't even know ever happened. People died and their loved ones never even got to really know what happened. So I want to know if the Order ever did anything good."

"Fighting in those wars was good, Maxim. We weren't out fighting for fun. We weren't trying to take over anywhere or capture any people. When we weren't in battle, we were protecting others on Uoria from threats that didn't need to involve all of the Mikana."

"Then what? How did it become like it is now?"

"You know the answer to that, Maxim. You know exactly what happened to change everything."

"Does the Order do good anymore?"

Athan drew in a breath.

"No. The Order does very little anymore. Even the things that we were always meant to do, the reasons that the organization came to be in the first place. It has all faded away. Those in the Order now have lost touch with what it means and aren't willing to do what it takes to guard and to serve."

"So why are you still a part of it?"

"Because I always have been. There is no leaving the Order. Once you are a part of it, you devote your life to it. No matter what I did, I would still be bound by the regulations and traditions of the Order, and that means that I would be in danger of their retaliation. I am still a part of the Order. I always will be. But I have turned my back on them, and because of that I will be in danger for the rest of my life."

"Or until we can fix whatever happened after the Klimnu."

11

Azrael gripped the strap of his bag that rested across his chest with one hand and a torch with the other. He turned to the gathering of Eteri that had come to say goodbye to him and raised the torch into the sky by way of tribute to them. Without a word, he turned back to the small group that was gathered at the wall. Lila and Zyyr stood closest to the wall, while Oro and Ariella stood slightly away from them. Ariella's young faced looked sad and Oro stroked it gently until she lifted her eyes to look at him again.

"I'm sorry that he isn't here," Oro said softly. "If this is too difficult for you, you don't have to come."

Ariella's eyes widened sharply.

"You don't want me to go with you?" she asked.

"Of course I want you to go with me," Oro said. "You are my mate and the reason for my every breath now. I don't want to spend a moment without you. But that love is why I would not force you to do something that you didn't want to do. If you can't leave your home and your family to come with me on a mission that I admit might be very dangerous, I understand. I would come back for you."

"You would?"

"Always."

"Then I could never consider staying. If you wouldn't abandon me, then I will never abandon you. I just wish that my brother was here so that I could say goodbye to him."

"Ariella."

Almost as if her sadness had acted as a lure for him, Anson's voice boomed behind Azrael. He turned to watch the massive man coming toward them. He eyed Oro with a look that was still uneasy, still suspicious of this creature that came in and claimed his younger sister for his own. Ariella ran up to her brother and embraced him.

"Will you be alright?" Anson asked.

"Yes. Oro will take care of me."

"And if he doesn't?"

"He will. I will be back to see you soon."

"Are you sure?"

"Yes, Anson. Haven't you learned by now? There's so much more out there. So many adventures and experiences. So much that should be and needs to be done. But we always find a way to come back to that which we hold most dear. I will always come back home. No matter how far I am or how long I stay, I will never be away from you."

Anson pulled his sister in for another hug and then released her so that she could return to Oro. Azrael could see that the soft glow from her skin had dulled slightly, showing the sadness that she was carrying within her. He didn't want to stand there any longer. He didn't want to hear any more goodbyes or wishes of luck. He didn't need luck. He only needed what he had searched and longed for, for so many years, and he wouldn't be able to find that until they left.

Finally he saw Lila turn to everyone and wave.

"Thank you all so much for everything. I mean that for myself and for Idella."

They had chosen not to have the gathering directly in front of the entryway to the underground realm and now they formed a line as they walked down the narrow path that curved slightly around the rocks to bring them to that place in the wall. When they arrived, he started toward the entry, but noticed that the others seemed to be staring at the wall with looks of concentration and vague concern.

"What's wrong?" he asked.

"We have to find the place in the wall that has the entry-way," Zyyr told him.

"What do you mean?" he asked. "It's right there."

He pointed to the gap in the wall, but the others stared at it and then turned to him blankly.

"You can see it?" they asked.

"What do you mean? Of course I can see it. It's right there."

"We know it's there," Lila said, "but we can't see it. It was the same way when we first came out of there. We knew that there had to be an exit because Loralia had talked about some of her people leaving their realm to come for food and supplies. We had to believe that we would find it, and we finally did. Now we have to find it again. Do you mean that you are able to see it now?"

"Yes."

"I don't understand," Lila said. "I thought that..."

"You know that that entryway is there," Azrael told her. "You went through it. You know that you have seen it, felt it, and used it. You just don't trust yourself enough to remember where exactly it was located."

"But you do?" she asked.

There was a touch of defensiveness in her voice and Azrael felt himself straighten and his fists clench slightly. He had to remind himself that she, too, had a link to this place and may feel it was just as strong, and just as important as the link that he had. She was too young to understand his frustration at her impatience and challenge.

"That's the point. I don't have to trust myself to know where it is. I have used it before and I know that I will use it again. I don't need to remember where it is because I believe that I am meant to go through it. I have to in order to find my daughter and understand what happened to her."

He saw the expression on Lila's face change and when she looked toward the wall again, her mouth opened slightly.

"It's there," she said.

Azrael nodded.

"You will learn that the world is a less frightening and overwhelming place when you choose not to waste your wonder on the things that you already know are and should be. Save it for those moments that really deserve it."

Stepping past the other four, Azrael continued forward toward the gap in the wall. It was smaller than he remembered, and he wondered if that was only a function of time or if his memories were skewed by the enormity of the first time that he had gone through that entryway so many years before with Aiyla at his side. It was before the horrors of the Valdicians, after the struggle with the Covra. They believed that peace had finally come to their homes and they were ready to announce that they were planning to bond the species forever through their union. There had been great joy among the Irisa and the women had immediately begun working on the preparations for their tying, the first ritual in what would be an unprecedented celebration combining the traditions of both species. It was a celebration that would never happen.

He reminded himself that he had promised his service and loyalty to these beings, promised to stand beside those who were the closest link that he had to the daughter he had never been able to hold. He stopped and waited until the others had joined him just inside the entryway. Together they moved deeper into the cavern, all of them seeming to sense a change as they looked around with deeper understanding of what had happened there. Azrael looked around the empty underground settlement that had once been so full. It was as though he could still hear the voices of the people living there and feel the energy that always seemed to surround the unique and beautiful Irisa. He had gotten to visit the underground realm only a few times after the Irisa left their original home and moved to protect themselves from the plague that was destroying them at a frightening pace. In that brief time between them going beneath the ground and the Irisa deciding that they had to guard themselves by completely locking themselves away, he had had the opportunity to watch this settlement grow and even envisioned himself spending his life here with his family.

Now the space looked cold and dark, reminding him of the devastation that had occurred there. It was as if the rocks themselves had died when the lives of the Irisa were lost, one by one, to the plague that they would never have the opportunity to understand.

"Can I have a moment, please?" he asked as they passed by the chamber where the Irisa had made their small homes.

The others nodded and Azrael put down his bags, walking reverently into the space. He made his way to the home where Aiyla had lived with her family. He didn't know what he would find inside, or even what he wanted to. He opened the door and stepped inside, letting the waves of memory wash over him. Unlike the rest of the realm, the house felt warm and comforting, almost as though it was still in the same moment that it had been when he walked out of it so many years before. Azrael felt as though he could stand in the middle of the room and wait for Aiyla to come in. He closed his eyes, imagining her there with him. He could almost smell the soft sweetness of her hair and the warmth of her skin. He could hear the flow of her breath in the air around him. He could nearly feel the touch of her fingertips on his face, wiping away the tears that slid silently along her cheeks and onto his lips.

"I love you," he whispered into the space occupied at once by this moment and one from long before.

He opened his eyes and walked slowly through the home. There were so many signs of them still there. It was obvious that it had been cleaned since the deaths of the family that had lived there, and he assumed that he was looking at the careful and loving attention of his daughter. Suddenly it occurred to him that it was unlikely Aiyla continued to live in the home with her parents after their child was born. She would have preferred to have her own space to raise the baby. He left the house and headed down the narrow, winding road that led through the homes toward the small home that he and Aiyla had once fanta- sized would be their own.

He paused in front of the home and stared at it for several long seconds, wondering if there was any chance that she had fulfilled at least that dream for them. Azrael flattened his hand on the door and tried to tune into the emotions that may still exist within the wood. Though they readily and easily felt the emotions and feelings of those around them when they wanted to, it was much more difficult to sense energy that still lingered long after the person was no longer experiencing them. Sometimes, though, those emotions seeped into the very walls and ground so that those surfaces held them and expressed them almost as the person themselves would have.

Focusing in as fully as he could, Azrael sought the feeling of Aiyla in the house. It came to him immediately. He could feel the energy of her at the home, sense the full range of emotions that she had experienced in the time that she spent living in that small but comfortable home. He felt sadness, fear, and loneliness that reflected what he had gone through in the days after she had walked away from him for the last time. He felt the excitement and longing that must have come when the baby was born and Aiyla embarked on raising her without her father. Finally, deep within the wall, he felt joy.

Azrael opened the door to the house and stepped inside. He was surrounded by the feeling of Aiyla, but as he wandered through the few small rooms, he felt more lingering emotions and energy that he knew didn't belong to her. The tight connection that he had with Aiyla made the feeling of her strong, but these others were harder for him to find. They came in layers and he realized that some were the energy of his daughter. He absorbed these as much as he could, trying in a way to live the moments that he should have with her through the feelings that she had experienced and left behind. The further he moved into the home, though, the more he realized that there was another person there and that that energy was linked strongly to

Aiyla. It wasn't until he reached the bedroom, still perfectly made up as if she had just walked out of it, that it really sank in that she had spent her life with someone else.

He struggled to process what he was feeling. He had never been able to imagine loving anyone else after the moment that he left Aiyla's side for the last time. Throughout those long years, though, he had often hoped that the woman he loved hadn't suffered the same deep loneliness and emptiness that he had. It made him ache to even think of her being completely alone and their child growing up without knowing the love of a father. He often hoped that she would find someone to care for her and help her to live her life without the sometimes overwhelming pain that he had dealt with. Now that he knew that she had, though, it hurt. He felt like that man had stolen the life that was meant to be his and he found himself resenting every emotion that he encountered.

Azrael walked out of the home and hurried back toward the main chamber of the realm. He swung his bags back up onto his back and strode silently across the chamber toward where he remembered the reflected sky would be. He had only gotten to see it once before the Irisa closed themselves off from the rest of the planet. It was the day that it was created and he still remembered it as one of the most beautifully moving moments of his life. He stood at the edge of the reflected afternoon sky staring into its depths until he felt Lila come up beside him.

"Are you alright?" she asked softly.

The genuine compassion that she had for him helped to ease some of the tension that he was feeling, but he was still too far within himself to really connect with her. He nodded.

"I always am," he said.

"How are we going to get across?" Zyyr asked as, he too, came to the edge of the sky.

Azrael looked at him.

"You didn't plan for the sky?"

"No," Zyyr said, his voice almost powdery as he realized the failure in his planning.

"You concerned yourself so greatly with a detail so small as finding the entrance to the tunnels that you nearly couldn't find it, but you didn't stop even for a moment to think of something so great as the sky."

He saw Zyyr looking around as if trying to find some way to traverse the open space. Suddenly Ariella rushed forward and leapt off of the bank of ground where they stood. Oro screamed as she disappeared out of sight briefly, but an instant later she reappeared. Her delicate wings were spread to either side of her and her body floated comfortably in the air.

"It's just the sky, Oro," she said. "There's nothing to be afraid of."

Her wings fluttered slightly and she rose up higher out of the reflection so that she was flying at their height. Azrael followed her, spreading his wings so that he came off of the ground and floated above the sky. He flew toward the trees on the other side of the sky and felt for the thick vines that he remembered hanging from them. Taking a knife from his hip, he cut one of the long vines from the tree and went to work knotting it tightly to the end of one of the other vines. He repeated the process once more and then gripped the vine, putting all of his weight on it to make sure that it was strong enough. Satisfied, he flew back over the sky and handed the end of the vine over to Zyyr.

"Swing," he said. "Hold on as tightly as you can and swing over to the other side. I'll be beneath you."

Azrael sank down until he was several feet beneath the level of the ground where the others stood and watched as Zyyr adjusted his grip on the vine. The Denynso looked down at him and Azrael nodded, but the warrior hesitated.

"You have to trust me," Azrael called up to him.

"Zyyr," Oro said from beside Zyyr, "think about Jem. What was the last thing that you ever heard him say?"

Zyyr drew in a breath and Azrael saw his hands tighten so hard on the vine his knuckles turned white.

"I always wanted to fly."

With those words, Zyyr jumped and swung with the vine across the sky. He grasped a vine on one of the trees, stabilized himself, and released the vine. Azrael flew up to grab it and pulled it back over to the other side to Oro. He coiled the vine around his arm and grasped it securely before taking the same jump that Zyyr had. Azrael flew up and stood on the ground beside Lila.

"Will you come with me?" he asked.

She looked up at him and he could see the swirl of emotion in her eyes.

"This is where they lived?" she asked quietly, as if she only wanted him to hear her.

"Yes. After the plague hit when they were above ground, they came down here and created this settlement. It wasn't long after that that they decided that they needed to cut off completely from everyone else to protect themselves."

"And they never came out?" she asked.

Azrael shook his head.

"The hope was that someday they would be able to go back to their original land, but the Denynso settled there and then the plague hit again. They didn't live to come above ground again."

"Except for Loralia," Lila said. "She survived because of you."

Azrael felt his heart tighten and he gave a short nod.

"I can see Idella in you," he said. "Obviously I didn't know her when she first came, but I remember her distinctly from when she would return from the Mikana kingdom to visit. You look like her and I think that if she were here, she would be proud of what you've done."

"I haven't done anything yet," Lila protested.

"Yes, you have. You have done so much more than you know."

He reached out for her and swept her into his arms like a child. Being as careful as he could not to dip too far and startle her, he flew her across the sky and placed her carefully beside Zyyr.

"Now all we have to do is climb," Oro said.

"Climb?" Lila asked.

"Remember the hole in the ground in the kingdom orchard? I told you that there are holes just like that in the Denynso orchard."

"I remember," Lila said.

"They are right above you."

Azrael watched Lila's eyes travel up the tree beside where they stood and then come back to Zyyr.

"Then we climb."

12

Creia walked slowly into the banquet hall and lowered himself onto his throne. His body ached and he was still struggling to clear his mind, but he was back in his own meeting hall and had never felt more grateful.

"I reached out to find a shuttle to get you to Earth as quickly as possible. I told them that it is an emergency of the highest order and they assured me that they would get a shuttle to us as fast as possible. There are several ships that are currently out on route already and they are going to contact them and find out if they can divert one of them here to make the trip faster. Now all we can do is wait."

The small gathering that was in the banquet hall with him nodded. None of them moved from their seats. It was as if they felt compelled to stay close to each other, worried that if they moved, something more could happen to them. Theia came to his side and rested her hand on his back.

"You will do some of your waiting in the bath," she told him. "You will feel better."

He knew that she was right, but he shared the desire of

the others to remain close. He felt like he had spent too much time away from his compound and his people as it was, and he didn't want to fail them again. The determination behind his mate's stare, however, told him that he really had no choice in the matter and he allowed her to help him stand and guide him upstairs into their private quarters. She had already run the bath for him and just the smell of the hot water and soap made the tension in his muscles start to slip away.

Creia undressed carefully, tossing aside the tattered, bloodied, and dirty clothes, and then stepped down into the sunken tub so that the hot water rose up around his chest. Theia knelt down beside him and reached down to run her hand along his chest.

"I love you," she said. "Thank you for coming home safely to me."

"I love you," he replied. "Thank you for giving me the strength to be able to."

Theia rested her lips on his and then stood, disappearing out of the room so that he could have a few moments to himself. It was a strange feeling. He had spent nearly all of the time that he had been imprisoned alone in that room, yet it had never felt like it. He could always feel Ryan's eyes on him, even when he was not on the screen, or the eerie, disconcerting presence of the thing in the tank in the lab. Especially once the screen was affixed in front of him not to be removed, it was as though there was never a moment when he wasn't being watched. Now that he was in his private quarters, he was finally alone. He finally felt like he could breathe.

When he was finished bathing, Creia got out of the tub and took his time dressing. The pain still radiated through his body where he had been injured, but he was thankful for the healing ointments that Maxim and Kyven had used for him. He knew that it was the ingenious creations that Ciyrs developed with the help of the human women and George that were allowing his body to heal. He would need to undergo a complete healing when Ciyrs returned to Uoria, but for now, the ointments were enough to ease some of the pain and protect the wounds from infection.

Feeling revitalized, Creia walked down the curving steps from his private quarters into the main meeting hall. He stopped short when he saw Zyyr and Oro standing in the middle of the room.

"Creia!" Zyyr said, rushing toward him. "Maxim told us what happened. Are you alright?"

"Zyyr?" Creia asked, feeling somewhat confused. "Oro? What are you doing back here? The others told me that you stayed in the Mikana kingdom when they left."

"We did," Zyyr told him. "We didn't even know that they had come back here or anything that was happening. Sir, we brought some people with us that you need to meet. They have information that you need to hear."

Creia followed their eyes as both warriors looked to the doors of the meeting hall and watched as a young woman came in followed by another young woman and a man only slightly younger than himself. It took a moment before it registered to Creia that they both had wings folded down beside them.

"Alright," Creia said cautiously, trying to process what was happening around him.

The man with the wings stuck a memory deep within him, but he wasn't sure what it was. He stared at him further as Zyyr took the hand of the woman in front of the two winged creatures and guided her forward a few steps.

"This," Zyyr said. "Is Lila. She is my mate."

"Hello, Lila," Creia said. "It is very nice to meet you. Welcome to our home."

"Thank you," Lila said.

The young woman was beautiful in an ethereal way and he felt himself tilt his head at her slightly. Zyyr obviously noticed the expression on his face and nodded.

"She is Mikana," he said, "but she has Irisa in her bloodline. Loralia's kind."

The word suddenly triggered the memories that were buried deeply within him. It was as if pictures flashed in the backs of his eyes and his ears were suddenly filled with the sounds of battle. He drew in a deep, shuddering breath.

"Azrael," he said, low in his chest.

The winged man's eyes snapped up to him and they stared at each other for several long seconds.

"Creia?" he said, taking a step toward him. "You..." his voice trailed off as he continued to look at the Denynso king. "It has been so long."

"Sir?" Zyyr asked, sounding confused.

Creia looked at him and gestured toward Azrael.

"I remember Azrael from many years ago. We went into battle together."

The two had not spent an extensive amount of time together, but even their brief encounter had left an impression on Creia. The horrors that he had witnessed during that battle had been hard on Creia in a way that he couldn't express, and he had pushed those memories deep into the back of his mind, hiding them away so that he could focus on leading his clan. Now that Azrael was standing in front of him, though, he couldn't keep the memories away from his thoughts. It was obvious looking at the man that he had gone through many more difficult times after the last time that Creia had turned his back and walked away from the battlefield. His wings were tattered and scarred, and eyes that once sparkled and danced were now dull and cold.

"Criea," Zyyr said, "Azrael is Loralia's father."

Creia looked at Zyyr sharply and then back at Azrael.

"Loralia?" he asked, dumbfounded by the revelation.

He couldn't understand. He knew Azrael when he was very young, long before Loralia would have been born, and had then encountered him again many years later. By then he had grown angrier and more bitter, but Creia had never known what had happened to him.

"Can we sit down?" Zyyr asked. "We have a lot we need to tell you."

13

"Are George and Zsilvia still not back?" Eden asked, handing Lysander up to Pyra. "The wedding is about to start."

Pyra shook his head as he took his infant son and bounced him lovingly in his arms.

"I haven't seen them since they left this morning," he said. "Have you asked any of the others? They might have already gone and sat down with the other guests."

Eden nodded. The absence of the couple made her uncomfortable. They had both expressed excitement to be guests at the historic celebration and had assured them that they were only going to be gone for a few minutes. She knew that the lab that he and Ivy worked in was very close to hers, so she could estimate how long it would take for him to get there and to get back. Even if he had had to search for whatever it was that he needed to find, they should have been back quite a while ago. She didn't understand why he would be gone for so long, or why he would risk missing the wedding.

"Eden?"

She turned toward the voice and saw Samira coming toward her. The gown that she had chosen was simple yet exquisite. It clung to her curves and pooled down at her feet like glittering cream. The entire gown was covered in tiny iridescent beads, giving her a sparkling look. She wore her thick hair up away from her shoulders and her makeup was smooth, delicate perfection. Eden's breath caught in her throat slightly and she felt emotion building up in her chest.

"You look so beautiful," she said.

"Thank you," Samira responded, glancing down. "So do you. I love the way that you look in that dress."

Eden looked down at the bridesmaid dress that she was wearing and smiled.

"I always dreaded being asked to be a bridesmaid because I figured that the dress was going to be horrible. I was so happy that you asked me, and I think that this dress is a big part of it."

She laughed and Samira joined her, stepping forward to gather Eden into a hug.

"Alright. I came to find you because we are about to get started. The men are already all lined up out there so we are supposed to head over to the tent now." Eden hesitated. "What's wrong?" Samira asked.

"Zsilvia and George aren't here," she said.

"What? Where did they go?" she asked.

"Early this morning George said he needed to run back by his lab because he needed to check on something, but that he would be back before the wedding. Zsilvia went with him. They should have been back a while ago, but no one has seen them."

Samira looked distressed as she gazed to one side like she was thinking. Finally she turned back to Eden.

"We can't really wait for them. I hate to have them miss it, but they aren't part of the wedding party, so we will just have to go ahead without them. They will catch up with us at the reception."

Eden nodded.

"I'm sure they'll understand." Eden smiled and took Samira's wrist playfully. "We can move ahead without them, but we can't move ahead without you. Come on. Your warrior is waiting for you. Let's get you married."

Together they rushed out of the building toward the tent where the ceremony was to be held. The coordinator had closed the flap so that no one would be able to see Samira until her walk and the other bridesmaids were gathered there. Zuri and Jane turned toward Samira and both women smiled broadly. Zuri reached out toward Samira and handed her the bouquet that she had been holding.

"Are you ready?" she asked.

Samira nodded.

"Absolutely."

The music inside the tent swelled and the two ushers opened the flap just enough for Eden to step through and start her walk down the aisle. She tried to remember how the coordinator had told her to walk, that she should seem casual but also dedicated to getting to the end of the aisle. It seemed like a fairly aggressive way of thinking about walking in a wedding, but she did her best to walk in exactly that fashion. She was halfway down the aisle when she finally glanced up from the long creamy white aisle runner to the men that were standing along one side of the officiant. Pyra smiled at her and she felt her heart melting. He looked incredible in his suit and she longed for more time alone with him.

Finally she got to the end of the aisle and took her place.

The other bridesmaids filed in and then there was the excited shifting and muttering as the guests gathered in the chairs flanking the aisle anticipated Samira coming down the aisle. As the music changed and all of the guests stood, Eden let her eyes fall on her infant son sleeping peacefully in his grandmother's arms in the congregation. Everything seemed peaceful, in control for that moment. This was something that she would never have expected to see and do when she first left for Uoria. In those days that she was traveling and even in the earliest time that she was on the planet, life was too painful and confusing to even begin to consider that such beauty and love could happen less than two years later.

Samira took her place across from Ty and rested her hands in his. Eden could see the lovely bride shaking slightly and felt a new sense of happiness in her chest. Even though Samira and Ty had been mated for some time, the idea of actually getting married was still meaningful enough to Samira that she looked both nervous and thrilled at the same time. The thought that maybe one day she and Pyra would have a wedding of their own skittered through her mind and she felt her lips curve up even more.

Samira and Ty had spent some time changing the standard wedding ceremony so that it more appropriately expressed their unique relationship and this momentous occasion, and Eden found herself lost in the words that the officiant said. He spoke in a voice that was low, slow, and gentle, lulling Eden into a sense of rapt attention that held her until he turned to Ty and asked him to repeat his vows. Though this ceremony wasn't something that Ty understood, the tone of his voice and the look on his face told Eden that he was just as filled with emotion as Samira.

Finally it was Samira's turn to recite the vows to Ty and slide the enormous golden band onto his finger. He gazed down at it and then back at Samira adoringly.

"You may now kiss your bride," the officiant said.

Ty gave Samira a gentle tug to pull her closer and leaned down toward her, his lips parting. Eden drew in the same anticipatory breath as the rest of the guests. Just before Ty's mouth touched Samira's, a scream tore through the tent. Eden suddenly felt like the world around her was moving in slow motion. She turned toward the scream and felt her hair tumble from the pins that had held it on her head. It fell across her eyes, making the growing screams around her even more frightening.

Eden pushed the hair away from her face and saw the wedding guests running from toppled chairs trying to get out of the tent. Chaos had broken out and for a moment Eden couldn't see what had happened to start it. Suddenly her eyes fell on a group of tall, cloaked creatures walking slowly down the aisle, slicing through the turmoil with unnerving calm. Pyra came toward her and she reached for him, but it still seemed as though she were struggling against the space around her and couldn't get to him fast enough. The bouquet fell from her hand and she turned toward the chair where she had seen her grandmother holding Lysander.

She tried to force her voice out of her throat to tell Pyra to get the baby, but she couldn't hear it over the oppressive noise around her. Before she could get any further, she saw one of the cloaked creatures approach her grandmother and reach out for Lysander. Her grandmother clutched him tighter to her chest and tried to climb over the fallen chairs around her to get away, but another creature jumped down in front of her, startling her so that she stumbled backwards. The warriors descending on them, but two of the other creatures stepped in their paths and drew swords from beneath their cloaks.

Eden forced her feet to move, demanding her body to go toward her son. She started to climb over a pile of fallen chairs, but she couldn't get to him. One of the creatures reached down and grabbed the baby out of her grandmother's arms, yanking his blanket from her clenched hands as she pleaded. A scream tore from Eden's mouth, finally breaking through the muffled, deadened sound of the world around her. There was nothing she could do. In an instant, the creatures swept Lysander back up the aisle and were gone.

"Prya!" she screamed. "They took Lysander!"

"I know!" her mate shouted back at her. "Ero, go after them!"

The warriors moved around the space, moving chairs out of the way and trying to calm the guests that remained, asking each of them if they had seen anything or might know who or what those creatures were. Ero ran out of the tent, but returned after only a few moments,

"They're gone, Pyra," he said, "I don't know where they went, but I can't see them anywhere."

"All of you, go. Find them. They have my son."

The warriors rushed out of the tent as the women came to gather around Eden. Her body was shaking and she felt tears pouring down her cheeks. Suddenly something popped into her mind and she whipped around to the bridesmaids behind her.

"Jane, do you still have that picture that you showed us?" she asked.

"Of course," Jane said in a shaky voice. "It's at the house."

"Will you bring me there?"

The panic that had taken hold of Eden drained away and was replaced by a sense of calm determination. She followed the other women out of the tent toward Jane's car.

When they got to Jane's house they gathered in the living room while Jane got the picture. Eden paced around, willing herself to believe that Lysander was still safe. The creatures had targeted him specifically, so there was a reason that they wanted him. Hopefully that meant that they would take care of him and keep him safe long enough for them to find him.

Jane came back into the room and handed Eden the picture. She stared down at it and the memory that she had been searching for since the first time that she had seen the picture formed in her mind. She looked up at Pyra.

"Ryan," she said.

"Ryan?" he asked, coming toward her to look at the picture with her.

"This picture," she said, pointing at the man who they had realized so strongly resembled a Denynso, "is in Ryan's office. I must have looked at it a thousand times and never thought about it. When Jane first showed us the picture I didn't remember it, but now I do."

"He has Lysander," Pyra said.

"And he might have George and Zsilvia, too," Eden said.

Pyra nodded.

"Reach out to Ciyrs, tell him that he and the other warriors need to get to the lab."

Eden felt her chest tighten. This was the first time that Pyra had actually asked her to use her ability to communicate with Ciyrs. The fact that she was able to connect with the healer in the same way that she could connect with Pyra had been a source of great turmoil and anger since they first discovered it when Ciyrs healed her after she nearly died from the Klimnu attack when she was first on Uoria. The ability to communicate with their thoughts was something precious and private that warriors shared with their mates and it pained Pyra to know that she shared the same type of link with Ciyrs. This hurt had caused Eden to close off that connection with the healer who had become the closest person to her other than Pyra.

Now, though, her mate was acknowledging not just the special bond that Eden and Ciyrs had, but also the value of their unique connection. She reached out for Pyra's hand and gripped it tightly as she connected with Ciyrs.

"Go to the lab," she told him without waiting for him to respond. "Ryan has Lysander and he might have George and Zsilvia, too. Get the others and get there as fast as you can."

They were running out of the apartment back toward the car when Elianna's voice came to Eden's mind.

"What's happening?" she asked. "Ciyrs said that you told them to go to the lab."

Elianna had stayed behind at the wedding tent, and Eden was more thankful in that moment than ever before that her unprecedented connection with Ciyrs also meant that she was able to communicate with his mate.

"Tell all the guests who are left to go home. Gather everyone from Uoria. Go change and then gather at the house where Pyra and I have been staying. Be ready. We'll let you know when you need you."

As the car rocketed toward the lab Eden reached into the small bag that she carried with a strap around her wrist and pulled out a clip for her hair. She twisted her hair back out of her face and clipped it into place.

"Do you have your blade, Pyra?" she asked.

Pyra handed her the dagger that he had taken to

carrying with him since the last battle with the Klimnu. She gathered the long skirt of her dress and tucked the blade beneath it, cutting up into the fabric to split the dress up above her knees. Handing the knife back to Pyra, she used her hands to tear the fabric off. Whatever was waiting for them at the lab, she was going to be ready.

14

The ship quaked beneath Elise's feet and she grabbed for the table beside her to prevent herself from stumbling. She looked up at the emergency lights that would signal if she and the other attendants needed to return to their pods, but they weren't signaling.

"What's going on?" she asked to one of the other attendants as he entered the room.

"I don't know," he replied. "The captain just said that we've changed course."

"Why?"

"He didn't say."

The ship was traveling smoothly again and Elise headed as quickly as she could toward the captain's control room.

"What's going on?" she asked. "Is something wrong with the ship?"

"No," the pilot responded. "We've received orders to deviate from our original flight course. Another ship will be utilized to complete our original trip. Please return to your responsibilities. There is nothing you can do."

As Elise turned to leave the control room and go back to

what she had been doing, she caught a glimpse of one of the monitors and noticed the path that they were currently on. Their original trajectory would have taken them to one of the remote moons at the corner of this segment of the galaxy, where a group of tourists waited their transport to the next stop on their extended vacation tour around the galaxy. Their new path was highlighted on the screen now and she realized that it looked familiar. Braving another moment in the control room, she took a step forward and looked at the top corner of the monitor where she could see their final destination: Uoria.

Azra climbed into the back of the car, but stopped before latching his safety belt. He could hear Elise's voice in his mind. Though he hadn't been able to keep his mate far from his thoughts ever since he had had to leave her on the shuttle so that she could return to her career while he was on Earth, he had not actually heard her. This was the first time that they were making their mated connection and even with the turmoil going on around them, he felt a sense of excitement rush through him. It took a few moments before he was able to focus in on what she was saying. He realized that she didn't know that she was communicating with him. Rather, she had let herself become vulnerable enough that he was able to tap into the line of communication and he was now listening to her thoughts.

"Uoria," she thought. "We're going to Uoria."

"Why?" he asked.

There was a long period of silence and then her voice, slightly nervous this time, came back into his mind.

"Azra?" Elise asked.

"Yes, my love. It's me. You can communicate this way with me."

"Can anyone else hear me?" she asked.

"No," he told her. "Only mates can communicate through their thoughts. The only exception is Eden and two of the three people that she can communicate with through her thoughts."

"I miss you," she said.

"I miss you, too. More than I could ever describe to you. Why are you going back to Uoria? I thought that your contract had you traveling on a vacation course for the next few weeks."

"It does," Elise told him. "The pilot just announced that we have been authorized to go off course for a special request. I questioned him about it and he told me that Creia requested an emergency shuttle to arrive on Uoria and bring passengers to Earth."

"Why did they choose your specific shuttle?" he asked.

"The shuttle that I'm on right now is equipped with special experimental technology that is meant for high speed travel. It can cut the trip between Uoria and Earth from five days to one."

"That sounds dangerous."

"It can be. That's why it hasn't be released to the public yet. We had only just mastered the new technology that shortened the trip, but now this one has been developed and could revolutionize travel."

"I don't need you to sell me on it," Azra said and immediately regretted snapping at her. "I'm sorry," he said. "The technology sounds amazing, really it does, and I'm happy that they chose your route to redirect to Uoria. I only wish that I was there. I miss you so much and with everything going on, I'm worried about why Creia would request an emergency shuttle."

"What's going on?" Elise asked. "Don't you know why he would ask for a shuttle? Are there others on Uoria that you left behind and may want to join you?"

Azra's mind traveled to Maxim, Ivy, Lynx, and Rain, as well as some of the other warriors who didn't make the trip with them.

"Yes, but that wouldn't be an emergency. He might request a regular shuttle if some of them changed their mind and wanted to come to Earth to be with us, but he wouldn't ask that one of the official specialized shuttles be redirected because of an emergency just to get them to Earth. Something else must be going on there."

"What's happening on Earth?" Elise asked.

Azra briefly recounted the events of the wedding and their current mission. She gasped, but before he could respond to her, the car stopped outside of the lab and the doors flew open.

"I have to go," he told her. "We just got to the lab. As soon as you find out what is going on with Creia and why he needed an emergency transport, please tell me. I love you."

"I will. I love you."

He had given her only the most basic of details, not wanting to upset her. Azra knew that if Creia had asked for an emergency transport, something very serious was happening. He couldn't let her know that, though. She needed to be able to focus, to be at her best so that when they did arrive on Uoria and prepared to return to Earth, she would be able to do her job as best she could so that they could handle this situation, whatever it was.

Closing off his mind so that Elise didn't accidentally

connect into him when he was inside the lab, Azra climbed out of the car, resting his hand on his dagger in the same way as the other warriors around him. In that moment, the brief second between climbing out of the car and actually storming into the lab, Azra remembered the days when the Denynso warriors left their weapons hanging in their homes and had no reason to carry them with them when they traveled.

15

E den could hear the other warriors stomping through the hallway when she ran into the lab.

"Here!" she screamed and she heard their footsteps pounding toward her.

When they got to her, they all started running, allowing Eden to guide them as they wove through the hallways to the door to the lab that she had once shared with Ryan. She had expected that she was going to be afraid when she arrived and was getting ready to be face to face with this man, but there was no sense of fear in her at all as she reached out and touched her hand to the handle on the door. There was only anger and disdain that compelled her to find Ryan and destroy him.

The door opened easily beneath her hand and they all rushed inside. Lysander's cries filled the space and Eden felt her heart swell with both happiness and pain. She was overjoyed to know that he was still alive, and yet the sound of his screams, knowing that he wanted her and that she wasn't there with him, was the most heartbreaking sound that she had ever heard. Eden ran toward the secondary lab that was attached to the first and immediately saw Ryan. He was standing in the back corner, holding Lysander in his hands as he looked down at him with an expression on his face that was truly indecipherable.

"Ryan!" she shouted.

He turned toward them and she saw a sickening smile cross his lips.

"Well, hello, Eden. How nice of you to drop by. And I see that you brought friends with you. I'm delighted to meet you all. "

Ryan was standing next to a tall tank, but all of the lights within it were out, making it impossible for Eden to see what was inside. She rushed toward the baby, but immediately felt herself forced backward. She tried again, but again it felt like a tremendous current of air was pushing her backward so that she couldn't get any closer to him. She lifted her hand and felt that there was a force field around her, preventing her from being able to cross the lab and get to Lysander. Pounding her hands against it, she screamed, the sound more like an animal cry than one coming from someone who was born human. She felt the Denynso strength and aggressive anger building inside her and wished that she could use them to push through the force field so that she could get to the baby.

She could hear Ryan laughing and the desire to destroy him only increased. Eden turned back so that she could talk to the other warriors and found that there was another force field behind her and Pyra, keeping them isolated in that small section of the lab. She turned around wildly, pacing in the small area and trying to find a way to get out so that she could get to the baby. She had turned around for a third time when her eyes suddenly fell on another of the large tanks along the wall. The lights were on in this tank and she could see George and Zsilvia lying on the ground, piled on top of one another as if simply tossed in there.

She gasped and pressed herself against the force field, trying to look closer and see if they were still breathing.

"No," she murmured.

"Don't worry," Ryan said viciously. "They're still alive. Barely just, I must admit, but they are alive. I took them as a failsafe. I figured that if I couldn't get my hands on your offspring and you and your mate were stupid enough to try to fight and we had to kill you, that at least I would have a breeding couple that I would be able to use."

"He's human," Eden told him, hoping that somehow that would make a difference to him. "He isn't like me. He hasn't been changed."

"That doesn't matter," Ryan told her. "After all, this child is half-human. Even though you are Denynso now, you conceived him when you were human. He is a hybrid just as any children that I could produce out of those two would be. They might not be as powerful getting their Denynso blood only from their mother and not the most feared warrior in the galaxy, but I'm sure once my army recovered Pyra's body we could do something to fix that."

Eden felt her body shaking and the hot tears returned to her eyes. This time, however, it was anger and disgust that fueled them.

"What do you mean?" Pyra asked through gritted teeth.

"It's so simple," Ryan said. He used the arm that wasn't holding Lysander to gesture at the lab and the tanks. "Hybrids. The future of armed combat. When Eden was here working with me she thought that I was creating some kind of mechanical weapon. She thought that I wanted Pyra's blood so that I could synthesize it and put it into those weapons. That was partially true, but it had nothing to do with mechanics. I was creating the weapons themselves."

"Keep him talking," Ciyrs's voice suddenly said in Eden's mind. "Do not let him leave the room with Lysander. The only way that we are going to get through this is if we all band together. We are going to go get the others."

Eden knew that the healer was right. The only chance that they had of rescuing Lysander, George, and Zsilvia, and getting out of the lab themselves, is if they kept Ryan distracted and didn't let him carry on with any of his plans. She glanced over her shoulder long enough to see Elianna and Ciyrs slip behind the other warriors and disappear out of the door to the lab. She turned back to Ryan.

"Why hybrids?" she asked. "Why did you want to blend Denynso and human? Why not just find a way to enslave the Denynso so that they could be militarized?"

"The Denynso will never be enslaved," Pyra growled.

Ryan laughed and carried Lysander over to a table. Fear overtook Eden's heart, but Ryan placed the baby in a basket and walked away from him. Her son was still screaming, but at least, for that moment, Ryan was not touching him and she had to imagine that that meant that he was safer. Ryan walked over to them, standing only inches from the force field as if taunting her.

"You truly believe that, don't you?" he asked, staring at Pyra.

Pyra took an aggressive step toward Ryan, but he couldn't get to him.

"The warriors would die before being captured". The warriors behind them roared in agreement, but Ryan didn't seem swayed. The block between them had seemed to take away the fear of the Denysno that his first encounter with

Pyra had instilled and now he felt secure enough to completely confront them.

"You've been captured," Ryan pointed out almost whimsically. "I have you right here and there is nothing that you can do about it. I could do whatever I want with you. I think that I will wait, though. Why spoil the fun? Soon all of the warriors will be here and I will be able to create everything that I have ever dreamed of."

"You never answered me," Eden said. "Why hybrids? Why blend the humans and the Denynso?"

"It's not just them," Ryan said.

"I don't understand."

"You have no idea who I am," Ryan told her. "My great-grandfather was the general of the Valdician army that controlled the prison colony before the Nyx 23 mission came. I spent my entire childhood listening to the stories that my parents would tell me of him and watching his banked memories, reliving every moment of what he went through."

"Banked memories?" Pyra asked.

Eden nodded.

"Some people can't handle the thought that what they have done in their lives won't be remembered when they die, so they have their entire consciousness preserved. This allows others to watch through their memories. Sometimes it is very important people who are banked so that future generations can know of the amazing things that they accomplished. Usually, though, it is just self-obsessed people who are too afraid of disappearing and think that everything that they have done is too noteworthy and impactful to ever be forgotten."

Ryan slammed his hands on the force field and Eden glared at him. They held each other's stare for several long seconds before Eden finally relented. No matter what she was feeling for Ryan in that moment, he still had her child and she needed to do everything that she could to make sure that he was going to take care of him.

"What my great-grandfather did was more impactful than anything that has been done since. Odan created something powerful and impressive, something that no one else had ever been able to create, and he was going to revolutionize the entire galaxy. He is the one who came up with the plans to have the Denysno captured from the compound and brought to Penthos. There he was training them to be slaves. He lured Nyx 23 to the planet knowing very well that the humans of Earth can't tolerate anything that they don't deem appropriate."

"What is appropriate about enslaving an entire clan?" Eden asked.

"It wasn't just them," Ryan said. "Nyx 23 was going to be the next step. They lured them to the prison planet with the intention of sending them to Uoria where their allies were waiting to imprison them in the compound now left behind. There they would be trained as enslaved soldiers and used to take over Uoria. The Valdicians and the Covra would then continue until they had the entire galaxy at their mercy. That plan, however, didn't work out exactly as they had envisioned. Nyx 23 came, just as they knew that they would, but when they sent them to Uoria, the ship somehow went just slightly off course. They ended up crashing in a different area of the planet than they were supposed to, so instead of them being captured instantly, there was confusion and they were able to escape the grasps of the Covra for a time. That is when it all changed."

"Earth sent the military," Eden said.

Ryan nodded darkly.

"The humans swarmed the planet and there was a brief but bloody battle. The humans destroyed what my great-grandfather had built. Everything that he had worked so hard for was now gone. The mission for the military was to come and kill off all of the Valdicians, and then liberate the remaining prisoners back to their original home. Of course, that didn't happen."

"The Denynso never returned to Uoria," Pyra said.

"No," Ryan said. "That's because they came here."

"How?" Eden asked. "I don't understand."

"A rogue member of the military immediately recognized the power and potential in the Valdicians. He went to my great-grandfather and asked for his cooperation. Odan obliged and together they brought the rest of the Valdicians and the surviving Denynso back to Earth. That man's name was Richard and though he served in the military, deep in his heart he was a scientist. As soon as he saw the Valdicians and the Denynso, he knew that he wanted to be able to use the incredible capabilities of both to breed a master warrior race. Odan told him of the plan to take over Uoria and they agreed to work together, shifting their focus away from just taking over Uoria and working from there. Instead, they would breed warriors powerful enough to take over Earth, the greatest conquest in this and any neighboring galaxy. From there, nothing would have stopped them."

"But something did," Eden said.

"Breeding warrior's takes time," Ryan snapped. "They had to create the hybrids and then further hybrids from there. Richard's wife agreed to be the first human incubator. She gave birth to a half-human, half-Valdician. At around the same time a Validician woman delivered a half-Valdician, half-Denynso. These were the first two hybrids, but Odan and Richard weren't satisfied. They knew that

they could do better, make even more incredible combinations to build armies that were stronger, more powerful, and
more fearsome than anything that the universe had ever
seen. They raised these children, grooming them always to
be their next breeding couple. When they came of age, they
bred and had a son. That was my father."

"You are a hybrid?" Pyra asked.

Ryan turned on him with fire in his eyes.

"Yes," he snarled, "but my father fell in love with a
human woman. Rather than breeding with one of the other
species, he bred with her and had me. I ended up with none
of the traits of the other species. That didn't stop me,
though. I spent my entire life watching my great-grandfather's memories and listening to the stories that my grandfather and father told me. I knew that one day it would be my
chance to continue their efforts. I would take everything
that they had learned and expand on it. I wasn't satisfied just
to stop with those combinations that they had been working
on. By the time that I was old enough to start with the
experiments, the original Valdicians and the Denynso we
had brought here had all died out. Though there were some
Valdician children that had been born pureblooded, they
hadn't had the foresight to have any pure Denynso bred. All
I had left was children of various degrees of diluted blood. I
knew that I needed more Denynso to work with. I am the
only one left in my bloodline. My family is now gone and I
have no children. It is up to me to complete what my family
started and created the ultimate race of warriors."

"But why did you send me after Pyra's blood?" Eden
asked. "I know that you just hoped that they would kill me
off, but you had to have some kind of contingency plan just
in case I did manage to get it and bring it back to you. You
couldn't have intended to use it to further your experiments.

That would require cloning the DNA from the blood and you would have to use a human woman as a carrier. That child would have been just as much a hybrid as the ones that you already had."

"Yes," Ryan said. "That's true. The blood was never meant to be used to clone, though. It was for something much more powerful. You see, my family was brilliant. They focused on the Valdicians, the Denynso, and the humans at first, but they had never forgotten where this all began and what opportunities awaited them. They continued to use their alliances on Uoria to collect other species to integrate into their experiments. Some bred more easily and willingly than others, while some turned against their own kind to offer up members into our experiments. My father, the last of my family, died when I was 16. That is when I took over. Within a year I had something in my possession that none of the others had ever had, something that would make my hybrids beyond anything that they were capable of creating."

Ryan walked back to the corner of the lab with the darkened tank and pressed a button beside it. Eden gasped as light flooded the tank, illuminating the bound creature inside. It reared back, letting out an angry roar, and she felt her heart pounding in her chest.

"Klimnu," she whispered.

16

Ryan laughed when he heard Eden and nodded.

"Please, feel free to continue to be as scared as you'd like. It only feeds him. It would be even better if you could muster up some anger. That really gets him going. Of course, it's nothing like blood."

Eden's eyes snapped to Pyra and saw that his eyes were closed, his face calm as he gripped the pendant that he wore around his neck. He was obviously struggling to stay calm, to control the emotions coursing through him so that he didn't further incite the Klimnu now thrashing in the tank.

"How did you get a Klimnu?" Eden asked, forcing herself to follow her mate's lead and stay as calm and even as she could even as she felt the terror of her son being vulnerable to Ryan

"When the experiments were just starting the Covra was still working closely with us. They sent my family members of other species, including one of a species that they had used many years before to build a prison."

"The Mikana," Pyra said.

"Yes. A beautiful, strong, and intelligent race. They

offered one of their kind to my family and through him they learned of an elite group known as the Order. It wasn't until years later that they discovered that the Mikana on Uoria had undergone an incredible change. We found out that after their conflict with the Covra some of their number had transformed into another species all together, a species that was cruel, vicious, and unstoppable. Exactly what we wanted for our warriors."

"They are stoppable," Pyra said. His voice was completely calm and even now and Eden knew that her mate had absolute control over his emotions now. "The Denynso stopped them."

"That's what you thought," Ryan said. "But you see, the Order had been struggling with the Klimnu for some time. What had once been one, powerful force had divided. Half embraced the changes of the Klimnu and wanted to utilize the power that those changes offered them to further their own control. The others continued to cling to their original Mikana roots and rail against what they thought was the cruelty and pointless brutality of this species. They went to war against each other, each with their own allies by their side. I knew that I had to have one of the Klimnu, but none were willing to participate in the experiments, and they were far too cunning for us to capture. I knew that I couldn't let another mistake happen."

"Mistake?" Eden asked.

"In the early stages of the experiments, my great-grand-father had used Mikana to breed an incredible hybrid. Unfortunately, she and one of the Mikana men escaped the lab and returned to Uoria. They worried briefly that she would tell others what she had experienced and that every-thing that they had worked so hard for would be destroyed. It never happened. They never heard from her again. Even still, by the time that I was old enough to be in control of the breeding, I knew that we couldn't let that happen again. I couldn't expect the most desirable of species be the one to choose whether to be a part of the experiments or not. I would have to take one for myself.

I learned of a man who was both adored and hated in the order. His family had been fighting the corruption in the Order for generations and was leading an ever-growing group of rogue followers into battle against the Klimnu supporters, all of which were now cooperating with me. This man was more powerful even than the leader of the Order and was willing to sacrifice anything in order to take down the corrupt members of the Order and end the breeding. He thought that he knew who he could trust, but he was betrayed. I found out that he was planning on faking his own death during a battle and then rising up against us with his army. In doing that, he essentially walked right into his chains.

You see, the Klimnu had begun fighting with the Denynso at this point, and that dwindled the numbers that were available to fight in the war. I knew that the chances of my allies overcoming the core Order members and their allies were little to none. But that was fine. I was willing to sacrifice numbers in order to get what I wanted. All I needed to do was wait."

"Why did it have to be him? Why didn't you just choose any of the Order members?" Eden asked.

"This man was special. His family had discovered that many years before, his grandfather's father had been claimed by the Order and offered to my family's cause. He became the father of the woman who escaped. Knowing that his family had been involved in the breeding infuriated him and he vowed to destroy me and everything that my family had created. Just as much as it made him hungry to take me down, though, it made me just as eager to get my hands on him. The corrupt members of the Order knew exactly what made a Mikana a Klimnu, and with the hatred and rage that surged through him, Aegeus would be the most powerful Klimnu ever created.

He was at once the greatest threat to me and the most desirable of conquests. I let him walk into battle believing that he was going to be able to follow through with his plan and conquer my allies. He didn't realize that we were ready for him. We brought him here. We forced his transformation. He has been here ever since."

"Why?" Eden asked. "Why bother to keep him? If he was such a threat, why didn't you just kill him?"

"Because the power that he has as a Klimnu is much more important than the threat that he posed to us. That threat was over the moment that I captured him. No one knows that he's still alive. Everyone believes that he was destroyed in that battle. That moment ended much of the conflicts and allowed me to work that much harder at creating my hybrid army. He has produced some of my most impressive hybrids. Not willingly, of course, but that is little of my concern. The only problem was that the last of my Denynso half-breeds had died. They had begun to fight the experiments and their numbers had dwindled. The newest creations of my army showed no sign of the Denynso that we had worked so hard to instill in them. I knew that I needed more. And so we are here. After years of seeking out the blood of the Denynso so that I could make Aegeus even stronger and feed the hybrids that have Klimnu blood, years of desiring the blood of the most powerful and feared of all of the warrior race, I discovered something even better." Ryan walked over to the basket and lay his hand on

Lysander's stomach. The baby had cried himself to sleep, but the silence was even more chilling to Eden. "This hybrid baby is special. He is the son of this most powerful warrior and of a woman who went to Uoria human and became Denynso. I can't even imagine the possibilities that lie within him."

"No!" Eden gasped, pressing against the force field.

The Klimnu Ryan had called Aegeus roared again and pulled against his chains. Eden knew that the rage inside Pyra was growing again, but now she wasn't afraid of it. This was not the Klimnu that they had fought against and that had tried to kill not only her, but Elianna, Leia, Zuri, and the rest of the clan as well. This was a man who had fought against them and tried to restore control to Uoria, but had been captured and tortured, forced to become exactly what he had hated. If anything, Eden wanted him to feed off of the anger that she and Pyra were feeling. She wanted him to grow stronger. Maybe then they would have a chance to overcome Ryan.

"Don't worry," Ryan said, touching Lysander's face gently. "I'm not going to do anything to harm him. He is much too precious to my cause. He is going to make the hybrids that my family dreamed of." He walked away from the baby toward Eden and Pyra again. "But before that can happen, I have to ensure that the legacy of my family is protected. I thought that all good within the Order had been eliminated, but I was wrong. One who was once the closest confidante of Aegeus is still alive and is now helping what is left of the family that had worked so hard to stop me. Their bloodline has to end. But once Maxim and Kyven are dead, there will be nothing more standing in my way."

17

"Are you sure that this is going to fit?" Jonah asked. "It's going to have to," Rain replied. "I don't know what's happened to the technology on Earth in the more than a century since we have been there, and I don't want to show up without anything that I am familiar with. I know this vehicle. I can operate it. Whatever we are going to face there, we are going to need the control that having it will give us."

Jonah nodded and continued taking bags out of the vehicle. The others were all gathered at the base of the landing platform staring up at the incredible ship that had just arrived. It was like nothing that she had ever seen before and the enormity of the time that they had lost truly hit her. At the same moment she felt a sense of gratitude for what had happened to them. Had it not been for the Covra locking them and leaving them to incubate their eggs for 100 years, she never would have been alive to meet Lynx or to be a part of the incredible changes that were going on around her all the time. Though she never thought that she would have chosen the pain and torment that they went through, had she known what awaited her just on the other side of the lock, it wouldn't have been so torturous.

The doors to the shuttle opened and a woman stepped out. She looked around the crowd at the base of the shuttle and when her eyes fell on Creia, she scurried down the stairs toward him.

"Sir?" Rain heard her say. "Are you Creia?"

"Yes," he said slightly suspiciously, "I am Creia, king of this compound."

"My name is Elise. Azra told me to tell you that I am his mate."

There was a moment of stillness and then Criea spoke again.

"You are the mate of my son, Azra?" he asked.

"Yes," Elise replied. "I met him on his journey to Earth."

"If you are his mate, why are you not with him now?" he asked.

"I have to complete my obligations to the fleet."

"Have you communicated with Azra recently?" he asked. "Does he know that you were coming here?"

The woman nodded.

"Yes. I told him as soon as I found out about the emergency transport request. He is extremely worried about you and the others, sir."

Creia nodded.

"Does he say that everything is alright on Earth?"

"Yes. At least, he didn't mention that there was anything that might be wrong."

"Then you need to hurry. Get to him before there is. How long will this shuttle take?"

"We have been authorized to use the fastest travel technology available. We will get to Earth within a day."

"Good." Creia turned to the others. "Move as quickly as you can. Get inside and be ready to go. There can be no delays."

"Excuse me," Rain said, rushing up to Elise. "I need to bring this with me."

She gestured toward the vehicle and Elise nodded.

"Absolutely. That's no trouble at all. Just bring it this way."

Rain's heart lifted in her chest. Though she knew that Jonah was probably right telling her it was ridiculous to want to bring their vehicle with them on their mission to Earth, she felt more comfortable knowing that it was with her. It felt like a bridge of sorts connecting the life that she once had with the one that was hers now. It comforted her to know that even in what she knew was going to be unfamiliar and potentially frightening surroundings on this evolution of the planet that she had always known, she would have some form of control.

Jonah got back in the vehicle and brought it slowly behind Elise and Rain. They walked around to the back of the platform and Rain saw the base of the ship settled nearly on the ground. Rain opened a metal hatch on the side and inputted numbers into a control panel. She pressed her hand flat to a sensor screen and a few seconds later a large bay door opened on the side of the ship.

"You can bring it in there. Once you're inside, I'll lead you to the pods."

Rain stepped out of the way and gestured for Jonah to bring the vehicle in. She and Elise followed behind him, and as soon as the vehicle was in place, the bay door closed. Chains came up from the floor and secure onto the bottom of the vehicle, securing it into place for the travel. Jonah climbed out of the vehicle and they quickly followed Elise through another door and into an elevator that lifted them to the floor of the shuttle where the others were boarding. Jonah ran out to gather the bags that he had left outside while Rain paced in the common room, unable to contain the uncomfortable blend of thoughts and emotions churning in her belly.

"If everyone will take their places in the pods," Elise said. "We will take off in just a few minutes. The pods will open once we are safely out of orbit."

Rain felt a touch on her back and turned to see Lynx standing behind her. He swept her into his arms and squeezed her tightly. His lips touched the side of her neck and she felt his breath running along her skin. She concentrated on the feeling, memorizing it so that she would be able to call it to mind during her time in the pod. Though she hadn't traveled in a pod on any ship, she had heard enough of the others talking about them that she knew that she wasn't going to like the feeling of being restrained in that way.

Lynx kissed her and released her.

"I love you," he said.

"I love you, too," she replied.

They walked together toward the pods and allowed Elise to guide them into them, adjusting their safety harnesses as she lowered the lids over them. Rain could feel the rumble of the ship beneath her and heard the roar of the engine as the ship took off. She closed her eyes, reminding herself that she had done this before. She went over everything that she had found out as she waited for the pod to open, using the information to distract her. Finally she heard the hiss and low pop of the lid opening and she scrambled to remove her harness so that she could climb out of the pod.

Elise was standing in the middle of the room when she

climbed out, a look of shock on her face. Eden rushed to her.

"What is it?" she asked.

"Azra," she said. "My mate. He just sent me a message."

Her voice was low and powdery, almost as though she didn't want to say the words that were coming out of her mind because she feared if she said them then they would be true.

"What did he say?" Eden asked.

Lynx came to her side, quickly followed by Jonah and then Maxim and Ivy. Elise looked at each of them.

"Pyra and Eden have been captured. Ryan has Lysander, George, and Zsilvia. He wants Maxim and Kyven." She looked at each of them again. "I don't know what it means."

Rain drew in a breath. She didn't know what she should say. Knowing that Azra was her mate meant that she was a part of the Denysno now, meaning that she had the right to understand what was happening. Rain started to explain, but Elise got a strange look on her face and started toward the large windows along one side of the ship.

"What's wrong?" Rain asked, following her.

Elise leaned against the back of the window seat and stared out into the darkness beyond the ship.

"It feels like we're starting to land," she said.

"That shouldn't be," Athan said, coming up beside them. "We've been traveling less than three hours."

"Even if the pilot activated the boosters as soon as we got out of the orbit of Uoria, we should still be traveling for several more hours."

The ship lurched slightly and Eden heard a hissing.

"We're entering the orbit of another planet," Elise said, sounding terrified. "This isn't right."

"Where were you supposed to be going before you got

redirected to Uoria?" Maxim asked. "Could the ship have just reentered that trajectory?"

Rain saw Elise shake her head almost violently.

"No. We were headed to a small moon. It was a tourist spot. This isn't it. I don't know where we are."

A sick feeling sank in Rain's stomach. She felt like she couldn't breathe. Something was wrong, but she didn't know what.

"Everyone back to your pods," Athan demanded. "Prepare to land."

Rain saw Elise continuing to stare through the window as the rest of the group scattered to get back into the pods before the ship landed. She grabbed onto the woman's wrist and pulled her gently.

"You need to prepare to land," she said. "Wherever we are, we're going to hit ground soon and you need to be safe."

Her words seemed to break through the fog that Elise was in and she looked at Rain for a few long seconds before nodding. Rain released her arm and ran back to her pod, locking the lid in place and fastening her harnesses. The ship trembled and then she felt it sinking rapidly toward the surface of the planet. She closed her eyes again, clasping the harness and wishing that Lynx was in the pod with her. What seemed like seconds later there was a hard bump and the ship fell still. Rain waited for a few moments and then released herself from her harness and opened the lid.

Several of the others were already filling the common space and Rain immediately pushed past them to the window. What had been a dark blanket of sky was now orange and brown. The planet looked desolate beyond the window, but Rain felt the shiver of fear in her heart as memories flickered through her mind. She knew the land that she was staring at, knew the seemingly endless sea of dry, burning sand and dust beyond the thick pane of glass. It was older now, darker and more war-torn than the last time she had stared down at it, but she knew it. They were on Penthos.

18

L ysander had begun crying again and Eden felt the heaviness in her breasts grow more intense. She looked at Ryan, who was standing near the tank staring in at Aegeus.

"Ryan," she said, trying to appeal to him as much as she could. "I need to take care of the baby."

He glared over his shoulder at her and scoffed.

"I'm not going to let you out so that you can take him back," he said. "Don't you think that I know by now that you can't be trusted?"

"He needs to eat, Ryan. If you want to be able to use him for your breeding, he has to be alive, and the only thing that will sustain him is me. I'm not going to try to take him back. I wouldn't do anything that might cause him to get hurt. I just want to feed him and change him. That's all. Please. He hasn't eaten in hours. He needs me."

Lysander screamed louder at the sound of his mother's voice and Eden felt as though her heart were tearing in two. Ryan turned to look at the baby and then finally back to her.

"Fine," he said. "I'll let you come in to take care of him. But only you. Pyra needs to be controlled."

"What do you mean?" Eden asked.

"If he will go into one of the cages willingly, I will allow you to come in and take care of the baby. I may even spare your life so that you can keep him alive as long as I need him."

The warriors behind them shouted their protests, but Pyra nodded.

"I will go," he said.

"Pyra, no," Eden said, reaching for him.

She now knew more clearly than ever what Ryan was capable of, and the thought of her mate being vulnerable to him in a cage was terrifying. Pyra leaned down and kissed her lightly.

"Don't be afraid," he told her. "As long as my family is safe, that's all that matters."

The force field lowered and Pyra walked willingly toward one of the tanks near the back of the lab. He stepped inside and immediately the door slammed closed in front of him. The lights inside the tank turned off and Eden gasped, closing her hand over her mouth. Across the room the baby cried again and she rushed toward him, gathering him from the basket and holding him close to her chest as she sobbed.

"I need something to change him with," she told Ryan. "A towel, a lab coat, anything."

Ryan brought her a towel and a washcloth and Eden carried the baby over to one of the sinks so that she could bathe him. As she settled him into the warm water, she held his head close to her chest so that she could nurse him, using the towel to block Ryan's view of her breast as her son ate.

"Where are you going to keep us?" she finally asked, still gazing down at Lysander as she gently bathed him.

"What do you mean?" Ryan asked.

"You said that you would spare my life so that I could take care of Lysander until he was grown so that he can be the beginning of the new hybrids. Where are you going to keep us?"

"No," Ryan said. "I said that I would spare your life so that you could take care of him for as long as I need him. He can be the beginning of my new army without having to wait to grow up."

"He's just a baby," Eden protested, pulling Lysander out of the water and using the towel to wrap him.

"For so long I have been creating hybrids the long, slow way, waiting for women to carry them and then having to have them grow up before they were useful. I am only just now getting to enjoy seeing some of my creations reach adulthood. Now, though, I don't have to wait that long. I have mastered the ability to splice DNA into an existing adult creature. That is how I have been using Aegeus. The angrier he gets, the more powerful he gets, and each time I notice a new level of fury within him, I withdraw DNA and splice it into some of my hybrids. I now have blends of Klimnu, Covra, and Valdician. Soon I will add Denynso. Don't fret too much, though. You have some time before your son becomes the...shall I say, bearer of good news? Your king tried to save you. He sent many of those who were left on Uoria here to rescue you and to stop me. He was even so kind as to send along Maxim and Kyven so I don't have to worry about hunting them down myself."

"What did you do to them?" Pyra demanded.

"Calm down," Ryan demanded. "You might have the most powerful blood in existence, but I don't need you alive to use it." He turned back to Eden. "As soon as I heard that Creia was seeking out an emergency transport for some of his people to come to Earth, I made a few little adjustments. As of right now they are on Penthos getting to know some of my hybrids. Soon, you will all be there. When the war is over, I will gather the bodies and use the DNA to create whatever I would like. Maxim and Kyven will be gone, no one will ever find out what happened to Nyx 23, and very soon I will have the army that I need to conquer the universe."

The door to the common area opened and a cloaked creature stepped in. Gasps rippled through the group and Elise let out a chilling scream.

"Everyone out," a voice demanded from within the hood.

"That is a Valdician," Rain whispered to Lynx.

"Are you sure?" he asked.

"I would recognize a voice like that anywhere. They must have taken over the shuttle."

They turned to Elise, who shook her head, holding up hands as if in surrender.

"I didn't know. Please, you have to believe me."

"Everyone out!" the Valdician demanded again.

"Resist," Rain heard Jonah hiss into her ear. "Keep them occupied."

She glanced over her shoulder in time to see Jonah, Azrael, Oro, and Ariella moving toward the back of the group. Another cloaked figure stepped out of the control room and Maxim suddenly lunged forward. In the chaos that ensued, Jonah and the others ran across the room and disappeared through the door that Elise had led him and Rain through when they first boarded. She didn't know what they were doing, but she had no time to react. Lynx suddenly grabbed her and started running toward the door to the shuttle. They ran down the stairs and out into the searing heat of the planet.

"What are you doing?" she asked. "Why are we out here?"

"We have no choice, Rain. Elise is the mate to one of the warriors. She is part of this now. They were waiting for us, just the same way that the Valdicians were waiting for you when you first came here. Now we have to do what you intended to do all along. We have to fight."

19

A crashing sound made Eden jump and she turned to see Pyra kicking the glass of the tank in front of him. Each smash of his enormous boot shook the entire cage and she could see that the glass was beginning to turn white, showing that it was weakening.

"Stop that!" Ryan demanded. "I could destroy your family in a matter of seconds."

All around Eden the sound of chanting began to swell. The warriors stood on the other side of the force field, shouting the way that they did when they walked into battle. The sound thumped through her, nearly overwhelming her. She gathered the baby against her chest and backed up, getting as far away from Ryan as she could. The more he screamed, the louder the chanting and the sound of Pyra's foot against the glass became. Eden grabbed the basket from the table and ran toward one of the tall metal shelves on the far end of the room. She kissed Lysander on his head and rested him into the basket, bringing the blankets inside tightly around him. Kissing him once more, she placed the basket on the highest shelf that she could reach and then walked around the side so that she could push the shelves against the opposite wall, wedging the unit between two walls and a cabinet to create a three-sided barrier around the baby.

Once she was confident that Lysander was safe and secure, Eden let out a yell and ran toward Ryan. Her sudden advance startled him and Ryan stepped back. The movement didn't deter her and Eden reached out to grab him, curling her hands around his neck. As they fought, the chanting only grew louder. In her mind, though, she could hear Pyra.

"Don't kill him. Keep him alive. We'll need him in order to save the others."

Eden heeded her mate's command and loosened her grip on Ryan's neck. At the same moment she lifted him up off of the floor, calling into use every bit of the Denynso strength that now filled her, and threw him toward the tank that held Pyra. Ryan's body crashed into the weakened glass, causing it to shatter. Just as Ryan tumbled out onto the floor in a sprinkling of shattered glass and Pyra stepped over him to gather Eden in his arms, Eden saw Ryan's coat move. It lifted into the air as if someone had grabbed it and she looked up to see Ty staring at it, manipulating it with the inborn power that he had gotten from his Valdician ancestor.

A second later the jacket fell back into place, leaving behind a slim control pad that Ryan had used to put the force fields into place. Eden reached out and grabbed it, pressing the button to release the fields. Ryan was trying to scramble to his feet as the shouting warriors flooded toward him.

"Stop!" Pyra demanded. "He stays alive until I say otherwise."

The warriors had created a circle around him and Eden stepped back away from it to run toward the tank that held Aegeus. She pressed her hands to the front of it and stared in at him. He strained against his chains and bared his teeth at her, but in his eyes she could see the desperation and pain.

"I'm not going to hurt you," she said. "You're going to have to trust me."

He thrashed against his chains more, but she stayed calm. Never would she have believed that she would have felt this much compassion toward one of the grisly creatures that had attempted to kiss her and that had killed Jem. Now that she looked closely at him, though, all she could think of was Maxim. She had seen him begin to go through the transformation of becoming a Klimnu and the horror of that memory was burned into her mind. This man was Maxim's father, and he had not become this willingly. She had to help him.

"I know your son," she told him. "Maxim."

Aegeus stilled and leaned toward her. She nodded.

"Where is he?" Aegeus asked.

It was the first time that she had heard him actually speak and his voice sent chills through her. It was the same unnerving voice of the Klimnu, but underneath there was a softer, warmer tone that proved to her how hard Aegeus had struggled against the transformation and how desperately he fought not to let it take over him completely.

"If Ryan is to be believed, he is with the others on Penthos."

"We need to get to him."

Eden nodded. She was reaching for the controls that would open the tank when she felt someone grab her from behind. She whirled around to see Loralia standing behind her.

"What are you doing?" Loralia asked, sounding horrified. "Ciyrs and Elianna came for us. We need to leave. Now!"

"Not without him," Eden said, gesturing toward Aegeus.

"What?" Loralia asked.

"This is Maxim's father," Eden told her. "He has been held captive since the battle when everyone thought he was killed."

Loralia stepped up to the glass and Eden saw her staring in at Aegeus. Her hand flattened on the glass and a tear streamed down her cheek.

"How could he do this to him?" she whispered.

"What do we do with him?" one of the warriors shouted.

The others yelled out suggestions, each more violent than the next, but Pyra put up his hands to stop them.

"No! I told you, he stays alive until I tell you."

Eden reached for the controls again, finally succeeding in opening the tank.

"He deserves exactly what he has done," Loralia said.

She took the compact from around her neck and opened it, holding it in place so that one of the mirrors reflected the tank where Aegeus was still chained. An instant later the tank appeared around Ryan, capturing him in the now-empty chains as if replacing Aegeus with him."

"You can't reflect people?" Eden asked, turning back to Aegeus.

"No," Loralia said.

"Why?"

"Because if I did, what would happen if, even for a

moment, you stopped believing in yourself? Which one of you would disappear?"

Eden felt her breath stream out of her. She reached out for the chains that held Aegeus and realized that she didn't have a key to release them.

"Gyyx, help," she called out.

Gyyx rushed toward her. He reached into the tank and grabbed onto the chains that held Aegeus. With a loud grunt he tore the metal away from its fastenings. Once broken from the walls, he picked up the cuffs around Aegeus's wrists and pulled the lock apart before moving on to the next one. Within moments Aegeus was free.

"Go get Zsilvia and George," Eden told Gyyx. She turned to Aegeus, "Come with me. I'm going to bring you to Ciyrs."

They were walking past Ryan chained in the tank when she heard his voice.

"You," he growled. "I know what you are. You are half Irisa, half Eteri. You must be the most unique hybrid that I ever created."

Eden felt Aegeus take a step back and looked up, startled to see a massive man with tattered blue wings standing at the doorway, flanked by a Denynso warrior and a man she had never seen.

"You did not create her," the man said in a voice that shook through Eden. "I did."

Loralia shook her head and stumbled back. Tears were sparkling on her cheeks as she reached for Eden. Not knowing what to do, Eden held her, supporting her as she seemed to dissolve in her arms.

"Pyra," Oro said, pushing past the other warriors to get close to their leader. "They have the others on Penthos. We got here as fast as we could, but I don't know what's happening to them there. We need to go."

Pyra nodded and they started to stream out of the room. Eden called to Ty to get the baby as she led Loralia and Aegeus out of the room, taking a moment before stepping out of the door to give one last look to Ryan. She wanted the memory of him that she carried in her mind to be him in chains.

20

M axim ran out of the ship and yelled down at Rain and Lynx.

"Get back inside," he screamed. "We need to stay together until we figure out what's going on."

Rain looked up at Lynx.

"Pyra put you in charge when he left the settlement," she said. "That means that it is your decision."

"No," Lynx said, shaking his head. "Not anymore. Creia chose Maxim. I am honored to follow him."

They climbed back into the shuttle and went to the common room where everyone else was gathered. There was a sense of confusion and tension in the space as everyone milled around, not knowing what they were supposed to do. Suddenly a bright light appeared on the far wall. Everyone stepped back and Maxim stood out in front, his hand rested on his dagger again. He watched as the light swirled and moved, then seemed to shatter into tiny flecks before coming together in the image of a face.

The man on the wall was bloodied and bruises were evident on his neck.

"Thank you for responding to my invitation," he said. "It was so kind of all of you to visit. I have to admit that I did make it fairly impossible for you to decline. Now that you are here, though, I should tell you that you will not be alone for long. My hybrids are coming and they will be delighted to have new guests to practice with. It has been so long since they have been able to fight against any real opponents. I suppose that you will have to do. By now the others are on their way to you. They thought that they had me captured. They didn't realize that I know all about the Irisa. Their reflections might seem intimidating to some, but they don't scare me. It was just a matter of waiting for them to leave and then knowing I could walk free at any moment. I can't say the same for you."

"Why are we here?" Maxim shouted at the image on the wall.

"I can't have you getting in the way of my plans. Your family has been interfering for years and it's time for that to stop. I thought that I ended it with your father, but then you came along and are causing trouble for me again."

"My father?" Maxim asked.

He felt his heart start to race in his chest.

"You didn't actually believe that he died, did you? The great Aegeus? No. Not then anyhow. But by the time that my army is done with you, you are going to wish that he had just died on that battlefield."

Athan rushed forward toward the wall and Maxim grabbed at the older man to pull him back.

"What did you do to him?" Athan screamed. "Where is he?"

"You'll know soon enough," the image that Maxim now realized was Ryan said. "But for now it's time to go. You are about to meet the beginnings of my army. They are the most powerful hybrids ever created, and once this is all over and I am able to stabilize the DNA from that hybrid baby and Eden's milk to splice into them, they will be invincible. They will have the ruthlessness of the Covra, the speed of the Klimnu, the power of mind of the Valdicians, the Irisa, and the Eteri, the cunning and organization of the humans, and now the power and bloodlust of the Denynso."

Maxim felt his blood boiling. He took a step closer to the image, his jaw set.

"If it is a fight you want, it's a fight you're going to get."

Ryan laughed and as the sound grew louder, his image blinked and flickered, then disappeared, leaving the empty wall again. Maxim turned toward the group.

"Nylek," he said. "I need you to contact Theia. Tell her that Pyra, Eden, Lysander, and the others are safe. Ask her to get Creia, Mina, and anyone else he can and go into the orchard. There are vehicles there. Use them to go to the Mikana kingdom and find Ellora. Ask her to show you to my father's room. I will guide them from there."

"What are you doing, Maxim?" Ivy asked, coming to his side and taking his hand.

"I am sending them to the weapons room to gather supplies, just as my father intended. We are raising up an army." He looked back at the wall and then toward the window at the emptiness beyond and the silhouettes of shadowy figures that had begun to form in the distance. "It's time to prepare for war."

TE

(THE END)